A HEART DIVIDED

ALSO BY JIN YONG

A Hero Born

A Bond Undone

A Snake Lies Waiting

JIN YONG

Legends of the
Condor Heroes IV

A HEART DIVIDED

Translated from the Chinese by
Gigi Chang and Shelly Bryant

ST. MARTIN'S GRIFFIN
NEW YORK

First published in the United States by St. Martin's Griffin, an imprint of St. Martin's Publishing Group

A HEART DIVIDED. Copyright © 1959, 1976, 2003 by Jin Yong (Louis Cha). English translation copyright © 2021 by Gigi Chang and Shelly Bryant. Illustrations © Jiang Yun Xing. All rights reserved. Printed in the United States of America. For information, address St. Martin's Publishing Group, 120 Broadway, New York, NY 10271.

www.stmartins.com

The Library of Congress Cataloging-in-Publication Data is available upon request.

ISBN 978-1-250-25013-1 (trade paperback)
ISBN 978-1-250-22064-6 (hardcover)
ISBN 978-1-250-22065-3 (ebook)

Our books may be purchased in bulk for promotional, educational, or business use. Please contact your local bookseller or the Macmillan Corporate and Premium Sales Department at 1-800-221-7945, extension 5442, or by email at MacmillanSpecialMarkets@macmillan.com.

First published in the Chinese language as *Shediao Yingxiong Zhuan* (4) in 1959; revised in 1976, 2003

First published in the English language in Great Britain by MacLehose Press, an imprint of Quercus Publishing Ltd., a Hachette UK Company

First U.S. Edition: 2021

10 9 8 7 6 5 4 3 2 1

CONTENTS

CONTENTS

CHARACTERS

As they appear in this, the fourth volume of
Legends of the Condor Heroes: A Heart Divided

MAIN CHARACTERS

Guo Jing, son of Skyfury Guo and Lily Li. He grows up with his mother in Mongolia, where they are looked after by Genghis Khan. He is now on his first journey to the Central Plains, the native land of his parents.

Lotus Huang, daughter of Apothecary Huang; recently named Chief of the Beggar Clan. Witty and mischievous, a skilled martial artist and extremely fast learner. She befriends Guo Jing early on in his travels, and they now journey together, sharing many adventures.

THE JIN EMPIRE AND ITS RECRUITS

Wanyan Honglie, Sixth Prince, also known as Prince of Zhao, has made conquering the Song his personal mission, in the hope of securing his reputation and legacy among his own people. He is an astute politician, using rivalries within the Song court and the *wulin* to his own advantage.

His recruits from the martial world include:

The Dragon King **Hector Sha** controls the Yellow River with his four apprentices, whose lack of skill infuriates their Master, even though it is most likely his foul temper that has prevented them from learning anything more than their rather basic moves.

Browbeater Hou, the Three-Horned Dragon, so named for the three cysts on his forehead.

Graybeard Liang, also known as Old Liang, the Ginseng Immortal and, more disparagingly, the Ginseng Codger. He comes from the Mount of Eternal Snow (Changbai Mountains) up in the northeast, close to the current border with Korea, where he has practiced kung fu for many years as a hermit, as well as mixing special medicinal concoctions with the aim of gaining strength and prolonging his life.

Lama Supreme Wisdom Lobsang Choden Rinpoche, from Kokonor, now known as Qinghai. He is famed for his Five Finger Blade kung fu.

Tiger Peng the Outlaw, Butcher of a Thousand Hands, has command of much of the mountainous region surrounding the Jin capital Zhongdu, which would later become Peking.

SUBJECTS OF THE SONG EMPIRE

Yang Kang, son of Ironheart Yang and Charity Bao, sworn as brother to Guo Jing while both are still in their mothers' bellies. He was raised as Wanyan Kang, the son of Wanyan Honglie the Sixth Prince of the Jin Empire, and only discovers the identity of his biological father at the age of eighteen.

Mercy Mu, god-daughter of Ironheart Yang, takes part in martial contests her godfather stages to find her a suitable husband and is defeated by Wanyan Kang.

Lily Li, Guo Jing's mother. After the attack on Ox Village, she ends up in Mongolia and lives among Genghis Khan's followers with Guo Jing.

THE MONGOLIANS

Genghis Khan, the Great Khan Temujin, is the mighty warrior who has united the various Mongolian tribes and conquered kingdoms to build an empire spanning Asia and Europe. He has many children, five of whom appear in this story:

Jochi, his eldest son.

Chagatai, the second son.

Ogedai, the third son.

Tolui, the fourth son, and Guo Jing's sworn brother.

Khojin, one of his many daughters whose names are mostly lost to history, betrothed by her father to Guo Jing.

Among Genghis Khan's followers, a number have fought alongside the conqueror since his humble beginning as a tribal leader. His most trusted retainers are the Four Great Generals—**Muqali**, **Bogurchi**, **Boroqul** and **Tchila'un**—and **Jebe**, who taught Guo Jing archery and wrestling.

THE SIX FREAKS OF THE SOUTH

Also known as the Six Heroes of the South when being addressed respectfully by other characters. They refer to themselves as a martial family, though they share no blood ties. They were known as the Seven Freaks until the death of Zhang Asheng the Laughing Buddha.

Ke Zhen'e, Suppressor of Evil, also known as Flying Bat. The oldest of the Freaks, he is often referred to as Big Brother. Blinded in a fight, his preferred weapons are his flying devilnuts, iron projectiles made in the shape of a kind of water chestnut native to China.

Quick Hands **Zhu Cong** the Intelligent is known for his quick thinking and even quicker sleight of hand. His dirty scholar's dress and broken oilpaper fan, really made from iron, belie his martial skill. He is particularly knowledgeable in acupressure points, using them to disable his opponents in a fight.

Ryder Han, Protector of the Steeds. Only three feet tall, but a formidable fighter and an expert horseman. His weapon of choice is a whip.

Woodcutter Nan the Merciful, known for his kind, if not shy, nature, fights with an iron-tipped shoulder pole.

Gilden Quan the Prosperous, Cloaked Master of the Market, is a master of the rules of commerce and is always looking for a good deal. He fights with a set of scales.

Jade Han, Maiden of the Yue Sword, is the youngest of the group and the only female. She is trained in the Yue Sword, a technique particular to the region surrounding Jiaxing, developed when the Kingdom of Yue waged war on the Kingdom of Wu in the fifth century B.C.

THE FIVE GREATS

Hailed as the five greatest martial artists in the *wulin* after they demonstrated their skills at the Contest of Mount Hua.

The Eastern Heretic **Apothecary Huang**. A loner and radical who practices his unorthodox martial arts on Peach Blossom Island. He holds traditions and their accompanying morals in contempt and believes only in true love and honor. His eccentricities and heretical views have earned him a dubious reputation, one that he himself cultivates.

Double Sun **Wang Chongyang**, also known as Central Divinity, founded the Quanzhen Sect in the Zhongnan Mountains, with the aim of training Taoists in the martial arts so that they might defend the Song against the Jurchen invasion. A real historical figure, he lived from A.D. 1113 to 1170.

The Northern Beggar **Count Seven Hong**, sometimes referred to as the Divine Vagrant Nine Fingers, was the Chief of the Beggar Clan, with authority over all the beggars in the Song and Jin Empires, until he appointed Lotus Huang as his successor after being wounded by Viper Ouyang. He is respected for his sense of righteousness, but few can point to his whereabouts at any given time, as he likes to roam the *jianghu* alone. He is also known for his great love of exceptional cooking.

The Western Venom, **Viper Ouyang**, is an expert in taming venomous snakes and developing lethal toxins. His martial skills, including his Exploding Toad kung fu, are inspired by the deadly creatures he keeps. He will stop at nothing to get his hands on the Nine Yin Manual.

The Southern King, **Duan Zhixing**, is the ruler of the Kingdom of Dali. He is known for his signature kung fu, Yang in Ascendance, a pressure-point locking system that also has great healing powers.

THE QUANZHEN TAOIST SECT

A real branch of Taoism, whose name means "Way of Complete Perfection."

The Seven Immortals, students of Wang Chongyang, are in fact real historical figures:

Scarlet Sun **Ma Yu**, the oldest of the Immortals, teaches Guo Jing internal kung fu based on breathing techniques.

Eternal Truth **Tan Chuduan** was a blacksmith in the Sect's native province of Shandong before he became a Taoist monk.

Eternal Life **Liu Chuxuan**, third student of Wang Chongyang.

Eternal Spring **Qiu Chuji** befriends Ironheart Yang and Skyfury Guo at the beginning of the series and vows to protect their unborn offspring. To this end, he devises a martial contest with the Seven Freaks of the South. He becomes teacher to Yang Kang.

Jade Sun **Wang Chuyi**, the Iron Foot Immortal, befriends Guo Jing after hearing of Qiu Chuji's contest with the Seven Freaks of the South.

Infinite Peace **Hao Datong**, born to a wealthy family in Shandong.

Sage of Tranquility **Sun Bu'er** is the only female of the Sect. She was married to Ma Yu before they both found their spiritual calling.

Zhou Botong the Hoary Urchin, sworn brother and student of Wang Chongyang, is a lay member of the Quanzhen Sect and the martial uncle of the Seven Immortals.

Harmony Yin is one of Qiu Chuji's students. He first met Guo Jing on the Mongolian steppe when he was sent by his Master to test Guo Jing's developing martial skills.

THE BEGGAR CLAN

The Beggar Clan is a fictional group that has appeared in countless works of martial-arts literature. Despite having members all over China, its strength lies mostly in the north—in territories already annexed by the Jin Empire at the beginning of this novel.

Beneath the Chief, who at the start of this volume is Lotus Huang, following Count Seven Hong's injury, are the three Elders, each in charge of Clan affairs in a different part of China: **Surefoot Lu**, Elder of the West; **Jian**, Elder of the East; and **Elder Liang**. The fourth Elder, **Peng**, was demoted for plotting against his new Chief, Lotus Huang.

IRON PALM GANG

Led by Iron Palm Water Glider **Qiu Qianren**, the Iron Palm Gang are known for their greed and willingness to collaborate with the enemy for strategic gain. Despite his terrible moral reputation, Qiu is regarded as a great fighter. And yet, others suspect these skills to be nothing more than a result of sleight of hand and treachery. Little do they know that Qiu has a twin brother, **Qiu Qianzhang**, who is an inveterate trickster.

THE INHABITANTS OF PEACH SPRING

Reverend Sole Light lives atop a mountain near Peach Spring, with his four disciples—the **fisher**, the **logger**, the **farmer** and the **scholar**—and his martial brother, who is visiting from Sindhu, which we know today as the Asian subcontinent. One of his serving men, **Old Yang**, lives in Peach Spring and brings food and other essentials to **Madam Ying** the Supreme Reckoner, who dwells in a swamp not far away.

CHAPTER ONE

THE BLACK SWAMP RECLUSE

I

THE CONDORS FLEW THROUGH THE DARK AND HEAVY NIGHT. Guo Jing, clinging to the bird's neck, called to Ulaan using his internal strength, urging the Fergana horse to keep pace on the ground.

The only light came from the mountaintop blaze they had fled. There was not a hint of the moon overhead. Not a single star in sight.

The condors were exceptionally strong, but soon the load of a fully grown human began to tell. As each flap of their wings grew more strained, they dipped lower and lower.

The moment they touched down, Guo Jing rushed over to check on Lotus. She was draped lifeless over the female condor's back. Qiu Qianren's Iron Palm strike had thrust her to the very brink of death. He quickly undid the sash that he had wound around the bird to keep Lotus secure in flight, and massaged her acupressure points. It was a long time before she opened her eyes.

Guo Jing stood rooted to the spot, cradling her in his arms, unsure what to do. He wanted to ask her for advice, but she was too groggy to speak.

He peered into the black wilderness, his wits still scrambled from their narrow escape. He wanted to summon Ulaan but feared giving away their position. The belligerent Qiu Qianren must still be hunting for them with his Iron Palm Gang followers.

At length, he took small, cautious steps, his legs swallowed up by dense undergrowth. There was no path, no trail, just thorns tearing at his trousers, scoring his skin, but pain was the least of his concerns right now. He trudged on, deeper and deeper into the inky night.

He forced his eyelids apart as wide as possible, yet he could make out little in the gloom. He advanced gingerly, worried that he might step into a void, a pit or a gorge. However slow his progress, he had to keep going, in case the Iron Palm Gang were still in pursuit.

He plodded on for more than two *li*, until a star twinkling at the sky's edge to his left caught his attention. He squinted at the faint glimmer, trying to work out its position in the heavens to get his bearings, and realized it was the glow of a lantern.

It could be a settlement! Guo Jing was overjoyed.

He shifted Lotus from his arms onto his back and broke into a jog, heading directly for the light. In no time at all, he had covered another *li*, and the shrubbery seemed to have thickened into a forest. The beacon, though dim, hailed him through the branches. He plowed on, and, before long, stumbled onto a track that twisted and coiled through the woods. Then, the flicker disappeared. He scaled the nearest tree to reorientate himself.

The lamplight had somehow moved. It was now behind him.

He hopped down and waded through the vegetation in the direction of the glow, only to stop when he realized it had moved again. He climbed up another tree, jumped down, darted ahead—again and again—but it kept shifting, so that it was always at his back.

No closer to the light than when he had first spotted it, Guo Jing discovered they were now buried so deep in the thicket that the condors would not be able to locate them. His head spun from running round and round after the elusive gleam, and then it struck him. He had been disorientated like this before. There was something strange about the paths in these woods.

Guo Jing ran through his options. I could jump from tree to tree. But what if I stumble? I've got Lotus on my back. She'll be scratched by the branches! Yet I can't sit here and wait for daybreak. Her injury needs tending . . .

One thing became apparent: bumbling around like a headless fly would achieve nothing. He stood still, collected himself and smoothed his breathing.

"Go right, at an angle," Lotus whispered.

"How are you feeling?"

Relief washed over Guo Jing. She's conscious! But all he got in reply was a worrying grunt into the back of his neck. He followed her directions without another word, and on the seventeenth step, he heard:

"Left. Eight steps."

He obeyed.

"Turn around. Thirteen steps."

Guo Jing forged ahead through the pitch-black forest, twisting and turning as Lotus instructed. Although shrouded in a fog of pain, she had gleaned enough about the trail from his blundering to realize that it was man-made and mapped out according to the principles of the Five Elements and the Mysterious Gates. If it were formed naturally, she would have been as hopelessly befuddled as Guo Jing was, but her father Apothecary Huang had devoted a lifetime of study to this very subject and taught her much about it. She had the ability to navigate a path through this wood with her eyes closed.

Lotus pointed left, then right; from time to time, they were forced to backtrack to make progress. Guo Jing felt they were meandering farther and farther from their goal, but, before long, he found himself clear of the trees and saw what he had been chasing.

Light, straight ahead. Not a lantern, but lamplight spilling from two thatched huts, diffused by a white mist.

He ran.

"No!"

Too late.

Aiyooo! Guo Jing found himself knee deep in mud, stuck fast in a bog. He mustered his *qi* and sprang, upward and back, freeing his legs from the mire. The stink of peat assaulted his nostrils.

"Sir, we beg you to grant us entry. One of us is grievously hurt," he said, projecting his voice. "We seek only a drink for our parched lips and a brief respite under your roof."

He waited for a reply. Nothing. Absolute silence. He asked again. Still no response. He restated his request for the third time.

"You've managed to get this far. You can surely find your way in," a woman answered, making no effort to hide her displeasure.

Guo Jing would rather camp in the wild than impose himself on an inhospitable stranger, but Lotus was in no state to brave the elements. She needed shelter. How were they going to cross this quagmire surrounding the shacks? He described their predicament to his half-conscious beloved.

"Tell me about the huts," she mumbled with difficulty. "One round, one square?"

Guo Jing strained to make out their silhouettes through the haze. A heartbeat later, he cried, "You're right!" She never ceased to surprise him.

"We can cross the bog from the opposite side," she said, wheezing. "Go all the way round." Once he reached the spot she knew to be the starting point, she stopped him. "Now, face the light and walk straight ahead, three steps. Next, diagonal left, four steps. Then, straight again, three steps. After that, four steps to the right, also at an angle. Weave your way forward, straight, left, straight, right. Count your steps. Don't get it wrong."

Guo Jing probed with his toes, and, as Lotus had foretold, he found a foothold—a wooden stake buried in the sludge. Feeling his way through the slough according to her instructions, he reached another post, then another. Some were at an angle, others wobbled. Were it not for his superb lightness kung fu, he would have toppled into the morass after a few steps.

Keeping his mind focused and his breathing under control, he managed to cross the swamp by the one hundred and nineteenth step, alighting on firm ground in front of the square hut, but there was no opening or entrance along the perimeter wall.

"Jump in from here. Land on your left," she breathed.

Guo Jing tightened his arms around Lotus, making sure she would not be jolted, and sprang over the wall as he had been told. When he touched down, he was awed by her ability to anticipate every detail of their new surroundings.

The courtyard was split in two. A pond to the right, and to the left, solid ground.

He crossed this unusual garden and headed toward the hut. The entrance was wide open; no doors guarded this circular moon gate.

"Go in. It's safe."

2

"MASTER, WE ASK FOR YOUR FORBEARANCE. CIRCUMSTANCES have compelled us to impose on you." Guo Jing allowed time for an answer that never came before stepping across the threshold.

The room's furnishings were spartan. Standing in his way was a long table, on which seven oil lamps were arranged in the shape of the Northern Dipper constellation. Beyond, a grizzle-haired woman sat on her haunches, a hemp robe draped over her shoulders. She had heard them come in, but her eyes did not wander for an instant from the clusters of bamboo slips that were spread out across the floor.

With great tenderness, Guo Jing placed Lotus on a chair. She looked waxen, even in the warm glow of the firelight, without a tinge of color to her cheeks. The sight made his heart sore. He wanted to ask the old woman for a cup of water, but the words caught in his throat—he could not bring himself to interrupt her.

Lotus, after a short rest, revived somewhat and grew curious about their reluctant host. The bamboo slips that so captivated the woman were all about the same size, each roughly four inches long

and one-fifth of an inch wide. They were counting rods, arranged in four rows to calculate—Lotus scanned the groupings—the square root of fifty-five thousand, two hundred and twenty-five. She could see that the woman had already worked out the first two numbers of the answer, two and three, and was moving the slips to determine the third and final.

"Five. Two hundred and thirty-five," Lotus blurted out.

The woman whipped around and fixed the intruders with a glare before turning back to her mathematical problem.

For the first time, Guo Jing and Lotus were able to see their host's face. Her forehead was marked by deep wrinkles, but the skin on her cheeks was smooth and unblemished. Her features were delicate and she seemed to be no more than forty years old, though the lines on her brow and the graying hair belonged to someone at least two decades older. They wondered what hardship could age a person so.

At length, the woman stopped working with the counting rods.

Five! The same as the little girl's guess. She glanced at Lotus in bewilderment; then her eyes hardened. You just got lucky! Now leave me in peace!

She turned away and noted "two hundred and thirty-five" on a piece of paper, then reset the slips to calculate the cube root of thirty-four million, twelve thousand, two hundred and twenty-four.

In the time it took the woman to place the counting rods into six rows and work out the first number, which was three, Lotus had reached the solution: "Three hundred and twenty-four."

The woman sneered in derision, assuming that she was spouting nonsense, and continued to switch the slips around for the time it takes to drink a pot of tea. At last, she arrived at the result.

Three, two, four.

She stood up, stretched and shot Lotus a black look.

"Come with me." She scowled, pointing to the inner chamber, then picked up an oil lamp from the long table and disappeared inside.

Guo Jing helped Lotus to her feet and guided her into the room. The wall was curved and a layer of sand covered the floor—vertical strokes, horizontal lines and circles were scratched into this temporary surface. There were also characters and short phrases inscribed around the marks, such as Supreme, Heaven Unknown, Earth Unknown, Man Unknown and Matter Unknown.

Guo Jing hovered at the entrance, unable to make any sense of the writing on the floor and wary of disturbing it if he took another step, whereas Lotus, who had been taught mathematics and advanced reckoning skills by her father, instantly recognized the symbols and words—they represented some of the more difficult calculations that were in the process of being solved. These equations, though complex, could be worked out methodically by anyone familiar with the Heaven Unknown technique.

Steadying herself against Guo Jing, Lotus pulled the Dog Beater from her belt and started scribbling in the sand. She solved the seven or eight questions marked on the floor in the twinkling of an eye.

The woman had been struggling with those equations for several months, and seeing them resolved with such ease sent her into a stupor. After a long silence, she asked, "Are you human?"

Lotus smiled, then tried to explain through ragged gasps for air: "The methods of the Heaven Unknown or the Four Unknowns aren't difficult. You do realize there are nineteen unknowns altogether, don't you?

"*Beyond 'Man' is Spirit, Luminance, Cloud, Nebula, Rampart, Tower, Height, Above and Heaven;*
Beneath 'Man' is Earth, Below, Decrease, Descent, Decease, Wellspring, Darkness and Specter.

"Well, things do get complicated when you try to solve the Nineteenth Unknown."

All color drained from the woman's face. She slumped on the sand and buried her face in her hands, struggling to wrap her mind around the implications of the girl's words. And yet, when she eventually looked up, she sounded almost glad. "You're a hundred times more skilled in reckoning than me. Now, how would you solve this? Line up the numbers one to nine in three columns of three. Whether down, across or diagonal, the sum must be fifteen."

Lotus chuckled to herself. That's a child's game! The Nine Halls Method is the foundation of Peach Blossom Island, and Papa applied it along with the interaction of the Five Elements.

> "*The significance of the Nine Halls,*
> *The method in the Hallowed Turtle.*"

Lotus chanted as she scrawled on the floor with the Dog Beater, her voice still weak from her injury.

> "*Four and two as shoulders, eight and six are feet.*
> *Three on the left, seven on the right,*
> *Nine as crown and one as shoe,*
> *In the center five sits tight.*"

Every last vestige of life now left the woman's already ashen cheeks. "I thought I invented this, but it's so common that there's even a verse about it."

"The Nine Halls Diagram is the most basic form. There are grids of four by four, five by five, even of a hundred, and none of them is that complex. Take the four-by-four as an example. First, you write down the numbers in four columns, then you start swapping positions, beginning with the four corners. One is moved to sixteen, four is switched with thirteen. Then the four numbers in the middle trade places: six with eleven, seven with ten. The sum of each row, column or diagonal line is always thirty-four."

The woman drew on the sand as Lotus explained and was startled by the simplicity of the solution.

"We can also replace the squares of the Nine Halls with the octagons of the Eight Trigrams, so eight times nine is seventy-two. We start by writing a number from one to seventy-two on each side of the octagon." Lotus illustrated her workings on the sand as she spoke, halting from time to time to catch her breath. "Done right, the total of each individual Eight Trigram will always be two hundred and ninety-two. And there'll be thirteen octagons together—the original nine converted from each square of the Nine Halls, plus four more that sit in-between. You've probably never heard of the Script of River Luo and its many variations. I wouldn't have known any of this without my teacher."

Gaping at the complex configuration of numbers on the floor, the woman hauled herself unsteadily to her feet.

"Who are you, miss?" Just as she uttered those words, her face contorted and she clutched at her heart. Reaching into the inside pocket of her robe, she found a vial and swallowed a green pill contained within.

It was some time before her discomfort eased.

"Never mind!" She sighed as tears rolled down her cheeks.

Guo Jing and Lotus exchanged glances, feeling a little awkward thanks to their host's odd obsession and extreme response. They waited for her to calm herself. Just then, shouts and cries rose from the forest.

"Friends or foes?" the woman asked.

"Foes," Guo Jing said.

"The Iron Palm Gang?"

"Yes."

The woman cocked her head and listened.

"Leader Qiu leads the pursuit personally . . . Who *are* you?" she growled.

Guo Jing stepped in front of Lotus protectively and said in a loud, clear voice: "We are disciples of Chief Hong the Divine Vagrant Nine Fingers. My martial sister was injured by Qiu Qianren of the Iron Palm Gang. If the Elder has dealings with the Gang and cannot offer us refuge, then we shall bid you farewell now." He bowed low and turned to support Lotus.

"So young. So headstrong. You may escape, but will she?" A faint smile played on the woman's features. "So, you're students of Count

Seven Hong. No wonder you have such skills . . ." She trailed off as her attention was drawn outside, to the noise the Iron Palm Gang was making. One moment they sounded deafeningly close, the next faraway and faint.

"They won't find the way in, don't worry. Even if they do, you are my guests, and I, the Supreme . . . Madam Ying, am not accustomed to being intimidated in my own home." For years, Madam Ying had been referring to herself as the Supreme Reckoner. Yet, confronted by this young woman, who was a hundred times more adept in the arts of mathematics, she was too ashamed to use that title.

Guo Jing wrapped his hand over his fist to show his gratitude. Madam Ying loosened the clothes around Lotus's shoulder to examine her wound. Frowning, she produced the vial again and dissolved a green pill in a bowl of water.

Lotus took the bowl, but did not drink from it immediately. She could not decide whether she was willing to trust this woman.

Madam Ying noted her hesitation and said, smoldering with injured pride, "You've been struck by Qiu Qianren's Iron Palm kung fu. You think you can survive without my help? If I want you dead, I just need to be patient for a few days. The pill is for the pain. If you don't want it, fine!" She snatched the bowl and splashed the content onto the sand.

"How could you!" Furious, Guo Jing lifted Lotus on his back and made for the doorway.

"My house is not an inn. You cannot come and go as you please." A counting rod in each hand, Madam Ying planted herself at the exit.

You've left me with no choice, Guo Jing thought, laden with guilt. "Elder, pardon my impertinence." He bent slightly from the knee and raised his arm. Tracing an arc in the air, he thrust. Haughty Dragon Repents.

The attack contained a mere fifth of his strength. After all, he just wanted to get out, he had no reason to hurt the woman. Her response would determine his next move—strike with more force or to pull back altogether.

Madam Ying leaned back a fraction and flicked her left arm up, brushing Guo Jing's blow aside.

Drawn in by her countermove, Guo Jing stumbled half a step forward. Madam Ying was also caught out, her footing slipping a little on the dry sand. Both were taken aback by the other's skill.

"Boy, show me everything your *shifu* has taught you." She aimed a counting rod at the Pool at the Bend acupoint in the crook of his right arm.

Sensing a deadly sting lurking in the strike, Guo Jing pulled away and launched another move from the Dragon-Subduing Palm. Several exchanges later, he recognized that Madam Ying's martial training—supple and yin to the extreme—was his exact opposite. Not a single one of her attacks was straightforward; there was always a malevolent twist. If it were not for the Competing Hands technique, which gave him the ability to cast two unrelated kung fu moves at the same time, he would have taken a nasty hit or two.

Proceeding with increased caution, Guo Jing put more strength in his palm thrusts, but to little effect. Each twirl of her arm seemed limp and weak, and yet her onslaught flowed like spilled mercury, slipping between the smallest gap, impossible to predict or to block.

Another handful of moves later, Guo Jing was forced to retreat two paces. Count Seven Hong's advice on tackling Lotus's Cascading Peach Blossom Palm came to his mind: *Ignore whatever she's doing. Every move that comes your way—feint or true—you answer with a Haughty Dragon Repents.*

Still, he wavered. It was not in his character to seek to hurt a stranger. Yes, this was a place of ill luck. Yes, she did not seem to be a kind person. But there was no reason for emnity between them. All he wanted was to get out. He had no wish fight her and absolutely no desire to hurt her. And so, he had been holding back, but he knew what the price for one passing moment of distraction would be— not only his life, but Lotus's too . . .

Guo Jing took a deep breath. Lifting his elbows slightly, he fired a right-handed punch while propelling his left palm forward. Swift and slow at once, this was the sixteenth move of the Dragon-Subduing Palm, Crunch Frost as Ice Freezes.

The movement contained an energy that was at once firm and supple, creating a tension of opposites that could fluidly adapt to counter any assault. Count Seven Hong's martial foundation was pure yang, as expressed by the supreme firmness of his strength, yet, like the saying from *I'Ching*—"From the aged yang, a youthful yin springs"—at the very extreme of this firm state was a strand of suppleness. In each of the eighteen Dragon-Subduing Palms, the two divergent forces coexisted and intermingled to a point at which they were indistinguishable.

Madam Ying sucked in a quick gulp of air and swiveled sideways. She managed to dodge the punch and the kick flying at her, but she could not move fast or far enough to avoid the horizontal swipe of his left palm that followed them. She was struck square on the right shoulder.

Guo Jing knew she would either be thrown against the earthen wall, and that part of the hut would collapse on impact, or her body would crash right through it to land in the courtyard outside. And yet, she defied him. The instant it made contact, his palm skidded off her robe.

As if she were slathered in a thick coat of grease.

The brunt of the blow might have missed its target, but it was still strong enough to rock Madam Ying to the core. The bamboo slips she had been clutching clattered to the floor.

Guo Jing pulled back, unnerved.

Nimble and deft, Madam Ying recovered swiftly. She touched her fingers together to form two beaks, pecking at the Spirit Seal and Jade Hall acupressure points on Guo Jing's chest.

Her technique is just like Brother Zhou's, Guo Jing thought, impressed by the level of skill on display. Having sparred with Zhou

Botong hundreds and thousands of times, he knew he would not be fast enough to block her, but he could steal in with a counterattack to push her away.

He tilted back marginally and swung his arm, driving an enormous force toward her shoulder.

Madam Ying realized her humerus would shatter if Guo Jung's thrust made contact. She skimmed away from it with the same Weatherfish Slip technique as before.

Guo Jing jumped back several steps. What fascinating kung fu, he marveled. My energy simply glides off her!

Madam Ying had retreated an extra few steps to put more distance between them. How has he mastered such intricate techniques at his young age? Is it because he was taught by one of the Greats? she thought sourly. I've been living here, alone, cut off from the world, for more than a decade. I've worked night and day on my martial capabilities. I thought I had invented an unassailable repertoire, that I was almost ready to leave this forsaken place to rescue him. Yet, it turns out that, next to this girl, I am a novice in reckoning, and, against this unweaned boy, I stand no chance, even when he is carrying the girl on his back; I cannot beat him, even when he holds his strength in check to avoid injuring me. Does it mean all these years have been wasted? That all the sacrifices I made are for nothing? Am I supposed to forget about vengeance, forget about freeing him? All these doubts and questions were resulting in a deluge of tears.

Guo Jing felt awful that he had made the woman cry. "This junior has been most impertinent. I did not mean to hurt you. Please pardon me, Elder. Please let us go."

Madam Ying marked, as the boy addressed her, how his gaze kept flitting back toward the girl, to check on her, and those glances contained so much love and concern. A flood of envy and rage overtook her—she who had suffered so many misfortunes, who had been torn from her true love. How dare these lovebirds invite themselves into her house and dash her hopes of ever being reunited with him!

"You don't need to guard her against me." Resentment sharpened her tone. "She was struck by Qiu Qianren's Iron Palm kung fu. A blackness has now shrouded her face. She's only got three days left."

Guo Jing whipped around to look at Lotus, who was still draped on his back. Just like the woman had said, a faint inky cloud had darkened her brow. The sight brought a chill to his heart, followed by a surge of hot blood. He wrapped his arms tighter over Lotus's back. "How . . . how are you feeling?"

Lotus knew the woman was telling the truth. She had been dogged by a burning sensation in her chest and abdomen, and yet, her limbs were ice cold. "Will you stay with me? Please?"

"I won't take even half a step away from you!" Guo Jing said, forcing down a sob.

Gently, he settled her by the wall and sat down to join her. Taking her right hand, he touched it against his left, thinking he would try the healing method in the Nine Yin Manual to smooth the erratic flow of her *qi*, though he could not be sure that this woman would not attempt to foil the endeavor. The slightest interference from her would mean instant death for Lotus and serious injury for him, but it was a risk he was ready to take.

Summoning his inner *neigong* strength, he sent it gently through his palm, but Lotus did not respond at all. Puzzled, he propelled a little more energy into her hand.

Wah!

Blood shot from her lips, staining the front of her dress.

"Lotus!"

Guo Jing could not take his eyes off the bright red splatters on the white fabric.

"I've no *neigong* left." Lotus's chest heaved laboriously. "This won't work. Don't—don't cry."

"Whatever you're doing with your internal force, it'll only kill her faster," Madam Ying sneered. "Say your goodbyes now. Even if you stay right by her, she only has three days."

Guo Jing turned his tear-filled eyes on their host, beseeching her to stop stinging them with her cruel words.

For more than a decade, Madam Ying had been curdling in shattered dreams of lost love, growing ever more embittered and spiteful. She was in fact thrilled to have the chance to bear witness to the catastrophe that was befalling these young sweethearts and she had many more scathing remarks in store for them.

Yet, that despondent look reminded her of . . . Wait . . . Had the heavens sent them here to deliver her revenge?

"Yes, it must be so," she muttered to herself. "At last! At last . . ."

3

The yelling and shouting grew louder again. After trekking round and round the forest all night, the Iron Palm Gang remained convinced that the young couple had taken refuge somewhere within it, but they were too disorientated by the landscape to tell left from right.

"Qiu Qianren, the Leader of the Iron Palm Gang, seeks an audience with Madam Ying, the Supreme Reckoner." A stream of powerful *neigong* carried his voice inside the hut, against the howling of the wind.

Madam Ying headed to a window and paused to gather her *qi* at the Elixir Field in her lower belly. "Pardon me, Leader Qiu, I do not receive visitors from the outside world. Death awaits those who venture into my black swamp." She sent her rejoinder far into the night.

"Madam, I am certain a boy and a girl have entered this swamp of yours. Allow me to deal with them."

"You have grossly underestimated my craft with that assumption."

A hollow laugh rang out, then the clamor of the Iron Palm Gang grew dim and distant.

Madam Ying turned to Guo Jing. "Do you want her to live?"

Caught out by the question, he stood gaping, then fell onto his knees. "If the senior Elder would offer help—"

"Am I so old as that?" A thick frost descended on Madam Ying's face, cold and hard.

"No, no, no, not at all."

Her eyes softened and her attention drifted over to the window. "'Not at all'... Still, I have grown old," she said in muted tones.

Guo Jing was now fretting over his clumsy attempt to show respect, which had clearly offended their host. Would she rescind her offer? He was desperate to explain himself, to let her know how much they would appreciate her assistance, but he had never felt more tongue-tied.

Madam Ying marked the mounting fluster in the boy, the beads of sweat forming on his forehead, which gathered speed as they rolled down. She sighed. If he had shown me even one-tenth of the affection this dolt is demonstrating now, she thought, this life of mine would not have been wasted. Then she began to hum:

> "For the fourth time the loom is ready,
> To weave a pair of lovebirds so they can take flight.
> Pity the hair that grows gray before its time!
> The ripples of spring among green grass,
> The chill of dawn lurking in the deep,
> In each other scarlet feather bathe."

The lyric poem sounded very familiar to Guo Jing, but he could not think where he had first heard it. His second *shifu* Zhu Cong? Lotus?

"Do you know who wrote that?" he asked under his breath. "What does it mean?"

"I don't know. I've never heard it before." Lotus shook her head. "'*Pity the hair that grows gray before its time.*' What a great line! Lovebirds, you know, mandarin ducks, have a streak of white on their heads..." She sneaked a peek at Madam Ying, awed by how her locks matched her song.

Then where did I hear it? And from whom? Questions whirled in Guo Jing's mind. Not Lotus's father. Or Squire Lu when we were at Roaming Cloud Manor. Yet, I know it... Why am I troubling myself over a poem when Lotus's life is at stake? The Master must know a way to save her. Why else would she pose that question? I will do whatever she asks, if it gives us hope.

Madam Ying had also retreated into her past—rapturous moments, heartsore encounters . . . Conflicting emotions bubbled in her chest. Joy and sorrow flitted across her features. Suddenly, she snapped out of her reverie and looked Guo Jing in the eye.

"Only one person in this world can treat her injury."

"Please, Elder—no, no—please, Master, please help her. We shall be forever grateful." He made three heartfelt kowtows.

"Don't bow to me. Do you think I'd be in this damp and dank place if I had the skill to revive her?"

Guo Jing had learned from his mistake and kept his mouth shut.

"Well, I must say you're blessed by the heavens," Madam Ying went on. "First, you stumbled upon me. And I happen to know of this healer and his whereabouts. And, as luck would have it, he lives within three days' journey of here. Whether he is willing to help . . . that, I cannot say."

"I'll beg him on my knees! Surely he won't stand by and let her die."

"It's human nature to stand by and do nothing. Any fool can beg. Is that enough to secure help? What can you offer him? Why does he have to help you?" Madam Ying's tone was full of bile.

Guo Jing bit his lips and nodded. He was afraid that he might speak out of turn again and crush this one chance Lotus had.

Madam Ying indicated a doorway to her left. "She can rest over there."

Thanking their host, Guo Jing helped Lotus into the side chamber and lifted her onto a bamboo daybed. The woman headed into the square room and sat down at the desk to write. She prepared three notes, wrapped them individually in cloth and sewed them shut with thread.

"Once you're out of the forest, head northeast for Peach Spring. I expect the Iron Palm Gang are waiting in ambush. If you manage to get away, open this white pouch when you get to the town. It has instructions on what to do next. You must not look into any of the pouches before the appointed time."

Promising to follow her instructions to the letter, Guo Jing reached out, but Madam Ying drew back. "Not so hasty. If he refuses to help, I won't ask anything in return, but if she lives—"

"We shall of course repay the gift of life," Guo Jing pledged.

"You must return within one moon's time," Madam Ying said to Lotus, "and live with me for one year."

"Why?" There was a trace of tension in Guo Jing's tone.

"It's got nothing to do with you!" she snapped. "It's her I'm asking."

"You want me to teach you the principles of the Mysterious Gates. I accept, of course. I give you my word."

Madam Ying handed the pouches to Guo Jing, one white, one yellow, one red. With gratitude, he tucked them into his inside shirt pocket for safekeeping and got down on his knees to kowtow, but Madam Ying hopped out of the way.

"No need to thank me. We don't know each other. We share no kinship. I have no need to help you. I wouldn't have spent all this energy even if we were acquainted. Let me be perfectly plain. I don't want your gratitude. I am doing this because it serves me. Only the self-seeking endure."

Her words grated against every fiber of Guo Jing's being. He gritted his teeth and put up with it for Lotus's sake, hoping his face did not betray him. He knew full well that this would not be the time to debate ethics, even if he had been born with a gifted tongue.

"You must be hungry. I'll bring you some congee." Madam Ying retreated from the room again.

Lotus was half dozing on the daybed, trying to conserve energy. Guo Jing sat next to her, besieged by a thousand thoughts. Madam Ying returned shortly with a wooden tray bearing two bowls of steaming hot sinica-rice porridge, a large plate of sliced guinea fowl and a small dish of cured fish.

Ever since he had realized there was hope yet for Lotus, Guo Jing had been aware of his grumbling stomach, and now the sight of food made his mouth water. He thanked their host and touched Lotus's hand. "Will you eat something?"

She parted her eyelids a fraction and shook her head. "I don't want to eat. My chest hurts."

"My pill would have helped."

Ignoring Madam Ying's provocation, Lotus said to Guo Jing, "Give me another Dew of Nine Flowers."

The precious panacea had been a parting gift from Zephyr Lu after their stay at Roaming Cloud Manor. Lotus had since kept them close to her person in an inside pocket. Though the pills had no healing power, they were effective in dulling pain and calming the nerves, helping both Count Seven Hong and Guo Jing when they were injured by Viper Ouyang.

Guo Jing removed a ceramic bottle from her robe, unscrewed its cap and took out one pill with great care.

"Is that the Dew of Nine Flowers? Let me see!"

Madam Ying's eyes were fixed on the crimson pills. Neither Guo Jing nor Lotus had noticed the tremor that passed through her when the restorative was first mentioned.

Alarmed by her cutting tone and the malicious glint in her eyes, Guo Jing handed the whole vial over to Madam Ying. A sweet scent drifted to her nose. The fragrance alone brought a sense of calm and coolness to the body.

"Where did you get these? From Peach Blossom Island? Tell me! Tell me!" She gave Guo Jing a deathly stare as she rasped in a voice hoarse with emotion.

Did she get tangled up with one of Papa's disciples? Lotus wondered. That would explain why she wants to learn the Mysterious Gates and the Five Elements.

"She is the daughter of the Lord of Peach Blossom Island," Guo Jing said.

"Old Heretic Huang's child?" Madam Ying jumped up, her eyes flashing with spite, ready to lunge.

Nodding, Guo Jing shifted over to shield Lotus.

"Give the pouches back to her," Lotus said. "We won't have anything to do with Papa's foe."

But Guo Jing could not bring himself to hand them over.

"Put them down, Guo Jing. I might yet live. And if I die, so what?"

Guo Jing set the life-saving instructions on the side table, for he would never presume to defy Lotus, but he could not hold back the flood of tears pouring down his face.

Madam Ying paid the young couple no heed. Gazing out of the window, she muttered "Heavens!" to herself again and again. Abruptly, she snatched up the pouches and rushed into the next room, still holding the bottle of Dew of Nine Flowers tight in her other hand. She scrabbled about for a while, keeping her back to the doorway, so Guo Jing and Lotus could not see what she was doing.

"Let's go. I can't bear the sight of her," Lotus said just as Madam Ying returned.

"I've been studying the art of reckoning so I can make my way across Peach Blossom Island." The woman seemed to be talking more to herself than to them. "But it's all been in vain—I could work at it for another hundred years and still I wouldn't be able to catch up, not even with the Old Heretic's daughter. I'll accept this as my lot and I shall not complain. Take them and go!"

She stuffed her instructions and the pill bottle into Guo Jing's hands. Then she looked Lotus in the eye.

"The Dew of Nine Flowers is harmful in your current state. Don't take them, and don't forget your promise. Your father ruined my life. I'd rather let the dogs eat this." She tossed the food out of the window.

Insulted as never before, Lotus could not let this crone have the last word. Then, an idea came to her, better than any retort. She took Guo Jing's arm, pulled herself onto her feet and wrote three reckoning questions in the sand with the Dog-Beating Cane.

The first was: "The Sindhu written calculation of the seven

brilliances and nine luminaries," which included the sun, the moon and the stars—Water, Fire, Wood, Metal, Earth, Rahu and Ketu.

The second was: "The problem of distributing silver and issuing rice to soldiers whose numbers are conscripted in cubic multiples."

The last one was the Problem of the Ghost Valley Sage:

Here are objects whose number is unknown: counted by threes two remains, counted by fives three remains, counted by sevens two again remains. How many are there?

Once Lotus had set down these cryptic words, she shuffled out of the hut, leaning on Guo Jing's arm. When Guo Jing got to the perimeter wall, he turned to take one last look at their eccentric host. She stood staring at the ground, clutching the counting rods. He then lifted Lotus onto his back and picked his way through the swamp and the woods at her promptings, placing his feet with care as he kept a tally under his breath.

"What did you draw on the sand?" he asked when they were clear of the strange landscape surrounding Madam Ying's huts.

"I've given her three problems to solve." A spark of the old, mischievous Lotus. "Which, I dare say, will take her more than six months to figure out. By then, all her hair will have turned white! Serves her right for being so rude!"

"Why does she bear such a grudge against your father?"

"Papa's never mentioned her . . . She must have been very beautiful when she was younger. Don't you think?"

Lotus wondered if there could be a romantic link. Maybe Madam Ying wanted to marry Papa! She snickered inside. That must be it. What a hare-brained woman. If he doesn't like you, throwing a hissy fit won't make him change his mind!

"Beautiful or not, I don't care. As long as she doesn't have second thoughts and come after us for the instructions."

"Let's take a look! I doubt she means us well."

"No! She said we have to wait until we get to Peach Spring." Guo

Jing was adamant that they should obey Madam Ying's strictures and Lotus soon relented.

As THE new day dawned, Guo Jing climbed a tree to check for any signs of the Iron Palm Gang. It appeared that they had given up. Relieved, he whistled several times, and soon he heard the beating of Ulaan's hooves. Not long after that, the condors were sighted on the horizon, winging their way toward them.

Just as Guo Jing had finished helping Lotus onto the Fergana horse, a clutch of trees not far away burst into life. Dozens of black-clad men jumped down from the branches. They had lain in wait all night, but Qiu Qianren was not among them.

"Fare ye well!"

A gentle squeeze from Guo Jing's legs and the colt took flight. He felt as if they were airborne, the wind rushing past his ears. In no time at all, the Iron Palm Gang were nothing but a smudge on the horizon.

4

By MIDDAY, ULAAN HAD COVERED MORE THAN A HUNDRED *LI*. Guo Jing stopped at a small roadside stall for a snack. The chest pains were still troubling Lotus and she could barely manage half a bowl of thin congee. Somehow, eating made her breathing short and shallow. She collapsed without warning.

Panic seized Guo Jing. He knew they could not travel with Lotus in this state, so he asked the stall keeper for a room.

"Sir, for years our soil has been depleted and our crops have failed. Poor country folks like us can barely keep a roof over our heads. If you go five *li* farther, you'll find a rice merchant. His shop is big, he may have a bed if you offer him silver."

Thanking him, Guo Jing carried the unconscious Lotus over to Ulaan. Before long, they arrived at a row of three sizeable houses behind a high brick wall. Wheelbarrows stood by an open main gate, one loaded with a dozen or so sacks of rice, one with firewood and black coal, and the last with vegetables, meat, sweet potatoes and seasonings.

Guo Jing approached the entrance and found an old man inside, drinking tea on a bench. Around sixty or seventy years of age, he had a kindly face and a headful of silver hair, but his cheeks and chin were perfectly smooth, unmarked by a single whisker.

"Master, we are travelers and my sister has been struck by a sudden illness. Might we beg a room to rest for the night? We can pay for our stay." He took out a large *sycee* ingot from his robe and presented it with both hands.

"Of course, I am happy to provide what I can, but this is too much."

"We are forever grateful, Master." Guo Jing set the silver down with a great show of courtesy. "Please take this for now. When we depart tomorrow, we shall present you with another to thank you." The stall keeper's words had stayed with Guo Jing, and he thought that, since the old man was a trader, surely the more money he offered, the more likely he was to find a bed in this place.

"Might I ask your name, sir?" the old man said.

"My surname is Guo, my martial sister's is Huang. How should we address you, Master?"

"Yang is my name. Please, have some tea," he said as he prepared the cups for his visitors.

While Guo Jing helped Lotus onto the bench and checked on her breathing, Old Yang took note of the mud caked on his trousers. It was much darker than the dust and earth staining his shoes and ankles.

"It is no mean feat to come through the forest at night without getting lost," the elderly man observed.

"We were lucky." Guo Jing was too preoccupied to notice the wheels of the handcarts were coated in the same black peat as his trousers.

"We supply food and other necessities to the people living in the forest," Old Yang explained.

Guo Jing nodded, realizing for the first time that Madam Ying might not be self-sufficient. He held a cup to Lotus's lips, helping her drink, before gulping down some tea himself.

The old man led them to a guest room, which was modestly appointed with an unvarnished wooden table and some chairs. Two beds were neatly made up, each with its own gauze canopy, straw mat and thin quilt.

Guo Jing supported Lotus as she lay down, keeping his palm on her back between the shoulder blades over the Spirit Tower pressure point, smoothing her *qi* slowly and gently. He carefully avoided using the healing method from the Nine Yin Manual, afraid that he might make her cough up blood again.

Some time later, a serving man came in with a simple meal of steamed rice and thin congee accompanied by cured fish and meat. Guo Jing fed Lotus some of the liquid from the gruel. With difficulty, she managed to swallow a few mouthfuls, but she could not bring herself to eat the other dishes.

Guo Jing wolfed down the rest of the food and stretched out in the other bed.

"Keep me company like this forever," Lotus said. "I'd be content even if I were sick for a hundred years."

"If you're sure you won't get bored of me, I'll stay with you for as long as you want."

"What about your Princess Khojin?"

Caught out, it took Guo Jing a short while to come up with a reply. "I might have agreed to marry her, but, first, I'll keep you company for a hundred years—for two hundred years. If she's willing to wait, let her wait." He sighed. "Lotus, I will not leave you, even in death. I'll just have to do her wrong—"

A voice ravaged by age began to sing softly outside, interrupting Guo Jing.

"Welcomed by clean breeze,
Loved by white clouds,
Dream not of silk robes and gold belts.
One thatched hut,
Wild flowers bloom,
Care not who rises or falls, who thrives or fails,
Alone on a humble path, merry am I.
Dawn, to the verdant hills!
Dusk, to the verdant hills!"

"Wonderful," Lotus said weakly. "I've heard many songs set to this 'Goats on the Hill' tune, but never one so well written. I wonder who came up with the lyrics—I'll learn it for Papa." Tapping out the rhythm, she hummed under her breath.

"You're a connoisseur, miss." The old man had overheard her quiet comment. "Do you know the story behind this version?"

"Can you ask him in?"

Guo Jing projected his voice. "Master, please come in."

Old Yang entered and sat on the chair by Lotus's bed.

"Do tell us, sir," Lotus said.

"The song is at least three hundred years old—it is from the Tian-bao era of the Tang dynasty."

"Really?" She had not expected such a provenance.

"You have probably noticed my accent. Perhaps you have even surmised that I come from Yunnan."

"We can tell that your enunciation is different from the locals of western Hunan. Softer, more malleable. So, this melodic tone is from Yunnan . . ." Lotus said, recalling the intonation of the detestable Madam Ying, which shared some similarities with that of this old man. Was she from Yunnan too?

"I was born in Dali, and that was where I grew up. I was sent here some years ago to plant trees and supervise a construction project. When that was completed, I was charged with staying on to supply the woods with essentials."

Lotus nodded, too unwell to speak. It occurred to her that they should not reveal too much about themselves to an associate of Madam Ying—they could not be certain if that woman was friend or foe.

"I could tell from your clothes that you rode through the forest in the night. And since I've had no word from those parts that I should not receive you, I am happy to tell you some old tales if you're interested. You've heard of the Dali Kingdom, have you not?"

Lotus nodded again, and the old man went on.

"During the Tianbao era of the Tang dynasty, Yunnan was known as the Kingdom of Nanzhao, ruled by a king called Geluofeng. He was a powerful man—the Tang Empire and the Tubo Kingdom both tried to win him to their side.

"At that time, the Xuanzong Emperor of Tang was more interested in his Noble Consort Yang than state affairs, and left the running of his country to his two Chancellors, Li Linfu and Yang Guozhong, who was the Consort's paternal cousin. Tempers soon flared at court.

"In the tenth year of Tianbao, Yang Guozhong sent the Governor of Jiannan, Xianyu Zhongtong, on a campaign against the Kingdom of Nanzhao, with an army of eighty thousand men. They rode south, taking Jingzhou and Quzhou, but were soon pushed back north, suffering a terrible defeat in Lunan, losing three-quarters of their number.

"In the thirteenth year of Tianbao, Yang Guozhong sent General Li Mi to attack Nanzhao. He also set off from Jiannan, leading seventy thousand soldiers. King Geluofeng was a skilled tactician, drawing his attackers deep into his own territory, capturing Li Mi and destroying the whole army. Not one man returned to his homeland.

"Thanks to these two aborted conquests, more than a hundred thousand Tang soldiers—prisoners and deserters—ended up in Yunnan. My own ancestor was a minor officer of the Tang army who settled down with a local tribeswoman. But, by my father's generation, our family fortune had dwindled. My father had no choice but to cleanse my body, and I became an eunuch in the palace of the Dali Kingdom."

"We've heard that King Duan of Dali is a wise ruler. It must have been a privilege to serve him."

"You are very knowledgeable, miss." The old man was pleased by her reply. "My ancestors have passed down several other versions of 'Goats on the Hill.' I was told that the tune was very popular in the Tang capital Chang'an. Everyone used to sing it—nobles and commoners alike. The Tang army came from all over China, some from Sichuan, some from Chang'an, and the songs took root in Yunnan with the surviving soldiers who could never go home. Of course, the music was also adapted to the Yunnan way of speaking." Realizing he might be interrupting the young woman's rest, Old Yang bade them farewell.

"Shall we look at Madam Ying's instruction?" Guo Jing asked when they were alone again. He took out the white pouch and unpicked the seam. It was a crudely drawn map inscribed with two short lines:

Follow the route as indicated until you reach a thatched hut next to a waterfall. Open the red pouch when you arrive at this location.

5

THE NEXT MORNING AFTER BREAKFAST, GUO JING PRESENTED Old Yang with another silver ingot. The elderly man resisted at first, but Guo Jing persuaded him to take it as payment for a few flatbreads for the journey.

Riding together on Ulaan, Guo Jing and Lotus followed the trail marked by Madam Ying for seventy or eighty *li,* until the road began to narrow. In the distance, eight *li* or so ahead of them, the hills grew mountainous and craggy, closing in around the track so only one person could pass at a time. Guo Jing had no choice but to leave

Ulaan at a nearby farmstead and continue on foot with Lotus on his back.

For two hours, he walked. At times, the pass was so narrow that he had to shift Lotus into his arms, and together they slipped through the gap sideways.

The fiery summer was still burning high in the seventh month and the sun continued to scorch everything it touched, yet it could not find its way into this gorge, so the air remained reasonably cool for the time of year.

Guo Jing soon heard his stomach rumble. Without stopping, he tore a flatbread into bite-size pieces for Lotus, before attacking the ones that remained. They disappeared in no time and he regretted his gluttony. His throat was parched; he was desperate for a drink of water. Was that the hum of a brook that he could hear? He picked up his pace.

What he had thought was a gentle trickle grew into a thunderous torrent, its roar amplified by the ravine. The path took him up to a ridge, and, across from where he was standing, a mighty white dragon swooped down from between two mountains. A magnificent waterfall.

He looked down. A small thatched hut sat close to the pool below the cataract, just as Madam Ying had described. He let Lotus rest on a rock, took out the red pouch from his inside shirt pocket and unpicked the thread. He found a short note within:

This injury can only be cured by King Duan . . .

He muttered the name in surprise as his eyes scanned the message.

Lotus had been drifting in and out of consciousness all morning, exhausted by the journey and numbed by pain, but the mention of King Duan seemed to revive her a little. It also brought to mind Viper Ouyang's words on the raft when they were making their way back to the mainland from the deserted Rosy Cloud Island. The Venom had hinted that King Duan could heal Count Seven

Hong's injury. She tried to recall what her father had said about King Duan . . . King of the South. One of the Five Greats. Ruler of the Kingdom of Dali in Yunnan . . . Which is many thousands of *li* yonder, in the southwest corner of the country, without doubt more than three days' journey from where we are now in western Hunan. She sighed in dejection, then leaned on Guo Jing's shoulder to read what that awful woman had written.

> *This injury can only be cured by King Duan. He has committed much wickedness and thus has retreated to Peach Spring to lead a life of seclusion. Hard it is for outsiders to gain an audience, and to admit to seeking treatment would cause great offense—you are likely to fall at the hands of the fisher, the logger, the farmer or the scholar before reaching his court. To gain an audience with the Southern King, claim that you have come at the bidding of your* shifu *Count Seven Hong with important news for his ears alone. In his presence, show him the contents of the yellow pouch. Life or death all hang upon this.*

Confused by the note, Guo Jing turned to Lotus. "What does she mean? What wickedness did he commit? Why would seeking treatment cause offense? Who are the fisher and the others?"

Lotus was equally perplexed. "I've no idea," she said, frowning. She hated to disappoint Guo Jing.

"Let's go and find out," he said, lifting her onto his back.

GUO JING found the descent quicker and easier than he had anticipated. As he picked his way down, he noticed a man perching on a rock, close to the waterfall and in the shade of a willow tree. His face was shielded by a conical bamboo hat, his body hidden under a straw cape.

When Guo Jing reached the valley floor, he was mystified to see the man fishing with a rod. Could there really be fish in the pool?

he wondered. Surely they would be too busy struggling against the currents to notice the bait? He studied the man. He seemed to be in his forties, his sun-scorched face dark like a cast-iron wok. Wiry whiskers bristled from his cheeks. Whatever he intended to catch had his full attention. His eyes did not wander from the depths for a single moment.

Guo Jing settled Lotus by the willow tree and tiptoed to the edge of the water, taking care not to disturb the man. He was eager to see what could be lurking at the bottom of such a fearsome waterfall. At length, he caught a flash of gold from deep in the plunge pool, and the fisher's face also lit up.

The rod bent and bucked against the man's grasp.

A golden fish had taken the bait.

Guo Jing watched in wonderment. The shimmery creature was neither fish nor snake, its head and body wide and flat. He had never seen a living thing quite like it.

"What is it?" he exclaimed, excited.

Just then, another strange golden fish clasped its mouth over the fishing line. The fisher was ecstatic, shifting his grip on his fishing rod, which was rapidly warping at ever more extreme angles. Any moment now, it would fly out of the man's hands . . . *Pak!* It snapped in two.

With the line now slack, the pair of curious fish managed to detach themselves from the hook and fishing line, swimming leisurely in circles in front of the fisher, as if to bait him. In the blink of an eye, they slipped into a gap between two boulders. Somehow, they seemed to be unaffected by the churn of the crashing flow.

"Stinker!" the fisher roared, glaring at the insolent boy. "All day, I've been sitting here. And you! You come by and scare them away!" The man jumped to his feet and raised his enormous hands—each as large as a palm-leaf fan—menacingly, ready to give the intruder a good swat. Then, after a moment's conspicuous internal struggle, he settled for clenching his fists, his knuckles popping audibly.

"Forgive me, Uncle," Guo Jing said. "What fish was that?"

"Haven't you got eyes? Fish? Do they look like fish? They're gold wah-wahs."

"What?" Guo Jing giggled at the funny name.

"Are you deaf, stupid boy? I said, gold wah-wahs!"

Guo Jing bowed and cupped his hand to apologize to the man and to appease him. He needed him to point them in the direction of King Duan's retreat.

Lotus could not stand the man's exasperated splutters anymore and said, "You mean golden salamanders, right? What's so special about them? I've got a few pairs at home."

"Oh, really? A few pairs?" The fisher snorted in disbelief and gave the impudent girl an appraising look. He would test her knowledge of these amphibians. "Do you know what they're used for?"

"Used for? Who cares? I like how they look and how they cry *wah-wah-wah* like a babe. So, I got hold of some to keep as pets."

All at once, the man's tone became almost civil. "If you really do have so many of them at home, lass, do spare a pair for me—for my loss."

"Why?"

"I caught one just now—" he jabbed his finger at Guo Jing— "and his shouting drew the other one out, snapping my fishing rod. These gold wah-wahs are clever. They never fall for the same ruse twice. You scared my gold wah-wahs away, and you need to put that right."

"You'd have only caught one, though. You said so yourself, they don't fall for the same ruse twice."

Scratching his head, but finding no answer for that, he said in a sulk, "Then give me one."

"If you split a golden salamander from its mate, both will die within three days."

"Alright, I was wrong." The fisher wrapped his palm over his fist and bowed three times. "Would you kindly gift me a pair, please?" He was now certain of the girl's familiarity with these unusual creatures.

"Tell me what you're planning to do with them."

"Very well. I'll tell you everything." The fisher realized nothing but the truth would convince this shrewd young woman. "My martial uncle traveled from Sindhu to visit my *shifu* and came upon this pair of gold wah-wahs on his journey. In his country, they have these venomous creatures that have been causing much harm to humans as well as livestock, but there are few humane ways to get rid of them. Gold wah-wahs happen to be their natural predators. He was going to bring this pair back to Sindhu and breed them. He's entrusted me to look after them during his stay, but—"

"You were careless and they escaped. Into this pool!"

"How did you know?"

"Anyone who's kept them knows how difficult it can be. I had five pairs and two escaped."

The man's eyes glowed with hope. "Give me a pair, please, good lady. You'd still have two pairs and you'll save me from the wrath of my martial uncle."

"Perhaps. Why were you so unpleasant just now?"

"I've got a short temper! I know! I should change. I really should!" It was the fisher's turn to be obsequious. "Brother, I apologize, forgive me. Miss, where do you live? Is it far? Mind if I come with you?"

"Not very close, but not that far. Three or four thousand *li*, maybe?"

"You're wasting my time, wench!" the fisher spat, waving his fist, which was almost as large as a vinegar vat. He so desired to give this impertinent girl a good thump, but then it occurred to him—she's a girl, a young, willowy girl, I'd kill her with a single punch—and he restrained himself.

"Relax, Uncle." Lotus grinned at the cantankerous man before turning to Guo Jing. She could tell he was ready to intervene if the man did turn violent. "Call the condors."

He did as she asked, unsure how the birds could help.

Guo Jing's whistle resonated in the valley and the fisher realized his lucky escape: Good thing I kept my temper under control. If we did come to blows, I'd suffer a beating at the hands of this lad.

Soon, the condors were in sight. Lotus pulled of a piece of bark from the willow tree and scratched a short note with a throwing needle:

Papa: Send me a pair of golden salamanders with the condors.
Your daughter Lotus presents this note with a bow.

Guo Jing cut two strips from his shirt and tied the message tightly to the male condor's leg.

"Fly to Peach Blossom Island and come back quickly," Lotus said to the birds.

Concerned that the condors would not understand, Guo Jing pointed east and repeated "Peach Blossom Island" three times.

The condors cawed and arched their wings. After circling a few times over their masters, they headed east and soon disappeared into the clouds.

The fisher eyed the boy and the girl. "Peach Blossom Island? Who is Master Apothecary Huang to you?"

"He's my papa," Lotus said, full of pride.

"Oh." The hot-tempered man said no more.

"The condors will be back with your gold wah-wahs in a few days."

The fisher looked the two of them up and down, doubt and suspicion clouding his face.

6

"WE HAVE NOT HAD THE PLEASURE OF LEARNING YOUR name," Guo Jing said with a bow.

"Why are you here? Who sent you?"

"We hope to seek an audience with King Duan." Guo Jing ignored the briskness of the fisher's questions, but he could not bring himself to lie, as Madam Ying had instructed, falsely claiming that they had been sent by Count Seven Hong.

"*Shifu* has no dealings with the outside world. What do you want with him?"

If it were up to Guo Jing, he would have told the truth, but what if honesty cost them the chance to meet the King of the South?

When Guo Jing hesitated, the fisher scrutinized Lotus and noticed how pale her cheeks were. "You want my *shifu* to heal you."

Guo Jing moved his head up and down as regret filled his heart. He should have lied from the start.

"He won't see you!" the fisher roared. "And I'll face chastisement. Forget your gold wah-wahs. Leave. Now!"

Surprised by the vehement refusal, Guo Jing stood there, unsure what to do next. At length, he cupped his hands and bowed low. "She is appealing for help as Apothecary Huang's only daughter and the Chief of the Beggar Clan. We hope Uncle would think on Lord Huang and Chief Hong, and show us the way so we can pay King Duan the respect due to a hero of his stature."

The mention of Count Seven Hong instantly calmed the irate man. "She's the Beggar Chief? I don't believe it," he said, shaking his head.

Guo Jing pointed to the bamboo stick in Lotus's hand. "This is the emblem of the Chief of the Beggar Clan, the Dog-Beating Cane. I am sure Uncle recognizes it."

A nod. "Who are you to the Divine Vagrant Nine Fingers?"

"He is our *shifu*."

"Oh, so you've come to see my *shifu* on his command?"

Noting Guo Jing's hesitation, Lotus cut in: "Yes."

The fisher looked at his feet and mumbled to himself, "What should I do? *Shifu* and the Divine Vagrant are very close friends."

Lotus could see that he was deliberating over his response. A little nudge now could open the way for them. "Master Hong asked us to seek an audience with King Duan, firstly to treat my injury, but also to pass on an important message."

"He told you to see 'King Duan'?" The man snapped his head up and glared at her.

"Yes."

"He said 'King Duan'?"

Lotus bobbed her head, realizing the title had roused the surly man's distrust, but she could not unsay what had been said.

"King Duan has long left this world of dust!" The fisher edged threateningly closer.

"He's dead?" Guo Jing and Lotus cried in unison.

"Your Master was with King Duan when he departed. Why would he, of all people, send you to see 'King Duan'? Who really sent you? Tell me why you're here!" He took another menacing step forward and raised his left arm—using it to mask his right, which was darting out to grab Lotus's shoulder.

Guo Jing had his eye trained for the slightest change in the man's stance, but held back from intervening until the attacking hand was no more than one foot from Lotus. Twirling his left palm, Guo Jing thrust his right forward in a Shun the Concealed Dragon.

The effect of this Dragon-Subduing Palm was akin to an invisible defensive wall falling between Lotus and her assailant. If the fisher's blow strayed into its path, it would trigger a burst of energy from Guo Jing. If the man stepped back, then the force contained in the palm strike would dissipate into the air.

Puzzled by the wayward aim of Guo Jing's counter, the fisher nevertheless kept his focus. The girl! His hand was now just inches from her shoulder. An acute pain jolted his arm. A searing heat sizzled his chest. He had not made contact with Guo Jing's palm, but the strength emanating from the young man was so strong that it thrust his attack aside.

The fisher jumped back and pulled his arms in to guard his torso, in antipation of a follow-up. Guo Jing surprised him by relaxing his stance before holding his palm over his fist in a gesture of respect.

Impressed by the boy's restraint, the fisher recognized that he had been thwarted by one of the eighteen Dragon-Subduing Palms, which Count Seven Hong had demonstrated for his *shifu*. He knew he should not offend a disciple of Chief Hong.

"I can see that you are indeed the Divine Vagrant's students, but your Master didn't send you, did he?" Much of the aggression had left his tone.

Guo Jing nodded, knowing he could not deny it, and wondered how the fisher had figured it out.

At this honest admission, the pugnacious man assumed an almost kindly expression. "Even if the Divine Vagrant himself had come to see my *shifu* for a cure, this lowly creature would have had to stand in his way. I hope you will pardon me."

"Really? You'd stop Chief Hong?" Lotus could hardly believe her ears.

"Yes. With my life."

What's going on? Lotus was intrigued. One moment he's saying Count Seven was present when King Duan passed on, the next he's saying he'll lay down his life to stop Count Seven from seeking treatment from his *shifu*, who is undoubtedly King Duan! It makes no sense! Well, one thing is certain. This *shifu* of his is somewhere up this mountain, and we *have* to see him.

But how?

She tilted her head back to see as high as she could, but she could not make out the summit. Even judging from where it tore into the clouds, it seemed higher than the middle crag of Iron Palm Mountain. Steeper too. There was hardly any vegetation on its rocky surface. Impossible to find a way up on foot. The waterfall looked as if it was cascading straight from the sky, reminding her of the poet Li Po's famous line:

From the heavens comes the water of the Yellow River.

As her eyes followed the cataract down into the pool, her mind searched for a plan to scale this obstacle. A glint. A swerve. Brilliant gold shooting from the dark depths. She edged toward the verge for a better look.

The golden salamanders! They had burrowed their way under a large rock, but the tips of their tails were still visible, swishing around. She beckoned Guo Jing over.

"Ah! I'll catch them."

"Don't be silly. The water's too fierce."

Without another word, Guo Jing took a deep breath and jumped into the plunge pool, fully clothed and still wearing his shoes. If he could catch these creatures, surely the man would take them to see his *shifu*. He would find a way to deal with whatever happened next. He could not bear the idea of standing by and doing nothing while the injury ate away Lotus's life force.

"Guo Jing!" Lotus shifted her footing too fast and stumbled forward.

Displaying well-honed reflexes, the fisher grabbed Lotus by the arm, in spite of his astonishment at Guo Jing's descent into the water. Once he had steadied the young woman, he ran into the thatched hut.

In the short time it took Lotus to sit down, Guo Jing had found a way to plant his feet firmly at the bottom of the pool. The plummeting water beat him incessantly, but his body did not even sway.

Slowly, he bent from the waist, arms reaching out. He closed his fingers around the tails of both golden salamanders at the same time.

He tugged. Gently. Terrified of hurting these strange creatures.

Their skin was smooth and slimy. A couple of wiggles and they slipped from his grasp. They delved deeper under the boulder, evading his second attempt at catching them.

Lotus gasped at the near miss. The fisher also sucked in his breath. He had resting on his shoulder a small rowing boat, exceptionally dark in hue, and in one hand, two iron oars. He was ready to launch the craft.

Guo Jing focused his energy in his feet and used the Thousand

Jin Load kung fu to root himself to the bed of the pool. Stilling his *qi*, he wedged his hands under the rock where the strange creatures had taken shelter.

Up, he heaved.

It moved.

Thrilled, he launched a Leap from the Abyss from the Dragon-Subduing Palm. Thrusting with both hands, he lifted the boulder clear.

He then let fly with a Dragon in the Field, hurling the rock sideways. The combined force of the waterfall and the Dragon-Subduing Palm sent it careering over the edge of the plunge pool into the gorge below.

Guo Jing now clutched a golden salamander in each hand. Holding them aloft, he trudged along the base of the pool, step by step, through the relentless thrashing of the cataract against his head and shoulders.

Over the years, the gushing water had gouged a trench of more than two *zhang* into the bedrock, and Guo Jing had dived right into its very depths. The fisher, amazed that anybody could swim up with the pressure of the waterfall beating down on them, dipped an oar as far into the water as he could so the young man could haul himself ashore.

But Guo Jing knew if he loosened his grip even slightly, it would give the salamanders a chance to escape. Lotus's life depended upon them. Rallying his *qi*, he flexed his right foot and shot up through the depths. Then he kicked high, planting his left foot on the side of the trench, and propelled himself onto the shore through the unrelenting rush of water.

Lotus was astounded by his control of breathing and strength—this feat was performed not just underwater, but while being battered by a mighty waterfall.

Though Guo Jing's kung fu had undergone marked improvement in the past weeks, it was his desperation to save Lotus that allowed him to tap into abilities yet unknown to him. Now that he was safely on the shore, the sight of the cataract frothing and spluttering was enough to make him dizzy. He could hardly believe that he had jumped in and grappled with it without a second thought.

The fisher was awestruck. All but the greatest martial Masters would have been trapped by the water pressure. To break free required supreme control of *qi*, exceptional agility in lightness *qinggong* and remarkable mastery of external kung fu—all at the same time.

The salamanders thrashed in Guo Jing's hands, screeching like bawling babies. Laughing, he thrust them at the fisher. "Now I see why they're called wah-wahs."

The man had just hauled the small boat ashore. He cast down the oars and reached for the precious creatures, but just before he touched them, he yanked his hands back.

"No, I can't. Throw them back into the water."

"Why?" Guo Jing could not understand his change of heart.

"I can never take you to *Shifu*. If I accept your gold wah-wahs without returning the favor, then I'll be an ingrate, despised by the world."

"They're just fish—nothing to be grateful for! You have your reasons why you can't let us see your *shifu*. We understand. We won't force you. Just take them, Uncle." Guo Jing bundled the salamanders into the fisher's hands.

Though clearly conflicted, the man held fast to the amphibians.

"Lotus, we both know the saying, 'Life and death are fated, age and year can't be foretold.' If we can't find a cure, I'll carry you on the road to the netherworld. Let's go." Somehow saying this out loud gave Guo Jing solace. In life or in death, he would stand by her.

His earnest words made Lotus well up, but she already had a plan. "Uncle, humor me, please. Or else I'll die wondering, unable to close my eyes, unable to find eternal rest."

"Huh?"

"This mountain is smooth like a mirror. I can't see any trail leading uphill. If you were to let us pass, how would we make our way to the top?"

The fisher hestiated, then decided that they could not ascend without his help, even if they knew the method. "Well, it's not as difficult as it seems. Just around this slope on the right, the water is less fierce. It comes down as rapids, rather than a waterfall. I can row one person upstream with each trip."

"*Ah!* Farewell, then." Lotus took Guo Jing's elbow to pull herself up, while he cupped his hands to say goodbye.

Relieved to see the young couple walking away, the fisher was reminded by the salamanders' squirming that he needed to secure them sooner rather than later. He rushed into the hut, muttering his thanks.

"Quick! Take the boat!" Lotus whispered in Guo Jing's ear.

He stopped dead. "That . . . that isn't right."

"Fine! Stick to your precious principles!"

What's more important? Principles or life? Guo Jing could not come to a conclusion. But Lotus had already let go of his arm and was trotting unsteadily, with the help of the Dog Beater, toward the rapids the fisher had just mentioned. Instinct kicked in. Guo Jing grabbed the little boat and hurried after her.

7

GUO JING TOSSED THE CRAFT INTO THE ROILING WATER, tucked the oars under his arm and scooped Lotus up, carrying her for the last few steps. Then he heard it. A faint fizzing sound, above the rumble of the rapids, something zooming toward them. Secret weapons. He ducked and lunged forward into the boat, pulling Lotus with him.

Lotus's reactions were slowed by the injury and she was hit on her back by one of the projectiles. Luckily, it was deflected by the Hedgehog Chainmail stowed in her knapsack.

The fisher raged and roared, but they could not make out his words above the din of the wild river.

The white water was sweeping them downstream at great speed, closer and closer to the precipice. If they were forced over it, they would be thrown into the ravine below, smashed to pieces. Guo Jing struck an oar into the water and hauled. The boat edged a few feet forward. He grasped a fleeting chance to help Lotus into a more secure position, then dug the blade in again. They gained another few feet against the current.

"Putrid hag! Devious vixen!" Snatches of the fisher's outrage cut through the howls of wind and water.

"I'm the only one being cursed!" Lotus was amused that the fisher refrained from insulting Guo Jing as he flung his land-bound abuse and punches at the air.

Her comment fell on deaf ears. All of Guo Jing's senses were engaged in the battle against the seething water. His arms, fortified with internal strength, struck back with the oars. The little boat's prow pitched violently in the swell. Inch by inch, they were making progress.

The water here might have been less angry than around the waterfall, but, nevertheless, Guo Jing was straining with every particle of his body to propel them forward. His breathing had grown shallow and his cheeks were hot and flushed. Several times he was overwhelmed and they were swept along by the torrent. Each setback proved to be instructive, and soon Guo Jing had worked out a pattern to combat the onslaught of nature: Dragon Whips Tail, launched simultaneously in each hand with the Competing Hands technique. When the might of the Dragon-Subduing Palm surged to the very tip of each blade, it was as if he were rowing on a calm lake.

Lotus laughed. "I doubt that odious man can row as fast as you."

AFTER TWO particularly treacherous stretches and a sharp bend, the stream started to gain in width and the landscape opened out. They could see the river meandering up the mountain, and, with each stroke of the oar, the water became less murky. Though they were still going against the flow, it was offering only mild resistance now.

Soon, the waterway had broadened to more than one *zhang* across. Lush peach trees lined the shore, interspersed with verdant willows, their tendrils teased by the increasingly gentle current. The banks would be ablaze with peach blossoms at springtide. Even now, clusters of small white flowers were dotted about at the edge of water, infusing the air with their sweet scent.

This calm, bucolic scene was a pleasant surprise, and both Guo Jing and Lotus felt refreshed. The stream was now a luxuriant jade green, veiling the riverbed. Guo Jing dipped an oar straight down to gauge the depth. Not only did it not reach the bottom, it was almost ripped from his grasp by the fierce undertow. He turned his mind back to the task at hand, guiding the boat leisurely upstream to the chirrups of hidden birds.

"If I can't get better, bury me here," Lotus said. "I don't want to go down again."

Guo Jing turned to face her, and was about to offer a few words of comfort when they were plunged into darkness. They had entered a cave. The floral fragrance grew more intense. There was also a renewed fury to the water, accompanied by a buzzing hum that was amplified by the rock all around them.

"What's that noise?"

Lotus shook her head. "I don't know."

Dazzling brightness. They reemerged into daylight.

"Wow!" they exclaimed in awe.

From the craggy ground ahead, two geysers of water shot twenty feet into the air, fizzing noisily. Sprays of droplets drifted like flurries of snow, refracting the sunlight into radiant hues.

Guo Jing hopped ashore, holding the boat tight against the bank while helping Lotus disembark. Then he pulled the craft out of water, propping the oars on the seat.

Together, they gazed at the wellspring of the river. They could have come up with many words of praise and admiration, but nothing came to their lips. They were content, sitting hand in hand, shoulder to shoulder, to share this moment of peace and clarity in silence.

A SNATCH of song drifted over from beyond the rainbow. "Goats on the Hill," the tune Old Yang had hummed the day before.

> *"The city laid waste,*
> *Did the heroes survive?*
> *How oft does the dragon with clouds mingle?*
> *Pondering the ebb and flow of power,*
> *Bitterness fills the bosom.*
> *The Tang Empire rose as the Sui fell.*
> *The way of the world an ever-shifting billow.*
> *Swift, fault the earth, the sky.*
> *Slow, fault the earth, the sky."*

Lotus was moved by the gravity of the lyrics. Most songs set to this melody were about ordinary things and everyday life—and there must have been thousands of renditions over time, for it had been sung up and down China for several centuries, since the Tang dynasty ruled the land. Yet, this was the first time she had come across one that reflected on matters of state and the inevitable rise and fall of empires.

She could now see the singer heading toward them. He carried an axe in one hand and a bundle of firewood under his other arm. Madam Ying's cryptic instructions came to her mind:

To admit to seeking treatment would cause great offense—you are likely to fall at the hands of the fisher, the logger, the farmer or the scholar before reaching his court.

They had just met the fisher, and now the logger was approaching. These four men must be King Duan's followers or disciples. The thought weighed on Lotus. They had enough trouble getting past the fisher, and she could tell from the logger's warm baritone that he would be a tough opponent . . . As she tried to picture the trials they were about to face, he broke into song again:

> "*On the Bridge of Sky Crossing,*
> *Resting on the balustrade, the eyes cast yonder,*
> *From this land, the regal air has long melted away.*
> *Overgrown trees,*
> *Overflowing water,*
> *No sign of the fortune-turning general, All to ruination at the turn of*
> *the head.*
> *Merit, long it never lasts!*
> *Fame, long it never lasts!*"

The logger cast a brief look at Guo Jing and Lotus as he walked by, continuing on his way toward a cluster of trees that stood beside a steep rise netted by climbers, where he began chopping wood, as if the strangers were not there at all.

The man's commanding presence exuded authority and gravitas. Though he was collecting firewood in rough-spun clothes, Lotus could imagine him marshalling soldiers on the battlefield. The mere sight of this formidable figure would cow his enemies. King Duan ruled the Kingdom of Dali in Yunnan, and it would not be outrageous to assume that this woodcutter was once his general, but what made him so partial to these statesman's laments?

> "*Mountains huddled,*
> *Torrents bubbled,*
> *Tong Pass sat aloft over river and ridge.*
> *Gazing toward the western capital,*
> *The mind dithers.*
> *Where the Qin and Han once passed, the heart hurts,*
> *Palaces, watchtowers, ten thousand rooms, to earth all returned.*

> *Thrive, the people suffer!*
> *Fail, the people suffer!"*

The last two lines brought to Lotus's mind a sentiment her father had often expressed: "Emperor, generals and chancellors, without exception, are the bane of the people. When kingdoms change hands, it is always the people who suffer."

"Well sung!" she cheered.

"How so?" The logger hung the axe from his belt and turned to the young woman.

Lotus decided to answer with lines sung to the same melody:

> *"Welcomed by clean breeze,*
> *Loved by white clouds,*
> *Dream not of silk robes and gold belts.*
> *One thatched hut,*
> *Wild flowers bloom,*
> *Care not who rises or falls, who thrives or fails,*
> *Alone on a humble path, merry am I.*
> *Poor, aspirations great as mountains!*
> *Rich, ambitions grand as mountains!"*

She thought Old Yang's lyrics would make a perfect rejoinder. On the one hand, it paid tribute to the logger's assumed past as a military man, on the other, it praised the pastoral simplicity of his new life. The only improvement she devised was adapting the last two lines to further compliment his choices—first serving King Duan as his general and now following his sovereign to lead a hermit's life.

Lotus's voice might have been weakened by her injury, but the song had won the logger's heart. For, as the age-old saying goes: "Everything wears out, but flattery never tires."

Pleased that the young woman had understood him so well, the logger pointed at a woody vine, as thick as his arm, leading up the vertiginous slope. "Go on!" He assumed the fisher had offered them the boat to come upstream. How else would they know where to launch the craft and how to combat the current?

Guo Jing craned his neck. Mist and clouds swallowed at least half the crag. How far would he need to climb? Unable to comprehend much of the lyrics, he had not realized Lotus's song was all it had taken for them to be granted passage.

"Thank you, Uncle," he said loudly, fearing the man would change his mind. He lifted Lotus onto his back and cut a thin but strong climber to use as a rope, binding her tightly to him in case she lacked the strength to cling on for the whole ascent. Then he took hold of the vine the logger had indicated. Inhaling deeply, he heaved, pulling himself and Lotus up, little by little.

In a trice, he was already a dozen *zhang* from the ground. The logger's voice could still heard:

> " . . . *Where were the battles bygone?*
> *Victory, to earth we return!*
> *Defeat, to earth we return!"*

Lotus tittered into Guo Jing's back. "Maybe we should listen to him. No. Let's not bother!"

"Huh?"

"Everyone dies one day." Then she broke into song:

> "*Healed, to earth we return!*
> *Failed, to earth we return!"*

"Pah! Don't listen to him!"

Lotus hummed to herself:

> "*Live, you will carry me!*
> *Die, you will carry me!"*

"That's more like it. In life and in death, I'll carry you!"

"Dying hasn't been so scary since you said you'd carry me on the road to the netherworld . . ."

They soon found themselves surrounded by a white haze so dense that not even the summer sun could penetrate it. Guo Jing could feel the drop in temperature in spite of all his physical exertions.

"Whatever happens next, this hasn't been a wasted trip," Lotus said. "We've seen so many sublime sights."

"Can you stop being so morbid?"

Chuckling, she blew on the back of his neck. Warm and ticklish.

"Hey! Behave! We'll fall!"

She laughed. "Now who's being morbid?"

Guo Jing gave her a smile and turned his mind back to the ascent, his arms working faster than ever. In no time at all, the vine was leading him forward instead of upward. They had reached the top.

8

JUST AS GUO JING HAD HAULED HIMSELF AND LOTUS ONTO firm ground, they were rocked by a loud crash as if the mountain had split open, followed by the whine of a distressed animal and the sound of a man shouting.

"An ox? On a mountain this high and steep?" Guo Jing was puzzled. Adjusting Lotus's weight on his back, he hurried over to see what had caused the commotion.

"Fisher, logger, farmer, scholar," Lotus reminded him. "Oxen plow fields."

On the slope ahead, the draft animal was howling into the sky, helpless. It thrashed on its back, contorting its body, flailing its hooves in a bid to right itself, while the boulder supporting it trembled under its weight.

Lotus chuckled as she marveled at the bizarre scene. "We were just singing 'Goats on the Hill,' now we've got an ox on the hill."

Holding up the rock—and the struggling animal—was a

bare-chested man with mud up to his knees. Arms thrust high over his head, he had planted his feet at right angles for maximum purchase. He too was in a precarious situation: the ground he stood on jutted out, with a sheer drop on three sides. If he were to sacrifice the ox and let go, he would still be crushed by the boulder, since there was nowhere he could go to avoid it.

Lotus supposed the animal must have climbed up the hill and slipped, causing the rockfall, while the farmer happened to be close enough to come to the rescue. Now, both man and beast were stuck.

She had not expected to find farmland at the summit of the mountain. Looking around, she estimated that there must be at least twenty *mu* of paddy fields, and at the edge of one patch of cultivated land was a pile of hastily discarded tools.

He must be the farmer, Lotus deduced. What a stupendously strong man. The ox is at least three hundred *jin*, and then there is the weight of the boulder! As she wondered how the man would get out of his predicament, she sensed Guo Jing undoing the vine that was tying them together, and the next thing she knew she was being placed lightly on the ground.

"No! Not so hasty!"

Always willing to lend a helping hand, Guo Jing was racing to the man's aid. "Go! Help the ox!" He positioned himself under the rock, half crouching, and pushed.

The farmer felt his burden ease, but was doubtful that this stranger could support the rock and the ox on his own. He let go with one hand.

Guo Jing secured his footing, pooled his inner strength and thrust upward. He was now supporting the boulder by himself, lifting it away from the farmer's hand. The man waited to make sure the stranger was strong enough before bending low to slip out from under the rock and help the ox.

Just as he reached for the beast, he realized the man who had come to his aid was a mere boy, no more than eighteen or nineteen. There was nothing distinguished about the lad, and yet he did not look as though he had any trouble bearing the rock's great weight. The farmer grew suspicious. This boy's strength was far superior to his own, which was considered exceptional. What had brought him here? He could not have stumbled across this place by accident. He cast his eyes around and saw a girl leaning against a rock. Even from a distance, he could tell she was grievous sick.

"What brings you here, friend?" the farmer inquired.

"To seek an audience with your honorable *shifu*," came the reply.

"What is your business?"

Guo Jing was at a loss for an answer.

"Lead the ox away," Lotus called. Her voice lacked power. "You wouldn't want them both to fall into the abyss, would you?"

There was no whistling arrow from my martial brothers below to say that I should receive them, the farmer thought as he scrutinized the girl. He must be a skillful martial artist to have forced his way up. I'll question them while he's stuck.

"Are you here to seek treatment?"

Guo Jing nodded. There was no point in lying, since they had already admitted as much to the fisher.

"Ah, let me make inquiries." An odd look flitted across the farmer's face. He bounded up the hill, leaving the ox to its thrashing and whining.

"Wait! Help me with the rock first!"

"I shall be back soon."

Lotus knew the man wanted to wear Guo Jing out until he was too weak to fight back. She wished she had the strength to help, but all she could do was watch in frustration as the wily farmer hurried away.

"Hey, Uncle, come back!"

"Don't worry," the farmer said with a simpering smile. "He's strong enough."

Guo Jing helps you, out of the goodness of his heart, Lotus grumbled under her breath. How dare you trap him like this? You won't get away with it!

"Uncle, we can appreciate your wish to ask your *shifu* first," she said as loudly as she could. "I have a letter here from our *shifu* Count Seven Hong, if I could trouble—"

"Are you both students of Master Hong?" the farmer asked as he went over to fetch the note. It now made sense that the boy was so strong.

She nodded. "Yes, he's my martial brother. But he's all brawn and no brains." She pulled out the Hedgehog Chainmail and rummaged through the knapsack for the nonexistent message. She then looked over at Guo Jing and horror marred her features.

"Help him, please, Uncle!" she shrieked. "His hands will be ruined!"

"He'll be fine." The farmer brushed off her concerns and reached for the letter.

"You don't understand. He's learning Splitting Sky Palm. He soaked his hands in vinegar last night. He's not supposed to strain them today. It'll ruin his craft forever."

There was a grain of truth to her lie, for she had described the actual training method devised by her father. Although the farmer had not heard of this kung fu, he knew enough to realize that she had cited an advanced method of martial cultivation.

If I hurt the Divine Vagrant's disciple, he said to himself, not only will I have to face *Shifu*'s wrath, but I won't be able to make peace with my conscience either, for the boy came to my aid. But what if the girl is trying to gull me into freeing him?

"This is Hedgehog Chainmail. No weapon can penetrate it," Lotus said, noticing his hesitation. She offered him the steel shirt. "Please, Uncle, could you kindly drape it over his shoulders? He could then support the rock without hurting his hands. I'm sure you wouldn't want to be the cause of bad blood between our Masters, right?"

The farmer was of two minds whether he should trust her as he reached for the treasure from Peach Blossom Island he had heard so much about.

"*Shifu* always entreats us to act in good faith," Lotus added, sensing his misgivings. "You can test its strength."

The farmer knew his Master thought highly of the Divine Vagrant's integrity. He had been studying the girl, a picture of earnest innocence, and was increasingly inclined to believe her. Still, he could not afford to be careless when his teacher's safety depended on his decision. He drew the short saber hanging from his belt and brought it down on the Hedgehog Chainmail. Indeed, as she had promised, it withstood his blade.

"I'll do as you say." The farmer went up to Guo Jing and laid the shirt on the young man's shoulders. Then he pressed his hands against the boulder. "Let your shoulders take the weight."

Lotus was paying close attention to the farmer's every move. Once she was certain he had taken the rock's full weight, she shouted, "Dragon Soars in the Sky!"

Guo Jing's body reacted automatically. He shot out from under the rock and propelled himself away from it, landing next to Lotus with the Hedgehog Chainmail draped snugly over his shoulders.

A stream of curses flowed from the farmer. His arms held high, he was once more stuck under the rock.

"Don't worry, you're strong enough," Lotus said, mocking him. "Let's go."

"You've tarnished the Divine Vagrant's reputation!"

"I doubt it. Can *Shifu* fault me for obeying my father? Papa says a little lie hurts no one."

"Who's your father?"

"Didn't I show you the Hedgehog Chainmail?"

"You're the Old Heretic's spawn!"

Giggling, Lotus took Guo Jing's hand and left the spluttering farmer behind.

CHAPTER TWO

REVEREND SOLE LIGHT

I

WITH GUO JING'S SUPPORT, LOTUS SHAMBLED ALONG THE trail through the paddies and soon they came to a narrow stone bridge spanning a deep valley. The structure was just over a foot wide and most of it was obscured by drifting clouds. They could not tell how far it extended or what was on the other side. If they were on firm ground, of course, a path that narrow would not have bothered them in the least. Yet, right now, one look at the nothingness below was enough to make their hearts quail.

"King Duan has done a good job of secreting himself away," Lotus remarked. "By the time his rivals have made it this far, I'm sure most of their grievances would have melted into the air."

"Why do you think the fisher said King Duan had left this world?"

"I can't work it out. I don't think he made it up to fool us, since he said our *shifu* was there when it happened."

"Well, there's only one way to find out."

Guo Jing stooped and lifted Lotus onto his back, then started to sprint across the bridge using the Fleet Foot Light Step technique.

The uneven paving stones, coated in condensation, were slippery in the extreme. He had to move fast to maintain his balance.

"Watch out!" Lotus yelled when they were seven or eight *zhang* across the bridge.

A gap yawned ahead. At least five feet wide.

Guo Jing heaved a deep breath and charged forward. At the very edge, where the gap yawned, he pushed off with his back foot and glided across on the momentum of his thrust.

"The condor was steadier," Lotus said when they touched down on the other side.

Guo Jing kept up his pace and leaped over another gap, then another, then another. After the seventh breach, he could at last make out through the mist the relatively flat ground at the far end of this dilapidated bridge. And yet, between where he was and where he needed to get to was a chasm of more than one *zhang*, perhaps even reaching a dozen feet. He was confident that he could jump over it, but, on the spot where he would land, a scholar sat cross-legged, and just beyond him was one last rift he would have to negotiate before they could set foot on firm ground.

"We are here to seek an audience with your honorable teacher." Guo Jing steadied his footing and projected his words. "We would be grateful if Uncle could guide us to him."

The scholar was reading aloud from a thread-bound volume rolled up in his left hand. He was so engrossed, bobbing his head to the sound of his own voice, that he did not seem to hear the young man at all.

Guo Jing asked again, even louder. No reaction.

"What should we do?"

Lotus answered with a frown. There was no question in her mind as to why the scholar had seated himself there—if they wanted to get past by force, they would have to push him from this foot-wide stump of the bridge into the abyss. But they were here to ask for help. To murder the man would not set the right tone. She needed to get him to acknowledge them. She listened to his recitation, hoping it would give her inspiration and help her find an opening that would spur the scholar into a response. Then it dawned on her that he was reading from the *Analects of Confucius*, a classic that all students know inside out.

"'In the twilight of spring, the season's garb completed,'" the scholar declaimed. "'With capped men five and six, and boys six and seven, bathe we in the water of River Yi and in the breeze among rain altars, and sing we on the way home.'"

The man gushed and gasped in delight as he read, as if he too was bathing in the spring breeze, singing and dancing.

Lotus wondered if she could provoke him with some outrageous comments about the classics.

"What's the point of reading the *Analects* a thousand times if you can't grasp the significance within?"

As she had predicted, the scholar lifted his eyes from the book.

"Do enlighten me."

He was about forty years of age, and wore his hair tied in a kerchief, in the style preferred by educated men. From his chin, a long black beard flowed. In his right hand, that ubiquitous accessory of a man of letters—a folding fan.

A Confucian literati, without a doubt.

"Does sir know how many disciples Confucius did have?"

"Of course I do. Three thousand students did Confucius have, of whom seventy-two were particularly distinguished."

"Of these seventy-two, how many had come of age? How many were still boys?"

The scholar was taken aback. "Such details were not recorded in the *Analects*, nor are they mentioned in other sources."

"I wasn't mistaken when I said you hadn't grasped the significance within. You just read the passage out loud: 'Capped men five and six, and boys six and seven.' Five and six is thirty, so that's how many capped men who had come of age. Six and seven make forty-two, that's the number of boys. Thirty plus forty-two is exactly seventy-two."

Chuckling at her brutish misinterpretation, the scholar had to give the girl credit for her quick thinking nonetheless.

"I am full of admiration for the young lady's learning. Might I inquire what business has brought you here to seek an audience with my teacher?"

Lotus deliberated over her riposte: *If we say we have come to seek treatment, he'll probably try to stop us as the others did, but I cannot ignore such a direct question* . . . *Let me reply with Confucius's own words.*

"'A sage, alas, is not in my lot to meet! If I could meet a man of virtue, that would suffice,'" she quoted. "'How can one not be joyful when friends come from afar?'"

The scholar threw his head back in laughter. "I shall take you to my *shifu* if you can give me satisfactory answers to my three questions. If you make one mistake, however, then I'm afraid I will have to ask you to turn back."

"Please don't make them too difficult. I am not at all learned."

"They shan't be too hard. The first is a poem, which contains one word—"

"Riddles! What fun!"

The scholar smoothed his beard and began:

> *"For years the six classics have guided this heart,*
> *One blade for ten winters this hand has honed."*

Lotus stuck out her tongue. "A man of letters and the sword. Impressive!"

He smiled and continued:

> *"Reclining, this one sprig of apricot blossom,*
> *Explain the heavens' mysteries these lips would not.*
> *Masterstroke from this great one,*
> *Obscures half a bed of naught.*
> *Set aside this courtier's cap to retreat with the name whole,*
> *This face, did you know how it once looked?"*

57

Lotus laughed to herself as she listened to his recitation: Papa told me all about this tired old acrostic when I was a child!

"Pardon our lack of manners," she said with exaggerated politeness. "We did not realize we were in the presence of one who has set aside his position in court to retreat to this idyllic country. Forgive us, please, *foremost* of scholars, as revealed by the first letters of your verse."

The man was dumbfounded by the ease with which she arrived at the answer. It rolled off her tongue as if it had required no thought at all! He had assumed the puzzle would occupy her for a good half a day. No matter how great the boy's kung fu might be, this bridge was too perilous a place in which to remain standing for long with another on his back. He thought they would give in and go back the way they had come.

"I am in awe of the breadth of your knowledge, miss. The verse is old and by no means a description of this humble scholar." He realized his next question would need to be exceptionally difficult if he wanted to get the better of this bright young woman. He cast his eyes around for inspiration and a row of palm trees swaying in the wind caught his attention.

That will do, he told himself with a flick of his fan.

"I shall share the first line of a couplet. Might I ask miss to match it with a second line?"

"Mmm . . . matching couplets isn't as fun, but I'll do as you say if it means you'll let us pass."

He pointed at the palm trees with his fan:

"Palm fronds sway in the wind, the thousand-hand Buddha waves his folding fans."

Lotus felt a grudging respect. Well, well, this stuffy old bookworm isn't as dull as he looks. He's not simply described the scenery, he's also elevated his own standing with a reference to the Buddha! Pairing words won't be enough. I will have to comment on his person too.

She looked around, searching for something in the landscape that would spark her imagination. Her eyes settled on a lotus pond in front of a small temple at the end of the bridge—perhaps the place where they would find King Duan.

In this part of China, summer heat still lingered at the end of the seventh lunar month, but up here in the mountains there was an autumnal edge to the air, which had caused the lotus leaves to shrivel and wilt.

"I have a second line, but I fear it might offend Uncle." She beamed at him.

"Please, go ahead."

"Promise you won't take offense?"

"You have my word."

"If you say so . . ." She began, motioning at his kerchief:

"Lotus leaves wilt in the frost, the one-legged phantom wears his scholar scarf."

"Marvelous!" Merry laughter. "A perfect match in every way!"

Guo Jing at last caught on to the joke when he saw the withered lotus leaves drooping over stalks that jutted from the surface of the pond.

"Stop laughing! I don't want to be a bareheaded wraith!" Lotus tittered at her own witticism.

The scholar realized she would find a rejoinder to anything he could devise, but a word game from his student days now came to his mind. It was the first line of a couplet that had stumped generations of literati—one he had no answer for. And as far as he was aware, no one had yet come up with a solution.

"Might I ask miss to complete another couplet?

"Timbre, tone, tune and toll, tumbling as they tut."

Lotus cracked a smile when she heard the first words, before scrunching up her face in an attempt to look perplexed.

Another ancient and stale puzzle. Lucky me! Yes, it's very hard to match all the layers of the wordplay, but Papa cracked it years ago! Well, I'll let you gloat for now . . .

She scratched her head and mumbled to herself, putting on a convincing act of agonizing over the test.

The man fell for her dramatics and allowed himself a short-lived smile, before the fear that she would ask his opinion overtook any sense of triumph. "This indeed is an impossible line to match, and I must confess that I do not have the learning to formulate a neat response. Might I remind miss that, if you cannot provide a satisfactory answer, you must go back the way you came."

"I wouldn't say it's impossible." Lotus flashed her most brilliant smile. "But I've already offended Uncle once, and if I reply, I shall insult all four of you in one breath. It is not befitting to let these words pass my lips."

Of course the scholar did not believe her. To come up with a match and taunt them at the same time? Never!

"If your line truly forms a couplet, then we will not mind being mocked."

"In that case, please accept my apologies:

"*Goblin, ghoul, ghost and ghast, grumbling in the gut.*"

The scholar climbed to his feet, flabbergasted by her flawless response. "I submit to your superior scholarship." He flicked his sleeves to extend them to their full length and bowed deeply with his hands together in a gesture of utmost respect.

"I wouldn't have had this idea if you and the other uncles hadn't tried so hard to stop us." Lotus returned the courtesy, grinning from ear to ear. She was delighted that she had put her father's witty jibe at his disciples to such good use.

The scholar hopped over the final gap and stood to attention. "Please."

He watched the young man leap over the widest breach to the

stump he had just vacated, effortless and sure-footed. The weight of the girl on his back did not affect his footwork at all.

I thought I had mastered the martial and the literary arts, and yet today I have been bested in both by these youths, the scholar said to himself, somewhat disheartened. Then he noticed Lotus's self-satisfied smile, and he could not refrain from taunting her.

"Miss has a great store of literary talent, but is perhaps somewhat wanting in deportment."

"Enlighten me, please."

"'A man and a woman should not touch when giving or receiving gifts, such is propriety.' I trust miss is familiar with this quote from the *Mencius*? Now, I gather you have yet to leave your maiden's chamber and thus could not have wedded this young man. Why do you allow him to carry you thus? Mencius also laid out the case of the drowning sister-in-law, exploring when it is appropriate for a brother-in-law to extend a helping hand. From what I can discern, miss hasn't fallen into water, nor are you this young man's sister-in-law. Surely it is not proper to permit such contact?"

How come everyone can tell that we're not married? Lotus was both intrigued and displeased by this phenomenon.

"Mencius is full of hot air. Much like yourself, sir," she shot back. "Why should I listen to him, or to you?"

"How can you dismiss the wisdom of the great sage as hot air?"

Smirking, Lotus recited in a sing-song voice:

> "*How come a beggar has two wives?*
> *How does the neighbor keep so many fowls?*
> *Since the King of Zhou still reigns,*
> *Why canvass the rulers of Wei and Qi?*"

The poem was another of Apothecary Huang's creations. He had made it his mission to satirize and mock the great thinkers like Mencius and Confucius, to express his contempt for the strictures the classics, which formed the bedrock of Chinese culture, had imposed on people's minds.

The scholar stood agape. He had no words with which to counter these logical questions. He could brush away the first two quips since they were querying parables Mencius set out to explain a philosophical point, but he had to concede that even the Master himself would not be able to justify the actions questioned by the final challenge. The Zhou dynasty, which had ruled China for six hundred years before Mencius's birth, was still in existence then, though greatly enfeebled and fractured into many fiefdoms and states. Why in sooth did Mencius offer his service to King Hui of Liang and King Xuan of Qi instead of the King of Zhou, who had the most legitimate claim to the realm? He could not fathom how this teenage girl had come to be so erudite and astute. He knew better than to challenge her again, so he led them forward without another word.

As they stepped onto the much smaller bridge that spanned the lotus pond, the scholar could not resist taking a stealthy look at the enigmatic young woman who had made such a fool of him. For once, Lotus looked away tactfully, though she could not stifle a giggle.

2

THE SCHOLAR GUIDED GUO JING AND LOTUS THROUGH THE temple's main gate and settled them in a chamber on the eastern side of the courtyard.

"Please, make yourself at home. I will inform *Shifu* of your arrival," he told them once a novice had brought tea for the guests.

"The farmer is trapped under a boulder," Guo Jing said, recalling Lotus's trickery. "You should help him first!"

"Let's see what's in Madam Ying's last message," Lotus said, when the scholar had left the room.

"It completely slipped my mind!" Guo Jing took the yellow pouch from inside his shirt and unpicked the seams.

It was a crude drawing on white paper. A man, clothed in the regal garb typical of the land of Sindhu, was cutting a piece of flesh from his chest with a dagger. A balance sat before him: on one side of the scale, a white dove; on the other, the skin and muscle the man had flayed from himself. The bird was small, but it outweighed what the man had offered. A raptor surveyed this scene from the sidelines.

Lotus studied the gruesome, crude image, but its significance eluded her. The one thing she could glean from it was Madam Ying's ignorance when it came to the art of painting, though her calligraphy was passable. Guo Jing folded up the image once Lotus was done. He was not going to burden himself with the task of deciphering its message.

When the novice returned, he touched his palms together, held them upright over his chest in a Buddhist greeting and bowed. "May I ask what brings sir and madam to this far-flung place?"

"We are here to seek an audience with King Duan," Guo Jing said.

The novice put his hands together in the same respectful gesture. "King Duan has long left this world of dust. I am sorry that you have come here for nothing. Might I invite you to a vegetarian meal before guiding you back down the mountain?"

Guo Jing was crestfallen. After all their efforts, they were still being sent away with the same frustrating and enigmatic excuse. Yet, things were coming together for Lotus—the temple, the novice and the way he talked . . . She prised the drawing from Guo Jing's hand and offered it to the young monk.

"We would be very grateful if you would deliver this note to your superior and let him know that Guo Jing and Lotus Huang humbly request an audience. We hope he will grant us one on the strength of his friendship with the Divine Vagrant Nine Fingers and the Lord of Peach Blossom Island."

Genuflecting, the boy accepted the paper, folded it up, then took his leave. This time, he returned almost straight away and indicated that they should follow him.

The temple turned out to be a far more extensive complex than the first courtyard had suggested. They followed a paved path through a bamboo grove before arriving at three stone cottages set in the peaceful embrace of lush greenery.

The novice walked up to one of the cottages, pushed the doors open with a light touch and stepped aside, standing with his body politely inclined to allow the guests to enter first. Guo Jing gave the boy a smile, moved by the courtesy they were being shown, and lent Lotus his arm so she could steady herself as she stepped over the threshold.

Two monks sat cross-legged on prayer mats in the middle of a sparsely furnished room. On the low table between them was a censer, from which the gentle scent of sandalwood filled the air. One of the monks had darker skin than was common for the people of this region, with a pronounced nose and deep-set eyes. Lotus knew he must be the martial uncle from Sindhu the fisher had mentioned.

The other man, she noted, had a regal presence that neither his rough-spun *kasaya* nor his flowing white beard could conceal. She also perceived a shade of sorrow between his graying eyebrows. Behind him, the scholar and the farmer stood in waiting.

Her intuition confirmed, she took Guo Jing's hand, led him before the kingly monk and lowered herself onto her knees. "Uncle, your juniors Guo Jing and Lotus Huang bow to you."

Guo Jing copied her stance without asking wherefore and kowtowed four times.

With a kindly smile, the monk got to his feet and helped the young couple up.

"I am delighted that Brother Seven has acquired such outstanding protégés, and Brother Apothecary is most blessed to have such a wonderful daughter. My indolent students —" the monk gestured at the scholar and the farmer—"told me that your martial and literary understanding far surpass theirs. My heartfelt congratulations." He followed these sentiments with a bout of effusive laughter.

Guo Jing could not make sense of this latest turn of events. *From the way he talks, he has to be King Duan. But how come the king is now a monk? Why did they all say that he'd left this world of dust? How can Lotus tell this monk is the man we've been seeking?*

"Tell me, how are your father and your *shifu* doing? They're well, I trust?" the monk asked Lotus. "It's hard to believe twenty years have gone by since we were at the summit of Mount Hua together. Your father wasn't even married then—and now he has such a beautiful, accomplished daughter! Have you got any siblings, my dear? Who is your grandfather? I dare say he's a great hero."

"I'm an only child." Lotus's eyes reddened and tears threatened to fall. "Mama left this world a long time ago. Her family name was Feng, but I don't know anything about her father."

The monk patted Lotus on the shoulder to console her. "Have you been here long? I have just emerged from the meditative state of *samandhi* after three days and three nights."

The monk's delight at their arrival was evident, and it was plain to Lotus that the trials they had to go through were all his students' doing. She would not let the affront pass without comment. "We have only just arrived. In fact, it is most fortuitous that the Uncles were so determined to hold us back and did everything they could to make our journey so very difficult. Or else, we would have been here much too early."

The monk chuckled. "They're worried about me being disturbed by the outside world. But how could you two ever be outsiders to me? I know you, my dear, have made sense of it all already. I am now known as Sole Light. When King Duan left this world of dust, your *shifu* was there—he was right by my side when I pledged myself to the *triratna* and received the tonsure. Your father doesn't know about any of this, does he?"

"No, Papa isn't aware and *Shifu* has never mentioned it to us," Lotus replied.

By now, Guo Jing had wrapped his mind around these latest revelations. The men were not making veiled references to King Duan's physical death; they had been referring to the oath a monk took to renounce the secular world. And if they had been sent by Count Seven Hong, they would be seeking Reverend Sole Light rather than King Duan.

Lotus is always so perceptive, he said to himself. She knew the second she clapped eyes on him.

"Good food is the only thing your *shifu* allows to pass his lips. He wouldn't waste his breath prattling about this aged monk. You must have had an arduous journey. Have you eaten—" The monk gasped and took Lotus by the hand, leading her to the open doorway, where the light was better. Grave concern clouded his features as he inspected her face in the sun.

Guo Jing might not be the shrewdest, but even he could not fail to realize that Reverend Sole Light had detected Lotus's injury. He fell to his knees and knocked his head loudly against the floor. Then he felt the monk's hand under his arm. A great force was peeling him off the ground. He went with the flow and stood up slowly, for it was rude to oppose one's elder.

Within Sole Light's polite gesture was a test of Guo Jing's internal kung fu. The monk had employed a mere half of his strength and was poised to pull back the instant the young man showed the first sign of being overwhelmed by his power. He would not dream of humiliating his guest by making him flip in a somersault.

By complying, Guo Jing had confounded all expectations, nullifying the monk's energy, which required a greater skill and control than direct opposition would.

No wonder my students were ashamed of themselves after their encounters with this young man, Sole Light reflected. Brother Seven has indeed trained a first-rate disciple.

"Help her, Uncle!" Guo Jing pleaded as he straightened up. Just then, a strong current coursed through his body, threatening to topple him. He stepped forward involuntarily as his own strength poured forth to root his feet.

I can't believe how long his energy stayed inside me. Guo Jing replayed the exchange in his mind, his heart pounding, his breathing unsettled by this disruption to his *qi*. *I thought I'd balanced out his strength when I stood up with him. Somehow, his power entwined with mine, so I ended up being tipped over by the rebound of my own force. I still have a long way to go before I can control my inner power like this. The reputation of the Five Greats is fully deserved.*

The awe and admiration Guo Jing felt for the monk's kung fu was evident on his face.

Smiling, Sole Light put a hand on his shoulder. "It is already no mean feat to have cultivated the skill you have just demonstrated."

All the while, the monk had kept hold of Lotus's hand. He led her to a prayer mat, his face somber despite his reassuring words. "Child, don't be scared, there's nothing to worry about."

His warm and sympathetic tone conveyed a tenderness Lotus had never before experienced. She knew her father doted on her, but he had always treated her as an equal, a close friend, pushing away paternal feelings and gestures because of his desire to defy social strictures. And now it was almost as if she were at last in the company of the mother she had never met.

The pain, the fear, the despairing thoughts she had desperately held at bay for the last few days burst forth with her sobs.

"Hush, my dear, hush," Sole Light cooed. "There's no need to cry. Uncle will make your affliction go away." The gentler his tone, the quicker her emotional defenses crumbled and the faster her tears flowed.

Guo Jing was jubilant that Lotus could be saved, but he was also growing self-conscious and shamefaced thanks to the hostile glares of the monk's followers, since it was only through chicanery that they had made it this far. At the same time, he could not understand why the scholar and his fellows were so resolute in preventing them from meeting this kindly monk, who seemed only too eager to help.

"My child, tell me what happened. How did you come by this injury? How did you find this place?"

Holding back her sobs, Lotus told Sole Light how she had mistaken Qiu Qianren for his martially inept twin brother and had been struck on the shoulder by his Iron Palm kung fu. She noted the little changes to monk's countenance as she spoke, catching a fleeting frown on his otherwise peaceful face when she first mentioned the name Qiu Qianren. Then she told him how they found Madam Ying in the swamp and how she gave them directions to the temple. Sensing a gloominess settling over the monk, as if he were gripped by woes from the past, she trailed off discreetly.

"What happened next?" he said with a sigh. Relishing the chance to get even with the scholar, the farmer and the fisher, Lotus recounted in grossly exaggerated detail the unsporting means they had resorted to in their attempts to restrain and discourage them, playing up the fact that she was a harmless, injured little girl. She painted the three men in such a bad light that even Guo Jing was moved to speak up in their defense. Only the logger was spared from her barbed tongue. Instead, she showered him with excessive praise for letting them pass freely.

The scholar and the farmer flushed red in fury, then went pale from fright at her inflated accusations. They would dearly love to refute her claims, but how could they act so discourteously in front of their teacher and liege? They had no choice but to suffer the indignity in silence.

To add insult to injury, Sole Light nodded in earnest at each of her denouncements. "How could we treat guests like this? You're right, they've been most rude. I will make sure they apologize to you in person."

Puffed up with triumph, Lotus swept her eyes over the scholar and the farmer as she continued her tale of how they strove to thwart them even once they had won entry to the temple. "And then I asked them to show you the drawing. Only then did they stop being truculent and allow us to receive your invitation."

"What drawing?" Sole Light sounded surprised.

"The one with the hawk, the dove and the flayed man."

"Whom did you give it to?"

The scholar took the piece of paper from his inside shirt pocket and offered it with both hands. "I have yet to present it, because *Shifu* was deep in meditation."

Sole Light gave Lotus a conspiratorial smile. "See, if you hadn't told me about this picture, I would have never got to see it." He unfolded the paper and understood at once. "Whoever gave you this thought I would refuse to help you and sent it to goad me. Well, they've underestimated this old monk!"

Lotus caught a strong whiff of panic emanating from the scholar and the farmer. Why do they act like I'm taking away everything they hold dear? she mused. All he said was that he would help. Maybe it will take some precious herbs to cure me and they don't want to part with them?

Sole Light lifted the drawing to the light to examine it, then flicked it with a finger, a quizzical expression on his face.

"Did Madam Ying draw this?"

"Yes."

The monk thought about her answer. "Did you witness her drawing it with your own eyes?"

Sensing that something was amiss, Lotus replayed the whole encounter in her head. "She had her back to us. I could see her brush move, but I couldn't see what she was putting down."

"You said she gave you three notes. Do you mind showing me the other two?"

Guo Jing removed them from his pocket.

One glance and a shadow crept over Sole Light's face. "Just as I thought," he said under his breath as he put the messages into Lotus's hands. "Brother Apothecary is a connoisseur of painting and calligraphy. I am sure he has passed his wisdom on to you. What differences can you discern between the three of them?"

Lotus ran her fingers over the notes. "These two are standard semi-processed jade plaque Xuan paper. The drawing is done on an antique silk paper. Mmm . . . that's a rare material."

The monk nodded. "I am no authority on the art of the brush. Tell me your opinion of the draftsmanship."

"Uncle, stop pretending," she said, after assessing the drawing with more care than before. "One glimpse was enough to tell you this wasn't painted by Madam Ying."

"So it really wasn't painted by her?" he asked with a slight quaver in his voice. "I made that deduction from the circumstances, not from any hint in the drawing."

Lotus took the monk's arm and patiently explained. "Look here, Uncle. The handwriting in these two notes. Soft, graceful, feminine. Now, look at the lines in the picture. Lean and hard, aren't they? The brush must have been wielded by a man. I know it. This is a man's hand, beyond doubt. He is unschooled in the art of calligraphy. He knows nothing about structuring strokes or controlling the brush, but there's a weighty, penetrating strength to his touch. It's reached all the way through the paper . . . The tint of the ink shows its vintage . . . This drawing was done a long time ago—it's probably older than me."

Sole Light turned to the scholar and indicated a bound volume on a small bamboo table. An elongated yellow label ran down the cover:

Sutralamkara Sastra
by the Bodhisattva Asvaghosha

Translated by Kumarajiva of the
Kingdom of Kucha, Master of Tripitaka

I hope he isn't going to start lecturing us on Buddhist scriptures, Lotus thought wearily.

The scholar brought the book over with great reverence. Sole Light turned a leaf and put the drawing next to it.

"The same!" Lotus gasped.

The monk nodded.

"What's the same?" Guo Jing whispered.

"The paper," Lotus said. "Feel the texture. Aren't they exactly alike?"

He could now see that the picture was sketched on paper as thick and stiff as the pages of the volume of Buddhist scriptures, and on closer inspection it was clear they shared a similar coarse surface, with flaxen strands running through it.

"Is this unusual?" Guo Jing asked Lotus, but she said nothing, so he turned to Reverend Sole Light.

"My brother-in-faith brought me this book from the Western Regions." At this, Guo Jing and Lotus took note of the other monk for the first time. He had not shifted position at all, and was still sitting cross-legged on the prayer mat, undisturbed by the conversation. "This scripture is written on paper from that part of the world, and this image is drawn on the same kind of paper. Have you heard of a place called White Camel Mount, out in the west?"

"Viper Ouyang, Venom of the West!" Lotus exclaimed.

Sole Light moved his head slowly in affirmation. "This picture came from his very hand."

Even Lotus was dumbstruck by the revelation.

"That far-sighted man put this plan in motion a long time ago." A faint smile drifted across the monk's features.

"I didn't realize this was painted by the Venom," Lotus said with disquiet in her voice. "This can only be villainy, Uncle."

"All this for a mere martial manual."

"So this is about the Nine Yin Manual too?" Agitation brought an unnatural high color to Lotus's cheeks.

She had been holding herself together with what little inner strength was left in her body for the past few hours and Sole Light could see that she was now on the point of collapse. "Let's get you better first. We can talk later." He took her by the arm and guided her toward a small side chamber.

"*Shifu!* Let us!" The scholar and the farmer groveled at their Master's feet, blocking his way.

The monk shook his head. "Can you heal her?"

"We'll try out best."

"Try?" Sole Light's face darkened. "This is a matter of life and death."

"They are here on the instructions of one with evil intent! They couldn't possibly mean you well, *Shifu!*" The scholar could not hold back any longer. "You can't let charity and compassion lead you into a trap."

"What have I been teaching you all these years? Here, take a good look." He handed the scholar the drawing.

"*Shifu*, you said this was painted by the Venom of the West. Surely, their coming here is part of *his* infernal plot!" The farmer kowtowed, anxious tears staining his face.

Guo Jing and Lotus were flummoxed. What harm could come from healing someone?

"Stand up. You're distressing our guests." Sole Light's soft voice conveyed absolute authority.

Unable to dissuade their mentor, the scholar and the farmer shuffled to their feet, heads hung low in dejection.

3

REVEREND SOLE LIGHT LED LOTUS INTO THE SIDE CHAMBER and beckoned Guo Jing over to join them. The small room was austere: three prayer cushions and a censer sitting on a squat table made of bamboo. The monk let down the blind over the doors—which was also of bamboo—and lit a stick of incense, planting it upright in the burner. He invited Lotus to take the mat in the middle and sat down cross-legged on the one to the right.

"Guard the entrance. Don't let anyone in. Not even my disciples." The monk closed his eyes to help him focus, but something drove him to part his eyelids again. "If they try to force their way in, fight back. Your martial sister's life depends on it."

"Yes, Uncle." The monk's solemn tone nagged at Guo Jing, though he could hardly imagine such defiance from Sole Light's followers, who had displayed nothing but utmost veneration and obedience in their Master's presence.

Sole Light then said to Lotus, "Do not let your body tense up at any point. Be it agonizing pain or unbearable itch, do not resist with your *qi*."

"I'll consider myself dead," Lotus said with a laugh.

The monk smiled, lowered his eyes and relaxed his brow. In this meditative state, he allowed his energy to course around his body.

An inch of the incense had turned to smoke. Sole Light touched his left hand over his chest and sprang to his feet. Reaching out slowly with the index finger of his right hand, he tapped the Hundred Convergences acupressure point at the crown of Lotus's head.

Her body spasmed at the contact, but Lotus was only aware of the warmth seeping through the top of her skull.

Without adjusting his stance, the monk prodded the pressure point an inch and a half lower, Rear Vertex, at the back of her head. At once, he moved on to the point below, Unyielding Space, then Brain's Door, Wind Mansion, Great Hammer, Kiln Path, Body Pillar, Path of Life Force, Spirit Tower . . .

In the time it took for half the incense to burn away, Sole Light had activated all thirty points that made up the Governing Vessel along Lotus's spine.

The astounding display left Guo Jing spellbound, his jaw hanging low. When Sole Light reached out, he was the embodiment of leisurely ease, yet as he withdrew his arm, he became a whirlwind of swift elegance. For each of the thirty acupressure points, he employed a different technique. Structured, expansive, full of character—no two moves were the same. Guo Jing could see nothing in common with the skills taught to him by the Six Freaks of the South, and, more surprisingly, he could not even find any similarity with the methods described in the passages entitled "On Locking Pressure Points" in the Nine Yin Manual. He realized he had been given the privilege to behold Yang in Ascendance in action, the kung fu that had established the King of the South's reputation, but he had no idea that Sole Light was pouring his own strength, accrued over a lifetime of training, into Lotus to reconnect the inner energy flow in her Eight Extraordinary Meridians.

The monk had Guo Jing change the incense and took the chance to sit down for a short rest. When he sprang into action again, his movements were lightning fast and marked by mesmerizing precision.

Guo Jing's eyes were not keen enough to discern the finger that was flitting between the pressure points, for it was as lithe and agile as a dragonfly dipping its tail in a pond. All he could make out were the tremors in the arm that preceded the actual prod.

One single exchange of breath and it was done. Twenty-five acupoints along the Conception Vessel, from the chin to the sternum in a straight line down Lotus's torso.

Guo Jing was awestruck.

Presently, Sole Light moved on to the fourteen points of the Yin Link Meridian, which ran from the inside of the right calf, along the leg and the right flank, terminating at the throat. Now he swooped like the dragon and prowled like the tiger, full of might and spirit. The religious garb could not mask the carriage of a king.

The monk continued, without taking a break, on to the thirty-two points of the Yang Link Meridian, which began on the outside of the left ankle, tracing the left side of the body, all the way to the head. This time, he stood one *zhang* away from Lotus, then, in a flash, whizzed up close to nudge the Wind Pool pressure point on her neck, just behind the ear. The instant Sole Light made contact, he zipped away as briskly as he had zoomed forward.

What a marvelous technique! Guo Jing was absorbing all he could. With deft footwork like this, one could spring on an opponent then sprint away speedily enough to keep out of harm's way.

He feasted his eyes on the swerves and swings that Sole Light employed to swoop in and out, and soon gleaned that the real difficulty lay in falling back with the same acrobatic lightness as darting forward—like the way a hare would shoot away from a predator. He was reminded of his fight with Madam Ying. Her slipperiness shared the same roots as what Sole Light was demonstrating, though her execution fell far short of his.

Two more sticks of incense later, Sole Light had triggered the acupressure points on the meridians of Yin Heel and Yang Heel, which ran alongside Yin Link and Yang Link.

The monk now reached for the Great Bone point on Lotus's left shoulder and a line from the Nine Yin Manual came into Guo Jing's head.

How thick can I be? he chided himself. Of course it's described in the Manual! It's just that I'm too brainless to connect words with motion!

He went over the relevant portions of the martial tract in his head and noticed aspects that matched what he was seeing. He began to grasp that, while the Manual outlined the fundamentals, Sole Light was illustrating the infinite variations, interpretations and mysteries hidden between the lines.

Of course, Guo Jing would not dream of attempting to learn Yang in Ascendance without express approval from the Master himself. He focused instead on the insights into the Nine Yin Manual he could glean. A picture began to form in his head of what happened when a person trained in internal kung fu was injured: the meridians in their body became blocked, which meant the flow of their life energy was disrupted. When he was injured by Viper Ouyang's Explosive Toad kung fu at the Imperial Palace in Lin'an, he could rally his strength through the healing method in the Manual because he was hardy enough to propel his *qi*—with Lotus's inner force as guidance—around every available path and acupressure point within his body to restore his circulation. But Lotus had been caught off guard by Qiu Qianren and her strength was too depleted to allow her to perform this act of self-preservation.

Now he registered what Sole Light was doing. The monk was

injecting his own store of *neigong*—a purely external energy—to reconnect the rivers of Lotus's life force.

There was only one meridian left to go, the Belt Vessel. Unlike the others, which guide the flow of *qi* along the length of the body, the Belt Vessel, as its name suggests, encircles the waist.

This time, instead of facing Lotus, Sole Light had his back to her, his arm twisted behind him. His finger crept ponderously toward her Camphorwood Gate, at the base of the right side of her ribcage.

There were eight acupoints on this channel, but the monk seemed to be straining to reach them. His movements were labored, his breathing ragged, his body trembling—he was on the brink of collapse.

Guo Jing was desperate to do something, to steady the monk, but what if he ruined everything? Sweat was now streaming from Sole Light's eyebrows. Lotus was also drenched in perspiration. She looked like she was trying to keep the torment inside her body from getting the better of her, her features were screwed up, her teeth clamped down on her lower lip.

4

"*Shifu!*" The bamboo blind was smacked aside.

Guo Jing swung his arm behind him toward the doorway in a Dragon Whips Tail. *Thwack!* His palm connected with a shoulder, sending the intruder stumbling back. He spun round to see who he had struck. The fisher.

Having lost his boat, he had had to take the circuitous land route to the temple, trekking more than twenty *li* up and around the mountain. He had learned of his teacher's offer to heal the injured girl upon arrival, and had barged in, blinded by rage, ready to give his life to stop his Master. The fierce palm thrust did not deter him. He braced himself to charge again, but was restrained by his brothers.

"It's done," the scholar snapped. "There's nothing you can do now."

Sole Light had returned to his prayer mat, sitting cross-legged once more, his face as white as chalk, his robe soaked. Lotus was splayed on the floor, stock-still, showing no signs of life.

Terrified, Guo Jing scooped Lotus up and was assaulted by an awful stench of rot and gore. Her face was deathly pale, without a trace of color, though the charcoal undertone had also faded. He put his hand under her nose. Her breathing was deep and even. Relief washed over him.

The monk's four disciples had gathered around their Master, hushed and grim-faced.

Guo Jing observed a rosiness returning to Lotus's cheeks, but no sooner were his hopes raised than they were cruelly dashed, for the pinkish tint began to burn a fiery red. Beads of sweat formed along her hairline. The flush of flaming scarlet blanched into cadaverous gray again.

Twice, the blood rushed to her face and ebbed after heavy perspiration. Then she groaned, and her eyelids fluttered. "Where's the fire? Where's the ice?"

"Huh?" Guo Jing had lost the ability to form actual words.

Lotus scanned the room and shook her head. "It was a dream. A nasty one with Viper Ouyang, Gallant Ouyang and Qiu Qianren. They put me in a furnace, then in ice." She shuddered at the memory. "I was burning then I was frozen. It was horrible . . . Uncle? Uncle, are you alright?"

Sole Light opened his eyes slowly and smiled. "Rest for a few days. Keep off your feet. Then you'll be fine."

"I haven't got a drop of strength left inside me. I don't even want to lift my finger." Her impish humor had returned and she refused to let the farmer's malevolent glare ruin her mood. "Uncle, you've worked hard to save me. You must be exhausted. I have some Dew of Nine Flowers that were made to my papa's recipe. Would you like some?"

"That's very kind of you. Your father shared this precious physic with us on Mount Hua when we were exhausted by the Contest. It has the most remarkable restorative effects."

Guo Jing took out the ceramic bottle from Lotus's knapsack. The scholar received it on his Master's behalf and emptied the contents into his palm, while the logger ran to the kitchen for a bowl of water.

"I won't need so many," Sole Light said with a laugh. "These pills aren't easy to come by. I'll just take half."

"But, *Shifu!*" the scholar implored. "All the world's magical remedies still won't be enough."

With his store of internal energy depleted, the monk was too frail to argue. He swallowed them all with a few mouthfuls of water. Then he turned to Guo Jing. "Make sure she rests for a couple of days. When you wish to leave, you don't need to come to me first, but there's one thing I would like to ask of you."

Guo Jing prostrated himself, knocking his head loudly on the floor four times to show his gratitude. Lotus also fell to her knees and bowed to Sole Light with a wholehearted deference that she had never demonstrated before, not even to her father or Count Seven Hong. "I shall never for a moment forget this gift," she swore.

"No, no, no, forget it all, don't let it become a burden." The monk turned to Guo Jing. "Please don't breath a word of this visit, including how you got here, to anybody. Not even your *shifu.*"

It was not a request Guo Jing was anticipating. In fact, he had been thinking how he might bring Count Seven Hong here for treatment. He was at a loss as to how to respond.

"And please don't trouble yourself with thoughts of coming this way to see me again. We'll be moving on quite soon."

"Where to?"

Sole Light gave an enigmatic smile.

Lotus understood the monk's silence. With the benefit of hindsight, she could almost sympathize with his disciples' desperation to thwart their endeavors to get here. This hermitage must have taken much planning to create and conceal. Now, because of her, the whole enterprise had gone up in smoke. They would have to abandon everything. Why on earth would they share their new location? Only now did she become conscious of the enormity of the kindness she had demanded of Sole Light and his followers. A debt she could never repay. Pangs of conscience weighed on her. Her eyes flitted to the four disciples. Perhaps she should apologize . . .

Sole Light swayed, then slumped to the floor, face down.

The six of them rushed toward the monk, crowding over him, aching to help, but all they could do was watch the muscles on his face convulse, watch him mask the great pain that was tearing up his insides. Nobody knew what to say or do.

After the time it takes to finish a pot of tea, Sole Light regained some of his faculties and gave Lotus a weak smile.

"Child, did your father make these Dew of Nine Flowers himself?"

"No, they were made by my martial brother Zephyr Lu, following Papa's formula."

"Has your father ever said that it is harmful to take too many?"

She felt winded by the question. Could something be wrong with the pills?

"Papa's told me its benefits are more prominent in concentration, but, because they are so hard to make, he takes them sparingly."

Frowning, Sole Light pondered and shook his head. "I'd never presume to divine your father's thoughts. Could he have given your Brother Lu an erroneous prescription? Could there be any ill will between you and Brother Lu that may have caused him to mix in some impure pills?"

A chorus of gasps.

"*Shifu*, have you been poisoned?" the scholar asked.

"Remember, your uncle-in-faith is here." The monk tried to calm his disciple. "He can find an antidote to the deadliest venom."

The four men beset the young couple. The farmer roared in Lotus's face: "How could you poison the man who saved your life?"

Guo Jing felt conflicted. Was he going to have to fight the students of Lotus's deliverer?

Lotus was too intent on determining what had happened to take much heed of the agitated men. She cast her mind back to every interaction related to the Dew of Nine Flowers since she was first given them at Roaming Cloud Manor. In the intervening months, not only had she taken the pills, so had Guo Jing and Count Seven Hong. The last time was . . . at Madam Ying's! The woman took the whole bottle to the next room, out of their sight . . .

"Uncle, it was Madam Ying!"

"Her?"

Lotus gave an account of that particular exchange. "She said they were bad for my injury and I shouldn't take them anymore. It must have been because she had already put in the poisoned pills."

"She was kind to you." The farmer could not hold off the snide remark.

For once, Lotus was not in the mood to engage in a battle of tongues. The news that she had been the conduit of Madam Ying's vile scheme was almost too much to bear.

"She wasn't kind to me. She was using me to get to Uncle. If I were poisoned, her plot would have unraveled."

"Sins of the past . . ." Sole Light muttered to himself. Soon serenity returned to his face and his voice grew in strength. "It is my fate to suffer. It has nothing to do with the two of you. This is between Madam Ying and me. Karmic retribution, bringing closure to entanglements of old. Now, be good, look after yourselves. Rest here for a few days, then leave this mountain and get on with your lives. I might well have been poisoned, but my brother-in-faith will find an antidote. There's no need to worry."

Guo Jing and Lotus took their leave, bowing on their knees once more. Sole Light waved away their gestures of obeisance and closed his eyes, turning his focus inward.

THE YOUNG couple edged out of the room, trying to create as little disturbance for the monk as they could. They found the novice waiting at the doorway and followed him to a small guest room furnished with two bamboo daybeds and a small table.

When they were settled, two elderly monks came in with a rustic vegetarian meal. "Please enjoy," they said in unison, their voices unusually high pitched.

"Is the Reverend better now?" Lotus asked.

"I regret that we are not privy to such information," one of them replied.

When they had left the room, Guo Jing said, "Judging from their voices, I'd think they're women."

"They must be eunuchs who once served King Duan in his palace. Like the rice merchant Old Yang at Peach Spring."

Weighed down by the day's events, they could find no appetite, so they sat in silence. The only sound in the temple was the occasional rustling of bamboo leaves stirred up by the breeze.

"Uncle Sole Light's kung fu is really remarkable," Guo Jing said eventually. "I don't think anyone we know could best him. Not *Shifu*, or your papa, or Brother Zhou. Not even Viper Ouyang or Qiu Qianren."

"So you think he's the greatest of them all?"

"Hmm . . . I can't tell. They each have a powerful signature kung fu, but none of them can get the better of the others' supreme moves."

"Then who has the most rounded comprehension overall?"

"Your papa, of course."

A smile bloomed on Lotus's face, but it soon withered away. "I don't get it."

"What?"

"Think about this. Uncle Sole Light is nigh on unbeatable. His disciples are no joke either. Why do they hide up this mountain? Why do they blanch at the mere mention of visitors? Of the greatest Masters in the world, Viper Ouyang and Qiu Qianren might be his enemies, but I doubt those two would work together to defeat him."

"Even if they do come at the same time, we don't have anything to fear from them."

"Really?"

Guo Jing felt his face burning up.

"Oi, what's going on? Why are you acting shy all of a sudden?" Lotus said, laughing.

He collected himself and explained. "Uncle Sole Light's martial prowess is equal to Viper Ouyang's. At worst, they would draw in a fight. Uncle has this backhanded way to lock pressure points . . . it looks to me like it could neutralize Exploding Toad kung fu."

"What about Qiu Qianren? The scholar and his fellows are no match for him."

"True. I could probably hold him back for fifty moves, but, by a hundred, I'd struggle too. Anyway, Uncle Sole Light's method of tapping your pressure points—"

"You've learned it? You can beat Qiu's rusty Iron Palm now?"

"You know how slow I am—I can't remember a move after seeing it once. Besides, Uncle hasn't agreed to teach me. It would be wrong to try to grasp it without his permission. What I'm trying to say is, observing Uncle Sole Light makes some of the passages in the Nine Yin Manual seem more comprehensible. I still won't be able to come out on top against Qiu Qianren, but I'll be able to hold out a bit longer. And you can join in to give that old fossil a good drubbing."

"You've forgotten one thing."

"What?"

"Uncle's been poisoned. We don't know when he'll get better."

That silenced Guo Jing for a good while. "Madam Ying is so unforgiving . . . Oh, noooo!"

Lotus's heart skipped a beat. "What?"

"You promised to live with her for a year. Are you going to keep your word?"

"What do *you* think?"

"If she didn't point us this way, we'd never have found Uncle Sole Light, and you might not—"

"Might not? Just say it as it is: I'd be dead! Unquestionably so. And since you're a great man and your *word* is as steady as a mountain, I dare say *you* want me to keep the promise." She turned away, recalling how Guo Jing had refused to renounce his betrothal to Khojin—even though he had no desire to marry the Mongolian Princess—just because he had given his word.

Guo Jing was hopeless when it came to matters of the heart, especially the intricacies of a girl's emotions. He was blind to the subtle shifts in Lotus's mood, and had not grasped that the conversation had moved on. "I don't understand why she wanted you to stay for a year. You could spend all that time teaching her, but she'd barely scratch the surface of your father's knowledge. Why bother?"

Lotus, by now, was cradling her head in her arms. Receiving no answer, the oblivious Guo Jing asked again.

"You know nothing! Blockhead!"

"I asked because I am a blockhead."

His pleading tone made Lotus rue her harsh words. She buried her face in his chest, fighting back tears.

Thoroughly confounded, he patted her lightly on the back.

"I'm sorry. It's my fault. I won't call you that again." She dried her eyes on his sleeve as a hint of a smile returned.

"I am a blockhead. I know it."

"You're a good soul. Kind. I'm neither." She sighed. "Madam Ying, well, it's obvious there's bad blood between her and Papa. She said so herself—she wanted to go to Peach Blossom Island to seek redress. Now she's seen with her own eyes that her reckoning skills are inferior to mine, and her kung fu weaker than yours, she must know she'll never get vengeance in the way she's been dreaming of. What she's going to do now is to hold me hostage to draw Papa out when he comes to my rescue. That way, she's in control, she can choose the ground and set a trap to snare him."

"Ahhh!" Guo Jing slapped his thigh. "You can't keep this promise."

"No, I have to."

"Huh?"

"Think about it. She planted the poison for Uncle Sole Light in the Dew of Nine Flowers. How many steps ahead does she have planned out? That's how calculating she is. As long as she lives, she'll be a threat to Papa. She wants my company. She'll get my company. She can scheme all she likes, but she'll never outsmart me."

Madam Ying doesn't know what she's got herself into! Guo Jing stopped himself from saying the thought out loud in case Lotus took it amiss.

"But it'd be like living with a tiger!" he protested.

They were interrupted by the sound of loud voices, coming from the direction of Sole Light's meditation room.

Exchanging glances, Guo Jing and Lotus tried to make out what had caused the commotion, but no further sound was forthcoming.

"I wonder how Uncle Sole Light is feeling," he said.

Lotus shook her head.

"Go on, have a bite to eat, then lie down and rest."

She repeated the gesture, then whispered, "Someone's coming."

Footsteps. Crossing the courtyard. Heading their way?

"The wench is full of tricks. Kill her first." It sounded like the farmer.

Guo Jing and Lotus had not expected so much vitriol from the monk's disciples.

"Don't be so hasty. Let's find out more." That was the logger.

"What more is there to find out? They're sent by *Shifu*'s enemies. We'll kill one and keep the other alive. If you have questions, ask that simple-minded fellow."

The fisher, the logger, the farmer and the scholar were now outside their room, blocking the doorway. They were making no effort to conceal their presence.

Guo Jing launched a Haughty Dragon Repents against the back wall, which crumbled outward with a thunderous thud. He then lifted Lotus on his back and made to hop over the rubble. Just as he leaped up, Lotus sensed someone grabbing at their legs from the left. There was little Guo Jing could do to protect himself midair, so she flicked her wrist in an Orchid Touch, her fingers glancing the Yang Pool pressure point on the back of the attacker's hand.

The farmer jerked away into a defensive block, startled by the breezy precision and lightning speed of Lotus's counterattack, though she lacked the internal strength to do him any real harm.

Her intervention allowed Guo Jing to hurdle the rubble, but moments later he was howling in frustration. An insurmountable barricade of thorns lined the perimeter wall. He turned to face his pursuers.

"Your honorable teacher gave us permission to leave, which you heard with your own ears. Why are you defying his wishes?" he asked Sole Light's four students, who had spread out in a line, cutting off any escape.

"Our *shifu* gave his life to save hers, and yet, you—"

Lotus interrupted the fisher. "What do you mean he gave his life?"

The ill-tempered man spat on the ground, refusing to dignify her with an answer.

"Can you truly be ignorant of the fact that our *shifu* exchanged his life for yours?" the scholar asked, incredulous.

"No! How?" Lotus exclaimed. "Tell us. Please!"

The scholar hestitated. The shock on their young faces seemed genuine. He cast a fleeting glance at the logger, who inclined his head to indicate that he was of the same opinion.

"Miss, your internal injury was healed by Yang in Ascendance imbued with Cosmos *neigong*," the scholar explained. "The damage was so acute that only the combination of those two kung fus could restore the flow of your *qi* and pull you back from the brink of death.

"Since the passing of Immortal Double Sun of the Quanzhen Sect, our *shifu* is the only person in command of both arts. The process sucks dry the healer's primal life force, to the point that he loses all his martial ability for five years."

The monk's selflessness took Lotus's breath away.

"For the next five years, *Shifu* would have needed to train rigorously night and day. A small mistake would not just have cost him a lifetime's cultivation of kung fu; he would also have suffered a crippling disability. A more serious misstep would mean death. *Shifu* sacrificed the most cherished part of his life to revive yours. How could you be so ungrateful? How could you repay his altruism with malice?"

Lotus lowered herself from Guo Jing's back and kowtowed four times in the direction of Sole Light's rooms.

"Uncle Sole Light, I did not know I was demanding such a rich and precious gift from you." She spoke softly as tears trickled down her face.

Her earnest gesture eased the tension a little.

"Tell us honestly," the fisher demanded. "Did you know that your father sent you to entrap our *shifu*?"

"Why would Papa do that?" Lotus was reaching boiling point. "How dare you slander him! The Lord of Peach Blossom Island would never sully himself with such a dishonorable, underhanded trick!"

"Forgive my unjust words." The fisher cupped his hands, backing down in the face of her fury.

"If Papa heard how you besmirch his name, he'd make you pay, disciple of Reverend Sole Light or not . . ."

"Your father is known as the Heretic of the East. We thought that, with such a title, he would behave in a . . . manner becoming the Venom of the West." The fisher offered a wry smile. "It seems that we have made a false assumption."

"How could you think my papa is anything like that shriveled old snake! And what has that stinky toad done to you?"

"Let's talk inside," the scholar said. "We will tell you everything."

5

The scholar led Guo Jing and Lotus back to the chamber on the eastern side of the temple's front courtyard where they had first waited for an audience with King Duan. As everyone sat down, Lotus noticed the scholar and his brethren chose places close to the window or the doorway, cutting off all direct routes of escape. She sniggered at their precautions, but decided not to draw attention to them—for now.

"Have you heard of the Nine Yin Manual?" the scholar asked.

"Yes, that book has brought nothing but harm to this world." Her mother's untimely death came to Lotus's mind. If she had not expended all that energy trying to recall its contents, she would most likely have survived childbirth.

"Presumably you are familiar with the Contest of Mount Hua too? The leader of the Quanzhen Sect not only won the respect of the other Greats, he also gained custodianship of the Nine Yin Manual. One year after the Contest, Immortal Double Sun came to the Dali Kingdom with his martial brother—"

"Zhou Botong the Hoary Urchin?" Lotus interjected.

"You are well-informed about Masters of the *wulin* for one of your tender years."

"Spare me your compliments."

"Well, Martial Uncle Zhou is indeed a most jocular fellow. I didn't know that he also goes by such a whimsical title. At that time, *Shifu* had not yet taken the vow."

"So he was still the king?"

"Yes, he was still our sovereign then. The reason for Immortal Double Sun's visit was the Yang in Ascendance kung fu. He had admired the technique at the Contest and traveled all the way to our court to learn more. Over a fortnight, *Shifu* shared everything he knew about the pressure-point locking system, and the Immortal taught *Shifu* his signature skill, Cosmos *neigong*. We four were tasked with waiting on the Immortal and his brother during their stay at the palace, and were privy to their discussions, but, alas, we were too ignorant to be able to benefit much from this treasure trove of martial insight."

"What about the Old Urchin? Did he learn anything? His kung fu is very good."

"Lengthy discourse did not interest Uncle Zhou, so he roamed every corner of the palace to keep himself amused. He even visited the women's private quarters—where the Queen and the other consorts lived. The eunuchs and ladies-in-waiting dared not bar him, as he was the king's honored guest."

Guo Jing and Lotus exchanged a smile. They knew this irreverent streak all too well.

"Toward the end of the Immortal's stay, he said to our *shifu*: 'I fear I don't have long in this world—my old ailment has returned—but it heartens me that the secrets of Cosmos *neigong* are now in your capable hands. No man shall be tyrannized by Viper Ouyang and his black-hearted ways: with my learning allied with Your Majesty's Yang in Ascendance, you can keep him in line. This impoverished monk is most blessed to be granted access to the Dali Kingdom's cherished martial secret, and I vow never to share my knowledge of Yang in Ascendance with anyone else.'

"Only then did *Shifu* apprehend the Immortal's true intentions. It was the prospect of an unchecked Viper Ouyang that had driven him to travel thousands of *li* to Dali. If the Immortal had come merely to offer his knowledge, it could have been misconstrued as an affront, but the Greats were martial equals, and it was not unheard of for Masters of their stature to learn from each other and to exchange one supreme kung fu for another.

"The Immortal departed this world not long after his return home. We heard that he stayed true to his word and did not teach his disciples Yang in Ascendance. Apparently he didn't even practice it himself. *Shifu* worked hard to attain mastery of Cosmos *neigong* and fulfill the duty entrusted to him, but before long misfortune struck our Dali Kingdom and *Shifu* renounced the trappings of the mortal world for the tonsure."

Lotus wondered what could have been so traumatic as to make a man give up his kingship. Much as she wished to find out, she was aware that being inquisitive right now might be taken amiss. She shot Guo Jing a withering glare to stop him from commenting, knowing his simple soul would not grasp the sensitivity of the situation.

Sorrows from a bygone time gripped the scholar. "Somehow, news of *Shifu*'s knowledge of Cosmos *neigong* got out," he said eventually. "One day, my elder martial brother –" he gestured to the farmer— "was sent by *Shifu* to gather medicinal herbs from a snow-capped mountain on Yunnan's western frontier. There, in the wilderness, he was attacked with Exploding Toad kung fu."

"Viper Ouyang!" Lotus exclaimed.

"Who else!" the farmer roared. "A foppish youth appeared from nowhere and railed at me for stealing herbs from his home. How could a whole mountain range—thousands of acres of land—be his? He was spoiling for a fight, but I wouldn't be provoked, because *Shifu* has always bade us to let peace be our guide. He grew bolder in his provocations and demanded that I should grovel for my freedom with three hundred kowtows. His insults got under my skin. It was a protracted fight, for I wasn't skilled enough to overpower him. The Old Venom came out of nowhere and ambushed me. The next thing I knew, I was being carried down the mountain to the Celestial Dragon Temple, where *Shifu* was residing at the time."

"You'll be pleased to hear that this rake, Gallant Ouyang, met his fate," Lotus said.

"What? Who slew him?"

"Why? Are you troubled by his death?"

"I'd hoped to wreak vengeance with my own hands."

"That satisfaction will never be yours, I'm afraid . . ."

"Who killed him?"

"A good-for-nothing. His kung fu was pathetic, but he outwitted that coxcomb."

"A deed most just," the scholar remarked. "Do you know why Viper Ouyang injured my brother?"

"Isn't it obvious?" Lotus replied. "The Venom would not hesitate to take someone's life, there and then, but he chose not to, because, by keeping his victim alive, he could impair Uncle Sole Light's elemental *qi*. Since it would take five years to recuperate from the strains of the healing process, the King of the South would lag far behind at the next Contest of Mount Hua."

"That was not the half of Viper Ouyang's infernal scheme. He intended to come for *Shifu* right away, when he was at his weakest—"

Guo Jing spoke up. "I don't see how someone as peaceable as Uncle Sole Light could have done anything to provoke such enmity from Viper Ouyang."

"Well, it is in the nature of men cruel and evil to hate anyone who is their moral opposite, and such men need no animus before they do harm. For Viper Ouyang, the fact that his Exploding Toad was vulnerable to Yang in Ascendance combined with Cosmos *neigong* was reason enough for him to act against our *shifu*."

Guo Jing nodded in agreement with the scholar's explanation. "How did Uncle get away?"

"The moment *Shifu* set eyes on the injury, he divined Viper Ouyang's purpose," the scholar replied. "That night, after tending to my brother, we abandoned Celestial Dragon Temple. The Venom wasn't able to track us down, but we knew he would not give up. We searched far and wide for a secluded location where we could resettle, and eventually came upon this place.

"My brethren and I wanted to take the fight to the Venom at White Camel Mount after *Shifu*'s recovery, but he was adamant that he would never grant us leave, for he has always believed that heaping wrong upon wrong would bring no resolution. So, for a few years, we enjoyed peace and stability—until your arrival. We had assumed that, as you are the Divine Vagrant's disciples, you could not harbor ill will for our *shifu* . . . 'The man has no mind to hurt the tiger, but it is in the heart of tigers to prey on men.' If only we knew, we would have laid down our lives to stop you from setting foot in this temple." The scholar rose to his feet menacingly. "We would have done everything in our power to stop *Shifu* from succumbing to your dark plots." He drew his sword from its scabbard with a *sha!* The cold glisten of polished metal filled the room. His fellows, weapons in hand, had also assumed fighting stances, hemming the young couple in.

"I sincerely had no idea that it would cost your *shifu* five years of training to heal my injury." Lotus still hoped she could talk them down. "I also didn't know that the pills had been meddled with—it was not my doing. But one thing is clear in my heart: Uncle's gift of vital growth is as expansive as the heavens and as nourishing as the earth. Not even the most heartless, unscrupulous person could reward such bounty with bale."

"Then why do you lead his enemy here now?" the fisher demanded.

"We didn't!" Lotus and Guo Jing protested as one.

"You didn't? *Shifu* was poisoned. Then, a jade bracelet arrived. It can't be a coincidence."

"What bracelet?" Lotus asked.

"Stop playing the innocent!" Armed with two iron oars, the fisher swept one sideways at Guo Jing and jabbed the other at Lotus.

Guo Jing leaped into action. He twirled his right arm, pushing aside the oar aimed his way, while his left hand grabbed the blade of the one threatening Lotus and jerked it up and down. A blast of his inner force tore it from the fisher's grasp. He immediately spun the makeshift weapon around and knocked its loom into the farmer's metal rake.

Sparks flew as the two met with a reverberating clang.

Then, with a twist of his wrist, Guo Jing slammed the oar back into its owner's hand, as swiftly as he had snatched it away.

A moment passed before the dumbstruck fisher gathered the

wherewithal to tighten his grip. Gathering strength to his arms, he raised the oar to bludgeon Guo Jing into submission. At the same time, the logger swung his axe at the young man.

Guo Jing let fly with a palm thrust from each hand, whipping up a storm that lashed into the men's chests.

"Back!" The scholar recognized the might of the Dragon-Subduing Palm.

The fisher and the logger were no common brawlers, having been trained personally by one of the Five Greats. They halted their offensive and stepped back, unflustered. As they did so, a jolt went through their bodies. They felt themselves being drawn forward, through their weapons, by the power in Guo Jing's palms. Only two options were open to them now: let go, or let that frightful strength forever knock the breath of life out of their rib cages.

Once Guo Jing had gained control of the oar and the rake, he tossed them back gently. "Catch!"

"Exquisite!" Even as the scholar was praising Guo Jing's kung fu, his sword was darting, at an oblique angle, toward the young man's right flank. The least martial disciple of Reverend Sole Light in appearance was turning out to be the most accomplished fighter of them all.

Startled by this brisk, incisive attack, Guo Jing's palms danced faster to create a shield of protection around himself and Lotus. This invisible line of defense was powered solely by his internal force, and yet it was like a mountain range had descended between the young couple and the scholar—not even whetted steel could find a way through. With each thrust and twirl of the hand, Guo Jing enlarged his circle of protection, turning an unbreachable barricade into a swelling tidal wave, pushing the four men back toward the walls, giving them no breathing space to launch any meaningful counter.

Hard-pressed to avoid being struck themselves, none of the four men could break through. When they attacked head-on, Guo Jing parried. When they tried to steal in, Guo Jing thrust back. They could not gain the upper hand, even though Guo Jing was keeping the keen edge of his palm strength in check, careful not to use more force than necessary.

The scholar's sword quivered and the air around it hummed. Its point danced like summer lightning, six high strikes followed by six low. Then it lunged dead on, seeking out Guo Jing's torso six times, before whizzing to his back with the same wicked precision. Now it aimed six probes at his left flank, now it flitted to his right side in a mirror image of what had come before. Six successive stings of the sword, repeated from six directions, in the blink of an eye.

The Thirty-Six Swords of Mount Hhaqlol. The most aggressive sword-fighting sequence under the heavens.

Despite the sustained onslaught from the other three disciples, Guo Jing dedicated one hand to fending off the scholar's sword, tracking it as its tip flittered up and down and around his body, throwing it off target with the power pouring forth from his palm. The dazzling variations failed to cut through this invisible barrier, the sword's point slipping and glancing off its mark. It could not even snag itself on Guo Jing's clothes.

As the scholar thrust the sword for the thirty-sixth time, its point hissing over Guo Jing's right side, the young man curled his middle finger under his thumb and—*clank!*—a jet of inner force struck the foible of the sword.

A Divine Flick.

Apothecary Huang's fight against the Quanzhen monks at Ox Village had come to Guo Jing's mind and he had copied the Heretic's signature skill. The attempt lacked finesse, but it was enough to send a shock of energy up the hilt, numbing the scholar's arm and weakening his grip. The sword almost flew out of his hand.

"Stop!" he ordered as he leaped back.

The other three disciples backed down.

"I told you their hearts are pure, but you all doubted me," the logger said as he tucked his axe into his belt.

6

THE SCHOLAR PUT AWAY HIS SWORD AND BOWED, HOLDING his palm over his fist. "I am most grateful for your forbearance."

Guo Jing returned the polite gesture, though he was thoroughly confused. Why did it take a fight to prove they meant no harm?

Seeing that the scholar's reasoning had eluded Guo Jing, Lotus whispered in his ear, "If you had impure motives, you would have injured these four by now. Then there would be no more obstacles between you and Uncle Sole Light, who is in no state to defend himself." She now turned to the four men. "Who is Uncle's enemy? Why did they send this jade bracelet?"

"I wish I could give you an answer," the scholar replied. "We are also very much in the dark. The only thing we know for sure is that it's related to *Shifu's* decision to renounce the secular world."

Just as Lotus parted her lips to ask another question, the farmer glared at the scholar and said, "How could you take such a risk?"

"What do you mean?" the fisher said.

The farmer pointed at the scholar. "He let them know that *Shifu's* elemental life force was drained. If they really did harbor dark thoughts and we four couldn't hold them back, then *Shifu*..."

The logger laughed. "If our dear Chancellor Zhu did not consider such things, would he have been offered the most prominent official post in the Dali Kingdom? He has long recognized that our guests are friends not foes. The scuffle just now was staged to gauge their kung fu training and to convince you."

The scholar smiled at his martial brother's outraged expression—a look of frustration mixed with admiration.

The novice appeared at the doorway and touched his palms together in a Buddhist greeting. "Brothers, *Shifu* asks that you see our guests off on his behalf."

The four disciples stood to attention the instant they heard the word "*shifu*."

"We can't leave when Uncle's enemy is on their way," Guo Jing said. "I wish to help you fight them."

The martial brothers were heartened by the offer.

"Let me ask *Shifu*," the scholar said.

When he eventually returned, Lotus could tell from his expression that Reverend Sole Light did not want his guests to become embroiled in the matter.

"*Shifu* asks me to convey his thanks," the scholar said, the disappointment in his voice clear. "He says no other soul can take our place when it comes to making peace with our karma."

Nodding at the scholar's words, Lotus said to Guo Jing, "We'll speak to Uncle directly." He supported her on the walk to Sole Light's rooms, but the doors were shut. He knocked several times. Not a sound came from within.

These two flimsy wooden boards would give in to the lightest shove, but who would dare use force to enter the Reverend's chamber?

"It looks like *Shifu* will not be receiving guests," the logger said. "Water runs far in mountains tall, our paths shall cross again."

"Lotus, let's fight anyone we run into on our way down." Guo Jing was fired up by the thought of the sacrifice Sole Light had made to save Lotus. "Whoever we find climbing this mountain must be Uncle's enemy. I don't care if he forbids us to stop them, it's the least we can do."

"Great idea!" Lotus replied loudly, to ensure the monk could hear her through the doors. "They may be every bit as terrifying as Viper Ouyang, but we can tire them out. If we die trying, we'll die reciprocating Uncle's great gift." She began to walk away, pulling Guo Jing along behind her.

The doors parted with a creak and the squeaky voice of an elderly monk came from within: "Please enter."

Sole Light was sitting on the same prayer mat as when Guo Jing and Lotus had first set foot in the room, as was his brother-in-faith from Sindhu. Drawn, with pale waxy skin, the monk looked like a different person—gone was the glow of health and strength.

The young couple prostrated themselves, too choked with emotion to form words.

"Come in, I want to speak with you all," Sole Light said to his disciples, who were loitering outside.

The four men paid their respects to their elders upon entering. The monk from Sindhu nodded in acknowledgment, then lowered his head in contemplation. Sole Light seemed to take little notice of his students. He looked blankly at the wisp of incense coiling up from the censer as he turned a jade bracelet round and round in his hands.

A woman's bracelet in mutton-fat white jade from Khotan? Lotus noted. How intriguing . . . What is its story?

At length, the monk heaved a sigh and turned to the young couple. "I am most touched by your kind offer of help. And now I realize that, if I withhold the full account from you, someone might be wounded as a result of my reticence, and that is not my wish at all. Do you know who I was before I became a monk?"

"The King of Dali, in Yunnan," Lotus replied. "Your name is known far and wide as the ruler of this southern realm."

"Kingship is but an illusion. This monk is but an illusion. Names, of course, are an illusion. Even you are an illusion."

Lotus's eyes widened at this cryptic statement. She could not grasp his meaning at all.

"The Kingdom of Dali was founded in the year Nine Hundred and Thirty-Seven, twenty-three summers before the Song Empire was established. Our seventh king, Bingyi, abdicated after a four-year reign to become a monk. His nephew, King Shengde, inherited the throne, and he, together with four of the kings who came after him, including my father, King Zhengkang, all gave up their secular lives for a monastic existence. I was the eighteenth monarch of our kingdom, and the seventh to be tonsured."

The four disciples were familiar with this story, but, to Lotus and Guo Jing, it was most curious. Reverend Sole Light's decision was odd enough in isolation. Why had so many of his regal ancestors given up their power? Could a monk's life be so much better than that of a king?

"We of the family Duan are minor rulers of far-flung borderlands, yet we have taken an disproportionately prominent place in the world," the monk continued. "Down through the generations, each ruler has been acutely aware of his inadequacy to take on this significant role, and we have all been cautious and careful—we were most apprehensive of succumbing to lofty ambitions and overreaching ourselves.

"Yet, as kings, we are fed without having to toil, clothed without having to work. We travel by horses and carriages, we sleep in grand palaces. Our whole existence is built upon the blood and sweat of our people. Many of us, in our dotage, grow repentant. We look back and see that our actions have done our people more harm than good. As such, many of my forebears gave up their power to embrace a spiritual life . . ."

Sole Light trailed off and turned his gaze to the window, a faltering smile on his lips, sorrow furrowing his brow. No one dared make a sound. The bracelet once more had his attention. He slipped it over his index finger and spun it around.

"But I became a monk for a different reason. If we are to trace back its origin, we will have to return to the summit of Mount Hua, to the fight for the Nine Yin Manual. The leader of the Quanzhen Sect, Wang Chongyang the Double Sun Immortal, took the honors and was named the Manual's custodian.

"The following year, he came to Dali to share with me his most famed technique: Cosmos *neigong*. For a fortnight, he stayed in my palace and we spent the days sparring and discussing the martial arts. Little did we suspect that his martial brother Zhou Botong, bored out of his wits, had taken to wandering every corner of my palace seeking diversion. It was during these explorations that he planted

the seed that has grown into the situation we find ourselves confronted with today."

Lotus tittered quietly to herself. It would have been most irregular if the Hoary Urchin had not managed to find a way to get himself into trouble.

CHAPTER THREE

THE HANDKERCHIEF
OF LOVEBIRDS

I

SOLE LIGHT SIGHED IN SELF-REPROACH. "STILL, THE ROOT of the problem lies with me. I was a minor king of a small fiefdom, and, like all overlords, I had my share of consorts and beauties in my private palace, though mine was by no means on as grand a scale as the Song Emperor's . . .

"Such a sin of mine, that was. My fascination with martial pursuits meant that I was rarely in the company of women. Days would often pass by without my setting eyes on the Queen. As for the rest of the consorts, I was rarely intimate with any of them." The monk looked up at his disciples. "I have kept this from you all these years, but you shall learn the whole truth today."

So they are as ignorant as we are, Lotus said to herself.

"My consorts often watched me working on my kung fu. Some found it riveting and entreated me to teach them. Sometimes, I obliged, since martial-arts training is beneficial to one's health. There was one, Consort Liu, who was particularly gifted. Though she was tender in years, she was focused, practicing all day, and showed vast improvement in very little time.

"It was all fated to come to this. On one of his explorations, Brother Zhou chanced upon her training in the garden. Now, Brother Zhou lived and breathed the martial arts. And, given his childlike naivete, it did not occur to him to maintain the proper distance between a man and a woman. He approached her and asked to spar with her. As you know, Brother Zhou was taught by Immortal Double Sun himself. A beginner like her did not stand a chance—"

"Oh dear, did he hurt her?" Lotus interjected.

"No, he didn't, but he locked her acupoints after a couple of moves and demanded to know whether she accepted her subjugation. Of course, she yielded. How could a newcomer to the martial arts not be enthralled by Brother Zhou's prowess?

"In the flush of his triumph, Brother Zhou unbound her and chattered away about the mysteries of pressure-point locking—the very skill she had been beseeching me to share with her. It goes without saying that I had refused. What might happen if I taught such an advanced method of control to the ladies in my private palace? So she seized her chance and bowed to Brother Zhou, hoping he would grant her that knowledge."

Lotus giggled. "It would tickle the Old Urchin to be so honored."

"You know Brother Zhou?"

"We're old friends. He lived on Peach Blossom Island for more than a decade—and he didn't leave once."

"What would make someone of his temperament remain in one place for so long?"

"He was locked up by Papa, but he's free now."

"I see." Sole Light nodded. "How is his health?"

"Oh, he's in rude health, but he does get more and more unhinged with age." She chuckled into her hand, then pointed at Guo Jing. "The Hoary Urchin swore brotherhood with him."

The idea of this outlandish fraternity brought a smile to the monk's somber face. "The teaching of pressure-point locking has always been guided by one unspoken rule, as ancient as the art itself. It should never be passed between a man and a woman, unless it is from father to daughter, from mother to son or from husband to wife. To share the knowledge with those of the opposite sex without blood or familial ties is a great taboo—"

"Why?" Lotus cut him off.

"I am sure you are familiar with Mencius's wise words: 'A man and a woman should not touch when giving or receiving gifts.' To learn this art, you have to touch every single pressure point on the other person's body with your hands—"

"Didn't you do just that with me?"

Irritated by her frivolous interruptions, the fisher and the farmer shot her a hostile look.

"What? Can't I ask a question?" she glowered.

"Pay them no heed. It was different—you were grievously injured."

"If you say so. What happened next?"

"So, Brother Zhou started to teach her in earnest. He was in his hot-blooded prime and she was in the full bloom of youth. Physical interactions grew into emotional connections . . . and it reached a point of no return . . ."

Lotus parted her lips, but bit her tongue in time.

"I was informed of their . . . I was outraged, but I hid it, I pretended I knew nothing. I couldn't allow Immortal Wang to lose face like that. But, soon, the Immortal became aware of it too. I guess Brother Zhou was a frank and honest soul and wasn't used to concealing—"

"What do you mean 'it reached a point of no return'?" Lotus could not hold back her question any longer.

Suddenly coy, Sole Light considered how he could word it within the bounds of decency. "They were not man and wife, but they committed the deed of a man and his wife."

"They gave birth to a baby?"

"They simply spent a fortnight together, it takes many months to reach childbirth." The monk skirted away from the awkward subject and resumed his tale. "Immortal Wang tied up Brother Zhou and brought him to me, to be dealt with as I saw fit. Now, for us martial men, the one thing we value the most is the upholding of righteous loyalty toward our kinfolk in the *wulin*. How could I let my petty personal attachment to a woman come between the friendship I shared with Immortal Wang?

"So, I untied Brother Zhou, summoned her and gave my blessing to their union. But he started to yell and bawl, claiming he did not know that what he had done was wrong. He now realized the deed was unworthy, and that I could have him beheaded, but nothing could induce him to take her as his wife.

"Immortal Wang was incensed. He said he would have cut Brother Zhou's throat the instant he discovered his shameful, immoral act, but for the knowledge that his brother could indeed be so ingenuous, so unworldly, so sincerely oblivious to the meaning and consequence of his actions."

Lotus stuck out her tongue. "What a close shave."

"I had never been so affronted. I was livid. I said to Brother Zhou, 'I am gifting you what I hold dear, willingly and with no ulterior motive. You know the time-honored saying, "Like limbs are brothers, like garbs are helpmeets." This is simply a matter with a woman, it is of no import.'"

"Fie! Fie! Uncle, how could you treat her like that? Your words are utter, utter hogwash!"

"Enough!" the farmer roared.

"Why can't I argue back when he's wrong?"

The four men stared at Lotus, stupefied. They had always venerated their teacher and liege with every fiber of their being. To take issue with him was simply unimaginable. The girl's flippancy was beyond the pale.

But her rebuke did not bother the monk. He continued his story: "Brother Zhou would simply shake his head at whatever I had to say, and that angered me further. 'If you love her, why do you reject her? If you don't love her, then why did you . . . ? Our Dali Kingdom might be inconsequential, but we will not be so insulted by outsiders under our roof.'

"My words sent Brother Zhou into a stupor. He stared at me, then fell to his knees and knocked his head against the floor. 'King Duan, it is my fault. Strike me dead. I deserve it. I won't raise a hand to defend myself. I won't dodge the blow. Just kill me now!'

"I was shaken by his reaction and asked him, 'Why would I kill you?' And he just said, 'Then I'll take my leave.' He took out a silk handkerchief from the inside pocket of his shirt and turned to her. 'Yours.' He extended his arm. She pulled a feeble smile, but made no move to take it. He let go. The handkerchief drifted down, landing by my foot.

"After that, Brother Zhou slapped himself across the face, over and over, so hard that his cheeks were bloodied. He kowtowed to me once more and then he was gone. That was the last I saw of him. Immortal Wang apologized and begged my forgiveness and left my court the same day. Not long after that, I received news of his departure from this world. The Immortal was unparalleled among men, a true hero, noble and benevolent . . ."

"Immortal Wang's kung fu might have been stronger than yours, but I doubt he was more noble or benevolent. His seven disciples are very average—utterly awful, in fact. They're nothing compared with your four students."

"The Seven Immortals of Quanzhen are known and admired by everyone under the heavens."

Lotus pursed her lips. "That's just plain wrong! Your protégés are more than a match for them—both as men and martial artists . . . Now, what happened to the handkerchief?"

Her praise cheered the four disciples, but they groaned inwardly at her girlish fixation on such trifles.

"I could not bear the sight that I was left with. She stood paralyzed before me. An empty shell, deserted by her soul and her spirit. It made me furious, so I picked up the handkerchief. A pair of mandarin ducks frolicking in water. Lovebirds. Embroidered by her. A token of her love for him. Scorn rose in me when I saw the lyrical poem sewn—"

Lotus supplied the words:

> "*For the fourth time the loom is ready,*
> *To weave a pair of lovebirds so they can take flight.*"

"Stop!" The farmer again. "Enough of your insolence!"

"You know it too?" Sole Light's question sent a jolt through his disciples.

"It's finally come to me!" Guo Jing straightened up in excitement. "I knew I'd heard this poem before, when we were at Madam Ying's but I couldn't place it. It was on Peach Blossom Island! Big Brother Zhou was bitten by a snake and the venom made him delirious. He kept rambling on about looms . . . and weaving birds . . . and graying hair! What are the rest of the words? Lotus, can you remember?"

She recited the verse in full:

> "*For the fourth time the loom is ready,*
> *To weave a pair of lovebirds so they can take flight.*
> *Pity the hair that grows gray before its time!*
> *The ripples of spring among green grass,*
> *The chill of dawn lurking in the deep,*
> *In each other scarlet feather bathe.*"

"That's the one!" Guo Jing struck himself on the thigh. "Big Brother kept saying that it's dangerous to clap eyes on beautiful women, because one look is enough to make you do bad things, and worst of all is that you do it without realizing that it's bad, so you end up offending good friends and angering martial brothers. He also said I must never let any woman touch my pressure points, or else awful, awful things will happen. He told me to stay away even from you."

"Pah!" Lotus pretended to spit. "I'll give that mooncalf a good twist of the ear the next time I see him." She collapsed into laughter. "Now I see why he got in such a sulk when I teased him about failing to find himself a wife."

Puzzlement clouded Guo Jing's face again. "Hang on. How come Madam Ying knows the poem?"

Lotus sighed, exasperated. "Because Madam Ying is Consort Liu."

2

"You certainly share your father's intelligence." Sole Light's expression was solemn. "Ying is her given name."

Among the four disciples, only the scholar had suspected there was connection between Consort Liu and Madam Ying, and he was only half convinced of his deduction. The other three stared at their *shifu*, open-mouthed.

"I tossed the handkerchief at her and never summoned her again. I wallowed in self-pity at being jilted, and ignored state affairs. Nothing but martial training could take my mind off—"

"You really loved her, Uncle," Lotus interjected. "You know that? Why else would you be so upset?"

"Miss!" the disciples cried in unison. How could she speak to her elder with such impudence?

"What? Am I wrong? Uncle, am I?"

The monk continued his story without commenting on Lotus's observation. "I did not send for her for almost a year. But I saw her often in my dreams. One night, her vision came again to haunt my sleep and I could no longer fight back the urge. I had to see her. I wanted to see what she had been doing. I went to her quarters in secret, hopping from roof to roof. Just when I landed on the ridge of the roof of her chamber, I heard it. The cry of a baby. I froze. I stood on the frost-coated tiles, utterly still, battered by a bitter cold wind. I didn't return to my rooms until daybreak, and shortly afterward I was struck down by a terrible sickness."

Lotus had heard many tales of kings and emperors, but not one in which the monarch set aside his regal pride to scale walls and traverse roofs in the middle of the night to see one of his consorts.

Sole Light's students remembered the illness well. Thanks to his martial stature, their *shifu* had long been immune to common colds and extreme weather. On the odd occasion that he was indisposed, his recovery was far speedier than that of the average person, thanks to his superior internal strength. Yet, this time, not only was he incapacitated, but the malady lingered for a long time. Now they finally knew why: he was heartbroken. He had let down all his defenses.

"Why were you sad? She gave you a child. That's a good thing, right?"

"My silly girl, it was not my child. It was Brother Zhou's."

"But he was long gone. Did he come back in secret?"

"No, he didn't. Have you not heard of the phrase 'ten moons with child'?"

"The little one must be the very image of the Hoary Urchin. Stuck-out ears. Snub nose. That's how you knew he wasn't yours."

"I didn't catch the newborn's face. And I didn't need to. I knew because it had been a very long time since I was last with her. The child couldn't have been mine."

Lotus still could not quite grasp the logic, but she had a feeling that to ask further questions might cause the monk embarrassment.

"It took me almost a year to recover from that illness. When I got better, I distracted myself with anything that could keep my mind from straying back to that night. Two years dragged by. One night, when I was meditating in my chamber, the drapes over the doorway were thrown aside. It was her. She had come to me. The eunuchs and sentries tried to stop her, but they were no match for her palm thrusts.

"The commotion drew me back to the present. I opened my eyes to see a child cradled in her arms, and sheer terror on her face. She knelt and kowtowed, wailing, sobbing, begging. 'Mercy, Great King! Mercy! Spare my child!'

"I got up to take a closer look at the toddler. His tiny face was flushed a feverish red, his little chest heaving and throbbing. I took him from her arms. I held him, my hands on his back. I could feel the fracture through his skin. Five ribs. Snapped.

"She pleaded with me: 'Your Majesty, I have sinned and I deserve to die, but please spare this child.' Her choice of words was curious—'spare'—so I asked, 'What has happened?' She just knocked her forehead on the floor, over and over again. I tried once more. 'Who hurt him?' She wouldn't answer, she simply cried, 'Mercy, Great King! Mercy!'

"I didn't know what to say or do. At length, she began to speak again between snivels and kowtows. 'Your Majesty . . . granted me death . . . no complaint . . . but the child . . . the child . . .' I was full of questions. 'Who granted you death? How did the boy—?'" For the first time, she looked me in the eyes and said in a trembling voice, 'Didn't Your Majesty send your guard to . . .'

"I realized at last that something sinister was afoot. 'My guard? Impossible! Who would dare?' She was overjoyed. 'If this wasn't your imperial decree, then my child is saved,' she cried. Moments later, she fainted.

"I carried her to my bed and placed the baby next to her. When she came to, a short while later, she took my hand and told me what had happened. She had been lulling the boy to sleep when a masked imperial guard jumped in through the window. He wrenched the child from her arms and aimed a slap at his back. She hurled herself at him, fighting tooth and nail, but he shoved her away and struck the child again, this time on the chest. Then he left, with a cackle. She'd assumed it was I who had sent him and came straight to my rooms to beg for the boy's life.

"I was bewildered by her account and examined the child again. I couldn't tell what kung fu had caused his injury, but I knew the attacker was no common thug. This infant had taken two powerful palm thrusts. He was still breathing, but his Belt Meridian was severed. Clearly, the masked man had wanted to hurt the boy without killing him outright. I went straight to her quarters to see if the assailant had left any trace. I found some very faint footprints on the roof tiles and the window frame.

"I told her what I could gather from them: 'The assassin was a Master, skilled in lightness kung fu. Not a soul in this Kingdom, besides myself, is at that same level.'

"Her face was ashen. 'Could it be him? Why would he want to hurt his own son?'"

"The Old Urchin wouldn't do that . . ." Lotus said.

"At the time, I believed he was behind this heinous act. Who else of his martial standing had reason to hurt this harmless baby? I assumed he didn't want his reputation tarnished by an illegitimate child. But, even as she uttered those words, she was full of shame and remorse. 'No! Never!' she shouted. 'It can't be him! That laugh. It wasn't his. It couldn't be him!' Struck by her conviction, I asked, 'How can you be sure? You're in shock.' She looked me in the eye and said, 'I will never forget that laugh. Even when I'm nothing but a ghost, I will remember it.'"

A shiver down ran everyone's spine. Lotus and Guo Jing's encounter with Madam Ying was just a couple of days old and her voice was still fresh in their minds. They could almost hear her spitting those words out through gritted teeth.

"She sounded so unshakeable in her conviction that I had no choice but to believe her, though I had no notion of who else it could be. For a time, I did toy with the idea that it might be one of Immortal Wang's disciples—Ma Yu, Qiu Chuji or Wang Chuyi. Perhaps they could have traveled thousands of miles to eliminate a toddler to preserve the Quanzhen Sect's . . ." Sole Light trailed off, catching Guo Jing's moving lips and his hesitation over whether to interrupt. "Go on, speak, I won't take offense."

"Elder Ma, Elder Qiu and Elder Wang are heroes who follow the moral code of *xia*. They would never do such a wicked thing."

"I met Wang Chuyi on Mount Hua. He seemed to be of sound character, but I don't know the others. But one thing has always puzzled me. Let's say it was indeed one of the Quanzhen Immortals.

They could have easily dispatched the child with one blow. Why leave him half dead?"

Sole Light gazed out of the window, loss and self-doubt darkening his face. This mystery had haunted him for more than a decade. After a short interval, he said, "Right, I should continue—"

"It can only be Viper Ouyang," Lotus declared.

"That occurred to me too, but she insisted that killer was shorter than the average man. And the Venom, like his fellows in the Western Regions, is well-built. He's at least a head taller than our men."

"Really? Hmmm . . ." Lotus was baffled.

"I couldn't think of anyone who had cause back then, and I still can't today . . . Her tears streamed down her face as she hugged the child. He wasn't as badly injured as you, but he was so young. He had nothing inside his little body that could help him bear such a blow. To heal him would cost all my primal strength. I was torn. Her anguish was so infectious that I was almost moved to grant her her wish, but, each time I was about to reach out for the boy, my mind strayed to the second Contest of Mount Hua. To the cold, heartless fact that, by saving his life, I would be forfeiting all hopes of becoming the Greatest Martial Master Under the Heavens, depriving these fingers of a chance to turn the pages of the Nine Yin Manual."

A profound sigh. "Immortal Wang said that the Manual was the greatest source of evil in the *wulin*. It is incontestably true—the slaughter it has caused, the lives it has destroyed. In the hope of possessing its secrets, I have abandoned compassion, charity, love. I dithered for almost two hours before I made up my mind to revive the boy. In those hours, I was not human. I was baser than fowl or beast. And the worst part is that I came to the decision to help because I could not withstand her pleading any longer. It was not because I'd had an epiphany that it was the right thing to do, something that any human with a heart would have done."

"See? I was right when I said you loved her very much, Uncle," Lotus said.

But Sole Light did not seem to hear her. "When she heard that I would help, she passed out from joy. I brought her round then untied the child's night clothes, so I could massage him using Cosmos *neigong*. I peeled open his little shirt and the sight of his undergarments stopped me in my tracks. I couldn't move, I couldn't say a word.

"Two mandarin ducks frolicking in water. The poem about weaving lovebirds. The handkerchief she gave Brother Zhou as a token of their love. She had fashioned it into a vest to keep their love child warm. She could see the change in my countenance. Her already bloodless cheeks turned whiter still. She pulled a dagger from her belt and pressed it to her chest. 'Your Majesty, I have done you wrong and I am ashamed to face this world any longer, but allow me to appeal to your magnanimity. Let me give my life in exchange for my child's. This lowly woman shall return in the next life as your dog or your horse, so I can serve you with one heart to requite your grace and benevolence.' With those words, she plunged the blade into her heart."

The knowledge that she had survived this could not prevent a sharp intake of breath from the listeners.

Sole Light continued, scarcely registering their reaction. He was now recounting the events for himself. Everyone else may as well have ceased to exist. "I plucked the dagger from her grasp. I was quick, but its point had already pierced the skin. Blood soaked her robes. I locked her pressure points in case she tried to take her life again, took care of the wound and carried her to a chair. She looked at me, her mouth clamped shut. Just her eyes. Fixed on me. Beseeching. No words. No one spoke. Only one sound remained . . . the child's wheezing.

"The past—our past—assaulted me through his labored panting. The days when she first came to the palace. When I taught her kung fu. Lavished her with attention . . . She waited on me. Always gentle, always eager to please, but she did it with respect, with trepidation. She had refused me nothing, but she had also never loved me. Not with her heart. Not with her soul.

"But I had not known that . . . Not until I saw how she looked at

Brother Zhou. Then I understood. Those eyes were drinking in everything about a man she loved with every fiber of her being. That was what love looked like.

"Her eyes took in, without blinking, how Brother Zhou let go of the handkerchief. Her eyes took in, without blinking, how he turned his back on her and walked away, out of the palace, out of her life.

"It was those eyes, that look, that had made my sleep fitful, my food tasteless. And now I was confronted with that look in those eyes once more. And now, for the second time, I was witnessing, through her eyes, the breaking of her heart. For another. Not her lover, this time, but his son. The son she'd had with him!

"Oh, for a man to be so begrimed, for a king to be so abused! The fire of hideous rage, the flame of grotesque wrath burned in me. I lifted my foot and brought it down on an ivory stool, breaking it into pieces. Then I saw something that shocked me more than anything else that night. 'What . . . what happened to your hair?' She didn't hear me. She only had eyes for her child.

"I had never known that one look could contain so much love, so much sorrow, so much longing. She knew I would never help his child. She knew each moment her eyes feasted on this little life while its chest still heaved, was a most precious moment for her, but it also brought her son a moment closer to death.

"I fetched a mirror and said to her, 'Look at your hair!' It had been mere hours since she had burst into my room with her babe, but in that short time she had aged by decades. She was just eighteen. Maybe nineteen. Yet, in those few hours of rage, distress and repentance, of hopes raised and dashed, of love, pity and heartsick, the onslaught of extreme emotions had turned her temples white!

"She cared not for the change in her looks, but she resented the mirror for blocking her view of her darling child. 'Take it away!' she barked. Forthright. Direct. She had forgotten that I was her king. Her lord and master.

"I was speechless. I knew how much care she took of her appearance. Why did it not matter to her now? I asked myself as I tossed away the mirror. I studied her. Her eyes never strayed from her child. I'd never seen such yearning. She was willing the boy to live. She was trying to inject her own life into his small body just by looking at him, to replace and to replenish the vitality that was seeping out of him."

Guo Jing caught Lotus's eye and knew the same thought was in her mind: That was how you looked at me when I was at death's door. They reached for each other's hand, holding tight. Their hearts throbbed, a warm tingle surged through their bodies. They had been blessed with such luck. They could sit next to the love of their life, no longer in danger, having made a full recovery. They would not have to watch the other die. They would never die. The love inside their hearts could never die.

"I reached out, again and again, intending to help the child, so I could chase that look from her face. But that handkerchief. Wrapped around his belly. Over his heaving chest . . . That pair of lovebirds. Mandarin ducks. Nuzzling. Leaning into each other. Mandarin ducks mate for life. Mandarin ducks have white plumes on their heads. Mandarin ducks are symbols of happy union, of fidelity, of growing old together. Why '*pity the hair that grows gray before its time*'?

"I saw the silver hair at her temples with new eyes. A cold sweat broke out, soaking through my robes. Spite numbed my heart. I said to her: 'Go on, you two. Grow old and grow gray together. Go on! Leave me here to play as king! Alone in the palace, without a soul! This is your spawn with him. Why should I waste my elemental strength to save it?'

"Her eyes flicked across my face. The last time I felt her gaze upon me. A look of hatred, of bile, of resentment, of abhorrence. I'll never forget how it seared my skin. I'll remember it until my day of reckoning. 'Unbind me. I want to hold my son.' Stern, cold, devoid of emotion. The voice you'd use for a subordinate. And there was something in her tone I could not refuse. I did as she commanded. I unlocked her pressure points.

"She scooped up the child and pressed him against her bosom. He was wracked by agonizing pain. He wanted to cry, but he couldn't make a sound. His little face had gone puffy and purple. His eyes were imploring, begging his mother to help him, to relieve him.

"My heart had turned to stone. There was not a drop of compassion left in my being. I watched her hair turn, strand by strand, from black to gray to white. I didn't know if I was hallucinating or if it was really happening before my eyes. She was cooing, trying to comfort him. 'My son, Mama isn't skilled enough to heal you. But Mama can stop the pain. Hush, my little love, hush . . . Sleep . . . Sleep . . . and never wake again . . .' She hummed a lullaby. She sang it so beautifully. It was such a lovely tune. Mmm . . . Yes, yes, that's it, that's how it goes. Hark!"

There was only silence in the room.

"*Shifu*, you've been talking for a long time. Rest now, please."

"A smile spread across the child's face." Sole Light carried on without heeding the scholar's words. "Then, his little body contorted. She murmured, 'My love, my heart, sleep. It'll stop hurting when you're asleep. Nothing will ever hurt you again . . .' Her words trailed off. She had driven the dagger into her son's heart."

Lotus yelped and grabbed Guo Jing by the arm. The faces of the four disciples were as white as a sheet.

The monk went on, oblivious to his audience. "I cried out and staggered back. I almost fell. In here –" he tapped his heart—"chaos. I watched her straighten up. Slowly. 'One day, I will plunge this dagger into your heart.' She spoke ever so quietly. Then she took a jade bracelet off her wrist. 'You gave me this the day I came to the palace. Wait for the day it makes its way back to you. That is when this dagger will find its mark. Wait for that day.'"

Sole Light twirled the bracelet over his finger. "This bracelet. I have waited for more than a decade. At last, it has returned."

"She killed her own son, Uncle. It's got nothing to do with you," Lotus said, in an attempt to console the monk. "It wasn't you who hurt the child in the first place. And she's already poisoned you.

Whatever blood debt existed has been crossed out. I'll go and send her on her way. I won't let her bother—"

She was interrupted by the novice, who had rushed in with a small parcel. "*Shifu*, this was sent from the foot of the mountain."

Sole Light opened the package to a chorus of mutterings.

The dead child's undergarments. The silk had yellowed with age, but the colored thread tracing the pair of mandarin ducks was still vibrant. A rent, caked with blackened blood, had torn the two lovebirds apart.

The monk stared at it for a long time.

"'*To weave a pair of lovebirds so they can take flight.*' To take flight! *Ai!* A dream, it was." At length, he resumed his tale. "She howled and howled, holding her lifeless child. Then she leaped out the window, jumped up onto the roof and disappeared into the night. For three days and three nights afterward, I could think of nothing else. I could not bear the thought of food or drink passing my lips. At last, I came to a resolution. I abdicated and passed the throne to my heir, my eldest son, so I could receive the tonsure." He pointed at the four disciples. "They had been by my side for many years and did not want to be parted from me. They too left court and followed me to the Celestial Dragon Temple outside the city of Dali.

"For the first three years, they took turns returning to court to assist my son. It did not take long for him to grow familiar with state affairs, and the country enjoyed peace. It was around that time we encountered Viper Ouyang. When they were searching for the Venom, Ziliu –" Sole Light pointed to the scholar—"discovered that Madam Ying was living as a recluse and practicing martial arts in a swamp near Peach Spring, in western Hunan.

"I was worried that she might hurt herself while training, and moved here from Dali so I could keep an eye on her. I arranged for trees to be planted, to fortify the woods surrounding her marshland, and provided her with food and supplies—"

"See, Uncle, I was right. You still love her. You don't want to be apart from her."

3

Sole Light drew in a breath and said, "These four were concerned about me and came with me to Hunan. We settled here and haven't been back to Dali since.

"For the sake of one marble-hearted moment, I have not found rest or peace for more than ten years. It was I who refused to save the child that night, and, since then, I have hoped to save others to atone for that sin. But my disciples have never understood. They keep trying to stop me. And, regardless of how many people I restore to health—a thousand, ten thousand—I can never bring back the child that I refused to help. I will not be absolved until I willingly give my life back to him.

"I have been waiting every day since for Madam Ying to come, for her to drive her dagger into my heart. My biggest fear was that I would die before her arrival, fated not to face my karmic retribution. Well, now, at last, she is on her way.

"There really was no need for her to tamper with the Dew of Nine Flowers. Had I known she would come so soon after I was poisoned, I wouldn't have imposed on my brother-in-faith and asked him to purge the toxins. I could have kept them at bay with my kung fu for a few hours until she arrived."

"This woman has a black heart!" Lotus was indignant. "She has long known your whereabouts and that you have been looking after her. The only thing stopping her from her vengeance is her mediocre kung fu, so she sits there, plotting and scheming, waiting for an opportunity—waiting for someone like me to direct here. It so happened that we stumbled across her after I was injured by Qiu Qianren. Since then, I've been her pawn and her weapon, first to weaken you, then to poison you. It makes my blood boil just to think about it! But, Uncle, you haven't explained how that drawing by Viper Ouyang ended up in her possession, and how it relates to everything you've told us."

Sole Light picked up the copy of *Sutralamkara Sastra* from the low table next to him and turned the leaves until he found the passage he was looking for.

"There was a king, whose name was Sivi," he read aloud. "And he followed the ascetic path and sought enlightenment perfect and supreme. It came to pass that he happened by chance upon a hawk chasing after a dove. And the dove hid itself under the arm of King Sivi, trembling and wounded.

"The hawk asked the king to return his prey unto him, saying, 'The king saveth the dove, the hawk dieth for hunger.' And King Sivi pondered the words of the hawk: To save one and hurt another is unrighteous. And he took a sharp knife and cut a piece of his own thigh for the hawk.

"The hawk said unto the king, 'The king's flesh should be the same as the dove by weight.' And King Sivi sent for a balance, and laid the dove on one scale and his flesh on the other.

"He trimmed all the flesh from his thighs, but the scale holding the dove was lower. He cut flesh from his chest, his back, his arm, his belly, but his offering still weighed less than the dove. And so the king stepped onto the scale.

"And the earth quaked and music sounded from the heavens. And celestial *apsaras* scattered petals and fragrance filled the roads. And *devas* and *yaksas* in the firmament sighed, crying, 'Rejoice! Rejoice! Such good courage has never before been seen.'"

The dignified and heartfelt reading moved all those present.

"She wanted to provoke you into saving me." Lotus had at last unraveled the final mystery.

"When she left Dali aggrieved, she must have roamed the *jianghu* seeking martial Masters who could train her so she could take revenge. I expect that was how she encountered Viper Ouyang. It is likely that the Venom helped her devise this plan and sketched the drawing for her. This scripture is well known in the lands of the Western Regions, so he would be familiar with the parable."

"So this is a sophisticated plot to hurt you . . . the Venom used Madam Ying and Madam Ying used me."

"Do not blame yourself. If you hadn't come across her, she would have hurt someone and sent them my way. It was just a matter of time. For the injured person to reach me, they would have to be accompanied by someone who is extremely skilled in the martial arts. As you rightly observed, this image was painted a long time ago, so this plan of the Venom's has been in motion for at least a decade. During all that time, she has not come across anyone who could help her claim her revenge—until now. It was destined to be so."

"It's because there was something else she cared about more than retribution."

"What could that be?"

"She wants to rescue the Hoary Urchin from Peach Blossom Island!" Lotus explained how Madam Ying had been trying to teach herself the art of reckoning and the principles of the Mysterious Gates. "Then she met me and realized she would never catch up with Papa, not in a hundred years. And since I happened to be injured—"

Sole Light laughed and got to his feet. "At last, everything has come together for her today." He turned to his disciples, adopting a stern expression. "Prepare to receive Consort Liu—no, Madam Ying—and guide her here. Treat her with the utmost courtesy."

"*Shifu!*" The four men fell to their knees, tears staining their faces.

"You've been with me for so many years. Can you still not understand what is in here?" The monk slapped his chest, then turned to Guo Jing and Lotus. "I hope I can ask one thing of you."

"Of course," they answered as one.

"Please descend this mountain now. The debt I owe Madam Ying is too great to be repaid in one lifetime. In future, if she encounters any difficulty or danger, I beg you to come to her aid on behalf of this aged monk. And if you could unite her with Brother Zhou, then I would be forever grateful."

Guo Jing and Lotus looked at each other, unsure how to respond.

"I hope I am not asking too great a favor."

After a moment of hesitation, Lotus said, "Your word is our command," and tugged Guo Jing's sleeve so he would join her in bowing low to take their leave.

"There is no need for you to see Madam Ying again. There is another way down on the other side of the mountain."

Acknowledging the monk's instructions, Lotus turned and headed out of the room, hand in hand with Guo Jing.

The four disciples threw curses at her back. How could she walk away, so calm and carefree, so callous and ungrateful, when danger was about to befall the man who had restored her life?

But Guo Jing knew Lotus would not stand by—she must already have devised a plan—so he followed her without a word. The moment they stepped outside the room, she whispered in his ear. He hesitated at the doorway, then nodded and turned around.

Seeing Guo Jing's approach, Sole Light repeated his request. "You are honest and loyal and you have a kind heart. You shall become a great man. I am counting on you in this matter concerning Madam Ying."

"I shall do everything I can to fulfill Uncle's command." While his pledge was still lingering in the air, Guo Jing's hand shot out to grab the Sindhu monk's wrist—the man had not moved from Sole Light's side all this time. A moment later, his finger landed first on the Florid Canopy pressure point on the monk's sternum, then on the Celestial Pillar at the back of his neck, locking the movement of his limbs.

"What are you doing?" Sole Light demanded. His students gaped, aghast, and scrambled to respond. None of them had envisaged this turn of events.

Guo Jing answered by reaching for the monk's shoulder, trapping him under the power of his palm thrust.

Sole Light flipped his hand and, brisk as lightning, had the young man's wrist in his grasp. A supreme counterattack. The crisp and precise reflex caught Guo Jing unawares, yet the contact also revealed the monk's depleted internal strength.

Guo Jing responded with a Reverse Grapple, twirling his palm around to lock onto a spot on the back of Sole Light's hand that would numb the whole arm, while he swung a Dragon Whips Tail to throw off the fisher and the logger, who were charging at him from behind.

"Forgive me, Uncle."

Guo Jing tapped twice on the monk's right flank, at the Essence Spur point under his armpit and the Phoenix Tail toward the base of his spine. Then he whipped up a storm of palm strikes to drive the fisher, the logger and the scholar out of the room. The air crackled with his *neigong*. The men tried to defend themselves, to hold their ground, but any contact with this force field numbed their arms and compelled their feet to shuffle in retreat.

"Stop! Please!" the scholar entreated, unable to fathom the boy's sudden aggression.

Lotus had also slipped back into the chamber and was chasing the farmer out with the Dog Beater. The big man charged like a maddened tiger, desperate to help his stricken Master. Thrice he pounced, and thrice he was pushed back.

Once all four of Sole Light's students had been forced to retreat to the courtyard outside, Lotus thrust the Dog-Beating Cane between the farmer's eyes. Swift, fierce, accurate.

"*Aiiiyaaaa!*" The man reeled backward and catapulted himself away from her.

"Nice move!" She spun round to pull the doors shut, then regarded the men with a smile. "Please, allow me to speak."

Guo Jing pulled back the palm thrust he was about to launch at the fisher and the logger. "Forgive us," he said, cupping his hands.

The four men gaped at each other.

"Please believe us that we mean no offense at all." Lotus spoke with humility. "We only wish to help. We could not possibly stand aside and do nothing when my savior is in peril."

The scholar stepped forward and bowed low. "Miss, we trust that you can find a way to keep our *shifu* safe. We could not defy his express command and prevent her arrival. Nor could we raise a hand against her, as she was our Master's consort and our Mistress. We are aware that he would have welcomed her knife without a murmur, even if he had his full martial strength, for he longs to be free from the torment caused by the . . . the child's death. But how could we live with ourselves if we stood by and let it happen? We would lay down our lives to do your bidding."

"We too are bound to Reverend Sole Light by a great debt of gratitude and will do everything in our power to avert the danger," Lotus replied, uncharacteristically solemn. "It would be best if we could keep Madam Ying from entering this temple, but I very much doubt that it will be possible. She has waited for more than ten years in her fetid swamp for this one chance—she must have planned for every eventuality and will not be easily dissuaded. There is one way we could resolve this situation once and for all, but it's a risky gamble since we are up against someone who is smart, cunning and determined. I wish there was another way."

"Please, tell us," they begged.

Lotus began to elaborate, her eyes alive with anticipation. Her audience exchanged glances, unsure what to think of her audacious plan.

4

THE SUN BEGAN ITS SLOW RETREAT. THE BREEZE STOLE IN with the night, swaying the rows of palm trees guarding the temple and rustling the wilted lotus leaves covering the pond. The half-light threw a craggy shadow across the temple, in the shape of a giant sleeping on the ground.

The four disciples sat cross-legged at the end of the broken stone bridge, peering into the gloaming, their hearts ill at ease. As twilight faded into gloom, a milky haze drifted up from the ravine. A murder of crows flew past, cawing, then dived into the murky darkness below.

No sign of anyone advancing toward their side of the bridge.

The four followers of Sole Light were each haunted by their own thoughts. The logger prayed that Consort Liu would realize at the last minute that his Master had not caused any of the misfortune she had suffered and would turn back in peace, whereas the fisher was certain that keeping them waiting was part of her infernal plot. The impetuous farmer just wished that she would appear that instant so this wretched business could be over—he cared little for the consequences for himself.

Foreboding clouded the scholar's mind. The longer it takes her to get here, the more treacherous our situation will be, he told himself. He had never felt this listless and helpless during his long years of service in the Dali court, where he had faced and overcome his share of crises.

A chill crept up his spine as the cry of a faraway owl sounded, just as the last trace of light was blotted from the sky. Is there really no way to resolve this amicably? he asked himself. Is it inevitable that *Shifu* will die at the hand of this woman?

"She's here!" The logger's whispered warning interrupted the scholar's thoughts.

A shadowy blur was speeding toward them, gliding over each gap on the bridge as if its body were immaterial. The improvement in her kung fu was frightening to behold.

The scholar and his fellows got to their feet and took up positions on each side of the bridge, ready to receive their Mistress.

Although she was robed head to toe in black, in stark contrast to the colorful finery of her imperial days, there was no mistaking it was her.

Consort Liu. King Duan's favorite from the palace.

The men fell to their knees, prostrated and chanted in unison, as though at court: "We bow to Your Highness."

"Your Highness? Consort Liu died a long time ago. I am Madam Ying." She surveyed the men kneeling to her left and right. "Here we meet again, Great Chancellor, Grand Marshal, Commander of the Navy and Captain of the Imperial Guard. I thought His Majesty received the tonsure because he had freed himself from the shackles of worldly affairs, yet in fact he has been holding court from this mountain hermitage all along."

The men shivered at the bile in her tone.

"His Majesty is much changed," the scholar ventured to reply. "Your Highness would not—"

"Your Highness, Your Highness..." Madam Ying scowled. "Enough of your derision! And enough of your kneeling too! I don't want your stiff respect for the dead."

The men glanced at one another and stood up, speaking in one voice in the palace tradition: "We wish madam peace."

Madam Ying waved their words away. "I know he has sent you here to block my path, so why bother with these courtesies? Go on. Show me your kung fu. I know how many lives you men—king and court—have ruined and destroyed. You don't need to put on an act for this common old crone."

"His Majesty loves the people as his own flesh and blood," the scholar said. "To this day, the people of Dali still praise his benevolent reign. His Majesty has also never been wanton with the lives of those under his rule, even those who have committed grievous crimes. He has often been lenient—"

"Enough!" Madam Ying's own trespass crept up on her like the blush darkening her cheeks.

The scholar lowered his head. "Pardon your humble servant."

"My servant?" she sneered. "I am here to see Duan Zhixing. Will you let me pass?"

Duan Zhixing. The sound of those three characters sent shock waves through the four former courtiers. They were aware, of course, that they represented the name given to their lord and liege, but, as they were his subjects, just to consider addressing him so directly would amount to an unforgiveable offense—to voice them out loud was unthinkable.

The farmer, who had once led the Imperial Guard, could no longer hold his temper in check. "Once a king, always a king! You cannot speak of him in such terms."

With a wicked screech of laughter, Madam Ying launched toward them at a run. The men repositioned themselves to block her path, their arms flung wide. They were confident they could hold her back. They would deal with the consequences of going against *Shifu's* orders later . . .

She charged headlong at their blockade, making no move to swing a fist or thrust a palm to scatter the men.

Fearing her body would slam into his, the logger skewed to the side and reached out to grab her shoulder. His fingers grazed her robes, slipping off the fabric as if he were trying to grasp a smooth flat surface.

The farmer and the fisher swooped in from either side, roaring and growling. She dived low and slid away from under the fisher's arm like a water snake.

A faint fragrance of orchid and musk wafted toward the fisher's nose and panic gripped his heart—it would break all rules of propriety if he brought his elbow down and trapped her in an embrace. He flung his arm higher, as far away from her body as he could.

But the farmer had no such qualms. He lunged, his hands opened wide—two clamps ready to close around her waist.

"Manners, Brother!"

The farmer ignored the logger's warning. He could already feel her beneath his fingertips. And yet she slid out of his grasp, as though he had taken hold of a handful of grease.

Weatherfish Slip kung fu, inspired by the black marsh she called home.

Confident that the disciples could not handle her, and having evaded three of them with little effort, Madam Ying was now ready to retaliate, aiming a backhanded slap at the farmer.

The scholar stepped forward to intercept, tapping at the pressure points on her wrist after twirling an arm past her guard. This simple maneuver harnessed the power of a lifetime's martial training.

Madam Ying's forefinger flew at the scholar's outstretched digit, and what began as a numbing sting from the touch of her fingertip became a jolt that ripped like a crack of lightning through his body. With a cry, the scholar crashed to the ground. The fisher and the logger rushed to his aid, while the farmer swung a left hook at Madam Ying.

Madam Ying watched the farmer's punch hurtle toward her face, heavy as a hammer blow, without so much as flinching. Her nonchalance gave him pause: I'll crack her skull and splatter her brains . . . He wanted to wrench away, but his knuckles were already skimming the tip of her nose. She cocked her head faintly and his fist glanced off her cheek. He knew he needed to pull back now that his strike had failed to land, but she was faster, trapping his wrist. He tugged and struggled, trying to free himself from her grasp. *Crack!* Shards of pain shot down his arm. She had knocked his forearm out of joint with an uppercut. Not one to yield easily, he clenched his teeth and poked his right index finger into the crook of her elbow.

The farmer and his peers had been taught the art of pressure-point locking by Sole Light himself. Though they had yet to reach the dizzying heights of their Master's skill in Yang in Ascendance, they were among the most accomplished practitioners of this combat technique alive.

Of course, Madam Ying had long known that, if she were to avenge her son's death, she would need to develop a way to foil these potent taps of the finger, and she had eventually found inspiration from embroidery, a craft at which she—like many women of her time—excelled. She had forged a golden band that fitted over the tip of her right forefinger. This ring held in place a needle, one-third of an inch long, which she laced with a deadly poison. Like all masters of needlework, she had keen eyesight and a steady hand. After several years practice, she could skewer a fly midair.

"The fingers to the heart connect." The well-known saying described the strong and immediate connection between the extremities and the core. At the very tip of the index finger is the Metal Yang acupoint, which is the first point in the Large Intestine Meridian that travels up the arm to the nose.

This was the spot where Madam Ying had struck the scholar, and now she was poised to do the same to the farmer. With a smirk, she curled her finger slightly, holding it still, directly in the path of his attack. She would let him prick himself on the waiting needle.

Like the scholar, the farmer had put all his strength into his strike, hoping to bring her down with him.

Stung on the fingertip, he howled in pain and slumped to the ground.

Sniggering, Madam Ying continued on her way to the temple.

"Your Highness, stop, please!" the fisher cried.

She halted at the foot of the small stone bridge spanning the lotus pond. At the far end was the temple's front gate.

"Or else?" She turned to face him. Her ice-cold glare cut through the darkness. "The Chancellor and the Captain have both been stung by my Needle of Seven Dooms, and nobody in this world can save them now. Do you wish to share their fate?" With those words, she strolled onto the bridge, unconcerned that she had left her back open to her enemies.

5

JUST AS MADAM YING WAS ABOUT TO STEP OFF THE BRIDGE, she heard a greeting.

"Master."

The faint outline of a man emerged from the shadows. He put his hand over his fist in respect, but he was standing in her way.

Madam Ying was shaken. How did I fail to hear him approach? It only took me twenty paces to cross this bridge. If he had launched an attack instead of cupping his hands, I would be dead or maimed by now. She peered at the shrouded form. Tall, broad shoulders, thick eyebrows, large eyes. The boy she had directed to this mountain sanctuary.

"Is the girl any better?" she asked.

"Thanks to Master's guidance, my martial sister was healed by Reverend Sole Light," Guo Jing replied.

"Then why isn't she here to thank me personally?" Madam Ying pressed ahead as she spoke.

"Master, please turn back."

She ignored him and pushed forward, swiveling slightly at the last moment to avoid running square into him. Deft and undaunted, she slipped past him in the blink of an eye.

Her maneuver put Guo Jing on the back foot, even though he had been anticipating it. He swung his arm in an ungainly arc behind him and sent forth a burst of internal power. Zhou Botong's Luminous Hollow Fist.

Madam Ying had already skimmed past the young man using her Weatherfish Slip technique, but now she was forced to scuttle backward, for there was a tenacity in the supple strength coming toward her that she could not counter. The retreat reminded her why she had come. There was no going back—come what may.

"Hey!" Guo Jing cried as Madam Ying pushed into him. In the shock of this unforeseen close contact, he felt her foot hooking his ankle. The next thing he knew, the two of them were tumbling into the lotus pond in a tangle of limbs.

Even as they were falling, Madam Ying snaked her arm under his armpit and grabbed him by the shoulder. She curled her middle finger and pressed down with her thumb. A Throat Sealer. Once her fingers locked onto his windpipe, she could cut off his breathing with one squeeze.

Acting on instinct, Guo Jing folded his arm over Madam Ying's neck and held her in a stranglehold. His counterattack, Neck Choker, also came from the Miniature Grapple and Lock repertoire she was drawing on.

Unable to match for brute strength, she released the clamp over his throat and threatened him with a pressure-point jab instead. He swiped his arm into her wrist, knocking her outstretched finger off target.

The bridge was no more than half a dozen feet above the pond. Three times she had tried to disable him as they fell, and three times he had parried with the same quick-fire, hand-to-hand combat technique.

Plop! They plunged chest-deep into muddy water.

Madam Ying scooped a handful of slush and made to smear it over Guo Jing's face. She had drawn him into this quaggy pond for the tactical advantage it would offer her—though she was the weaker party, she had lived on marshland for more than a decade and her fighting style was inspired by the slithery movements of weatherfish gliding through the mire.

Guo Jing managed to duck away from the handful of mud, but his footwork was hampered by the three feet of clay lining the pond. Madam Ying, meanwhile, was at home in her natural environment, skimming, skating, sliding over the silt. Her already speedy onslaught was now swifter than ever, a blur of stabs and slaps as she scooped up sludge to sling in her opponent's face.

They had barely exchanged five moves, but Guo Jing was struggling. He would have been in a better position if he let more strength flow into his strikes, but he did not want to hurt her. His sight stolen by the night, his feet bogged down by the mud, he had to rely on his ears to pick out the buzz of her blows and his nose to sniff out the handfuls of stinking sludge coming his way. He slogged this way and that, dodging two clumps of slurry by a hair's breadth. When he thought he was in the clear, a third slapped into his face, covering his eyes, nose and mouth.

Guo Jing threw three consecutive palm thrusts, not in retaliation, but to push Madam Ying back by at least five feet and give him time to wipe his face. This instinctive response had been drilled into him by the Six Freaks of the South. To allow oneself to be paralyzed by an injury mid-fight, especially one from a secret weapon, would be to invite a lethal follow-up.

6

MADAM YING HAD NOT COME ALL THIS WAY TO FIGHT GUO Jing. Once she had temporarily blinded him with mud, she hopped back onto the bridge.

If it were not for the pond, I wouldn't have a hope of subduing that boy, she thought as she rushed toward the entrance to the temple. The Lord of the Heavens is granting me my revenge.

She thrust her hands into the temple doors. *Creeeeaaak!* They flew open.

Not bolted? She halted, in case someone lay in ambush.

Nothing. No movement at all.

She stepped across the threshold, her eyes drawn to the main hall of worship. The Buddha's serene face glowed warmly, illuminated by a single oil lamp. She felt a pang in her heart and knelt on the prayer mat before the deity to ask for a blessing.

Then came the sound of light musical laughter. Right behind her.

Madam Ying swung her arm backward to shield herself as she pressed her hand down on the mat to propel her to her feet, spinning midair to face her opponent.

"Lovely kung fu!" A young woman dressed in a green robe fastened by a red belt grinned at Madam Ying. The golden hoop in her hair glistened in the dim light. She held a glossy green bamboo stick in her hand.

Madam Ying recognized her at once.

"I thank you for saving my life."

"No need to thank me. I sent you here to hurt another, not for your own good."

"The line between friend and foe is never clear cut. Papa held Zhou Botong on Peach Blossom Island for five and ten years, but it couldn't bring Mama back to life."

Madam Ying twitched at the mention of the Hoary Urchin's name. "What has he got to do with your mother?"

Lotus noted Madam Ying's jealous tone. So, she still has feelings for him. Why else would she assume there was a dalliance between him and Mama? I'll toy with her a little first.

Lotus bowed her head and sighed. "He was the reason she died."

Madam Ying eyed the girl, her suspicions confirmed, it seemed. Such smooth, unblemished skin. Such grace and beauty.

My looks, even in the full bloom of youth, would seem homely by comparsion, she thought bitterly. If she takes after her mother's appearance, he might well . . .

"Don't get any ideas. My mother was celestial and that Zhou Botong is as boorish as a bull. Only a blind woman would fall for him."

The insult set Madam Ying's mind at ease, but she could not resist a caustic remark. "Since love has favored that boy of yours, thick as a pig as he is, why would it not smile on a boorish bull? How did . . . How did he cause your mother's passing?"

"I'm not talking to you anymore. You're mean!" Lotus flicked her sleeve and stormed off.

"Wait! I take it back. He's very, very smart." Madam Ying would do anything to appease the girl if it meant a chance to learn more about Zhou Botong's fate.

Lotus turned her eyes on Madam Ying. "He's not smart at all, but he's honest and true-hearted. He'll always be good to me, even if the heavens come crashing down. The Old Urchin didn't set out to hurt Mama, but if it weren't for him she wouldn't have died. My father shattered the Urchin's legs and locked him up, but later he regretted it. A culprit to every wrong, a lender to every debt. Who killed your child? You should go to the ends of the world to seek them out. What's the point of shifting the blame onto another?"

The words hit Madam Ying like a blow to the head. She stood on the spot, dazed, utterly lost for words.

"Papa came to understand that, and freed the Hoary Urchin—"

"So, I don't need to rescue him . . ."

"You think you could free him if Papa didn't want to let him go?"

After Madam Ying had left Dali and made a new home for herself in the dark swamp, she had searched high and low for Zhou Botong without any luck. One day, the whispers reached her—he might be imprisoned by Apothecary Huang on Peach Blossom Island.

His resolute departure was branded on her memory, and she knew that, without a seismic change of circumstances, he would not consider a reunion. Though she was afraid for him, the rumors gave her hope. Of course, she did not wish ill on the love of her life, but this could be a chance to turn his heart toward her. If she rescued him, surely he would look back on their brief moment of bliss . . .

So, she set off for Peach Blossom Island and found herself trapped in the mazelike landscape for three days and three nights. Far from freeing him, she almost starved to death and needed rescuing her-self—by mute servants sent by Apothecary Huang, who guided her safely off the island.

When she returned home, she focused her mind on learning the art of reckoning, so she could overcome the complex defenses that protected the island. The news that Zhou Boutong had been released shook her to the core. Her heart was tugged in all directions by a conflict of emotions—a simultaneous assault of sweet joy, bitter pangs, sour stings and fiery rage.

"The Urchin has always done what I ask of him without ques-tion," Lotus said with a smirk. "If you want to see him, come with me. I will act as your matchmaker as a thank-you for saving my life."

Heat rushed to Madam Ying's cheeks as her heart hammered in her chest.

A loud clap snapped Lotus out of her self-congratulatory mood.

She thought a few well-chosen words had turned bloodshed into wedlock, but the hard frost on Madam Ying's face and the violence with which she struck her hands together behind her back said otherwise.

"A half-grown wench like you has his ear?" Madam Ying scoffed, her voice shrill. "Why does he listen to you? Because you're pretty? I've done you no kindness, and I seek nothing from you in return. Step aside, now. If you drag your feet—"

"Oh dear, you want to do away with me!"

"Old Heretic Huang might intimidate a lot of people, but not me—I fear nothing and no one. Not the heavens; not the earth."

"If you kill me, who will give you the answer to those three questions?"

Madam Ying had lost sleep and appetite over the reckoning problems Lotus had left her with. She first came to her studies as a means to save Zhou Botong, but soon, it was sheer curiosity that was propelling her forward, even though she knew her ability to solve such puzzles was of little use, for Apothecary Huang's understanding would always be heavens beyond hers. At Lotus's prompting, the questions returned to her, word for word, and she was once more overcome by the urge to get to the bottom of them.

"I'll explain, if you let me live." Lotus reached for the oil lamp by the Buddha and placed it on the ground. Then she took out one of her throwing needles and scratched its point against the floor tiles.

Madam Ying watched in awe as Lotus arrived at the solution, step by step, to "The Sindhu written calculation of the seven brilliances and nine luminaries." She then moved on to the second, more complicated, puzzle: "The problem of distributing silver and issuing rice to soldiers whose numbers are conscripted in cubic multiples."

"Wondrous!" Madam Ying gushed as Lotus scratched out the equation. "The answer to the last question is twenty-three, but, however hard I tried, I could not come up with the formula that leads me to that number."

She repeated the question under her breath:

"Here are objects whose number is unknown: counted by threes two remains, counted by fives three remains, counted by sevens two again remains. How many are there?"

"Let me show you," Lotus said. "Reckon, here, means divide. Divide by three, then multiply what remains by seventy. Divide by five, then multiply what remains by twenty-one. Divide by seven, then multiply what remains by fifteen. Add these three numbers together; if it's not larger than one hundred and five, then it's correct. With larger numbers, you can then minus one hundred and five or a multiple of one hundred and five."

Madam Ying mumbled Lotus's explanation under her breath as she tried it out.

"You don't have to swallow that whole, there's a poem that explains it:

> *Three walk in the rare age of seventy,*
> *Five plum trees with twenty-one sprigs,*
> *Seven sons united at half-moon,*
> *Take five and a hundred and you shall see."*

Madam Ying fumed as she listened. This imp must have learned my past and composed this verse to mock me. The first line is insinuating that I have served two men, and the third line is a swipe at the fact that I only spent half a month with Zhou Botong . . . She was wary of anything that could be construed as a reference to her ignominious past.

"Enough of your prattling!" Madam Ying barked. Though she could see little through the gloom, she had gained a sense of the temple's layout and concluded that King Duan's chamber must be in a courtyard beyond this one. She had also realized the girl's aim was to slow her progress, and she had no desire to dally with Apothecary Huang's daughter, who, despite her tender years, was as full of tricks as her father.

Why am I wasting time on these stupid reckoning problems when I've got a much more important task to attend to? She marched forward, stepping around the Buddha and making for the doorway behind the altar.

Pitch black. Not a speck of light.

"Duan Zhixing, come and meet me. Why hide in the dark?" Madam Ying shouted. Deep in hostile territory, she would rather err on the side of caution.

It was Lotus, not Sole Light, who replied. "He had the lamps extinguished so you wouldn't be nervous."

"Huh!" Madam Ying narrowed her eyes in suspicion. "I am destined for hell. Why would I cringe from a little light?"

Lotus took out a tinderbox from her dress and bent down by Madam Ying's feet, cradling a flickering flame.

A clay teacup, half filled with oil and with a twine of cotton for a wick. Next to it, a bamboo stick jutted out of the earth, its end filed into a spike. Madam Ying had not anticipated anything like this.

While Lotus flitted around the courtyard kindling the makeshift lamps, Madam Ying was counting. One hundred and thirteen cups, each accompanied by a spike. The ground glowed like the starry night sky.

Madam Ying was mystified. What is this configuration? The Plum Blossom Stakes? But that kung fu is usually practiced with either seventy-two or one hundred and eight spikes. These aren't organized in any discernible order. Not the Nine Halls. Not the Eight Trigrams. Not the Five Petals of the Plum Blossom. Could she be wearing shoes with metal soles? That must be it. How else would she be able to walk among them without getting hurt? I can't outmaneuver her when she's so well prepared . . . I'll push my way through, pretending I haven't noticed them.

Madam Ying strode forward, but it was difficult to avoid the stakes.

"What's all this? I haven't got time to play." A swipe of her foot knocked over five or six spikes.

"Hey! You can't do that!"

She took no notice of Lotus and continued kicking left and right.

"Fine, if you're going to be a brute, I'll extinguish the lamps. I hope you can remember where the spikes are."

This gave Madam Ying pause. What if they all come out now and attack me? she thought. They know the layout of the stakes, but I'll be skewered alive! I need to cross this courtyard now! She summoned her *qi*, urging herself on.

"You really know no shame." Lotus planted herself in Madam Ying's way, armed with the Dog Beater.

The bamboo cane, wielded sideways, whirled toward Madam Ying's face in an emerald blur. The older woman chopped a palm down, expecting to split the flimsy weapon in two. She had never considered the teenage girl a martial threat, yet, little did she know, she was facing a move from the Block permutation of Dog-Beating kung fu, which would morph into a ruthless counterattack the second it was challenged.

The tip of the cane rapped sharply on the back of Madam Ying's hand. Although no acupoint of note was hit, it was a painful blow, and her fingers were instantly numbed. But she would not let this momentary setback cloud her judgment. Assuming a defensive stance, she appraised her opponent.

How come this waif is so skilled? Her father must have taught her all he knows, she said to herself, as she recalled the trip to Peach Blossom Island and how she had been pushed to the brink of death without ever setting eyes on the Master himself. She did not know that Lotus was tapping in to a repertoire known only to the chiefs of the Beggar Clan, and that, if Apothecary Huang were on the receiving end, he too would be stumped by its intricacies.

In this short moment while Madam Ying stayed on the defensive and deliberated her next move, Lotus had been maintaining the Block variation with her hands, while flitting between lamps and spikes like a butterfly, kicking out more than half of the one hundred and thirteen lights with the tip of her shoe. It was a marvelous display, for she extinguished the flames without toppling the cups, spilling the oil or dislodging the bamboo stakes.

This fleet footwork was one of Apothecary Huang's cherished inventions, Swirling Leaf Kick. Lotus's demonstration was neat and tidy, but Madam Ying could tell that the girl had yet to harness the technique's full potential, for these movements were more predictable and straightforward than her work with the cane.

She's only just recovered from her injury. Her primal qi is still impaired, Madam Ying reminded herself. *If I focus on her footing, I can take her out in a few dozen moves.*

Only a handful of lamps in the northeastern corner of the courtyard were left flickering in the night breeze. The rest of the temple grounds had been plunged once more into darkness.

The cane flashed twice. Madam Ying shuffled back, scanning the yellowish gloom for a safe place to take shelter. Taking advantage of her opponent's retreat, Lotus vaulted high with aid of the Dog Beater and whirled a sleeve in the direction of the only source of light remaining. The fabric unfurled with the full force of Splitting Sky Palm. The last few lamps went out instantly.

How do I fight in the dark? Every step I take, I run the risk of my foot being impaled, Madam Ying said to herself. Then she groaned as she heard Lotus's voice ring out once more.

"Now, let's play! I hope you've memorized the position of the spikes. If you subdue me in thirty moves, I'll let you see King Duan."

"You've spent hours training here," the older woman retorted. "I've only caught a glimpse."

"In that case, light a lamp, rearrange the stakes, and then we'll fight." Lotus relished the thought of triumphing over Madam Ying on her terms.

So we're competing on powers of recall, now . . . I haven't come here to play games, Madam Ying told herself. *I need to preserve my strength for taking vengeance. I know what to do . . .*

"Very well. This old crone will play with the little fledgling." She took out her own tinder and flint, and lit an oil lamp on the ground.

"Why do you call yourself an old crone?" Lotus was making conversation to slow Madam Ying down. "You're more alluring than most girls of sixteen. I can see why King Duan was so smitten, back then, and why his heart is still yours, all these years later."

Madam Ying had repositioned a dozen or so bamboo spikes by now, but she faltered at Lotus's words. "Smitten? He barely noticed my existence in the palace."

"Didn't he teach you kung fu?"

"Ha, what a great honor!"

"I know why! He was practicing Cosmos *neigong*. He couldn't get too close to you."

Madam Ying snorted. "What do you know, little girl? Where do you think the Crown Prince came from?"

Lotus cocked her head, considering the question. "Hmmm . . . It was before Cosmos *neigong*."

Madam Ying curled her lips and said no more, busying herself with the rearranging of the stakes, though the exchange continued to swirl around in her mind.

Lotus paid close attention, committing every new position to memory, since one false step, even by a couple of inches, would mean a bloody hole in her foot.

"King Duan didn't save your son because he loved you," Lotus said, out of the blue. "That's the reason why."

"What do you know? He loved me, did he?" Pure vitriol dripped from her words.

"He was jealous of the Hoary Urchin. Why would he feel that way if he didn't love you? He would have saved your child, but he saw the handkerchief with the lovebirds wrapped over the baby's belly. *Pity the hair that grows gray before its time!* You wanted to grow old with the Urchin and that broke King Duan's heart. He wanted death to end his pain!"

Madam Ying had never imagined that a king could harbor such

feelings for a consort. For a moment, she stopped what she was doing, lost to the past.

"You should turn back," Lotus said, breaking the silence.

"Are you going to make me?"

"Your wish is my command. If you can get past me, I won't stand in your way. But if you can't . . . ?"

"I'll never come back. And you won't have to live with me for a year."

"Agreed! I must say, though I rather enjoy your company, I wasn't looking forward to staying so long in that stinky mucky place."

All the while, Madam Ying had not stopped repositioning the spikes. About three score of them had now been moved.

"I'm done." She extinguished her lamp and slashed her claws at Lotus through the blackness.

Sensing the danger, Lotus swiveled at an angle, placing her foot down precisely between two spikes that Madam Ying had just redeployed, then speared the Dog Beater at the woman's shoulder.

Madam Ying took no notice of her counterattack. She marched forward—*clack, clack, clack*—crunching the spikes underfoot.

Argh! Lotus realized she had been outsmarted. The woman had snapped the sticks when she replaced them. How did I not foresee that?

7

A GLIMMER OF LIGHT SHONE FROM A ROOM AT THE FAR SIDE of the rear courtyard. Madam Ying pushed open the doors.

An elderly monk sat on a prayer mat. He was wrapped in a thick *kasaya* that reached up to his cheeks, and a silvery beard flowed down his chest. His head was bowed, his eyes lowered. He was meditating. The four disciples, together with a handful of aged monks and young novices, stood to attention at his side.

The logger went up to the seated monk when Madam Ying entered and touched his palms together in a Buddhist greeting, "*Shifu*, Consort Liu is here."

The monk gave a slight nod, but said nothing.

A single oil lamp burned in the chamber, but its wavering flame was too weak to highlight the details of the monk's face. Madam Ying was aware that King Duan had cut himself off from the secular world, but she could not have predicted that a mere decade of seclusion would turn a strapping, regal man in his prime into this wizened, withered old thing. Lotus's words came back to her mind.

Perhaps he did feel something for me, she whispered to herself, and her grip on the dagger slackened.

Spread on the floor in front of King Duan was her son's undervest, refashioned from the love token she had bestowed on Zhou Botong. The handkerchief with the lovebirds. Her jade bracelet had been placed upon it. Her first gift when she entered the palace. Her time as a consort in the Dali court flashed before her eyes. Arriving at the palace. Learning kung fu from the king. Meeting the love of her life. Her heart being trampled by that very man. Though he left her, she bore him a son—his birth, his death . . . his pleading eyes as his insides were ripped apart by pain. He was just a toddler, but that look conveyed a thouand, ten thousand words, each of them reproaching his mother for doing nothing to ease his suffering.

Her heart hardened.

She raised the dagger. Strength coursed to her wrist.

She thrust. At his heart. Until the whole blade was buried in his chest.

The moment the knifepoint pierced his flesh felt a little strange to Madam Ying. Given King Duan's martial sophistication, she knew one thrust might not be enough to finish him off. She tightened her grip on the hilt, ready to pull the dagger out and plunge it into his heart again.

She tugged. Once. Twice. The blade would not budge. Was it caught in his ribs?

Madam Ying had rehearsed this one stab to the heart tens of

thousands of times. She wielded the deadly weapon in one hand, while the other wove an unremitting defensive pattern to protect her flanks and her back.

A king would inevitably be surrounded by dozens of guards.

She pulled again. The dagger simply would not shift.

The four disciples were lunging at her, howling, outraged.

She had done what she had set out to do. This was no place to tarry. She let go of the blade and leaped out of the room.

She stole one last look from the doorway.

King Duan was clutching his chest with one hand. He was in agony.

Revenge was hers at last, but she felt nothing. No elation, no relief.

He never uttered a word of reproach—about my faithlessness, about the son I bore my lover. Madam Ying was considering the past in a way she never had before. He freed me from my obligation and offered his blessings for my marriage to his rival. He didn't try to stand in the way of my happiness—it was that whoreson Zhou Botong who spurned me. He even let me stay on in the palace. He could have punished me. He could have sentenced me to death. But he didn't. Instead, he gave me a richer allowance from the palace treasury. He ordered men to plant trees to shield my hermitage in the black swamp. He has been sending food and supplies so I won't go without. All these years, he hasn't stopped looking after me. He has made sure I want for nothing. He has treated me very well—better than I deserve . . .

For more than a decade, the only memory she had kept of King Duan was his flint-hearted refusal to save her son's life, the only feeling she had had for him was rancor, and yet, this one stroke of the knife had revealed all the kindness he had shown her.

Sighing, she tore her eyes from the dying king and dragged her mind from her memories to focus on her escape.

She came face to face with another monk standing in the courtyard just outside the room. Hands held together in a Buddhist greeting. Looking at her with affection.

She knew that high nose bridge and strong jawline well. The

lamplight from the room might have been weak, but there was no mistaking that she was looking at her king.

Could he be a ghost?

No, he is real and he is King Duan.

Her skin prickled and she let out a scream.

Did I kill the wrong man?

Madam Ying turned to look at the monk she had just stabbed. He was climbing to his feet and shrugging off his vestments. He gave his beard a tug and it fluttered to the floor.

Guo Jing!

Lotus's gamble was inspired by an age-old stratagem known as Cicada Sheds Skin, for, when that insect moults, the empty shell hanging on the branches still retains the outline of its shape, as though it had never left the tree. In her version, the hollow slough was Guo Jing, disguising himself as Reverend Sole Light so he could take Madam Ying's blade on the monk's behalf.

To put the plan in motion, Guo Jing ambushed the Martial Great, locking his pressure points. He also neutralized the monk's brother-in-faith from Sindhu, in case he turned out to be well trained in combat, though in reality the man knew no kung fu at all.

Lotus's role was to delay the vengeful woman long enough for the four disciples to dress Guo Jing as their *shifu*, which involved helping him wash off the mud from the lotus pond, shaving his head, attaching their master's beard to the young man's face and wrapping him in a monk's habit.

The four men carried out Lotus's instructions to the letter, but they were laden with guilt. Not only were they openly defying their *shifu*'s command to let Madam Ying take her revenge, they were also forced to manhandle him and remove his beard to provide Guo Jing with a credible disguise. The worst part of all was having to let the young man risk his life as the body double—all because of their own martial shortcomings. To falter even slightly when struck with Madam Ying's dagger would mean certain death.

Guo Jing had devoted much thought to what he would do when the moment came. He took advantage of the swathes of fabric enveloping him to conceal his arms within the garment's folds. He caught the flat surface of the blade between his fingers, but even his powerful inner strength could not hold back Madam Ying's determined thrust. The point of the dagger sank half an inch into his chest, narrowly missing his ribs. He could have worn the Hedgehog Chainmail, but they could not risk Madam Ying realizing that she had driven the dagger into metal instead of flesh. Every last detail had to be carried out to perfection if they were to deceive her, for she would return if she thought her revenge had failed.

Sole Light's appearance now upended Lotus's meticulous plan.

It turned out that Guo Jing, wary of causing the monk harm, had only locked the least important of his pressure points. In spite of the day's exertions and the aftereffects of the poison, Sole Light still had some command of his inner kung fu. While everyone was busy with Madam Ying, he was willing his energy around his body in an effort to free himself, returning to his chamber just as the woman was making her escape.

"GIVE THE dagger back to her."

Reluctantly, Guo Jing handed the weapon over.

Ashen-faced, Madam Ying received it, unsure what this gesture meant.

What punishment will he mete out? she asked herself, staring at the blade in her hand. When she looked up, she was surprised to see him unwrapping his *kasaya*.

"Let her leave in peace," he ordered his disciples as he pulled open his undershirt. Then he turned to Madam Ying, his countenance serene. "Here, plunge your knife where you will. I have waited a long, long time for this."

His gentle tone struck her like a thunderbolt. She could even detect tenderness in his eyes. Once more, she was reminded of the magnanimity he had shown her, and the thought of it was washing away the bile she had wallowed in for so many years.

"I have wronged you." The dagger slipped from her fingers, clattering to the ground.

She ran into the night, her face buried in her hands.

8

NO ONE MADE A SOUND AS THEY LISTENED TO MADAM YING'S fading footsteps, bewildered by her reaction. Without warning, the scholar and the farmer collapsed at the same time, one facedown, the other on his back. They had been holding the toxins from Madam Ying's needle at bay with their inner strength, but now their *shifu* was safe, their bodies gave in.

"Please invite—"

Lotus was a step ahead of the logger, entering the room with the monk from Sindhu. The skilled healer gave the two men a theriac then sliced open their fingertips to let out blood blackened by venom. He looked at Sole Light with concern and spoke in a language only his brother-in-faith could understand: they were not in immediate danger, but the bane had taken root and would take two months of treatment to purge.

By now, Guo Jing had changed back into his own clothes and tended to his wound. He kowtowed, begging the Martial Great for forgiveness.

Sole Light reached out to help the young man to his feet. "You risked your life for me. I don't deserve your generosity," he said with humility, before turning to his brother-in-faith to explain what Guo Jing had done.

The Sindhu monk nodded with approval and said something that sounded very familiar to Guo Jing.

"*Sirahstha hahoramanpayas . . .*" the young man chimed in.

Sole Light could not believe his ears. He asked Guo Jing how he was able to recite these words, for they were in a curious form of Sanskrit inflected by the Chinese language. Guo Jing explained he had spoken out loud without thinking and that he was quoting a line from a nonsensical passage at the end of the Nine Yin Manual. He told the monk how Zhou Botong had tricked him into learning the whole Manual by heart, and then recited the jumble of random characters in full to illustrate his point.

Amazed by the words coming out of Guo Jing's mouth, Sole Light said, "The Double Sun Immortal once told me that Huang Shang, the Master who wrote the Manual, had not only read every single Taoist Canon in existence, he was also a scholar of Buddhist scriptures and the Sanskrit language from which the texts were translated.

"What you have just shared is the conclusion to the Manual. It contains the most profound content in the whole treatise and is the key to interpreting cryptic elements in the preceding chapters.

"It also tells us why it was written in cipher. Huang Shang feared that his work might fall into the hands of unscrupulous men—for the techniques detailed in the Manual would make them unassailable. He considered destroying this concluding statement, but he couldn't bring himself to obliterate his own work, so he rewrote it in a code that is drawn from the tradition of setting down Sanskrit words phonetically in Chinese characters.

"He realized that by doing so he would make it difficult for the Manual to be understood in full, for knowledge of Sanskrit has always been rare in the Central Plains, and even rarer among those with sophisticated martial skills. Of course, the reverse is also true: few from Sindhu know Chinese characters. He must have thought that if a martial Master were acquainted with both languages, they could hardly be a rascal knave, for they would be steeped in both Buddhist and Chinese cultures.

"This arrangement made the contents of the final portion nigh on incomphrensible: even Immortal Double Sun could not decipher it. Oh, the heavens' intent is in sooth wondrous. You have no grasp of the Sanskrit language, yet you were able to memorize this long, incantation-like passage. A karmic coincidence!"

He asked Guo Jing to repeat the passages from the Manual's final section again, slowly, line by line, so he could write down the meaning in Chinese. When he had finished, he said, "I hope you will stay with us for a little while. I'd like to study this text and share its wisdom with you." Even a Master as learned and skilled in *neigong* as Sole Light had struggled to grasp the full profundity of the Nine Yin Manual.

Martial arts rooted in the Taoist school of thought had always been characterized by the supple quality of yin, and yet, this very belief system also propagated the idea that the proliferation of anything, even if it was fundamentally positive, would grow into something negative and ultimately be the cause of its ruination. This was the reason Huang Shang named his opus "Nine Yin"—yin to the utmost—as a reminder that, if the balance between yin and yang tips over to one extreme, it is inevitable that calamity will ensue.

In the Manual's final statement, he summarized this understanding and detailed a technique that would ensure the mutual replenishment and harmonization of yin and yang, as a corrective to the Taoist overemphasis on the suppleness of yin in all matters martial. This metaphysical coda was of greater importance than all the kung fu that came before it.

Sole Light shook his head, marveling at the knowledge set down in the manuscript. "If I followed the method described here, I could restore my primal energy and recover my kung fu in less than three months—a process that would take at least five years without the Manual's help.

"My martial arts stem from the Buddhist tradition, which is rather different from the Taoist internal-strength system, but the Manual explains that, at the very heights of martial learning, everything comes together—the distinctions between diverging schools are negligible."

Lotus wondered if this miraculous method could help Count Seven Hong. Sole Light was visibly concerned when she described how the Beggar had been injured at the hands of Viper Ouyang, but his response was reassuring: "Your *shifu* won't need my help. He can restore himself with this –" he gestured at the text—"all by himself."

IN THE days that followed, Guo Jing and Lotus stayed close to Reverend Sole Light, learning from his insights into the final paragraphs of the Nine Yin Manual. Lotus felt stronger with the arrival of each new dawn. One morning, as she strolled arm in arm with Guo Jing by the lotus pond outside the temple, she heard the condors' cries.

She clapped and cheered. "The gold wah-wahs are here!"

The birds were flying in from the east, and, when they landed the couple were disconcerted to find that there were no salamanders to be seen, the female condor had a gruesome wound on her chest, while the male condor had a strip of green fabric tied around one leg.

Lotus recognized the cloth as her father's preferred material for his outer robes. It had been ripped from a garment and fastened to the bird in haste . . .

So, the condors did reach Peach Blossom Island, she said to herself. Could Papa be under attack? Perhaps there was no time to deal with my request. Is that what he's trying to tell me?

She examined the female condor's wound as Guo Jing applied a salve to it. It looked as though she had been hit by an arrow, which she had pulled from her breast herself. Whoever had managed to hurt this magnificent creature must have been well trained in the martial arts.

These clues were not enough to give a clear picture of what had happened on Peach Blossom Island, but she knew in her gut that, taken together, they spelled trouble. She wished the condors could articulate what they had witnessed.

Weighed down by foreboding, Lotus and Guo Jing went at once to Reverend Sole Light to take their leave.

"I wouldn't try to keep you here in Peach Blossom Island's hour of need, though I do wish we could spend more time together," the monk said. "Yet, fret not, I don't believe any living soul is capable of causing harm to our erudite Brother Apothecary." He sent for his disciples and sat the young couple down, teaching them one last lesson from his lifelong practice of the martial arts.

Two hours later, Guo Jing and Lotus bade the monk farewell, each with a heavy heart. The scholar and the farmer, still weakened by Madam Ying's poison, saw them off at the temple's main gate. The fisher and the logger accompanied them all the way to the foot of the mountain, staying with them until they found Ulaan, before clasping the young couple's hands in a warm gesture of farewell.

GUO JING and Lotus rode together, back toward Peach Spring, on the same trail as they had taken days before. The scenery had not changed, but their hearts were lighter than when they had last set eyes upon it. Thinking of the great gift Reverend Sole Light had bestowed upon them, Lotus dismounted and knelt on the road, bowing toward the mountain where the monk resided. Moments later, Guo Jing joined her in the dust to express his gratitude.

Then they resumed their journey, laughing and talking, the condors leading the way from high amid the clouds. Lotus was still worried about her father, but she felt reassured by Reverend Sole Light's words. Whatever had happened, she had faith that her papa's extraordinary martial prowess would keep himself safe.

"It's funny to think, we've gained something from every danger we've faced," Lotus said. "That old codger Qiu Qianren's rusty Iron Palm hurt a lot, but it gave us the *neigong* method concealed in the funny passage at the end of the Nine Yin Manual. Now we know something not even Wang Chongyang could work out, and he was the Greatest Martial Master Under the Heavens!"

"I'd rather know no kung fu, if it means you'll be safe."

"*Aiiiyoooo*, are we learning to sweet talk?" She laughed, though inside, she felt warm and fuzzy. "If you knew no kung fu, you'd just be dead. Any old Iron Palm Gang minion could've lopped your head off with a swing of his saber. You'd never get to exchange blows with Viper Ouyang. Actually, no, not even with Hector Sha!"

"It doesn't matter. I won't allow you to be hurt again. When I was injured in Lin'an, I didn't think it was so bad, but watching you suffer . . . my heart really ached."

"You're a heartless beast!"

"Huh?"

"You just said it's fine for me to watch you suffer, for my heart to ache!"

Guo Jing gave a sheepish grin and touched the tip of his toes on Ulaan's flank, since he had no response to that. The colt lifted his muzzle high, whinnied and off he flew in a gallop.

They arrived at Peach Spring just after midday. A couple of hours on horseback had proved to be more tiring than Lotus had anticipated. Her flushed cheeks and irregular breathing drove home the fact that her primal power had yet to fully regenerate.

Peach Spring was a very small town and there was only one hostelry worthy of the name, called the Tavern to Avoid the Qin, which referenced Tao Yuanming's tale about the discovery of Peach Blossom Spring, a forgotten but prosperous community that had found refuge from war and strife by hiding deep inside a mountain for generations, shielded by peach trees.

Once they had sat down and ordered, Guo Jing said to the waiter, "We would like to charter a boat for Hankow. Could you send a boatman here to discuss the journey?"

"It costs a lot to hire a whole barge just for two people. You'd save money sharing," the man said.

Lotus rolled her eyes and threw a silver ingot weighing five *taels* on the table. "Is this enough?"

The man bowed apologetically—"More than enough!"—and scurried downstairs.

When the food arrived, Guo Jing realized he should not have ordered wine as alcohol might hamper Lotus's recovery. He stopped her from drinking and abstained himself, so she would not feel left out. They had barely touched the meal when the waiter returned with a boat-master. It would cost three *taels* and six *candareens* of silver to sail directly to Hankow. The price included rice, but not the dishes to go with it.

Lotus handed the ingot over without haggling. The man took the payment with a grateful incline of his head and waved his hands over his mouth, letting out a raspy *ahhh* sound followed by more exaggerated gesticulations to ensure he was understood. Lotus nodded and signaled back, moving her arms and shaping her fingers in increasingly complex, expressive and elaborate combinations. The mute wagged his head happily at her reply and took his leave.

"What were you two saying?" Guo Jing asked.

"He said he would wait for us to finish our meal, so I told him to use the time to buy a few chickens, several *taels* of meat, some good wine and other provisions. I'll pay him back when we go aboard." Lotus grew up around servants made deaf and mute by her father, and had been conversant in sign language by the age of three.

"I dread to think what would happen if it were just him and me." Brimming with admiration, Guo Jing spoke through a mouthful of steamed honey-cured fish. The more he sampled this flavorsome dish, the more he wished he could pack it up and take it to share with the gourmandising Count Seven Hong.

"I wonder where *Shifu* is now," he said. "I hope he's coping with the injury. I worry so much about him."

The sound of footsteps coming up the stairs drew Lotus's attention away. A Taoist nun appeared on the landing. Her slight frame was engulfed in a gray habit, her face veiled by a thin cloth. Lotus could only see her eyes, but something about them—not to mention her gait and her figure—felt familiar. Where have I seen her before? She watched as the waiter took the nun's order and brought her a bowl of plain noodles.

Guo Jing, by now, had noticed that Lotus was fixated on the newcomer and threw the nun an apparently disinterested glance.

The woman whipped her head away. She must have been watching him . . . Catching her reaction, Lotus whispered with a giggle, "The nun's heart is all aflutter. She thinks you're very dashing."

"Stop your nonsense! You can't joke about that. She's taken an oath."

"I don't care if you don't believe me."

When they headed downstairs to pay their bill, Lotus lingered on the landing to steal one last look. The nun, who seemed to have anticipated Lotus's curiosity, lifted a corner of her veil. Lotus almost cried out but for the nun's quick wave to forestall her reaction. Then she covered her face again and turned her attention back to the noodles. Guo Jing, a few steps ahead of Lotus, was oblivious to the exchange.

Lotus found the boat-master standing outside the tavern and signaled that he should wait for them onboard since she wanted to buy a few things. The man nodded and pointed at a good-sized riverboat capped with an awning woven with strips of bamboo, but he continued to loiter in the area, making no move to head for the waterfront.

Noting the man's reluctance to make himself scarce, Lotus led Guo Jing eastward into an alleyway, where they would be out of sight of anyone at the tavern's doorway, but could still get a good view of any comings and goings. Before long, they saw the Taoist nun emerge, her eyes lingering on the Fergana horse and the condors. She looked around, as if to check if their masters were nearby. Finding no one she recognized, she headed west.

"Yes, that's how it should be," Lotus said aloud to herself as she tugged Guo Jing's sleeve, dragging him in the opposite direction from that taken by the nun.

Perplexed, Guo Jing followed without question.

A few streets later, they reached the town walls and left Peach Spring by the East Gate. Now Lotus marched south, skirting the town's perimeter until they reached the South Gate.

Realizing they were going in the same direction as the nun, Guo Jing asked, "Are we chasing her? This is no time for games!"

"Who's playing games?" Lotus chuckled. "You'll regret not chasing this celestial creature."

Guo Jing stopped dead. "Lotus, I'll be cross with you if you keep talking like this."

"Go on, show me how cross you are."

Once more lost for words, Guo Jing fell in step after Lotus as she hurried on.

Five or six *li* later, they at last caught sight of her. They could make out her gray outline, sitting under a scholar tree. But, when she detected their approach, she hurried off down a trail that descended into a valley.

Lotus took Guo Jing's hand, leading him on in hot pursuit.

"Lotus, if you insist on being silly, I'll carry you back."

"Good idea, I'm exhausted. You can follow her."

Guo Jing crouched down to let her climb onto his back. "You mustn't tire yourself out. Hop on, I'll carry you."

"I'll show you her face first." Letting out a peal of laughter, she took off, closing in fast. The nun had also stopped. She turned to face Lotus and waited for her to draw near.

Lotus pounced and threw her arms around the woman, pulling off her veil.

"Lotus! No!"

Guo Jing stopped in his tracks when he saw the nun's features.

Mercy Mu.

"Big Sister, what happened?" Lotus wound an arm around Mercy's waist. "Has that louse Yang Kang been beastly to you again?"

Mercy lowered her head, her eyebrows knotted, her eyes teary, her expression doleful.

"Sister," Guo Jing said in greeting when he caught up.

Mercy muttered a quiet *hmm* in acknowledgment.

Lotus took Mercy's hand and led her to the creek. They sat down, side by side, beneath a weeping willow. "What did he do this time, Sister? We'll make him pay. He played an abominable trick on us too—almost got us killed . . ."

Mercy's head remained bowed. She stared at the reflection of her and her friend in the stream. Fallen petals drifted over their faces, carried by the current.

Guo Jing perched on a rock a few feet away, mulling over a series of questions. Why is Sister Mu dressed as a Taoist nun? Why didn't she join us at the tavern? Where is Yang Kang now?

Sensing the pall of despondence that had fallen over her friend, Lotus fell silent. She would just sit and hold her hand—she would talk when she was ready.

At length, Mercy found the strength to speak. "Little Sister, Brother Guo, the boat you hired belongs to the Iron Palm Gang."

Guo Jing and Lotus both drew in a deep breath.

"Your riverman has the full power of speech and is known to be one of the most accomplished martial artists in the Iron Palm Gang. He acts mute so you can't gauge the extent of his kung fu from the timbre of his voice."

"Well, he had *me* fooled. He signs so well! This is not the first time he's played this role."

Guo Jing had scaled the willow tree the instant he had heard the words Iron Palm Gang. Apart from a couple of farmers working the fields in the distance, there was not another person to be seen in the valley. He now understood why Lotus and Mercy had taken such a roundabout route to meet in secret. It had given them a chance to shake off anyone tailing them.

Mercy heaved a sigh and spoke slowly, as what she was about to say clearly pained her. "After we parted in Baoying, I went north to collect my godparents' remains and escort them south. I ran into him again at Ox Village, in Lin'an . . ."

"We know. We saw him take Gallant Ouyang's life."

Mercy looked up, her eyes wide with disbelief. How did they know? Lotus gave a brief account of their stay in the secret chamber in the dilapidated inn while treating Guo Jing's injury, then told her how they had unmasked Yang Kang as a charlatan at the Beggar Clan Assembly.

"He has committed vile and wicked deeds," Mercy said through gritted teeth. "I hate myself for being so blind. I am cursed that I ever met him."

Lotus dabbed her handkerchief on Mercy's cheeks to dry her fast-flowing tears, but she had little sense of the turmoil in her friend's heart—the regrets, the self-reproach, all originating from her liaison with Yang Kang. Mercy needed to tell her friends all that had happened, to warn them of what was to come, but she knew not where to begin.

CHAPTER FOUR

RAGING RIVER,
TREACHEROUS SHOAL

I

DRAWING STRENGTH FROM LOTUS'S WARM GRASP, MERCY was at last ready to share her tale. She kept her eyes focused on the flowers floating over water so clear she could see the riverbed.

"I thought he had changed his ways," she said. "And then the two Masters from the Beggar Clan appeared. They were the men I had helped all those years ago, and they were trusted by Master Hong. They traveled with us to Yuezhou for the Beggar Clan Assembly.

"On the way, he told me that Master Hong, as he breathed his last, had asked him to take over as Chief of the Clan, but that I must keep it a secret. Of course, I found that hard to believe, but part of me was thrilled. I had seen with my own eyes the deference shown to him by Clan members, and, by the time we reached Yuezhou, the idea didn't seem so far-fetched.

"On the night of the meeting, I stayed behind in the city because I wasn't part of the Clan. I was so full of hope for the future. I thought that, once he was named leader, he would at last be able to do something great—for our people and our country. And, one day, he would avenge his parents with his own hands. I couldn't sleep. Everything was finally coming together in perfect harmony. I had never been happier in my life. I eventually dozed off when it was almost dawn, and that was when he jumped in through the window.

"I was still half asleep. I thought he was being reckless again. Then I heard him whisper: 'Something terrible has happened. We must go now.' I asked him to explain. 'The Unwashed refused to accept Chief Hong's last command,' he told me. 'They fought with the Washed over who should be the new leader and many died . . . I couldn't stand by and watch them slaughter each other, so I offered to give up the title. But the Elders of the Washed wouldn't let me go. Luckily, Leader Qiu of the Iron Palm Gang happened to be there and he helped me get away. We have to go now. To Iron Palm Mountain, where we can lie low for the time being.'

"Of course, it wasn't welcome news, but I thought it was noble of him to step down so he could stop the fighting. I didn't know if the Iron Palm Gang was a force for good or evil, but, the way he put it, we had no choice, so I went with him.

"When we got to Iron Palm Mountain, we were told that Leader Qiu was away traveling. I started to notice the furtive ways his men crept about their business, and it didn't feel right, so I said to Yang Kang, 'You can't walk away from the Beggar Clan. Why don't you seek out your *shifu*, Reverend Qiu the Eternal Spring? He can gather influential heroes from the *jianghu* to talk to the Beggar Clan and persuade them to select someone well respected in their ranks as chief. By stopping the bloodshed, you will still be honoring Master Hong's last wish.'

"He didn't answer me directly and kept changing the subject to our union. I told him off and he got upset. We ended up arguing. The next day, I regretted my harsh words. Although his priorities were misplaced—for he cared more about his private emotions than avenging his parents—he had always been good to me.

"By nightfall, I was so troubled I decided to write him an apology.

I tiptoed to his room. I was about to slip the note through a gap in his window, when I heard voices within, so I peered through the opening. There was a little old man in his chamber. Small, speckled beard. He wore an arrowroot shirt and he was waving a palm-frond fan."

Guo Jing and Lotus exchanged glances. Qiu Qianren or Qiu Qian-zhang?

"The man took a ceramic flask from inside his shirt and put it on the table. 'Brother Yang,' he said, 'worry not about your wife-to-be. She may be shy now, but, with a smidgeon of this powder in her tea, I guarantee you shall enjoy nuptial bliss tonight.'"

Qiu Qianzhang! The young couple shared a grin.

"Yang Kang was all smiles. He seemed so grateful to this old fox. I almost fainted from rage. The fossil took his leave not long after and I followed him. I punched him in the back and he fell. He'd have tasted my saber if I were somewhere safe, but instead I gave him a good beating, then I emptied his pockets. He had all manner of queer contraptions in them. Rings, bricks, sword stumps . . . I didn't know what he used them for, but I knew it was for making mischief. There was also a thread-bound notebook. It looked important. I got more and more cross as I went through the old man's things and I decided that I had to confront Yang Kang about the flask and every-thing else—we needed clarity between us.

"He was expecting me. I found him standing at the door with a smile on his face. 'Sister, please come in.' I stepped inside, and he pointed to the flask on the table. 'Guess what's in the bottle?' I was seething, so I said, 'Who knows what vileness it contains!' He was in excellent humor. 'A friend gave it to me earlier,' he said. 'He told me to put a little of this powder into your tea and everything would go as I wish.' This was not how I had expected our exchange to go and I felt my outrage slipping away. I picked up the bottle, opened the window and threw it out. 'Why did you keep it?' To which he replied, 'I respect Sister as I would a celestial being. How could I commit such a base crime?'"

Guo Jing nodded with approval. "Brother Yang did right."

Mercy scoffed, but said nothing more.

Lotus thought back to when she had seen Yang Kang and Mercy on Iron Palm Mountain. They were sitting side by side on the edge of the bed. His lips were brushing her ear, whispering, and his arms were pulling her close. Mercy was smiling, bashful.

We must have come upon them after this episode, Lotus said to herself. I bet Yang Kang saw her beating up Qiu Qianzhang, and that's why he came clean, the snake!

"What happened next?" Guo Jing asked, just as Zhou Botong had taught him. Always show interest and prompt the storyteller to continue.

Mercy's response was not one he had ever seen from the Hoary Urchin.

She flushed crimson and twisted away, her head bent even lower.

"Oh, Big Sister, I know!" Lotus cried. "You bowed to the heavens and earth and became man and wife!"

Mercy's head snapped up, her gaze fixed on Lotus. She had gone as white as a sheet, biting down hard on her lip. There was a peculiar glint in her eyes.

Lotus knew she had spoken out of turn. "I'm so sorry, my tongue ran away with me. My dear sister, please don't take it to heart."

"Your tongue didn't run away," Mercy muttered. "It was my senses that took their leave. I—I became . . . man and wife with him . . . but we—we didn't . . . didn't bow to the heavens and earth. I detest myself for my lack of self-control . . ." She trailed off as tears coursed down her cheeks.

Lotus put her arm around Mercy's shoulders, trying to find some soothing words for her friend. A moment later, she pointed at Guo Jing. "Sister, don't feel bad. It's nothing to be ashamed of. Not long ago, in Ox Village, he wanted that with me too."

Now it was Guo Jing's turn to feel awkward. "We . . . didn't . . . I . . ."

"You thought about it, though?"

Even the tips of Guo Jing's ears were burning a fiery red. He bowed his head and whispered, "I was bad."

Lotus patted him on the shoulder. "It makes me very happy that you want me to be your wife. Nothing bad about that."

This little exchange made Mercy ache deep inside. *She may be smart, but she's too young to really grasp that . . . Still, she's very blessed to have met someone so pure of heart.*

"What happened afterward, Sister?"

Mercy was staring vacantly at the stream once more. Her voice was very small. "Afterward . . . I heard yelling. Orders being bellowed out. It was chaos. He told me to keep quiet and said it had nothing to do with us—it was an Iron Palm Gang matter. Men began to assemble in the courtyard outside our room and they were told to fetch weapons and prepare torches so they could capture the trespassers.

"I looked out the window. The man issuing commands turned out to be that old fossil I had beaten up. I had not realized he was the leader of the Iron Palm Gang. I was worried that he would come in and confront me. And how . . . how could I face anybody after what had just happened? But, once his men were ready, they marched away."

"That old codger isn't the one you punched, Sister," Lotus said.

"What do you mean?"

"There are two of them. Twins. They look exactly the same. The one you beat up was called Qiu Qianzhang. Awful kung fu, nothing but a trickster. The one giving orders was Qiu Qianren, the actual leader of the Gang. One wave of his Iron Palm and you wouldn't be talking to us now."

"Really? If I had met him and died at his hands, everything would've been so much simpler."

"But our Brother Yang would miss you."

Mercy twisted away from Lotus's touch with disgust.

Lotus stuck her tongue out. "Then *I'd* miss you."

"I should go now," Mercy said, standing up. "Take care of yourselves. Beware of the Iron Palm Gang."

Lotus shot to her feet and grabbed Mercy's hand, pleading, "My dearest, dearest big sister, please don't be angry with me. I won't talk nonsense like that again."

"It's not you I'm angry with. It's . . . it's just that my heart hurts."

Lotus pulled Mercy back to their seat under the tree. "What did that villain do to upset you?"

"When the old man and his followers were gone, I asked him about our plans. He said, 'Since we are now man and wife, I'm not going to hide the truth from you. The army of the Great Jin Empire will soon march south, and, with the Iron Palm Gang's help from this side of the border, the Two Hus will be ours.'

"He was so excited by this grand plan. He said that once they had destroyed our Song armies, his father the Prince of Zhao would ascend the throne as the Great Jin Emperor, and he would be named the Crown Prince.

"And then he said to me, 'And you—you will become Her Highness the Consort.' I . . . I slapped him, very hard, and I ran. I ran out of the room and down Iron Palm Mountain. No one paid me any attention, they were all rushing the other way. Toward the summit.

"Every spark of life in here –" she put her hand over her bosom— "had gone out. Only ash remained. I didn't want to live anymore. I kept running. I didn't know where I was going. I just ran. Then I came upon a Taoist nunnery and barged inside. I stepped through the gate and I fainted. The old abbess took pity and let me stay. I succumbed to an illness and was bed-bound for days. When I recovered, she gave me this gown for the road, so I could return to Ox Village . . ."

"We're going in the same direction. Let's travel together!" Lotus said. "We're heading to Peach Blossom Island. I can share some kung fu with you along the way."

Mercy shook her head. "No, I—I'm fine. Thank you for thinking of me." She got to her feet and took a bound volume from inside her robe. "Big Brother Guo, this notebook contains affairs related to the

Iron Palm Gang. Please pass it on to Master Count Seven when you see him. Perhaps it could be of some use."

"Of course."

She pressed the book into Guo Jing's hands and disappeared between the weeping willow branches without saying goodbye.

2

"I HOPE NO WICKED MEN BOTHER HER ALONG THE WAY," GUO Jing said, a little while after Mercy's abrupt departure. "She has to travel alone for thousands of *li* to reach the Two Zhes. At least she knows enough kung fu to deal with any common rogues she comes across."

"Mm . . . hard to say. Even we get plagued by wicked men."

"Second *Shifu* has often said, 'In times of chaos, men are less than curs.' Maybe that's why?"

"Perhaps. Now, let's deal with that mute dog!"

"We'll still sail with him?"

"Of course! I suffered so much at the hands of that old fossil Qiu Qianren. I can't let him get away with it. We may not have the kung fu to beat him, but we can start by taking out a few of his minions."

So, they returned to the tavern, where they found the boat-master still skulking around the entrance. He spotted his passengers and bounded over to greet them. Guo Jing and Lotus acted as though they did not know his secret and followed him down the quay to the canopied riverboat he had pointed out earlier. Vessels of this size dominated the Yuan River, cruising down with produce from the hills in western Hunan and sailing up with rice from paddy fields downstream.

Two youths, stripped to the waist, were scrubbing the deck as they boarded. The boat-master waited for his passengers to settle in, then unmoored the craft, sculled to the middle of the river and raised the sail. Propelled by a brisk southerly wind, the barge shot downriver like a singing arrow.

Lounging on the deck under the awning, Guo Jing could not take his mind off Yang Kang and Mercy. We have sworn to share our blessings and hardships as brothers, he said to himself. I can't stand by and watch him take a wrong turn. I should make him see his mistake and bring him back to the path of righteousness . . .

"Can I see the notebook Sister Mu gave you?"

Absentmindedly, Guo Jing pulled the thread-bound volume out of his inside shirt pocket.

Lotus flipped through the pages, her eyes scanning their contents. "*A-ha*, that's how it got there! Come, look."

Guo Jing pushed himself up and read over Lotus's shoulder, but he was more taken by the view before him. The eventide sun floated just over the river surface. The water, mirroring the rosy clouds overhead, painted everything—Lotus's face, her clothes and the book—with a rippling, rubescent glow.

THE VOLUME turned out to contain a chronicle of the Iron Palm Gang, penned by Qiu Qianren's *shifu* and predecessor, Shangguan Jiannan.

Before Shangguan became the Gang's thirteenth leader, he was an officer serving under General Han Shizhong, a Song patriot. Han, like Yue Fei, had successfully stemmed the encroachments of the Jin Empire and believed in actively repelling the Jurchen army, instead of angling for a fragile peace by making treaties and paying tribute.

And yet, with the rise of Qin Hui to the post of Chancellor, it was the faction that preferred peaceful negotiations which gained power in court. Qin Hui used his influence to recall General Yue Fei from the frontline and thereafter engineered his demise. Han Shizhong, who held a lower official rank, was demoted and his troops were taken away. The majority of units under his command were disbanded, the soldiers sent back to their old lives, toiling once more in the fields.

When Shangguan Jiannan was released, he traveled to Jinghu with his decommissioned brothers-in-arms, so they could be closer to the war against the Jin. They were all furious that their homeland was in the grip of treacherous officials. Some volunteered to join the force defending the city of Xiangyang, a strategic stronghold near the border, against the Jin's invasion from the north, while Shangguan became a member of a small local outfit known as the Iron Palm Gang.

When the Iron Palm Gang leader passed on, Shangguan was named as his successor, though he was relatively new to the group. He took on this duty with great zeal, improving the members' discipline and encouraging them to act in ways that were moral, righteous and good for the country. Soon, heroes and patriots of the Two Hus were flocking to join the Gang, and, within a few years, its influence in the south was compared to the Beggar Clan's hold on the north.

Although Shangguan Jiannan was no longer a soldier, he held fast to his responsibilities as a loyal son of the Song Empire: to protect the homeland, to vanquish its foes, and to restore lost territories. He often sent men to the southern capital of Lin'an and through the enemy lines to Bianliang—the Song Empire's main capital, now under Jin occupation—to gather intelligence so he could keep abreast of the latest news and troop movements, looking for a chance to strike back at the invaders.

Some years later, Shangguan was told that an Iron Palm Gang member had befriended a jailer who had stood guard over General Yue Fei in his last days of imprisonment. According to this man, the General wrote a military tract while confined and it was among the objects interred with him when he passed on. Shangguan made it his mission to track down this text and later discovered that it was most likely hidden within the grounds of the Imperial Palace in Lin'an.

Shangguan summoned every capable fighter in the Gang to go

east with him. They stole into the royal complex under the cover of darkness and were able to find *The Secret to Defeating the Jin* without any complications.

Shangguan then went straight to his old commander Han Shizhong, who was leading the life of a hermit by the shore of West Lake after his forced retirement from the Imperial Court. The sight of Yue Fei's handwriting brought back a flood of reminiscence for the aged warrior—the patriot's unjust death and his thwarted dreams of freeing his people from their Jurchen shackles. Han was so roused by his memories that he drew his sword and swung it at his desk.

When the older man had collected himself, he said to Shangguan that he was too old to make use of the military treatise, but insisted that it could be a powerful weapon in the hands of a younger man. He then took out a bound volume and gave it to Shangguan. It contained General Yue's poems, letters, memorials to the Emperor and other writings that Han had compiled and copied out by hand to commemorate his old friend. He bade his former officer to take on General Yue's mantle, to rally the heroes of the Central Plains, repel the invaders and restore the realm to its rightful ruler.

For it occurred to Han Shizhong that Yue Fei would not have written the military text just for it to keep him company in the grave. The General had never been one for empty words and gestures, and the book stressed the importance of serving one's country with loyalty and righteousness—it must have been intended for a practical purpose. Perhaps Qin Hui had kept the General guarded so closely that the writings failed to make it out of his jail.

Still, Han Shizhong was certain that the General would have made provision to get his vital work into the right hands. Could it be that the news had never reached the intended recipient? What if they had come to the palace but could not find the treatise because Shangguan Jiannan had already taken it?

The two men decided to leave a message in its place. Shangguan painted a landscape of Iron Palm Mountain, and within the mounting concealed another piece of paper with a message of sixteen characters:

> *Yue Fei's final writings*
> *In Iron Palm Mountain*
> *Beneath the Middle Crag*
> *In the Second Segment.*

Han Shizhong added a poem by his old comrade, in case the painting alone was too cryptic a clue. He believed that Yue Fei must have set down the military strategy for his officers, and hoped that the presence of the General's verse would prompt them to study the painting, thereby discovering the hidden message. And so, Shangguan went back to the palace and placed the hanging scroll where he had found Yue Fei's book.

Shangguan Jiannan then returned to Iron Palm Mountain and studied General Yue's guide to training troops and vanquishing the enemy on the battlefield. In those years, the Jin army's incursions were increasing in frequency and ferocity, but the Iron Palm Gang barely had enough strength to protect itself, let alone rally patriots to mount a campaign north to repel the Jurchens. His dream of chasing the Jin from Song territory was never realized.

Decades later, Shangguan Jiannan departed this life a disappointed man, and the leadership was passed on to his disciple Qiu Qianren. The older man had no illusions about his student's nature. Qiu cared only for the martial arts and had no interest in any higher principles. The fate of his country had never concerned him, so, although Shangguan shared all his knowledge of kung fu, he never instructed him in the art of war and battle formations, or told him about Yue Fei's writings, since it would mean nothing and served no function for a man of Qiu Qianren's inclination.

When Shangguan Jiannan realized his end was nigh, he took Yue Fei's military tract with him on his final journey—to the cave in the middle crag of Iron Palm Mountain—to prevent it from falling into the hands of false-hearted men.

"LEADER SHANGGUAN held Yue Fei's writings close to his chest as he breathed his last," Guo Jing said with a sigh. The sun had now dipped below the horizon and dusk was fast descending.

"I assumed he had conspired with the Jin, like the Qiu brothers. If I had known, I would have shown his remains the respect he deserved. I can't imagine how aggrieved he must feel in the underworld right now. The once patriotic Iron Palm Gang is now made up of double-dealers."

Their boat was now moored by a village and the boat-master was busy slaughtering a chicken for dinner. Worried that their food might be tampered with, Lotus snatched the ingredients from him, grumbling about his unhygienic cooking area. The man glared at her as she went ashore with Guo Jing. He had no hope of browbeating the eloquent girl using sign language, but nor could he blow his cover by regaining the use of his tongue. All he could do was storm into the cabin to let out a string of profanities and groans of frustration the instant they stepped off the boat.

Lotus found a farmstead whose owners allowed her to use their kitchen, and, after they had eaten, they sat under a tree to enjoy the evening breeze.

"What do you think Qiu Qianzhang was planning to do with Leader Shangguan's chronicle?" Guo Jing asked. "How did he get hold of it?"

"It wouldn't have been difficult for the old swindler to steal the book, since he looks exactly like his brother. And he's been posing as the leader of the Iron Palm Gang, so he'd need to know their history, or else people would see through his act . . . I bet Brother Tempest Qu knew nothing about his great contribution to the cause."

Guo Jing looked at Lotus in confusion.

"Remember the cave behind the waterfall? By the Hall of Wintry Jade in the Imperial Palace in Lin'an?"

He nodded.

"That was where General Yue Fei's last writings were believed to be hidden. And wouldn't Shangguan Jiannan have put the painting back in the place where he found the book?"

"Yes . . ."

"Brother Qu was banished from Peach Blossom Island by Papa, but he always hoped he would be allowed back one day. He knew how much Papa loves painting, calligraphy and antiques. Tell me, where in the world has the best collection of such treasures? The Imperial Palace in Lin'an, of course. So, Brother Qu stole into the royal residence and carried off many great works of art—"

"I see what you mean now. It was one of the paintings your Brother Qu took. He kept everything in the hidden room in Ox Village. He was planning to present them to your father one day, but he died at the hands of the Imperial Guard before he was ready to make the journey. And, when that scoundrel Wanyan Honglie came after General Yue's writings, all he found was an empty casket. The book was long gone, and the painting that would have pointed him to its new location had been taken too . . . If we'd known, we wouldn't have needed to fight so hard outside the cave. I wouldn't have been injured by the Old Venom, and you wouldn't have had to worry for seven whole days."

"There, you're mistaken. If we hadn't spent all that time in the secret chamber, we'd never have found the painting, and we wouldn't have . . ." Lotus trailed off. Her eyes were drawn to the newly risen moon and her heart ached at the memory of that fateful encounter with Khojin. "I wonder how Papa is . . . We haven't got long until the fifteenth. Moon Festival. The mid-autumn full moon. We'll be at the Tower of Mist and Rain in Jiaxing, fighting Tiger Peng and his motley crew . . . After that, you are going back to Mongolia, aren't you?"

"No, I have to avenge my father and Uncle Yang first. I have to take Wanyan Honglie's life."

Lotus was still gazing at the luminous crescent in the sky. "And then?"

"We have to help *Shifu* heal his injury, we have to make sure Brother Zhou meets with Madam Ying, we have to visit my *shifus'* homes in Jiaxing, all six of them, one by one, and we have to find my father's grave."

"When we have done all those things, you'll have to go back to Mongolia, won't you?"

"No . . ." But he could not come up with another excuse. He would have to return for his mother, so she could at last come home to the South, where she was born.

"Guo Jing, listen. I know you're trying to delay the inevitable, I know you don't want to be parted from me." A sigh. "I don't want it either . . . But why are we being so foolish, dwelling on it? We should enjoy each moment together to the full. One merry day lived is one merry day less. Let's head back to the boat. We can have some fun with that imposter."

When they boarded, the boat-master and the two deckhands were already asleep in the stern.

"I'll keep watch." Guo Jing kept his voice low.

"Let me teach you a few signs to show them tomorrow," Lotus whispered back.

"Why don't you do it yourself?"

"They're too foul for a maiden's hands."

Guo Jing was amused by the thought of cussing with gestures. "Teach me tomorrow. It's late."

Lotus was more tired than she would admit, since she had yet to fully regain her elemental power. She laid her head on Guo Jing's lap and was soon dozing off. She was careful not to press her shoulders or back into him, for fear of pricking him with the Hedgehog Chainmail.

Guo Jing wanted to meditate and work on his internal strength, but he knew that if he sat cross-legged in the usual position, he might arouse the boat-master's suspicion. So, he lay flat on his back and channeled his energy according to the instructions from the final section of the Nine Yin Manual, as interpreted by Reverend Sole Light. An hour later, he sensed an invigorating pulse coursing through his limbs and reverberating in his bones.

Satisfied by these results, he was brought back to the present by Lotus's voice. "Don't marry her, please," she murmured. "I want to marry you . . . No, no, ignore me. I was wrong. I won't ask anything of you. I know I'm the only one in your heart. That's good enough."

"Lotus, Lotus . . ." Guo Jing whispered.

The soft breathing of slumber was her only reply.

He watched the pale moon caress her face, with a heavy heart. The rosy glow had yet to return to her cheeks, so her skin was almost translucent. He did not know how long he had been gazing at her when a light frown creased her brow and a tear rolled from the corner of her eye.

She must be dreaming about our future, Guo Jing thought. Her carefree giggles are just an act. She laughs to hide the great weight she carries, and I'm the cause of it. It would be better for her if we hadn't met in Kalgan. What about me? Can I bear to cast her aside?

The sound of water sloshing against the side of the boat broke into Guo Jing's thoughts. He was astounded that anyone would be so reckless as to raise their sail in the dark, especially as the Yuan River was notorious for its rapid currents and treacherous shallows. It sounded to him as though the craft was coming downriver toward them. He was just about to push himself up so he could peer through the gap between the gunwale and the awning, when three muffled claps from the stern gave him pause. The dull noise carried a long way in the dead of the night. Suddenly, the slop of an oar slipping into water and the rustle of sails being lowered could be heard. Moments later, the unknown vessel drew abreast.

Guo Jing woke Lotus up with a nudge as their boat bobbed in the water. He peeled back the canopy in time to catch a glimpse of a black silhouette—their boat-master, perhaps—hopping across onto the barge that had just arrived.

"Stay here, I'll take a look."

Lotus nodded.

Crouching low, Guo Jing tiptoed to the prow. The other craft was still swaying from the boat-master's impact, providing the perfect cover for him to come aboard without being detected. He leaped high and touched down in the middle of the crossbeam up on the mast. The vessel dipped a little from his weight, but otherwise remained steady. He waited a little before climbing down and finding a gap in the woven canopy he could spy through.

Three men. Clad in black, in the manner typical of the Iron Palm Gang. One of them wore a blue-green kerchief over his brow. Burly and tall, he seemed to be in command, for the boat-master was bowing to him.

"Fort Master Qiao," the boat-master said in a deferential tone.

"They're both aboard?"

"Yes."

"Do they seem wary?"

"No, but they won't eat what we cook, so we can't—"

"*Huh!* We'll finish them on Blue Dragon Shoal. When you leave Blue Dragon Market, the day after tomorrow, smash the tiller three *li* from the shoal, at precisely midday. We will take over from there. Remember, these two are very skilled in kung fu. Be vigilant. When the deed is done, our leader will reward you handsomely. Go back by water and take care not to rock the boat. You don't want to wake them."

"Yes, Fort Master Qiao." The boat-master retreated with a bow and slipped into the river, portside.

Guo Jing flexed his toes and landed lightly back on his own craft. He told Lotus what he had heard.

"Blue Dragon, White Tiger, we won't be cowed by a shoal. We rowed up raging rapids to get to Uncle Sole Light. Now, bedtime for us both!"

They slept soundly through the night, safe in the knowledge that they would not be attacked and thus had no need to keep a lookout. The next day, they sat on the deck to admire the landscape as they sailed past.

On the morning of the third day of the voyage, Lotus signaled to the boat-master as he weighed anchor and prepared to set sail: "Put the horse ashore. I don't want him to drown if we capsize at Blue Dragon Shoal."

The man shot her an odd look, but promptly recovered from his slip, feigning incomprehension. Lotus threw her hands up, overwhelmed by the urge to swear at him. She had picked up a most colorful repertoire of curses from the servants of Peach Blossom Island, who were all fearsome criminals made deaf and mute by her father. She touched two fingers to form a circle and decided it was too unbecoming. She abandoned the gesture with a giggle and led Ulaan onto dry land with Guo Jing.

"Lotus, let's ride away."

"Why?"

"I want us to be together always, safe and sound. What's the point of getting even with these scheming crooks?"

"Together always?" she scoffed.

Smarting from this snub, he watched her let go of the reins and point north. Ulaan understood that he would be reunited with his masters soon and galloped off, disappearing into the distance.

"Back to the boat."

"Why take such a risk? You haven't regained your strength."

"It's fine if you don't want to come." With that, she returned to the barge and went aboard. Guo Jing had no choice but to follow her.

As he climbed over the gunwale, she gave him a radiant smile. "You really are a dolt sometimes. The more adventures we share, the more memories we'll have of our time together. So, when we part, we'll have plenty to remember each other by—that's good, isn't it?"

"Do we—do we have to part? I don't want to—I won't. No matter what!"

She just looked at him in silence.

Her blank expression elicited a wretched feeling in his heart. A giant hammer was pummeling the core of his being out of shape and he knew not how to stop it. He had promised Tolui on a hotheaded impulse that he would honor his betrothal to Khojin, but now he had to live with the bitter agony he had inflicted upon Lotus and himself.

3

STANDING TOGETHER ON THE PROW, GUO JING AND LOTUS surveyed the undulating hills, which were fast growing into jagged mountains as they sailed closer to noon and Blue Dragon Shoal. While they were being swept downriver at dazzling speed, the upstream traffic struggled against the strong current, even though the vessels were being hauled along with thick ropes from the shore. The larger barges they passed could only make progress thanks to the combined strength of several dozen men, and lighter craft still required a minimum of three or four pairs of hands. Often a vessel would appear nailed to the riverbed, beaten about by the frothing waves, for just to stay where it was already took its best efforts in this tug of war against the power of nature.

The tow-men trudged forward, one step at a time, huddled and bent low, their foreheads almost scraping the uneven path. Stripped down to the waist, they had each wound a flimsy piece of white cloth around their heads. Glistening sheets of sweat clung to their sun-scorched backs, making their skin iridescent in the midday sun. They howled with each heave of the rope. A cacophony of cries rose and fell, unceasing, echoing between rock and river.

Trepidation mounted in Guo Jing as their barge washed downstream. "We've misjudged the Yuan River. This stretch of dangerous water seems to go on and on." He was careful to keep his voice low. "What if we *do* capsize? You've yet to regain your strength. The risk is too great."

"What do you think we should do?"

"Take out the boat-master and steer the boat ashore."

A shake of her head. "That's no fun."

"This isn't the time for fun."

"But I like fun!" Lotus said, giggling into her hand.

The sight of the waterway ahead being squeezed ever narrower by steep slopes either side disturbed Guo Jing. What could he do to make sure they got through safely? He asked himself over and over again, but his brain failed to offer up a solution.

After a bend in the river, cottages could be seen dotted high and low on a mountain in the distance. The boat raced along with the fast-flowing water like a galloping horse, and, in a flash, they were bearing down on the settlement. Scores of burly men stood on the waterfront awaiting their approach. They caught the hawsers tossed their way by the boat-master and looped them onto a large capstan. It took fifteen men turning the winch with all their might to pull them to shore.

At the same time, a second vessel of a similar size was being dragged to the dock from downstream. The moment its anchors were dropped, the tow-men flopped to the ground, puffing and panting, unable to move.

Guo Jing eyed the exhausted men with alarm, for it could only mean one thing: the stretch of river ahead was more treacherous. He also noted there were graybeards among the laborers, as well as teenage boys of no more than fourteen or fifteen. Young or old, they were, without exception, jaundiced and stick thin, their ribs protruding out so prominently that he could count them from afar. He felt a lump in his throat to witness the harsh conditions endured by the common people.

By now, their barge had also set anchor among the twenty or so vessels lining the dock of this hillside village.

"Brother, what is this place?" Lotus called to one of the men who had hauled them in.

"Blue Dragon Market."

She nodded in acknowledgment and edged toward the back of the boat with Guo Jing to keep an eye on their boat-master. He was gesturing at a brawny man on the water's edge. Then, a hatchet appeared in his hands. He swung, once, twice. The mooring lines were cut clean through. He dropped the hatchet and yanked both anchors out of the water.

The boat careened sharply, caught in the grip of the raging river, before spinning a full circle. Seized by the brute force of nature, the craft tore downriver to cries of dismay from the dock. In a trice, the shrieks died away, as they were swept out of earshot of Blue Dragon Market and over a steep drop in the watercourse. The barge plunged and plummeted. Water sprayed and splashed. The boat-master clasped both hands over the tiller, his eyes reading every crest and billow. The two deckhands, each clutching a barge pole, flanked their captain. There was no way to tell whether they were poised to fend off boulders or to guard the boat-master from Guo Jing and Lotus.

The river boiled with relentless fury. The craft hurtled onward, as if flung over a cliff, in free fall. They could crash into rocks and be smashed into a thousand pieces at any moment.

"Take the helm, Lotus!" Guo Jing bellowed as he made for the stern.

The deckhands raised their poles, ready for combat, but what chance did they have against Guo Jing?

Rushing after him, Lotus yelled—"Wait!"—then dropped her voice to a whisper and pointed to two white dots in the sky. "The condors."

Guo Jing at last understood why Lotus had been so composed. They could fly off on the birds' backs when the boat crashed. He beckoned the raptors down to join them.

The boat-master allowed himself a smile at Guo Jing's aborted attack. The unweaned wretch must be scared stiff by the turbulence, he told himself.

The distant rhythmic chants of a tow party could now be heard above the river's rumble. Presently, a canopied boat came into view, inching steadily forward against the current. A black flag flew from the mast.

The boat-master brought down the hatchet, slicing through the tiller handle. The foaming water instantly devoured the splintered wood as he readied himself to leap onto the oncoming vessel.

The condors were now perched on the gunwale. Guo Jing held one hand out toward Lotus and pressed the other down on the female condor's back to keep her steady.

"Not yet!" she called. "Grab an anchor. Smash that boat!"

With the tiller sabotaged, leaving no way to control the rudder, the river was hurling them into the other craft. They were just one *zhang* apart and closing fast. The helmsman of the oncoming vessel pushed the tiller as far as it would go and managed to edge his barge a fraction to port, avoiding a head-on collision.

Right then, Guo Jing launched the anchor. It ripped through the air, powered by a Drawn by Six Dragons from the Dragon-Subduing Palm.

Screams and shouts sounded above the roar of the river.

The anchor's metal bulk crashed into the other boat's bow, where a half dozen or so bamboo cables were fastened to the vessel's tow pole.

Already strained out of shape by the opposing forces of the roiling river and the hauling men, the post exploded on impact. Taut towlines fell slack. The laborers tumbled headlong to the ground.

Like a kite with its string snapped, the barge swiveled round and round, then rushed stern-first toward Guo Jing's and Lotus's boat.

The shrieks of men, rising above the bellowing of the river, reverberated between the cliff faces either side.

"Heeeelp!" the boat-master cried.

"The mute speaks!" Lotus could not pass up the chance to mock him.

Taking a deep breath, Guo Jing gripped the second anchor rope with both hands and tossed the metal weight into the air with a

Dragon in the Field. He whirled it over his head as he wheeled round three times to build momentum.

Then he let go, propelling the heavy load with a blast of his *neigong* power. This time, he aimed for the rudder.

A man shot out of the cabin, snatched up a barge pole and swatted it down on the airborne anchor's shank. The bamboo shaft bent and arced—*crack!*—and broke in two.

Still, the contact was enough to deflect the anchor away from the boat. It crashed into the river, where it sunk without trace.

The man stood at the stern, steady, in control, unaffected by the violent lurching of his vessel. Gusts of wind tugged at his arrowroot short jacket, sweeping his speckled beard to one side.

Qiu Qianren!

4

Paaaang! Guo Jing and Lotus were thrown into the air, their backs slamming against the cabin doors. Their boat had rammed into a cluster of rocks. In a trice, they were ankle-deep in water. Too late to escape on the condors now—they had flown away in fright at the impact.

"Follow me!" Guo Jing called to Lotus and he stamped his feet against the deck.

Up he shot in a Dragon Soars in the Sky, angling his body so that he was hurtling his full weight into Qiu Qianren.

A desperate gambit, but in this life-and-death moment, what option did he have?

If he tried to land anywhere else on Qiu's barge, the martial Master would strike at him before he could touch down, and there would be nothing he could do to defend himself.

But, if he launched his body at Qiu Qianren in a frontal assault, he might be able to force him back on his heels, which might give him the chance to gain a foothold.

Yet, Guo Jing's reasoning was apparent to Qiu Qianren too. The seasoned fighter brandished the broken bamboo pole. Its jagged point ripped through the air in a succession of feints and firm thrusts.

Rather than trying to fend off the sharp severed pole, the airborne Guo Jing hit back with a Thick Clouds Without Rain, striking his hands in quick succession at the crown of Qiu's head. Then he swiped his arm against the makeshift weapon, pushing its vicious point aside as he dived toward the deck.

With a howl, Qiu let go and drew his palms together, propelling them toward Guo Jing's chest. Once he made contact, he would send the boy flying into the bubbling water. After all, his feet were firmly planted, and the whelp had nothing to stand on but the wind.

Just then, Lotus hopped up and tapped the Dog Beater against the broken barge pole as it fell through the air. Riding on the residual internal force contained in the discarded weapon, she vaulted over to Qiu's vessel, raining down three ferocious jabs with the cane as she descended.

The rapid-fire onslaught almost caught Qiu Qianren out, very nearly striking him in the eye, and he turned away from Guo Jing to deal with Lotus.

As Guo Jing landed on the deck, he sent forth a Withdraw to Gain, a Dragon-Subduing Palm move rarely used in combat.

Qiu twisted away from the Dog-Beating Cane and swept his foot sideways, forcing Guo Jing to take a step back. Instantly, Qiu thrust out his palms—*swoo-oosh*—one after the other.

For centuries, the Iron Palm Gang's fame had been sustained by this very kung fu, which took the group's name. When it was passed down to Shangguan Jiannan and his disciple Qiu Qianren, they had enriched the repertoire with their own interpretations. Although the Iron Palm was less powerful than the Dragon-Subduing Palm, it had the advantage of greater variety.

Half a dozen moves were exchanged in the twinkling of an eye. Confined to the barge's narrow deck, Qiu Qianren and Guo Jing fought warily, pulling back before their moves reached their full potential. Still, the deafening rush of the river could not mask the shrill hiss that followed each lash of their palms.

Qiu's helmsman had regained some control of the vessel, in spite of the initial chaos and the ongoing fight, wresting the boat the right way round as it reeled downstream.

The other craft, by now, had been ripped in two by the angry river. Spars of wood, stretches of sail and the three-man crew were churned about in circles, dragged deeper and deeper into a whirlpool.

Lotus had her hands full tackling the crew of Qiu Qianren's barge, but, when the boat-master's shrieks reached her ears, she felt compelled to fling a hurried insult his way as he and his two deckhands thrashed and flailed. It did not matter how hard they paddled, they could not escape the pull of the vortex. They were sucked down to the riverbed together with what was left of the wreckage. Meanwhile, the condors wheeled in the sky, cawing in distress.

Barely any time had passed and the rapids had already carried them a couple of *li* from where the other boat had sunk. All the while, Lotus had been jabbing and thrusting with the Dog-Beating Cane, forcing Qiu's minions back through the cabin, toward the bow, so she could help Guo Jing deal with their leader. Just when she was about to join the fight, she caught the glint of steel from the corner of her eye.

One of the retreating men. Hacking down with his saber.

Lotus could not see who the man was attacking, but time was of the essence, so she flicked her wrist and sent a handful of sewing needles flying into his arm. The blade fell from his hand as he uttered a blood-chilling wail. Lotus darted into the cabin and, with one swift blow, sent him sprawling. Then she turned to check on his intended victim.

Madam Ying. On the floor. Her arms and legs bound. The only acknowledgment she gave her rescuer was a cold glare.

Lotus was astonished to find the vindictive woman here, of all places. She picked up the saber and hacked through the rope binding her wrists.

The moment her hands were free, Madam Ying snatched the blade from Lotus's grasp.

It flashed once.

The man was left twitching in his own gore. She now turned the bloodstained weapon on the restraints around her ankles.

"You saved me, but don't hope for anything in return."

"Fine, we're even now."

Lotus hastened back to the deck. She had no time for petty wrangling with the likes of Madam Ying. Whirling the Dog-Beating Cane, she wove a web of attack over Qiu Qianren's back.

The martial Master was not particularly concerned by Lotus entering the fray; he merely responded by channeling more *neigong* power into his palms. He had been dominating the boy. What could a teenage girl bring to the fight?

But, as he listened to his followers being chased overboard by Madam Ying, their muffled screams swallowed by the river, a thought chilled his heart: No human being, not even an expert swimmer, would stand a chance in this water.

A dozen moves in, he also had to face a rude awakening. The girl's little green stick was peskier than he had assumed. Feeling the strain of the double onslaught, he edged backward and hopped onto the gunwale. With the wild waves at his back, he no longer had to worry about being harassed from behind.

Guo Jing let rip with a series of his most potent strikes, but Qiu Qianren held his ground without shifting half an inch, as though his feet were nailed in place. It gave Lotus an idea: You call yourself Iron Palm Water Glider, let's see if you can really walk on water!

She renewed her attack, but Qiu's risposte was calm and precise, his palms a blur of motion as he kept one eye on the river.

Expecting reinforcements? She continued to taunt him in her head. Well, your kung fu may be better than ours, but there are three of us! Together, we can throw you overboard.

"Step aside, little girl," Madam Ying said. She had been keeping track of the battle as she swept the Iron Palm Gang members off the boat, sparing only the helmsman.

Annoyed by her disparaging tone, Lotus thrust twice with the Dog Beater, forcing Qiu Qianren to twist away and disengage. She grabbed the chance to jump back a couple of paces.

"Let her have a go." She gave Guo Jing's robe a tug and he also gave ground.

"Master Qiu, I never imagined that a celebrated personality of the *jianghu* would stoop so low as to use a doping incense on a sleeping woman," Madam Ying said in her haughtiest tone.

"Had I time to deal with you myself, you would know I have no need of incense," Qiu Qianren shot back. "I can catch ten of you with my bare hands."

"How might I have offended the Iron Palm Gang?"

"These two befouled our hallowed site. And you gave them shelter."

"Oh, them? Do what you like. They're nothing to me."

Madam Ying's prickly antagonism vanished as swiftly as it had surfaced. She perched on the gunwale, ready to enjoy the spectacle.

Under normal circumstances, it would not have been possible for the mistrustful woman to be abducted by the mediocre martial men of the Iron Palm Gang, whom she had just cast into the river, but, since her descent from Sole Light's mountain sanctuary after her failed attempt at revenge, she had been in a state of intense distraction.

The way Guo Jing took the knife for Sole Light and the monk bared his chest for her, had awakened the natural sympathy she had suppressed for so long. And yet, as she made her way down the mountain to find a guest house for the night, the memory of her infant son's death came flooding back—his face distorted by pain, his eyes pleading—and her heart had turned to stone again. Sitting alone in her room, haunted by her past and tortured by her fleeting weakness, she failed to detect the waft of incense smoke laced with incapacitating herbs.

Now she redirected her bile at Guo Jing and Lotus, hoping she would see them dragged away by the current along with Qiu Qianren.

Lotus glared at the capricious woman. Once we've dealt with him, you'll be next! She stood shoulder to shoulder with Guo Jing, and together they rained down a torrent of flying palms and sweeps of the Dog-Beating Cane.

Madam Ying soon came to the conclusion that Qiu Qianren, despite his superior strength, could not outlast the young couple in a battle of attrition. Then she noticed that he seemed to be changing his tactics, shifting his footing along the narrow gunwale. Could he be trying to find a way to catch the young couple unaware?

"Don't overstretch yourself. Rest a little."

Guo Jing's tender concern filled Madam Ying with a bitter pang of longing.

Nobody ever treated me how he treats her, she said to herself. Envy warped into jealousy and, once more, hate consumed her.

"What kind of fight is this, two against one? Let's make it fair." Madam Ying pulled a pair of bamboo slips from her robe, and, without another word, began to jab and swipe at Lotus.

"You really are a mad crone. Now I know why the Hoary Urchin wants nothing to do with you!"

Thus provoked, Madam Ying attacked so viciously that Lotus struggled to defend herself, even with the aid of the sophisticated Block technique from the Dog-Beating repertoire, for her agility was still hampered by her damaged inner strength. Madam Ying had many years of training over her, and the efficacy of the woman's kung fu—inspired by the slick movement of fish—was amplified by the unpredictable motion of the barge.

"I know you miss the Old Urchin, but you can't win him back by acting like him." Lotus hoped to buy time by poking at the woman's sore spot. "He doesn't care for the deranged."

Guo Jing, for the time being, was just about scraping by on his own against Qiu Qianren, drawing on Reverend Sole Light's instructions to maintain an uninterrupted circulation of *neigong* energy around his body between each chop of his palms.

Buoyed by Madam Ying's support, Qiu Qianren struck back with renewed vigor. He did not understand her change of heart, but that did not concern him, since he knew it would not be long before he had sapped the boy's strength.

He avoided a razor-sharp slice from his opponent with a nimble twist of his waist, then thrust his palms out, his right above his left.

Guo Jing twirled his hands and pushed back with a Withdraw to Gain.

A clash of inner forces.

Huh! They each grunted as they scuttled back by three steps.

Qiu Qianren promptly regained his balance, but Guo Jing tripped over a coiled rope. He went with the fall, flipping into a roll to give himself time to find his footing, while drawing his arms in to protect his chest.

Cackling at the clumsy tumble, Qiu closed in to secure his victory.

5

LOTUS, MEANWHILE, WAS HARD PRESSED BY MADAM YING'S relentless assault. Her breathing was getting shallower and beads of sweat were forming on her hairline. She knew she could not hold out much longer, and that fact was obvious to Madam Ying too, judging from the way she was relishing their duel.

Then, the sound of Qiu Qianren's laughter boomed above the roaring torrent, the creaking timbers of his battered vessel. Abruptly, the flush of victory was wiped from Madam Ying's face and she froze mid-move. She had just stabbed a bamboo slip at Lotus, and, though she should have pulled back to guard against a counter-thrust, she let her arm remain extended, leaving her core exposed.

Seeing her chance, Lotus speared the Dog Beater toward Madam Ying's heart, aiming for her Spirit Repository pressure point.

The woman took no notice.

"It was you!" Madam Ying shrieked. A shudder racked her body, as though she had been swept by a demonic gust.

Then she pounced, arms flung wide, teeth bared, at Qiu Qianren.

To lock the man in her arms and tear at his flesh.

Qiu leaped sideways and barked, "What are you doing?" His heart quailed at her wild eyes and fearsome countenance.

Growling like an enraged tiger, Madam Ying launched herself at him again, without a thought for her own safety.

Qiu hammered a heavy blow down on her shoulder, one he was sure would shock her into drawing her arms up to block. Nay, he was wrong. She had only one concern: to seize him.

If she gets me in a body lock, the boy can strike me at will . . . A sudden fear for his life compelled Qiu to cut short his attack and scuttle portside, away from the possessed woman. An undignified retreat unworthy of a great Master, but, right now, staying alive mattered more than saving face.

Lotus took Guo Jing's hand and pulled him aside to give Madam Ying more room.

Qiu ducked and dodged. His sophisticated skills had little chance to shine against an opponent who cared nothing for her own life.

She lunged. She clawed. Forcing him back toward the stern.

Her eyes bloodshot. Her face twisted in a mask of rage.

She sprang. She swiped. She had him trapped by the tiller.

This is it! This mad hag is my reckoning! The martial Master resigned himself to his fate as he shrank back.

She raised her hand again. *Thump!* The helmsman flew into the white water. A kick. The tiller splintered.

The boat began to whirl in wild circles.

Lotus groaned. Why does she have to go berserk now? She'll kill us all! She pursed her lips to whistle for the condors.

Paaang! The vessel slammed sideways into a cluster of rocks.

A breach in the hull.

Qiu Qianren took a deep breath and got ready to jump. They were not that far from the shore. He might be able to leap all the way to safety. Either way, he would sooner try his luck with the rapids than let this demented woman drag him down to the netherworld.

He pushed off with all his might, but his momentum was spent one *zhang* from land. He plunged down and was dragged to the riverbed by a fierce undertow. Next thing he knew, he was spat out and swept downstream. It was his good fortune that spars of wood from his barge had been scattered far and wide by the collision. He grabbed hold of the first piece of flotsam that came his way, and kicked and splashed with every last drop of his *neigong* as the current churned him about. He was not a good swimmer, drinking a bellyful of murky water with each breath he took, but decades of martial training had fortified his strength and resilience. He fought tooth and nail against the rapids and eventually crawled ashore, bone-weary.

He slumped against a rock, gulping as much air as he could. When he looked up, he realized he had been washed a dozen *li* downriver. The wreck of his boat was a mere dark spot on the horizon, but he was convinced that he could still make out the bloodthirsty face of Madam Ying flashing her teeth and snapping her jaws at him.

"You can't run from me!"

Madam Ying prepared to cast herself overboard after Qiu Qianren. Guo Jing could not bear to see her drown, so he dashed forward, pulling her back by the hem of her robe. The boat lurched, drawn by the turbulence into the heart of the river. She swung her palms in fury. He ducked, but held on tight.

"Leave her be! We have to go!" Lotus called, gesturing at the condors perched on the gunwale.

Guo Jing let go and all resistance went out of Madam Ying. She flopped onto her knees, her tearstained face buried in her hands.

"My son! My son!"

The wild water, sloshing around their ankles, was fast claiming the barge. Lotus urged Guo Jing once more to escape while he still could.

"Go!" he cried. "Send the condor back."

"There isn't time!"

"We promised Reverend Sole Light. We can't leave her. Go!"

Lotus wavered. The monk had given up years of martial training to bring her back to life . . .

A thunderous crash. The barge groaned and shuddered. They had crashed into another cluster of boulders. The impact almost sent them flying.

Water gushed in from every joint and crack.

They were going under. Fast.

"The rocks!" Lotus cried.

Guo Jing nodded and pulled Madam Ying to her feet. She complied, her body yielding and pliant, her blank eyes fixed on the swirling billows. He looped his arm around her back and heaved.

"Jump!" he said.

The three of them landed on the boulder at the same time.

The rapids lashed at the rock, drenching them with spray. In the short time it took them to secure their footing on the slippery surface, the barge was devoured by the ravenous torrent.

The condors had flown over, following Guo Jing's call, but they too were intimidated by the feral river and would only circle overhead.

Lotus was no stranger to fierce currents, having grown up on an island, yet even she felt faint and dizzy at the sight of the water tearing past. She held her eyes averted to keep her head from spinning. Once she had steadied herself somewhat, she scanned the shore in search of a way out of their predicament.

A stout willow tree. About ten *zhang* from their refuge.

"Hold tight!" She grabbed Guo Jing's hand, slipped into the water and dived down toward the sunken vessel.

Guo Jing wedged his feet into a crevice and lowered himself into the water, stretching as far as physically possible. He clutched Lotus's wrist with his *neigong* strength, praying that his grip was firm enough and trying not to think about what might happen if . . .

Lotus unwound the halyard connecting the sail to the mast and tugged it free. With Guo Jing's help, she climbed back onto the boulder and hauled in the rope.

"Dagger," she said, when she had gathered a coil about twenty *zhang* in length. She cut the line and whistled, beckoning the female condor to land on her shoulder, but Guo Jing reached out and intercepted the bird, worried that his beloved's small frame could not take the weight.

Lotus tied one end of the rope around the condor's leg and pointed at the willow, gesturing that she should fly across to it and then come back.

The condor spread her wings and circled over the tree several times before returning.

"No! Loop it around the tree!" Lotus hissed, but, of course, the bird could not comprehend her words or her frustration.

Lotus sent the condor to the tree again and again, and each time it wheeled high above the branches. But, on the eighth attempt, she succeeded in persuading the raptor to fly low enough so that, when she turned back, she looped the rope around the willow's robust trunk.

Thrilled, Lotus pulled the line taut and secured it with Guo Jing's help.

"Go on," he said to her.

She gestured at Madam Ying. "Let her go first."

Glowering, the woman grabbed the rope and hauled herself forward, one hand at a time, wading through the water at first, before hoisting herself above it.

Lotus cast Guo Jing a knowing grin. "Great Lord, if you enjoy this little trick, be generous with your tip." With those words, she leaped up and landed on the line, holding out the Dog-Beating

Cane to keep herself steady. Then, like an acrobat, she tightrope-walked over to the willow tree using lightness *qinggong*.

Having never before attempted such a feat himself, Guo Jing decided to imitate Madam Ying's more down-to-earth method, trusting to his grip rather than his balance.

He was a short distance from the shore when he heard Lotus yell, "Hey! Where are you going?"

He pulled himself forward faster, afraid that Madam Ying, in her frenzied state, might rush headlong into harm's way, then he swung down to the ground.

"She's gone."

Guo Jing looked toward where Lotus was pointing. Madam Ying was scuttling south over rocks and boulders.

"We have to follow her," he said. "She's not in her right mind. She may run into danger."

"Of course." Lotus tried to take a step forward, but her legs buckled and she sank to her knees. Shaking her head, she realized that the escapade had been too much for her recovering body.

"Rest here, I'll find her." Guo Jing took off after Madam Ying, but soon he came to a gully full of craggy rocks and chest-high weeds. Three paths fanned out before him, and there was nothing to indicate which of them she had taken.

As light began to fail, Guo Jing thought of Lotus, alone and defenseless by the river, and turned back.

6

GUO JING AND LOTUS SPENT A FITFUL NIGHT ON THE ROCKY shore, their empty stomachs growling in protest. Once it was light enough, they picked their way along the river, calling for Ulaan. On and on they walked, but there was no sign of the horse. It was past midday when they came across a small tavern, where they bought three roosters from the innkeeper. They gave the condors one each, while Lotus roasted the third over a fire—their first meal since the wreck of their barge.

The birds flew up a nearby tree with their roosters and tore at the flesh with glee, raining down a shower of fluttering feathers. Then, out of the blue, the female condor screeched and took to the sky, flinging away the half-eaten carcass. The male raptor arched his pinions and joined his mate, filling the air with urgent caws.

"They sound tetchy." Guo Jing had never seen them act like this.

"Let's see what they're up to."

They hurried after the birds, which were now wheeling high in the sky some distance away. The condors swooped in a synchronized dive, plunging beneath the treeline before shooting back up wing to wing.

"They're attacking something on the ground!" Guo Jing exclaimed.

Two or three *li* later, they found themselves at the edge of a market town. The condors flew back and forth over the houses, searching for their prey.

Guo Jing whistled, but they ignored him.

"What has upset them so much?" He was perplexed.

At length, the birds returned to them, though they were in a troubling state. Blood streamed from a deep cut on the male condor's foot. A lesser creature would have lost it altogther.

The female condor was clutching something in her talons. It took Guo Jing some time to coax her into letting go of it, and, when she finally relented, he was aghast to find a gory, hairy mess in his hand.

"The condors have never attacked anyone for no reason. What do you think happened?" He turned the freshly torn scalp this way and that, unable to fathom what would have made the bird sink her claws into someone's head.

"We'll know when we find whoever it belongs to," Lotus said as she tended to the male condor's cut.

They found a guest house for the night, then split up to search for the scalped man. The market was bustling and full of people—they combed every street and alleyway until sundown, but found nothing.

"I looked everywhere, but I didn't see anyone with a raw wound on his head," Guo Jing said, dejected.

"He probably covered it up."

"Oh!" He had seen many men in hats . . . but he couldn't have gone up and ripped a stranger's cap off, could he?

THE NEXT morning, they woke to find Ulaan outside the guest house, having been guided there by the condors. Although they still wanted to know who the raptors had mutilated, there were more pressing matters at hand and they knew they should not tarry in the town. They had to get to Lin'an to find Count Seven Hong so they could share the method that would allow him to recover from his injury, then to Peach Blossom Island to check on Lotus's father, and then to Jiaxing in time for the martial contest with Tiger Peng and his cronies on Moon Festival, which was less than a fortnight away.

Lotus was in high spirits, chuckling and chattering away as they were whisked along on Ulaan's back. The condors watched over the three of them from the sky. Each night, she sat on the bed in their inn or guest house, hugging her knees, and prattled on about nothing in particular until it was long past midnight. Guo Jing could see that she was exhausted, but she ignored his pleas to get some sleep and kept drawing him into conversation.

Several days of hard riding later, they found themselves within reach of the Eastern Sea, crossing from West Jiangnan to the eastern part of the Two Zhes, where they found an inn for the night. After a short rest in their room, Lotus asked the innkeeper for a basket so she could shop for dinner.

"Let them bring us our meal," Guo Jing said. "We've been on the road all day. You must be exhausted."

"But I want to cook for you! Don't you like my food?"

"Of course, I love all your dishes, but, right now, you need rest. There'll be plenty of time to cook for me when you're better."

"Plenty of time . . . ?" Lotus froze in the doorway, one foot in the courtyard outside. A faraway, vacant look in her eyes.

Guo Jing took the basket from her arm. "We'll find *Shifu* and the three of us will enjoy your wonderful cooking together."

A moment later, she turned back and cast herself facedown onto the bed.

Guo Jing had not the faintest idea what was going through Lotus's mind. He assumed the journey was catching up with her and she was having a nap, but, in actual fact, tears were staining her cheeks and the bedclothes. He stayed still and quiet, lest he woke her, and only tiptoed over when he heard the call for dinner.

"We're not eating here. Come with me." She gave him a broad grin and jumped to her feet.

Lotus wandered through the town until they heard blaring trumpets and crashing cymbals coming from an imposing mansion guarded by white walls and a sturdy gate. She observed the steady stream of guests flowing in through the wide-open main entrance and led Guo Jing along the perimeter until they arrived at the rear garden. Without a word, she leaped over the wall and marched across the courtyard, making straight for the main hall. Guo Jing trailed after her, out of habit.

The main hall was the grandest part of the house and it glittered with candles and lamps. Inside, a magnificent spread of food and drink was laid out on three round tables, each seating ten to twelve men, merrily feasting.

A banquet in full swing.

"Marvelous! We've come at the perfect time," Lotus said aloud to no one in particular.

She strolled in, giggling to herself, then announced to the whole room: "Begone!"

The host and his thirty-odd guests just stared at the teenage girl.

Lotus pulled the man sitting closest to her from his chair and hooked her foot against his ankles. His fleshy bulk crashed to the floor. The guests needed no further persuasion. They shot to their feet, knocking over chairs and each other in the scrum to get away.

A dozen men armed with sabers and spears rushed into the hall in response to their master's cry of distress. Lotus turned to face them, beaming, and, within two moves, she had subdued the two brawlers leading the ragtag band and snatched up one of their blades. Brandishing the weapon, she charged at the rest of the men. They pushed and shoved their way out of the banquet hall, shrieking for clemency.

Spying that the aged master of the house was attempting to slink away, Lotus darted after him and grabbed him by his grizzled beard. She held the saber menacingly over his head.

"K-kind and merciful miss!" The man fell to his knees. "I-i-if you want gold . . . take it! Spare this old fellow. Please . . ."

"Who says I want gold? Get up and drink with us." Still gripping his beard, Lotus pulled him to his feet. His chin and cheeks burned with searing pain, but he dared not make a sound in protest. She beckoned Guo Jing to join her at the head table, in the place set for the guest of honor.

"C'mon, sit!" She grinned at the shivering merrymakers who had remained in the hall, paralyzed with fear.

"Why are you all standing?" A flourish of her hand. The saber stood quivering, its point driven into the tabletop.

The guests fell over themselves in their haste to sit at the unoccupied tables.

"You don't want to sit with us?" Lotus's eyes swept over their stupefied faces before settling on the blade. It was still trembling from the force that had planted it upright in the wood.

Now, the men jostled for a place at the head table, sending chairs crashing to the floor as they fought for a seat.

"A pack of three-year-olds would have better manners than you lot!"

More shoving and elbowing. At last, the guests were evenly spread among the three tables.

Lotus poured herself a cup of wine. "What's the occasion? Why this banquet tonight?"

"Ummm . . . i-it-it's for my s-s-son. B-b-born one m-moo-moon ago," the master of the house stammered.

"A newborn babe at your ripe old age! Aaah, how sweet! I want to meet him."

The man's face turned an earthen hue. What if she . . . ? But, after a quick glance at the saber sticking out from the table, he sent for the wet nurse.

Lotus cradled the baby and studied his chubby little face by the candlelight, then, tipping her head to the side, flicked her eyes up to take in his father's features.

"Can't see any resemblance. He can't be yours."

Mortified, the man muttered, "Yea—yes . . ."

It was impossible to tell if he was agreeing with her, or if he was trying to say that he had indeed sired the boy.

"The kind miss speaks the truth," he added after a pause, quaking in terror.

There were some among the frightened guests who were sorely tempted to make a joke at the man's expense, yet they were also aware that the slightest reaction could provoke the mercurial girl, so they tried to remain as still and as silent as possible.

Lotus took out a *sycee* ingot of gold, pressed it into the nurse's hand then returned the child to her trembling arms.

"A little gift from your grandmama," she cooed.

The guests were gobsmacked. Such generosity! But why did she call herself grandmother when she was not much older than a child herself? None of it made sense.

The boy's father thanked the kind miss profusely, relieved that danger had passed.

Lotus picked up a large bowl and set it before him with an exaggerated show of good humor.

"A toast to you!" she said, filling it to the brim.

"Begging your pardon, Auntie." The host, assuming that the girl liked being treated as a senior, decided to play along. "I don't have the constitution for drink."

But that was not what Lotus wanted to hear.

"Is this a birthday or a funeral?" She yanked his beard. Her arched eyebrows mirrored the aggression in her tone.

The man raised the bowl and glugged down its contents.

"That's more like it!" She nodded her approval. "Shall we play a drinking game?"

The guests were eager to obey, but this bunch of moneyed merchants, landed gentry and minor scholars, though literate, did not possess the mental dexterity or poetic flair for clever puns and wordplay required for the kind of literati drinking games Lotus had in mind.

Irritated by the uninspired responses they were cobbling together, Lotus jabbed her finger toward the back wall. "Stand over there!"

The sound of chairs scraping the tiled floor gave way to the patter of scrabbling feet. A sense of relief filled the room. The men felt like they had been granted a stay of execution.

Just then—*thump!*—the master of the house crashed backward in his chair. He had succumbed to the wine.

Lotus roared with laughter and turned to a bemused Guo Jing. She helped herself to food and wine and began chattering about everything and nothing, as though they had the hall to themselves.

The guests, afraid to utter a sound, stood on ceremony. The young couple drank and feasted until well into the second watch of the night. Only then, after repeated pleas from Guo Jing, was Lotus ready to leave.

When they were at last back at the guest house, Lotus asked with a cheeky smile, "Did you have fun?"

"I don't see the fun in frightening those poor souls."

"I do what gives me peace. It's not my concern if other people live or die."

Guo Jing was struck by her strange tone, and he could not fathom the meaning of her words.

A moment later, she said, "I'm going for a walk. Are you coming?"

"Now? It's late."

"Grandmama can't stop thinking about her cute little babe."

"You can't—"

She cut him off. "Stop fretting! I'll bring him back. In a few days. When I'm done playing with him."

Laughing, she bolted through the doorway and hopped over the guest house's outer wall.

Guo Jing hastened after her and seized her by the arm.

"Lotus! Enough!"

"No!" She whipped round to confront him. "Not enough! I only have fun when I'm with you, but you're leaving—leaving me—in a few days. You're leaving me to spend your life with Princess Khojin. She'll stop you from seeing me. I know she will.

"Each day I spend with you is one less I have in your company. That's why I'm cramming so much into every moment. I want to do two, three—nay—four days' worth of things with you in just a single day. Yet, I still want more, it's not enough, do you understand, Guo Jing? Do you see why I won't go to sleep? By staying up late, I get to talk with you that little bit longer . . . Do you get it, now? Do you still want to stop me?"

"You know I'm a muddlehead, Lotus." Guo Jing clasped his hands over hers. "I—I'm sorry that I didn't realize this is how you . . . I—I . . . I can't leave you . . ." He did not have the words to make sense of this jumble of feelings.

Lotus gave him a rueful smile. "Papa taught me so many lyric poems and I never grasped why they always seemed to be about some kind of anguished woe. I thought perhaps they spoke to him because he missed Mama. Now I understand what they're trying to say: joy and good spirits are fleeting, but gloom and misery stay with you for a lifetime. And now I see why Papa keeps telling me, 'None in this world lives with a heart unhurt.' Because that's how it is . . ."

The tips of the willow trees shimmered in the silver moonlight. A gentle breeze tugged at their robes, washing over their skin like cool water.

Guo Jing had never been perceptive when it came to feelings—his own or another's. Although he was aware of the depth of Lotus's affection for him, he had never imagined that, when love took root in the heart, it could wreak such havoc. Her words made him see the last few days in a different light.

Yes, I'll miss her very, very much when I'm back in Mongolia, but I'll find ways to cope, he told himself, because I'm rough-hewn and thick-skinned. What about her? She's nothing like me. She'll be on her own on Peach Blossom Island, with just her father for company . . . and, one day, he'll leave her for the next world. Who will she have then? Just a handful of deaf and mute servants. And her own thoughts, turning round and round in her head, day after day. That's the fate I've condemned her to—I'm burying her alive.

The realization cut deep, making his whole body tremble. He clasped her hands tighter, his eyes drinking in her forlorn face.

"Lotus, let the heavens crash down, I'll keep you company on Peach Blossom Island all my life."

His words sent a jolt through her body.

"What—what did you say?" she asked in a quavering voice, meeting his eyes.

"I don't care what Genghis Khan wants. I don't care what Khojin wants. I want to spend my life with you."

Since he had agreed to honor his promise to marry Khojin, he had been plagued by his decision. Now that he had cast off his scruples to follow his heart, he felt unfettered for the first time in weeks.

Guo Jing clasped Lotus close to his chest. She melted into his embrace, and her breath caught in her throat. The world fell away when they were in each other's arms.

They stayed like that for a long time without exchanging a word. At length, Lotus muttered into his chest, "But your ma . . ."

"I'll bring her back south, and she can live with us on Peach Blossom Island."

"And your teacher, Jebe? Your sworn brother, Tolui?"

"I'll just have to owe them a debt of friendship. I can't split my heart into two."

"What would your six *shifus* say? What about Reverend Ma and Reverend Qiu?"

"I'll live with their scorn and implore them to accept us." Guo Jing heaved a sigh. "Lotus, you won't part from me, and I'll never part from you."

"I have an idea." She broke into giggles. "We'll stay on Peach Blossom Island. They can come looking for us, if they wish, but they'll never find you, if you don't want to be found. They'll never work out the labyrinthine layout Papa designed."

Guo Jing was about to protest that it would be disrespectful to hide from his elders, when he heard the sound of distant footsteps. Two men, a dozen *zhang* or so south of them, hurrying northward with the aid of lightness kung fu.

CHAPTER FIVE

CALAMITIES TO COME

I

JUST AS THE YOUNG COUPLE HAD AGREED, WITHOUT A WORD spoken, to enjoy their moment together and resist their natural curiousity, they heard snatches of conversation drifting over from the martial strangers:

"... Urchin ... duped by Brother Peng ... nothing to fear ..."

Could they mean the Hoary Urchin? Guo Jing and Lotus leaped into action.

The men's kung fu was average at best, so they were oblivious to the travel companions they had gained. The landscape grew hillier as they followed the men farther and farther from the market town. After five or six *li*, they arrived at a valley where echoes of obscenities and insults could be heard ringing in the night.

A couple of torches flickered in the pitch-black wilderness, picking out a group of shadowy figures gathered around two men sitting crossed-legged on the ground. Guo Jing recognized Zhou Botong straight away in the half-light, but it took him a little longer to place the bulky form wrapped in crimson vestments ... Lama Supreme Wisdom! The two sat facing each other, stiff and catatonic, without the slightest hint of movement. Nothing to suggest that either man was still breathing.

Never had Guo Jing seen the Hoary Urchin so still . . . so corpse-like. His appearance, along with the exchange they had overheard earlier, led the young man to assume the worst. He tensed, ready to jump to his sworn brother's aid, but Lotus seized his arm and yanked him back down behind a rock.

"Wait," she said quietly. "Just watch."

The slurs they had overheard were being hurled from the mouth of a cave to the left of Zhou Botong. The opening was so small that an adult man would have to bend double to venture inside, and yet the foul-mouthed men kept their distance, visibly wary of what was lurking within.

It took some time for Guo Jing and Lotus to pick out the detail of what they were seeing in the gloom, and, when they did, they could hardly believe their eyes. So many familiar faces: the Ginseng Codger Graybeard Liang; Hector Sha, Dragon King of the Daemon Sect; Tiger Peng, Butcher of a Thousand Hands; Browbeater Hou the Three-Horned Dragon, who had lost an arm and gained three more cysts on his forehead since they had last come across him, in Ox Village, a month before.

The group was completed by the two men who had unknowingly guided the young couple to this valley. When they turned toward the firelight, Guo Jing recognized them as Old Liang's students, one of whom he had sent flying with a Haughty Dragon Repents when he had first learned the Dragon-Subduing Palm.

A sense of unease gnawed at Lotus as she peered around, trying to make out if anyone else was skulking in the darkness.

How come they've got the Urchin in their power? she asked herself. He could handle this lot with one hand tied behind his back. For a Master like him, they're mere playthings.

"I think Viper Ouyang is here," she whispered into Guo Jing's ear.

She was trying to think of a way to confirm her suspicions when she heard the guttural growls of Tiger Peng:

"Come into the open, dog, or we'll smoke you out!"

"Go on, do your reeking worst!" came the booming retort.

A voice Guo Jing knew well. His first martial teacher, Ke Zhen'e, the eldest of the Freaks.

"*Shifu*, I'm here!"

Guo Jing darted out of his hiding place, without a care for Viper Ouyang or anyone else who might be lurking nearby, for protecting his Master was his only concern. He grabbed the man nearest to him—Browbeater Hou—and tossed him aside.

Though taken by surprise, Hector Sha and Tiger Peng were the quickest to recover and react. They pounced as one, while Graybeard Liang sneaked into position behind Guo Jing a moment later, poised to deal a stealthly knockout blow. But, before he could raise his hand, he sensed the air near his back parting and he ducked.

Ke Zhen'e had heard, from inside the cave, the sound of footsteps circling his disciple and let fly a poisoned devilnut.

The projectile whizzed by, passing just above the crown of the Ginseng Immortal's head, scorching his skin. In one great leap, Graybeard Liang distanced himself more than a *zhang* from the fight and examined his scalp gingerly. He heaved a sigh of relief. No blood, but the brush with danger had shaken him—his undershirt was drenched in sweat. The memory of Tiger Peng falling victim to the potent poison delivered by the blind man's secret weapon was fresh in his mind.

Not one to let an affront pass, he pulled several Bone-Piercing Needles from his robe and tiptoed over to the cave. He extended his arm across the entrance, taking care not to make a sound, and readied himself for sweet vengeance.

A numb spot appeared on his wrist. Needles clinked as they hit the ground.

Girlish giggles. "On your knees, or taste the cane."

Old Liang snapped round and found Lotus grinning at him, bamboo stick in hand. Growling, he thrust his left hand at her shoulder and grabbed her weapon with his right. She veered away from the palm strike, but did not shift the cane, so he was able to wrap his fingers around its tip.

Ha! Let go, little girl, or I'll pull you in too! he thought with glee.

He tugged, drawing her weapon toward him. The instant he thought he had taken control of it, the bamboo cane juddered to life and slipped from his grip. Rattled, he flapped his arms to bat it away, but it was a futile gesture, for he had brought her weapon inside his circle of defense himself. All he could do was to follow with his eyes an emerald blur he had no hope of catching, for the tip of the cane was closer to his core than his hands. *Thwack!* A crack on the head.

He let his legs buckle, then tucked himself into a roll, going along with the force of the clout out of instinct. Once he had pulled away by ten paces or so, he sprang to his feet and gaped at the bright-eyed girl who had just made a fool of him—his head smarting, his mind a whirl, his body awash with shame.

"You've been graced by my cane technique, now tell me what that makes you," Lotus said, beaming. "I know you're familiar with the name of this kung fu."

Beaten like a mangy cur . . . Graybeard Liang thought as he rubbed his sore head. His body convulsed at the reminder of his mortifying treatment at the hands of Count Seven Hong and that very same Dog-Beating Cane.

"We shall give Chief Hong face and retreat." He signaled to his disciples and the three of them melted away into the darkness.

Guo Jing, meanwhile, was having no trouble repelling the joint assault from Hector Sha and Tiger Peng. A jab of his left elbow, and Sha shrank three steps back. Guo Jing, riding the impetus of that attack, then swung his forearm out, aiming for Peng.

Tiger Peng dodged the blade-like edge of the flying palm and shifted his stance for a counterattack, but Guo Jing was faster. A hook of his right wrist, and he had the Butcher of a Thousand Hands hoisted up by the back of his collar.

The stout man's legs dangled in the air. He punched and kicked, but his blows contained no sting. His strength seemed to be blunted by the way he was being held up and he could do nothing but watch as Guo Jing's fist fell like a hammer blow on his chest.

This is it . . . He braced himself as he squealed, "What day is it today?"

"Huh?"

"Aren't you a man of your word?"

"What do you mean?" Guo Jing's fist hovered above Peng's sternum, but he was not ready to let him touch firm ground just yet.

"Is it Moon Festival today? Are we in Jiaxing? Have you forgotten our contest? We agreed to test each other's kung fu on the fifteenth day of the eighth moon, at the Tower of Mist and Rain, in Jiaxing. How can you hurt me now, before the appointed day and time?"

There was a logic to his argument that Guo Jing could not dispute. He was about to set the Butcher down when the fragments of conversation that had brought him here surfaced in his mind.

"What did you do to Brother Zhou?"

"Nothing. The Urchin made a wager with the lama. The first to move loses."

Guo Jing regarded his sworn brother with relief and called into the cave, "First *Shifu*, I trust you are safe and well."

All he got in reply was a grunt.

He flung Tiger Peng ten paces away from him, so the mean-spirited man could not deliver a sneaky kick to his abdomen.

But Peng was in no mood to prolong their scuffle.

"The winner of this fight shall be decided on the fifteenth, in Jiaxing," he said after jumping farther back. Then he cupped his hands in farewell and took off with the help of his fastest lightness *qinggong*. As he cursed Hector Sha and Graybeard Liang for deserting him, he wondered what it was that was making the young upstart's kung fu improve by leaps and bounds each time they met. Could he have uncovered some magical elixir? Perhaps there was sorcery at play . . .

2

LOTUS STOOD BETWEEN ZHOU BOTONG AND LAMA SUPREME Wisdom, desperate to know why the lama had not made off with the rest of his cronies. They were glaring at each other. Not so much as a flicker of recognition or a flutter of their eyelids as her face loomed over theirs.

Duped by Brother Peng . . . The words echoed in her head.

This must be Tiger Peng's ploy to deprive the Old Urchin of his martial abilities, she said to herself. How else could the lama and his lackluster skills hold the legendary Zhou Botong the Hoary Urchin back—all on his own—giving the others the chance to harass Ke Zhen'e? The Urchin, being the Urchin, must have regarded it as an amusing game. He would never have guessed their nefarious motives. That must have been the reason why, when the brawl broke out just now, he sat as steady as Mount Tai and did not deign to lift even his little finger.

"Holla! Urchin!" Lotus bellowed into Zhou Botong's face.

Of course, he could see her and hear her very well, but he could not picture a fate more tragic than losing a wager.

"Isn't it tedious, just sitting there? We're still hours from declaring a winner. Let me make this more exciting. I'll tickle your laughter pressure points. And I'll be fair, triggering them at the same time, with the same force. Who laughs first, loses. Agreed?"

Lotus's suggestion could not have come at a better time for the Hoary Urchin. Sitting still for so long had stretched his patience to breaking point. He was desperate to shout in agreement, but, after some fierce mental wrestling, he managed to suppress the urge.

Not expecting a reply, Lotus sat on her haunches halfway between the two men, set down the Dog-Beating Cane and extended her arms, aiming her index fingers at the acupoints on their waists. For once, she managed to be impartial and let an equal amount of internal energy flow into each hand. She knew the Old Urchin's *neigong* was far superior and would be able to withstand her probing, yet she was mystified as to why she was unable to elicit even a hint of reaction from the lama.

If I were in his place, I'd be bent double and howling in hysterics by now. Eyeing the monk with grudging respect, she channeled more power into her fingers.

Zhou Botong bore down with all his inner strength, but Lotus was poking her fingers into the very base of his rib cage where the muscles were the softest, and, as a result, the least receptive to his inner power. He could push out his midriff a touch as a countermeasure, but what if he misjudged the minute adjustment and ended up shifting his whole torso? He could not risk losing the wager that way. The only option left to him was to gird his mind against the onslaught, but his young friend would not ease off, piling on more and more force.

At last, the Urchin could tolerate it no more and flexed his tummy, bouncing Lotus's finger away. He sprang to his feet with a guffaw.

"Fat monk, you've trounced the Hoary Urchin!"

Lamenting her uncharacteristic impartiality, Lotus straightened up and turned to Lama Supreme Wisdom. "You've won. We won't make trouble for you, this time. Off you go!"

No response. No movement.

She gave him a tap on the shoulder. "Get up!"

It was a light push, without any internal strength, and yet it was enough to topple his hefty bulk over. As he lay on his back, facing the heavens, the monk's hands were touched together as before, and his legs were still crossed midair, as if he were a painted clay statue of the Buddha.

Did he suffocate himself keeping his pressure points sealed? Lotus put a finger under his nose. She could feel his breath.

"Urchin, oh Urchin, you've been tricked."

"What?" Zhou Botong's eyes bulged at the news.

"Unbind him and I'll tell you all about it."

It took the Old Urchin a few moments to comprehend her words. He bent down to feel the lama's body. Eight major acupressure points had been bound.

"It doesn't count! It doesn't count!" Zhou Botong yelled, hopping from foot to foot. "Those scoundrels locked his movement when he sat down. The fat monk could stay like that for another three days and three nights!" He squatted on his heels and called to the lama. "Come, come, come, let's do it again!" But the man was still stuck on his back in the same position, unable to move, unable to respond. Muttering about a rematch, the Old Urchin worked to remove the binds, his hands flitting over the monk's pressure points.

Lotus's eyes followed him as he bustled about. "Hey, what happened to my *shifu*? What did you do with him?"

"Oh!" The Urchin shot to his feet and scampered into the cave, almost running straight into Guo Jing, who was guiding Ke Zhen'e out. Once the youth had heard his sworn brother prattling away in boisterous spirits, evidently unharmed by the antics of the night, he had slipped inside to check on his teacher.

When they were outside, Guo Jing was shocked to see in the gloom that the First Freak was donned in mourning white, with a strip of cloth the same color wound around his head.

"Master, did someone pass away in your family? Where are my other *shifus*?"

Ke twisted his face toward the heavens. Two streams of tears coursed down his withered cheeks. Guo Jing had never seen his mentor so distraught and he swallowed his follow-up questions.

Just then, Zhou Botong emerged with someone else on his arm, who had a drinking gourd in one hand and a half-eaten chicken in the other.

"*Shifu!*" Guo Jing and Lotus cried in unison, and they rushed over to greet Count Seven Hong.

The Divine Vagrant Nine Fingers nodded at his students, grinning through the chicken thigh clamped between his teeth.

Darkness descended over Ke Zhen'e's features. He swung his metal staff down, swift and savage. The Exorcist's Staff technique he had perfected in Mongolia as a means to tackle Cyclone Mei. Designed to bludgeon with blistering, ferocious force, it made a terrifying sound as it descended on its victims, but left them no time to evade its wrath—it was his wish that the blind woman would hear the coming of her end.

Needless to say, Lotus had let her guard down since Tiger Peng and his pack had fled the valley. Why would anybody here wish her harm? By the time she sensed the gust whipped up by the staff, it was already too late.

Guo Jing reached out without a second thought. He knocked the heavy weapon off target with one hand and grabbed it with the other. How could let it crush Lotus's skull? He intercepted his mentor's strike on instinct, not realizing how much his strength had improved in recent weeks, or that the simple move contained all the power of the Dragon-Subduing Palm.

A mighty wave of energy crashed into Ke Zhen'e. It tore the staff out of his hands and swept all anchorage from his feet, throwing him facedown to the ground.

"*Shifu!*" Guo Jing stooped to help his teacher. He felt sick to see what he had inflicted upon a man he held in the highest regard.

Ke's nose was bruised and swollen. His lips, bloodied. In his mouth, a dark gap where his two front teeth had been.

The sightless man shook off his student's arms and spat into his open palm. "Yours!"

Guo Jing stared at the grim mess in his *shifu*'s hand and cast himself to his knees. "Your student deserves the harshest punishment!"

"Take them!" The eldest Freaks shoved his hand toward Guo Jing.

"Master!"

Guo Jing collapsed into panicked sobs, while Zhou Botong burst out laughing. "*Shifu* beating his disciple, a common sight. Student thrashing his teacher, a special treat!"

"Very well . . ." Ke Zhen'e tossed the teeth into his mouth and threw his head back, gulping them down.

The Hoary Urchin cheered, applauding the Freak's literal demonstration of an age-old martial saying: Teeth smacked from the mouth, knock them back with blood.

Shaken to the core, Lotus shuffled over to Count Seven Hong to cling to his arm. She could not fathom why Ke Zhen'e wanted her dead, but she could sense the grief and bile seeping from every pore of his person.

Guo Jing was still kowtowing fervently. "I would never dream of striking you, Master. It was a sincere mistake. Please, chastise me."

"Master? Who are you calling Master? Now that you've got the Lord of Peach Blossom Island for a father-in-law, you need no other! The tricks of the Seven Freaks of the South are too trifling for a great man like yourself, Lord Guo."

Guo Jing knocked his head hard against the ground, but it did not soften the wrath of the man who had initiated him into the world of kung fu. The man whom he held in the same high esteem as his own father. The man who was his teacher, his mentor, his *shifu*.

"Great Hero Ke." Count Seven Hong at last opened his mouth to speak. The chicken thigh he had been savoring fell from his lips and he caught it in the same hand that was holding the rest of the bird. "The boy is a novice. Students sometimes fail to control their strength and hurt their master. I taught him that move, so this Old Beggar is at fault too. Please accept my humble and heartfelt apologies." He finished with a bow, bringing his gourd and the chicken carcass together in some rough semblance of a gesture of respect.

Zhou Botong, fearing that he might be left out, parroted Count Seven Hong's words and action, substituting "Old Beggar" with "Old Urchin" and explaining that he had given Guo Jing lessons in channeling his energy. But his playful echo of Count Seven's words turned the well-meaning remark into a grating scoff in the blind man's ears.

"Pah! You Greats are powerful, but to what end? Not one of you acts with righteousness, and that will be your downfall!" And, in the heat of his fury, Ke Zhen'e cursed the Heretic, the Venom, the King and the Beggar—the four most powerful Masters of the *wulin*.

"Wait, why do you curse the King of the South? Has he wronged you too?" Zhou Botong never knew when to keep quiet.

"Hey, Old Urchin, someone's here to see you!" Lotus was aware that Ke Zhen'e's ire would be hard enough to quench without Zhou Botong's meddling, and it would be a hopeless task if he were around. "The lovebird has taken flight."

"What?" The shock of those words sent the older man three feet into the air.

"She's here to bathe your scarlet feather in the chill of dawn." Another reference to Madam Ying's poem.

"Where?" the Urchin shrieked.

"Just over there."

"I won't see her—never, never, never, never, never. Good Miss Huang, dear Miss Huang, please don't tell her you've seen me," Zhou Botong begged. "I'll do anything you ask of me . . ." His voice trailed off. He had already sprinted so far north, he was almost out of earshot.

"I'll hold you to your word!" Lotus shouted after him.

"When a word bolts from the Hoary Urchin's mouth, not even eight horses can chase it down!" The ghost of his voice was the only part of him that remained in the valley.

Lotus found Zhou Botong's reaction unsettling. It was extreme, even by his standards. She had hoped to coax him into seeking Madam Ying out. Who would have thought he would be so terror-stricken by the mere mention of her? Well, at least she had succeeded in getting rid of him before he could cause more trouble.

Kneeling by Ke Zhen'e, Guo Jing was speaking through his tears. "*Shifu* left the comforts of home and moved to the wilderness of Mongolia, all because of me. This kindness I can never repay, even with my death. Today, this hand injured you, and I will have nothing more to do with it!" He pulled out the golden dagger and chopped down.

Hearing the blade cut through the air, the sightless man twisted his staff sideways. Sparks flashed as the weapons clashed.

The boy put all his force into the blow, Ke told himself as numbness dulled his grip.

"I know you speak from the heart," he said, somewhat breathless from the exchange "I hereby ask you to do one thing for me."

"I shall most certainly oblige," came Guo Jing's eager reply.

"If you refuse, the bond between us shall be severed for eternity."

"Your command will be my lifelong mission."

Ke struck the Exorcist's Staff against the ground. "Bring me the heads of Heretic Huang and his daughter Lotus."

Reeling, Guo Jing spluttered, "What hap—how—?"

The Freak cut his student off with a snort. "I wish the heavens would grant me sight for this one moment. I would love to see the face of this ungrateful little bastard!"

He swung the metal staff at the crown of Guo Jing's head. The young man stayed on his knees, rooted to the spot.

Lotus had had an inkling of what Ke Zhen'e might demand of Guo Jing and was poised for action. She thrust the Dog Beater in a Rabid Dog Blocks the Way. The instant it made contact with the metal staff, the bamboo cane slipped a touch to the side, twirled round and flicked out. The intricate move turned Ke's force back onto him, flipping the staff to the side and rocking his footing.

The eldest Freak made no attempt to disguise the impact of Lotus's intervention. Instead, he beat himself in the chest twice in anguish and took off in the same direction Zhou Botong had taken.

Guo Jing went after him. "*Shifu! Shifu!*"

The old man halted, turned back and snarled, "Does the Great Lord Guo wish to take my life?"

The savageness of Ke Zhen'e's tone stopped Guo Jing dead in his tracks. Head hung low, he listened to the diminishing thud of the metal staff against the ground as his First Master hobbled away. Re-calling their years together in Mongolia, Guo Jing curled up on the ground and wept.

3

Taking Lotus's hand, Count Seven Hong approached Guo Jing. "Another bitter feud between Hero Ke and Heretic Huang," he sighed, "fueled by their fiery tempers. This Old Beggar will do his best to bring peace."

Guo Jing dried his tears and sat up. "*Shifu*, do you—do you know why?"

"My stomach has been growling most of the day. We'll talk after I've had a good meal."

They walked Count Seven to their guest house. Lotus found some meat and wine in the kitchen and conjured up a quick but delicious late-night feast. When the Beggar was sated, he began to tell them how the scene they had happened upon had come about.

"You saw the Hoary Urchin just now. He was gulled into that bet with the lama. With him out of action, the gang was ready to do away with me, but the stars were on our side. Your first *shifu* came across us and stood by me until we found refuge in that cave. The villains were wary of his poisoned devilnuts and did not try to force their way in, which gave us a reprieve. And then you two arrived.

"Master Ke stands firm by his principles. He stayed by my side, putting my life before his, ready to defend me to the death." Count Seven heaved a sigh and glugged down two large gulps of wine. After that, he stuffed a chicken drumstick into his mouth. A couple of chews later, he spat out the bone. Satisfied, for the moment, he wiped his greasy lips on his sleeve and resumed his tale.

"Things were rather precarious until you came along, and obvi-ously I was no help at all in my current state, so Master Ke and I didn't have time for idle conversation. But this much I know for sure:

his rage doesn't stem from that simple fall. He's a hero and adheres to the moral code of *xia*. He wouldn't be so small-minded. There must be another reason. Well, we're only days away from Moon Festival. Once we've taught those blackguards a lesson at the Tower of Mist and Rain, I'll speak to Master Ke and resolve this misunderstanding."

Waving Guo Jing's tear-flooded gratitude away, the Beggar said, with a twinkle in his eye, "Now, tell me everything that's happened to you two in the past weeks. How come your kung fu has improved so much? Master Ke is much admired in the *wulin* for his craft, and yet one wave of the hand from you young 'uns sent him tottering!"

It was too complex a story for Guo Jing to tell, and he was still haunted by the disgrace he had subjected his teacher to, so Lotus happily brought Count Seven up to date with their adventures. He applauded Yang Kang for ridding the world of Gallant Ouyang, but let rip a succession of expletives when he heard what had happened at the Beggar Clan Assembly.

"That knave! And the Four Elders—woolly old clods! Surefoot Lu has dung for brains! I'll squeeze the life out of Elder Peng!"

He grew subdued and distant when Lotus told him how she had been brought back to life by Reverend Sole Light and how Madam Ying came to take her revenge in the dead of night. He sucked in a breath when she described how the former consort of the Dali Kingdom went berserk at Blue Dragon Shoal.

"Do you know her?" Lotus inquired, noticing her Master's odd reaction. Perhaps he too had been seduced by her charm. Is that why he never married? What's so special about Madam Ying? She's obsessive and odd. How did she make so many martial Masters fall for her? Was it her beauty? Her intelligence? Maybe she cooks well? I wonder how we compare . . .

"No, I don't know Madam Ying." Count Seven's voice interrupted her musings. "But I was there when King Duan took his monastic vows—I was standing right next to him.

"He wrote to me one day, inviting me to Dali. I knew it must be for a matter of great import. He wouldn't have got in touch about a mere trifle. Anyway, the thought of Yunnan dry-cured ham, crossing-bridge soup noodles and pounded rice cake sent me on my way instantly.

"When I got there, King Duan looked wretched. Wasted away. A changed man. He was so full of life and energy on the summit of Mount Hua, just a few years before. A couple of days into my stay, he invited me to spar, but, in fact, he wanted to teach me Cosmos *neigong* and Yang in Ascendance.

"This Old Beggar is no dullard. We are martial equals. Each of us Greats has an unparalleled skill that no ordinary man can withstand. I have the Dragon-Subduing Palm; King Duan, his Yang in Ascendance acupressure jabs; the Venom, the Exploding Toad; and the Heretic actually has two, Splitting Sky Palm and the Divine Flick.

"Now, King Duan had been granted the knowledge of Cosmos *neigong* by Wang Chongyang. There was no doubt who would claim the title of the Greatest Martial Master Under the Heavens when we all met again. Why on earth would he want to teach me those two supreme repertoires? And why didn't he want me to demonstrate the Dragon-Subduing Palm in return? Something was amiss. I made up some excuse about needing time and privacy to think things over, and held a secret conference with his four disciples. I worked out what he had been planning: he would commit suicide once he had finished teaching me. We had deduced that he was heartsick, but the why and wherefore eluded us."

"King Duan feared that no one would be strong enough to face Viper Ouyang after his death," Lotus commented.

"Yes, I had inferred that too, so I stood my ground, refusing to learn anything from him. In time, he started to open up. He told me that, although his four students were earnest, loyal and hardworking, their hearts were torn between running the kingdom and kung fu training. And that, though they were born with some martial intuition, they were not truly gifted and would never become supreme

Masters. As he understood it, the Seven Disciples of the Quanzhen Sect were much the same—they would never attain the heights of their mentor Wang Chongyang. He could live with my refusal to learn Yang in Ascendance, but, if he did not share Cosmos *neigong* with a Master worthy of it, how would he face the Double Sun Immortal when he passed on to the next world?

"It was clear that he'd thought the matter through and there was nothing I could say to change his mind, other than digging in my heels and rejecting his offer. That was why he abdicated and became a monk—it was a way to leave this life without physically killing himself. I was right by him when he received the tonsure—and that was more than ten years ago . . ." Count Seven's tone was uncharacteristically wistful. "Well, it's for the best that this tangled affair has at last been resolved."

"Now it's your turn to tell us your adventures," Lotus urged.

"My adventures? Well, I enjoyed the Contrast of Five Treasures four times in the imperial kitchens, which, I have to say, did satisfy my cravings. I was also treated to lychee pork kidney, quail potage, goat tongue slips, ginger and vinegar whelks, and goat tripe stuffed with oysters—" As Count Seven rattled off the palace's most famous delicacies, he could feel his mouth watering and the glorious flavors came flooding back.

"How come the Old Urchin couldn't find you?"

Count Seven chuckled at the memory. "The imperial chefs started to notice their prized creations going missing, and rumors that the fox demon had returned to haunt the kitchens began to circulate. They offered me a great deal of candles and incense sticks in homage. Not long after that, the stories of the fox demon reached the commander of the Imperial Guard, and he sent eight of his men to the kitchens to catch the crafty old thing.

"Now, as you will recall, this Old Beggar has lost his kung fu, and the Old Urchin was nowhere to be seen, so these guards were very bad news. I scuttled off and found a quiet part of the palace, to lie low. I ended up in a place called the Hall of . . . Virescent

Sepal. That's it. Virescent, ha! It's got a courtyard full of plum trees. Our weedy Emperor comes here every winter to admire the blossoms. Of course, not a soul goes anywhere near this spot at the height of summer, apart from a few old eunuchs who come every morning to sweep and prune.

"Beautiful, delicious food could be found in every corner of the palace. You could let loose a hundred Old Beggars in there and none of us would ever go hungry. The perfect place to convalesce in peace. I ate like the Emperor, I slept like the Emperor, but I had an even better life than the Emperor himself, because no one troubled me about anything. Until I heard the Old Urchin's voice in the middle of the night, that is. He shrieked like a vengeful ghost, screeched like a cat in heat and bayed like a pack of mad dogs, rousing everybody from their beds, turning the palace upside down. Amid this chaos, I heard men shouting: 'Master Hong! Count Seven Hong!' I tiptoed out of my little paradise, and who should I find? Tiger Peng, Hector Sha, Graybeard Liang and their cursed little throng of flunkies."

"Huh? Why were they looking for you?" Lotus asked in surprise.

"I was as baffled as you are now. One peek at those faces was enough to send me scurrying back to my courtyard, but the Hoary Urchin had already spotted me. He ran up and folded me in his arms. 'Thank the heavens and earth! I've found you at last,' he cried into my ear. Then he yelled at Graybeard Liang and his wretched mob to bring up the rear—"

"He was commanding them?"

Count Seven laughed. "Yes, it was incredible. I couldn't make head nor tail of what the devil was going on. The scoundrels seemed to be scared witless and followed the Urchin's every word. With the Ginseng Codger and his ragtag rabble standing guard, he slung me on his back and off we went to Ox Village look for you two.

"On the way, he told me how he'd panicked when he couldn't find me, and, when he came across Graybeard and his posse, he beat them into submission and made them search every lane and alley of the capital, day and night, until they'd tracked me down. He told me he had also searched the palace high and low several times, but it was such a sprawling complex, and I had hidden myself so well, they hadn't been able to locate me until that night."

"I can't imagine the Urchin bossing anyone around. How did he tame those dogs and keep them on a leash?"

"The Hoary Urchin has his ways and means. He rolled little balls of grime and dead skin from his body and stuffed three of them into each of their mouths. He then claimed that he had force-fed them a deadly toxin that would only reveal its potency after forty-nine days, and he was the only person in the whole world with the antidote. If they behaved and obeyed him, he would grant them the cure on the forty-eighth day. To be honest, they weren't entirely convinced, but when your life is at stake . . . Well, you know the saying, 'Better to believe the worst will happen than assume it can never come to pass.' So, they swallowed the Urchin's tall tale and ended up at his beck and call, running around to placate his every whim."

At this point, even the stricken Guo Jing managed a smile.

"Once we left the city, the Old Urchin decided to put them to use searching for you two. But, earlier tonight, when they returned once again without any news, the Urchin got carried away berating them and gave the game away. 'If you don't find my little brother Guo Jing and the lass Lotus,' he said, 'I'll feed you a few more pills of piss and grime!' They hounded the poor man with trick questions and eventually pieced together the truth. There had never been any poison. They had been duped.

"Those rascals would never let such an affront slide, and I told the Urchin quietly that he needed to dispatch them once and for all. We all knew it would take the lot of them to get the better of the Urchin, and, even then, it might not be enough. It was Tiger Peng who came up with the ploy you happened across. Tricking him into a wager with the fat monk from Kokonor.

"Of course, I tried to stop the Urchin from taking the bait, but can you imagine him saying no to the chance of winning a bet? So,

I ran—as fast as I could—and, as luck would have it, I came across Hero Ke. He offered me protection and kept me company as we fled from Tiger Peng and his cronies to the cave where you found us. The Urchin might be foggy in the head sometimes, but he did realize that he shouldn't let me stray too far, so he hurried after us too. But the swine wouldn't let him be and heckled him into taking part in the contest."

"It's lucky we overheard those students of Graybeard Liang, otherwise the Urchin would have wagered your life away." Lotus found herself amused and annoyed in equal measure by the infantile martial Master.

"It's a marvel that I'm still clinging on to life. It makes no difference who gives it away."

"Ah! Remember when we were sailing back to the mainland from Rosy Cloud Island—"

"Ghost Crushing Island," Count Seven corrected her.

"Alright, whatever you say. Ghost Crushing Island it is . . . I suppose it's more fitting now that Gallant Ouyang has become a ghost in every sense of the word. Anyway, when we fished the Ouyangs onto our raft, the Venom said that your injury could only be healed by one person under the heavens, but you refused to tell us his name. Now that we've been to western Hunan, we know you were talking about King Duan—or Reverend Sole Light, as he is now known."

"He could reconnect the energy flow in my Eight Extraordinary Meridians using Yang in Ascendance and Cosmos *neigong*, but it would damage his elemental *qi* and he'd need at least three years to recover from the exertion. He may not be weighed down by the troubles of this world. He may not care about winning the next Contest of Mount Hua. But he is in his fifties. How many more years has he got left in which to recover? Could this Old Beggar demand that from a friend?"

"*Shifu*, you can reconnect the meridians by yourself, without anyone's help," Guo Jing said.

"Really?"

"Remember the gibberish at the end of the Nine Yin Manual? Reverend Sole Light has translated it for us," Lotus explained. "He bade us tell you that you can use the method to heal yourself." She then recited a portion of the translation, followed by the explanation the monk had shared with them.

Count Seven sat pondering her words for a long time. "Yes!" he cried, jumping to his feet. "It'll work, but it'll take a year or so."

"I suppose Tiger Peng will get Viper Ouyang to help them at the contest on Moon Festival," Lotus said, changing the subject. "The Urchin's kung fu is every inch the Venom's equal, but we can't guarantee he won't have one of his episodes. We should get Papa to come, so victory is assured."

"You're right. I'll go to Jiaxing. You head to Peach Blossom Island to fetch your father."

Guo Jing wanted to escort Count Seven to Jiaxing, but the Beggar brushed aside his concerns. "Time is of the essence. I'll take Ulaan. I couldn't possibly run into any trouble with him. One little tap on his rump and no living creature can keep up with us."

4

THE NEXT DAY AT DAWN, COUNT SEVEN GOBBLED A BIG BOWL of noodles and guzzled an equally sizeable bowl of wine to fuel him for the road. He mounted Ulaan and tensed his legs ever so slightly. Sensing the subtle change in pressure, the colt neighed at Guo Jing and Lotus, as if to bid them farewell, and sped north.

Guo Jing stood in silence, long after the Beggar had disappeared over the horizon. Everything that had happened the night before was gnawing at him. Why did First *Shifu* want to kill . . . ?

Lotus left him to his thoughts and went to the waterfront to arrange their passage to Peach Blossom Island.

The voyage did not take long. This time, she sent the boatman back to the mainland once they had disembarked.

"Guo Jing," she asked, when they were alone. "Will you grant me one thing?"

"Do you mind telling me what it is first? I don't want to make a promise I can't fulfill."

"I'm not asking you to bring me the heads of your six *shifus*."

"Why do you have to bring that up?"

"Why can't I? You can push it to the back of your mind, but I can't. I like you, but not enough to let you cut my head off."

Guo Jing heaved a sigh. "I don't understand why First *Shifu* was so angry. He knows I love you more than anyone. He knows I'd rather die a thousand, ten thousand times—or let you cut my head off again and again—than do anything to harm even a hair on your head."

Moved by this earnest admission, Lotus took his hand and leaned into him.

"Do you think it's pretty here?" She pointed at a line of weeping willows by the water.

"If I were to picture the home of celestial immortals, it would look like this."

"I want to live, and I want to live here. I don't want you to kill me . . ."

He stroked her hair to reassure her. "Why would I ever do that?"

"What if your *shifus*, your mother and all your good friends wanted me dead? Would you listen to them?"

"The whole world could want you dead, but I'll always be on your side. I will always protect you."

"So, you're willing to give up everyone—for me?" She gripped his hand tighter.

Hesitation. Silence.

She looked up, into his eyes. Yearning for an answer. Frightened of what it would be.

"Lotus, I told you I want to spend my life with you. Here, on Peach Blossom Island. I meant it when I said it. They weren't just empty words."

"Good. Then, from now on, from today, you will stay on the island."

"Today?"

"Yes. Today. I'll ask Papa's help with the contest in Jiaxing. I'll get Papa to kill Wanyan Honglie with me, so we can avenge your father. I'll go to Mongolia with Papa to bring your mother here. I'll implore Papa, I'll persuade him to apologize to your *shifus*. I'll make sure nothing's left undone—you'll never be bothered by any unfinished business. There'll be nothing to disturb your peace of mind."

Recognizing the note of peculiar desperation in her tone, Guo Jing tried to dispel her fears. "Lotus, you know I'd never break any of my promises to you. You don't have to be like this. You can set your mind at ease."

She sighed.

Silence.

At length, she said, "It's hard to speak with certainty about anything that happens in this world. When you accepted your troth-plight to the Mongolian Princess, you didn't imagine that you would break it one day. All my life, I've always done what I want, whenever I want, but now I realize . . ." She trailed off and lowered her head as her eyes welled up. "You think you've got it all planned out, but the heavens will always trip you up."

Guo Jing had no answer. His heart was going through the same upheaval. On the one hand, he wanted to spend his life with her on the island, as he had pledged, to honor her love; on the other, he could not simply cast aside every association with the outside world, every human connection in his life, though he could not explain to himself why it would not be possible for him to meet that demand.

"It's not that I don't believe you." Lotus's voice was barely above a whisper. "It's not that I'm forcing you to stay, it—it's just—I'm . . . terrified." She buried her face in his chest, and her body quivered as she sobbed.

Guo Jing had not realized how much she was troubled by the

uncertainties ahead. After a moment's thought, he asked, "What's disturbing you?"

Her tears just fell faster.

He thought of their time together, the dangers and difficulties they had lived through by each other's side. Never once was she afraid. She had taken every situation in her stride, with a giggle and a rejoinder. Yet, right now, on her beloved island, about to see her father, she was in floods of tears. Why?

"Are you worried something bad might have happened to your papa?"

A shake of the head.

"Are you scared that, if I leave this island, I'll never come back?"

The same response.

Four or five questions later, he was still nowhere near the answer.

At last, she turned to face him. "I can't put into words what terrifies me. It's just, whenever I think of your first *shifu*—when he was attacking me—something in his eyes makes me flinch, even now Something makes me think that, one day, you'll heed his words, and take my life. That's why I beg you to stay on the island. Do it for me, please!"

"Is that it? I thought it was something really bad." He gave her a smile. "Remember when we were in Zhongdu? My *shifus* called you 'she-demon' at first, but they relented afterward. They may seem stern on the outside, but they're really very gentle and kind. Once you get to spend more time with them, you'll see, and I know they'll like you very much. You've seen Second *Shifu*'s sleight of hand; I'm sure he'd be thrilled to teach you a trick or two. And Seventh *Shifu* has the sweetest temper—"

"So you're determined to leave?"

"No, we'll leave together, and we'll kill Wanyan Honglie together. After that, we'll go to Mongolia together for my mother, and we'll all come back together. Wouldn't you like that?"

"That means we'll never come back together. We'll never spend our lives together." Her enunciation was slow and dispassionate.

"Why?"

"I can't explain it." She shook her head. "It's something I saw in your first *shifu*'s face. And I knew then. Killing me isn't enough for him. He loathes me from the core of his being. It comes from the marrow of his bones."

Guo Jing could feel her heart cracking a little more with each word she uttered. Even though her features were unchanged, the twinkle of carefree mischief had been dulled by a shroud of brooding anxiety, as if she could already see with her own eyes the horror that was to come.

Her intuition has never failed us. If I don't listen to her now, and something bad happens later, what will I do then?

Guo Jing's heart tightened at that thought and the words rolled off his tongue before he realized what he was saying.

"Come what may! I won't leave."

Lotus gazed at him, her cheeks marked by two bright rivulets of tears.

CHAPTER SIX

UPHEAVAL ON
THE ISLAND

I

"Is there anything else—?"

"No, nothing," Lotus whispered, then her voice grew strong with certainty. "If I ask for anything more, I know the heavens will not grant it."

She flicked her sleeves skyward and began to dance. The golden band over her hair gleamed in the sun. Her dress fluttered in a breeze of her own making. She twirled with more urgency, unfurling her sleeves at the trees around her, sending a flurry of petals into the air. Red, white, yellow, purple, they flittered around her like so many butterflies. She sprang up, leaping from tree to tree, capering in the footwork and postures of Wayfaring Fist and Cascading Peach Blossom Palm. She was euphoric.

This scene reminded Guo Jing of a story his mother used to tell him when he was small, about a celestial mountain in the Eastern Sea.

Peach Blossom Island is more wonderful than that fabled place, he said to himself. And Lotus more beautiful than any heavenly creature.

"*Yi?*" Lotus let out a quiet note of apprehension and put an end to her frenzied dance. She jumped down, beckoned Guo Jing to follow her and sprinted into the woods.

Guo Jing made sure he was never more than a step behind. The last thing he wanted was to get lost on this island again.

Lotus zigzagged through clumps of vegetation at top speed, then came to a halt without any warning.

"What is that?" She was pointing at a sandy brown lump ahead, her tone ominous.

Guo Jing ventured closer.

A horse.

One he knew very well. Wind Chaser, his third *shifu* Ryder Han's beloved companion. She had traveled to Mongolia with her master almost twenty years ago, and Guo Jing had known her since he was a little boy.

He reached out to touch her belly. The warmth of life had long deserted her. Finding his old friend's lifeless body in this unlikely location hit Guo Jing hard.

She might be in her twilight years, but the last time he had seen her she had been as robust and as fleet of foot as ever. How come she lay dead, here, of all places? Third *Shifu* must be devastated.

Then it occurred to Guo Jing that she had not collapsed sideways, as he would expect from a horse that had died from natural causes. Her great form was crumpled over her buckled legs. He had seen this pose once before . . . Khojin's steed, when it was struck dead by Apothecary Huang.

Gathering his inner energy, he cradled the mare's neck and heaved, so he could reach under to feel her forelegs. The bones were shattered. Gently, he set her down and felt her back and loin. Her vertebrae, crushed. He examined her golden coat, turning her over, as a sickening dread took hold of his stomach. He could not find a single scratch on her body.

Who killed Wind Chaser? Where is Third *Shifu?* The questions haunted Guo Jing as he sat heavily on the ground. Then he remembered where they were.

Only one person on this island had the ability to strike dead a horse this way. And this person was known to be cruel and cold-hearted enough to do such a thing to a harmless creature.

Apothecary Huang.

Lotus had been observing Guo Jing, keeping her thoughts to herself.

"Don't jump to conclusions," she said, after giving him a moment to work through his thoughts. "We'll search the area carefully and find out what actually happened."

With those muted words, she flicked away stray branches and leaves to inspect the marks left on the trail, moving forward slowly.

When Guo Jing realized Lotus had found footprints in the sodden earth, he pushed past her to follow them. He blundered onward without a care, as if he had forgotten that he could end up hopelessly enmeshed in this labyrinth of an island.

The footprints came and went, just like the paths Guo Jing had been speeding along. Each time, it was Lotus who rediscovered the trail by backtracking, probing between rocks and through the undergrowth. Sometimes, no impressions were left on the ground, but she would spy faint lines scored by weapons on tree trunks, or other signs of human activity among the vegetation.

Several *li* later, they came upon a sea of flowering shrubs, with a mound bulging from its center.

This time, it was Lotus who darted ahead.

Guo Jing had stumbled across this site on his first visit. Lotus's mother was interred among the blossoms. He recalled bowing at her perfectly tended memorial, but the scene before his eyes now diverged from the image in his memory.

Here lies Madam Feng,
Mistress of Peach Blossom Island

The same characters were now lying sideways. The headstone had been knocked to the ground.

He lifted it the right way round.

Lotus, meanwhile, was staring at the exposed tomb entrance. She knew in her gut that something monstrous had happened. She battled the urge to rush inside, and forced herself to take in the surroundings first.

The lawn to the left of the entrance was badly trampled. The stone portal bore marks from a clash of weapons.

She stepped inside the tomb passage and listened. Deathly silence. Unable to make out any sound from within, she began to venture forward.

Guo Jing hurried after her, feeling nervous about the hidden threats they might find lurking underground.

Lotus proceeded with caution, her mind reeling at the cracks and chips on the masonry lining the walls. Testament to the fierce tussle that had taken place in the narrow passage.

Several *zhang* into the tunnel, a cudgel lay in her way. She picked it up and held it to the last of the light reaching in through the unguarded entry.

One half of a steelyard. Gilden Quan's weapon. The balance beam, wrought from refined iron, was as thick as a child's arm. It had been snapped at the midpoint.

Lotus caught Guo Jing's eye and saw what was on his mind. A possibility she dared not voice.

Only a handful of martial Masters in this world had the strength to snap the sturdy instrument in two with their bare bands. Considering where they were now, this list narrowed down to one candidate.

Her own father.

Guo Jing seized the broken weapon from Lotus's shaking hands and stuffed it into his belt. He then crouched low and felt his way along the progressively gloomy passageway. His heart was a string of buckets dancing up and down the shaft of a well, as he searched for the rest of the weapon, at the same time desperately hoping that he would find nothing. The sounds of his robes dragging on the paving stones masked neither the sniffles from his nose nor the whines from his throat.

He crawled. He groped. He stopped. He had come into contact with something hard and round. The counterweight. The flying bludgeon his sixth *shifu* used to devastating effect in combat.

He scooped it up and placed it in his pocket. It was too dark to see, so he let his sense of touch guide him. His fingertips brushed against something less hard than iron or stone, but as cold as both. The undulating surface was almost waxy . . .

A face?

He jerked back—*pang!*—and smacked his head into the marble-lined vault of the passageway. He was too busy fumbling in his shirt for his tinderbox to feel any pain. As the small flame burst into life, he felt the last vestige of air being punched out of his lungs. Inside, his head was being pounded into pulp. Outside, the corridor spun before his eyes.

Blackness was all that remained.

Guo Jing had fainted, but the match was still burning in his hand. Lotus was now confronted with the sight that had knocked him out cold.

Gilden Quan's glassy eyes stared into hers. The missing half of his weapon protruded from his chest.

The truth, right there, in her path. A reality she had no choice but to face head-on. She tried to keep calm, mustering what courage she could find within and taking a step closer to Guo Jing. She pulled the tinder from his hand and held it under his nose.

She watched the coil of smoke worm its way into his nostrils, making him sneeze. She watched his heavy eyelids part with reluctance, his unfocused eyes taking in her face before flitting away to anywhere else but her. She watched him clamber to his feet and step mechanically around his sixth *shifu*'s remains, heading further into the sepulcher.

She staggered on behind him.

Her mother's burial chamber.

Chaos.

A chunk of stone was missing from the offering table. Hacked away in battle.

In the corner to their left, someone lay on his side, his back toward them. He wore a headscarf. He was in the shadows, but it was clear who he was. Zhu Cong the Intelligent, the second of the Freaks.

Guo Jing crossed the room and reached out to his Master, helping him onto his back. His body was as cold and lifeless as the stone chamber it lay in. His shoes had slipped off his feet. Yet, a phantom smile lingered on his face, a harrowing expression under the flickering flame.

"Second *Shifu*, I'm here," Guo Jing said as he cradled his teacher, shifting him into a sitting position. A series of soft clinks. Gems and precious trinkets were tumbling from inside the dead man's robes.

Lotus picked up a piece of jewelry that had rolled close to her and let it slip between her fingers after a quick glance.

Sighing, she said, "That's Mama's—"

"You—you think my *shifu* came here to steal? How—how dare you!"

She felt Guo Jing's glare and turned to him. She would not be cowed. Not by that hate-filled look. Not by the menace in his growl. She held his gaze, looking deep into his wild, bloodshot eyes.

"My second *shifu* is a hero. A man of virtue! He'd never steal from your father. A-a-above all else, he'd never steal from your mother's tomb!"

Despite this outburst, Guo Jing could see that there was no hint of an accusation in the eyes looking back at him. Just woe, he said to himself, and his rage fizzled out. He took in the jewels on the floor. These glittering objects had spilled from his mentor's clothes. That was something he could not deny.

Second *Shifu* was known in the *jianghu* as Quick Hands for his superb sleight of hand. He could empty any pocket and take any object from a person without being detected, and, over the years, even the most sensitive and guarded of martial Masters had been caught out.

Could he really have come here to steal? Guo Jing began to doubt himself.

No! Never! A voice shrieked inside. Second *Shifu* was an honorable man. He had never craved riches and wealth. He had only used his skill against wrongdoers. Never for personal gain. He could never do something so despicable. There has to be another reason. It has to be so.

Torn between the facts before his eyes and the memory of the man he loved and revered, Guo Jing felt a throbbing pressure mounting in his skull. It was playing tricks with his vision, making the room dark one moment and blinding bright the next. He screwed his fists into tight balls, his joints popping and cracking with tension.

Lotus could see that he, like her, was wrestling with this grim new chapter in their existence.

"If you want to take my life, do it now." Her voice was almost inaudible. "The other day, when I saw the look on your first *shifu*'s face, I knew we could never find happiness together. Mama is over there. Please, lay my body next to hers, then leave this island as fast as you can. Don't let Papa find you here."

Guo Jing did not seem to have heard a word. He started to pace back and forth, sucking in big mouthfuls of air and emptying his lungs noisily.

Lotus left him to it and went to seek solace from her mother. She parted the drapes behind the offering table and made for the sarcophagus, only to find—*ah!*—yet another grisly tableau displayed before her.

Ryder Han was slouched over the far end of the casket, facedown. Five bloody holes in the crown of his head, dug by human fingers, yawning at her.

Slumped close to him was his cousin Jade Han. She too was supported by the coffin. It looked as though she knew she stood no chance and could not bear the thought of being mutilated by the person who had caused this carnage, instead taking the matter into her own hands, slitting her throat with her sword and clinging to her trusty blade, even in death.

But, before she had expired, she had dipped her fingertips in blood and made a mark on the top of the casket.

On the slab of lustrous white jade that adorned the precious container, carved from a golden-hue *nanmu* laurel tree.

This was how Lotus found the youngest Freak. Her fingers splayed in the midst of writing a character. Death had claimed her before she could complete her task.

A little cross on the luminous nephrite.

Whether Jade Han had used her own vital fluid or her cousin's as ink, there was no way to tell, yet, in the five bloody streaks dragged across the white surface by her fingers, Lotus could see the life sapping from the woman as she was pulled down by the weight of her own body. It was a gruesome sight, but she could not tear her eyes away until she was shoved aside.

"Seventh *Shifu*, I know what you're trying to write," Guo Jing croaked. "'Apothecary Huang'! I know. I will bring you revenge."

He stole over to Ryder Han's body, speaking softly as he settled the diminutive man on the floor. "I saw Cyclone Mei die with my own eyes, Third *Shifu*. Her Master is the one person left on this earth who could have done this to you. I will give you revenge."

He turned his attention back to the youngest Freak, arranging her body into a more dignified and restful position. He then marched past Lotus and across the burial chamber, disappearing up the passageway.

Lotus was rooted to the spot, her heart frozen stiff. Twice had he pushed past her . . . She was invisible to him.

What little light Guo Jing's tinderbox offered had departed with him, leaving her in the murk of the tomb. An unspeakable fear gripped her, even though she had spent many hours on her own down there and knew every inch of the place.

Not anymore. Not when there were four extra bodies.

The thought sent her scrambling up the tunnel, almost tripping over in her desperation to get out. When she was back in the warmth of daylight, she realized what must have made her stumble. The corpse of Gilden Quan.

2

After taking a moment to pull herself together, Lotus reached automatically for the mechanism to shut the entrance to the tomb. She had always done so after visiting her mother, and so had her father . . .

Why hadn't Papa closed it this time? The question dispelled some of the fog that had been blurring her mind since she had first set eyes on the dead horse. Was he in a great hurry? But he'd never leave Mama unguarded and exposed to the elements . . . Wait, there were three dead *men* inside. Papa would never, ever let *them* keep Mama company—under no circumstances would he allow that. Could . . . could he have fallen prey to . . .

She shifted the gravestone to cover the tomb entrance, tapped each side of the portal thrice to seal it and ran to investigate their living quarters.

Although Guo Jing had come above ground earlier, he was ensnared by the island's meandering paths within a few dozen paces. It was sheer luck that Lotus was heading in the same direction. He waited for her to overtake him and tailed her closely, but neither chose to acknowledge the other's presence. After burrowing through a bamboo grove and skirting a lotus pond, they arrived at a rustic complex built from unstripped pine—Apothecary Huang's chambers.

"Papa! Papa!" Lotus ran inside.

Here too, violence had left its mark. Cracked columns standing askew. Tables and chairs upended. Books and writing instruments scattered on the floor. Hanging scrolls ripped and torn.

Papa? Where are you? She gripped the upturned desk for support,

to cling on to what little control she had left. No, this can't be—she tried to convince herself—this isn't right . . .

She rushed to the servants' lodgings. Not a soul in sight. The stove was cold. Dirty bowls cluttered the worktop. Some contained congealed leftovers, as though they had been abandoned mid-meal. If anybody had survived the attack, they were long gone.

Guo Jing and Lotus were the only people left alive on the island.

She trudged back to the main house and found Guo Jing standing in the middle of the study, exactly where she had left him. His unseeing eyes were fixed on an imaginary spot; his face was wooden, blank.

"Cry, Guo Jing. Go on, cry."

She could imagine the depth of his grief, for the bond he shared with the Freaks was as profound as that between any parent and child. She was also aware that he needed to find a release for the emotional pressures mounting inside him, since abrupt swings of extreme feelings could cause serious internal injuries to one who had attained an advanced level of *neigong*.

But, as soon as Lotus uttered his name, she felt herself overwhelmed by all that she had seen and felt. Her knees gave way and her voice faltered. When she finally got a grip of herself, the thought came to her that, if she could find some clues to explain what had happened, perhaps she could jolt him out of his catatonic state . . . She pushed herself to her feet and started rummaging through the desk drawers. In the top right compartment, she found a note written in a hand she did not know, but, just as she was unfolding the paper, it was snatched away from her. Guo Jing had recognized the calligraphy as his second *shifu*'s:

The lowly wanderers of the South—Ke Zhen'e, Zhu Cong, Ryder Han, Woodcutter Nan, Gilden Quan and Jade Han—bow to Master Huang, Lord of Peach Blossom Island.

The letter flapped in his shaking hands as his eyes ran over it.

We have come across the hearsay that the Six Masters of the Quanzhen Sect have been provoked by slanderous tongues and laid blame upon Peach Blossom Island. We know in our hearts that they are mistaken in this matter, but the voice of base vassals such as we is inconsequential, we could not hope to win the serious hearing of both parties and bring peace.

The Master is one of the greatest heroes of our age, in the same league as the Double Sun Immortal Wang Chongyang. For a surety, it would not befit your honor to yield to or to grapple with those who are your junior.

The praises of a thousand ages were heaped upon Chancellor Lin Xiangru, for he halted and turned back his palanquin to give way to General Lian Po, and thus avoided confronting might with might.

Among great heroes thence and now, is there one who does not boast a bosom as wide as the sea? To breed quarrels as trifling as that of chickens pecking at worms is beneath the Master's repute and, in troth, is unworthy of the Master's standing.

For one day shall the disciples of Quanzhen come to the steps of Peach Blossom Island carrying canes on their backs, like General Lian Po when he at last saw the error of his haughty spirit, and the Master's great virtue would be known and admired by every man of honor under the heavens. A noble conclusion that would be.

The note brought Guo Jing's mind back to the battle between Apothecary Huang and the Seven Immortals of the Quanzhen Sect in the dilapidated inn at Ox Village, when Viper Ouyang dealt Eternal Truth Tan Chuduan a secret death blow and laid the blame on the Heretic. In his recollection, the Lord of Peach Blossom Island was too proud to clear up the misunderstanding and seemed to revel in the Quanzhen Masters' hatred for him.

Guo Jing attempted to make sense of what he had witnessed so far. My *shifus* must have discovered that the Quanzhen Sect were going to Peach Blossom Island to seek revenge, and sent this letter to dissuade Apothecary Huang from engaging them in a direct confrontation, so there would be a chance for both sides to see the truth one day. They did this out of the goodness of their hearts to prevent bloodshed, and yet that heartless man thanked them with murder!

But why come to Peach Blossom Island when they had already sent this letter? They must have heard that the Quanzhen Sect were already on their way, and feared that their note was not persuasive enough. They must have wanted to talk both sides down, to stand between them and stop them from fighting . . .

Oh Heretic, you beast! Guo Jing cursed. I know how it went! You thought my *shifus* came to help the Quanzhen monks and you unleashed your evil on them, not bothering to confirm whose side they were on.

Timidly, Lotus peeled the letter out from between Guo Jing's fingers. He did not seem to register her action at all. She tried to rein in her galloping thoughts so she could take in the content with a clear head.

They had come with good intentions, but the wretched Quick Hands was too set in his thieving ways, she concluded as she put the note back into the drawer. He could not resist the temptations of Mama's treasures and did the unspeakable, so Papa . . .

SHE HAD been standing in silence for some time when she heard Guo Jing muttering under his breath: "I won't kill her. I won't kill her . . ."

"You should cry."

"I won't cry. I won't cry . . ." he repeated in a whisper, until the only sound was the murmuring waves.

The song of the sea had been a constant companion in Lotus's life, and memories of her first fifteen years on the island swelled like a rising tide. They splattered against the fringes of her mind, like the billow's sprays, vanishing as swiftly as they had appeared.

"I should bury my *shifus*. Shouldn't I? Is that what I should do?" Guo Jing's voice brought her back to the present.

"Yes, you should," she answered, though she knew he was not speaking to her. She headed back to her mother's grave with an impassive Guo Jing trailing at her heels.

LOTUS WAS reaching for the mechanism to open the mausoleum when a mighty force pressed into her. She leaped to the side to find an airborne Guo Jing sweeping his foot into the headstone.

Carved from the hardest granite, the stone slab stood in defiance. The full force of Guo Jing's martial prowess only succeeded in knocking it a fraction askew, while bright red blood was fast staining his sock, his shoe and the hem of his trousers. Undeterred, he pummeled his fists against the rock, before pulling out Gilden Quan's fractured steelyard to aid his attack on the stoic memorial. Shards of stone flew in a shower of sparks, yet the only thing that succumbed to his strength was what remained of his sixth *shifu's* weapon. He flung the battered iron beam away and thrust with both palms, drawing on his *neigong* without holding anything in reserve. The recalcitrant rock finally snapped in half, revealing a metal rod running through its core. He grabbed it, twisting and wresting, and the tomb tunnel revealed itself with an agonized creak.

Guo Jing stood motionless, staring into the place of death.

"Only he knows how to open the tomb. Only he could have tricked my teachers inside. It has to be him! It can only be him! It's him!" With a wild howl to the skies, Guo Jing sprinted down the dark passage.

Lotus stared at her mother's headstone, which had stood over the tomb's entrance just moments ago. Now it lay shattered and scarred, the once pristine surface marred by bloody handprints. The animus that had fueled its destruction lingered in its debris.

If he tries to defile Mama's casket, it will be over my dead body! She braced herself to go underground again.

Just then, Guo Jing emerged with Gilden Quan's remains. He set his mentor down with reverence and went inside again, bringing up the bodies of Zhu Cong, Ryder Han and Jade Han, one by one, with solemn ceremony.

Lotus let him perform his labors uninterrupted. She could sense that his smallest movements conveyed his wholehearted devotion to his Masters.

He loves them far more than he will ever love me, she realized, as a biting chill spread from her core to her extremities. The urge to find her father grew stronger still, and yet somehow she was unable to tear herself away. She shadowed him as he carried his *shifus* one by one into the woods, some hundred paces from her mother's tomb.

Guo Jing thrust Jade Han's sword into the ground to dig a burial pit, plunging the sharpened steel with increasing force and velocity, until—*pak!*—it could not withstand his crazed fury any longer, breaking off at the hilt.

A burst of anguish surged up from Guo Jing's chest. He opened his mouth in a voiceless cry and out shot fresh blood. Not once, but twice. He paid no attention. He simply cast what was left of the sword aside and squatted on his heels, tearing up soil with his bare hands, flinging it away in a manic frenzy.

Lotus fetched two spades from the gardener's hut and threw one to him. Guo Jing caught it without a word or a look of acknowledgment. Yet, the moment she planted hers in the ground, it was ripped out of her hands and tossed away in two pieces.

Lotus backed away from him. Her legs fell out from under her. She had no more tears to shed.

Guo Jing attacked the earth with every fiber of his being, and, in no time at all, he had two graves ready. He cradled Jade Han's body and laid it in the smaller pit before kowtowing to his seventh *shifu*. He stared at her for a long while, then, with utmost tenderness, he covered her with earth.

He lifted Zhu Cong into his arms, but paused when he noticed the bulge in his mentor's shirt. Jewels from the tomb.

How can I let that man's filthy gems keep Second *Shifu* company for eternity? The idea turned Guo Jing's stomach. Balancing the body against his own with one arm, he removed the trinkets from his teacher's pockets and tossed them away without a second glance. Once his Master's corpse was free from their contamination, he set the Second Freak down and noticed that there was still something in his left hand. Guo Jing wrested the fingers open and found a jade shoe, just over an inch in length. He hurled it on the ground with a *fie!* He had nothing but revulsion for these pointless, pretty things.

Although Lotus could not see very well from where she was sitting several steps away, she was certain that it did not belong to her mother. Where had Zhu Cong found this exquisite plaything? she wondered. Even from a distance, she could discern the masterful craftsmanship and the lifelike details of this dainty miniature maiden's shoe, captured in the highest quality green jade.

Guo Jing stared vacantly into the pit he had prepared for his mentors, and, with reverent care, he laid Zhu Cong, Ryder Han and Gilden Quan to rest. He scooped up a handful of earth but he could not bear the thought of scattering it.

"Second *Shifu*, Third *Shifu*, Sixth *Shifu*!" he cried in the same respectful, loving tone he had always used to address his Masters, taking in their faces one last time. Then the glinting jewels caught his eye again. He dropped the spade, swept up the offending items and took off for the tomb.

Lotus rushed after him, fearful that he might further deface her mother's memorial, and threw herself, arms wide, in front of the undefended entrance.

"What are you doing?"

He pushed her aside and hurled the gems into the dark tunnel. Most of them clinked and tinkled their way down toward the burial chamber, but the jade shoe landed by Lotus's feet. She picked it up and saw the character *zhao*—beckon or recruit—carved on the heel, and the character *bi*, which means compare or compete, on the insole.

"This does not belong to my mother," she said, holding it up.

Guo Jing stared past her, then turned away without a word. He ran back to his teachers and covered their remains with earth.

3

DUSK WAS APPROACHING. ALMOST HALF A DAY HAD PASSED since the traumatic discovery and Guo Jing had yet to shed a tear or show any emotion but rage. Lotus, who had grown ever more concerned about his internal state, thought perhaps he would be able to vent his pent-up feelings in private. She left him at the burial site and went back to the main house to look for some food. She returned an hour later with a slapdash meal of dried fish and cured ham, and found Guo Jing standing in exactly the same place and in the same posture as when she had left him, a statue in the encroaching gloom.

"Guo Jing," she said, her voice quiet and timid. He did not hear her. "Please, you haven't had any food all day."

"I'd rather starve than eat anything from this island."

Lotus was relieved to have elicited a response, but she also knew his character well—he would be as good as his word. She let the food box slide from her arm and sat down.

One standing on his feet, one sitting on the ground, both stationary. The only movement was the moon's, as it crept over the waves and climbed through the sky, peering down from above.

Their hearts, like the meal Lotus had prepared, had gone cold.

A blood-curdling cry blew in with the breeze, breaking the monotonous lapping of the sea.

Lotus could hear pain and anguish in the voice, but she could not tell if it belonged to man or beast. It sounded like a howling wolf, a growling tiger and a groaning man, all at once.

When the wind died down, the wailing died with it.

She parted her lips to call Guo Jing, but thought better of it. Whatever it is, it doesn't bode well. I shouldn't add to his burden.

All her life, she had roamed the island alone at night. She had known every leaf on every tree and every blade of grass, and yet tonight she could barely master her nerves as she stepped into the darkness, heading in the general direction of that fearful sound.

A dozen paces later, a gush whipped past her. Guo Jing streaked by in a straight line, then began kicking and striking at trees and shrubs that stood in his path.

Watching him tear blindly ahead, Lotus sighed. Not only had he lost his way, he had probably lost his mind too.

"Follow me," she said weakly.

Guo Jing trailed behind her, crying, "Fourth *Shifu*! Fourth *Shifu*!"

Woodcutter Nan, the fourth of the Freaks.

The moon provided enough light for Lotus to make out the harrowing marks along their meandering route. Branches crudely hacked and snapped. From time to time, they found the flower bed or the strip of lawn flanking the track trampled twice over. Whoever had passed this way before them had strayed from the trail, only to double back when they realized their mistake. Then, she saw, a hundred feet or so before them, a stake planted in their path.

Guo Jing recognized it immediately. Woodcutter Nan's weapon—an iron shoulder pole. He barreled ahead and plucked it from the earth.

When Lotus had caught up with him, she pointed to the ground. "Three sets of footprints."

"Apothecary Huang!" he rasped. "I'll kill you for what you've done to my *shifus*!"

"You'll have to kill me first."

Ignoring her, Guo Jing knelt down to study the impressions. One set were heavy and haphazard, drifting off the path and wandering back. They must be Woodcutter Nan's. The footprints of the other two, who were traveling in tandem, were swift and sure. They knew where they were going.

Only Apothecary Huang could navigate this island.

Only Apothecary Huang had the lightness *qinggong* to move this fast.

"Fourth *Shifu*'s prints have dried, but the others are fresh," Lotus noted. "He must have gone down this path quite some time before they did."

"My *shifu* has taken refuge in this quiet part of the island, but your father won't let him be. He's tracked him down and he's going to kill him. Go on, lead the way!" he hissed, before projecting his voice: "*Shifu*, Guo Jing's coming!"

Lotus knew that, when they reached Woodcutter Nan's hiding place, he would ask for her head, but what could she do—nay—what did she care? She was aware that, with each step she took, she was one step closer to meeting her end. She had made peace with that. But what if she found Papa there, as Guo Jing had predicted? What would she do then?

Then they saw him. A man writhing and thrashing around under a peach tree.

Guo Jing rushed forward and threw his arms around the man, overjoyed that his Master was alive. Woodcutter Nan looked up, a manic grin plastered on his face. An eerie noise—*hoorrrrr-hoooorrrrrr*—rasped from his throat.

"Fourth *Shifu*! Fourth *Shifu*!" Guo Jing burst into tears.

Nan answered with a palm strike and the same painful growl.

Out of instinct, Guo Jing ducked, only to find a fist hurtling his way.

After a split second's reflection, Guo Jing decided the blow was a teacher's chastisement for his pupil, and he welcomed it. He held still and allowed the punch to connect. *Thump!* His feet left the ground and he flipped head over heels in a backward roll.

Guo Jing thought he was familiar with his mentor's strength, having sparred with him countless times since childhood, but the raw power in this blow took him by surprise.

Just when he had steadied himself, a second strike came, more potent than the first. No, he would not shy from it. A burst of stars and sparks clouded his vision, and he almost blacked out.

Woodcutter Nan picked up a large chunk of rock and lifted it high above Guo Jing's head.

Lotus could tell that Guo Jing would not evade his *shifu's* wrath, nor raise a hand against him. He was waiting for the rock to fall, for his skull to be smashed in, his brains splattered on the mud.

She could not stand by and let that happen. She lunged, striking Woodcutter Nan on the arm. He teetered, then crashed to the ground, yowling, flailing, unable to get up again.

"Why did you push my *shifu?*"

Lotus may have been heavy-handed in her desperation to save Guo Jing, but she was not prepared for the Fourth Freak to be so unsteady on his feet. She extended her hand to pull the man up and, as she bent low, she saw his face clearly for the first time.

Dyed white by the cold moonlight, his smile was forced and unnatural.

She gasped in fright and recoiled at the spine-chilling sight, unwilling to touch him.

The man threw a jab, hitting her square on the left shoulder.

A dull pain spread through Lotus's chest, throwing her back by a couple of steps. Woodcutter Nan howled as his fist was torn by the Hedgehog Chainmail.

"Fourth *Shifu!*" Guo Jing pleaded, while Lotus and the Freak shrieked.

For the first time, a flicker of recognition flashed in Nan's eyes. He opened his mouth to speak, but no sound came, despite the visible exertion that was making his facial muscles twitch and twist as sorrow and frustration mounted in his eyes.

"Take your time, Master. Who did this to you?"

Woodcutter Nan threw his head back, desperate to speak, but this time he could not even move his lips.

"*Shifu!*" Guo Jing screamed.

"He wants to write."

Following Lotus's gaze, Guo Jing saw that his mentor was dragging a trembling finger through the earth, making a cluster of disjointed slashes and strokes.

Lotus's heart thumped, fearful of the revelation to come, then something occurred to her. Wait, he's on Peach Blossom Island. Any idiot would assume it was Papa who did this. So why is he wrestling so hard with death for one extra moment to set down the name of his killer? Could it . . . could it be someone else?

Her eyes followed the jerking finger. She could tell the little strength he had left was seeping away fast.

Write it down quickly, please! she prayed.

The Fourth Freak pulled his finger across, then down, before looping it upward. Then a tremor ran through his hand and it moved no more.

Guo Jing had been holding his teacher's body while he tried to write. He felt, through his chest, the final spasm as Woodcutter Nan's life was snatched away. Now all that remained was an inanimate shell in his arms.

"*Shifu,* I know what you're trying to write." Guo Jing squinted at the incomprehensible mark. "The character *dong,* for east. Eastern Heretic. Apothecary Huang. This is his island and there's no one else as evil and cutthroat as he."

He cast himself on Woodcutter Nan's body, bawling his eyes out and beating his chest.

A DAZZLING light prised open Guo Jing's eyes. It took him a little while to register that it was now morning and the sun had risen fully. He had a vague memory of crying over Woodcutter Nan's body, but he did not know that he had passed out in exhaustion over the corpse. He looked around. No Lotus. Just an empty vessel in the form of his teacher and a pair of vacant eyes gazing into nothingness.

Eyes staring in death.

The old saying brought on another downpour of tears. He could now understand what it meant to depart unwillingly and with grievances, unable to find peace as one drew one's final breath. He reached out with unsteady hands and placed his fingers on his fourth *shifu's* eyelids, renewing his vow of vengeance, before guiding them shut.

The physical signs of Nan's last struggle—particularly that sinister smile—were seared on Guo Jing's mind. What kind of injury had caused them? He unknotted the ties that held his Master's robes together and examined his body. Other than the little bloodstained pricks on his knuckles from punching the Hedgehog Chainmail, he could not find a single scratch on his skin and there was no sign that he had been struck by inner *neigong* power.

It must be the Divine Flick! Guo Jing told himself. I've seen enough of that kung fu to know that it can kill without drawing blood. I'll hunt you down and kill you, Heretic! For my *shifus*!

He scooped up the Fourth Freak and tried to retrace his steps back to where he had buried his other teachers. But, within a few dozen paces, he could no longer pick out the footprints on the indistinct path. Deflated, he gave up, burying Nan under the peach tree where he had found him.

Guo Jing then hurried down the first track he stumbled upon, determined to make his own way to the shore to find passage back to the mainland, but, before long, he found himself turned around and around, robbed of his sense of direction.

He sat down to rest and collect himself. It had been a whole day since his last meal and his stomach was complaining loudly.

I'll ignore the paths and head east, following the sun, he decided. That way, I'll get to the sea at some point.

Yet, he was soon faced with a dense forest, one that he could not force his way through, for barbed vines were choking every branch of every tree.

Onward! No turning back! he told himself, climbing up the nearest tree. As he leaped forth to take the first step of this treetop march, he heard fabric ripping and felt a burning pain in his calf.

The thorns had shredded the legs of his trousers. Angry red lines appeared on the exposed skin.

Undeterred, he braced himself and jumped. Once, twice, but he could not make a third spring. The creepers had coiled around his ankles. He pulled out the golden dagger and hacked them away. He looked ahead to map out a route, but the jungle of spikes spread as far as the eye could see, layer upon layer, into the horizon.

"I'll cut my legs off to leave this damned island!" he yelled at the forest as he prepared to vault to the next tree.

"Come down. I'll take you to the shore."

He could see Lotus looking up at him through the canopy, by a row of trees to his left, and he jumped down to join her. He had made up his mind not to speak to her again, but, when he saw her bloodless pallor, he wanted to know if there had been a set back in her recovery. His lip quivered—images from the day before flashed by—and he bit his tongue and twisted his head to look the other way.

Lotus, of course, could read his conflicted emotions from his features. She waited, hoping that he would turn to meet her eyes, but he kept his face averted.

"Let's go," she breathed out with a heavy heart.

The dreadful discovery had struck Lotus as hard as it had Guo Jing, especially since she was yet to wholly regain her strength after the internal injury caused by Qiu Qianren's Iron Palm kung fu. She had not managed to snatch a moment's rest all night, and her insides were still twisting in knots as she tried to come to terms with that fact that she could not blame anyone for what had happened. Not Guo Jing. Not Papa. Not even the Six Freaks of the South. But why did the Lord of the Heavens insist on punishing her so? Why her, of all people? She had never done anything particularly bad or wrong. Why? Was He jealous? Could He be resentful of the happiness she had found?

With each step she took, she knew the rift between her and Guo Jing was getting wider. To the point where it could never be bridged. When they arrived at the shore, they would part for the last time. Never would she see him again in this life.

With each step she took, she felt a part of her heart crumble away.

Still, she forced herself to walk on.

Out through the trees and onto the beach.

The sea. She had nothing left inside to hold herself together. She swayed, planting the Dog Beater for support, but her arm was as drained and spent as the rest of her body.

Guo Jing reached forward to steady her, but, just as his fingertips grazed her shoulder, he recalled whose daughter she was, and swung his other arm.

Thud! A punch to the helping hand. Zhou Botong's Competing Hands kung fu.

While his heart, his mind and his two palms struggled between love and hatred, Lotus fell facedown in the sand.

A rush of remorse and anguish filled Guo Jing's bosom, even though it might have been forged from iron and stone right now. He caved in at the sight of her so helpless, and scooped her up. He looked around to find somewhere soft to set her down, and saw a green cloth flapping in the wind amid an outcrop of rocks to the northeast of where he was standing.

Lotus opened her eyes to find herself in Guo Jing's arms as he peered at something in the distance. She turned to see what had captured his interest.

"Papa!"

Upon hearing her cry, Guo Jing started to run, still carrying her. As they drew near, they realized the green robe was caught between two rocks, and next to it lay a mask made from human skin.

Apothecary Huang's disguise.

Guo Jing lowered Lotus onto the rock with a gentleness he had not shown since this wretched affair had come to light, and held on to her hand while she reached for the robe.

A bloody palm print marred the fabric.

Nine Yin Skeleton Claw! Guo Jing saw Ryder Han's gory end in his mind's eye again. That fiend was wearing this robe when he butchered Third *Shifu!*

A rush of hot blood flooded his chest. He flung Lotus's hand away, tore the robe from her grasp and ripped it in two. That was when he noticed a strip of fabric missing from the garment's hem. About the same shape and size as the piece that had been tied around the condor's foot.

Before he could give much thought to that, his eyes were once more drawn to the gruesome handprint.

So crisp was the impression that even the lines on the skin were preserved. It was reaching out of the cloth, slapping him in the face.

Rage boiled and bubbled within him.

He tossed away the vile garment, bunched up his own robe over his abdomen and jumped into the sea.

A boat was moored nearby. He waded toward it and vaulted aboard. The crew were long gone, but it did not matter. He could work out what to do. With the golden dagger gifted to him by Genghis Khan, he cut the dock lines and weighed anchor.

He did not look back.

Lotus watched the sail billow as the wind carried Guo Jing westward. She clung to the hope that he would turn back and take her with him, but, as the vessel pulled away, resolutely and without hesitation, her heart succumbed, bit by bit, to a biting frost until it was frozen into one solid block of ice.

She watched the craft disappear into the horizon, where the sea blended into the sky. Then it struck her. She, abandoned here, on her own. Guo Jing, gone. Papa might not come back. This, her present, her future. Never-ending days on this island, alone, forsaken . . .

Am I to stand here by the sea for eternity? she asked herself, as a small voice inside implored, *Don't, Lotus, don't.*

4

IN NO TIME AT ALL, GUO JING WAS A DOZEN *LI* WEST OF Peach Blossom Island. Suddenly, condors' caws cut through his black mood and brought him back to the here and now. They were winging his way and soon they were perched on the yard.

We've left Lotus behind, without a living soul to keep her company. The thought of her standing alone on the shore compelled him to turn the boat around.

As he rode the waves, making slower progress with the wind no longer in his favor, his mind drifted back to the scene outside the cave, when they were reunited with Zhou Botong, Count Seven Hong and Ke Zhen'e. I know now, I know now, Guo Jing said to himself, remembering how Ke Zhen'e had swung his staff at Lotus. First *Shifu* was on the island. His eyes can't see, but his ears are keen. He heard Apothecary Huang carrying out his evil deeds. Somehow, he survived and escaped unharmed. That's why he tried to take Lotus's life. That's why he wants me to take her life. That's why he told me to bring him her head as well as her father's. Because he was here. Because he knows the truth. But I can't do that to Lotus. She didn't hurt anyone. She has nothing to do with . . . And yet, how can I ever be with her again? Wait . . . When we found Fourth *Shifu*, he was still alive . . . so that monster couldn't have gone far. I'll catch up with him. I'll cut off his head. I'll bring it to First *Shifu*. I'll die trying!

Now he had a clear sense of what he needed to do, he pulled the tiller and turned west toward the mainland again, with vengeance at the forefront of his mind.

Before guo Jing went ashore, he scuttled the boat by swinging the anchor into the hull. He could not bear the sight of anything associated with Peach Blossom Island now that his Masters were lying cold in the ground. The vessel rolled onto one side. He watched it for a long time from the beach as the waves dragged it under, as though it were carrying the last traces of his five *shifus* to the seabed with it. When no trace of the boat was left above the surface, he set off on foot, heading west, until he came upon a farm. There, after asking for directions to Jiaxing, he bought some rice and had his first meal in more than a day.

When he reached the Qiantang River, he decided to stop for the night. A glorious moon, almost completely full, shimmered on the water. As he gazed at it, humbled by the grandeur of nature, a thought suddenly occurred to him. Could it be Moon Festival already? Had he missed the contest at the Tower of Mist and Rain? He asked the innkeeper for the date and was relieved to hear that it was only the thirteenth day of the eighth month. He would make it in time, but he decided to travel through the night to be sure. He crossed the river and purchased a horse, arriving at Jiaxing just after noon the following day.

Once he entered the city, Guo Jing asked for the way to the Garden of the Eight Drunken Immortals. He had heard so much about the tavern from his *shifus*. They would recall with relish every detail of the fight against Qiu Chuji, giving him a blow-by-blow account of how they had tested each other's wit and kung fu with a bronze censer full of wine, and he had always longed to see the legendary drinking house with his own eyes.

It was just as his seventh *shifu* Jade Han had described it. The ornate building stood on the shore of South Lake, its eaves curling up into the sky as if taking wing, and its supports intricately carved and painted. Overhead, hanging outside, above the top floor, was a horizontal plaque. Though the black lacquer background was peeling in places, the gilded characters reading *Garden of the Eight Drunken Immortals* still gleamed bright and untarnished. They were written in the hand of Su Dongbo, one of the Song Empire's most admired poets, statesmen and calligraphers. Inside stood a large wooden sign that read *Li Po's Legacy*.

Guo Jing's heart throbbed to at last set foot in this fabled establishment, and he bounded up the stairs.

A waiter ran after him. "Sir, I'm afraid the upper floor has been reserved. Please take a seat downstairs."

A voice boomed from above. "Guo Jing, you're here!"

The young man looked up. A Taoist monk drinking alone. The

lush beard reaching down to his chest could not mask the glow from his cheeks. Eternal Spring Qiu Chuji.

"Elder Qiu!" He sprinted over the final few steps and knelt before the Taoist, touching his forehead to the floor.

"How wonderful! You're here early." Qiu Chuji helped Guo Jing to his feet in good cheer, oblivious to the tearful croak in the young man's voice. "I look forward to feasting with your *shifus* tonight, before we fight Tiger Peng and his horde tomorrow. Are they here yet? I have the banquet prepared already." He gestured at the eight tables around him. Only one pair of chopsticks and one wine cup graced each large round surface, except for his, which had a place laid for every seat.

"Eighteen years ago, I first encountered your seven *shifus* here, and this was how they arranged the reception. Over here, vegetarian fare was served for Abbot Scorched Wood. It's such a shame that neither the Reverend nor your fifth *shifu* will be able to join us today."

Guo Jing turned away. He could not look Qiu Chuji in the eye.

"I've even brought the censer from Fahua Temple," the unobservant Taoist continued merrily. "When your *shifus* arrive, we shall drink to our hearts' delight!"

Guo Jing eyed the large bronze container looking rather out of place next to the painted screen. From where he was standing, he could see that, although the outside of the vessel had oxidized over the years into a mottle of greens and blacks, the inside had been scrubbed shiny and clean for this occasion. The aroma of a good vintage wafted through the air.

First *Shifu* is the only one who can take part in this reunion, Guo Jing thought darkly. I would give my life away—willingly and happily—this very moment, if I could see all seven of my teachers here, drinking, chatting, laughing—alive!

"As you know, your *shifus* and I pledged to meet here this year, on the twenty-fourth of the third month, for your duel with Yang Kang," Qiu reminisced. "To be honest, I always hoped that you'd win, ever since I made the wager with your *shifus* eighteen years ago. I've always held their principled ways in the highest esteem, and your victory would have brought further glory to the reputation of the Seven Freaks of the South.

"I might have taught Yang Kang for years, but I must confess that I never put my whole heart into the matter; I was more interested in roaming the world and ridding it of evil. That young man, alas, did prove our ancient wisdom—'Ink blackens all that is nigh'—with his upbringing in the Jurchen palace.

"His substandard kung fu is my fault, of course. I'm not ashamed to acknowledge my shortcomings as a teacher of the martial arts, but where I truly floundered was with his education. I have failed to instill in him the principles that shape a man of honor and virtue, and, in doing so, I have done your Uncle Yang a grievous wrong. I've heard that Yang Kang has changed his ways, but foul air can never be fully purged, and I deeply regret my oversight."

Guo Jing wondered if he should share the deceitful deeds Yang Kang had committed since Qiu Chuji had last seen him, but there had been so many, he did not know where to start, even if he did manage to get a word in edgeways.

"To make one's way in this world, one must always live by the principles of loyalty and righteousness. Achievements in literary or martial matters are trifling in comparison—they represent the very tips of branches, whereas our integrity is the trunk of a tree.

"Even if Yang Kang were a hundred times more skilled in kung fu, you would still have claimed victory for your *shifus* on the strength of your moral fiber. And Qiu Chuji admits his defeat not just with words, but from the depths of his heart." The monk chuckled, recalling the misunderstandings and misjudgments that had led to a lasting friendship.

"What's wrong, my boy?" He at last noticed that Guo Jing, instead of laughing along with him, was crying, and his question made the young man's tears flow faster.

Guo Jing cast himself to the floor and sobbed, "F-f-five of my *shifus* . . . gone . . ."

"What do you mean? Gone?" Qiu Chuji prayed that his ears were deceiving him.

"Only First *Shifu* . . . is still with us," Guo Jing choked out the words.

Qiu felt like he had been struck over the head by a crack of thunder. His powers of speech deserted him. He had been looking forward to a joyful reunion and he was expecting his friends to arrive at any moment. How could they have been snatched away so cruelly? He had spent only the briefest time with the Seven Freaks of the South over the past eighteen years, but the connection they shared was as close and inextricable as that between vital organs in his body. He had long considered them brothers, with whom he would stand shoulder to shoulder through life and unto death.

This unbidden news was a knife to the heart. He could not bear to sit at the feast he had prepared for his friends any longer, and he strode to the window. He leaned against the balustrade, the rippling expanse laid out before him, the faces and features of the Seven Freaks flitting through his mind. Tilting his head back, he yowled at the heavens.

"What's the point of this hateful thing when they're gone?" He wrapped his arms around the bronze censer and hurled it out over the lake with the full power of his inner strength. It crashed into the water with a mighty splash, sinking into the bottom in the blink of an eye.

"How did they die?" Qiu Chuji seized Guo Jing by the arms.

The young man was about to answer when he spotted a tall and lean man dressed in a green robe out of the corner of his eye. The man ascended the wooden staircase without making the slightest sound.

Am I seeing things? Guo Jing blinked. No . . . It's him! Apothecary Huang!

He pulled away from Qiu Chuji and sent his palm flying across the banquet table in a ferocious attack. This Haughty Dragon Repents contained every last drop of his *neigong*. He was holding nothing back—he did not care if he died, so long as he could drag Apothecary Huang down to the underworld with him.

Thrown by this unexpected aggression, the Heretic twisted a fraction to one side and reached out with his left arm. An adroit deflection.

Since Guo Jing had no reserve energy in his body, he had nothing left to deal with the Heretic's counter, and—*craaaaack!*—he hurtled through a wooden partition and plunged toward the ground floor.

THIS WAS not a lucky day for the Garden of the Eight Drunken Immortals. Guo Jing landed on its store of crockery.

Earlier, during the lunch trade, when the tavern's elderly manager saw Qiu Chuji arrive with the bronze censer and heard his unusual requests about the table settings, his heart trembled at the memory of the fight that had almost destroyed this establishment eighteen years before. Now, with the crash of cracking ceramics assaulting his ears, he entreated every deity for help. "O, Guanyin the Observer of Sound, deliver us from this ordeal . . . Jade Emperor, City God, help us . . ." But the hundreds of bowls and plates and saucers and cups that had broken Guo Jing's fall ignored his prayers and shattered into thousands of pieces.

Guo Jing held his hands high, as far away from the shards as he could, and flexed from his core to flip onto his feet. He charged up the stairs, only to catch a blast of green shooting out of the window in the wake of a gust of gray.

I can't subdue the Heretic barehanded, but I'll risk any number of blows to stick this into him. With that thought, Guo Jing whipped out the golden dagger tucked in his belt and jumped after Qiu Chuji and Apothecary Huang.

The streets of Jiaxing were always bustling at this time of the day, and, the moment two martial men were seen leaping out of the windows of the Garden of the Eight Drunken Immortals, a crowd began to gather, hopeful of catching some action. They were thrilled to witness the spectacular feat of a fighter gliding down from the tavern's first floor—until they saw the glinting knife in his hand. Screams broke out, and those closest to the armed warrior jostled to get out of his way, almost causing a stampede in their panic.

Apothecary Huang and Qiu Chuji were nowhere to be seen amid the crush of onlookers.

"Where did they go?" Guo Jing barked at an old man standing close to him.

The sight of the shiny blade had reduced the whitebeard to a trembling mess.

"Great sir, I know nothing! Let me live!"

Guo Jing repeated his question, but only the word "Mercy!" came forth from the aged man's lips.

Extending his arms before him, Guo Jing parted the throng, but could find no sign of either man. He ran back into the drinking house, sprinting upstairs to gain a better vantage point, and saw a skiff speeding toward the Tower of Mist and Rain—Apothecary Huang was sitting under the canopy, while Qiu Chuji worked the scull.

Elder Qiu won't stand a chance in single combat against the Heretic! he thought, and he hurried down to the waterfront, hopping on the first boat he came across. Seizing the oar, he threw the boatman ashore, keeping his eyes fixed on his *shifus'* murderer as he stabbed the scull into the lake with all his strength. But, on water, frantic and fraught motion can only impede one's progress. After one particularly violent twist of the blade, it snapped off and floated away. Groaning in frustration, Guo Jing peeled a plank from the deck and thrust that into the water, but his frenzied haste only resulted in him lagging farther and farther behind. When he had finally slogged his way to the quay beneath the Tower, the two men were long gone.

Calm down! You can't lose your head before you've had your revenge, Guo Jing told himself, filling his lungs slowly. He then exhaled in the same controlled way and repeated the breathing exercise three times. His mind became clear and his senses sharpened. His ears could now pick out the faint clanks of clashing weapons, as well as the swishing of blades cutting through the air. He could even make out occasional faraway huffs and growls.

There are more than two fighters! he noted in surprise, and he looked around to get a good grasp of his surroundings before approaching the Tower as stealthily as he could. The ground floor was deserted, but a familiar figure was perched on the banister at the top of the vertiginous staircase leading to the first floor.

"*Shifu!*" Guo Jing ran up and bowed.

Chewing loudly, Count Seven Hong nodded at his disciple. He then jabbed the leg of mutton in his hand at the courtyard below, indicating that Guo Jing should take a look, before bringing the juicy meat to his lips for another bite.

Guo Jing joined his Master and saw, amid flashes of steel, Apothecary Huang surrounded by . . . he counted eight men. However, the flush of elation that came with seeing the vile beast so beleaguered fizzled out when he took a closer look at the besiegers.

His first *shifu* Ke Zhen'e was among them. Swinging his metal staff, he stood back to back with a young Taoist armed with a sword. The rest of the fighters were clothed in similar gray robes—the Six Immortals of the Quanzhen Sect. Guo Jing knew them all and he could not bear the thought of losing yet another person he cared about to Apothecary Huang's cruel ways.

Guo Jing soon realized that they had assumed the Heavenly Northern Dipper formation, and Ke Zhen'e was at the Heavenly Jade position, the place once taken by Eternal Truth Tan Chuduan. The young monk paired with him was Harmony Yin, Qiu Chuji's disciple.

Even with Yin's help, it was obvious that his first *shifu* was unfamiliar with the Taoists' tactics and was struggling to keep up with them. Guo Jing could also see that his mentor was less skilled than the Quanzhen Masters, and that his sightlessness was hampering his ability to adapt to the ever-changing formation.

The monks' swords danced as one, lunging forward, pulling back, drawing apart and gathering close.

It was as fierce a battle as Guo Jing had ever seen.

A month ago, in Ox Village, the Quanzhen Taoists had deployed two swords against Cyclone Mei and her *shifu* Apothecary Huang to extraordinary effect. Now, with seven blades and an iron staff, they were an awe-inspiring sight.

Meanwhile, the Heretic was armed only with his bare hands. He seemed to be on the back foot, for all he had done since Guo Jing's arrival was dodge his opponents. He had not found a chance to raise a palm or aim a kick over the space of several dozen moves.

Justice is catching up with you today! Guo Jing observed with satisfaction.

But, just then, Apothecary Huang pivoted on his left leg and spun, swiping twice at each of his attackers with his right foot. All eight men were forced to take three steps back.

Guo Jing had to give the man credit for this flawless demonstration of the Swirling Leaf Kick.

At this point, Huang looked up at Count Seven Hong and gave him a wave and a nod.

He seems so relaxed! I thought he was hard pressed . . . Guo Jing shook away his bewilderment as the Heretic raised his left palm, cleaving it down at an angle toward Eternal Life Liu Chuxuan's head.

He was indisputably on the offensive now.

An assault on Liu's position, the Heavenly Pearl, should have been countered by the Taoist's neighbors on either side, Qiu Chuji at the Heavenly Power and Ke Zhen'e at the Heavenly Jade. Qiu's sword flickered instantly at their assailant's right armpit, but Ke was a beat slower—he thrust his staff only at Harmony Yin's prompting.

Under normal circumstances, the eldest of the Freaks was able to compensate for his loss of sight with his keen hearing, locating friend and foe alike from scratching footsteps, rustling clothes and other noises they made as they moved. Up against Apothecary Huang's nimble feet and lightning strikes, which left no sonic trace and little stirring in the air, he was truly left in the dark.

The Heretic's blow lashed down at Liu Chuxuan. The formation's interlocking defensive system had failed. And yet, for reasons unbeknownst to the Taoist, the attacking hand hovered for a split second, a hair's breadth from the crown of his head.

The monk grabbed his chance, flopping to the ground and rolling out of the way. At that same moment, Ma Yu and Wang Chuyi thrust their swords at the Heretic.

Liu Chuxuan might have escaped certain death, but the Heavenly Northern Dipper had lost a vital component.

Cackling, Apothecary Huang rammed into the Sage of Tranquility Sun Bu'er, shooting beyond the formation by three steps, then suddenly plowed backward into Infinite Peace Hao Datong.

Why is he running into me with his back exposed? Surprise at the Heretic's unusual move slowed Hao's blade by a beat.

The Heretic whizzed past, as agile as a darting hare. He stopped, twenty paces away from the Quanzhen monks.

He had broken through the formation.

Count Seven chuckled in approval. "What a handsome performance!"

"They need help!" Guo Jing cried, making for the stairs.

"Not so hasty!" the Beggar cried after him. "I was concerned for your *shifu* at first, when your father-in-law wouldn't fight back. You can never presume to know what the Heretic has up his sleeve. But now I can see that he's not in the mood to hurt anyone today."

"Really?" The young man halted, curious to learn how his Master had come to that conclusion.

"If he wanted bloodshed, do you think that skinny monkey of a monk would still be alive? These little Taoists are no match for him. Not at all." He sunk his teeth into the mutton leg, tearing off a large piece, and explained through a mouthful of meat: "The Quanzhen lads were teaching your first *shifu* the Heavenly Northern Dipper before your father-in-law and Qiu Chuji arrived. Yet it's not something you can pick up in just a few minutes. They tried hard to persuade Master Ke to stay out of the fight, but he wouldn't take no for an answer. I don't know what could've happened to sow such enmity between him and the Heretic. Anyway, that's why he's now sharing the Heavenly Jade position with the young 'un, but, of course, they aren't strong enough to block your father's killer moves."

"He's not my father!"

"Eh? What do you mean?"

Guo Jing glowered, too angry to speak.

"Where's Lotus? Did you lovebirds fall out?"

"Nothing to do with her," he answered curtly. "That beast—he— he killed my *shifus*—"

"What? Are you sure?"

But Guo Jing's attention was drawn away by the intensifying tussle below. Apothecary Huang had now turned to his signature kung fu, Splitting Sky Palm. The air shrieked with each slice of his hand. None of his opponents could get within a dozen paces of him.

The Martial Great's kung fu was formidable, but not to the extent that he could keep skilled fighters of Ma Yu, Qiu Chuji and Wang Chuyi's level at a distance, barehanded, under normal circumstances. However, the Heavenly Northern Dipper's power came from the relationship between the seven positions, and, if one fighter were pushed back, the rest would have to retreat alongside them.

Right now, Hao Datong, Sun Bu'er, Ke Zhen'e and Harmony Yin were the weak links. Each step they gained, they were sent back by two.

The Quanzhen monks were preserving the outline of the formation, but Apothecary Huang was able to slip between their well-honed blades at will nonetheless.

"A-ha! I see what he's doing," Count Seven said aloud to himself.

"Tell me, please!"

"Our Heretic is a sly old fox. He's pushed them back so he can tease them into showing him the inner workings of the formation. Within ten moves, he'll bring them close again."

Count Seven Hong's martial abilities might have been diminished by the injuries he had suffered at Viper Ouyang's hands, but the Venom could not destroy the martial acumen he had acquired through a lifetime's practice.

Apothecary Huang did exactly as the Beggar had predicted. Each thrust of his palm grew weaker than the last as he drew the Quanzhen Taoists and Ke Zhen'e closer and closer in, until the eight of them were clustered around him.

Four swords speared as one.

To fail to draw blood at such close quarters was unthinkable, and yet, somehow, the blades all glided past, missing the Heretic by a hair's breadth.

If Liu Chuxuan, Qiu Chuji, Wang Chuyi and Hao Datong were any less agile, they would have each received a gaping wound by a brother's hand.

Guo Jing could see that Apothecary Huang had grasped the underlying principle behind the formation, and that he would not hesitate to strike at its weakest point—Ke Zhen'e and Harmony Yin.

I can't do any good from up here ... With that thought, he flew down the steps, calling out, "I'm going to help them," over his shoulder.

5

THE CONTEST HAD TAKEN A DIFFERENT TURN BY THE TIME Guo Jing reached the courtyard. Having allowed the Taoists to close in on him, Apothecary Huang was now trying to get to the left of Ma Yu.

Clutching the golden dagger, Guo Jing readied himself to pounce the second the Heretic broke through.

Wang Chuyi whistled, then rushed forward, bringing Hao Datong and Sun Bu'er with him. Together, they curled to the left, making up the Dipper's handle, and wrapped Apothecary Huang back into the Taoists' midst.

He shifted his footing again and again, and, each time, he was brought back into the fold by Wang Chuyi, or by Qiu Chuji, who led the four positions that formed the scoop of the constellation. But the stubborn Heretic would not give up, aiming once more to get to the left of Ma Yu.

On the fourth attempt, Guo Jing finally realized what the Martial Great was striving for.

The position of the North Star.

GUO JING had first seen the Heavenly Northern Dipper in action in Ox Village, when the Quanzhen Masters were pitted against Cyclone Mei and Apothecary Huang. With no knowledge of astronomy, he had barely been able to keep up with what was going on, but, since then, as they observed the night skies together, Lotus had told him more about the seven stars that made up the constellation.

Now he knew how to find the North Star, by linking the Heavenly Jade and the Heavenly Pivot in the scoop of the Dipper and extending that line northward. He had also learned that the North Star's position was fixed—it was always in the same place, and the constellation rotated around it each night.

When he was held by the Beggar Clan on the Jun Hill islet in Dongting Lake, he had compared the stars shimmering in the sky to his memory of the Ox Village fight, and gained an insight into how the formation utilized the connection between the astral positions to amplify the power of an offensive or defensive move. He tested out his new understanding with success that night, when he was beset by swarms of angry beggars.

It went without saying that Apothecary Huang was not only a hundred times smarter than Guo Jing, he was also learned in astromancy and reckoning, as well as Yin Yang and the Five Elements— all of which informed the principles behind the Heavenly Northern Dipper. In Ox Village, he was not able to overcome the formation there and then, but since then he had replayed the confrontation in his head many times over, to look for fatal flaws.

While Guo Jing was eager to learn from Wang Chongyang's

invention, the Heretic was only interested in defeating it. He had come to the conclusion that, if he could take the place of the North Star, the formation would disintegrate on its own. If the Taoists insisted on prolonging the fight, he could manipulate them from his position of power, and never be ousted, according to the eternal forces guiding the stars in the heavens.

THE TAOISTS too understood the implications of Apothecary Huang's bid to shoot past Ma Yu at the Heavenly Pivot position. They knew he had discovered the key to neutralizing the formation.

If Tan Chuduan were still alive, they would have been able to charge as one. They may not have been able to subdue the Lord of Peach Blossom Island, but they could have ensured he could never occupy the North Star. But instead the Heavenly Jade position was guarded by Ke Zhen'e and Harmony Yin. Not only were their martial skills inferior to Tan's, their understanding of the formation was also limited.

Ma Yu was conscious that this fight would not end well if they continued in this way, especially with Guo Jing standing by, poised to enter the fray. If they put Apothecary Huang in real danger, the young man would surely come to his father-in-law's aid. But how could they shirk the grave responsibility of avenging Zhou Botong and Tan Chuduan's deaths? Moreover, their late teacher Wang Chongyang was the Greatest Martial Master Under the Heavens. If six of his disciples could not overpower Apothecary Huang, they would be shredding, with their own hands, the hard-earned reputation of the Quanzhen Sect as the orthodox school of kung fu.

"I THOUGHT the students of Wang Chongyang would put up more of a fight," Apothecary Huang jeered as he charged at Sun Bu'er.

Woo-ooo-oosh! Three blistering cuts from his palm.

Ma Yu and Hao Datong thrust their swords at him in response. Huang swiveled away from the steel points with a slight twist of his torso.

He arced his palm at Sun Bu'er again.

Woo-ooo-oosh! Another three strikes at breakneck speed.

The Lord of Peach Blossom Island had found fame with the torrential way he rained down brisk attacks, relentless in their intricacy. Right this instant, Wang Chongyang could come back to life and Count Seven Hong could recover all his kung fu, and yet, were they in Sun Bu'er's shoes, both would struggle to evade the knife-edged fury of Apothecary Huang's palms.

The Taoist nun, needless to say, had no hope against this succession of quick-fire blows from such a formidable opponent. She raised her sword to protect her face, but the Heretic had already changed tactics. He swiped his foot left and right, one sniping strike after another, six times in total.

The Supreme East Wind. An unstoppable amalgamation of two of Peach Blossom Island most famed martial secrets: Cascading Peach Blossom Palm and Swirling Leaf Kick.

Six moves from one kung fu, then six from the other, whipping up a whirlwind onslaught that swirled ever faster as the sequence wore on. By the sixth set—after thirty-six moves altogether—even a first-rate martial artist would have inevitably taken a hit.

The Quanzhen monks closed ranks to come to their martial sister's aid, but, at high-pressured moments such as this, one small slip can jeopardize the whole enterprise.

Ke Zhen'e was half a beat too slow when his side of the Dipper closed in.

Snickering in triumph, Apothecary Huang slipped past the blind man. Immediately, there came a cry of *aiyooo!* that instantly began to fade away, as though the soul that uttered it had been snatched by a gust of wind.

The Heretic had grabbed Harmony Yin by the back of his robes and flung him high onto the roof of the Tower of Mist and Rain. And, now that he had at last forced a breach in the formation, he was not going to allow his opponents any respite or a chance to re-group.

Squaring his shoulders, he charged headlong into Ma Yu, expecting the Taoist to skip aside. But the most senior Master among the Quanzhen Seven stood his ground.

Holding his blade in a high guard, Ma extended the index and middle fingers of his left hand in the Sword Sign and speared them at Apothecary Huang, aiming for between his eyebrows, steady and firm with the strength of *neigong*.

The Heretic veered a little to the side.

"Impressive! You live up to your reputation as the foremost disciple of Immortal Wang."

Huang twisted around as he spoke, sweeping his foot at Hao Datong and sending the man flying backward in a somersault as his sword clattered to the ground. The Heretic snatched it up and plunged it toward the Taoist's heart.

Liu Chuxuan dived forward to intercept.

Steel clashed with steel.

"He may yet live." A burst of laughter exploded from Apothecary Huang, accompanied by a savage pulse of his wrist.

Pak! Both swords snapped at the foible.

A swirl of green. The Lord of Peach Blossom Island was making for the North Star.

THE TAOISTS knew there was no way to keep the formation intact. This day would mark the end of the Quanzhen Sect.

With a sigh, Ma Yu steeled himself to throw his sword down and yield, but, for some strange reason, the green whirl was heading his way again.

Someone else was standing in the North Star position.

Guo Jing!

Qiu Chuji was thrilled. He had seen how the young man had lunged at Apothecary Huang earlier, at the tavern, with no regard for his own life.

Ma Yu and Wang Chuyi, although unsettled by Guo Jing's intervention, had faith in the young man's pure heart. He would never do harm to anyone on the same side as his first *shifu*—even if he had a duty to help his father-in-law.

But panic mounted in the remaining Taoists. It was only natural that the son-in-law should side with his father. They resigned themselves to a brutal end.

Apothecary Huang, meanwhile, was at a loss. He had assumed that, if he broke the formation and took the North Star, the Quanzhen Masters would be forced to surrender and beg for mercy. It had never occurred to him that the North Star would be taken already.

The Taoists were still bearing down on him with their full force, so, without turning to look, he flung a backhand from Splitting Sky Palm at whoever it was who had secured the position he needed.

It was blocked.

Huang was startled. Who can this be? Only a handful of fighters can withstand such a blow. He fended me off with one hand and held his footing.

He glanced back. Guo Jing?

The Heretic reassessed the situation. He would need to deal with the boy at once, or the Quanzhen monks would steal up from behind and trap him in the formation again.

He chopped, hacked and thrust, each move more brutal and rapid than the last, but Guo Jing dispelled them with his *neigong*.

Next came a fierce strike lurking within a feint. He tried to draw Guo Jing into attacking him by showing a momentary weakness, but the boy maintained his defensive posture.

Guo Jing held the dagger sideways to guard his chest and drew his other hand slowly across his lower abdomen, deflecting the Heretic's two-pronged attack.

This considered response alarmed Apothecary Huang further. The busybodies from the Quanzhen Sect must have shared the secret to their formation with the lad, he concluded. That's the only way this blockhead would know about holding the North Star position. Yes, that must be it—he's joined forces with them to subdue me!

Not in his wildest dreams would the Heretic have guessed that the youth had worked out the essence of the Heavenly Northern Dipper formation all by himself, thanks to the Nine Yin Manual.

Guo Jing knew that, if he was to avenge his *shifus*, he would have to resolutely hold the North Star and resist the temptation to chase after the weaknesses Apothecary Huang might feign to lure him out of position. He steeled himself and focused his all his energy on keeping his feet firmly planted, as if nailed to the ground.

You've made up your mind, haven't you? To oppose me! *Huh!* the Heretic grumbled silently as he appraised the situation. Just know this—you're forcing me to incapacitate you. Well, as you wish, boy! I'm going to break free and I'll just have to brave Lotus's wrath.

Huang raised his left arm, tracing a neat arc. When he reached a spot seven inches in front of his chest, his right palm smacked against the back of his outstretched hand. Together, they flew toward Guo Jing's face—at double the strength.

If he refuses to move . . . Lotus will be miserable for life, the Heretic thought, wavering.

Guo Jing knew he could swerve to avoid this powerful blow, but it would mean giving up the North Star, and, if the Heretic got into position, nothing would compel him to give up his place. The young man tried to shut out the voice telling him that his *neigong* was not up to the task and that fighting in this bull-headed manner would cause nothing but harm to both parties. If he wanted revenge, he had no option, he could not budge, even if it meant serious injury or worse.

Tightening his jaw, he launched a Dragon in the Field and braced himself for impact.

"Move, foolish boy. Why do you stand against me?"

It was Apothecary Huang's voice, instead of his palms, that struck Guo Jing in the face. *He's holding back from hurting me . . .* The youth shook away the thought and kept his eyes locked on his mentors' murderer, the golden dagger raised.

The Quanzhen Taoists and Ke Zhen'e had resumed their formation. They were now closing in on Apothecary Huang from behind, biding their time, waiting for an opportunity to strike back.

"Lotus—where is she?"

The longer Apothecary Huang observed Guo Jing, the more unsettled he grew. *Why did he have this dark cloud over him? Why such anger in his eyes? Could something have happened to . . .*

"What did you do to her? Tell me!"

He was now looking out for every tiny change in the young man's bearing, noting how his jaw twitched and his knife hand was beginning to tremble.

"Why is your hand quivering? Why won't you speak?"

Images of his *shifus'* horrific deaths rose up to haunt Guo Jing once more. Grief and anger caused his body to shake and the rims of his eyes to redden.

Apothecary Huang understood from the boy's silent agitation that something was terribly wrong. He remembered how heartbroken Lotus had been when they had discovered Guo Jing's betrothal to the Mongolian Princess. *Why was she not here with him, right now? Could she have offered up her life to lost love . . .*

The Heretic flexed his toes and pounced.

Qiu Chuji charged, his sword whirling, as Wang Chuyi too swung his blade and Hao Datong thrust his palms, their combined efforts trapping Apothecary Huang between them. The full force of the Heavenly Northern Dipper was once more unleashed.

With a swipe of his palm, Guo Jing parried the brunt of the Heretic's lunge, and followed up with a stab of his dagger, swift and shrill, like a flash of lightning.

But Huang was undeterred. He redoubled his offensive, clawing at Guo Jing with a backhand slash, his aim precise and vicious.

Just as he was about to trap the young man's wrist, he sensed the sting of a sword buzzing over his back. He sheered away with a twist of his waist, turning to find that it was Wang Chuyi who had thwarted him, for his minute adjustment had robbed him of the chance to disarm Guo Jing by a mere two inches.

Guo Jing twirled the knife around, hacking, slicing.

The battle was now reaching boiling point. The Quanzhen Masters had joined the conflict intent on avenging the deaths of Zhou Botong and Tan Chuduan, but as it dragged on, and the Heretic time and again held back from hurting them, the Taoists felt their animosity draining away.

Apothecary Huang was also aware that a feud born of misapprehension had been brewing between him and the Six Freaks of the South since they had first set eyes on each other. The haughty man had considered it beneath his status as their martial senior to explain his position. Instead, he had planned to give the upstarts a good thrashing to instil some manners. Once they had been thoroughly trounced—and had admitted as much to themselves—he would clear the air once and for all.

Sun Bu'er and Harmony Yin would not be standing and breathing right now if he were not inclined to mercy. Yet, he had not factored Guo Jing's unforeseen appearance into his calculations, nor imagined that he would fight tooth and nail against him. The only possible reason for Guo Jing to act this way was that the young man had done Lotus wrong, that his insistence on honoring his word had shattered her heart, destroyed her will to live and caused her to . . .

Yes, that would explain everything. He would take the little rat alive and wring the truth out of him.

Meanwhile, with Harmony Yin still clambering down from the roof of the Tower of Mist and Rain, Ke Zhen'e was left to fend for himself. Neverthless, the Heavenly Northern Dipper was rolling staunchly forward, exerting more and more pressure on Apothecary Huang as Guo Jing kept him busy from the North Star.

The Heretic had tried several ways to shift Guo Jing—from out-flanking him using his superior *qinggong* to shoving him aside with brute force—but the Taoists always came to the young man's assistance at the right moment. By the time Huang had dealt with the monks, Guo Jing was firmly in position once more.

As the fight wore on, Apothecary Huang started to feel increasingly cramped—he knew that, if he was not careful, he could find himself hemmed in before long.

He also had to admit that he felt a certain relief when Ma Yu shouted "Stop!" and pointed his sword to the heavens.

His martial siblings halted their advance, but remained on guard, maintaining their positions in the formation.

"Lord Huang, you are a grandmaster of the martial arts, and we mere students would never set out to cause you offense." Ma Yu spoke with humility. "Forgive us for using our numbers against you. Might we ask your opinion on how you propose to settle the blood debt we are owed for the deaths of Martial Uncle Zhou and Brother Tan?"

Apothecary Huang scoffed. "What is there to say? Deal your death blow! Kill Heretic Huang to secure the Quanzhen Sect's reputation. Isn't that what you want? Let me help you." Without shifting his feet or lifting his arm, he hacked at Ma Yu's face with his right hand.

Ma Yu slewed away, shocked that an attack of such complexity and ferocity could be launched with so little warning. It was the ultimate move in the Cascading Peach Blossom Palm, a single swipe of the arm that channeled a torrent of feints and firm strikes in infinite combinations. Huang had been honing this skill for a decade, hoping to use it to win the title of the Greatest Martial Master at the second Contest of Mount Hua. It was developed for use in a one-on-one duel, so he had not used it in the melee, but against Scarlet Sun Ma Yu alone, it could reach its full potential, and nothing the Taoist had learned in his decades of training could help him.

If Ma Yu had held still, he might have suffered only a glancing blow, but instead he swiveled squarely into a palm thrust aimed at his back. He raised his arm to block, only to find the Heretic's other hand inches from his chest.

My insides will be scrambled by his internal energy, Ma Yu said to himself, feeling no fear, only a strange resignation.

His martial brothers lunged with their swords, but it was too little too late. They were already steeling themselves to witness their eldest brother's death. Yet, at the last moment, Apothecary Huang pulled back, letting out a savage bark of laughter.

"I know you won't back down, even if I destroy you one by one. So, come, together, all of you. Do your worst!"

Snorting at the man's conceit, Liu Chuxuan threw a punch, which Wang Chuyi followed with a sweep of his sword. The Heavenly Northern Dipper was now in its seventeenth permutation, with Ma Yu next in line to thrust with his blade, but the Scarlet Sun Immortal took two steps back instead.

"No! Stop!" He signaled for his martial siblings to lower their weapons. "Lord Huang, we thank you for your clemency."

Apothecary Huang accepted the humble words with a nod.

"By rights, I should be dead," Ma Yu continued. "And since you have found the flaw in the formation created by our late Master, we should have the self-awareness to cast down our weapons and acknowledge our defeat, submitting ourselves to your will. However, since a blood feud binds our two martial branches, we have no choice but to seek redress. Once our task is fulfilled, I shall draw my sword across my neck and give my life to thank you, Lord Huang, for the mercy you have shown me."

The Heretic took a moment to consider Ma Yu's grave words, then waved them away. "Hard it is to untangle the knots of amity and enmity. There is no need to explain. Make your case with your sword."

The exchange presented Guo Jing with a quandary. Elder Ma and his brethren are here to avenge their martial uncle and brother, he said to himself, but Brother Zhou is alive and well, and Reverend Tan's death had nothing to do with Lord Huang. But, if I'm honest about what happened, the Reverends will step aside. Without them, First *Shifu* and I have no chance of taking our revenge. And yet, to keep that knowledge to myself, would make me the worst kind of scoundrel. My *shifus* told me many times: we can lose our heads, but never our sense of what's right.

So he decided to speak up. "Reverend Ma, Reverend Qiu, Reverend Wang," he cried. "Martial Uncle Zhou is well, and Reverend Tan was killed by Viper Ouyang."

"What do you mean?" Qiu Chuji asked.

Guo Jing recounted the events he witnessed from the secret room inside the desolated inn at Ox Village as he treated the injury he had sustained at Viper Ouyang's hands. Unlike Lotus, he was not gifted with words and in the art of storytelling, but he was able to explain with sufficient clarity how Qiu Qianzhang's lies had led to a fierce fight, how Viper Ouyang had ambushed Tan Chuduan, then Apothecary Huang, and how Cyclone Mei had sacrificed her life to protect her teacher.

The Quanzhen monks might have taken an active part in the events Guo Jing had just described, but their memory of them was rather different. Seeing the doubt on their faces, Guo Jing added, "I want nothing more than to tear this man's throat out with my teeth, yet I cannot withhold the truth from you."

Faced with the hatred still burning in Guo Jing's eyes, Apothecary Huang could not understand why the young man would speak on his behalf. "Why do you hate me so much?" he asked sharply. "And where's Lotus?"

Ke Zhen'e answered for his disciple. "You know full well what you've done. We may not be able to bring him to his knees," he called to Guo Jing as he swung his iron staff at Apothecary Huang, "but we'll die trying."

Tears burst forth as joy gushed through Guo Jing's heart—First *Shifu* has forgiven me!—then the gut-churning scenes from Peach Blossom Island came flooding back.

"Second *Shifu* and . . . they met such a gruesome fate . . ."

Apothecary Huang took hold of the end of Ke Zhen'e's staff, halting his attack, and turned to Guo Jing. "What do you mean? Zhu Cong and the others were enjoying themselves on my island. What are you saying, boy?"

Ke tugged with all his strength, but it had no effect whatsoever.

"Is that why you raise your fists and fill my ears with nonsense?" the Martial Great demanded.

"I know you killed my *shifus*! I know those hands of yours are covered in their blood!" Eyes wild, Guo Jing hacked down with the dagger, his bloodlust drowning all caution.

Apothecary Huang thrust Ke's staff into the knife's path.

Claaang! An explosion of sparks.

"Did anyone see me do it?"

"I buried my five *shifus* with these hands. I know what I've seen."

"Do you?" he sneered. "Very well. I, the Heretic, have always stood by my deeds. So, yes, you're right. I killed them!"

"No, Papa! You didn't! You didn't kill anybody! Don't claim what you didn't do!"

6

EVERYONE TURNED TO LOTUS, AMAZED THAT THEY HAD NOT noticed her entering the courtyard.

Guo Jing gaped at her, his heart torn in two.

Apothecary Huang let out a belly laugh. The vitriol he felt for Guo Jing was washed away by relief. "Come, my dear. Let Papa hug you," he said, spreading his arms wide.

They were the first kind words Lotus had heard since the carnage on Peach Blossom Island. She threw herself into her father's embrace.

"Pa, he's wronged you . . . and he—he's mean to me," she said between sobs.

Holding his daughter close, Apothecary Huang said, "For decades, pious fools have piled the wrongs of the world onto your pa.

A handful more trespasses make no difference. The Freaks of the South were the nemesis of your martial sister Mei. Why should I not avenge her death?"

"Nooooo! No, no, no! It wasn't you. I know it wasn't you!"

"Has that clod been mistreating you?" A cold smile. "Pa will get you justice." He twirled his hand and—*smack!*—boxed Guo Jing on the ear. The slap was as swift as lightning, impossible to block.

In the split second it took Guo Jing to register the stinging heat on his cheek, the offending hand had already returned to caressing Lotus's hair. Guo Jing touched his fingers to his face, at a loss how to respond, for he knew the strike was just for show.

"Guo Jing, are you alright?" Ke had heard the smack and feared the worst.

"I'm fine."

"Don't listen to the demon and his evil spawn. I'm blind but I'm not deaf. I heard him with these ears. He snatched the steelyard from your sixth *shifu* and snapped it in two with his bare hands. Who else on Peach Blossom Island has the skill to do—?" Sensing movement from Guo Jing, Ke Zhen'e swung his Exorcist's Staff.

Apothecary Huang pushed Lotus to safety, sidestepped Guo Jing's attack and made a lunge for Ke's weapon in one fluid movement.

But, this time, the First Freak was prepared, slipping his staff out of his opponent's grasp. Master and disciple stood side by side, united against the Heretic. But, though Guo Jing had encountered many exceptional martial artists and learned some of the most powerful kung fu under the heavens, his skills still lagged far behind that of the Greats. After two dozen moves, he was already struggling, even with the help of his teacher.

Qiu Chuji was racked by indecision. Guo Jing and Ke Zhen'e had extended a helping hand in the Quanzhen Sect's time of need. Can we stand by and watch their blood be spilled? he asked himself. The answer was self-evident. They could ascertain if Martial Uncle Zhou was still alive after they had beaten the Heretic.

"Master Ke, please return to the formation," Qiu called.

By now, Harmony Yin had climbed down from the Tower, and he hurried over to stand protectively behind the Freak, sword drawn. Though his face was bruised and swollen, he did not appear to have suffered any serious injury.

Once more, the Heavenly Northern Dipper formation was on the move, closing in on Apothecary Huang and his daughter.

The Heretic was incensed. You stinking monks are determined to make an enemy of me, aren't you? Do they think numbers alone can intimidate me? Do they really suppose that I would hesitate to kill them if need be?

One glimpse of her father's face and Lotus's heart sank: He won't hold back now . . .

Apothecary Huang pounced, hurtling to the left of Ke Zhen'e, but his charge was blocked by Wang Chuyi and Ma Yu.

Meanwhile, Ke took the chance to swing his staff down at Lotus's shoulder, accompanied by a string of curses: "You sinful witch! You hag of hell! You harlot strumpet!"

Lotus, who never let anyone get the better of her in an argument, was consumed with a burning rage. "I dare you to call me more names!"

The Seven Freaks of the South were descended from butchers, innkeepers and other common folk of the marketplace; insults were a craft they had perfected since childhood. Emboldened by her challenge and fueled by hatred for anyone associated with Peach Blossom Island, Ke Zhen'e hurled yet more vulgar abuse her way.

Even Lotus's ready wit was no match for the Freak's profanities, and her sheltered upbringing meant she was largely unfamiliar with such obscenities. It often took a moment or two for her to feel the sting of Ke's words as they grew increasingly unwholesome.

"Fie! Call yourself a teacher? Such language befouls the lips!"

"I save pleasantries for good people. To a filthy whore, I speak foul!"

Lotus replied with the Dog Beater, jabbing it at the blind man's face. Ke Zhen'e answered with his Exorcist's Staff, but, after a brief exchange of cuts and parries, the bamboo cane was dragging the iron staff east and west with the aid of the Draw technique. Not only had Lotus taken control of Ke's weapon, she had also disrupted the Heavenly Northern Dipper by neutralizing the Heavenly Jade position occupied by the Freak.

Qiu Chuji flashed his sword, spearing its point into Lotus's back. But the young woman paid him no heed, confident that the Hedgehog Chainmail would protect her, instead unleashing three more moves from the Dog-Beating repertoire on Ke Zhen'e.

Qiu hesitated—What kind of man am I to lay hands on a girl thus?—leaving the hard-pressed Freak without support.

Taking advantage of his indecision, Lotus touched her weapon against Ke's and twirled her wrist, latching on to an outburst of energy from the Exorcist's Staff, then flicked her cane to the left. The metal pole shot out of Ke's hand and plunged into the lake.

Wang Chuyi planted himself in front of the sightless, defenseless old man, sword raised against the Dog-Beating Cane. He had seen many superb martial displays in his time, but nothing as effortless and effective as the one Lotus had just staged.

"First *Shifu*, let me take over. You need a rest," Guo Jing called, giving up his place at the North Star. Once he took over the Heavenly Jade position, the formation gained a new edge—and not merely from his kung fu, for he had by now outstripped the Quanzhen Masters, or his familiarity with the principles that underlined the Heavenly Northern Dipper. Guo Jing's presence at Heavenly Jade shifted the formation's driving force from Qiu Chuji's Heavenly Pearl to him, and this new focus, though it left the formation less secure than before, confounded the Heretic with its unfamiliarity. It would take him a good few moves to figure out its flaws, and, even with Lotus's help, he was beginning to struggle.

Guo Jing was fighting without a care for his life. He prowled forward, flanked by the Quanzhen disciples, who, though happy to lend their support, had no wish to maim or kill. Nevertheless,

Apothecary Huang was feeling the pressure, flitting from danger time and again with the aid of his superb lightness *qinggong*.

Lotus regarded Guo Jing's demented onslaught in disbelief. Murderous bloodlust was clouding his normally friendly face. I don't know this Guo Jing, she thought, heartsick, and she threw herself in front of her father, arms flung wide.

"Kill me first!" she cried.

A cold glare as she was shoved out of his path. "Move!"

Is this how you treat me now? she lamented as she stumbled aside.

"Brother Apothecary, I'm here to help!" This greeting was followed by a harsh, metallic cackle.

The Quanzhen Masters knew it would be unwise to simply turn around, for they could find themselves trapped between the newcomer and their opponent. Working their way to the far side of Apothecary Huang in formation, they saw half a dozen men standing on the lakefront. In their midst, the wiry figure of Viper Ouyang, Venom of the West.

The Taoists howled at the sight of their brother's murderer.

"Guo Jing, let's have our reckoning with the Venom first!" Qiu Chuji cried, brandishing his sword and advancing on Viper Ouyang with his martial siblings in tow.

The young man did not hear the monk at all. He lunged at Apothecary Huang, exchanging five or six blows in a trice, then leaped back to catch his breath. Glaring at the Heretic, he lowered his shoulders and drew in his chest, ready for the next round.

Ke Zhen'e listened closely with his head cocked. He was waiting for a chance to lock his arms around Apothecary Huang so Guo Jing could finish him off.

Resigned to the fact that neither Guo Jing nor Ke Zhen'e would help them complete the formation, Qiu Chuji beckoned Harmony

Yin to take the Heavenly Jade position. Once the novice was in place, Ma Yu quoted Tan Chuduan's final words:

"The Way is found not in beads or brush.
Nature's music comes not from the flute."

A storm of thrusting palms and slicing swords, fueled by grief and vengeance, whipped into Viper Ouyang.

The Venom's Serpent Staff darted left and right. The Taoists drew back. Viper recalled the formation's might from Ox Village and proceeded with caution, waiting for them to betray any weakness. It did not take long for him to gather that Harmony Yin's position was the least fortified. If he could get rid of the young monk, he would dominate the battle. Heartened, he focused his assault on the boy, while keeping an eye on the other fight.

Guo Jing and Apothecary Huang were now tussling at close quarters. Lotus was able to keep Ke Zhen'e at bay with the Dog-Beating Cane, but her pleas of "Stop!" and "Listen to me!" fell on deaf ears.

By now, Guo Jing had sheathed his dagger and was fighting with his bare palms. Thrusting, swiping, striking, an incessant bombardment. At first, Apothecary Huang held back for Lotus's sake, but he was soon irritated by the constant buzzing, and his responses grew harsh as his heart hardened.

One small mistake now would prove fatal. As panic began to rise up in her throat, Lotus noticed Count Seven Hong observing the fight from the first floor of the Tower of Mist and Rain.

"*Shifu!* Help! They'll listen to you!"

Count Seven had been an anxious onlooker, frustrated that he could do nothing thanks to his diminished kung fu. Lotus's cry gave him an idea. Perhaps the Old Heretic still considers me a friend . . .

He hauled himself up onto the balustrade and jumped, gliding down to land on the battlefield.

"Oi! Hark the Old Beggar!"

The reputation of the Divine Vagrant Nine Fingers still carried weight. The fighting ceased.

Viper Ouyang was shaken to the core by Count Seven's dramatic intervention. How had he managed to regain his kung fu?

Over the last couple of days, Count Seven had been using the secret method from the Nine Yin Manual to reconnect his Eight Extraordinary Meridians, and the results had been incredible—he had repaired one energy flow, and, with it, a third of his lightness *qing-gong*. His internal strength in combat was still no more than that of a heavyset man new to the martial arts, but he could appear as fleet of foot as before. Even the hawk-eyed Viper was unable to tell that his sprightliness contained no substance at all.

Count Seven was gleeful to see that, in his weakened state, he still had the authority to command an audience, but what could he say to calm the Quanzhen monks and convince the Venom to retreat? He threw back his head and laughed. It was simply an act to buy some time, but his eyes alighted on the newly risen moon and . . .

Not quite a perfect circle yet . . .

"I can see some of the greatest fighters of the *wulin* before me," he said. "But now I realize you're just a bunch of rogues and knaves—you give your word as casually as you break wind."

Count Seven Hong was known for his forthright attitude, so no one took offense at his crude chastisement—he would not have offered it without good cause.

"We beg the Master to enlighten us." Ma Yu cupped his hands in respect and bowed.

"I heard there'd be a fight by the Tower of Mist and Rain on Moon Festival and decided to turn up early to have a nose around. And, since the crack of dawn, I've been treated to this constant shouting and banging—you lot running about with your soil-bucket formations and pissy urinal lineups, husbands beating wives, sons-in-law fighting fathers, screeching and shrieking like pigs to the slaughter. All day long and none of you thought about granting this Old

Beggar a moment's peace—I was so looking forward to a nap after my mutton leg. Look up. Look! What day is it today?"

Indeed, the moon was not yet full—it was only the fourteenth of the eighth month. The mid-autumn contest with Tiger Peng and the others, who had yet to arrive, was not due to start until the next day.

"Master is right—we should not be causing a disturbance here," Qiu Chuji said. "Viper Ouyang, let's take this fight elsewhere."

The Venom smirked. "It would be my pleasure."

"The Quanzhen Sect is truly a mess without Wang Chongyang," Count Seven said to himself in a stage whisper, making sure everyone could hear his aside, before addressing the monks. "Let me share an uncomfortable truth. You can put five monks, a nun and a novice together, and they still won't be a match for our Old Venom. I don't owe Wang Chongyang any favors and I couldn't care less if his tawdry little followers are wiped out, but I do want to ask you one question: In what form will you take part in the contest tomorrow? Do you plan to fight as corpses?"

Of course, the Quanzhen Masters recognized that these jibes were a kindly reminder that they had no hope against Viper Ouyang, for they had just failed to best Apothecary Huang, who was his equal in reputation. And yet, how could they back down when they were seeking to avenge one of their own?

Count Seven had also been keeping an eye on his two disciples. Guo Jing was staring daggers at the Heretic, while Lotus was on the verge of tears. What could he say to smooth over this shambles?

When the Hoary Urchin gets here, he can keep everyone in a line with his kung fu, and I'll be able to say my piece, Count Seven said to himself, pinning his hopes on Zhou Botong's impish nature—after all, missing the fun of such a fight would be most out of character for that overgrown child.

"This Old Beggar is going to sleep now," he announced. "If I hear so much as a peep out of you lot, I'll consider it an act of war. Tomorrow night, you can turn the world upside down and I'll watch from up there. And don't expect me to lift a finger to help any of you.

"Ma Yu, Qiu Chuji, get your little brothers and sister in order, sit them down and start channeling your *qi*. What meager inner strength you can gather now will be to your benefit—clinging onto the Buddha's legs for help at the last minute is better than nothing at all.

"Guo Jing, Lotus, massage my legs."

"Brother Apothecary and I have scores to settle with the Quanzhen Sect," Viper Ouyang said to Count Seven. "We all know that the Divine Vagrant Nine Fingers' words are as immovable as a mountain. I shall let things pass today out of respect for you, but, tomorrow, you will have to abide by your word and stand aside." He wanted to make certain that the Beggar would not step in, now that he had miraculously regained his martial prowess.

Count Seven giggled inwardly at the Venom's wary tone. *If only you knew! You could knock me down with your little finger right now.*

"This Beggar's farts have more substance than your vows. As I've said, I won't help anybody, but are you so sure you'll come out on top?" Without waiting for an answer, Count Seven Hong flopped on the ground, lying flat and resting his head on his gourd of wine. "Kids, massage, chop-chop!"

The mutton leg in Count Seven's hand had long been reduced to a stick of bone, but the gourmand was unwilling to relinquish it, licking and sucking in search of the last morsels of flavor.

"The weather's going to turn." The Beggar eyed the thickening clouds on the horizon and the mist clinging to the water. He sucked in a few big gulps of air and shook his head. "Stifling! Brother Apothecary, you'll give your permission, won't you? These tired old legs could really do with a massage."

The Heretic smiled as Lotus sat down, gently hammering her martial teacher's thigh.

"*Aaaahhhh*, these old bones have never had such a treat . . ." He glared at Guo Jing. "Oi, silly lad, the Heretic hasn't broken your paws, has he?"

"Master," Guo Jing mumbled as he sat opposite Lotus, mirroring her motions.

Ke Zhen'e slumped against a willow tree by the water, his unseeing eyes fixed in the direction of Apothecary Huang, his head turning left and right as his nemesis paced up and down, his ears picking out the light scratching of his footsteps.

The Heretic paid no attention to the blind man, a vague smile hovering on his lips.

The Quanzhen Taoists followed Count Seven's advice and sat cross-legged on the ground, eyes lowered, brows relaxed, working on their internal energy while maintaining the layout of the Heavenly Northern Dipper formation.

Meanwhile, the Venom's snake herders had set up a table and chair for him on the ground floor of the Tower of Mist and Rain. The Martial Great sat with his back to the others, picking at the food and drink spread out before him and pondering what miracle had allowed Count Seven Hong to recover from the crippling injury he had dealt him.

The heat was suffocating. Insects zoomed hither and thither. The mist over the lake was turning milky.

"Oh, the ache in my joints. They're sensing a storm. If we can see the full moon tomorrow night, I'll cut these legs off."

The Beggar had been observing Guo Jing and Lotus. The young lovers let their eyes rest everywhere but on each other. For a man as straightforward as he, suppressing his curiosity was out of the question. He asked several times, but they both just ummed and ahhed, refusing to give him a straight answer.

"Brother Apothecary, does South Lake have another name?" he called.

"The Lake of Mandarin Ducks."

"How romantic! Now, why are you two lovebirds ignoring each other by this lake of lovebirds? And why aren't you—father to them both—stepping in to stop this silly business?"

Guo Jing leaped to his feet, glaring at Apothecary Huang. "He—he killed my five *shifus*. He's not my father."

"So?" Huang sneered. "There's still one Freak left, though the blind bat won't live another day—"

Ke Zhen'e lunged, but Guo Jing was faster. The Heretic raised his arm in retaliation. Their palms thudded together—*pang!*—and Guo Jing stumbled two steps back.

"Oi! Do you think this Old Beggar's words are empty farts?"

Still glowering at Apothecary Huang, Guo Jing stepped down obediently.

"Old Heretic, the Six Freaks of the South live by the moral code of *xia*. Why would you hurt good people? I must say, I don't like the sound of it."

"I slay as I see fit. What can you do about that?"

"Pa! You didn't do it. I know you didn't. Tell them the truth!"

Huang looked at his daughter. In the pale moonlight, her complexion seemed more sallow than the last time he had seen her. He was almost swayed by pity, until he met Guo Jing's glare and saw the thirst for blood on his young face. His heart stiffened.

"I killed them."

"Pa, why?" Lotus sobbed. "Why do you have to claim things you didn't do?"

"Have you forgotten that the world has always seen your pa as a heretic and a miscreant? How can someone like me ever do good? All the evil under the heavens is my doing."

"I admire your honest admission, Brother Apothecary." Viper Ouyang cackled, raised his cup in a toast and drank it dry. "And I have a gift for you."

The two men were several *zhang* apart, and yet one small flick of his wrist was enough to send a sizeable bundle flying through the air to reach the Heretic.

Apothecary Huang caught the parcel and immediately knew that he was holding a human head. He peeled back the layers of fabric and was confronted by an unfamiliar face. The square headscarf of a learned man. A wispy beard covered his chin . . . freshly harvested.

Viper cackled in delight. "I entered the city from the west this morning and rested my feet at a school. This stuffy bookman was droning on about loyal subjects and filial sons. He was so tiresome, I had to cut his head off to shut him up. You the Heretic, I the Venom, we hold the world in the same disdain."

Apothecary Huang regarded the martial Master with contempt and distaste. "I have nothing but the utmost respect for loyal subjects and filial sons." He dug a hole in the ground with his bare hands and laid the head to rest, bowing three times before the fresh grave.

"So, your name is an empty title—the Heretic is also bound by convention," Viper said with a mocking laugh.

"Loyalty, filial piety, benevolence and righteousness are principles, not conventions!"

Thunder cracked. Storm clouds obscured the sky. Drums echoed around the lake. The splash of oars. Half a dozen stately boats, glittering with red lanterns, heading their way. Standing proud on the prow were colossal signs reading *Silence* and *Turn Away*, warning all onlookers of the arrival of an official retinue.

Someone of high rank and great import was approaching the Tower.

CHAPTER SEVEN

IRON SPEAR TEMPLE

I

TWO DOZEN OR SO MEN DISEMBARKED, AMONG THEM TIGER Peng and Hector Sha. Then, a tall, broad-shouldered man stepped ashore, accompanied by someone older, slight but nimble—Wanyan Honglie, the Sixth Prince of the Great Jin Empire, and Qiu Qianren, leader of the Iron Palm Gang. Now that the Jin Prince had gained the support of both Viper Ouyang and Qiu Qianren, he was confident that his cortège would win the contest, and felt safe venturing south again.

"Pa, that old fossil almost killed me with his palm thrust," Lotus said, pointing at Qiu.

Apothecary Huang had met the man twice before, at Roaming Cloud Manor and at Ox Village, and, both times, he had scampered away whimpering. How could that imbecile be capable of hurting his daughter? Of course, he had yet to realize that his dealings had been with the impostor and identical twin Qiu Qianzhang.

The Venom got up from his feast to welcome the new arrivals, conversing with the Prince in hushed tones, then approached Count Seven Hong.

"Brother Seven, you said you wouldn't take sides in the upcoming fight. Does that hold true?"

The Beggar sighed. *I'm in no state to help, even if I wished to.*

"What upcoming fight? I said I wouldn't help anyone on the fifteenth of the eighth moon."

Viper ignored his response and turned to the Heretic. "Brother Apothecary, neither the Quanzhen Sect nor the Seven Freaks of the South appear to know their place, offending a paramount master like yourself. It is beneath your status to raise your hand against such feeble warriors. Allow your brother, here, to deal with them, while you watch."

Apothecary Huang weighed up the situation. *If Count Seven Hong stayed true to his word and refrained from taking part, then the Quanzhen Sect would be annihilated by Viper Ouyang; though, if Guo Jing took the position of the Heavenly Jade, there would be a good chance that the formation could vanquish the Venom. And yet, the boy had been so single-minded about attacking* him . . .

How ironic that the future of the Quanzhen Sect rests upon the whim of this unweaned idiot, he thought. *If Wang Chongyang could see us from the world beyond . . .*

From Apothecary Huang's blank look, Viper knew his words had not had the desired effect. But he could not miss a chance to obliterate the Quanzhen Sect before Zhou Botong could come to their aid.

"What are you waiting for?" he taunted the Taoists. "Make your first move!"

"What did you just promise?" Count Seven roared.

Viper pointed to the sky with a smirk. "Midnight has passed. We're now in the early morning of the fifteenth."

Count Seven looked up. The moon had indeed crept westward, though half obscured by clouds. He could not deny that they had entered a new day.

A tap of the Serpent Staff against the ground and the Venom was suddenly standing right in front of Qiu Chuji. The Martial Great unleashed one deadly kung fu after another, keen to show off his signature techniques in the presence of such an illustrious audience.

The Quanzhen monks knew that the slightest error would spell the end—for themselves as well as their martial branch. Steeling their hearts, they engaged Viper Ouyang head-on, employing all their learning to maximize the power of the Heavenly Northern Dipper formation, but, within a handful of moves, they were straining to cope with the Venom's onslaught.

Guo Jing was scarcely aware of the Taoists' struggles. His eyes were trained on the murderer of his *shifus*. He would be battling him even now if he had not been forced to stand down by Count Seven Hong.

Lotus had been wondering how she could break Guo Jing's fixation on her father. The arrival of Wanyan Honglie gave her the perfect diversion.

"So, all your talk of revenge turns out to be mere empty words," she said, her voice ringing with derision. "Your father's murderer has come to you, and yet here you sit, doing nothing."

Giving her a baleful look, Guo Jing drew the golden dagger and charged at Wanyan Honglie.

I'll kill the Jin dog, then I'll kill the Heretic, he swore to himself.

Hector Sha and Tiger Peng planted themselves in Guo Jing's path. The young man hacked his dagger at them an angled backhand slash. Peng crossed his Scribe's Brushes—*claaang!*—and blocked the blade, but his numbed arms could not hold Guo Jing back. Sha swiveled to check his progress, employing Shape Changing kung fu to bar his way, but the young fighter pushed past him with ease.

Graybeard Liang and Lama Supreme Wisdom joined the effort to halt Guo Jing, brandishing their weapons. Old Liang threw two Bone-Piercing Needles, which the young man sidestepped smoothly before retaliating with a move known as Horns in the Fence, launching palm, dagger and body at his opponent. Graybeard cast himself to the ground and rolled out of harm's way—he knew he had not the skill to counter such a powerful attack.

Lacking Liang's agility, the fleshy Lama Supreme Wisdom knew he could not get away in time, so he held his cymbals firm against the assault. After all, he was the last line of defense for his patron Wanyan Honglie, the Prince of Zhao. *Bong, bong* . . . both cymbals flew straight up into the air as a gust whipped into his face. The lama thrust out a palm in reply, assuming that his great strength and the poison on his skin would make his attacker think twice, and yet, moments later, he felt his breath catch in his lungs, his arm racked with pain and his hand flopping uselessly as his wrist was knocked out of joint.

He stood stupefied, deserted by his supreme wisdom, his toxic touch nullified. The two copper-coated discs descended, one after the other, leaving a glistening, golden trail. The first landed square on the lama's glossy pate. If it had not fallen flat, its razor-sharp edge would have split his skull down the middle. Its fellow followed soon after. The steel plates clashed with a resounding crash and a deafening hum that traveled far into the night.

If Guo Jing wished to dispatch the lama, he could have done so with ease, but he had no quarrel with the man. He made straight for Wanyan Honglie, the golden dagger leading the way.

The Jin Prince stood petrified. He had counted on the four martial Masters in his employ to keep him safe, but they had been shoved aside in an instant. Not a single fighter now stood between him and Guo Jing.

Aiiiyaaaa! Shrieking, he bolted.

Dagger held high, Guo Jing followed in hot pursuit. Two palms materialized from a blur of earthy yellow, striking at him from the side. Guo Jing slewed away and arced the blade in retaliation, only to realize his body had been drawn into the wake of the powerful ambush. He took a step forward to steady himself and turned his eyes on this new opponent: Qiu Qianren.

Guo Jing drew in a deep breath to focus his mind. If he wanted to get past the leader of the Iron Palm Gang, he would need to forget about Wanyan Honglie and push aside any thoughts of revenge, for the time being. He readied himself, shifting his grip on the dagger in his right hand.

With Guo Jing now occupied and Wanyan Honglie once more under the protection of Graybeard Liang and Hector Sha, Tiger Peng allowed himself a sigh of relief. The danger had passed. He approached Ke Zhen'e and asked with mock concern, "Master Ke, where are the rest of you Freaks?"

Ke flicked his wrist, letting fly a poisoned devilnut, and settled into a defensive stance. Peng had suffered the effects of this secret weapon before and knew it would be too risky to try staving off the projectile in the dim moonlight. He jabbed both Scribe's Brushes into the ground, using them for leverage to vault up high, like a bird frightened by an arrow's song.

Swash! The devilnut zoomed by, passing under his feet.

Once safely back on firm ground, Peng noticed that the Freak had no weapon to defend himself. He lunged, thrusting his brushes, his jaw set tight.

The Exorcist's Staff was more than a weapon to Ke Zhen'e, for he was lame in one leg and relied upon its support to move around. At the sound of his enemy's approach, the Freak half hopped, half hobbled two paces to the side, but, as he took the last step, his legs buckled and he toppled face-first to the ground.

Peng speared one of the brushes at Ke's back, while holding the other close to his chest in case the blind man still had another trick up his sleeve.

Hearing the attack, Ke rolled sideways and the metal brush struck the ground, raising a smattering of sparks.

"You can't flap away from this, blind bat!" Peng roared, thrusting the other brush forward.

Still lying prone on the ground, Ke evaded the blow and—*hiss!*—flung another devilnut. Then he heard a muttering of insults and sensed a rush in the air, as it was first sucked upward, then pushed down toward him.

In his bid to escape Tiger Peng, the First Freak had dragged himself into Lama Supreme Wisdom, who had been nursing his injured wrist and cursing Guo Jing. Ke pressed a hand against the ground and propelled himself to the side. Although he managed to avoid the lama's descending foot, he felt a prick on his back. There was nothing more he could do, now, to escape Peng's brushes. He readied himself to face his fate, and yet, what followed was a girlish cry of *shoo!* then a gruff voice bellowing *aiyoooo!* before it was cut short by a thump.

Lotus had come to the rescue, sending Tiger Peng flying with the same technique she had used to disarm Ke Zhen'e earlier. Unlike the Freak, Peng held fast to his weapons, and so his stocky form took to the air along with the brushes.

"No one wants your help, she-demon!" Ke hissed as he climbed to his feet.

"Pa, look after this blind buffoon. Don't let him get hurt!" Lotus cried, and sprinted over to Guo Jing's side to fight Qiu Qianren.

Stunned, Ke Zhen'e stood alone in the midst of fierce fighting, struggling to grasp the meaning of Lotus's behavior.

Tiger Peng hauled himself back onto his feet, shamefaced but determined to get even. He sized up Apothecary Huang, who was facing the other way and did not seem to have heard his daughter. Peng crept up behind Ke, preparing to strike. Even if the Freak somehow recovered his sight and his staff, he would not be able to ward off this assault.

But, just before the brush had found its target, Peng heard a *swoosh*. A small speck of earth smashed into his weapon, dissipating into a puff of dusty smoke. A great force tore at the skin between his thumb and forefinger, knocking the brush out of his grasp. Peng could not understand where the projectile had come from or how it could make such an impact. He glanced at Apothecary Huang. His hands were clasped behind his back, his eyes fixed on the dark clouds on the horizon.

Ke Zhen'e recognized the unique fizz in the air. He had heard it once before, when Guo Jing fought Cyclone Mei at Roaming Cloud Manor. The Heretic's Divine Flick. How could he accept help from the murderer of his siblings? He threw himself at Apothecary Huang.

"What's the point of living when my brethren are dead?"

The Heretic did not seem to have heard the outburst, but when Ke Zhen'e came within three feet of him, he wafted his hand sideways across his back. A wave of energy surged toward the Freak, pushing his body to the ground until he found himself sitting on his rump. This strange force continued to pin him down, causing a curious sensation in his chest, as if his blood and breath were churning like a tempestuous sea.

2

The skies had grown darker. The thick mist was now creeping onto land, shrouding everyone's feet.

With Lotus's help, Guo Jing was able to hold his own against Qiu Qianren, but the Quanzhen monks were making their last stand. Hao Datong had suffered a blow from the Serpent Staff and Sun Bu'er's outer robe was ripped in two. Wang Chuyi realized that one of his siblings would be grievously wounded or worse before long, and pulled out a flare during a fleeting respite when it was the turn of Ma Yu and Liu Chuxuan to bear the brunt of the Venom's wrath. A flash of light, whistling, drew across the night sky.

Over the years, the Seven Immortals of the Quanzhen Sect had each taken on a sizeable number of disciples, and this third generation included a number of particularly skilled novices. Tiger Peng and his fellows were also known to have a multitude of students. Apprehensive that their unsporting opponents might try to carry the day through sheer weight of numbers, the Taoists had ordered their most accomplished protégés to wait on the far shore of South Lake. Should they see a flare, they were to cross the water to come to their teachers' aid. Yet, Wang Chuyi feared he might have sent his signal too late, for they were now completely engulfed by a pall of dense fog and could barely see a few feet ahead.

By now, the brume was clinging to their bodies like a white film, suffocating in its dampness. The gathering clouds crowded around the full moon, dimming its glow, and soon blotting out all light. In the gloom, caution was the watchword. The intensity of each fight dipped as they all drew back to focus on defense.

Since Guo Jing could only catch occasional glimpses of Qiu Qianren's fading form, he decided to take advantage of the mist's hazy cloak to seek out Wanyan Honglie once more. He opened his eyes as wide as he could, trying to catch a glint from the Jin Prince's golden coronet, but he could make out nothing in the muggy darkness. He dashed east and darted west, searching blindly, finding nothing.

"I'm Zhou Botong. Who wants to fight?" His voice sounded just a couple of steps from Guo Jing.

"Uncle Zhou!" Qiu Chuji called back, also close by.

For an instant, the clouds parted and a shaft of moonlight sliced through the mist to gasps of alarm as the combatants suddenly realized their enemies were no more than an arm's length away.

"Oooh, how wondrous! You're all here!" Squealing with excitement, the Old Urchin pulled up his sleeve and rubbed the skin over the crook of his left arm with vigorous relish.

"Deadly poison for you!" He cried, slapping his hand over Hector Sha's mouth.

The Dragon King responded with a Shape Changing move as he tried to flee, but he could not outrun the Hoary Urchin. An iron grip closed around his wrist and a ball of dead skin was forced between his lips.

Hector Sha had spent enough time with the irreverent martial Master to know that, if he spat out the revolting pellet, a worse fate would follow, so he kept it on his tongue, choking back the humiliation, waiting for an opportunity to get rid of it. Nobody has ever died from a bit of grime and dirt, he repeated again and again under his breath.

"Uncle Zhou, we're so pleased you're alive!" Wang Chuyi was as delighted as he was relieved that Zhou Botong had appeared at this crucial juncture.

The Urchin glowered. "Who said I was dead?"

"We heard that you'd been killed by the Heretic—"

"The Heretic?" A derisive snort. "Well, *try* he did. And for fifteen years, too. But, as you can see, he failed . . ." He let out a burst of gleeful laughter. "Hey, Heretic Huang, would you like to try killing me again?"

Apothecary Huang answered the Urchin's playful but powerful punch at his shoulder with a Cascading Peach Blossom Palm.

"Your martial nephews have been hounding me because they thought I killed you. They wanted to avenge your death."

"What? You killed me? When? Don't blow your own trumpet! Look! Am I the Hoary Urchin or the Ghostly Urchin?" His palms flew as fast as his words.

Apothecary Huang growled silently as he devoted his full attention to countering Zhou Botong's intricate rapid-fire onslaught.

The Quanzhen Masters looked on aghast. They had taken it for granted that their martial uncle would help them subdue Viper Ouyang, but here he was already sparring with Apothecary Huang.

"Uncle Zhou, stop! Don't fight Lord Huang!"

Ma Yu's entreaty fell on deaf ears.

"Urchin, listen to your nephew, leave Lord Huang alone," Viper echoed slyly. "You're no match for him. Run for your life. Run!"

Of course, Zhou Botong took the bait, bedeviling the Heretic further.

Lotus made her own attempt to break up the fight. "Old Urchin, you promised your martial brother Wang Chongyang never to learn kung fu from the Nine Yin Manual! Why are you fighting Papa with those skills? What would Immortal Wang say?"

"Kung fu from the Nine Yin Manual? No, no, no, no, no, watch me closely! See, I'm not! You don't know how much trouble it took to purge the Manual from my head! It was so easy to learn, but so hard to forget! Look, I'm using Luminous Hollow Fist, all seventy-two moves invented by me, and now this is Competing Hands, an original Urchin boxing technique." He gave Lotus a running commentary as he demonstrated his kung fu. "Can't you see? It's all my own invention. Not a stinking whiff of the Nine Yin Manual!"

Their last exchange on Peach Blossom Island was still fresh in Apothecary Huang's mind. This time, the overwhelming strength derived from the Nine Yin Manual that had so surprised him back then was missing from the elaborate moves, so the Urchin was once more his martial equal.

What strange methods had this man employed to unlearn something so entwined with his core? Huang wondered.

Satisfied by the sight of Zhou Botong wrangling with Apothecary Huang, Viper Ouyang redoubled his attack on the Quanzhen monks. He needed to break their formation before Zhou Botong came to his martial nephews' aid. His merciless assault, led by sweeps and thrusts of his Serpent Staff, put the Taoists in mortal danger.

"Uncle Zhou!" Wang Chuyi cried.

It finally cut through to Zhou Botong how much his brethren were suffering, but he was not ready to abandon his game with Apothecary Huang just yet. Left palm hacking sideways while his right fist jabbed straight ahead, he darted up to the Heretic's face and burst into laughter. In that moment, left flipped into right and right into left, the hack became a jab and the jab became a hack— what had been chopping athwart was now thrust forward.

Apothecary Huang had never encountered such a mercurial move. He flung his arms up to protect his face, but he was a fraction too slow. A sting at the end of his left eyebrow, where the skin was grazed by Zhou Botong's fingertips.

"Damn, damn, damn! That's from the Nine Yin Manual!" The Urchin slapped the offending hand.

Apothecary Huang saw his chance. His palm shot forward, swift and silent, striking at Zhou Botong's shoulder.

"*Aiyoooo!* Retribution comes apace!" the Hoary Urchin cried as he hunched his back and doubled over.

The mist had grown yet more impenetrable. Concerned for his

two *shifus'* safety, Guo Jing helped Ke Zhen'e to his feet and led him over to Count Seven Hong.

"Masters, please rest in the Tower until this fog passes," he said under his breath.

"Old Urchin," Lotus called. "Will you do as I say?"

"Don't worry, I can't beat your father."

"I want you to deal with the Old Venom. But you mustn't take his life."

"Why should I?" The Urchin was still engaged in a fierce battle with Apothecary Huang.

"If you refuse, I'll tell everybody about your dirty past."

"Hogwash! What dirty past?"

"As you wish!" And she began to chant in a sing-song voice:

> *"For the fourth time the loom is ready,*
> *To weave a pair of lovebirds so they can take flight."*

"Anything you say!" the Urchin shrieked. "Venom, where are you?"

"Uncle Zhou, take the North Star!" Ma Yu called through the haze.

Once Zhou Botong had joined his martial nephews' formation, Lotus cried out, "Pa, Qiu Qianren is a traitor to our country. We can't let him live!"

"Come to me, child." But the leader of the Iron Palm Gang had melted into the thick mist. The only figure Apothecary Huang could identify was the Hoary Urchin, thanks to his constant chortling.

"Venom, oh, Venom, bend the knee and Grandpa will let you live."

3

ONCE GUO JING HAD SETTLED COUNT SEVEN HONG AND KE Zhen'e inside the Tower, he resumed his search for Wanyan Honglie, but, in those few dozen steps between the courtyard and the Tower, he had lost the Jin Prince, who, along with his henchmen—Hector Sha, Tiger Peng, Qiu Qianren and the others—had simply vanished.

All that remained was Zhou Botong's booming voice. "Huh? Venom? Where are you? Have you run away from me?"

The weather that mid-autumn night was most peculiar. So dense was the fog that it had obscured the full moon as well as the faces of those standing hard by, leaving nothing but vague shapes in the murk. Voices were dulled by a dampness so palpable that it seemed to be forming a physical barrier. The curious weather had robbed everyone of their sight. Lotus stayed close to her father. Ma Yu muttered instructions to draw in the formation. Everyone listened out for the enemy, on their guard and ill at ease.

Utter silence.

Then, a low rustling. Growing louder, growing closer.

"Hark! What noise is this?" Qiu Chuji asked.

"Snakes!" Lotus cried. "The shameless old toad!"

"Come up," Count Seven shouted from the first floor of the Tower. "The Venom has let loose his snakes."

Yelping, Zhou Botong scrabbled toward the Tower as quickly as he could. He might be the most powerful martial artist present, but these creatures had always terrified him. He would not even risk the stairs, in case he got waylaid and bitten on the ankle. He sprang up using his lightness kung fu and landed, shivering, on the highest ridge of the roof.

The serpents slithered ever closer. Lotus clung to her father as they raced for the Tower. The Quanzhen monks felt their way up the stairs, hand in hand, but Harmony Yin stumbled and fell, bumping his head. When he rejoined them, moments later, he was sporting a huge lump.

LOTUS WAS keeping count of who was ascending the Tower's stairs but she did not hear Guo Jing's footsteps. "Guo Jing? Are you here?"

Her concern was apparent. She asked several times, but received no answer. "Pa, I'll go down to look for him."

"There's no need." A frosty reply. He was just a few steps away. "Don't use my name again. I won't answer."

"How dare you speak to my daughter thus!" Apothecary Huang swung his arm out. Guo Jing ducked away from the blow and twirled his palm, ready to fight back.

Tak, tak, tak! Arrows. Lodging into the window lattices.

"Catch the rebels!"

War cries rose from every direction. Bolts thudded into the woodwork of the Tower. There was no telling how many soldiers were out there.

"The Jurchen dogs must have bribed the governor of Jiaxing to send his army!" Wang Chuyi growled.

"We'll slay the turncoats, every last one!" Qiu Chuji roared in reply.

"Wait! There are snakes down there," Hao Datong reminded his hot-blooded brother.

The Venom's minions had almost reached the Tower and the archers were firing with increasing rapidity. It was clear that this was a planned ambush. Wanyan Honglie must have sent his soldiers out in small boats to surround the Tower, but he could not have predicted the weather. The fog might be giving his men cover, but it was also frustrating their aim—their only target was the hazy outline of the building.

Zhou Botong, alone on the exposed roof, was shouting curses at the snakes. He had caught two long bolts and was waving them around to ward off any others that came his way.

"We can't deal with both snakes and arrows up here," Count Seven said. "We have to retreat . . . Let's head west. We can take the land route." As the Chief of the largest gang under the heavens, he had a compelling way of speaking that commanded attention, and even the respected characters of the *wulin* gathered in the Tower were willing to lend him their ears.

The Tower of Mist and Rain jutted out into South Lake, embraced by water on three sides. When approached by boat, the Tower appeared to be floating on the ripples, and yet there were footpaths connecting it to the city.

The Quanzhen Taoists led the way, groping through the mist down the stairs. They could barely make out their own hands. How were they supposed to find a path to safety?

Qiu Chuji and Wang Chuyi twirled their swords in tandem to deflect as they picked their way through a torrent of missiles to find the route least bedeviled by archers. The rest of the group ventured forward hand in hand, reaching out to friend and foe alike, lest anyone got left behind. Guo Jing held Count Seven's hand in his right and extended his left to grab the person next in line. The fingers were dainty and the skin soft and smooth. He felt a pang of longing and let go immediately.

"Who wants to hold your hand?" Lotus muttered.

"Turn back! Turn back!" Qiu Chuji shouted. "Too many snakes ahead! There's no way through."

Apothecary Huang and Ma Yu had been bringing up the rear of the column, guarding against an attack from behind. At Qiu's cry, Apothecary Huang broke off two long branches of bamboo and brushed them against the ground. Hisses. The way back was blocked by serpents. An awful stench filled the air. Lotus tried to stop herself retching, but soon succumbed.

"There's nowhere to go. It's time to submit to our fate." Apothecary Huang threw the bamboo sprigs down and lifted Lotus into his arms.

Archers alone could not have stopped these martial Masters, but the Venom's snakes were another matter. One bite meant instant death. And there were hundreds and thousands of the creatures. All their martial learning was no use against serpents, since Apothecary Huang had snapped his jade flute and Count Seven Hong was not yet capable of launching his Skyful of Petals technique. Blinded by the brume, they stood on the spot, listening to the slither and hiss as the snakes closed in. Even if there were a way out, they could not see through the haze to find it.

"Little witch, give me your cane."

Lotus immediately handed the Dog Beater over to Ke Zhen'e. The blind man prodded the ground with the stick—"Follow me!"—and hobbled ahead, muttering as he made his way forward. "What's so surprising about a bit of fog? How do you think the Tower got its name?"

A native of Jiaxing, he had explored every single trail around the Tower in his childhood, and, for a sightless man, day, night, mist and fog were all the same. He could tell from the whistling of the arrows and the hissing of the snakes that a path he knew that led to the west was unobstructed, and was now heading confidently in that direction. Yet, seven or eight steps later, he found himself marching into a dense bamboo grove. Of course, he had not known that, in the intervening years, the track had become overgrown with vegetation, which was why it was not infested with snakes.

Qiu Chuji and Wang Chuyi slashed and chopped a way through with their swords, while Ma Yu called for Zhou Botong. The Hoary Urchin sat tight-lipped on the roof, scared of making the slightest sound. What if the wriggly creatures heard his reply and swarmed up the Tower to devour him? He knew they loved the taste of his flesh. It was not a risk he was willing to take.

4

THE GROUP EMERGED FROM THE BAMBOO GROVE A HUNDRED or so paces later to find a footpath. The rustling of snakes was behind them, but the thunder of soliders on the march was drawing near. The governor of Jiaxing's men were hurrying overland to outflank them. But what harm could crudely trained men-at-arms inflict upon warriors skilled in kung fu?

"Brother Hao, shall we?" Liu Chuxuan said.

"Marvelous!" Hao Datong hefted his blade and charged with his martial brother. Arrows buzzed in the mist, like swarming locusts. The Taoists beat them back with their swords.

Soon, the rest of the group found themselves on the main road. The heavens opened, tipping down buckets of water amid wild flashes of lightning and continuous cracks of thunder, washing the fog away in a trice. Still, with the moon blanketed by layers of clouds, the night was dark and everything was an indistinct blur.

"The danger has passed, fare thee well." With those words, Ke Zhen'e shoved the cane into Lotus's hand and limped eastward.

"*Shifu!*" Guo Jing called.

"Take Great Hero Hong to a safe place to rest, then come and find me at Ke Village."

"Yes, Master!"

Apothecary Huang plucked a stray arrow from the air and approached Ke Zhen'e. "I did not intend to spell it out, but, since you saved my life today—"

The Freak spat in the Heretic's face. "This day will be the reason I can't face my six siblings when I die!"

Apothecary Huang had bent low to speak to Ke Zhen'e, so their faces were less than a foot apart. Despite his extraordinary reflexes, he was caught out and the spittle skimmed across his cheek. He raised his hand, ready to strike the offender dead.

Guo Jing had been keeping an eye on his *shifu*, but, from a distance of twenty paces, all he could do was watch the exchange turn sour—he ran, knowing he would never make it in time, that he was about to witness the death of yet another of his teachers, but the next thing he heard was a dry chuckle.

"How could a man of my status behave like one of your ilk?" Apothecary Huang let his arm sink slowly and wiped the spit away with his sleeve. "Let's go, Lotus."

The Heretic's words and tone gnawed at Guo Jing, giving him pause. He could feel in his gut that something did not quite fit, but the notion in his head was so muddy and undefined that he could not say what it was he was unsure about. Before he could untangle this mystery, a scud of thick mist enveloped him and war cries could once more be heard. The Quanzhen monks raised their swords and charged at a squad of soldiers storming their way.

Apothecary Huang had no interest in tussling with lowly conscripts. "Brother Seven, why don't we find a tavern where we might enjoy a few drinks?"

"Perfect!" It was just the thing the Beggar had been craving, so the two Martial Greats disappeared into the gloom, arm in arm.

Guo Jing was a few steps away from Ke Zhen'e when a small band of soldiers rushed into him, separating him from his mentor. Never one to wish harm upon another, he used minimal force to repel them, but they turned out to be tougher than he had anticipated, for Jurchen soldiers and Iron Palm Gang members had been embedded into the ranks of the Song army.

"First *Shifu*! First *Shifu*! Where are you?" he cried, afraid that his teacher, without his sight or his weapon, would be hurt in the chaos, but he could not make out his Master's voice in the din, only the Quanzhen Taoists calling to each other amid the cacophony of battle.

LOTUS WAS standing close to Ke Zhen'e when her father approached him. She had followed their exchange with cautious optimism, but, in the blink of an eye, her heart was crushed and trampled. The Freak had not merely spat at her father, he had spat on all her hopes and dreams, and her one chance of finding happiness.

Numbed, she stood fixed to the spot, unaware of the men and horses tearing around her, until a cry of *aiyoo!* brought her back to the present.

She knew that voice. Ke Zhen'e.

She peered through the louring half-light to see an officer chopping his saber at the blind man from behind.

Ke rolled away, straightened up and threw a punch. He knocked the man over, but, when he pushed himself onto his feet, he fell back down. Lotus was much closer now. She could see something sticking out of his thigh. An arrow. She seized his arm and hauled him up. He flung her helping hand away, but the bolt was lodged in his good leg and he could not support himself on the lame one. He swayed and fell.

"Don't play the hero." Lotus caught him by the back of his collar and flicked at the True Shoulder pressure point above his right armpit with her Orchid Torch. Then she let go and grabbed him in a slightly more dignified manner, by the left arm. Ke desperately wished he could free himself from her grasp, but, having lost command of half his body, he could not resist her assistance, so he settled for demonstrating his displeasure with a mouthful of vulgarities.

Lotus half dragged, half carried Ke Zhen'e a dozen paces to a nearby tree, which provided some meager protection from the chaos around them. But, before she could catch her breath, they were spotted by soldiers and a shower of arrows rained down. Lotus stood in front of Ke Zhen'e and flourished the Dog Beater to protect her face.

"Leave me. Save yourself!" Ke grunted, grappling with the fact that she was shielding him with her body. Then he heard the arrows glancing off the Hedgehog Chainmail before clattering to the ground.

Lotus snorted at the old man's sentimental plea. "I won't desert you. I'll make sure you owe me your life. And there's nothing you can do to stop me."

She hauled him over to a low wall that would shelter him from the archers. Once they had traversed the short distance, she slumped against the barrier, panting hard, her heart hammering. Ke Zhen'e was a heavy load.

"Let any feud between us be crossed off." Ke heaved a sigh. "Go on your way! Consider this blind man dead."

"How am I supposed to consider you dead when you're very much alive? You can choose not to seek revenge from me, but I'm going to hound you for retribution." As she spoke, she thrust the Dog Beater at the Bend Middle acupoint behind each knee.

Ke cursed himself for letting his guard down against the she-demon, as he flopped helplessly onto his backside. As he berated himself, picturing the horrendous ways in which she would torment him, he picked out the sound of her nimble feet as she skirted around the wall, hurrying away from him.

The roar of battle was growing faint and distant. The Quanzhen monks must have scattered the troops, unwittingly chasing them away from Ke's hiding place. He thought he could hear Guo Jing calling his name, but his disciple was also moving farther and farther from him. He wanted to respond, but all his strength had been drained by the night's exertions, and he was further weakened by the injury he had just suffered. He could not summon the *qi* to project his voice far enough to reach Guo Jing's ears above the tumult.

Before long, silence returned. No more soldiers. No more fighting. A cock crowed in the distance and another replied, the heralds of dawn crying out.

On the morrow, the cocks will still crow in Jiaxing, Ke Zhen'e said to himself, but this life of mine will have been snuffed out by that she-demon. Never again will I hear the call of a new day.

Footsteps interrupted his morbid thoughts. Three people. One light and fleet. Lotus. The other two . . . their feet thumped heavily and dragged on the ground before each new step. Untrained.

"Here he is. Lift him up. Quickly!"

Lotus was standing right over him as she spoke those words. Then he felt her hand kneading his flesh as movement and control returned to his body—the binds on his pressure points removed. Immediately, he was taken by the shoulders and legs, lifted up and placed on a stretcher. Bamboo, he noted. A little jostling. The heavy-footed men lumbered forward.

What's going on? The question whirled in Ke Zhen'e's mind, but he knew better than to invite another tongue-lashing from the girl.

Thwack! The bearer at the front yelped in pain. Did she just cane him?

"What was that mumbling?" Her tone was pure menace. "Faster! I know what you soldiers are like. You fleece the common people. Not a single one of you has a shred of decency." *Thwack!* The man at the back this time, but he had learned from his comrade's mistake and he swallowed his groan.

Now Ke was beginning to wrap his mind around what was going on. She had captured two soldiers to carry him. Only this little witch could have come up with such a plan. The pain in his leg was getting worse. He could feel the arrowhead scraping and digging in deeper as the men carried him along the increasingly rugged path. He clenched his jaw and gritted his teeth. He would not give her any excuse to turn that barbed tongue of hers on him.

Soon, branches and leaves began to brush against his face and body. They were in a forest now. The men staggered and stumbled their way forward in fear of the cane, wheezing, huffing, out of breath.

Ke Zhen'e reckoned that they must have covered around thirty *li* and that it must be around midday by now, for his clothes were almost baked dry by the sun after being drenched by the predawn downpour. He could hear the tireless chirping of cicadas and the occasional barking dog. There was also singing, men and women conversing in song across the fields. This pastoral harmony was worlds away from the clash and clamor of the battle on South Lake just hours before.

They stopped, and he was lifted onto a bench. He could hear Lotus asking for two pumpkins and some rice, and then she disappeared for some time. They must have found a farmhouse they could rest in. When she came back, she set a steaming bowl down beside him.

"I'm not hungry," he croaked.

"I know your leg hurts, but I'm not going to help you just yet. I want you to suffer a bit longer."

He grabbed the bowl and splashed its contents at her. Snickers and shrieks. She must have skipped away, only for the scalding congee to catch one of the soldiers instead.

"Stop that racket! Master Ke has gifted you lunch! Lick it up."

Cowed by the girl's cane, the man threw himself down and picked up pumpkin pieces from the ground, stuffing them into his mouth. His face was stinging from the hot liquid, but it had been a day since his last meal.

Ke Zhen'e felt remorse. His rage had ended up hurting and humiliating an innocent man. The arrow was still embedded in his thigh and the wound would need tending soon. He felt around the shaft. He could pluck it out, but what if he could not stem the flow of blood? It went without saying that she would stand by and watch him bleed dry with relish, most likely mocking him as he faded away. As he debated what to do, he heard her say:

"Get me a basin of water. Double quick!"

Smack. The unmistakable sound of a box on the ear. Her orders were always underlined by a physical threat, he noted.

"Take the knife. Cut the fabric around the wound." He sensed the leg of his trousers being sliced open.

"I'll warn you now, old codger, I can't stomach screaming. If you're a proper man, you'll be able to handle this."

Before Ke Zhen'e could retort, a searing pain shot from the wound. She had jammed the bolt deeper into his leg. He threw a punch at her as a second shock of pain rocked him.

"If you move again, I'll cuff you too!"

He knew the she-demon was not making an empty threat. He could not bear to suffer the shame of being slapped at death's door. No, he would not allow himself to be so debased. For now, he would keep his face stony and submit to her—he knew he was no match for her in his current state. He only hoped she would finish him off with one clean blow.

The next thing he heard was the ripping of fabric. Was she making bandages? Confirmation came when a strip of cloth was bound tight around his thigh above the lesion, then another above his knee but below the gash. Very soon, it was no longer warm blood he felt trickling down his skin but something fresh and cooling. She was rinsing the wound.

Ke was perplexed. Why would she do this when she wants me dead? She can't mean well, not where I am concerned, not when she's the spawn of that bastard. How can either of them ever do any good? This must be one of her infernal schemes—she's always plotting.

The Freak tried to persuade himself that she was sowing evil as she applied a curative for blade cuts and bandaged his leg. Before long, the wound had stopped throbbing and much of the pain had eased. His stomach groaned loudly.

"What's that noise coming from your belly? Didn't you say you weren't hungry? Well, there's nothing left now." *Pak, pak.* "Move!" She rapped the soldiers over the head with the cane and, instantly, he was lifted onto the stretcher and carried off.

THEY TRUNDLED on for another thirty or forty *li*. Ke Zhen'e reckoned that it must be dusk, for he could hear crows squawking and croaking. But wait . . . He listened; this was no ordinary murder of crows. He could hear hundreds and thousands of them, flapping their wings, cawing, shrieking. They must be in the vicinity of Iron Spear Temple. Nowhere else near Jiaxing was home to so many of the birds.

The temple had been built to honor General Wang Yanzhang, who lived three hundred years ago, during the Five Dynasties era. Near the main temple complex there was a pagoda, in the roof of which crows had nested for generations. The local people believed these birds were soldiers and generals from the heavens, so their habitat was never disturbed and the colony thrived.

"Hey, you're from this area." Lotus's voice interrupted his thoughts. "Where should we spend the night? It's getting dark."

Ke weighed up their options. The army might still be looking for them and he could not trust the local people not to give them away.

"There's an old temple up ahead," he said.

"Oi, have you never seen a crow before? Move!"

The soldier yowled, but Ke did not hear the swish of the cane. She must have jabbed him with her finger or kicked him with her dainty foot.

They walked on for a little while before stopping. He heard doors being kicked down. A cloud of dust mixed with the stench of bird droppings drifted overhead. The temple must have been abandoned for years. He was waiting for her to give orders to move on and find a less filthy place to stay, but instead she barked at the men to sweep the floor and boil water. While they busied themselves with their tasks, she also bustled around, humming a song about lovebirds taking flight and growing gray before their time.

Soon, Ke Zhen'e was settled on the floor of the temple's main hall, with a prayer mat to use as a pillow. When the soldiers returned with hot water, she first tended to his wound and changed the dressing—to the Freak's great surprise—before turning her attention to herself, washing off the grime from the road.

"Are you looking at me? Do you want me to pluck out your eyes?"

Dok, dok, dok, dok . . . One of the men was knocking his forehead very loudly on the floor to show his remorse.

"Why do you watch me wash my feet?"

"This lowly man deserves to die," he mumbled through his kowtows, answering honestly. "My lady's feet are as white and beautiful as snow . . . and the pink toenails . . . like Guanyin the Observer of Sound . . ."

Ke Zhen'e was flabbergasted. What a stupid man! Who in his right mind would admit impure thoughts about such a sadistic captor? He wondered what gruesome punishment she would devise for him. Flay him alive? Cut his tendons and leave him to die?

No. She tittered!

"A cretin like you has seen Guanyin's feet?"

The soldier flipped in a somersault and—*pang!*—crashed to the floor. That was it. She did not take the matter any further. The two men scampered over to the rear part of the temple and were not heard from again.

Lotus paced the room, muttering to herself. "The name of the Iron Spear General intimidated and inspired during his lifetime, and yet, he was still caught and beheaded in the end. Being a hero can't save your life. Being a great man can't stop people mutilating your body. Hmm, this spear looks like it could be cast from iron."

"Of course, it is!" Ke Zhen'e could not stop himself answering her. He had spent many a happy hour with Zhu Cong, Ryder Han, Woodcutter Nan and Zhang Asheng in this temple, decades ago. Back then, he still had his sight. They were all children, but they were strong, and one of their favorite pastimes was to play fight with the spear forged in honor of the deified General.

Lotus pulled the weapon from the rack. "This should work. Feels at least thirty *jin*," she said aloud to herself, before turning to Ke Zhen'e. "I hurled your staff into South Lake and there isn't time to get a new one made for you. Take this spear. You'll need a weapon to protect yourself when we part ways on the morrow." She went into the courtyard. He sat up and listened. Loud banging, stone on metal. When she came back, she pressed the iron shaft into his hand—she had knocked the spearhead off.

Ke Zhen'e had never been alone. His elder brother Ke Bixie had been there with him all his life, until his untimely death at the hands of Twice Foul Dark Wind. He had also had his six sworn siblings— they had always been by his side . . . Now he knew they were to part ways, Ke realized he would miss Lotus's company—even though they had spent a mere day together. This feeling of loss baffled him. He took the spear. It was a little heavier than his staff—not that he had a choice right now. Her handing him a weapon, he had to admit, al- beit grudgingly, showed that she did not harbor any ill will toward him. Why would anyone arm an enemy?

"This shark gall and notoginseng powder will help the healing of your wound." She reached out, offering him a small envelope.

"Papa made this. It's up to you what you want to do with it. I know you hate the two of us."

Ke Zhen'e took the packet and put it in the inside pocket of his shirt. He wanted to say something, but he could not form the words. He secretly hoped that she would keep talking.

"Go to sleep."

Ke lay back obediently, setting the iron spear down next to him. A thousand thoughts ran through his mind, chasing sleep away. He listened to the crows perched atop the pagoda. They had quieted down with the deepening night, and yet Lotus did not fall asleep. It sounded like she was just sitting still, doing nothing.

After some time, she began to mumble to herself.

> "*For the fourth time the loom is ready,*
> *To weave a pair of lovebirds so they can take flight.*
> *Pity the hair that grows gray before its time!*
> *The ripples of spring among green grass,*
> *The chill of dawn lurking in the deep,*
> *In each other scarlet feather bathe.*"

She chanted the verse over and over again, savoring the words. Ke was not educated in literary matters and could not understand the poem's meaning, but he was moved by the melancholic note in her voice and was shaken by the depth of her despondency.

At length, she got to her feet and arranged the prayer mats into a makeshift bed. She lay down on her side and soon her breathing slowed. She was deep in slumber.

Ke put his hand on the spear shaft; and childhood memories came flooding back. Zhu Cong clutching a tattered old book, reading out loud and nodding in appreciation. Ryder Han and Gilden Quan climbing onto General Wang's statue, tugging the deity's beard for fun. Teaming up with Woodcutter Nan to play tug-of-war with Zhang Asheng, using this very same iron spear. Jade Han, a small child of four or five, clapping and cheering, the red ribbons on her two pigtails bobbing up and down . . .

Blackness. Once more, he could see nothing. His sworn siblings, his own brother, all of them taken from him, from this world, by Apothecary Huang and his disciples. The fire of hatred was rekindled in his heart. There was nothing he could do to quench it.

With the iron shaft's support, he limped softly over to stand before Lotus. She was fast asleep, her breathing light and even.

One strike. She won't know what killed her, he said to himself. I will never beat Apothecary Huang one-on-one. This is an opportunity granted by the heavens. This is my one chance to get revenge, so he can taste the pain of losing his own blood! And yet, she saved me. How can I repay the gift of life with death? Yes, that's what I'll do. I'll kill myself afterward, to thank her for today.

His mind made up, he raised the shaft.

I, Ke Zhen'e, have followed the path of righteousness all my life, he silently intoned to the gods above. I have not done a single deed that would be considered shameful to the heavens or the earth in all the decades that I have been alive. Tonight, I shall strike this maiden while she dreams. It is a reproachable act, but, when the deed is done, I shall atone for my trespass with my own death.

5

A GRUFF CACKLE RANG IN THE NIGHT, JOLTING LOTUS FROM her sleep. She jumped up to see Ke Zhen'e standing over her and at once understood what he must be contemplating.

"Viper Ouyang," she whispered, recognizing the spine-chilling laugh.

Hearing her scrabbling to her feet, Ke knew he could not follow through and he lowered his weapon, focusing on the noise coming from outside the temple instead. He heard voices, but they were too far away for him to make out what they were saying. Soon, he was able to pick out footsteps . . . a large group, at least thirty or forty men, some on horseback, heading his way.

"They must have seen the pagoda and decided to take shelter here. We should take cover." He held out his hand, waiting for Lotus to kick the prayer mats into disarray. The last thing they wanted was for the new arrivals to realize someone had been sleeping there. Ke could still see in his mind's eye every nook and cranny of this place, and he was confident he could find somewhere to hide. What about the doorway at the back of the main hall that led to another part of the temple? He tried the doors. They were barred.

"Damn those soldiers," he rasped. They must have bolted them when they scrambled away earlier.

They were trapped in the hall.

The main gate creaked as it was pushed open. Too late to break down the doors now. The Venom would hear them . . .

"Behind the statue," he whispered.

They were only just in time. The second they crouched down beneath the colossal effigy of General Wang, a dozen men walked into the hall. A scraping sound. The smell of sulfur. A torch had been lit.

"Your Highness, even though we could not claim a victory at the Tower of Mist and Rain, we have crushed our enemy's morale." Viper Ouyang's metallic voice.

"Thanks to the Master's foresight." This was Wanyan Honglie, without a doubt.

The same grating laugh. "It was all thanks to your son the young Prince's clever plan to deploy Jiaxing's army. We would have annihilated the rogues—if it weren't for the fog."

"With Master Ouyang on our side, we shall, for a surety, crush them another day," Yang Kang said. "But it's a shame I arrived too late and missed the chance to witness Master Ouyang in action."

Ke Zhen'e was simmering inside: Yang Kang was still consorting with his father's killer and his country's enemy!

Graybeard Liang, Tiger Peng, Hector Sha and the others took turns to heap praise upon Viper Ouyang, following the young Prince's example, making exaggerated claims for his martial flair and the ignominy to which he had consigned the Quanzhen Taoists.

And yet there was not one mention of Qiu Qianren. Ke Zhen'e surmised that he must be elsewhere. Still, there were enough *wulin* masters present to make him wary of breathing too freely, lest it expose their hiding place. He was fully aware of the contradiction inherent in the fact that, just moments ago, he was going to kill Lotus and then himself. He thought he had made peace with death, but now he could not stop praying that they would not be discovered and that no harm would come to either of them.

He wanted to live, and wanted her to live too.

A servant came up timidly to the Princes and Viper Ouyang, informing them that their beds were ready.

Once the man had been dismissed, Yang Kang sighed. "Master Ouyang, though my acquaintance with your nephew was short, we shared something of a rapport and I hoped we would become great friends, for he was not only cultivated in the martial arts, he was also learned in all things scholarly. Whenever my mind turns to his memory, such pain and anger grips my heart. I have sworn to slay each and every one of those loathsome Taoists of the Quanzhen Sect with my own hands, to bring peace to the spirit of Brother Ouyang in the heavens, but I am also aware of the limitations of my own power. I might have the heart, but I do not have the skill."

Yang Kang was hoping that Viper Ouyang would dispatch his *shifu* Qiu Chuji so nobody would question him again over his loyalty to his adopted father. So, at every given opportunity, he had been reinforcing the idea that the murder of Gallant Ouyang in Ox Village was committed by the Quanzhen Sect.

There was a long silence before Viper Ouyang responded, sounding more subdued than usual. "I have always suspected that odious boy Guo Jing of having a hand in my nephew's death. I did not realize it was the evil doing of the Quanzhen Taoists, until you told me about Qiu Chuji earlier. Do not doubt that I will have my revenge.

But, for now, I have a proposal for you, young Prince. Since White Camel Mount has lost its heir, I will take you on as a disciple."

"*Shifu*, please accept your student's kowtows!"

Yang Kang's joyous tone and the audible knocks of his forehead on the floor as he bowed to Viper Ouyang filled Ke Zhen'e with repugnance. Although the young man was descended from a line of patriots and honorable men, he had not only denied his birth father and chosen to side with his country's invaders, he was now happy to call a wicked, unscrupulous man his mentor.

He's on the path of no return, Ke thought, feeling a great contempt for the young man's lack of judgment.

"We have no suitable gifts with which to honor the teacher today, but I shall make sure our respect is shown handsomely in due course," Wanyan Honglie said.

"White Camel Mount has a small store of treasure already," the Venom replied. "I have come to realize how clever this child is and I simply wish to have someone to inherit my martial knowledge."

"I beg your pardon, Master. I spoke out of turn." Wanyan Honglie's painfully polite apology came amid a chorus of congratulations from the rest of the retinue.

"I'm hungry! I want food!"

Wait! Was that the girl from Peach Blossom Island? Ke Zhen'e could not believe his ears. How did she end up here, and in such company?

"It's coming, it's coming," Yang Kang soothed, placating her with good humor. "Quickly, bring something for the lady."

A little while later, Ke was treated to the sound of the Qu girl smacking her lips, devouring whatever she had been given with great relish.

"Nice brother, you said you'll take me home," she slurred, her mouth full. "I'm a good girl and I listen to you. Why am I not home yet?"

"We'll be there tomorrow. Just make sure your tummy is full so you sleep well." Yang Kang was exceedingly patient with her.

She wolfed another helping of food. "What's that swishing noise? It's coming from the big building."

"Birds? Mice?"

"Scary!"

"Nothing to be scared of."

"They're ghosts. I know. I'm scared."

Chuckling, Yang Kang replied, "Look how many of us there are. Ghosts and monsters are too scared to come out."

"I'm scared of the tiny fat ghost."

"Now you're being silly!" His mollifying tone was cracking, and irritation was beginning to show through. "There's no tiny fat any-thing, here."

"*Huh!* I know the tiny fat man died in Grandma's tomb. Grand-ma's ghost will chase him out. She won't let him live with her, so he'll come and haunt you."

"Another word from you and I'll tell your grandpa and he'll drag you back to Peach Blossom Island!"

The threat silenced the girl, but now Ke heard a scuttle of scur-rying feet.

"*Ow*, you stepped on me!" Hector Sha barked. "Stop running around. Sit down!"

Questions and doubts gnawed at Ke Zhen'e. The tiny fat man must be Third Brother, he said to himself. Ryder Han was killed by Apothecary Huang on Peach Blossom Island. Why would his ghost haunt Yang Kang? He knew that the girl did not have all her wits about her, but she must know something to have come to that con-clusion. How he wished he could go out and question her, but what could he achieve on his own with so many martial masters about?

Now the last thing Apothecary Huang said to him came to his mind: "How could a man of my status behave like one of your ilk?"

He had brushed it off, at the time—he thought the Heretic was simply being his usual condescending self—but it chimed with a different tone now. If he deigned killing me to be beneath him, then why would he lower himself to butcher my little brothers and sister? But, if it wasn't Apothecary Huang, then why did Fourth Brother say he saw him murder Second Brother and Seventh Sister?

As uncertainties continued to chip away at his prior conviction, he realized Lotus had taken his left hand and was tracing a character on his palm, stroke by stroke.

P-L-E-A-S-E

She paused and waited for his reaction before continuing.

DO THIS FOR ME

He took her hand and wrote: *YES.*
She was scrawling faster now.

TELL PA WHO KILLS ME

Dumbfounded by her request, Ke reached out for her hand to seek clarification, but all he caught was a breeze on his fingertips. She had leaped out from their hiding place.

"Good evening, Uncle Ouyang."

Her unheralded appearance was greeted by cries of "Who goes there?" and "Assassin!" accompanied by the swish and clinks of weapons being unsheathed and the shuffle of footsteps. Ke could tell she was surrounded.

"Papa sent me to wait for Uncle Ouyang here. Why are you all so on edge?" She sounded unfazed. There was even a hint of amusement in her tone.

"How did your father know we'd be here?" Viper sounded tense.

"Papa is an expert in medicine, divination, astrology, physiognomy and many other things. All he needs to do is to consult the heavens using the King Wen's Afore Heavens method."

The Venom chuckled. He did not believe a word of it, but he also knew that the young woman would not tell him the truth, however much he threatened her.

Hector Sha, who had taken several men to check the temple grounds, now returned, having found nothing irregular. They clustered protectively around Wanyan Honglie.

Lotus, meanwhile, had made herself comfortable on one of the prayer mats. "Uncle Ouyang, you've put Papa in a very awkward position," she said, with a wide grin.

A thin smile hovered on Viper's lips. He knew better than to give her a verbal response—he could not outwit her, and anything he said would provide her with more material to tease and taunt him with. He could not allow that to happen in front of this audience.

"Uncle Ouyang, Papa is trapped by the Quanzhen mob on the Little Island of Fleabane and Goosefoot in Xincheng Town. He can't get away without your help."

"Indeed?"

"Yes! A real man owns up to his deeds. It was you who killed the Quanzhen monk Tan Chuduan, but those stinking Taoists won't stop pestering my father about his death. And when you add in the meddling Hoary Urchin and Papa's refusal to explain himself . . . It's one big mess!"

"Your father's kung fu is unparalleled. Surely those Quanzhen fledglings could not possibly inconvenience him." The Heretic's tribulations were welcome news to the Venom.

"True, but the cow muzzles have the Urchin on their side, so Papa's really struggling. And he also bade me tell you this. He has beening poring over this one text for seven days and seven nights, and he's at last unraveled its meaning."

"What are you talking about?"

"*Mahaparas gatekras suryasanyanagha sirahstha hahoramanpayas . . .*"

No one present could understand a single word, including Viper

Ouyang, but he knew she had just quoted the first line of the incomprehensible passage at the very end of the second volume of the Nine Yin Manual. He had read those pages over and over again to the point where he almost had them memorized, and yet he could not unlock their meaning at all. Could Apothecary Huang really have worked it out? The thought excited him, but he made sure he did not betray a smidgeon of agitation or curiosity in his reply.

"Is this what little wenches like to joke about, these days? Who can understand such a random collection of characters?"

"Papa has translated it, line by line. It makes perfect sense. I saw it with my own eyes. Why would I jest with you?"

"Well, he deserves my congratulations, then." The Venom tried to sound nonchalant. He would never admit it out loud, but, deep down, he had always admired Apothecary Huang for the breadth of his accomplishments and expertise beyond matters martial. If anyone were to make sense of that passage, it would be him.

Lotus could tell that she would have to work harder to catch him in her snare. "I can still remember a few lines. Would you like to hear them?"

Without waiting for an answer, she began:

"*Sometimes the body aflutter stirs; sometimes the body heavy as if weighed down; sometimes the body light as if to take flight; sometimes as if restrained and bound; sometimes in curious cold or harsh heat; sometimes in merriment gambols; sometimes as if touched by matter malevolent, in alarm, the hairs stand on end; sometimes in great joy inebriated. All such many states with the method below can be guided into the mystic marvel.*"

Lotus had cited a few lines from the passages Reverend Sole Light had deciphered. These states and sensations, strange and indescribably wonderful, were familiar to anyone who had reached the higher levels of internal *neigong* training. These were moments when a practitioner should proceed with the greatest caution to ensure that heart and spirit were calm and in control, or else one could easily misfire into the demonic way. If there were methods to rein in and tame the heart-fiends she had just cited into the mystic marvel, then they would represent the most precious, treasured wisdom under the heavens.

A master of internal cultivation himself, Viper Ouyang recognized that the author must have achieved and experienced the supreme state to be able to pen such vivid descriptions. There was no doubt about its authenticity—the little girl could not have made it up, and indeed she had not.

"What comes next?" He was eager to hear more.

"Oh, there's a huge chunk I can't remember . . . but this line sticks in my head:

Each and every pore on the body clear and wide, and with the eye in the heart sees the thirty-six matters inside the body, as if opening up the garner and catching sight of the grains and pulses within, to the heart's wondrous joy, quiet calm and carefree stillness."

Viper regarded Lotus with distrust, trying to guess at her intentions. Why does she tell me about this now? he asked himself. She clearly knows the whole passage from top to bottom, but she chooses to play dumb, giving me the symptoms and the results, and skipping the portion in the middle that explains the process of cultivation.

"Papa also instructed me to ask Uncle Ouyang this: would you prefer the five-thousand-word version or the three-thousand-word one?"

"Do explain."

"If you help Papa, and together you destroy the Quanzhen Sect, then he will share with you the full translation of this mystical method from the Nine Yin Manual."

"And if I don't?"

"Papa entreats you to avenge him. Once you have killed Zhou

Botong and the Six Immortals of the Quanzhen Sect, I am to recite the three-thousand-word version for you."

"Your father and I have never been close friends. What makes him think so highly of me?"

"Papa says, firstly, he knows your nephew's murderer was a disciple of the Quanzhen Sect, and he believes that you will be keen to take vengeance."

It is well known that I'm Qiu Chuji's disciple . . . Yang Kang shuddered at the sly, insinuating expression on her face.

"Are you cold?" The Qu girl, sitting next to Yang Kang, noticed his reaction. He mumbled a few words to humor her. He could not let her tongue run wild and draw attention to him.

"Secondly, the fight with the Quanzhen monks started very soon after Papa had finally made sense of the text," Lotus continued, pretending that she had not noticed the exchange between Yang Kang and the girl. "He hasn't even had a chance to explain the details to me and he feels it would be such a shame if this amazing martial formula were to die with him.

"Now, of all the great masters in the world, he considers you a kindred spirit, not just his equal in martial learning, but alike in temperment also. He still remembers the honor you bestowed upon us, coming to Peach Blossom Island personally to ask for my hand for your nephew. It was a great misfortune that he was set upon by a disciple of the Quanzhen Sect, but my papa hopes that you will remember the bond you shared with your nephew and teach me this mystical method, once you have mastered it."

Viper's heart softened at the mention of Gallant Ouyang. She's not lying, he decided. Without the guidance of a master, a little girl like her can't possibly make sense of the method, even if she can quote it back to front. Still, he couldn't let her off the hook just yet . . .

"How do I know your version is genuine?"

"You've got the text with you, right? Once I explain the cipher, you'll be able to check, and you'll see for yourself."

"We'll rest here for the night. I'll help your father tomorrow."

"There's no time to lose. Tomorrow might be too late."

"Then I'll avenge him—it's all the same to me." Viper smirked. The translation of the Manual's final section was now firmly in his grasp, for it would merely be a matter of time before the girl was compelled to share its key, and, after that, he was confident that he could interpret its content fully. If Apothecary Huang and those Quanzhen Taoists were to hurt each other in the meantime, it would only be to his benefit.

"Will we leave first thing in the morning?"

"Of course. You should get some rest too."

6

KE ZHEN'E HAD BEEN PAYING CLOSE ATTENTION TO EVERY word exchanged and yet he could not make sense of how this talk of the Nine Yin Manual related to the grave message Lotus had written in his hand.

TELL PA WHO KILLS ME

What did she mean? The conversation with Viper Ouyang had reached its natural conclusion and what she had foretold had not come to pass. He could hear her dragging a prayer mat to another spot.

"Hey, Grandpa took you to Peach Blossom Island. How come you're here now?" he heard Lotus ask softly.

"I don't like being around Grandpa. I want to go home."

She's moved over to speak to the girl from Peach Blossom Island, Ke said to himself, still unable to fathom why Lotus thought she would be killed.

"So, Brother Yang sailed to the island and took you away on his boat. Is that how you got here? Am I right?"

Ke's ears pricked up. When did Yang Kang visit Peach Blossom Island?

"Yes, he's very nice."

"Where's Grandpa?"

"Don't tell him I ran away. He'll beat me."

"I won't tell—if you're a good girl and answer my questions nicely."

"You mustn't tell Grandpa. He'll drag me back. He'll force me to read."

"I won't, I swear. Grandpa teaches you to read?"

"Yes, he makes me read in the study. He makes me learn Papa's family name. He said it's qu-chirp-chirp, like a cricket, and that's my name too, qu-chirp-chirp. He drew it on the paper and said I must memorize it. He also said Papa's called . . . some kind of wind. I can never remember what it is. Grandpa got so cross. He shouted at me for being silly. But I *am* called Silly."

"Grandpa is very bad for shouting at you."

The Qu girl agreed vehemently.

"What happened next?"

"I said, 'I want to go home.' Grandpa shouted some more. Then, a funny man came in. He couldn't speak. He just waved his hands and made this *yeeee-yaaa* noise. Grandpa said, 'I'm not receiving visitors. Tell them to leave.' He came back with a piece of paper, not long after. Grandpa looked at it, then told me to follow the funny man and welcome our guests." She laughed at the memory. "The tiny fat man was so ugly. I glared at him and he did the same to me."

Her words brought Ke Zhen'e back to that fateful trip. They had heard that the Quanzhen Taoists were on their way to Peach Blossom Island to seek revenge, and took it upon themselves to warn Apothecary Huang. Their plan was to persuade the Heretic to avoid direct confrontation and let them mediate on his behalf. They were pinning their hopes on the friendship between the Six Freaks of the South and the Seven Immortals of the Quanzhen Sect, which went back almost two decades. He recalled that, when they presented themselves on the island, Apothecary Huang refused to grant them an interview, but, once he had read Zhu Cong's letter, explaining the reason for their visit, he sent the girl to receive them. Her trivial little exchange with Third Brother was etched on his mind.

And now he's gone forever . . . His heart contracted at the thought.

"Did Grandpa meet with them?"

"Grandpa told me to eat with them, then he went off somewhere. I didn't like looking at the tiny fat man, so I went to play on the beach. Grandpa was sitting behind a rock and looking at the sea, so I looked at the sea too. A boat! Coming to us. Grandpa called the people in the boat cow muzzles." She bent over in laughter. "Cow muzzles!"

How come she saw their boat? Fresh questions whirled in Ke Zhen'e's mind. We never saw the Quanzhen monks on the island.

"What did Grandpa do?"

"Grandpa waved at me and told me to come over to him. I was so scared. He caught me playing. He caught me not doing what he told me to. I stayed where I was. I didn't want to be caned. But he swore he wouldn't hit me, and said I should come over so he could talk to me. So I did. He told me he was going on a boat to go fishing in the sea. He had an important task for me. I was to tell the cow muzzles: Grandpa is not at home. He is out at sea. They should turn back. They won't know the way around the island. So, when the cow muzzles arrived, I went up to them: 'Grandpa is not home. Grandpa doesn't like looking at cow muzzles. *Ha ha!* Cow muzzles. Is that a cow muzzle on your face? I think it looks more like a pig's snout!' They glared at me. So I glared back at their pig snouts. Then they went back to the boat."

"And then what happened?"

"Grandpa went behind the big rock and got on his boat. I know Grandpa didn't want to see them, because the cow muzzles were ugly!"

"Yes! You're right! When did Grandpa come back?"

"Huh? He didn't."

Ke Zhen'e felt his body spasm at that answer.

"Are you sure?" There was a quiver in Lotus's voice too. "What happened next?"

"Grandpa was just about to set sail when two big birds flew in from the sky. Your white birds. Grandpa whistled at them and they came to him. They had something tied to their feet. I liked the look of it, so I shouted, 'Grandpa! Give me! Give me!'" The Qu girl was yelling as loudly as she had on the island.

"Shush! We're trying to sleep!" Yang Kang hissed.

"I want to know what happened next," Lotus whispered.

"I will speak softly," the girl replied under breath. "Grandpa ignored me. He tore off a piece of his robe and tied it to one of the big birds' feet. Then he let them fly away."

"Who fired arrows at the birds?" Lotus whispered back.

Now she understood why her father sent her that cryptic piece of cloth instead of the golden salamanders.

"Arrows? No one." The girl's expression was more blank than usual and she seemed to be far, far away from the present.

"Alright . . . and then?"

"Grandpa took the robe off and told me to get him a new one. By the time I came back, Grandpa was gone. The cow muzzles' boat was gone too. The only thing left was the torn robe on the ground.

This time, Lotus did not urge the Qu girl to continue. Ke speculated that her mind—like his—was racing through these revelations.

"Where did they go?"

"I could see them in the sea. I shouted for Grandpa, but he didn't answer me. So I climbed up a tree to get a better look. Grandpa's little boat was on this side. The cow muzzles' big boat was on that side." She demonstrated with her hands. "They moved slowly, slowly, slowly, and then I couldn't see them anymore. I didn't want to look at the tiny fat man, so I stayed on the beach, picking pebbles and playing in the sand until evening, when I took Grandpa, here, and nice brother back to the house."

"This Grandpa is not the one who makes you read?"

The Qu girl giggled. "No, this Grandpa doesn't make me read. He gives me cake."

"UNCLE OUYANG, have you got more cake? Give her another piece," Lotus said.

Viper cackled. "Gladly."

Ke Zhen'e was certain that his heart was about to leap out of his mouth. Viper Ouyang was also on the island that day? The Qu girl's screech cut through his shock, and his mind was forced back to the present. He heard a scuffle, more squealing from the Qu girl, and then Lotus asking, in a voice of calm authority, "Are you trying to silence her?"

The Venom's raspy laugh rang out again. "What's the point? She's a silly girl, and I do realize that I can't very well hide what happened from your father, even if I can fool everyone else. If you want to question her, go ahead, get to the bottom of it."

But the girl was groaning and whimpering, making a string of unintelligible sounds. She must have been struck at a point that impeded her speech.

"I don't need to; I've worked it out already. I just wanted it to hear it from her mouth."

"You are indeed your father's daughter," Viper said with a sneer. "Do enlighten me . . ."

"To begin with, I also thought Papa had killed five of the Freaks, but, once I had a moment to think about it, I knew it couldn't possibly be him. Do you think he'd leave three dead *men* behind in my mother's tomb? Do you think he'd leave the tomb entrance ajar?"

"*Ahhhh.*" Viper slapped his thigh. "We've been careless indeed, haven't we, Kang?"

Ke Zhen'e thought his heart was about to explode. He had finally unraveled the full meaning behind the words she had written in his hand.

TELL PA WHO KILLS ME

She had known it was Viper Ouyang and Yang Kang who murdered his siblings all along. She went out to confront them—laying down her life to reveal the truth, to prove that her father was innocent. That was why she wrote that message.

Oh, miss, you could have just told me who the murderers were! There was no need to throw your life away like this! But would I have listened to her? No! I've always been rash, always jumping to conclusions. Now I know the Flying Bat isn't just blind in the eyes but in the heart too . . . I've wronged Apothecary Huang and I've wronged his daughter. I'd have never believed her if she'd told me the truth to my face . . . Ke Zhen'e, oh, Ke Zhen'e, you're no Suppressor of Evil, you're a Suppressor of Good that deserves to be hacked into a thousand pieces! You're a blind fool and you've condemned a good woman to death!

Wallowing in self-loathing, Ke raised his hand, about to slap some sense into himself, only remembering at the last moment that he was in hiding. Viper Ouyang's grating voice assailed his eardrums once more.

"What made you think of me?" he asked Lotus.

"Not many people in this world have the skill to dispatch a horse with just one palm strike, or to snap a steel pole as thick as a child's arm with their bare hands. But, as I said, I didn't think of you at first. It was when we found Woodcutter Nan that I grew suspicious. Guo Jing asked the poor man who had hurt him, but he couldn't speak. He tried scoring the name of his murderer into the ground, but he expired after scratching three strokes."

"Woodcutter Nan was a tough man to have lasted so long." Viper laughed in cruel appreciation. "He was hiding from us. When we left the tomb, we found we had one body fewer than anticipated. We couldn't leave anyone behind, could we? We looked for him for several days. Luckily, Kang, here, has a map of Peach Blossom Island, with every strange twisting path and every trap and snare

323

clearly marked. We searched the island section by section and eventually we found him."

It was Lotus's turn to be baffled. How did the map fall into Yang Kang's hands? Papa gave it to Gallant Ouyang for one month as a consolation prize when his suit for my hand came to nothing . . . Yang Kang must have seized it after he stabbed Gallant in Ox Village. That's how they were able to open Mama's tomb. I see how it all happened, now.

"When I saw how Woodcutter Nan died," she said aloud, "I thought he must have been poisoned. The toxin had such strange effects . . . It was probably the handiwork of Qiu Qianren. That old man's known for his poisonous palms." Lotus said this to rile Viper Ouyang, and to gull him into confessing his crimes. She knew exactly what Qiu's kung fu could do, having suffered at his hands herself.

"Qiu Qianren's martial learning is superb, but the power of his palms comes not from poison. In fact, there's no deadly substance in his touch, though he makes use of toxins in his training. It's a way to cultivate strength—pushing venom out through the palms. Tell me, when Woodcutter Nan died, was he howling, trying to speak, but no words would come? And, rather than groaning in misery, he was smiling, was he not?" The vain man had fallen for her ruse, for Viper Ouyang would never concede that someone else possessed knowledge superior to his, nor let another person take credit for his handiwork.

"Yes, that's right! What poison could have done that?"

"He was twisting and rolling on the ground, and he struck with great strength—greater than he had ever known. Am I right?"

"Indeed! I thought such an unusual poison must surely be the work of Qiu Qianren. Who else under the heavens could have achieved such a thing?"

Lotus was openly baiting Viper Ouyang now, and the martial Master knew it.

"Why do you think I am called the Venom of the West?" he roared, thumping the butt of his Serpent Staff against the floor. "He was bitten on the tongue by one of the snakes in this very staff! That's why you couldn't find a mark on his body. That's why he could not speak."

Hot blood rushed to Ke Zhen'e head. He swayed and almost collapsed. Lotus thought she could hear a faint sound coming from behind the statue and she coughed loudly to drown it out.

"So, that's what happened!" She made a show of finally figuring out the last piece of a fiendish puzzle. "You slaughtered five of the Freaks, but somehow Ke Zhen'e managed to escape. And, since he can't see, he had no way of knowing who had done the foul deed."

At first, Ke Zhen'e wondered why she was stating the obvious, and then it came to him. She's reminding me to stay put, not to do anything rash. There's no point in us both dying, and for no reason, at that!

"You think that blind bat could slip from my clutches?" Viper crowed. "I let him go. Woodcutter Nan saw me in the act. He hid from us, but for how long? We could never let him live, and, if it took a few days to find him, so be it. As for the sightless old fool? We could afford to show some mercy."

"Ah, I understand. You let Master Ke believe that my father murdered his brethren. You wanted him to spread word throughout the *jianghu*, turning all good men and heroes under the heavens against Papa."

"It wasn't my idea. Kang came up with the plan. Didn't you?"

Yang Kang grunted his assent with reluctance, since it would be a great offense to the bond of *shifu* and disciple to ignore a direct address.

"What a clever strategy. I am full of admiration," Lotus jeered.

"You haven't explained what made you think it was I?" Viper was itching to find out what clues he had left for her to find, since he thought he had been very careful in planning the perfect crime.

"We fought Qiu Qianren in North Jinghu. He could have made straight for Peach Blossom Island, but could he outstrip our Fergana horse? Not very likely, is it? And then there were the three strokes

Woodcutter Nan managed to write on the ground—a horizontal, a short vertical and an enclosing hook. He could have been writing the character *dong*—east—for Eastern Heretic, but then it could also have been the character *xi*—west—for Western Venom, couldn't it? I realized that when I was on Peach Blossom Island, but I had yet to comb through all the details."

"I thought we'd been meticulous, but still, so many traces were left . . . Woodcutter Nan must have sensed something. He tarried and dragged his feet when we entered the tomb. When he saw me set upon Gilden Quan, he ran."

"Master Nan was a man of few words, but he noticed everything." Although Lotus and the Freaks had not got along at first, she had always had genuine respect for those upright heroes, since they were Guo Jing's teachers, and, as such, her seniors too. "I spent a lot of time wondering about the little cross Jade Han wrote on my mother's sarcophagus, trying to work out what the character could be.

"I know the young Prince is still a novice in all things martial, and he doesn't have the skill to have finished off the five Freaks by himself, so I never suspected him." She spoke as if Yang Kang was not there and took no notice of his indignant grunt.

"I was left all alone on Peach Blossom Island and I was in a stupor. I kept dozing and waking, my mind wouldn't stop, but I couldn't think clearly. I dreamed of a great many people. One of them was Sister Mu. I dreamed of her in the Duel for a Maiden. Suddenly, I was wide awake and everything became clear—I knew who the second killer was." For the first time, she acknowledged Yang Kang's presence and looked him in the eye.

Her words and her tone had long since conjured a cold sweat on Yang Kang's back. "Are you saying Mercy Mu spoke to you in a dream?" he said with a sneer, attempting to belittle her.

"Yes, she did," Lotus replied with a straight face. "If it weren't for the dream, I would never have thought of you. Now, tell me, where's your little jade shoe?"

Yang Kang gaped at her before assuming a haughty tone. "How do you know about that? Did Mercy mention it in your dream?"

"For that, I have no need to dream." A triumphant smile. "After you struck Zhu Cong down, you stuffed gems and jewels from the tomb into his robes, so it looked like he'd come to steal my mother's offerings and got himself caught and put to death by my father. I have to admit that it was a very clever plot to frame him. But you forgot one vital detail. Zhu Cong was known as Quick Hands."

"So?" Viper asked.

"Well, you thought you were planting the proof of his greed on him, but you had no idea he'd pilfered the proof of your guilt from you."

"What do you mean?"

"Zhu Cong's kung fu might have seemed insignificant to you." She inclined her head toward Viper Ouyang. "But, with his last breath, he lived up to his name, and picked the young Prince's pocket, clinging tight to his prize. His sleight of hand was so swift that neither of you—to this day—ever realized. If not for this object, I'd never have imagined that a young prince of the Great Jin Empire would deign to grace Peach Blossom Island."

"This is most amusing. So, Zhu Cong spoke to the living from beyond the grave." Viper laughed. "I did indeed underestimate the might of his quick hands. I presume the object he took was this jade shoe?"

"That's right. I know every single offering that was interred with my mother, and I had never before set eyes on the jade shoe clasped so firmly in Zhu Cong's hand as he died. There had to be a reason why it was there. The little shoe has the character *bi* on the sole and the character *zhao* carved on the heel. I couldn't make any sense of it—they don't form any comprehensible sequence. But then, that night, when I dreamed of Sister Mu fighting in the marketplace, that's when I saw the characters on a banner flapping by the stage. *Bi wu zhao qin.* Duel for a Maiden. That was when everything became clear."

"I wouldn't have suspected there was such a romantic story behind this little jade shoe." Viper laughed once more, greatly entertained.

"When Uncle Yang organized the Duel for a Maiden in Zhongdu, our young Prince, here, showed off his skills against Sister Mu, and I was lucky enough to catch the display," Lotus explained. She knew the Venom was not interested in such details, but Ke Zhen'e needed to understand how she worked out who was responsible for the massacre. "The young Prince pulled off Sister Mu's shoe, and that was enough to win the duel. How he treated his prize of the maiden later . . . Well, that's another story entirely."

And, indeed, much had stemmed from the Duel for a Maiden. The martial Masters in the service of Wanyan Honglie were present at this fight—Graybeard Liang, Hector Sha, Tiger Peng . . . They had also witnessed the Consort's death and Yang Kang's attitude toward his birth father and the maiden's godfather, Ironheart Yang. Thinking back on all that had occurred since the duel on that snowy, wintry day, just six months or so ago, even these battle-hardened men felt almost wistful.

"Thanks to the duel, everything fell into place. It made sense that, when the young Prince and Sister Mu promised themselves to each other, their love token would be a pair of jade shoes. I expect they each kept one. This one has the characters *bi* and *zhao*, and I imagine Sister Mu's has the characters *wu* for martial and *qin* for familial. Am I right, Your Highness?"

Lotus waited for a reply, but Yang Kang was not prepared to grant her the satisfaction.

"Now, it really can't be more obvious and straightforward. Ryder Han was taken by the Nine Yin Skeleton Claw. Twice Foul Dark Wind were the only two warriors in this world who knew that kung fu, and they are both gone. It's assumed that their teacher would've been skilled in the technique, but few know that Papa has never practiced a single technique described in the Nine Yin Manual—or that Iron Corpse Cyclone Mei actually took a disciple.

"Jade Han saw with her own eyes the young Prince kill her cousin Ryder Han with the Nine Yin Skeleton Claw. After she put the sword to her throat, she dabbed her fingers in her own blood to write the name of the killer. Alas, life left her before she could set it down. All she bequeathed us was a small cross. A horizontal line intersects with a vertical one. The muddle-headed Guo Jing insisted it was the first two strokes of Huang, but she was actually trying to write down the character of Yang, which begins with the same stroke order . . ."

Lotus tailed off, subdued by the thought of the irreparable breach between herself and Guo Jing, but Viper Ouyang was in exceedingly good humor, roaring with mirthless laughter.

"I was going to wipe away this little cross, but Kang knew better. 'This could be the first two strokes of the character Huang,' he said. So I let it be. No wonder the Guo boy fought your father with so little thought for his own well-being."

"I cannot deny the ingenuity of your plan, and poor Guo Jing did not have the capacity to discern the truth in his state of extreme grief. You know, I had assumed that you'd coerced the servants into showing you around the island. I'd never have guessed that she was your guide, but seeing her here, I imagine that Your Highness must have promised to bring her back to Ox Village. That's why she likes you and calls you her 'nice brother', obeying your every command.

"Actually, even without her, you'd be able to navigate the island, since you've got the map. I dare say you were hiding near the tomb, and you told her to tell the Freaks that my father would meet them there. With Uncle Ouyang on your side, what chance did they have? It's a perfect plan—like catching turtles in a tank."

Ke Zhen'e was amazed. Her description was so close to what he had experienced, it was as if she had been there with him. How well he remembered being ambushed in the antechamber, and how he had hobbled up the passage from the subterranean room with Woodcutter Nan . . .

"Uncle Ouyang must have picked up Papa's discarded robe when he disembarked. In the dim light of the tomb, if he donned the garment, he might pass for him, especially when several of the Freaks were already seriously wounded. Woodcutter Nan, being the vigilant one, must have entered the tomb passage last, and when he heard

Gilden Quan's steelyard being snapped, he pulled Ke Zhen'e along with him. At the time, he believed it was my papa who had dealt the death blow. But, in fact, Gilden Quan and Zhu Cong were killed by Uncle Ouyang, and the young Prince killed Ryder Han, while Jade Han slit her own throat. You always intended to let Ke Zhen'e live, but not Woodcutter Nan. His escape wasn't part of your plan. He managed to find a secluded spot on the island and cheated death for a few days, but eventually you caught up with him and killed him with your snake.

"After your killing spree in the tomb, you went to Papa's study and turned the place upside down, so it looked like Papa and the Freaks had had a nasty fight. But, Uncle Ouyang, if Papa wanted to do away with them, do you think they could put up enough of a fight to leave the room like that? Don't you think you were trying too hard to cover up your tracks and ended up flaunting your crime instead? I sensed something was wrong the moment I stepped into Papa's study."

"I cannot fault your version of the events," Viper said, impressed by her account. "Though, I must say, it was the Freaks who sealed their own wretched fate. Kang and I didn't know they would be there when we set off for Peach Blossom Island."

"Well, to be honest, I suspected that too."

"I can't hide anything from you, you clever little thing."

"Let me guess—and please don't be offended if I get it wrong. When you first came ashore, you were hoping that the battle between the Quanzhen Immortals and Papa would end in injuries or worse for both parties, so you could rid yourself of both the Quanzhen Sect and Peach Blossom Island in one fell swoop, just like how Bian Zhuangzi slayed the war-wearied tigers.

"But, as it turned out, you arrived too late. The Taoists and Papa had left the island. Then, the young Prince found out from the Qu girl that the Freaks were there, and that was when you hatched your plan, and showed off your cunning, framing my father for the death of five of the Freaks. Once the deed was done, you slaughtered every single servant on the island and disposed of their bodies, so no one could dispute your story. Then you spent a few days hunting down Woodcutter Nan.

"Your hope was that, when word of the atrocity spread, Count Seven Hong and King Duan would have to stand against Papa. The young Prince was worried that, when Papa returned, he would see through your ploy and destroy the incriminating evidence, so, as insurance, you let Ke Zhen'e get off the island alive. He's lost the use of his eyes, but not the use of his tongue, and you wagered that his blindness would prevent him from seeing the truth and that he would make the necessary accusations for you."

Ke Zhen'e had never felt more ashamed or angry at himself. He really had been as blind as a bat!

"I truly am envious of the Old Heretic that he should sire such a daughter," the Venom said admiringly. "You have worked out every twist and turn of the whole sorry business as if you were there. Young lass, I don't enjoy acknowledging this, but you are incredibly bright."

CHAPTER EIGHT

THE ARMY MARCHES WEST

I

"UNCLE OUYANG, YOU'RE TOO KIND." THERE WAS A TINGE of sadness to her tone, and none of the satisfaction Viper had been anticipating. "Guo Jing has fallen for your ploy and vowed to kill my father, even if it costs him his life, severing all ties . . ." She trailed off, struggling to maintain her composure. "When you save Papa tomorrow . . . Were your nephew still with us . . . our troth-plight . . ." A heavy sigh, conveying all that she was unable to put into words.

Why does she bring up my boy and that business again? Viper Ouyang's natural suspicion sprang into life.

Lotus turned to the Qu girl. "Hey, your nice brother treats you very well, doesn't he?"

"Yes! He's taking me home. I didn't like the island. I want to go home!"

"Why do you want to go home? It's haunted. Someone died there."

The girl gasped and screamed. "Ghost! A ghost in my home! I don't want to go back!"

"Who killed that man?"

"I saw nice brother—"

Clink, clink, something clattered to the floor.

"Why did you try to hurt her, Your Highness? Why won't you let her speak?"

"The idiot girl talks nonsense!" Yang Kang squawked.

"You know this grandpa wants to hear your story," Lotus cajoled.

"No, I'm not talking. Nice brother doesn't want me to."

"There's a good girl," Yang Kang said in a honeyed tone. "Lie down now and sleep. If you open your mouth and say even one word, I'll tell the ghost to come and eat you alive!"

Cowering, the Qu girl muttered her assent and wriggled back into her bedding, pulling the blanket over her head.

"Hey, if you won't talk to me, I'll get Grandpa to drag you back," Lotus said darkly.

"No! No!" the girl yelled through the coverlet.

"Then tell me who the nice brother killed in your home."

The specificity of her demand left everyone open-mouthed.

Yang Kang pooled his strength in his right hand, ready to plunge his fingers through the Qu girl's skull with the Nine Yin Skeleton Claw if she breathed a word of what he had done in Ox Village. He could not allow Viper Ouyang to learn the truth.

I should've got rid of her on Peach Blossom Island. He rued his soft-heartedness. I thought there were just the four of us at the inn—me, Mercy and the young couple. This half-wit must have been hiding somewhere.

Everyone waited for the Qu girl's answer with bated breath. Ke Zhen'e scarcely dared to inhale. Time passed, and soft breathing, then snores, began to fill the silence.

She's fallen asleep! Yang Kang let out a sigh of relief, his palm sweaty from the tension. She's a threat to me as long as she lives, he said to himself as he stole a glance at Viper Ouyang. The Martial Great was sitting with his eyes closed. Moonlight, reaching through the window, bathed one side of his face in its cool wash. He looked detached, unconcerned by the exchange that had just taken place.

Since the Qu girl was deep in slumber, the men settled down with their makeshift bedding and closed their eyes, drifting off.

Then the Qu girl cried out in a drowsy haze—"*Ow!* Who pinched me?"—and jumped up.

"A ghoul!" Lotus shrieked. "A ghoul with broken legs! It's you! You killed him. He's coming to take your life!"

"No! Not me!" the Qu girl screeched. "Nice brother—"

A hiss then a thump. Yang Kang's attempt to dig his fingers into the Qu girl's crown was forestalled by Lotus. She had flipped his legs out from under him with the Dog-Beating Cane.

Hector Sha and his companions scrambled to their sleepy feet and surrounded Lotus.

She took no notice, pointing at the temple gate. "Come. Your kill-er's here."

The Qu girl followed Lotus's finger, but could see nothing in the dark. Still, the thought that there could be a ghost lurking nearby was enough to terrorize her. She pulled Lotus's sleeve and cried, "Don't come for my life. It wasn't me! It was the nice brother. He killed you with his spearhead. I saw it. I was hiding in the kitchen. I saw everything . . . Legless ghoul, don't, don't come for me!"

It had never occurred to Viper Ouyang that Yang Kang might be his son's murderer, yet he knew the Qu girl was not clever enough to lie. He let out a shrill laugh of grief and wrath.

"Your Highness, my nephew deserved his fate." He glared at Yang Kang. "You did well in killing him. My congratulations!"

His words pierced the ears of all within hearing, like a thousand tiny needles. They tried in vain to stop their bodies from shuddering and their teeth from chattering. Even the crows in the pagoda were roused by his voice, croaking and flapping their wings in fear. Some took to the sky in fright.

Yang Kang knew that, if he stayed put, he faced certain death. He cast his eyes around the main hall, searching for an escape route.

Wanyan Honglie began pleading with the Venom when the crows had calmed down enough for him to be heard. "This girl is not of her right mind. I trust Master Ouyang does not believe her words. It was I who invited your nephew to join my enterprise, and both myself and my son came to rely on his wisdom and knowledge. Why would we wish harm upon him?"

Viper had been sitting on the floor, but, with one flex of his toes, his whole person flew up into the air. Then, without straightening his body, he leaped across and was suddenly sitting next to the Qu girl in the same cross-legged posture. He grabbed the girl by the arm.

"Why did he kill my nephew? Tell me!"

"I didn't kill him. Don't come after me!" She thrashed around, but she could not free herself from the Venom's iron grip.

"Pa! Pa!" she wailed.

Viper hissed his question again and again, to the point where the Qu girl ceased to cry and simply stared blankly.

"Hey, don't be afraid," Lotus cooed. "Grandpa just wants to give you some cake."

Viper fumbled in his robe at this reminder—fear would only make her clam up—and pulled out a *mantou*. He let go of her arm and stuffed the cold bun into her hand. "Here! Cake!" A grim approximation of a smile.

The Qu girl clung to the bread, still terrified. "Grandpa, it hurts!"

"I won't do that again. You're a good girl." Viper spoke in a gentle voice that was almost laughably out of character.

"That day, the sir with the broken legs was holding a girl in his arms, wasn't he? Was she pretty?" Lotus asked.

"Very! Where is she now?"

"You don't know who she is, do you?"

The Qu girl clapped and smiled smugly. "I do! I do! She's the lady-wife of my nice brother."

This was all the confirmation Viper Ouyang needed. He had always known of his boy's fondness for women, and was not surprised that a woman was the cause of his downfall. And yet one thing nagged at him. Even though Gallant had lost the use of his legs, he was still the superior fighter of the two. Yang Kang did not have the skill to cause him harm. How had it happened? He snapped around to face Yang Kang. "My nephew gave offense to the young Consort, and for that he deserved a thousand deaths."

"No . . . no . . . it wasn't me . . ."

"Who, then?"

Viper's roar scattered Yang Kang's wits and left him limp and weak. Drenched in sweat, he could not string two words together.

"The Heretic gave the map of Peach Blossom Island to my nephew," the Venom went on. "I asked how it came into your possession, and you told me you were good friends and that you'd borrowed it to learn about the Five Elements and the Eight Trigrams. I must say, I was not entirely convinced at the time, and now I know why. You killed him and took it from him, didn't you?"

Terror had reduced Yang Kang to a mute, shivering wreck.

"Uncle Ouyang, you mustn't blame His Highness for his cruelty, or your nephew for his wanton ways. You only have your kung fu to blame," Lotus said with a sigh.

"What do you mean?"

"When I was in Ox Village, I heard an exchange between a man and a woman. I haven't been able to place the speakers, until now."

"Huh?" Viper had not the faintest idea what she was talking about.

"Let me repeat what I heard word for word. I wasn't able to see their faces, so I didn't know who they were. The man said, 'They saw me kill Gallant Ouyang. What if they tell someone?' And the woman replied, 'Real men are brave and get things done. You shouldn't have killed him if you were going to worry so much . . .'" Lotus let the words hang in the air.

"She's right," Viper said a beat later, realizing that she was not going to continue. "What did he say to that?"

Forced to listen to his own words from Lotus's lips, Yang Kang could barely contain his panic. The moon, reaching in through the doorway, was now shining on the floor before the statue of General Wang the Iron Spear. He skirted around its sheen and tiptoed into position behind Lotus.

"He said, 'I have another idea. I could make his uncle my master. The idea first came to me a while ago. But his school of martial arts has a very strict rule: only one student per generation. Now that his disciple is dead, however, he might consider taking me on.'"

Lotus had not said outright who the speaker was, but, from her tone and accent, it had to be Yang Kang—a mix of northern and southern sounds: that of Daxing in Zhongdu, where he grew up, and the melody of Lin'an, where his mother Charity Bao was born.

Chuckling, Viper turned to where Yang Kang had been sitting, but he was nowhere to be seen.

A smack sounded, followed by a howl of pain.

Yang Kang, standing in the moonlight, his right hand bloody, his face drained of all color.

When Lotus began to mimic his way of speaking, he knew he had to silence her at all costs. He leaped up and plunged his talons down at her head. Needless to say, Lotus had been expecting this very reaction and had been on her guard, her senses attuned to the slightest change in the air. The instant she sensed him above her head, she sheered off to the right. His fingers dug instead into her left shoulder, and were pierced all the way through by the prickles of the Hedgehog Chainmail. The pain had almost knocked him out cold.

In the gloom of the main hall, no one was sure what had happened. They only knew that Yang Kang was hurt. Whether by Lotus Huang or Viper Ouyang, they could not tell, but they all decided it was best to keep quiet, in case the Martial Great was responsible. All but Wanyan Honglie, who rushed up to steady his son.

"Kang, what happened? Where are you hurt?" He pulled out his saber and put it in his son's hand. He knew Viper Ouyang would not let his nephew's murder pass, but he had numbers on his side—perhaps he and his son still had a chance.

"I'm fine," Yang Kang replied, clenching his teeth against the pain as he closed his fingers around the saber's hilt. It slipped from his grasp and clattered to the floor. He stooped to pick it up, only to find his arm hanging stiff and unresponsive. He pinched the back of his hand. Nothing. He could feel nothing on one side of his body.

He looked up at Lotus. "You—you poisoned me!"

Tiger Peng and his fellows had instinctively held back, daunted by the idea of standing in opposition to Viper Ouyang. Yet, having considered the situation, they all came to the conclusion that, as a prince of the Great Jin Empire, Wanyan Honglie would have the power and resources to resolve the unfortunate incident involving Gallant Ouyang, and they should really be seen acting on the young Prince's behalf. So, some of them rushed to Yang Kang's side with reassuring words, while the others bullied Lotus for the antidote, all making sure to give Viper Ouyang a wide berth.

"The Hedgehog Chainmail has never been laced with poison," Lotus shot back. "And, considering the company we are in, there are others who are more keen on seeing the back of you than I am."

"I ... I ... can't move!" Yang Kang's knees gave way and his body drooped. An animalistic growl rumbled in his throat.

Lotus could not fathom how her Hedgehog Chainmail could have elicited such a reaction. And yet there was no mistaking the surprise on Viper's face. By now, Yang Kang's features were twisted by merriment rather than pain. His spine-chilling countenance was accentuated by the silvery moonbeams. She had seen that same grotesque expression once before.

"It must have been Uncle Ouyang ..." she said.

"Well, it does look like the venom of my serpent." There was a note of astonishment in his voice. "I was thinking of giving him a taste of the very same poison, so I must thank you for doing the hard work, young lady. Tell me, how did you get hold of it?"

"You're the poisoner, not me, but you might not be aware of it."

"How can that be?"

"Uncle Ouyang, remember your bet with the Hoary Urchin? You fed your serpent's venom to one shark. When a second shark ate the poisoned carcass, it too succumbed to the toxin. When a third shark came to feast on the second victim, it fell prey to the same fate. This bane you've created can spread its lethal effects without losing any of its power. Am I right?"

"Why else do you think I am called the Venom of the West?"

"Indeed, and Woodcutter Nan was the first shark."

Yang Kang was in a frenzy, rolling back and forth on the floor. Graybeard Liang wanted to restrain the young man, but he was flinging himself about so wildly that no one could get close.

Viper pondered her words, his brow furrowed. "Can you elaborate?"

"You said you set your serpent on Woodcutter Nan, and, when we found him on Peach Blossom Island, he punched me. On my left shoulder. His poisoned blood was left on the prickles of my Hedgehog Chainmail, and so the steel shirt became the second shark. Just now, when His Highness struck me, by some divine justice, he was pricked by the very spikes stained with Woodcutter Nan's blood. So, he's is the third shark."

A chill passed through the temple. The hardened martial men grew ever more wary of Viper Ouyang, having witnessed the horrifying effects of the venom. They also noted how fast retribution came—it was just days since Yang Kang had plotted to butcher five of the Freaks, and now he was tainted with Woodcutter Nan's contaminated blood . . .

Wanyan Honglie approached Viper Ouyang and fell to his knees. "Master Ouyang, please spare my son's life. I shall be forever in your debt."

Though Yang Kang was no kin of blood, the boy had called him Papa all his life, and Wanyan Honglie had doted on him, treating him as his own issue. He had been so captivated by Charity Bao that his love extended to those dear to her.

"Are you saying your son's life is worth more than my nephew's?" Viper cackled, sweeping his eyes over the Prince's entourage. "If any of the heroes gathered here disagree with me, let them make themselves known."

Silence. Just then, Yang Kang vaulted up from the temple floor and—*pang*—punched Graybeard Liang, sending the old man flying in a somersault.

Wanyan Honglie had also climbed to his feet. "We leave for Lin'an now. We will find the best physician for the young Prince."

"Do you think a doctor—even the very best—could find a cure for my poison? Do you think a medical man would risk his life to thwart my will?"

"Help His Highness!" Wanyan Honglie ordered his guards.

Yang Kang hopped away from the hands reaching for him, jumping so high that he almost hit the rafter above. He jabbed his finger at Wanyan Honglie. "You're not my father. You killed my mother. Now you want to kill me."

The Jin Prince recoiled, stumbling several steps back.

"Your Highness, focus your mind!" Hector Sha cried, striding up to take Yang Kang by the arms.

The young man, with faster reflexes than anyone knew he possessed, flipped his right hand into a backhand hook and seized Sha's left wrist, digging his nails deep into the exposed arm. Stunned by the uncalled-for violence, the Dragon King's only thought was to free himself from Yang Kang's grip. Until the pain struck him. A numbing itch began to spread across his skin.

"The fourth shark."

Tiger Peng, a skilled user of poison himself, caught on to Lotus's meaning. He pulled his saber free from his belt and—*sha!*—hacked off his good friend's left arm.

Browbeater Hou lunged at Tiger Peng. "I'll kill you!"

"Stop! He saved me!" Hector Sha yelled at his martial brother.

Yang Kang's mind was completely gone now, leaving him a pointing, striking, kicking, biting, maddened thing. Not one man dared approach him after what had happened to Hector Sha. Shrieking, they all fled. The commotion woke the crows once more, and they circled the pagoda, casting ominous shadows on the clearing outside the temple, their caws clashing with Yang Kang's growls.

Wanyan Honglie was ushered into the open by his guards, though they could not prevent him from looking back and calling for his son. "Kang! Kang!"

Somehow, his cries managed to get through to the young man. "Father! Father!" he wailed as he ran toward the Jin Prince.

Overjoyed by the lucid response, Wanyan Honglie folded his arms around his boy. "Son, are you feeling better?"

A gnarled face and snapping white teeth answered his question. Terrified, Wanyan Honglie flung his son away from him and Yang Kang toppled to the ground, all strength drained from his body. There, he flailed on his back, unable to get up again. Wanyan Honglie could not bear to watch his son suffer any longer. He leaped on his horse and galloped into the night, his retinue straggling behind him.

Viper and Lotus watched Yang Kang writhing on the ground, each lost in their own thoughts. Before long, a final spasm seized the young man and then he was still.

It was Viper who broke the silence. "It's almost dawn. Let's see how your father fares."

"What's there to see? He must be back on Peach Blossom Island by now."

It took a moment for the Venom to collect himself. The smirk returned to his face. "So, the little wench has been lying all along."

"Well, only at first. Do you honestly think those stinking Quanzhen Taoists could trap my papa? Would you have let me question the Qu girl if I hadn't mentioned the Nine Yin Manual?"

Ke Zhen'e now had a new admiration for Lotus. He almost felt protective of her, and he prayed that she would come up with a clever ploy to get away from Viper Ouyang.

"Your lies were rooted in truth, or else I would never have fallen for them. Now, recite for me your father's translation of the final passage in the Manual—every last word."

"What if I don't remember it?"

"It'd be a shame if my snake were to bite a pretty girl like you."

Lotus had been prepared to die when she stepped out from the statue, and yet, having witnessed Yang Kang's agonies, she was not so certain anymore.

He might not let me go, even after I've told him everything Reverend Sole Light has shared with us, she realized, but she had no better plan right now than trying to string him along for as long as possible.

"If you recite the original, it may remind me of the translation. Give me the first line."

"Don't try to hoodwink me. Who on earth can remember such gibberish?"

Hang on . . . If he can't remember that passage, then he must value the manuscript as highly as his own life, she concluded. Yes, I can use that to my advantage.

"In that case, read it out and I'll translate it for you."

Viper Ouyang went back inside the temple and lit a candle stump from the altarpiece. Then he produced a parcel, carefully wrapped in three layers of oilpaper, from the inside pocket of his shirt, eager to at last make sense of the Manual's final pages.

Lotus suppressed a giggle. Look how he treasures the nonsense Guo Jing put down for him!

Viper read aloud: "*Mahaparas gatekras . . . habhaya kazidada sagalopa.*"

"Herein lies the key to the Manual: make good use of the observation of appearance in order to channel twelve kinds of suspiration."

Excited, the Venom continued, "*Jaramanas haho.*"

"Able to overcome a multitude of maladies, gradually enter the mystic marvel."

"*Siddhabhasita aneka.*"

Lotus pondered for a few moments, then shook her head. "That's not right. You've got it wrong."

"That's how it's written down."

"But it makes no sense . . ." She rested her chin in her hand, as though deep in thought.

Impatience screamed inside the Venom, but he dared not interrupt her.

At length, she said, "Guo Jing must have got it wrong. Can I see?"

He handed the manuscript over obediently. She took the pages and grabbed the candle to take a better look in its flickering light. Without warning, she jumped back a dozen paces, letting the flame lick close to the pages.

"Uncle Ouyang, this is fake!"

"Oi! What are you doing? Give it back!"

"Do you want to take the Manual or take my life?" She grinned, threatening to set fire to his treasure.

"What am I to do with your life? Give it back!" he snapped, ready to pounce on her and take the papers by force.

"Stay where you are!" She held the pages even closer to the flame. "One tiny movement and I'll burn them all!"

"*Huh!* I can't outwit you, you little imp. Put it down and go!"

"As a Martial Great, you'll honor your word, won't you?"

"I said, put it down and go," he repeated darkly.

Lotus set the Manual and the candle on the floor with a chuckle. "Sorry, Uncle Ouyang." With the Dog Beater in her hand, she turned to leave.

Though entirely unscrupulous, Viper did care deeply about losing face, so he stuck to his word and let her go. But, as she walked out of the temple's main hall, he leaped up and swung a vicious backhand. *Pang!* The statue of Wang Yanzhang the Iron Spear broke in half.

"Blind Bat, come out!"

Lotus whipped around and saw Ke Zhen'e jump out, twirling the spear shaft in an arc of protection. She realized her oversight. Anyone with the Venom's martial abilities would have heard Master Ke's breathing. He had not mentioned it because the Freak was too minor an opponent to be worthy of the trouble. She rushed back and reached out with the Dog-Beating Cane in Ke's defense.

"Uncle Ouyang, I'm staying, let him go."

"No, Lotus, go!" Ke cried. "Find Guo Jing. Tell him to avenge his *shifus.*"

"He won't listen to me, Master Ke. If you won't go, Papa and I will forever be wronged. Tell Guo Jing, I don't blame him. Tell him, don't dwell on the past."

But how could Ke Zhen'e let her risk her life a second time to save his? He stood his ground.

It was Viper Ouyang's turn to show impatience. "Wench, I agreed to let you go. Why did you come back?"

"I've decided I prefer your company, Uncle Ouyang. Let's be rid of this blind old fool. I'll stay with you, but you mustn't hurt him."

Viper was pleased by Lotus's suggestion, since he could not care less whether Ke Zhen'e lived or died. He strode forward and grabbed the front of the Freak's robe. Ke swung the spear shaft sideways to protect himself. Viper pushed back, his force numbing Ke's arms as a dull pain gripped the Freak's chest. With a clang, the spear shot upward through the roof.

Ke Zhen'e jumped back, but, before his feet touched firm ground, he felt his collar tighten and his body was lifted once more into the air. But he had been in enough fights to know this was not the time to panic. With a flick of his left wrist, he let fly with two poisoned devilnuts aimed straight at the Venom's face.

Viper had not imagined the Freak would have the skill to retaliate so effectively from such a compromised position. The projectiles were shooting toward him at great speed. At such close proximity, the only way he could dodge them was to bend backward. He used the momentum generated by his evasive maneuver to flip the blind man overhead and hurl him away, sending him through the temple doors. In fact, he was now flying faster than his own secret weapons, which had sailed just above Viper Ouyang's head.

"*Aiyoo!*" Lotus gasped. Any moment now, the poisoned darts would hit Ke Zhen'e.

Somehow, the Freak twisted his body midair and caught the two devilnuts in his palm. He could indeed see better with his ears than most people can with their eyes.

Viper applauded his display. "Impressive. I'll let you go, this time, Blind Bat."

Ke Zhen'e landed on his feet, but gave no response.

"Master Ke, Uncle Ouyang is going to bow to me, so I'll be his *shifu* and teach him from the Nine Yin Manual. Why are you dallying? Do you want to call me *Shifu* too?"

Ke was still standing, dazed, on the spot. He knew, despite her jovial tone, what grave danger she was in. He could not desert her.

But then, he heard Viper's voice. "The sky is light. Let's go." The Martial Great took Lotus's hand and pulled her along after him.

"Master Ke, remember what I wrote on your palm." Lotus's fading voice drifted back to him, already several *zhang* from the temple.

Flocks of crows rushed past Ke Zhen'e. The sound of them pecking and squawking over Yang Kang's body jolted him out of his stupor. He hopped onto the temple roof and groped around for the iron spear shaft.

Where should this blind old fool go? he asked himself when he had found his makeshift weapon.

Before he could come up with an answer, a wave of desperate screeching assaulted his ears, followed by a scramble of flapping wings. Then, *thud, thud, thud,* crows were dropping out of the air, one after another. The first group that had been feasting on Yang Kang's remains were now dead. Killed by Viper Ouyang's poison.

The Freak let out a long sigh and jumped down from the slanting tiles. He would head north, for now.

2

Ke Zhen'e had been on the road for three days when he picked out the caws of the condors. His disciple must be nearby.

"Guo Jing, my boy!" he called. "Guo Jing!"

Soon, the clatter of hooves echoed in the empty wilderness.

"*Shifu!*" Guo Jing cried, elated to see his Master unharmed. Almost a week had passed since they were separated in the skirmish with the Song army, near the Tower of Mist and Rain, in Jiaxing. The young man leaped from the saddle before Ulaan had come to a stop. Just as he was about to embrace his mentor, he felt a box on the ear. And then another.

Guo Jing's arms fell slack at his sides. He made no move to dodge the blows, letting his *shifu* hit him again and again. The next thing he knew, Ke was slapping himself on the face too.

"*Shifu?*" he asked, mystified by his teacher's actions.

"You are a young fool and I am an old idiot!" Ke Zhen'e struck Guo Jing and himself a dozen more times, until their cheeks were red and swollen. Then he cursed their stupidity once more, before recounting in detail how, in the Iron Spear Temple, Lotus had staked her life on revealing the truth behind the massacre on Peach Blossom Island.

Guo Jing tried to wrap his mind around the many twists and turns in his *shifu*'s story, while confronting a barrage of emotions—joy, shock, sorrow, shame, remorse.

I have sorely wronged Lotus, he said to himself.

"Our lives should be forfeit. How could we be so gullible?" Ke Zhen'e yelled into the desolate landscape.

Nodding vehemently, Guo Jing replied: "First *Shifu* is not to blame. You can't see. It's all my fault."

"No. I am not just blind in the eyes, I am blind in here too." Ke thumped his chest.

After a moment's pause, Guo Jing said, "We need to rescue her."

"Where is her father?" Ke asked.

"He took *Shifu* Hong back to Peach Blossom Island. Where do you think Viper Ouyang has taken Lotus?"

Ke Zhen'e had no answer for him. After a short silence, he said, "The Venom is sure to use torture. He won't be gentle. Go and find her, quickly. I will take my own life to thank her for uncovering the truth about my siblings' death."

"No, *Shifu*, you mustn't!" Guo Jing cried, though he knew his Master's temperament: no one could sway the eldest Freak when his mind was made up. "Please hurry to Peach Blossom Island. We need Apothecary Huang's help. I'm no match for Viper Ouyang."

Guo Jing's words spurred Ke Zhen'e into action. Clutching his spear, he adjusted his course and stumbled off in the direction of the coast, but, before long, he realized that his student was trailing after him. Ke swung his spear shaft backward in a blind arc. "Why are you following me? Why aren't you looking for Lotus? I'll kill you with my bare hands if you fail to find her!"

Shocked by the anger in his mentor's voice, Guo Jing halted and watched as Ke continued on his way east, eventually disappearing into a mulberry grove. At a loss as to how he might find Lotus, he eventually decided to start from her last known location, Iron Spear Temple. He leaped onto Ulaan and, with the condors flying overhead, made his way back toward Jiaxing.

It took Guo Jing no time at all to cover the distance it had taken his teacher three days to cover on foot. All around the abandoned shrine, he found dark clumps of lifeless crows. A pile of bones picked clean by the now lifeless scavengers lay outside the main hall of worship, their bleached white appearance a stark contrast to the black feathered bodies surrounding them.

Guo Jing loathed Yang Kang for causing the death of his five *shifus*, but the sight of his pitiful remains took the edge of his hatred—after all, they had been sworn brothers. He collected what was left of the young man and buried it at the rear of the temple.

"Brother Yang, I've given you a final resting place," Guo Jing said, bowing on his knees. "Please, help me find Lotus, to atone for your wrongs."

Autumn hardened into winter and winter melted into spring. Six moons had passed, and yet Guo Jing had found no trace of Lotus. He had asked many *wulin* Masters for help, including those of the

Quanzhen Sect and the Beggar Clan, tapping into their vast networks of associates and contacts.

Nothing. Not a single sighting. Not a whisper of her whereabouts.

The thought of the hardships Lotus must be enduring sliced through Guo Jing's heart like a keen blade. He was determined to find her. He would travel to the heavens' edge and the ocean's end if need be.

He went to Zhongdu, the Jin capital. He went to Bianliang, the Song Empire's former seat, stolen by the Jurchens. He went to Peach Blossom Island, where he found no sign of Lotus or her father. He even went to Roaming Cloud Manor. The grand estate had been razed to the ground, but he had no time to ask around and find out what disaster had befallen Zephyr Lu and his son Laurel Lu.

Guo Jing ventured north once more, entering Shandong province. Desolation met him along the way. Houses and villages stood empty and abandoned. Roads were packed with people fleeing from bloody clashes between the Mongolians and the Jurchens. The latter had been routed, and what was left of the Jin forces had taken to pillaging as they retreated, committing every manner of evil.

For three days, Guo Jing rode through war-torn landscapes, and the further north he went, the more heartbreaking the devastation. He was witnessing firsthand how the common people paid the greatest price when two armies met in battle. As the Jin soldiers moved south, they killed, burned, raped and looted. The Mongol troops were perhaps less brutal, but the difference was negligible to those who came across them. Though he had no love for them, Guo Jing had to admit that, for the time being, the Jin were keeping the Great Khan's cavalry away from the diminished Song Empire, delaying the horrors that were heading its way.

On the fourth day, Guo Jing crossed the border of East Shandong into territory still occupied by the Jin. He rested for the night in the town of Juzhou and continued north until he reached a village outside Mizhou. Just as he was about to ask the locals for a place to water

Ulaan and prepare some food, the neighing of war horses and the murmur of gruff, threatening voices filled the air. A company of Jurchen soldiers, several dozen strong, torched their way through the settlement, forcing the villagers from their burning homes. Young women were taken prisoner, their hands bound; the rest—including children and the elderly—were cut down on sight.

Outraged by the savagery on display, Guo Jing urged Ulaan forward, galloping straight at the leader of this cruel troop, and snatched his spear from his grasp. At the same time, he swiped his other hand at the Great Sun acupressure point on the man's temple. The officer's eyes bulged and he dropped dead. His followers roared in fury, leveled their weapons at Guo Jing, and charged.

Sensing the excitement of combat, the Fergana horse burst forward at such speed it was as though he had taken wing, bringing his master into the fighters' midst. Guo Jing seized a broad saber from a nearby soldier. He was still surprised by his own strength, for he had not intended to kill their officer with a single blow. Thrusting the spear with his right hand and swinging the blade with his left, he unleashed the Competing Hands technique on the rogue platoon. The ferocity of the onslaught crushed the men's fighting spirit. They wrenched their horses around, fleeing the same way they had come. And yet, at that same moment, a banner was sighted beyond the fire and smoke. A small division of Mongol riders was galloping toward the village. The Jurchen cavalry had already been crushed by the Mongolians on the battlefield, and they had no desire to face them again, so they pinned their hope on their strength of numbers, reasoning that they might stand a chance against a lone warrior, and spurred their mounts back into the settlement.

But Guo Jing was not prepared to let these soldiers terrorize the helpless farmers any further. Sitting astride his proud steed, he blocked the path leading into the village. A dozen of the braver men led the first charge, and a handful of them fell to Guo Jing's spear in a matter of moments. The rest remained rooted to the spot, too cowed to advance and too frightened to retreat.

The Mongol riders, who had not expected to receive help in enemy territory, now launched a decisive offensive to finish off the remaining Jin soldiers. When the fighting was over, the commander turned to Guo Jing, but, before he could address him, one of his subordinates recognized the young man and hailed him—"Prince of the Golden Blade!"—as he prostrated himself on the ground. Realizing he was in the presence of Princess Khojin's betrothed, the commander scrambled down from the saddle to pay his respects, sending his fastest rider to inform his superior.

While the Mongol soldiers were busy extinguishing fires, on Guo Jing's orders, to a chorus of gratitude from the surviving villagers, a thundering rumble of pounding hooves approached the settlement. The appearance of a yet another cavalry force, and a sizeable one at that, had the locals exchanging looks of fear and dismay.

A magnificent steed with a rich chestnut coat broke out from the newcomers' ranks, as fleet as the wind, and his rider—a strapping young general—asked, "Where is my *anda* Guo Jing?"

"Tolui!" Guo Jing rushed over and joyfully embraced his sworn brother. Recognizing a familiar figure, the condors swooped down to greet the Mongolian Prince, nuzzling him affectionately.

Once the two *anda* had greeted one another, Tolui sent a company to round up the Jin stragglers in the area and arranged for a tent to be set up on the hillside, so he and Guo Jing could catch up in comfort on all that had happened since they had parted.

The last few times these childhood friends crossed paths, circumstances had not allowed them much time to speak. Tolui now filled his *anda* in on developments over the past year or so since Guo Jing had left for the Central Plains with his *shifus*, the Six Freaks of the South. He had followed his father Genghis Khan on campaign after campaign, riding eastward and west, as had his three brothers, the Princes Jochi, Chagatai and Ogedai; the Four Great Generals, Muqali, Bogurchi, Boroqul and Tchila'un; and less-exalted generals, such as Jebe and Subotai. Together, they won many glorious victories for the Great Khan, greatly expanding Mongol territory—even the

Tangut state would soon fall to their might and become a part of their realm. Now he and Muqali were tasked with the conquest of the Jin Empire, and they had been routing the Jurchens in Henan and Shandong. The defeated soldiers—along with other remnants of the Jin army—had retreated to Tong Pass, taking refuge in the mountain stronghold, too afraid to venture into Shandong to face the invaders.

3

SEVERAL DAYS LATER, AN URGENT MESSAGE ARRIVED AT Tolui's camp. Genghis Khan was summoning all his Princes and generals to the northern part of the Mongolian desert. Tolui and Muqali handed the banners of command to their deputies without delay and set off that very night. Guo Jing decided to join them since he had not seen his mother for more than a year and had no clear idea where he should go next in search of Lotus.

After several days of intense riding, they arrived on the banks of the majestic Onon River. Looking out over the vast plains, which stretched from horizon to horizon, as far as the eye could see, Guo Jing saw thousands of war horses roaming between rows and rows of *gers*, as countless spearheads and weapons glistened in the spring sunlight. In this makeshift city of tents, one magnificent example fashioned from beige felt stood out from the tens of thousands in modest gray. The tip of its canopy was crowned in solid gold, and a banner made from the tail hairs of nine yaks was planted beside its entrance.

As Guo Jing took in this grand view, he could feel the might of the Great Khan's army and the authority that the golden *ger* exuded reaching far across the steppes into distant lands. He could imagine Genghis Khan issuing an order from his tent, and a herald carrying it to the swiftest horse, to be passed from rider to rider, until the Khan's words were received by a Prince or a general ten thousand *li* away. Bugles would sound. Beacons would be lit. Smoke signals would rise from the grasslands. Arrows would fall as dense as a locust swarm. Swords and sabers would flash as iron hooves pounded through plumes of dust.

What are the Great Khan's plans for these lands and people? Guo Jing wondered, but he was soon distracted from his musings by the cloud of fine earth kicked up by the cavalrymen spurring over to welcome them.

Tolui, Muqali and Guo Jing followed the soldiers to the golden *ger* to greet Genghis Khan. They realized they were the last to answer the summons, for all the other Princes and generals were already standing in two rows inside the tent.

Genghis Khan was pleased by their arrival. He listened to Tolui and Muqali's report on the situation in Henan and Shandong, before turning to Guo Jing. The young man knelt and said, "The Great Khan sent me to take the head of the Jin Prince Wanyan Honglie, but I failed and let him slip away several times. I accept my punishment willingly."

"Why would I wish to punish you? When the condor comes of age, it will catch the fox," Genghis Khan replied with a smile. "I am glad you are back. I have thought of you often."

The conversation soon moved on to the next steps in the campaign against the Jin. The majority of their remaining elite troops had taken refuge at Tong Pass, and it would be nigh on impossible for the Mongolian forces to breach its natural fortifications. But, if they could not subdue its garrison, they would not be able to vanquish the Jurchens once and for all. Muqali proposed they seek alliance with the Song Empire and join forces with their army to launch a pincer attack. Genghis Khan put the proposal into action instantly, ordering a scribe to draft a letter to the Song court and appointing an ambassador to ensure its safe delivery.

The meeting went on for some hours before they adjourned for the day. Guo Jing left the *ger* to be greeted by the spreading hues of dusk, and immediately went in search of his mother. He had barely walked a few steps when he sensed two hands reaching from behind to cover his eyes. Someone of his martial stature could not possibly fall for such an ambush. He leaned a fraction to the side and was raising his arm to push the attacker away when he caught a sweet fragrance. He pulled back immediately and cried out, "Khojin!"

Genghis Khan's favorite daughter regarded him with a hint of a smile. She had grown taller since their last meeting, near Ox Village, half a year ago. She stood proud over the windswept grasslands, her long-limbed, athletic frame accentuated by her spirited nature.

"Sister," he said, greeting her again.

"You've really come back!" Khojin burst into joyful tears.

This unguarded display of emotion touched Guo Jing. He could tell that she had a thousand things to say to him, but no idea where to start.

"Go and see your mother," she said after a long pause. "Who do you think will be more delighted by your return—me or her?"

"I'm sure Ma will be very happy."

"You mean I'm not?" A playful admonishment.

Guo Jing felt a pang of familiarity at Khojin's frank response. Though he had grown accustomed to the more roundabout way in which people expressed themselves in the South, it warmed him to experience Mongolian forthrightness again, to hear someone state outright what they were feeling in their heart. He was indeed back in the land of his boyhood.

Khojin took his hand and led him to Lily Li's *ger*. She was overjoyed to be reunited with her son, though the sight of him could not chase away the lonely months she had had endured while he was away.

Within a week of his return, Guo Jing was summoned by Genghis Khan.

"Tolui has told me about your decision. You chose to abide by your word, and that pleases me more than you can know, child. You shall wed my daughter very soon."

Shocked, Guo Jing's first instinct was to refuse. He had yet to find out whether Lotus was dead or alive. How could he marry some-one else behind her back? Faced with the imposing Genghis Khan, however, he could only stammer incoherently, unable to string half a sentence together.

The Khan thought the artless young man was struck dumb by excitement. He made him a gift of a thousand household slaves, a hundred *jin* of gold, five hundred horses, five hundred oxen, two thousand goats and three hundred camels, then ordered him to make preparations for the ceremony.

Khojin was the youngest daughter of Genghis Khan and his first wife and Consort, who had the highest status among all his women. The Mongol Empire had grown prosperous, its might reaching far and wide. Genghis Khan was indefatigable in battle; he could con-quer any state or kingdom. When the khans and chieftains of other local tribes learned of the forthcoming nuptials, they all came with congratulations and precious gifts, enough to fill dozens of *gers*. Khojin was radiant with joy, but Guo Jing's face was drawn with worry, his belly full of troubles.

As the day of their union approached, Guo Jing was increasingly weighed down by dejection, and his whole person was haunted by a cloud of gloom.

Lily Li noticed his demeanor and decided to probe him one eve-ning. Guo Jing told her all about Lotus, holding nothing back, from how they first met to how they had parted. She considered for a long time how she should respond, but, before she could share her thoughts, Guo Jing said, "Ma, I'm really torn. I don't know what to do. I don't even know if she can forgive me for how I treated her."

"We can't repay the Great Khan's kindness with ingratitude. But, as for Lotus . . ." She sighed. "Though I haven't met her, I can tell she must be very charming."

"What would Papa do?"

It was not a question Lily Li had expected. She cast her mind back to the brief years she had enjoyed with Skyfury Guo, recalling his character and values.

"Your papa would rather suffer for a lifetime than break his word," she said with pride.

Guo Jing got to his feet solemnly, his mind made up. "I have never met Papa, but I will live as he did. If Lotus is unharmed, I will keep my promise and marry Khojin. But if something bad has happened to Lotus, then I will not take a wife in this lifetime."

Lily Li was taken aback by his decision, for it meant that, if the worst were to happen, the Guo bloodline would end with him. And yet, she understood her boy. He was stubborn to a fault, just like his father, and she knew there was nothing anyone could say to sway him.

"How are you going to break the news to the Great Khan?"

"I will tell him the truth."

"Then we can't stay here any longer." Lily Li would stand by her son, no matter what. "After you thank the Great Khan, we will go south immediately."

Guo Jing nodded and started to help his mother pack a few changes of clothes and a small amount of silver for the journey. Everything else in the *ger* had been a gift from Genghis Khan and she left it all where it was.

When they were ready, Guo Jing said, "I want to bid Khojin farewell."

"Are you . . . able to say it to her? We should just go quietly . . . spare her the heartache."

"No, I must tell her myself." With these words, he took leave of his mother and went to find Khojin.

KHOJIN AND her mother were bustling around the *ger* they shared, getting ready for the impending marriage ceremony, when they heard Guo Jing's arrival.

Khojin's mother chuckled. "The wedding is just days away, and he can't get through a few hours without seeing you."

The young woman blushed. "Ma!"

"Fine. Off you go!"

Beaming, Khojin headed out of the tent.

"Guo Jing." Her voice was softer than usual.

"Sister, I need to speak to you."

Guo Jing led the way. They walked westward for several *li*, until they were some distance from the camp, then sat down on the ground. Khojin shuffled close and leaned against Guo Jing.

"I have something to say to you too," she said under her breath.

"*Ah*, you know?" Guo Jing gasped. Perhaps he would be spared the burden of delivering his heavy message?

"Know what? I wanted to tell you . . . I am not the Great Khan's daughter."

"Huh?"

Khojin turned her face skywards and gazed at the crescent moon that had risen above the horizon while they were walking. "Once we are married –" for once, she was taking her time over her words—"I will forget that I am Genghis Khan's daughter. I will just be Guo Jing's wife. If you wish to beat me, berate me, you can do as you wish. You don't have to hold back because the Great Khan is my father."

Guo Jing's chest tightened at her words. He could feel blood surging through his veins, and the heat that went with it. "Sister, you've been very good to me, but I fear I'm not good enough for you."

"No! You're the best in the world. Only Papa is better than you. My four brothers aren't even half the man you are."

Hearing this, Guo Jing realized that his lips would not be able to form the words he had come to say—that he was leaving Mongolia for the South first thing in the morning.

"I'm so happy," Khojin went on, unaware of the storm churning inside Guo Jing. "When I heard you had died, I just wanted to kill myself so I could be with you, but Tolui made me put the sword down. If it weren't for him, I wouldn't be here to marry you . . . Guo Jing, if I can't be your wife, I'd rather be dead."

He sighed, thinking of Lotus. He knew he would never hear Lotus speak to him in this way . . .

"Why are you sighing?"

". . . Nothing."

"I know Big Brother and Second Brother don't like you. But I'll keep reminding Papa that they're not to be trusted. And I'll say nice things about Third Brother and Fourth Brother, because they're fond of you. You have nothing to worry about."

A self-satisfied grin spread on Khojin's face. Guo Jing's confusion was clear to see. He did not understand why she had shifted the conversation on to her brothers. "Mama says that Papa has been thinking about his heir because he's getting old. Who do you think he'll name?"

"Jochi, surely? He's the eldest, and he's won the most battles."

Khojin shook her head. "I don't think so. Most likely, it'll be Third Brother. And, if not, then it'll be Fourth Brother."

"The Great Khan won't change his mind because of a few words from you, will he?" Guo Jing was not convinced by Khojin's predictions. He knew all four Princes. Jochi, the firstborn, was a fierce warrior, indomitable on the field, and Chagatai, the Khan's second son, was astute and capable—it was hard to say who had the greater potential. They were always in competition, each trying to outshine the other. The third son, Ogedai, was a drinker and a hunter, generous and easygoing. It was widely held that either Jochi or Chagatai would succeed, though it was common knowledge that the youngest, Tolui, was the Khan's favorite. As such, Ogedai knew that it was unlikely the title of the Great Khan would be passed on to him. Since he was no threat to them, he was able to maintain a close relationship with all his brothers.

"I don't know," Khojin replied. "It's just my guess. But, even if Big Brother or Second Brother becomes the Great Khan, there's no need to worry. If they make trouble for you, I'll take a blade to them myself."

"You don't have to do that." Guo Jing smiled. He knew it was no empty promise. She was dearest to Genghis Khan's heart, and even her battle-hardened brothers let her have her way.

"True, we can always run away to the South."

"I'm going south," Guo Jing blurted out.

Taken aback, Khojin said after a pause, "Papa and Mama won't let me—"

"It's just me . . ."

"But I'll always do what you want me to. If you say we're going to the South, that's where I'll go. If Pa and Ma try to stop us, we'll run."

"It's just me and my ma." Guo Jing hopped to his feet in agitation. "The two of us. Going home."

They looked into each other's eyes. One standing, the other sitting. Neither made the slightest movement, as if they were sculptures fashioned from wood or clay.

Confusion flooded Khojin's features. She could not understand his words.

"I'm sorry, Sister. I cannot marry you."

"Have I done something wrong? Are you upset that I didn't kill myself for you?"

"No, no, no, it's not you. You've done nothing. I don't know who's in the wrong. I suppose it's me."

He opened up to her about Lotus, telling her that she had been captured by Viper Ouyang more than six months ago, and that he had failed to find any trace of her. The Mongolian Princess was moved to tears by the grief in his voice.

"Forget me. I have to look for her."

"Will you come to see me when you've found her?"

"If she's safe and unharmed, I'll come back. If you'll still have me then, we'll get married. I won't break my word."

"I know you always keep your word. You should know that I've only ever wanted to marry you. Go find her. Ten years, twenty, as long as I'm alive, I'll be waiting for you here on the steppes."

Sobbing, Khojin leaped up to embrace him. Guo Jing folded his arms lightly over her body, his eyes red-rimmed. They held one another in silence. They both knew anything they said now would only inflict further pain.

4

Four horses charged past Guo Jing and Khojin, galloping toward the camp. One of the beasts collapsed ten *zhang* from Genghis Khan's golden *ger*. The rider scrambled to his feet and ran into the tent without casting a glance at the animal, which had dropped dead from exhaustion.

A moment later, ten buglers emerged and arranged themselves in formation to face all four directions, sending steady blasts of their horns out to the furthest reaches of the camp. This unrelenting alarum was Genghis Khan's most urgent summons. All Princes and generals were required to be present. Any who failed to attend or arrived late would be beheaded, with no exceptions.

"The Great Khan's call!" Guo Jing rushed back to the camp, using his fastest lightness kung fu, without bidding Khojin farewell, the thunder of galloping hooves sounding all around him.

Though he had strayed far from the camp, Guo Jing was not the last to enter the golden *ger*. And, before long, all those expected to attend were gathered before the Great Khan.

"Does that dog Ala ad-Din Muhammad have such fleet-footed princes? Such brave generals?" the conqueror asked with pride.

"No!" the men roared as one.

The Great Khan thumped his chest, pleased with the enthusiastic response then, in a furious tone, he cried, "Look how that dog treated my loyal servants! Look at the men I sent to protect our emissary to Khwarazm!"

Every eye turned in the direction he was indicating and howls of fury erupted as a knot of soldiers entered the *ger*. Lush beards should have adorned their faces, but all that was left of them was burned stubble that could not conceal the disfiguring swellings and bruises on the skin. Facial hair was a symbol of a Mongol warrior's dignity—it was considered a great insult to touch another man's beard. This was an unforgiveable affront.

"Khwarazm may be large, with a powerful army, but do they intimidate us? We left them alone because we were busy thrashing the Jin dogs. Jochi, my son, tell us what that cur has done."

Jochi stepped forward and said in his booming voice, "Some years ago, Father sent me to quell the cursed Merkits. On our return, flushed with victory, we came across a sizeable army sent by that Khwarazm dog to fight these same Merkits. Our forces met, and I sent a herald to convey Father's wish to establish an alliance, but that red-bearded dog refused, saying, 'Genghis Khan ordered you not to fight us, but Allah demands we fight you.' It was a fierce battle. We had the better of it, but they outnumbered us ten to one, so we had to retreat under the cover of darkness."

"Despite this provocation, the Great Khan continued to be courteous," Boroqul added. "When they robbed and murdered our merchants, we sent an envoy to repair relations, but that dog Muhammad is doing the Jin mongrel Wanyan Honglie's bidding. He had our brave ambassador killed, together with half his guards, then he scorched the beards of the rest of the men and sent them back to us."

A chill went through Guo Jing's heart at the mention of his father's murderer. "Wanyan Honglie is in Khwarazm?"

Growling, one of the survivors answered, "I saw him sitting next to the Shah, whispering in his ear."

"The Jin are working with Khwarazm. To trap us between their armies. But are we afraid?" Genghis Khan asked.

"No!" A collective cry, then one of the generals spoke up. "Invincible is our Great Khan. We will take the fight to Khwarazm, capture their cities, torch their houses, slaughter their men and seize their women and livestock!"

"We'll take Shah Muhammad! We'll take Wanyan Honglie!" Genghis Khan declared, and the generals chanted as one, filling the grasslands with their battle cry and making the candles in the *ger* flicker.

Genghis Khan unsheathed his saber and brandished the blade,

then rushed outside and vaulted onto his steed. The generals followed suit and together they rode until they reached a hill several *li* away. The Khan galloped to its crest, but his men stayed put at its base to give their leader the space to think in solitude, forming a circle around the mound instead.

Spotting Guo Jing down below, the conqueror called out, "Come here, son."

When the young man reined in next to him, Genghis Khan pointed his horsewhip at the view before them. The entire camp of the Mongolian army. By each *ger*, a fire was burning. They twinkled on the steppe like stars in the sky.

"My boy, remember what I said to you on that day when we were surrounded by Senggum and Jamuka on the hill."

"Yes, you said we Mongols have many brave men, and, if we were united, we could make all the world's grasslands ours."

Genghis Khan waved his whip over his head. A sharp crack sounded in agreement. "And now, we Mongols are united, and we will catch Wanyan Honglie."

Although Guo Jing had made up his mind to return to the South the next morning, he knew he could not let a chance to avenge his father pass him by. And he would also be eliminating one of Mongolia's enemies, thereby repaying some of the kindness the Great Khan had shown him and his mother over the years.

"We'll catch the Jin dog, this time!"

"Khwarazm claims to have a host one million strong, but I think they only have six or seven hundred thousand men. Still, that is a sizeable number. Our whole army amounts to two hundred thousand, and I have to keep some men back to fight the Jin. Now, do you think one hundred and fifty thousand of us can beat seven hundred thousand of them?"

"Yes!" Guo Jing was unfamiliar with the art of war, but he had the headstrong boldness of youth and he could not imagine shrinking from adversity.

"Indeed, we will triumph." Genghis Khan was infected by the young man's conviction. "That day on the hill, I said I'd treat you as my own son, and Temujin always remembers the promises he makes. Ride west with me. We will take Muhammad and Wanyan Honglie together. And, when we return victorious, you can marry my daughter."

Genghis Khan spurred his horse downhill, his voice booming in the night: "Muster the troops!"

A blast of bugles passed on his command.

As Guo Jing rode back by Genghis Khan's side, he saw soldiers rushing by and warhorses racing ahead, but there was not a hint of chatter or confusion—men and beasts prepared for the Great Khan's inspection with exemplary discipline and efficiency. Three divisions of ten thousand cavalrymen, sabers glistening in the moonlight, had arranged themselves in neat rows on the grassy plain in the short time it took the conqueror and his generals to return to the golden *ger*.

GENGHIS KHAN sent for his scribe. He was ready to declare war on the Shah of Khwarazm. The clerk selected a sizeable piece of lambskin parchment and set down a long message. When he finished, he read it aloud on his knees.

> "*Appointed by the heavens above to rule over the tribes of the earth, the Great Khan hath claimed lands stretching ten thousand* li *and conquered kingdoms beyond number. No sovereign hath since time immemorial reigned over an empery as vast and glorious as does the Great Khan. When the Great Khan strikes, he dazzles like thunder and lightning, and none living can withstand his fury.*
>
> "*The fate of thy state, whether mercy or desolation, depends upon thy resolve today. Think thrice with care. For, if thou wilt not submit and pay tribute, the great Mongolian troops thou shalt face . . .*"

Wrath spread over Genghis Khan's face as he listened. He gave the white-whiskered man a taste of his boot, sending him flipping over in a sprawling roll.

"Who are you writing to? Does Genghis Khan waste his words on a Khwarazm dog?" The conqueror picked up his horsewhip and lashed the scrivener over the head a dozen times. "Listen well. Write down my exact words."

Quaking in pain and fear, the man scrambled into a more dignified kneeling position and produced a second parchment, his eyes trained on his liege's lips.

The Great Khan gazed at the thirty thousand soldiers visible through the open flap of his *ger* and spoke in a deep bass: "Just six words."

He paused and declared in a voice loud and clear: "You want war. Here we come."

The startled scribe had never imagined penning a message for the conqueror so lacking in decorum, but he had suffered enough from the whip and his face was still burning from its sting. He held his tongue and set down the blunt words in his largest hand, filling the whole parchment.

"Put my gold seal on this and have it delivered right away."

Muqali stamped the letter with the symbol of Genghis Khan's authority and beckoned over the commander of a thousand-strong battalion, who he ordered to act as courier. The bold message roused the spirit of the warriors inside the *ger*, and, as they listened to the beating of hooves speeding westward across the open country, they chanted in one voice:

"You want war. Here we come."

"*Ho-hu! Ho-hu!*" The thirty thousand soldiers outside answered with the Mongol rider's war whoop. Horses huffed and neighed in excitement.

The battle call shook the grasslands and rattled the heavens, as though the fighting had already begun.

FROM HIS golden throne, Genghis Khan dismissed his generals, and, in their absence, he was soon lost to his memories. The ornate chair was once the Jin Emperor's personal possession, a prize the Khan had seized when his riders entered Zhongdu. On its back, carved dragons chased after a pearl. The conqueror rested his elbow on an armrest adorned by a fearsome tiger and cupped his chin in his hand. He thought of his youth, those distant days of hardships and trials. He thought of his mother, his first wife, his four sons and his beloved daughter. He thought of his countless concubines, his undefeated armies, his vast empire and the mighty enemy he was about to face.

He might have been getting on in years, but his hearing was still keen. He picked up the cry of a horse in distress in the distance and the lifeless silence that followed it. He was familiar with the scenario that had just played out. An aged horse, an incurable ailment, one hack of a saber to end all suffering.

I too am growing old, he admitted with a sigh. Will I come back from this campaign? If I die in the field, will my four sons turn the realm upside down fighting over this throne? . . . Can I escape the clutches of death?

He had always been fearless, indomitable, a great hero, but the days of waning strength were looming and thoughts of death were never far away, bringing a shiver to his heart. His mind turned to a group of people from the South that he had heard about. Taoists, they were called. It was said that they had ways of becoming an Immortal, of living forever without growing old. Could this be true?

Genghis Khan clapped twice and ordered a guard to send for Guo Jing, so he could ask the young man about the matter.

"I don't know if what you describe is possible," Guo Jing answered. "But lengthening one's life by training the *qi* and controlling your breathing—that can be done."

"Are you acquainted with anyone with such skills? Find them for me."

"Those who possess such knowledge are not easily summoned."

"True . . . I can send a high-ranking official with gifts to entice them north. But who should I approach?"

Guo Jing pondered the question. The Quanzhen Sect was the most orthodox school, and Reverend Qiu was not only the most skilled among his five martial siblings, but also the most interested in worldly matters. Maybe he could be persuaded?

Delighted by Guo Jing's suggestion, Genghis Khan called the scribe into his *ger* again, instructing him to write to Qiu Chuji the Eternal Spring Immortal inviting him to visit Mongolia. The man thought hard about how to word this letter, his skin still hot from the beating earlier. He decided to model it on his last composition and set down seven simple words:

I seek your knowledge. Come at once.

The man was confident the note would please the Great Khan by emulating his forthright style, but the moment the words came out of his mouth, he felt the horsewhip again.

"You think I'd address a learned man in the same way I do a Khwarazm dog. Start again. This letter must be long, respectful, polite."

The scrivener was unfamiliar with Chinese writing, so he sent for a Han clerk, relaying the Khan's instructions, and soon Genghis Khan was presented with a parchment filled with columns of neat calligraphy.

The heavens look askance at the tendency for haughty extravagance among those of the Central Plains, and I, who live in the northern wilderness, harbor no such sensual passions, but wish to return to honest simplicity and to forswear luxury for frugality. My every garment and my every meal are the same as that of a herdsman or a stableboy.

I see the people as my own children, I nurture talents as if they were my own brothers, seeking harmony in our principles and abundance in our gratitude. In drills, I step out first before divisions of ten thousand; on the field, I have survived more than a hundred confrontations and never lagged back. In seven years, I have succeeded in my great endeavor, uniting all between the heavens and earth and within the four breaths of the wind.

It is not my behavior that is deemed virtuous, but that the Jin lack constancy in their governance, and thus I have been blessed by the heavens to inherit the empery supreme. To the south, Song of the Zhao clan; to the north, the Uyghurs; to the east, the Tanguts; to the west, petty barbarian tribes. They all pledge loyalty as clients. Such power has never been known to the many Khans who have led our kingdom for thousands of years and hundreds of generations.

Yet, as I strive to maintain this great and weighty responsibility, I fear I am lacking the ability to instill orderly rule. Just as men have known to carve wood into boats when they wish to cross a river, thus must one hire wise men and choose capable aides when one wishes to settle all under the heavens. Since my ascendance, I have put my heart into every aspect of governance, but the places of the three chancellors and the nine ministers are still to be filled.

From my inquiries, I have heard that Master Qiu lives in truth and walks with integrity, is learned and experienced and has studied the laws of the world in depth. As such, the Master is rich in virtue and the Way, with the lofty airs of upright men of old and the graceful demeanor of noble men untainted by guile; and, for a long time, the Master has lived in valleys of rocks, hiding his body and shielding his form.

I have also heard that the Master has been disseminating the teachings of his forebears, drawing men who have attained knowledge in the Way, gathering like clouds in numbers uncountable on the path to seek Immortality. It has come to my knowledge that, since the clash of shields and dagger-axes, the Master has continued to live in the same place of old in Shandong, and my heart has much admired and thought often of the Master.

After reading out what he had written, the Chinese clerk asked, "Is this letter long enough?"

Laughing, Genghis Khan replied, "Yes, it is! Just add that I will send the Han Chinese official Liu Zhonglu to escort him, and insist that he must come."

The man touched his brush to the parchment again:

Of course, I am familiar with the lore of King Wen of Zhou finding Jiang Ziya fishing on the bank of the Wei River and bringing him back in his carriage to assist him at court, and the tale of Liu Bei visiting Zhuge Liang's thatched hermitage thrice to invite the master tactician to aid him in winning the throne.

Frustrated by mountains towering and rivers wide, I am unable to perform the courtesy of bowing low and entreating you in person, but I have descended from the seat imperial and stood to the side, fasted and bathed, before sending my close and trusted officer Liu Zhonglu to travel with the swiftest horses and an unadorned carriage, undeterred by the distance of many thousands of li, to humbly invite the Master to grant us his Immortal steps for a time. Think not of the far-flung sandy desert, but of affairs concerning vast multitudes, and of the skills that would help me preserve this body.

I shall personally wait on your Immoral seat, in hope that the honorable Master will deign to spare a word for me between a cough and a hawk, and I shall be satisfied. And now, this letter merely represents not one ten-thousandth of my intent. I sincerely hope, since the Master is at the forefront of the Great Way, that he would respond always to kindness and oblige the wish of the multitude, and this is why I am sending this invitation.

Once Genghis Khan had heard the additional content, he bestowed on the clerk five *taels* of gold and ordered Guo Jing to write a personal note to add weight to the letter. And, that same night, Liu Zhonglu traveled south to seek out the Taoist.

5

THE FOLLOWING DAY, GENGHIS KHAN GATHERED HIS PRINCES and generals to discuss their campaign in the west. In the sight of his most loyal followers, he named Guo Jing *Noyan* and allocated him a division of ten thousand soldiers. The title was Mongolia's highest official honor, granted only to those closest to and most trusted by the Great Khan.

Guo Jing might have been a capable martial artist, but he was a novice when it came to warfare. So, he turned to his sworn brother Tolui and the Generals Jebe, Subotai and Boroqul for help. He had never been a quick learner, and battle formations were full of subtleties and variations. How could he cram knowledge accrued over years of fighting on the field into a matter of days? Even organizational and administrative duties like inspecting soldiers, preparing provisions and selecting horses and weapons were beyond him. All he could do was to delegate work to the ten captains under his command, while Jebe and Tolui kept an eye on his progress and gave him advice and reminders along the way. After all, there was plenty to be done before one hundred and fifty thousand men were ready to march westward across frozen, barren landscape, and every man, whatever their rank, had their share of responsibility.

A month into the campaign, Guo Jing was feeling more and more uncertain in his role. He was under no illusions about his lack of strategic acumen, and, against an army of a million men, the eighteen Dragon-Subduing Palms and the Nine Yin Manual would be no use at all. One ill-advised command could spell total defeat. Not only would he tarnish Genghis Khan's good name, he would be personally accountable for the deaths of the ten thousand men under his banner. He resolved to resign his commission and fight instead as a regular soldier—a single rider breaking through the enemy lines to cause havoc. Just as he was about to head to Genghis Khan's golden *ger* to give him the news, one of his guards reported that more than a thousand Han Chinese had come to seek an interview with him.

Excited that Qiu Chuji had arrived sooner than expected, Guo Jing rushed out of his tent to find a large group of men in patched rags.

Three stepped forward, each greeting him with a deep bow. Jian, Liang and Surefoot Lu—Elders of the Beggar Clan.

"Have you had any news of Lotus?" Guo Jing asked, after taking a moment to gather his wits.

"We have been searching, but have yet to find the Chief," Surefoot Lu replied. "We are here to offer assistance on your campaign."

"How do you know about it?"

"We heard it from the Quanzhen Sect. A herald from the Great Khan was in contact with them concerning an invitation for Reverend Qiu Chuji."

Guo Jing stared at the wisps of white cloud in the south. The Beggar Clan has eyes and ears everywhere, he said to himself, and even they have no idea where Lotus might be. This can't bode well. The rims of his eyes turned red at this thought, but he quickly mastered his emotions. He ordered his guards to help the beggars settle in, then he went to the golden *ger* to inform Genghis Khan of the new arrivals, who were given permission to serve under his banner. After a moment's internal struggle, the young man broached the subject of his intention to step down.

"No one understands warfare from birth!" the Great Khan barked, clearly furious. "You'll learn after a few battles. How can someone who grew up under my care be afraid of leading troops? How can Genghis Khan have a son-in-law who can't cope with command?"

Guo Jing knew there was nothing more he could say on the matter and returned to his *ger*, weighed down by worry. At nightfall, while posting sentries, he came across Surefoot Lu, and, when the beggar learned of his troubles, he said, "If I'd known, I would have brought a copy of Sun Tzu's *The Art of War* or Grand Duke Jiang's

Six Secret Teachings from the South." He offered a few more words of consolation, then took his leave.

The Beggar Clan Elder's comment reminded Guo Jing that General Yue Fei's final writings were in his possession. *The Secret to Defeating the Jin.* A military treatise! How could he have forgotten? He took the thread-bound volume from the small parcel of clothes and personal belongings he had brought with him from the South and read through the night until noon the next day.

Even though he felt a little tired, he was also invigorated, for the book discussed in detail every aspect of military action—devising strategies, analyzing situations, launching assaults, maintaining a defense, training soldiers, deploying captains, assigning formations and leading guerrilla operations. Whether one was on the march or stationary, or in a secure or precarious position, it offered tactics that could confound an opponent's expectations. Guo Jing had leafed through the text when he was sailing down the Yuan River with Lotus; now that he had a use for it, he began to understand the true value of its contents.

Whenever he reached a section he could not comprehend, he would invite Surefoot Lu to his *ger* and seek his opinion. Each time, the Beggar Clan Elder would say, "I don't have an answer, right now. Let me think on it," and take his leave. Yet, moments later, he would return with a lucid, thorough explanation. Delighted, Guo Jing would ask the beggar follow-up questions, and the same thing would happen again. Surefoot Lu never had a response on the spot, but, once he had stepped outside to consider the issue, he was guaranteed to return with solutions, as though he had an extra store of intellectual power beyond Guo Jing's tent. At first, the young man thought little of it, but, when the same interaction recurred time and again over the next few days, even he sensed that there was something peculiar at work.

One night, Guo Jing pointed out a character he did not recognize. Surefoot Lu glanced at it and said he would step outside to consider the matter.

How odd, Guo Jing said to himself. You either know a character or you don't! How can you work out its meaning by just thinking about it? This isn't a question on the book's content.

Driven by the curiosity common to young men of his age, this commander of ten thousand soldiers sneaked out the back of his *ger* the instant Surefoot Lu left through the main entrance. He lay flat among the tall grass to spy on the beggar, determined to find out the source of his secret knowledge.

The older man scuttled into a nearby small tent, emerging again just moments later. Guo Jing rushed back to his *ger* and pretended that he had never left it.

"I recall now," Surefoot Lu said, and he stated the character's pronunciation and meaning.

"Elder Lu, why don't we invite your teacher to join us?" Guo Jing said with a chuckle.

The reply came a beat too slow. "I have no teacher."

"Let's see, eh?"

Grinning, Guo Jing took the Beggar Clan Elder by the arm and led him to the tent he had just ducked in and out of. The two Clan members standing guard by the entrance coughed as one the moment they saw Surefoot Lu was not alone. Recognizing it was a warning to whoever was inside, Guo Jing ran ahead and flung the tent open, but found it empty. He caught a slight movement of the felt on the far end and lifted the material to look outside. Just grass. Not a soul in sight in the gloom. Guo Jing fixed Surefoot Lu with a suspicious look, but the beggar insisted that he was the sole occupier of the *ger*.

Unconvinced, Guo Jing raised another question about General Yue Fei's writings in hope that he could lure out this mysterious fount of knowledge, but Surefoot Lu replied that it was one he would have to consider overnight. When Guo Jing received the answer the next morning, the only information he could glean from it was that this teacher was most likely a learned man of the *jianghu*, and that they held no ill intent toward him. He had decided to respect their wish to remain anonymous, and, since there was still much to be done to get his troops in order, he soon put the matter out of his mind.

Every night, Guo Jing studied the military tract, and through the day he drilled his soldiers using the methods described in its pages. The Mongol cavalry had always charged in a free-flowing, irregular horde and were unaccustomed to formal battle arrays, but they followed their commander's orders without complaint. In a little more than a month, the supplies for the whole army were ready, and the ten thousand men led by Guo Jing had also learned eight key tactical formations: Shielding Sky, Embracing Earth, Rising Wind, Hanging Cloud, Soaring Dragon, Winged Tiger, Gliding Bird and Coiling Snake. These combat arrangements were invented by the military strategist Zhuge Liang, based on ancient patterns, and General Yue Fei had enhanced them with his own interpretations.

In *The Secret to Defeating the Jin*, General Yue not only explained these formations in detail, he also gave an account of how he had come to appreciate their value on the field. In his early career, he had demonstrated a preference for guerrilla tactics, but his superior Zong Ze warned him: "You are as courageous, wise and talented as the great generals of old, but a fondness for irregular battle plans makes you vulnerable."

Once Yue Fei had mastered the art of tactical deployment, he came to a conclusion that had Zong Ze nodding in approval: "It is standard practice to assume a formation before battle, but tactics are only as good as the men you command." As General Yue gained experience fighting campaign after campaign, he realized that battles could not be won by simply deploying existing structures. He began to drill his soldiers relentlessly, until their familiarity with the maneuvers allowed them to adapt them as the situation required, giving them a tactical edge that all but ensured victory.

6

On a brisk, crisp morning, under a jade-blue sky stretching ten thousand *li*, fifteen divisions of ten thousand men lined up in neat rows on the steppe. Genghis Khan made offerings to the heavens and earth, and addressed his troops.

"Stones have no flesh, human life is finite," he cried. "My hair and beard have grown white. I may not return from this campaign. So, today, I will name the son who will raise my banner after I am gone."

The Khan's generals stirred, eager for the announcement. Many had fought hundreds of battles at the conqueror's side, giving their youth and blood to forge his empire, and for the most part they had likewise gone gray.

Genghis Khan continued: "Jochi, you are my firstborn. Who should I name as my heir?"

The Prince's heart skipped a beat. It was not a question he was expecting and not one he could answer comfortably. Brave, warlike, the eldest son with the most battle honors, he had always assumed that he would be the natural choice to ascend the throne.

It was the fiery Chagatai who answered. "*Huh!* Let Jochi speak? Let this Merkit bastard rule over us?"

In Genghis Khan's early days, when his followers were few, the Merkits had abducted his wife. By the time he rescued her, several years later, she had given birth to Jochi, but the Khan had raised him as his own blood.

Jochi threw himself at Chagatai and seized the front of his robe. "Father has never treated me as an outsider, and yet you insult me thus! You're no better than me, you arrogant cur! I challenge you. If you best me at archery, I'll hack off my thumb. If I lose in a duel, let me stay in the dirt forever." He then turned to Genghis Khan. "Father, give us permission to fight!"

The brothers had always had a fractious relationship, and now, with each clutching a fistful of the other's clothes, it seemed certain they would come to blows. The Khan's generals rushed over to restrain the pair. Bogurchi took hold of Jochi's arms, while Muqali dragged Chagatai back.

Genghis Khan was unusually subdued, reminded of how helpless he had been, so young and so weak that he could not even protect his own wife, thus sowing the seeds of the present discord. When he heard the generals chiding Chagatai for his rash words, for bringing up painful, buried ghosts of the past, he issued a calm but firm command: "Let go, both of you. Jochi is my firstborn, and I have always loved and valued him. There is nothing more for anyone to say on this matter."

Grudgingly, Chagatai released his brother. "It is known that Jochi is strong and capable, but he has none of Third Brother's finer qualities. Let Ogedai be your heir."

"Jochi, what say you?"

The question made it clear to Jochi that he would never be Khan. But he had always been friendly with Ogedai, and given the younger man's charitable nature, he would not have to fear future plots against his life.

"Excellency, I concur," he said, accepting his fate.

Tolui, the Fourth Prince, had no objection either, but Ogedai declined the honor.

"Do not refuse me," Genghis Khan said to his third son. "You may not be as skilled in warfare as your older brothers, but you are kind and generous. When you are the Great Khan, you will keep the peace between your princes and generals. So long as we don't turn against each other, we cannot be vanquished. Do not look so troubled. You are more than worthy."

A feast was held to celebrate the naming of the Crown Prince and everyone drank late into the night. By the time he reached his *ger*, Guo Jing was himself a little tipsy, but, before he could undress for bed, one of his guards rushed in.

"General! The First Prince and Second Prince have called their men to arms!"

"Tell the Great Khan immediately!"

"We can't wake him. He's passed out from the wine."

Jochi and Chagatai both had many loyal followers who had been fighting under their banners for years. If they were to meet in battle, it would do irreparable damage to the core force of the Mongolian army. The Princes had almost come to blows before the Great Khan during the day, and now, with their wits addled by drink, Guo Jing knew it was a clash he had little hope of averting. He paced around, slapping himself on the forehead and wishing he could think of a plan.

"If Lotus were here, she'd tell me what to do," he mumbled with mounting anxiety as he listened to the rumble of distant war cries. Any moment now, the Princes' men would be plunging their blades into their own countrymen.

Just then, Surefoot Lu rushed into the *ger* and handed him a note:

Keep the two forces apart with Coiling Snake.
Round up those who resist with Winged Tiger.

In the past weeks, Guo Jing had studied *The Secret to Defeating the Jin* so thoroughly that he knew it almost by heart. One glance at the message, and he could already visualize how he should deploy his soldiers to prevent bloodshed, but why had he not come up with the idea himself? What was the point of learning battle tactics when he was too slow-witted to apply them?

Guo Jing ordered a bugle to be sounded. Although his men were still half drunk from the feast, the iron discipline of the Mongolian army was drilled into their very bones. At the first blast of the horn, they were pulling on their armor and mounting their horses, and, before long, ten thousand men were lined up in orderly ranks.

Three beats of the drums, followed by a resounding fanfare. The vanguard roared, then spurred northeast, leading the charge. Several *li* later, a scout returned to report that the Princes' forces were drawn up in battle lines and the first skirmishes had already broken out. The war whoops of *ho-hu, ho-hu* were growing louder.

Am I too late? Can I stop them? Guo Jing asked himself as he signaled to his captains. On his command, ten thousand men instantly split into dozens of companies and began to arrange themselves in the Coiling Snake formation.

Three battalions from the Right-Rear Earth Axis company charged ahead, and the same number of troops from the Right-Fore Earth Axis drew back to form the snake's tail. Units from the Right-Rear Celestial Balance, the Right Earth Rear-Surge, the Right Celestial Rear-Surge, the North-Westerly Wind and the North-Easterly Wind took up positions to the right of this central force, mirrored by an identical deployment on the left flank.

By now, Jochi and Chagatai's advanced guards were already crossing swords. Guo Jing's troops drove a wedge between the two factions, separating them. Each of the Princes commanded more than twenty thousand men, but not a single soldier on either side had ever seen such a tight formation move so rapidly. Even seasoned fighters hesitated and began looking around in confusion for fresh orders.

"Are you here to help me or the Merkit bastard Jochi?" Chagatai yelled.

Ignoring the question, Guo Jing signaled to his flag-bearer, and the Coiling Snake morphed seamlessly into a Winged Tiger. Now the main strength of the formation faced to the left, led by four units from the Right-Fore Celestial Balance. Further companies moved to outflank Chagatai's force, while two units from the Left Celestial Fore-Surge stood ready to repel an assault from Jochi's forces.

At last, Chagatai caught a clear view of the banner of the commander who had dared come between him and Jochi. "I always knew southern barbarians weren't to be trusted," he hissed.

The Second Prince ordered his soldiers to attack Guo Jing's men, but the Winged Tiger, devised by the military tactician and general Han Xin during the decisive battle at Gaixia against the warlord Xiang

Yu, was adaptable, powerful and difficult to outflank. Though it was widely held, as decreed by Sun Tzu, that a commander should only consider encircling an opposing force if he outnumbered them ten to one, the flexible Winged Tiger formation defied this rule. A smaller army could employ it to get the better of a much larger opponent.

Guo Jing's soldiers began to weave through gaps in Chagatai's ranks in small units, making it difficult for them to determine how many men and horses they were up against. Fear and doubt started to spread through the Second Prince's troops as they were cut off from support and forced into isolated, disorganized groups, their already weak fighting spirit waning fast. After all, they understood they had been ordered to attack their own tribesmen, friends and brothers-in-arms, and feared the Great Khan's wrath.

"We are Mongolians. We are brothers. We shouldn't turn our blades on each other," Guo Jing's deputy cried. "Throw down your weapons if you want to keep your heads."

The majority of Chagatai's men dismounted at once and tossed their sabers aside, but a thousand of the Second Prince's most loyal and trusted fighters, following their commander's lead, charged at the heart of Guo Jing's formation.

A gong sounded three times, and eight companies of Guo Jing's soldiers galloped over from all directions to intercept Chagatai's small force. Ropes were stretched out across the ground to trip the horses, sending men flying from their steeds. Each of Chagatai's defiant soldiers was subdued by three or four of Guo Jing's men and pressed into the ground, their hands tied behind their backs.

Delighted to see Chagatai's troops quelled, Jochi urged his horse forward and hailed Guo Jing, but his call was drowned out by a blast of the horn. Guo Jing's rear guard was suddenly his front line, and they were closing fast on Jochi's men. The First Prince had studied tactics, but he had never seen anything like this. He ordered his riders not to engage, as he watched Guo Jing's force split into twelve groups, but now, instead of advancing, they were retreating. Jochi was flummoxed. He had no way of knowing that the mercurial formation was inspired by the twelve hours of the day. The groups—*Zi* of Great Black, *Chou* of Foe Crushed, *Yin* of Left Breakthrough, *Mao* of Green Serpent, *Chen* of Evil Smashed, *Si* of Forward Surge, *Wu* of Great Red, *Wei* of Advance Spur, *Shen* of Right Strike, *You* of White Cloud, *Xu* of Victory Claimed, and *Hai* of Rear Guard—alternated between launching assaults and holding their ground, charging back and forth in unpredictable patterns, always confounding expectations. Sometimes the companies on the right surged toward the left, and at other times those on the left cut across to the right. In no time at all, Jochi's ranks were broken, morale shattered, and any who resisted were subdued in the same way as Chagatai's loyal followers.

Outfought and outthought by Guo Jing, the Princes turned their minds to the indignities they had subjected the young man to at their first meeting, almost fifteen years before. Jochi had whipped the six-year-old Guo Jing half to death and Chagatai had set his mastiffs on him. Surely he would now seize his chance to take revenge. As their heads cleared, the Princes began to rue their drunken impulse and dread the punishment their father would mete out.

Although Guo Jing had broken up the battle and captured the two culprits, he was unsure if he had put himself in greater trouble, for he understood his place as an outsider. He was about to seek out Ogedai and Tolui for advice, when he heard a bugle's call. The Great Khan's white yak-hair banner, illuminated by torchlight, was approaching.

Genghis Khan had been incensed when he was at last roused from his drunken stupor to be greeted by the news that his two eldest sons were leading their armies against one another. He galloped over in his nightclothes, without stopping to arm himself, his loose hair flowing in the wind.

To his great surprise, he found the two forces sitting on the ground in neat rows, watched over by Guo Jing's cavalrymen. The Princes sat astride their steeds, but their helmets and weapons had been taken away, and they were each surrounded by eight warriors with gleaming sabers. On the gallop over, he had expected to find a bloody scene—his finest soldiers slaughtering each other and his two eldest sons slain. He had not imagined that such a disaster could be averted without casualties.

After hearing Guo Jing's account of the event, Genghis Khan summoned all the generals, publicly chastised Jochi and Chagatai, then he turned to his future son-in-law.

"You told me you knew nothing of leading armies, but you have done a greater deed tonight than if you had vanquished the entire Jin force. If we fail to capture a city, we can lick our wounds and return another day, but if I had lost my sons and my best soldiers, nothing we could do would bring them back."

The Great Khan rewarded Guo Jing with a generous gift of gold, silver and cattle. The young man took nothing for himself and gave the bounty to his soldiers, who rewarded his generosity with deafening cheers. Later that day, a stream of generals dropped by his *ger* with congratulations, and, when the last of them left, Guo Jing heeded his old mentor Jebe's advice and called on Jochi and Chagatai to apologize for any affront that he might have caused. He need not have worried. The Princes were genuinely grateful for his prompt and decisive action. After years of bad blood and resentment, they were at last warming to the young man, though the animosity between the two brothers still bubbled away beneath the surface.

When Guo Jing was alone at last in his *ger*, he took out Surefoot Lu's note and studied the calligraphy. Awkward, clumsy, likely to be the beggar's hand. Questions began to fill his head.

I've never mentioned the formations by name to Elder Lu, he reminded himself. And I've never asked him to explain them either. Has he somehow been reading General Yue's writings behind my back?

He decided to send for the beggar and discover the truth.

"Elder Lu, if you're interested in warfare, I can lend you the book."

Surefoot Lu laughed. "I have no desire to be a general, and I don't need military tactics to lead my brethren. Your book is of no use to me."

"Then how did you know about the Coiling Snake and Winged Tiger formations?" Guo Jing pointed at the note.

"You told me. Have you forgotten?"

Guo Jing knew it was not true, but he could not imagine what Surefoot Lu was trying to hide from him.

The next day, Genghis Khan summoned the Princes and generals to inform them of their roles in the upcoming campaign. Chagatai and Ogedai were to lead the vanguard, while Jochi was given the left flank and Guo Jing the right. Each of these armies would be made up of three divisions of ten thousand men. Genghis Khan would preside over the main army of sixty thousand with Tolui. Every soldier was allotted several horses, which they rode in turn to preserve the animals' strength. Officers and generals were given a greater number of steeds, so this army of one hundred and fifty thousand men marched with more than a million war horses, as well camels and horse-drawn carts carrying provisions for men and fodder for beasts. They traveled with more livestock than could be counted, for the troops were to venture deep into the western wilderness and they had to bring sufficient supplies for the whole journey.

At the urging of drums and bugles, the vanguard—thirty thousand men and many more horses—took the first steps westward, followed by the rest of the army. The Mongol riders journeyed farther into Khwarazm's territory than ever before, capturing cities and settlements with the ease with which one splits bamboo along its grain. They had mastered the art of forging and casting iron, which had reached them from the Song and Jin Empires, and were able to produce weapons and armor of unparalleled quality. Taken together with Genghis Khan's brilliance on the battlefield, it made them an unstoppable force. Shah Muhammad might have more troops under his command, but, man for man, they were no match for the Mongolians.

CHAPTER NINE

DESCENDING
FROM THE HEAVENS

I

AS THE MONGOL HOST MOVED WEST, WINNING GLORY ON THE field, taking cities and quelling foes, Guo Jing was gaining in confidence as a general. By the time the army reached the Sughd River, his initial doubts were almost forgotten. Nonetheless, when his men had finished making camp, Guo Jing retired to his *ger* to study military tactics, as he had every evening since he had assumed command.

Suddenly, a quiet flapping noise reached his ears. The tent's flies parted. A man darted in, followed by a few heavy-footed sentries. The intruder waved his hand, and, though the tip of his finger merely grazed the soldiers charging after him, it was enough to send them sprawling, one after another.

The trespasser cackled and turned to Guo Jing, his face catching the candlelight.

Viper Ouyang.

Guo Jing leaped to his feet. "Where's Lotus?" He could not decide if he was shocked or relieved to find the Venom in this far-flung foreign land, thousands of *li* away from the Central Plains.

Does it mean she . . . He dared not get his hopes up.

"That's what I've come to ask you. Where is the wench? Hand her over!"

A smile spread across Guo Jing's face. Lotus is alive! She escaped!

"Where is she?" Viper Ouyang demanded.

"Wasn't she with you? You took her in Jiaxing. Is she . . . well?" Guo Jing bowed, tears of joy and relief rolling down his cheeks.

Could he really have no idea? Puzzled, Viper Ouyang sat down cross-legged on the rug, as if it was his own *ger*. He knew the young man was too principled to lie to him, but all the clues indicated that Lotus Huang was hiding somewhere among this army.

Guo Jing, meanwhile, had dried his eyes, unlocked the guards' acupressure points, and called for drinks to be brought.

Viper picked up a bowl of *koumiss* and drained it. He had decided to tell the truth. "I found the wench hiding in the Iron Spear Temple in Jiaxing, but she ran away not long after."

"How?" Guo Jing was thrilled. Lotus was the cleverest person he had ever known. Of course she would find a way to escape.

"We were at Roaming Cloud Manor on Lake Tai . . ." Viper trailed off and gritted his teeth. "*Pah!* . . . What more can I say? She got away." The proud martial Master could not bear to explain how he had been outwitted by a teenage girl.

"Oh, thank you, thank you!" Those few words were enough for Guo Jing, for they confirmed that Lotus was safe. He could never forgive the Venom of the West for killing five of his *shifus*, but he was grateful that he had not harmed Lotus.

"Why thank me? I'm still hunting her. She got lucky and slipped away from me like a hare, but I made sure she couldn't get back to Peach Blossom Island. I tracked her as far as the Mongolian border . . . well, since you're here, she must be nearby—"

Guo Jing's heart leaped. "You've seen her?"

"Would I be talking to you now if I had? I've been watching your troops, day and night, but I haven't seen so much as a shadow resembling her. Tell me, where in hell have you hidden her?"

". . . You've been watching us . . . and I had no idea . . ." Guo Jing stammered.

"Why would a mighty general notice a lowly soldier from the Western Regions in the Celestial Fore-Surge company?"

The idea that Viper Ouyang had been lurking among his men sent a chill through Guo Jing, though he had to admit that the martial Master, with his angular facial features and knowledge of the languages of the Western Regions, would blend in very well, especially since the army had been taking prisoners and recruiting surrendered soldiers along the way.

Had he wanted to kill me, I'd be dead already, Guo Jing said to himself. Then he asked, with an unmistakable note of hope in his voice, "Why do you think Lotus is here?"

"You couldn't have subdued the Khan's two sons or taken so many cities without her help. Since she won't show herself . . . well, I'll have to use you to get to her."

"I want nothing more than to see Lotus again, but why would I let you near her?"

"You don't have a choice. You might be a general with a large army, but I –" he sneered—"can come and go as I like. Who can keep me out of your *ger*?"

Viper took Guo Jing's silence as an acknowledgment of his words and continued: "Let's make a deal."

"What kind of deal?"

"I promise not to touch a single hair on her head, if you tell me where she is. Or, I can look for her myself, and when I find her . . . I can't guarantee I will be so . . . pleasant."

Guo Jing knew this was no empty threat, and, since Lotus had not been able to return to Peach Blossom Island, it would only be a matter of time before he found her.

"Very well," he said after a pause. "We'll make a pact. But not on your terms."

"What do you propose?"

"Master Ouyang, your kung fu is far superior to mine, but I am much younger. One day, you will grow old and grow weak, and you'll be outmatched."

Guo Jing had previously called Viper "Uncle Ouyang" out of respect, but, with his *shifus'* blood on the Venom's hands, he would never address him with such familiarity again.

Viper Ouyang was startled by Guo Jing's comment, for it had never crossed his mind that he should consider the day when his physical prowess began to decline. Perhaps the boy was smarter than he seemed.

"And?"

"And, one day, I will find you, even if you hide at the heavens' edge. And I *will* avenge my *shifus.*"

"Then I should kill you now, before I get old and weak."

Cackling wildly, Viper Ouyang took one step to widen his stance, crouched, and sent both palms hurtling at Guo Jing with a mighty surge of inner strength that could topple mountains and upend oceans.

Guo Jing shifted his footing a fraction, avoiding the blow, and countered with a Dragon in the Field. By now, he had mastered the Transforming Muscles, Forging Bones section of the Nine Yin Manual, and the power of those techniques had been boosted by Sole Light's interpretation of the Manual's final chapter and his growing familiarity with the other kung fu techniques described in the martial tract. His internal force had developed a new purity and strength.

The Venom threw up his arms and blocked Guo Jing's attack head-on. He was no stranger to Count Seven Hong's signature repertoire, Dragon-Subduing Palm, and knew the young man's *neigong* was no match for his; yet, still, a quiver went through his body at the contact. He had been careless and underestimated his opponent. It had almost cost him dearly.

This boy will catch up with me long before I am old and weak, Viper Ouyang thought warily as he swiped his left hand at Guo Jing.

The young man swerved away and thrust out his palm to parry.

This time, Viper avoided a direct confrontation and twirled his wrist to dissipate the force of the boy's counter. But, though it appeared to be a straightforward defensive move, it concealed a sting in its tail. As the Venom's hand hooked over Guo Jing's, it unleashed a great burst of power into Guo Jing's face, compelling him to push back with his right arm.

Viper was reminded of the time they had fought palm to palm in the cave behind the waterfall, in the grounds of the Song Emperor's palace in Lin'an. Their two inner forces had clashed directly then, and, of course, his had proved stronger. He could sense that Guo Jing now had far greater powers of endurance; though, if it came to a battle of attrition, the young man would still end up dead or seriously injured.

So, the Martial Great tried the same maneuver he had pulled in the cave, luring his opponent into a trap. Just as he expected, Guo Jing drew his palm back slightly—a clear sign he was weakening. Viper summoned more strength to his arms, only to find his hand slipping. His young foe had evaded the brunt of the attack.

Roaring in fury, Viper sent forth a burst of *neigong* power, launching his palm into Guo Jing's chest as he made a silent promise. You will die today, boy!

And yet, before his fingertips could reach their target, Viper noticed that Guo Jing had lifted his left arm horizontally over his chest to guard it. The next thing he saw was the young man's right index finger spearing toward the side of his head. At the Great Sun pressure point on his temple.

Yang in Ascendance!

Guo Jing had seen Reverend Sole Light employ this technique to heal Lotus, and, in this desperate moment, he sought to emulate it, using the Competing Hands method to launch two different moves at the same time, guarding against Viper's attack while probing with his own.

It just so happened that Yang in Ascendance was the one skill that could counter the power of Viper's deadly Exploding Toad kung fu. How could the Venom fail to be alarmed by Guo Jing's imitation?

Leaping back, he yelled, "Even that old bore Duan Zhixing wishes to make trouble for me?"

In truth, Guo Jing's jab only superficially resembled the King of the South's signature move, for he had not been taught the skill and had no grasp of its subtleties. Moreover, it was not imbued with Cosmos *neigong*, so it could do no harm to the store of energy, accumulated over many years, that Viper used to launch the Exploding Toad.

From a safe distance, the Venom asked himself why Guo Jing had given up after a single attempt. Maybe the boy has not learned the whole repertoire? The thought reassured the martial Master, and he raised his palms. He held one hand above the other in front of his chest and let his energy pour forth for a brief moment before withdrawing it.

An attack with explosive speed.

Guo Jing threw himself to the side, his body reacting quicker than his brain to dodge the blow.

Crack! A low table behind the young man shattered.

In control once more, Viper Ouyang aimed a follow-up palm thrust. Just then, a gust of wind whipped into his back. Sneering at the attempted ambush, the Martial Great kicked out with his left foot without turning—making contact with the leg that was sweeping into him, striking it on the shin.

The assailant was sent flying, but, to the Venom's great surprise, he failed to break the man's bone. He snapped around. Three bearded vagrants stood in the *ger*'s entrance. The Beggar Clan Elders: Lu, Jian and Liang.

Surefoot Lu had recovered from the exchange with Viper Ouyang and was now clasping arms with Jian and Liang in a wall formation, the Beggar Clan's technique for overcoming a stronger opponent by making use of their numbers. Guo Jing and Lotus had been given a taste of its potency at the Beggar Clan Assembly at Jun Hill, when dozens of human walls, formed by hundreds of Clan members, had almost driven them off a cliff.

Viper Ouyang had never fought these three men before, but, judging from the strength contained in the kick he had deflected, they were a force to be reckoned with. He reappraised the situation: he could easily handle Guo Jing in single combat, but if, these stinking beggars insisted on meddling, it would be more trouble than it was worth . . .

"Your kung fu has improved a lot, lad." He let out his metallic laugh and sat down on the rug in the same cross-legged posture as before. "So, tell me about your terms." He resumed the conversation as if no blows had been exchanged and the beggars were not present.

"You want Lotus to explain the Nine Yin Manual," Guo Jing said. "Whether she's willing to help you is up to her. You must not harm a single hair on her head."

Viper chuckled. "Why would I, if she's compliant? After all, who wants a quarrel with Old Heretic Huang? And the silver-tongued little thing makes an amusing companion. However, if she insists on being difficult, it is only fair to use a little . . . persuasion."

"No!" Guo Jing shook his head.

"What do I get in return?"

"The next three times you fall into my hands, I will spare your life."

Viper Ouyang rose, drawing himself up to his full height. A grating, high-pitched laugh erupted from his belly, ringing out across the steppe. Hundreds of horses whinnied uneasily.

Guo Jing merely fixed his eyes on the Venom and said in a quiet voice, "It's not a joke. You know our paths will cross again."

The Martial Great had not, in truth, found Guo Jing's words amusing. He was wary of this boy, who knew the secrets of the Nine Yin Manual, and whose kung fu improved by leaps and bounds each time they met, because of this knowledge. This was a foe he could not afford to underestimate. And so, he laughed and calculated his options.

"Why would I, Viper Ouyang, need mercy from a runt like you?" The Venom paused. "But, so be it. We shall see."

Guo Jing reached his hand out. "The word of a gentleman—"

"—is as true as a horseman's whip."

Sniggering, Viper slapped his hand against the open palm, before flipping it around, allowing Guo Jing to strike the back of it, and then with a quick flick of his wrist, their hands met for the third time as the pact was sealed with three ceremonial claps, in the Song custom.

The Venom was about to question Guo Jing further about Lotus, when he caught a fleeting form through the gap between the *ger*'s flies. Recognizing the figure's swift footwork, he rushed outside, but there was not even a shadow in sight. He cast one final look at Guo Jing. "I will be back within ten days. Let's see who spares whose life then." And, in a flash, his cackle was jangling from more than a dozen *zhang* away.

Elders Lu, Jian and Liang stared in wonder, finding astonishment in each other's eyes. They now understood why this man's kung fu was ranked alongside that of their former chief, Count Seven Hong.

2

"NONSENSE!" SUREFOOT LU EXCLAIMED AFTER GUO JING told them that Viper Ouyang thought Lotus was hiding in the army. "How would *we* not realize our Chief was here? After all—"

"Actually, I think it makes sense." Guo Jing sat down and rested his chin in his hand. He was speaking slower than usual. "I've often felt Lotus was by my side. Every time I was out of my depth, I was given the cleverest advice, like she was with me. But, however much I miss her, I don't get to see her." Tears were threatening to fall.

Surefoot Lu consoled the young man. "Take heart. This separation is temporary. You will be reunited."

"I've wronged her. She probably doesn't want to see me ever again. I don't know what I can do to make amends."

The three Elders exchanged glances, but made no reply.

"I don't mind if she won't speak to me," Guo Jing continued. "I just want to see her one more time."

"We should let you rest," Elder Jian said. "As for Viper Ouyang . . . We can discuss tomorrow how to deal with him when he returns."

In the morning, the army resumed their march west, and, at sundown, they set up camp again. Surefoot Lu came into Guo Jing's *ger* and laid a scroll on the table. "I came across this painting in the South, but I don't know how to appreciate this kind of art. I thought it might find a better home with the General than with a humble beggar such as myself."

Guo Jing unrolled the artwork and stared agape at the image. A young woman sat at a loom, weaving, her hair fastened with a floral hairpin. She had Lotus's features, but she looked drawn and waxen, her eyes vacant, her brow creased. His gaze lingered on her face for some time before turning to the two lyric poems inscribed alongside the image:

> *For the seventh time the loom is ready,*
> *The silkworm spits the last thread of its life,*
> *Let not silk sheer or twilled be cut wantonly.*
> *Sundered for no reason,*
> *The colored phoenix and its immortal mate,*
> *Split apart on different sides of the robe.*

> *For the ninth time the loom is ready,*
> *Flying as one, leaves conjoined, branches entwined,*
> *For the fickle, partings aplenty since times bygone.*
> *From the beginning to the end,*
> *Through one strand of silk,*
> *Are the hearts linked and interwoven.*

The verses were modeled after the one Madam Ying had embroidered on the handkerchief she once gave Zhou Botong, but the sentiment conveyed was more heart-wrenching and the allusions more subtle. Guo Jing could not fathom the depths of every word, but the meanings of the more straightforward lines were obvious enough.

He was certain that the painting was Lotus's work, but the key question remained: how had Elder Lu come by it? He looked up to ask him, but the beggar had withdrawn from the *ger* while he was reading. Guo Jing immediately sent for him and was told that it was purchased from a bookseller in the South.

Now even Guo Jing could tell that something was amiss. What use would a man like Surefoot Lu—a beggar, after all—have for such a painting? And why did the woman look so much like Lotus? The only plausible explanation was that Surefoot Lu was hiding something from him, but Guo Jing was reluctant to question him further. He decided to bide his time.

As these thoughts were running through Guo Jing's mind, Elder Jian entered the *ger* and said in a low voice, "I just saw a shadowy figure flitting past the northeast corner of the camp. Viper Ouyang may be coming tonight."

"Good. The four of us will wait for him here," Guo Jing replied.

"Might I propose a plan of action?"

"Of course."

"We dig a deep pit in the ground here, and have twenty men stand ready outside with bags of sand. If the Venom falls into our trap, we'll make sure he can't get out again."

Guo Jing smiled. It was a brilliant idea. Given Viper Ouyang's arrogance and disdain for others, he would not suspect such a simple, old-fashioned ruse. Guo Jing let the three Elders take charge and called in soldiers to start the digging. When the pit was ready, they covered it with a rug and placed a light wooden chair over it, while twenty soldiers lay in wait outside with sandbags. It was common for armies advancing through arid terrain to dig wells for water, so what they had done did not draw any attention.

Once everything was ready, Guo Jing settled down to wait by candlelight, but Viper Ouyang did not make an appearance. In the morning, the troops were on the move again, and, as evening fell, when Guo Jing's *ger* was being set up, another team of men prepared a second trap. Again, there was no sign of Viper Ouyang.

The fourth night. Guo Jing sat in his tent, listening to the tolls of the *diaodou*, a cooking pan that doubled as the nightwatchman's gong. His thoughts were surging and ebbing to its undulating tones when a rustling sound like a falling leaf broke the pattern, and Viper Ouyang's unmistakeable cackle filled the air. Moments later, he strode in and sat down on the chair over the rug.

With a clatter and a crash, the Venom of the West hit the bottom of the pit, crushing his seat beneath him.

Even a martial Master of Viper's stature could not overcome the shock of falling into a narrow shaft, seven or eight *zhang* deep, quickly enough to jump straight out. And, at Guo Jing's signal, the soldiers rushed in and threw forty large sandbags into the pit.

Surefoot Lu chuckled merrily. "Just as Chief Huang—" He caught Elder Jian's glare and swallowed the rest of his words.

"What did you say?" Guo Jing asked brusquely.

"Chief Hong. I meant Chief Hong. It would tickle Chief Hong to see the Venom like this."

Guo Jing eyed Surefoot Lu suspiciously, but shouts of alarm outside the *ger* cut his interrogation short. He rushed out with the Beggar Clan Elders and found his guards staring with apprehension at something on the ground. He pushed through to see a mound of sand growing higher. He understood instantly—Viper Ouyang was using his kung fu to burrow out!—and ordered a troop of horsemen to ride over the pile of loose earth.

The Venom's strength, however potent, was no match for the weight of dozens of cavalrymen on galloping horses. The first heap began to collapse in on itself as a new one bubbled up elsewhere. The horsemen hastened over to trample the rising ground. Several more dunes emerged, only to be flattened, then all was quiet for some time. Could it be that Viper Ouyang had suffocated?

It was close to midnight. Guo Jing ordered the riders to dismount and dig for the Venom's body. A dozen soldiers surrounded the location of the last mound with torches, while the same number of men worked with shovels. When the pit was one *zhang* deep, they found

Viper Ouyang, stiff and unmoving. It was staggering how far the Martial Great had managed to tunnel from the *ger*, with very little air and just his bare hands to work with—like a mole. It was a testament to his great inner strength, and, for soldiers who knew no kung fu, it was an almost unimaginable feat. In awe, they pulled him out of the ground and laid him down on his back.

Surefoot Lu placed his hand under Viper Ouyang's nose. Nothing. He touched the martial Master's chest. Still warm. The beggar shouted for iron chains. And, with the words still hanging in the air, the Venom drew a few quick but undetectable breaths, leaped to his feet, and seized Surefoot Lu's right wrist with a howl of rage, locking his pulse to cut off his strength. Realizing that he could not break through beneath the pounding hooves, he had decided to feign death, since Guo Jing would be certain to dig him out. Once he was above ground, he reasoned, he would have a fighting chance of getting away.

The soldiers were horrified to see the stranger rise from the dead, but Guo Jing had kept his guard up all along. At the first sign of movement, he pressed his left palm against the Kiln Path acupoint on the martial Master's back and thrust his right into the Spinal Center point on his waist.

Although unsettled, the Venom readied himself to swipe a backhand slash at Guo Jing. However, before he could even lift his arm, he felt a faint numbness spreading through his body. He cursed. The boy would not have got near his vital pressure points if he had not been half crushed by the weight of the sand and exhausted from trying to burrow his way out.

A cold fear gripped him. If he lets his strength flow, my inner organs will be turn into pulp. Even if I keep his hands away from my pressure points, I can't be sure that I can subdue him in my weakened state.

With that thought, Viper Ouyang let go of Surefoot Lu and concentrated on standing upright and steady to mask the lethargy in his limbs.

Guo Jing was the first to speak, breaking the hushed silence surrounding them. "Master Ouyang, have you seen Miss Huang?"

"I caught a glimpse of her earlier. That's why I'm here."

"Are you sure?"

"Could you have come up with this scheme without the vixen's help?"

Guo Jing wavered for a moment. "Go on your way. I said I would spare you."

With a light shove, Guo Jing sent the martial Master more than one *zhang* away—a necessary precaution, given the Venom's unscrupulous nature.

Viper Ouyang was content to keep his distance for now, simply fixing his young opponent with a baleful stare. "It is not my habit to use weapons against a junior in single combat," he said in a frosty tone, "but, since the devious little witch is helping you, I am going to make an exception. I will be back within ten days with my Serpent Staff. You have witnessed the power of the poisonous snakes inside. Don't say I didn't warn you."

Guo Jing watched the Venom glide off into the darkness with the aid of his lightness *qinggong*. A northerly gust of wind swept across the steppe and he shivered involuntarily, though whether at the chilly air or from memories of the Serpent Staff's might as a weapon, he could not tell. He cast his mind over the armed fighting techniques he had learned from the Six Freaks of the South, but none could be considered a supreme kung fu and wielding weapons had never been his strong point. Still, facing the Serpent Staff barehanded was unthinkable.

He gazed into the night sky, at a loss what to do. Snowflakes began to drift down, gleaming in the moonlight. He headed back into his *ger* and was struck by the bitter cold inside. An attendant was stoking the coal fire; all throughout the camp, soldiers were busy bringing their horses into the tents for shelter.

This unexpected drop in temperature caught the Beggar Clan members out, for they had not brought furs or warm winter clothes with them and had nothing but their *neigong* power to keep them warm. Guo Jing gave orders for sheep to be slaughtered and skinned. There was no time to treat the pelts, so, once the blood had been cleaned off, they were distributed to the beggars.

3

IT WAS BITING COLD THE NEXT MORNING. THE SNOW HAD been packed into ice overnight. The Khwarazm army took advantage of the extreme weather to mount an assault, but Guo Jing was prepared, breaking their charge with the Soaring Dragon formation and hunting the survivors through the night.

Although the Mongolians were victorious, it did not lessen the harsh realities faced by soldiers as they battled in the icy and windy Western Regions, which have captured many a poet's imagination over the centuries:

> *The general keeps his armor on all the time,*
> *The soldiers' dagger-axes clank in the night march,*
> *The wind like a razor cuts and slashes the face.*
> *The steed's mane weighed by snow, their sweat turns to steam,*
> *The warhorse's coat hardens into ice, hiding the clipped pattern,*
> *Inside the tent the writing ink freezes on the inkstone.*

> *The fighting spirit of enemy soldiers soars to the sky,*
> *White bones on the battlefield twine with roots of weeds.*
> *In Jianhe, the wind urgent, the snow falls fast,*
> *In Shakou, the stones cold, the horses' hooves split.*

The piercing cold did not affect Guo Jing much, since he had grown up in the northern deserts, but how could Lotus—if she really was with the army—endure the bitter weather, when she had only known the mild climate of the South? The thought of her discomfort ate away at the young General, so, the day after the surprise attack, when the march was halted for the night, he went in secret around the whole camp, checking every *ger*, but he did not find a single sign of her presence.

With a heavy heart, Guo Jing went back to his tent, and was surprised to find his men digging a pit, under Surefoot Lu's supervision.

"Surely Viper Ouyang is too cunning to fall for the same trick twice?"

"Well, the Venom will expect us to come up with a different ploy, so we're giving him another taste of what he enjoyed so much." The Beggar Clan Elder then added mysteriously, "In artifice there is substance, in substance there is artifice. Whether artifice or substance, it cannot be augured."

Guo Jing shot Surefoot Lu a sideways glance. The man who said he had no need of military tactics to lead beggars was now quoting battlefield wisdom.

"But, if we try to catch him out with sand again, he will find a way around it," Surefoot Lu went on, paying Guo Jing's reaction no heed. "So, this time, we'll use boiling water."

Guo Jing recalled passing a cluster of cauldrons when he had entered the *ger*. He stepped outside again. The Beggar Clan Elders had arranged for twenty large iron pots to be set up outside. Dozens of soldiers were bustling around them. Some were building fires, while others broke large mounds of packed snow into smaller chunks with axes and shoveled them into the cauldrons.

"Wouldn't that kill him?"

"You promised to spare his life the next three times he falls into your hands. If he's boiled alive by scalding water, he didn't exactly fall into *your hands*, and no one could accuse you of breaking your word."

When the pit was ready, it was masked by the rug, on which a wooden chair was placed, just as before. Outside, fires were lit and the snow started to melt in the cauldrons, though the air was so cold that thin layers of ice would form on the surface if the fuel was not replenished fast enough.

"More firewood here! Quick!" Surefoot Lu shouted as a dark figure flashed across the white landscape.

Viper Ouyang parted the *ger*'s flaps with the Serpent Staff and strode onto the rug, crying, "I don't fear your traps!" Then he plunged, rug, chair and all, uttering a string of curses.

The Beggar Clan Elders listened in alarm to the commotion inside the tent. They had not anticipated the Venom would come so early in the night. The snow in the pots had only just melted; it was not even warm enough to use as bathwater. There were no sandbags close at hand. And they knew the martial Master could leap out of the pit with the same ease as he might turn his palm upside down.

"Guo Jing, run!" the Elders cried, just as a voice from behind them hissed, "Pour!"

Surefoot Lu caught the command and bellowed the word out loud: "Pour!"

The soldiers grabbed the cauldrons and rushed into the *ger*.

Viper Ouyang was already midair, halfway up the shaft, when several potfuls of water crashed onto him. The shock caused him to gasp, letting out the breath he had been holding. In free fall, he struck the butt of his staff against the base of the pit, sucked air into his lungs and pushed, propelling himself once more toward the opening.

A second wave of water lashed down onto him, but he was prepared this time, and it did not arrest his explosive upward motion. Yet, in this numbing cold, much of the water froze the moment it left the cauldron, and the Venom found himself hurtling painfully into fragments of ice as they rained down on his head.

And little did he know that the water at the bottom of the pit was also freezing fast. Having fallen short with his second leap, Viper was about to launch himself a third time when he sensed something pulling at his feet—they were trapped in a block of ice. Howling, he channeled his inner strength along his legs to the tip of his toes and broke through with a violent burst of energy, but, seconds later, more water cascaded down, solidifying around his upper body. In panic, he flung a sleeve over his face and managed to trap a pocket of air before his whole person was encased in ice. He then slowed his breathing using the Resting Tortoise technique, in the hope of preserving his life.

Although the water had failed to reach boiling point, the way in which the twenty cauldrons had been deployed was well planned out and rehearsed. Each vessel was manned by four soldiers, whose faces and forearms were wrapped in layers of cloth to protect against what would have been scalding splashes. The teams moved as one and stepped smartly aside once the load was discharged, to make way for the next group, sending down an all but constant stream of water. In no time at all, the pit was entirely filled.

The freezing water turned out to be an effective deterrent, securing Viper Ouyang in an ice pillar nearly five *zhang* in height and seven *chi* in diameter. Thrilled by their unintended success, the Beggar Clan Elders ordered men to dig around the block of ice and loop thick ropes around it, then had it dragged out of the ground by a team of twenty horses.

The news of this unusual sight spread like wildfire and soldiers from all over the camp gathered outside their commander's *ger* to marvel at it, lending a hand to help pivot the giant block of ice upright. By torchlight, it was apparent that Viper Ouyang had been frozen mid-action, one arm and one foot raised, his lips curled in a snarl and his eyes blazing. The crowd cheered at the spectacle, but Surefoot Lu feared that the martial Master might use his *neigong* to melt the ice and ordered more water to be brought to strengthen it.

But Guo Jing would not allow it. "I promised to spare him three times," he said. "Break the ice. Let him go!"

Though the Beggar Elders felt it would be a pity to set the Venom loose, they understood it was important for martial men to abide by their word. Surefoot Lu fetched a hammer, but, just as he was about

to swing it down, Elder Jian held him back and turned to Guo Jing. "How long can Viper Ouyang survive like this?"

"Perhaps two hours? Not much longer than that."

"In that case, I suggest we free him then. I don't think it would be amiss to subject him to a little hardship before we spare his life."

Guo Jing nodded. He had not forgotten that this man was responsible for the deaths of five of his *shifus*.

By now, word had spread to nearby camps and soldiers from other parts of the army were coming to see the man in the ice for themselves. Surveying the growing mass of onlookers, Guo Jing turned to the beggars. "As the saying goes, 'A man would sooner be killed than be mocked.' The Venom may be a villain, but he is also a grandmaster of the martial arts. He should not be reduced to a laughing stock." With that, he sent soldiers to set up a *ger* over the ice pillar and assigned men to keep watch, with firm orders that absolutely no one was allowed inside.

The three Elders released Viper Ouyang two hours later. Although the Venom had managed to survive on a small amount of air, thanks to the Resting Tortoise method of breathing, his primal *qi* was badly damaged. He sat cross-legged on the ground and channeled his energy around his body. Eventually, he coughed out three mouthfuls of blackened blood and left without a word, his countenance waxen but his movements unaffected by the ordeal. Guo Jing and the beggars watched in awe, impressed by the depth of his kung fu.

For the whole duration of Viper Ouyang's imprisonment, Guo Jing had felt unsettled. At first, he thought it was because he was threatened by the Martial Great's presence, but the agitation did not diminish when he was gone. He made a conscious effort to gather his spirit and quiet his mind, and, in the time it takes to drink a pot of tea, he managed to silence his emotions and empty his head. Then it dawned on him. The reason he had been so restless. The voice that had prompted Surefoot Lu to pour the ice-cold water on Viper Ouyang was one Guo Jing knew very well. It was Lotus's. He was almost certain of it. The Venom might have had his full attention at the time, but he could still hear that one word—"Pour!"—lingering in his ears . . . Only, he could not quite catch it in his heart. It was not possible for Guo Jing to sit still any longer. "Lotus *is* in the camp," he said aloud to himself. "I'll summon all my troops for inspection. That way, she'll have nowhere to hide . . . But I shouldn't force her to reveal herself to me if she doesn't want to . . ." He unrolled the painting Surefoot Lu had given him. The sight of the young woman in the picture filled him with a bittersweet longing.

4

GALLOPING HORSES BROKE THE SILENCE OF THE NIGHT. THEIR hurried approach was greeted by shouts from Guo Jing's guards. Presently, a herald entered his *ger* with orders from Genghis Khan.

The Mongolian army had been divided into four smaller forces when they had embarked on their western campaign, each riding unimpeded and victorious along a different route into Khwarazm. But now the Great Khan's sights were set on Samarkand, a new city that had replaced Gurganj as the capital. It was garrisoned by more than a hundred thousand Khwarazmians, their artillery primed, their grain stores full. The city's fortifications were sound: no defensive wall under the heavens was known to be thicker or better equipped. When his reconnaissance units had returned with their findings, Genghis Khan issued an urgent summons, recalling his men from different parts of the country to mount an assault on the city with the full might of the Mongol cavalry.

Guo Jing led his division south the next morning, following the Sughd River. Ten days later, they reached Samarkand, the first Mongols to arrive. The city gates opened and out poured the entire garrison. The Khwarazmians thought they could crush this little Mongolian detachment with ease, but, within half a day, more than five thousand of their soldiers had fallen to the Rising Wind and Hanging Cloud formations employed by Guo Jing's riders. The battle-weary defenders scuttled back behind their city walls, their fighting spirit crushed.

On the third day, Genghis Khan, Jochi and Chagatai arrived with their armies. The full Mongolian force of more than a hundred thousand men had come together to put Samarkand under siege. Several days of intense attacks did little to damage the sturdy city walls or force the defenders from their ramparts. The casualties mounted and still the Mongols failed to make a breach.

The sun rose on another day. Chagatai's eldest son, Mutukan, led the charge this time, eager to secure honor on the field. An arrow flew from the battlements and pierced his skull. Genghis Khan, overwhelmed by grief and fury, sent his personal guards to retrieve the body. With tears streaming down his cheeks, he clasped his favorite grandson to his chest and plucked the arrow from the boy's head. A barb shaped like a wolf's fang, fletching made from condor feathers, and the shaft—gilded in gold—had words inscribed on it. An officer recognized the characters as Jurchen script and relayed their meaning:

PRINCE ZHAO OF THE GREAT JIN

"Wanyan Honglie!" the Great Khan howled as he leaped onto his steed's back. "Hark, my brothers-in-arms! Whosoever breaches this city and captures Wanyan Honglie to avenge my grandson will be rewarded with all the silks and jade and men and women behind these walls."

A hundred riders of Genghis Khan's personal guard stood on the backs of their horses and echoed his words in one voice, rallying the army into action. Arrows buzzed through the air like swarms of locusts. War cries shook the heavens. Some units worked together to scale the walls, heaping mounds of earth, raising cloud ladders and throwing grapnels. Other teams brought a battering ram to bear upon the city gates. From the ramparts, the Khwarazmians worked tirelessly to repel the invaders, and, by sundown, Genghis Khan had lost more than four thousand soldiers, yet Samarkand stood as firm as a mountain. The Mongolians had not suffered such a thorough defeat since they had first marched into the country. When the Great Khan returned to his *ger* that night, his rage erupted like a burst of thunder, fueled by the pain of bereavement.

Guo Jing consulted *The Secret to Defeating the Jin*, hoping to find a way to take the city, but the fortifications of Samarkand were very different from those of the great cities of the Central Plains, so the methods of siegecraft set down by General Yue Fei were of little use to him.

He understood that, when an army besieged a city, their food and fodder would dwindle with time, and that the quickest way to replenish one's provisions was to take the city and plunder its stores, but that did not seem likely in the current situation. If the defenders sallied out, he was confident that the Mongolians would crush them with the ease with which one snaps a wilted twig or crumbles rotten wood, but there was nothing they could do if their enemies stayed behind their thick walls. As time wore on, they would soon be plunged into the depths of winter, and with the cold would come anxiety and impatience—the first signs of an army disintegrating from within.

Frustrated, Guo Jing called Surefoot Lu into his *ger* and explained his concerns, knowing the beggar would go straight to Lotus for guidance. Once Lu took his leave, Guo Jing tiptoed after him, but his plan was thwarted the moment he left the tent. Surefoot Lu was surrounded by a great mass of his clansmen, and they greeted Guo Jing as loudly as their voices would allow.

This must be another one of Lotus's ploys, Guo Jing thought with a sigh. She anticipates my every move and she can always come up with new ways to avoid me.

Surefoot Lu returned two hours later. "Such a large city cannot be taken in a rush," he said. "I can't think of any good strategies at present. Let's observe the defenders for a few more days. Perhaps they'll reveal a weakness."

Guo Jing nodded and the Beggar Elder took his leave. The young man's mind drifted back to Lotus again, and to the verses on the scroll painting. When he had left Mongolia for the South, more than a year ago, he had been a simple, unworldly boy, but the adventures and hardships along the way had made him more perceptive. Tonight, he felt he could almost grasp the affection that flowed through the poems and he grew more certain that Lotus still had feelings for him.

She's probably waiting for me to apologize. What can I do to make it up to her? he asked himself, wishing that he were not so dull-witted.

The question continued to plague him, keeping him awake well past midnight. When he at last dozed off, to fitful dreams of Lotus, he grabbed the chance to ask her what he should do. She gave her reply in hushed tones in his ear; yet, when he woke up, he had no memory of the words exchanged. No matter how hard he tried, nothing she said would come back to him. Joy turned to exasperation. He thought perhaps Lotus would appear in his dreams again, but sleep would not return to him. Knocking himself on the head in frustration, he suddenly had an idea.

I can't recall what she told me in the dream, but I can ask her! With that thought, he cried, "Send for Elder Lu!"

Surefoot Lu threw on a sheepskin and ran into Guo Jing's *ger* barefooted, thinking there had been urgent developments on the frontline, only to be greeted with a startling request.

"Elder Lu, I need to meet with Lotus tomorrow night. I'm giving you until noon to tell me where to find her."

"How . . . how's that possible? Chief Huang isn't here."

"You're smart and you'll find a way. If I don't get the answer I expect by noon, you'll be sorry." Guo Jing laughed silently at his unreasonable demand and turned to call in a guard before Surefoot Lu could argue back. "I want a team of executioners outside my *ger* at noon tomorrow," he told the man.

With the soldier's affirmative reply ringing loudly in his ears, the beggar left the tent, his face a picture of misery.

5

HEAVY SNOWFALL ARRIVED WITH THE NEW DAY. THE CITY walls, now coated in ice, were extremely slippery, as though they had been greased with oil. With no hope of scaling them until it thawed, Genghis Khan had the troops stay in the camp. The impasse weighed on him. Winter would soon be upon them. It would only grow colder in the coming months, and the temperature would not start to climb until the arrival of spring, in the second or third moon after the turn of the year. If they gave up on capturing Samarkand and continued to march west, they would leave their rear open to a hundred thousand enemy soldiers who could cut off their route home. If they stayed in the field and maintained the siege, they might end up trapped between the city walls and Khwarazmian reinforcements, horribly outnumbered. The likely outcome of either scenario was the complete destruction of the Mongolian army—not a single horse could hope to escape.

Genghis Khan paced back and forth outside his *ger*, his hands clasped behind his back. For once, he had no idea what to do. He stared with a frown at the towering snow-capped mountain that anchored the city's fortifications. It was a curious sight, rising up from the flat grassland like a tree trunk with neither branches nor leaves. The sheer craggy surfaces were of the hardest, most impenetrable rock; no vegetation could take root; not even monkeys or apes could find a foothold. The local people called it Bald Tree Peak.

It had been a masterstroke to build the city against this mountain, making use of the unusual terrain to form the western side of the city walls. This effective natural defense was not only impregnable, it had also lightened the burden of the capital's construction on the Shah's coffers.

Outside the walls, the Mongolian camp, its tents, horses and camels, were covered in a blanket of snow; within the city, cooking smoke rose from every household, curling up into the sky. The sight fueled the conqueror's black mood. *Through all the hundreds of battles I have fought, never have I been in such a desperate situation. Is this the end the heavens have in store for me?*

GUO JING had problems of his own. *What if Surefoot Lu kept his lips sealed regarding Lotus? He could not go through with his threat to have the Beggar Elder beheaded. Could he really hope to outsmart Lotus with this heavy-handed scheme?* He knew full well he had no hope of besting her in a game of wits.

Midday was approaching. He sat sullen in his *ger*, the executioners, with their broad sabers, lined up outside. A horn blast signaled that it was noon.

Surefoot Lu entered and announced, "I have a plan, but it may be too difficult to put into practice."

"Tell me! I'd give my life. I'll do anything."

The beggar pointed to Bald Tree Peak. "Chief Huang will meet you at the summit at midnight."

"Is this a jest? How do we get up there?"

"That's why I said it might be too difficult to realize." With that, Surefoot Lu bowed and left Guo Jing to his thoughts.

One word from Lotus and I'm stumped. The dejected young man sighed, staring vacantly at Bald Tree Peak. *It's several times higher than the middle crag of the Iron Palm Mountain, and far more treacherous than the Mongolian cliffs. If only there were a deity up there to throw me a rope . . .*

Guo Jing dismissed the executioners and rode glumly to the foot of the Peak. The mountain rose straight from the ground like a column—its bulk did not seem to taper as it reached for the sky. Its frozen surface glistened like polished crystal, reminding Guo Jing of the block of ice in which they had trapped Viper Ouyang.

He tilted his head back and fixed his eyes on the summit, where no man or beast, except those with wings, had ever set foot. His fur hat fell to the ground with a gentle thud.

I'd rather fall to my death than miss a chance of seeing Lotus, Guo Jing told himself. The ascent may be dangerous, but I'll stake my life on the attempt. If I fail, at least I'll be dying for her.

His mind made up, Guo Jing returned to camp feeling lighter, and he ate heartily that evening.

The sky was clinging to the last vestiges of light when Guo Jing stepped out of his *ger*. He had the golden dagger tucked into his belt and a long coil of rope wound around his waist. He found the three Beggar Clan Elders waiting for him.

"We're here to escort you up the mountain," Elder Jian said.

"Huh?" Guo Jing was at a loss for words.

"Don't you have an appointment with Chief Huang?" Surefoot Lu asked.

So, Lotus wasn't deceiving me! Giddy with anticipation, Guo Jing followed the Elders to the foot of Bald Tree Peak. A small company of a few dozen warriors was waiting for their arrival. They were accompanied by scores of oxen, sheep and goats.

"Begin!" Surefoot Lu ordered.

A soldier swung his saber, cut off the hind leg of a goat, and pressed the bloody flesh to the cliff face. The warm blood froze instantly, attaching the limb firmly to the icy surface, as if it had been nailed in place.

Guo Jing could not understand what they were doing. He watched as the soldier's action was repeated. The second stump was attached four *chi* higher than the first, and he suddenly realized they were building a makeshift stairway. This was indeed a shrewd solution, given the freezing cold. Surefoot Lu leaped up onto the highest goat's leg and caught a shank thrown by Elder Jian, affixing it to the rock.

Soon, the grisly ladder was more than a dozen *zhang* high. At first, the soldiers slaughtered the animals on the ground and tossed the limbs up to Guo Jing and the three Elders. But, as they climbed higher, they found the warm flesh was frozen stiff by the time it reached them, so ropes were let down to hoist the livestock up, and the four men prepared the footholds themselves.

Before long, they were approaching the halfway point, where the lashing of the wind was far more intense than on the plain below. Fortunately, the four men were martial Masters, so, although their bodies swayed with the gusts, their feet remained firmly fixed on the improvised perches. Still, to guard against plunging to their deaths should they slip, they looped a rope around their waists, tying themselves together for additional support. They reached the top just before midnight; the Beggar Elders were exhausted and Guo Jing was drenched in sweat.

Once Surefoot Lu had caught his breath, he said with a laugh, "Will you let me keep my head, now?"

"I don't know how to repay this kindness." Guo Jing wrapped his palm over his fist, feeling both wretched and grateful.

Surefoot Lu bowed, moved by the respectful gesture. "We have to obey our Chief's every order, even the impossible ones. What can we say? We have a very mischievous leader."

Laughing, the three Elders took their leave and began the long descent. Guo Jing watched them go, until they were halfway down the crag, then turned around to take in the magnificent scenery on the mountaintop. A crystalline world that had stayed frozen in the same state for tens of thousands of years. Some of the ice clusters looked to Guo Jing like flowers and plants made of jade. Others were shaped like exotic birds and beasts, or mirrored rugged mountain rocks, or were gnarled and twisted like twigs and branches. Enchanted, Guo Jing could feel that the prospect of being in Lotus's company was causing his body temperature to rise, his blood to bubble in anticipation, and his cheeks to flush red.

A giggle sounded from behind him, soft, almost inaudible, but it hit Guo Jing like a thunderbolt. He spun round. A young woman, gilded by moonlight, offering him an elusive smile.

Lotus!

Although Guo Jing knew that the only reason he had climbed the mountain was to meet with her, to actually find himself in her presence struck him as unreal, and he feared it was all a dream. Their eyes met, the joy of the moment mingling with the sorrows of the past months. They ran toward each other with no regard for the ice underfoot. They slipped and skidded at the same time, but, before Guo Jing hit the ground, he summoned his internal strength and propelled himself forward, wrapping Lotus in his arms. He could not bear the thought of her falling and hurting herself. It had been nigh on a year since they had parted, and the longing had driven them almost out of their minds. Now that they were reunited, how could they let go again?

It was a good while before Lotus wriggled out of the embrace and found an ice mound that was a convenient shape to sit on.

"I wouldn't have agreed to see you if you hadn't been so miserable."

Guo Jing gazed at her, unable to utter a word. After a long pause, he murmured, "Lotus . . ." His voice gained strength through his joy and he forced her name past his lips again.

She chuckled. "How many times have you said my name already? You've been calling it at least three dozen times a day."

"How do you know?"

Lotus gave him an impish smile. "You can't see me, but I see you all the time."

"Why didn't you let me see you sooner?"

"How dare you ask that? Do you take me for a fool?" Lotus pretended to chide him. "If you'd known I was alive, you'd have married your Princess Khojin! That's why I kept it a secret."

The mention of Khojin dampened Guo Jing's mood, reminding him of the promise he had made.

"Let's talk in that crystal palace." Lotus took Guo Jing's hand and led him to a huge, hollowed-out ice block a few paces away. Gleaming in the moonlight, it looked as though it was carved from crystal. They sat down, Lotus pressing close to him. "Should I forgive you for how you treated me on Peach Blossom Island?" she asked.

Guo Jing stood up and faced Lotus solemnly. "I will kowtow a hundred times to beg your forgiveness." He knelt and knocked his forehead on the ground, counting earnestly, "One, two, three, four . . ."

"Get up." Lotus reached out, beaming. "If I weren't ready to forgive you, you could behead Surefoot Lu a hundred times and I still wouldn't bother to climb this cliff."

"You're so good to me, Lotus."

"Am I? You thought only of avenging your *shifus*. You didn't have room for even my shadow in your heart. Why would I not be furious? But, when I saw you make that pact with Viper Ouyang, that you were willing to spare him three times if he promised not to hurt me, I realized I meant more to you than revenge."

"Did it take you so long to know my heart?" Guo Jing dipped his head in disappointment.

"Look what I'm wearing," Lotus said, hiding a shy smile.

Guo Jing's focus had not strayed from her face all this time, and only at her prompting did he recognize the black sable coat—the one he had given her when they first met in Kalgan. His heart quickened at the memory, and he clasped her hands in his.

They sat leaning against each other for a while, feeling no need to speak. At last, Guo Jing broke the silence. "How did you get away? First *Shifu* said you were taken by Viper Ouyang at Iron Spear Temple."

"Thanks to Brother Zephyr Lu's Roaming Cloud Manor . . . What a pity, though." Lotus sighed. "The Old Toad wanted me to explain the secrets of the Nine Yin Manual, but I told him I needed a quiet and peaceful environment. He thought we should go to a secluded temple, but I refused, saying I couldn't stand monks and their dreary vegetarian fare. Eventually, I managed to coax him into asking me where I wanted to go. That was when I mentioned Roaming Cloud Manor, telling him how it was built on the shore of the beautiful Lake Tai and how refined the food and drink were in that grand house. And then I brought up the sticking point: the master of the estate was my friend."

"He wouldn't like that."

"Have you forgotten how conceited the man is? He holds everyone else in disdain. The more I talked about Roaming Cloud Manor, the more he wanted to go there. He said it mattered not how many friends I could call on, he'd be able to deal with them all. And so we went to Wuxi, but Brother Lu had already left for Baoying with Laurel and Emerald, to visit her parents. I'm sure you remember that the Manor's grounds were designed according to Papa's interpretation of the Five Elements and the Eight Trigrams. The moment the Venom set foot inside, he realized he'd been fooled and tried to drag me out, but I turned a couple of corners and disappeared. He couldn't find me, so, in his rage, he burned the whole place to the ground."

"Ah!" Guo Jing gasped. "That's why all I found was ruins when I went there looking for you."

"I knew he'd do something like that, so I found a way to warn the household staff before I led him inside. But the crafty Venom kept watch over the route from Lake Tai to Peach Blossom Island and very nearly caught me several times. That was when I decided to head north to Mongolia. The whole time, he was hot on my heels. It's lucky that you aren't as sharp as he is, otherwise I'd have been hunted from every direction, with nowhere to hide."

Guo Jing gave a sheepish grin.

"But you're clever in your own way. You made Surefoot Lu come up with this plan for you."

"You showed me how."

"Did I?"

"Yes, you told me what to do," he said, and he went on to describe his dream.

Moved by his account, Lotus's smile turned solemn and her words came slowly. "People have said of old, 'True faith splits metal and rock.' I should have agreed to see you sooner, knowing how much you've missed me."

"Don't leave me again. Please."

Lotus gazed at the sea of clouds swirling around the peak and muttered, "I'm cold, Guo Jing."

He untied his fur cloak and wrapped it around her. "Let's go down."

"Meet me here tomorrow night. I have something to tell you about the final section of the Nine Yin Manual."

"Huh?"

Sensing Guo Jing's confusion, Lotus gave his hand a squeeze. "Papa worked out the meaning of the mysterious language at the end. I'll tell you all about it tomorrow."

Guo Jing was even more perplexed. Why would she claim her father was the translator, when it was Reverend Sole Light who had deciphered it? But, before he could raise this question, he felt her grip tightening again. He told himself there must be a reason for her strange behavior and agreed to return the next day.

The two of them climbed down from Bald Tree Peak and headed to Guo Jing's *ger*. Only when they were inside did Lotus whisper under her breath, "Viper Ouyang was spying on us."

"He was!?"

"He was hiding behind our crystal palace, but the Old Toad overlooked the fact that ice isn't opaque, even in the dark. When the moonlight fell on him, I caught a glimpse of his silhouette."

"That's why you brought up the Nine Yin Manual."

"Yes. We're going to trick him into going back. Then, we'll remove the footholds. He can stay up there working on his *qi* until he becomes an Immortal."

6

THE NEXT DAY, GENGHIS KHAN RESUMED THE ATTACK ON Samarkand, and, before long, more than a thousand of his best soldiers lay dead before the city walls. The Khwarazmian troops jeered and hurled abuse from the battlements, making the Great Khan curse and spit with rage. Fear began to creep into the great warrior's heart. In the wilderness all around their camp, the ground was littered with the carcasses of oxen, goats and horses that had frozen to death. If he failed to breach the city within ten days, at least half his army would perish in the bitter cold. He could not come up with a strategy to turn the situation around, and nor could he escape the idea that he, Genghis Khan—who had led a hero's life beyond compare—would meet his end here.

That night, Guo Jing, Lotus and the Beggar Clan Elders made preparations to quickly take down the makeshift footholds once Viper Ouyang had ascended Bald Tree Peak. They waited and waited, but there was no sign of the Martial Great. The Venom was keeping watch from a distance for any movement at the summit. He would not commit himself until he was certain that Guo Jing and Lotus were up there.

Eventually, Lotus realized they would have to take the initiative to lure the Old Toad out. She adjusted their plan, asking for several long ropes to be soaked in rock oil.

Found below the ground in Khwarazm, rock oil had first been discovered more than a thousand years before. When the locals dug wells for water, they came across a dark liquid that ignited readily. Ever since, they had been using it to cook and light fires, calling it fire oil. The Mongolian army had been seizing stores of it on their march through the country, amassing their own supply of fuel.

After securing the oil-soaked ropes on their backs, Guo Jing and

Lotus made their ascent. Once they reached the summit, they concealed the coils behind a rock and sat down in the same ice cave as the night before. Viper Ouyang followed the young couple in absolute silence, confident that they would be unable to detect his movements thanks to his supreme lightness *qinggong*, though in fact they had already spotted his indistinct outline through the ice.

Lotus began to explain a passage from the Nine Yin Manual and Guo Jing played along by prompting her and asking questions. It was all for show, but she was quoting directly from the martial tract. Viper listened intently, overwhelmed by the wisdom that was reaching his ears. Even if he did manage to cow the wench into sharing these martial secrets with him, she would never go into such detail. How fortuitous that he had this opportunity to spy on them instead. And yet, the Venom soon grew frustrated at Guo Jing's endless questions. This boy is indeed awfully stupid, he concluded.

Suddenly, urgent horn blasts filled the air, making Guo Jing jump to his feet. "The Great Khan's summons! I have to go."

Of course, the bugle call was part of Lotus's plan.

"Let's meet here tomorrow."

"Can't we talk in my *ger*? It must be tiring for you to climb up and down."

"The Venom has been searching for me all over the camp. There's nowhere to hide down on the ground, but even he wouldn't think to look for me up here."

Hearing this, Viper Ouyang could not resist a smirk. You think this little hill can stop me? You can run to the sky's edge and I'll still find you.

"Wait for me here. I'll be back in an hour."

At a nod from Lotus, Guo Jing began his descent. He was anxious about leaving her alone with Viper Ouyang, but, since the Martial Great wanted to listen in on their discussion about the Nine Yin Manual, it was unlikely that he would reveal himself or do anything untoward. As he made the long climb down, Guo Jing coiled the oil-soaked ropes around each frozen foothold.

Viper watched as Lotus appeared to grow increasingly restless, until she stood up and began pacing and muttering to herself. "Why's Guo Jing taking so long? This place is probably haunted. What if the ghosts of Yang Kang and Gallant Ouyang appear? I should go down. I can always come back up with him later."

Fearing that he would be discovered, Viper stayed huddled behind the ice block, utterly still, watching her disappear from view over the edge of the cliff.

Guo Jing and the Beggar Elders were waiting for Lotus at the foot of the mountain. The moment she was safely on firm ground, they lit the ropes. The flames licked higher and higher, feeding greedily on the rock oil and melting the frozen blood that had kept the severed animal legs affixed to the cliff face. They fell to earth, one by one, as the fire devoured the ropes, slithering toward the summit like a blazing snake. Against the inky sky and the brilliant white snow, it was a magnificent sight.

Lotus clapped and cheered, then turned to Guo Jing. "Are you going to spare him again?"

"Yes, but this is the last time."

"I know a way you can stay true to your word and claim his life to avenge your *shifus*."

"Lotus, you really are full of ideas!" Guo Jing gushed.

She gave him a smile. "It's just a simple plan. We'll let the Old Toad eat a bellyful of icy wind up there for ten days and nights. When he's hungry and cold and exhausted, we'll build a new stairway to bring him down. And that will be three times you've spared his life, won't it?"

"Yes."

"So, once he's back on the ground, we won't have to be courteous to him anymore. The two of us can dispatch a sickly, half-dead man, can't we? With the Elders' help, of course."

"We can . . . but finishing him off like that wouldn't be very honorable."

"What's the point of being honorable with a scoundrel like him?

Did he show mercy to your *shifus*? Was he honorable when he made his snake bite your fourth *shifu* in the tongue?"

White-hot rage flooded Guo Jing's veins at this reminder of the Venom's cruelty. He knew he might not get another chance to claim revenge.

"You're right. Let's do it," he said, his jaw clenched.

Lotus accompanied Guo Jing to his *ger*, where they resumed their discussion of the Nine Yin Manual, only, this time, they could throw themselves into it without the need to put on an act. Throughout their exchange, they were both thrilled to discover how much the other's martial understanding had improved over the past year. Unlike Guo Jing, Lotus had never memorized the original Sanskrit-inspired passage, and, since Reverend Sole Light's translation had been in Guo Jing's possession, her grasp of the Manual's key tenets was incomplete. Now that she at last got to see the full picture, she felt energized, despite the late hour.

After a time, Guo Jing turned the conversation to another of his sworn enemies. "Wanyan Honglie is hiding in Samarkand, but we're stuck outside the city walls. We can't get to him. Have you got any idea how we can breach the city?"

"I've been thinking about that ever since we got here, but none of the plans I've come up with guarantee success."

"What if *we* scale the walls? Among the Beggar Clan brothers, there must be at least a dozen with good enough lightness *qinggong* who could join us. Would that work?"

Lotus shook her head. "Archers are positioned almost shoulder to shoulder all the way along the ramparts. And, even if we managed to dodge the arrows on our climb and find a way into the city, how could so few of us tackle an army of a hundred thousand? We wouldn't be able to force the gates open."

The young couple were still talking at dawn the next day when Genghis Khan launched another attack on Samarkand. Thousands of soldiers manned his catapults, raining boulders down on the city. They also brought to bear the numerous cannons they had seized from the Jin and the Song armies. The bombardment, however, did little damage to the Khwarazmian troops taking shelter inside their barracks, and it was the common people who suffered, with many homes destroyed. The artillery assault continued for three days, but to little effect.

On the fourth day, snowflakes the size of goose down tumbled from the heavens. Guo Jing looked toward the mountaintop and shivered. "Viper Ouyang may not last ten days, in this weather."

"He'll live. Don't forget his supreme *neigong*—" Lotus's reply was swallowed by a gasp. Was that the Venom she could see jumping from the summit? "The Old Toad must have had enough. He's seeking solace in death," she said, pointing out the faraway speck in the sky.

She was just about to applaud his courage, when she noticed something strange about the distant figure. "How curious!" she muttered.

Rather than plunging straight down, Viper's body was drifting and gliding like a kite. Could he have employed sorcery to slow his descent? Was that why he was floating to earth in such a leisurely manner? He was now closer to the ground, and Lotus could see him more clearly. The martial Master was stark naked, holding two conjoined balloons above his head.

"Pity!" Lotus sighed, realizing what he had done.

For all his martial prowess, Viper Ouyang had been dismayed to find himself trapped on Bald Tree Peak, a thousand *zhang* above the ground, with no way of getting down. But, after several days, chilled to the bone and with nothing to warm his stomach, he fixed upon a desperate idea. He took off his trousers and tied a tight knot at the hem of each leg, then removed the rest of his clothes, using them to reinforce the fabric. Gripping it by the waistline, he swung his creation windward and watched as it filled out with air. Gritting his teeth, he leaped from the mountain.

It was an extremely risky endeavor, a wild attempt to cling to life by embracing death, but Viper had no choice. The trousers billowed out as he had hoped, greatly reducing the downward pull of the fall. With nothing to protect him from the bitter cold, he was almost frozen stiff. All he could do was to draw on the full depths of his inner strength, forcing his *qi* around his body to resist the icy air and numbing snow.

Lotus could not decide if she found the Venom's escape amusing or infuriating, but one thing was certain: she could think of no way to thwart his attempt. Meanwhile, every soldier in the two opposing armies, altogether several hundred thousand men, was staring up at the sky to marvel at the descent of this airborne figure. Many even prostrated themselves on the ground to greet what they believed to be the coming of a divine Immortal among men.

Studying the trajectory of Viper's flight, Guo Jing realized that he would land within Samarkand's walls, and, when the Martial Great was just several dozen *zhang* from the ground, he took an iron bow from a nearby soldier and let fly a number of arrows in quick succession. He guessed that the Venom would have difficulty twisting out of the way midair, but he was careful to aim for a part of his body that would not be susceptible to fatal injury, honoring his promise to spare the villain's life for a third time.

Blessed with unrestricted sightlines as he glided down, Viper spotted the arrows hurtling toward his lower body and tucked in from the waist, hunching his back and kicking out with both feet to knock them off course.

Amid the general hubbub, Genghis Khan received a brief report from Guo Jing about the mysterious figure in the sky and ordered his archers to bring the Venom down. Ten thousand bows were drawn at once, and arrows flew across the sky like a meteor shower, every single one aimed at Viper Ouyang. Even if he had a thousand arms and ten thousand legs, he could not have deflected them all. And, since he was using every stitch of his clothing to slow his descent, he had nothing to twirl as a soft shield—and there was nothing he could dodge behind in the sky. The martial Master knew he needed to change his course drastically before he was impaled by countless arrows and reduced to a flying hedgehog.

Viper let go of his inflated trousers and immediately found himself flipped upside down, plummeting head first.

Every soldier cried out in shock, their voices shaking both heaven and earth.

The Venom flexed his stomach and launched himself toward a large banner flying from the ramparts, just as a blast of wind pulled the fabric taut, stretching it from west to east. Viper shot out his left hand and caught a corner of the flag. This brief contact allowed the Martial Great to transfer the force of the fall, tearing the banner in two and buying himself time to flip into a somersault, hook his feet around the flagpole and slide down, disappearing behind the defensive wall.

Awed by this amazing feat, the soldiers took to discussing at great length what they had just witnessed. Indeed, for a time, both sides seemed to have forgotten that they were in the midst of war.

Guo Jing watched the display in frustration. Lotus won't be pleased that I'll have to spare the Venom on our next encounter, he said to himself, and yet, when he turned to her, she was grinning radiantly. "Why are you so happy?"

She clapped her hands. "I've got a present for you. Are you excited?"

"What is it?"

"The city of Samarkand."

Guo Jing was flummoxed.

"The Venom has shown us the way into the city. Get your soldiers ready. We will win a great victory tonight." She then leaned close, speaking in a whisper. Her words had him applauding in delight.

7

GUO JING'S MEN RECEIVED THEIR COVERT ORDERS IN THE early afternoon. They were to cut up their *gers* to fashion circular canopies on which they would fasten strong leather ropes. And they had just three hours to produce ten thousand of them. The soldiers were hesitant. If they dismantled their shelters now, how would they survive the bitter cold at night? And yet there was no question of defying their commander.

Meanwhile, Guo Jing arranged for all the cattle in the camp to be herded to the base of Bald Tree Peak. Then, he gave his men their orders. Ten thousand men were to wait out of arrow range in sight of Samarkand's north gate, split into four formations: Shielding Sky, Embracing Earth, Rising Wind and Hanging Cloud. They were warned to be on the lookout for enemy generals and other high-ranking officers coming their way. Another ten thousand fighters would conceal themselves at the foot of the wall either side of the north gate, divided into Soaring Dragon, Winged Tiger, Gliding Bird and Coiling Snake battle arrays, responsible for driving enemy soldiers into their brothers-in-arms facing the gate. A third unit of ten thousand was told to arm themselves lightly and wait for his instructions.

At nightfall, after the troops had filled their bellies, the two divisions marched for the north gate. Three hours before midnight, Guo Jing sent word to Genghis Khan that Samarkand's defenses would soon be breached and that the whole army should be ready to storm the city. Stunned by Guo Jing's claim, the warrior demanded that the young commander explain himself in person, but the messenger simply replied, "The Prince of the Golden Blade has already set off. He looks forward to toasting your victory."

Guo Jing sounded the bugle from the base of Bald Tree Peak, and a thousand of his men began to slaughter the cattle, pressing warm, bloody flesh to the icy crag to construct the makeshift stairways. The martial Masters from the Beggar Clan hopped up and down using their lightness kung fu, passing around animals and body parts, and, in no time, several dozen ladders were ready.

At Guo Jing's command, ten thousand soldiers clambered after their General, scaling the cliff, each man fastened to the next by a length of rope. Despite their numbers, they ascended in absolute silence, for they had been warned not to make the slightest sound. From afar, it looked as though dozens of dragons were winding their way up the mountain on this cold, dark night.

The summit was just about large enough to accommodate ten thousand men tightly packed together. Guo Jing ordered the soldiers to attach the canopies they had made that afternoon to their shoulders and jump down into the city, weapons at the ready. Their target was the south gate.

Striking his hands together, Guo Jing gave the signal to commence and leaped from the cliff, followed by several hundred Beggar Clan members. The Mongolian troops were known for their exceptional courage, so, despite the obvious dangers of jumping from such a great height, they boldly followed their commander's lead. After all, they had seen Viper Ouyang's graceful descent, and his equipment had been far less sturdy than what was now strapped to their backs. As the soldiers stepped off the edge of the mountain, the canopies billowed out like ten thousand flowers blooming all at once, allowing the men to drift steadily down.

A flush of excitement washed over Lotus as she watched the successful realization of her plan. She cared little if Genghis Khan took this city, for the Mongolians' military exploits meant nothing to her, but, if Guo Jing were victorious, he could ask for something that meant a great deal to both of them—if he were willing to listen to her advice.

The moment Guo Jing's feet touched the ground, he ripped the canopy from his back and swung his saber at a knot of enemy soldiers. By now, a small portion of the city's troops had woken to the sight of the Mongols descending from the heavens. As they registered the scale of the aerial assault, their fighting spirit instantly dissolved and mass panic took hold.

The first group to land were the Beggar Clan members. Well trained in the martial arts, they did not take long in battling through the demoralized defenders to close in on the city's south gate.

Although most of the Mongolian troops survived the descent,

only one or two thousand managed to land near the assembly point, and several hundred men perished because their canopy failed or they were hit by arrows. More than half were scattered by the wind to different parts of the city, where, outnumbered by the Khwarazmians, many were captured or killed. Guo Jing split the warriors he had on hand into two groups: one to seize control of the south gate, the other to protect their comrades, fending off attacks from their foes.

Astonished and delighted by the sight of Guo Jing's troops descending into Samarkand, Genghis Khan mobilized the whole army. They arrived to find the south gate already open, guarded by several hundred Mongolians. Battalions of a thousand men filed in, one after another, joining their brothers-in-arms inside to subdue the city's garrison.

The Khwarazmian army, though more than a hundred thousand strong, was fast collapsing. As the Mongolians advanced, they doused buildings with rock oil, and soon the city was ablaze, which only added to the chaos. Assured that his men still held the city's north gate, Shah Muhammad decided to flee in that direction, emerging to find Guo Jing's men waiting for him outside. The Shah had no desire to engage them. He sent word ordering Wanyan Honglie to maintain a rear guard and spurred ahead, surrounded by his personal guards.

Guo Jing caught a flash of Wanyan Honglie's golden helmet in the midst of the retreating troops and led a unit in pursuit. He was determined to capture the Jin Prince, but although the Khwarazmian army had suffered a crippling defeat, they were still a force to be reckoned with. They threw themselves at Guo Jing's soldiers outside the north gate like cornered beasts, for breaking through seemed their only hope of getting out alive.

Word soon reached Guo Jing that the Khwarazmians were pushing back the two divisions he had ordered to lie in ambush. The situation brought to mind an ancient Chinese military maxim that urged commanders to show mercy when they held the advantage: "Fall not for bait, strike not those in retreat, trap not those under siege, chase not the desperate." With this in mind, Guo Jing called for a change in tactics.

Responding to a wave of the signal flag, the four formations facing the north gate—Sky, Earth, Wind and Cloud—parted to allow their fleeing adversaries through. Once the majority of Samarkand's routed troops had charged past, the flag was raised and cannons sounded to call the four formations back into position, ready to face the last remnants of the Khwarazmian rear guard. Despite their fearsome reputation, these elite troops had lost all desire to fight after the city's fall, and, since they were also heavily outnumbered, they were quickly surrounded and disarmed. Guo Jing personally inspected the prisoners, one by one, but he did not find the Jin Prince hiding among them. He might have won the day, but he did not feel the flush of triumph, for his two arch enemies, Wanyan Honglie and Viper Ouyang, had evaded him amid the chaos of battle.

8

SAMARKAND'S LAST REMAINING FORCES HAD BEEN MOPPED up by the time the sky was fully light. Genghis Khan installed himself in Shah Muhammad's palace and summoned his generals.

Guo Jing was visiting the wounded when he heard the Great Khan's golden bugle. He immediately followed the sound of the call, which brought him to the square outside the royal residence. By its grand entrance stood a small knot of warriors, among them Lotus and the Beggar Clan Elders. Spotting Guo Jing, Lotus clapped her hands and two soldiers dragged forward a large sack, setting it at her feet.

"Guess what's in here," she said with a chuckle.

"How can I? This city has everything."

Lotus gave the sack a tug and out rolled a man. Disheveled hair, a split lip—he was wearing the standard-issue fur coat worn by the

Khwarazmian soldiers, but it was a face Guo Jing knew well. The Jin Prince Wanyan Honglie.

"Marvelous! Where did you find him?"

"I spotted a unit with the Prince of Zhao's banner among the troops fleeing through the north gate. A general in a gold helmet and brocade robe led them east. I didn't believe that someone as calculating as Wanyan Honglie would withdraw under his own flag, so I knew they were a decoy. Since they were heading east, it meant the cunning fox must be going west—and he ran straight into my ambush."

Lotus produced a dagger and held it out solemnly. It was the one given to Skyfury Guo by Qiu Chuji when the Taoist came up with Guo Jing's name, carving it on the hilt. Another, presented to Ironheart Yang, was inscribed with the characters *Yang Kang* and was now in Mercy Mu's possession.

"My congratulations," she said, "for you shall avenge your father today. Use this," she added as she handed over the dagger. "It will please his spirit in the heavens to know that it dealt the fatal blow."

Guo Jing took the weapon and bowed low. "Lotus, I don't know how to thank you for helping me in this matter."

She smiled. "It was just luck. Now listen, you've won a major victory today, and the Great Khan is sure to reward you handsomely. You should think about what you'd like from him."

"There's nothing I want."

"Come here." She beckoned him over, taking a few steps away from the others, so they would not be overheard. Once Guo Jing was up close, she said in a quiet voice, "Is there really nothing in the world that you'd like?"

Guo Jing thought hard, sensing there were hidden depths to her question. "There is one thing," he said eventually. "I never want to be parted from you again."

"Considering what you've achieved today, I think the Great Khan will overlook any offense your request may cause."

Guo Jing grunted in vague agreement, but he did not seem to have grasped her meaning. Lotus was forced to spell it out: "If you ask him for any rank or title, he'll agree to it, but you can also ask him to take away any rank or title already granted. It will be hard for him to refuse—so long as you first get him to give his word that he'll grant you anything you ask."

"Right . . ."

The sluggish way he uttered this one-word reply and the sheepish manner in which he scratched his head infuriated Lotus. "You rather enjoy being the Prince of the Golden Blade, don't you?"

"Oh!" At last, Guo Jing caught on to what Lotus was trying to get at. "You want me to ask the Great Khan to free me from my betrothal to Khojin."

"That's your decision. Maybe you do really want to be a Prince." Lotus's displeasure was apparent.

"Khojin's feelings for me are genuine, but I've only ever thought of her as a sister. If the Great Khan agrees to call off the engagement, it would be for the best."

Smiling, Lotus gave him a sidelong glance, but at that moment the golden horn sounded for a second time. Guo Jing took Lotus's hand and gave it a squeeze. "Wait for my good news," he said, before turning away to drag Wanyan Honglie into the palace.

The moment Genghis Khan saw Guo Jing, he came down from the throne and took the young General by the hand to lead him inside. Then he asked an attendant to bring a brocade stool and set it down next to the royal seat for the hero of the hour. Guo Jing briefed the conqueror on the capture of Wanyan Honglie, who was prostrating himself in utter subjugation on the floor.

Genghis Khan strode up to the Jin Prince and planted his foot on the man's head. "Did you imagine you'd end up like this when you first came to Mongolia to show off your might?"

Knowing that his death was assured, Wanyan Honglie fixed his eyes on Genghis Khan. "It is regrettable that we failed to wipe out your measly tribe when we Jurchens were at the height of our power. If we had, we would not be here today."

Laughing, Genghis Khan ordered his men to get Wanyan Honglie out of his sight and behead him in the square before the palace.

The command aroused mixed feelings in Guo Jing. On the one hand, he was pleased that his father's death would at last be avenged; on the other hand, he had always imagined exacting this vengeance himself, using the dagger Qiu Chuji had given his father. And yet, the despondent look on the face of the once haughty Prince dulled the hatred and anger he had nurtured for so long, and he realized that he did not need to dispatch the man by his own hand.

Genghis Khan turned to Guo Jing. "I decreed that the man who gave me this city, along with the head of Wanyan Honglie, would be rewarded with all the silks, jade and men and women within its walls. Send your men to claim your prize."

Guo Jing shook his head. "My mother and I have long enjoyed the Great Khan's generosity. We want for nothing and can find no use for more servants, gold or silks."

"You have the character of a true hero. Tell me, what do you want, then? I shall grant you anything you name."

Guo Jing stood up and bowed deeply. "I do have one thing to ask of the Great Khan, and I beg him not to be angry with me."

"Speak your mind," the conqueror said with a smile.

But, just as Guo Jing was about to make his request, a gut-wrenching wailing rose up from somewhere beyond the palace, reaching as far as the heavens and rocking the earth, making the hearts of all those within earshot skip a beat. The generals leaped from their seats and drew their weapons, thinking that the locals they had just subdued had risen up against their invaders. But Genghis Khan stopped them before they could rush out of the hall.

"All is well," the conqueror said, with a dry chuckle. "This cursed city refused to bend to the heavens' will, costing me not just soldiers and generals, but my dear grandson too. It deserves a thorough purge. Come, let us watch."

Genghis Khan led his generals out of the palace, where they

mounted their steeds and rode for the nearest gate, the shrieks growing ever more piercing and desperate. Once outside the city, they
saw thousands of Samarkandians on the run, crying, screaming, shoving each other, falling to the ground, all trying to avoid the galloping Mongol riders and the long sharp sabers that were slicing into
them.

When the Mongolians entered Samarkand, they ordered its people to leave the city. At first, the locals thought they were being sent
outside the walls to help the conquerors flush out any soldiers lurking among them, but the Mongols began to confiscate all items that
could be used as weapons, then to single out all the skilled crafts-
men and select the good-looking women and girls from the masses
gathered, binding their hands with ropes. The Samarkandians at last
understood the disaster that was about to befall them. Some resisted
and were cut down by sabers or run through with spears. Then, a
dozen battalions roared and charged into the crowd, hacking and
slashing with their blades. A massacre most brutal and savage. Men,
women, children, the elderly—no one was spared. Trembling white-
haired ancients, infants who had never left their mother's embrace,
all butchered without a second thought. By the time Genghis Khan
arrived with his generals, more than a hundred thousand had been
slaughtered. Mutilated bodies carpeted the ground in all directions.
The iron-shod hooves of the Mongolian horses thundered indiscriminately, treading them into the blood-soaked earth.

"Excellent! Kill them all!" Genghis Khan roared in good humor.
"Show them the might of Genghis Khan."

Unable to witness this carnage any longer, Guo Jing urged his
horse over to the conqueror's side. "Great Khan, spare them, please!"

But the warrior waved him away testily and shouted, "Slay them
all! Do not leave a single soul alive."

Guo Jing bit his lip and swallowed his words. A child of seven
or eight broke away from the crush of shivering, defenseless bodies
and threw himself at a woman who had just been knocked over by
a warhorse. "Mama!" he screeched as a rider charged at them. One

swing of the saber and mother and child were cut clean in two, the boy's lifeless arms still wrapped tightly around the woman.

The sight made Guo Jing's blood boil. "Great Khan!" he called at the top of his voice. "Didn't you say that the silks, jade, men and women of this city were mine? Why did you order this massacre?"

"What concern is it of yours?" Genghis Khan replied, with a cackle. "You said you didn't want them."

"And you said you'd grant me anything I name. Is that true?" Once he had the conqueror's affirmation, Guo Jing went on: "The Great Khan's word is as immovable as any mountain. I beg you to spare the people of this city."

Genghis Khan's expression hardened. He had never imagined Guo Jing would ask for clemency, but the boy had the right of it. He had given his word, and he could not take it back. Fury burned in his chest and fire glittered in his eyes as he glared at Guo Jing, clutching the hilt of his saber. "Is this really what you want from me, boy?"

The generals flanking Genghis Khan had fought shoulder to shoulder with the warrior through countless campaigns, and never once had they feared for their lives, for they saw death as nothing but a homecoming. And yet, at this moment, their commander's bitter wrath sent a chill through their hearts, leaving them quaking in terror.

Guo Jing had never been regarded by Genghis Khan with such severity, and he could not stop himself from shuddering with trepidation. He steeled himself to repeat his demand. "I beg the Great Khan to spare the people of this city."

"You won't come to rue this decision?" the warrior growled.

Guo Jing recalled Lotus advising him in the square outside the palace to use this opportunity to end his betrothal to Khojin. He was aware that he only had one chance before he lost the Great Khan's favor for good—a loss he could accept, if it weren't for the fact that his future with Lotus would flow by like running water along with it. And yet, how could he stand by and listen to the screams of tens of thousands of common people? How could he watch them be brutally butchered?

"I will have no regrets," he said, trying to sound certain.

Even so, Genghis Khan could detect the tremor in his voice. The young man was frightened, but he acted according to his heart, and the conqueror felt a grudging admiration for his stubborn courage. He unsheathed his saber and shouted, "Stand down!"

At the call of the bugle, the blood-soaked Mongolian riders withdrew from the terrified Samarkandians, and lined up neatly in columns, forming several divisions of ten thousand men.

No one had gone against the wishes of the Great Khan since he had earned that title, and to have his bloodlust so frustrated filled him with an unaccountable rage. He let out a howl, hurled his saber to the ground and galloped back to the palace. The generals glowered at Guo Jing. They had thought that taking such a grand city would offer them several days of plunder and bloodshed, but now all they would receive as a reward was their commander's black moods and the unknowable ways in which he might lash out. The exhilaration of taking Samarkand had come to naught.

GUO JING was conscious of the resentment from those close to Genghis Khan, but he paid them no heed, instead urging Ulaan to carry him farther into the wilderness beyond Samarkand. During the siege and the assault on the city, tens of thousands of houses on both sides of the city walls had been torched, and now the earth was littered with countless bodies, staining the snowy plains red with blood.

There is no escaping the cruelty of war, Guo Jing thought as he rode through the devastation. To avenge my father, I brought an army here and killed all these people. In conquering the world, the Great Khan has butchered many more. But what sins did these tens of thousands of soldiers and common people commit to deserve such a fate? To have their brains and innards smeared on the ground, their bones abandoned in the wastes? Was I right to help breach the city in my thirst for vengeance, and bring death to so many?

The more Guo Jing turned over the events of the recent past in his mind, the more unsettled he became. He wandered aimlessly, with only his anguished reflections for company, and did not return to the city until long after dark, when he found two of Genghis Khan's personal guards waiting for him. They bowed, and one of them said, "The Great Khan requests the company of the Prince of the Golden Blade."

Guo Jing was uneasy about the summons, and told his own guards to inform Surefoot Lu of where he was headed.

I went against his wishes today. Perhaps he will have me beheaded for insubordination, he said to himself. He may try to intimidate me into changing my demands, but whatever happens, I must save the people of Samarkand. He is the Great Khan—he cannot go back on his word.

Guo Jing arrived at Shah Muhammad's palace expecting to find Genghis Khan in a foul mood, but the sound he heard echoing through the building was the conqueror's ebullient laughter. Surprised, he quickened his steps, entering the hall to find the Great Khan had company. Khojin was sitting on the floor at his feet, leaning against his knee. And by his side was a Taoist monk with a glossy black beard that flowed down his robes—Eternal Spring Qiu Chuji.

Delighted, Guo Jing hurried over to pay his respects, but Genghis Khan snatched a halberd from his attendant, twirled it around and swung its blade down at Guo Jing's skull with his full strength. Startled, the young man tilted his head to one side. The shaft struck his left shoulder—*thwack!*—and split in two.

Laughing, Genghis Khan said, "There, boy, I shall let it pass. I would have taken your head today, were it not for Master Qiu and Khojin—and the victory you won."

Khojin jumped up to her feet. "Pa, if I weren't here, you would've been nasty to my Guo Jing!"

"Who says so?" Genghis Khan threw the broken weapon down in good cheer.

"I saw you! Don't try to deny it. I was worried—that's why I asked Master Qiu to come with me."

Smiling, Genghis Khan took his daughter's hand, and reached out for Guo Jing's. "Enough of your chatter, let's hear Master Qiu's poems."

AFTER THE fight at the Tower of Mist and Rain in Jiaxing, Qiu Chuji and his brethren apologized to Apothecary Huang, for they had then seen with their own eyes that the Heretic had not harmed their martial uncle Zhou Botong, and they had also learned that Viper Ouyang was behind their brother Tan Chuduan's death. Some days later, they came across Ke Zhen'e, who gave them a detailed account of how Yang Kang had accompanied Viper Ouyang to Peach Blossom Island and played a part in the murder of his five martial siblings, describing also the young man's untimely end.

Yang Kang's fate hit Qiu Chuji hard. He rued his negligence regarding his disciple's training. He might have taught the boy kung fu, but he had also let him stay on in the Jurchen palace. It was the Taoist's fault that the young man had become accustomed to rank and wealth, causing him to lose his way. Qiu Chuji had only himself to blame for Yang Kang's tragic end.

As such, when he received the letters from Genghis Khan and Guo Jing inviting him to Mongolia, he accepted the offer readily. He was aware that, at the rate the Mongol Empire was expanding, it would not be long before they were masters of the whole of China. If he could win Genghis Khan's ear, he might be able to rouse the conqueror's sense of charity, sparing tens of thousands from slaughter. If he were successful, it would be a deed of immeasurable worth. Besides, he was eager to see Guo Jing again. And so, he led a dozen disciples and traveled westward, despite the approach of winter.

Now sitting in comfort in the Shah's palace, Qiu Chuji was delighted to at last set eyes on the boy. He had grown stouter and stronger than when they parted, a year before, and the wind and snow had lent him a tawnier complexion. Before Guo Jing's arrival, the Taoist had been regaling Genghis Khan with tales of all he had seen and heard on his journey, telling him how the scenery and changing customs along the way had inspired him to pen some verses. Now invited to share them, with a stoke of his beard, the monk began to recite:

> "*A decade plagued by war, the sorrow of the common men,*
> *Of the many thousands, no more than one or two remain.*
> *Last year with fortune received the kindly summons,*
> *This spring a trip despite the cold is to be made.*
>
> *Shirk not from the three thousand* li *of ranges north,*
> *Thinking still of the two hundred townships of mountains east.*
> *The poor and desperate, eluding slaughter, gasp under strain,*
> *Here's hoping the strife of the people will soon cease.*"

Urtu Saqal, an official with a sound grasp of the Chinese language, translated the poem into Mongolian. Genghis Khan acknowledged it with a nod, but made no comment.

Qiu Chuji turned to Guo Jing. "When your seven *shifus* and I fought at the Garden of the Eight Drunken Immortals, your second *shifu* picked the inside pocket of my robe and found an unfinished poem. On my way here, I thought often of my old friends, and at last I completed it." And he began to chant:

> "*Since ancient times mid-autumn's moon,*
> *Radiant, as icy winds clean the night;*
> *Heavy hangs the Milky Way*
> *As water dragons vault the seas.*

"Your second *shifu* saw these lines all those years ago, and now I've written four more to go with them. But, alas, he'll never get to read them . . .

> *Songs fill the towers of Wu and Yue,*
> *Wine flows among the armies of Yan and Qin.*
> *My emperor, residing beyond Linhe,*
> *Wishes to end war and bring peace."*

Tears filled Guo Jing's eyes at the thought of his martial teachers.

At last, Genghis Khan threw off his silence. "Master Qiu, you must have seen the might of my army on your journey here. I wonder if you have verses to praise them?"

"Along the way, I did indeed witness the force with which the Great Khan breaches cities and claims land," Qiu Chuji replied. "And I was moved to write two poems. This is the first of them:

> *The gray heavens look down on the earth*
> *Why does it not save ten thousand souls in pain?*
> *These souls, day and night, in suffering and torment,*
> *Hide their gasps, swallow their voices, die in silence.*
>
> *Howling at the heavens, they answer not,*
> *A matter too minor, too small, too futile.*
> *Let not the many thousand worlds return to chaos,*
> *Let not the divine maker create more spirits."*

Urtu Saqal hesitated, asking himself whether he dared to provide a translation. It was obvious that the content would not please his commander, but, before he could make up his mind, Qiu Chuji began again:

"The second poem was:

"Ah, the heaven and earth split wide apart,
Granting life to creatures in thousands and millions.
Brutal violence invades without pause,
The cycle of suffering without end.

Heaven and earth are both divinities,
Why look on the dying without giving help?
Minor officials have compassion but not the blessing,
Night and day, fruitless labor in aching grief."

Though the prosody of the poems was not particularly neat, the compassion and humanity they conveyed shone through. Guo Jing thought of the scenes of carnage that morning and sighed with the full weight of a heavy heart.

Genghis Khan turned to Urtu Saqal. "The Master's poems are surely most excellent. Quickly, tell me what they say."

The official considered how he should respond. Many times have I entreated the Great Khan to avoid killing innocents, but he has never heeded my words. Maybe the Taoist's benevolent heart as expressed through these poems will move him. With that thought, he went on to translate the poems faithfully.

Genghis Khan was visibly vexed. "I have heard that the Chinese have a method for living long without growing old. I hope the Master will teach me," he said, changing the subject.

"Such a method does not exist in this world," Qiu Chuji responded flatly. "But the Taoist training of one's *qi* can help guard against illness and prolong one's life."

"What is the key to this practice?"

"'The Way of the heavens is impartial, yet on the benevolent it always bestows.'"

"And who are deemed 'benevolent'?"

"'The sage has no fixed intent, his heart follows the people's needs.'" Qiu Chuji continued, ignoring the Khan's question. "We have a revered text known as the *Classic of the Way and Virtue*. It is particularly cherished by us Taoists. What I quoted just now is from this book. It also says, 'Soldiers and arms are instruments of ill portent, not tools of the noble virtuous. Only to be resorted to when there is no other choice, and with calm composure. Delight not in victory, for those who find delight, find pleasure in slaughter; and those who find pleasure in slaughter will never realize their ambitions under the heavens.'"

Genghis Khan had been greatly pleased by the Taoist's arrival, thinking he was soon to learn the secret to immortality—or at least a way to extend his years—for, in recent months, he had been feeling his age, keenly aware of his waning strength. But all he had heard so far were entreaties to refrain from waging war and slaughtering innocents . . . It was not a conversation he was interested in continuing. Before long, he turned to Guo Jing. "Accompany the Master to his quarters so he can rest."

CHAPTER TEN

SECRET ORDERS
SEALED IN SILK

I

EIGHTEEN OF QIU CHUJI'S DISCIPLES HAD ACCOMPANIED HIM on his journey west, among them Li Zhichang, Yin Zhiping, Xia Zhicheng, Yu Zhike, Zhang Zhisu, Wang Zhiming and Song Defang. At Genghis Khan's request, Guo Jing showed them to their quarters, and, once they had rested, they joined the conqueror at the victory feast. Qiu Chuji answered his questions with patient courtesy, explaining in detail the Taoist methods for strengthening the body and extending one's years, while emphasizing that they were related to protecting the people and performing good deeds. By the time the banquet was over, the skies were beginning to grow light.

Lotus was waiting for Guo Jing at the palace gates with the Beggar Elders and her thousand clansfolk, all mounted on their steeds. She urged her horse forward the moment she saw him emerge.

"Did it go well? I was worried that the Great Khan would try to behead you in his rage, so I brought everybody here in case we needed to rescue you. What did he say? Did he agree?"

"... I didn't ask him."

"Why?"

"Don't be angry. It was because—"

"Guo Jing!"

Lotus blanched at the sound of Khojin's voice.

The Mongolian Princess sprinted from the palace, making straight for her betrothed. "Are you happy to see me?" She clasped her hands over his. "You didn't think you'd find me here, did you?"

Guo Jing nodded, then shook his head. He turned back to explain to Lotus what had happened, but she had slipped away, leaving her horse behind.

Khojin chattered away, telling him how much she had missed him. She did not realize that she had interrupted a conversation, or that Guo Jing was incapable of paying attention to what she had to say.

The young man was in turmoil. *Lotus must think that I didn't ask to cancel the engagement because Khojin was there. What can I do to remedy the situation?*

At last, Khojin noticed that Guo Jing was distracted. "What's wrong with you? I've come all this way to see you. Why are you ignoring me?"

"Sister, I have to see to an important matter now. We'll speak later."

Guo Jing pulled his hands away and rushed back to the camp. When he entered his *ger*, he asked his guards if they had seen Lotus.

"Miss Huang was here not long ago," one answered. "She took a painting and rode off with it."

"A painting?" Foreboding seized Guo Jing.

"Yes, the one you often look at."

She took her portrait ... Does that mean she wants to cut all ties with me? Guo Jing thought with alarm. *I'll leave everything behind and go south with her.*

He scribbled a note for Qiu Chuji and vaulted into Ulaan's saddle. The swift Fergana horse took him beyond the walls of Samarkand in no time at all. Fearing he might already be too late, Guo Jing urged his steed on, again and again. Before he knew it, he was dozens of *li* from the city. The ground, no longer strewn with the bloody corpses of men and horses, was covered by a blanket of pristine white snow. He spotted a distinct trail of hoof prints heading eastward in a straight line.

No horse on earth is faster than Ulaan. It won't be long until I catch up with her, Guo Jing told himself to bolster his spirits. Then, we can fetch my mother and return to the South together. I don't care if the Great Khan and Khojin resent me for the rest of their days.

Another dozen *li*. The marks now led north, and appearing alongside them was a line of footprints that were unlike any Guo Jing had seen before. This person had an exceptionally long stride—each step spaced almost four *chi* apart—and yet, his tread was light, the indentations in the snow no more than a couple of inches deep.

No one but Viper Ouyang has this level of lightness kung fu out here, Guo Jing noted with apprehension. Could it be him? Is he tracking Lotus? A heavy sweat dampened his clothes, despite the wintry air.

Having followed the hoof marks for some time, Ulaan now understood what his master was seeking and galloped after the spoor left by Lotus's horse, without needing to be prompted. For several *li*, the footsteps stalked the horse's path, in a straight line at first, until both sets of tracks veered west, then south, twisting and turning.

Lotus must have discovered the Venom and tried to shake him off, Guo Jing concluded. But how can she lose him when her horse leaves such an obvious trail?

He shadowed the tracks for yet another dozen *li* before noticing that they had begun to merge with some other impressions in the snow. He dismounted to take a better look. A similar trail of hoof- and footprints heading in the same direction, but one set of marks seemed to have been made before the other.

Maybe Lotus's evasive maneuvers were based on her father's interpretation of the Mysterious Gates? And, here, she seems to have returned to her original course . . . This line of reasoning reassured Guo Jing somewhat, for he had faith in her knowledge and believed that it could help her confound the Venom, but, at the same time, he worried about losing track of her amid the confusion of prints. He stood rooted to the spot, trying to work out how he should proceed, until it occurred to him that, however roundabout her route, ultimately she would have to head east to get back to the Central Plains. He mounted Ulaan once more, double-checked his bearings and set off, riding resolutely east.

AFTER GALLOPING for some distance, he came upon footprints again and caught sight of the silhouette of a man where the blue sky met the white snow. He urged Ulaan toward it, and as they approached he realized that it was Viper Ouyang. The martial Master had also seen him. "Hurry!" he cried. "She's in trouble!"

Guo Jing tensed his legs and the Fergana horse darted forward like an arrow, yet, when they were within several hundred paces of the Venom, Ulaan's gait changed. His hooves seemed to be sinking into the snow, as though there was a swamp underfoot rather than solid ground; then, snorting in agitation, he took off at an angle before circling back.

Mystified by his mount's behavior, Guo Jing noticed something even stranger. Viper was running in circles around a small tree. Guo Jing tugged at the reins, urging Ulaan to stop so he could speak to the man, but, for the first time, his prized horse defied him, making another loop without slowing down.

Have we wandered into a marsh? Is that why both Ulaan and the Venom won't stop moving? Is it to avoid being dragged down? he asked himself. But what about Lotus? He said she was in trouble. "Where's Miss Huang?" Guo Jing yelled in Viper's direction.

"I followed her prints here, then I lost all trace of her." The Martial Great pointed to the tree he was circling. "Look!"

Guo Jing spurred Ulaan over, managing to regain some control over him, and his attention was gripped by something hanging from a branch—it was glistening in the crisp sunlight. He snatched it up as they raced past. The golden band Lotus wore in her hair. Guo Jing's heart was in his throat. Not knowing what else to do, he headed east once more, galloping for several *li*, until he spotted a glint in the snow. Still in the saddle, he stretched his arm out, reached down, and picked up the gold and pearl brooch Lotus often pinned to her lapel. His despair intensified.

"Lotus! Where are you?"

A sea of white. In every direction. As far as the eye could see. He longed to catch a dark smudge speeding across this bleached expanse. He pushed on a few more *li*. And then he saw it.

Ahead of him, to the left, the black sable coat he had given her in Kalgan.

"Lotus!"

As Ulaan trotted around the coat, Guo Jing stood in the stirrups, his cries rippling out across the frozen plain. No reply. The flat terrain would not even grant him an echo. Sobs distorted his voice as he shouted her name.

Soon, Viper Ouyang drew up alongside him. "We'll look for her together. Let me rest for a moment and take a turn on your horse."

"She wouldn't be out here if it weren't for you!" Guo Jing tightened his thigh muscles and Ulaan took off.

Incensed, Viper flexed his back foot and sprang forward. In three great leaps, he was looming over the Fergana horse and reaching for his tail.

Unnerved by the Venom's explosive turn of pace, Guo Jing swung his right arm back in a Dragon Whips Tail, channeling his full strength. Palms clashed. He was sent shooting into the air, but thankfully Ulaan maintained a straight course. As Guo Jing fell, he stretched out and tapped his left hand on his horse's hindquarters, vaulting back into the saddle.

The force of Guo Jing's blow, meanwhile, had pushed Viper back by two steps. In a bid to counter the backward thrust, the martial Master planted one foot with a touch more force than was advisable. It was immediately gobbled up by the mud, leaving him shackled to the spot, with one leg knee-deep in the mire. Viper was well aware that, if he pulled the trapped limb out upward, he would end up driving his other foot down. Each fresh attempt to extract himself would only result in him being sucked in further, to the point where not even his superb martial skills could help. So, he drew himself up to his full height and tipped himself onto his back. As he touched the ground, he rolled sideways and swiped his free leg up in a Mandarin Duck kick. Drawing on the move's momentum, he dragged his other foot through the slurping mud in the same direction, plucking it out in a spray of sludge.

By the time Viper had extricated himself and flipped upright, Guo Jing had covered more than a *li* on his swift mount, shouting "Lotus! Lotus!" all the while. The Martial Great studied the horse's gait, which seemed to be getting increasingly balanced and even. Thinking that they must now be clear of the swamp, he hastened after Guo Jing, following the hoof prints, and yet the ground felt spongier with each step he took.

Viper suspected that he had been led from the edge of the marsh to its heart, and was reminded of the snares Guo Jing had laid for him in their last three encounters. The most recent of them was especially galling. The humiliation of exposing his unclothed body before the eyes of several hundred thousand men, no matter how awed they had been by his martial skills, was a burning shame he could not forget. He was determined to get retribution at all costs, so to find Guo Jing all alone in the wilderness was an opportunity too precious to miss. And he needed to ascertain if Lotus was still alive, for with her died his chances of discovering the secrets of the Nine Yin Manual. Gathering his *qi*, he deployed his fastest lightness kung fu, covering several *li* in an instant, swifter than a galloping horse.

The faint crunch of snow alerted Guo Jing. He looked back to find the Venom only a few *zhang* behind. Disconcerted, he urged Ulaan forward, and his pounding hooves had soon covered another dozen *li*.

All the way, the Fergana horse was keenly aware of the dangers lurking in the landscape. Feeling the soft ground give way beneath each thud of his hooves, he increased his speed, stretching his limbs

441

as though he had taken flight and was coursing on the wind. The magnificent steed charged ahead, as quick as lightning, working up a coat of sweat the color of blood. Droplets of perspiration sprayed along his trail, splashes of crimson scattered like peach-blossom petals on the snow.

Viper Ouyang's lightness *qinggong* was exceptional, but, having maintained top speed for an extended period, he sensed his breathing getting ragged and the strength in his legs waning. Soon, his pace slackened.

Guo Jing continued to call for Lotus, his voice growing ever more hoarse and husky. The gloom of the night thickened. The chances of finding her were getting slimmer by the second.

It was now pitch black. Ulaan had taken Guo Jing safely out of the swamp, leaving Viper Ouyang far behind.

A thought began to whirl in the young man's mind: I will give my life to find Lotus. Her horse can't compare to Ulaan. It probably got stuck half a *li* into the marsh.

On the one hand, Guo Jing understood that, if Lotus had indeed been swallowed by the bog, it was unlikely that he would be able to locate where it had happened, and, even if he succeeded, his only reward would be a cold body that was beyond all help, for he was painfully aware how long he had been searching. On the other, he found it comforting to cling onto the impossible idea that he could save her from the swamp.

Guo Jing dismounted and gave voice to his resolve, stroking the Fergana horse's back. "Oh, my trusty friend, I know it has been a hard day for you, but we have to turn back—even if it means death." He climbed wearily into the saddle and twitched the reins to indicate that they should return the same way.

Ulaan was frightened, unwilling to step into the marsh again, but Guo Jing insisted. Grunting, the celestial horse launched into his widest stride and headed back without further resistance. Knowing the great distance he had to cover, he built up his pace with every step, galloping faster and faster.

"Help! Help!"

Guo Jing had not long ventured back into the mire when Viper Ouyang's cries reached his ears. He followed the sound and saw, in the dim glow of the snow, two flailing arms raised high, grasping uselessly at the air. The bulk of the martial Master's body had been claimed by the bog, and the mud was creeping up his chest before Guo Jing's eyes. It would soon reach his mouth and nose, and, when that happened, his fate would be sealed along with them.

Guo Jing thought of Lotus suffering the same plight in her last moments, and hot blood surged and roiled in his breast. He almost jumped from Ulaan's back and plunged into the sludge himself . . .

"Help me! Quick!"

"My *shifus* died because of you. Lotus died because of you. I'll never help you!" Guo Jing spat the words out between gritted teeth.

"You swore to spare me three times."

"Lotus is gone! What's the point of our pact now?" Guo Jing yelled through his tears, riding off to a string of curses from Viper Ouyang. But, before long, he turned Ulaan around with a sigh. He could not steel his heart against a cry for help. The mud was already up to the Martial Great's neck.

"I'll pull you out, but I can't take you on the horse. We'll be too heavy and we'll sink."

"You can drag me along."

Guo Jing did not have a rope with him, so he took off his robe, dangled it from the saddle and galloped close to Viper Ouyang. The moment the martial Master grabbed the other side of the garment, Guo Jing squeezed his thighs and roared a command. Ulaan burst forward with all his strength and—*plop!*—pulled Viper out of the mire, onto its snowy surface.

If they were to head east now, they would soon be out of danger, but Guo Jing was not ready to give Lotus up and went west, farther

into the swamp. Viper lay on his back and let himself be towed along at great speed, taking the opportunity to smooth his breathing and channel his *qi*.

Guo Jing had Ulaan traverse the bog through the night, only reaching the far side when the new day began to dawn. There, he found the hoof prints left by Lotus's mount when she had first chanced upon this dreadful place. Guo Jing leaped from his horse and stared at them, fresh tears pooling in his eyes.

Standing in the snow, he held Ulaan's reins in one hand and cradled Lotus's sable coat in the other. He gazed vacantly into the distance, as if in a trance. His heart ached so much that he forgot his arch enemy was directly behind him. All of a sudden, a light touch between his shoulder blades jolted Guo Jing back to the here and now, but, before he could twist away from it, the pressure increased by a fraction. He realized the Venom's hand was over his Kiln Path acupoint.

Viper Ouyang cackled wildly, ecstatic that he had Guo Jing's fate in his hands, just as he had been at the boy's mercy when he was buried in the sand at the Mongolian camp.

"Kill me if you like. You've never said you'd spare me."

Guo Jing's disregard for his own life unsettled the Martial Great. He had intended to humiliate the boy before dispatching him, but the despair in his voice surprised him.

I didn't realize their ties were so strong. He wants to die for love, but I won't grant him his wish . . . After all, he also holds the key to the secrets of the Nine Yin Manual.

His mind made up, Viper locked Guo Jing's acupressure points, slung the young man across his horse's back and rode the beast south.

2

By mid-morning, they came upon a deserted village choked with frozen corpses. Guo Jing could tell from their horrific wounds that they were victims of the Mongolian invasion.

Viper Ouyang urged Ulaan through the settlement, calling out to see if any villagers were left alive. No answer but the grunts and snuffles of cattle. Pleased that they were otherwise alone, he dismounted and dragged Guo Jing into a stone hut.

"You're my prisoner now, but I won't kill you. In fact, I'll let you go, if you can best me in a duel."

With that, he tapped the young man's pressure points to restore his movement and left the hut to look for food. Soon, he returned with a goat, slaughtered the animal and busied himself in the kitchen. When the meat was ready, he threw Guo Jing a shank.

"Fill your belly, then we fight."

"Why do you care if I'm hungry?" Riled by the Venom's self-satisfied expression, Guo Jing leaped up and hacked his palm at the martial Master's face.

Viper raised his arm to block and retaliated with a punch. The table and chairs in the house were sent flying in the blink of an eye.

After three dozen moves had been exchanged, Guo Jing, not yet recovered from the journey, began to feel stretched. Viper seized his chance, stole half a step forward and lashed out with his right palm. The strike threatened Guo Jing's abdomen, aimed at a point just under his rib cage. The young man knew he had no hope of evading this attack and forced himself to hold still, waiting for the burst of energy that would kill him, but all he received was a smirk.

"That's enough for today," the Venom said. "We'll resume tomorrow, after you've practiced a few moves from the Nine Yin Manual."

"Pah!" Guo Jing spat, righted a stool that had been flipped over during the fight and settled down to eat. He tore off a large mouthful of meat and pondered the Venom's words as he chewed.

You want me to show you moves from the Manual. Do you realize that will make me your *shifu*? Ha! He was amused by the thought. I won't fall for your tricks. You can kill me. I don't care! Because you'll never find out the Manual's secrets from me . . . Now, what can I do to fend off that move of yours, just now?

Guo Jing considered all the different palm- and fist-fighting systems he had learned, but none seemed capable of countering the move that had undone him. Then he recalled a technique called Willow Catkins, from the Nine Yin Manual, which was a method for ratcheting up one's strength. Maybe it could help neutralize the force contained within the Venom's vicious swipe?

But I'll practice it in my head, Guo Jing thought, aiming a silent jibe at his captor. You can try reading my mind, if you want to learn it! Once he had picked the mutton leg clean, he sat cross-legged on the floor and tried to visualize the relevant passage from the Manual, picturing the flow of energy in action. His familiarity with the Transforming Muscles, Forging Bones chapter in the martial tract had provided him with a solid foundation in advanced methods for controlling his body, and that understanding had been further augmented by the key tenets interpreted by Reverend Sole Light. In less than four hours, he was able to master the theory of Willow Catkins.

Guo Jing stole a sideway glance at Viper Ouyang, who was seated in a similar posture and appeared to be working on his *neigong*.

"Let's fight again!" the young man cried, leaping to his feet, the edge of his hand already slicing down at the Venom.

Viper Ouyang twirled his palm to parry the strike. After several minutes' back and forth, he repeated the same jab at Guo Jing's midriff. This time, his hand slipped as he made contact, and as a result, he was drawn forward. Sensing a palm chopping down at his neck, Viper let himself be carried by the momentum of his aborted attack, gliding out of reach.

"Excellent move! Is it from the Nine Yin Manual? What's it called?" The Martial Great was impressed by the effectiveness of Guo Jing's maneuver.

"*Sacayotu amukta.*"

Unable to make head nor tail of Guo Jing's reply, the Venom assumed that the young man must be quoting the strange passage at the end of the Manual. This bull-headed boy won't bend to my will, he said to himself, suppressing a cackle of triumph, but I can trick him into revealing the Manual's secrets.

Spurred on by that thought, Viper altered the flow of energy to his palms and the contest resumed. Each time Guo Jing sensed that he was about to be overpowered, he halted their duel and sat down to practice a new skill. That night, he lay on his back and slept soundly, without a care, while the Venom tossed and turned, apprehensive that the boy might use the cover of darkness either to ambush him or to escape.

A MONTH flew by. Half the livestock in the village had ended up in the stomachs of Viper Ouyang and Guo Jing, as the pair continued to coexist in a delicate balance, sparring every day. Guo Jing had to admit that such close proximity to his arch enemy had forced him to practice kung fu as never before and learn new techniques.

As one of the greatest Masters of the age, Viper was able to glean much insight into the Nine Yin Manual by monitoring the young man's advancements, though when he compared his observations with the text in his possession, they never aligned. This greatly perplexed him. Indeed, the more he thought about it, the less it made sense, so he pressed Guo Jing harder. As a result, the young man improved by leaps and bounds in a matter of weeks.

At this rate, the boy's going to get the better of me before I've fathomed the secrets of the Manual, Viper realized with alarm.

In the beginning, Guo Jing had fought back full of resentment, but, as time went by, he was gripped by the desire to win and a determination to see their contest through to the bitter end. The young man wanted to dispatch the Venom using his martial knowledge, even if that seemed nigh on impossible. The challenge spurred him on, inspiring him to keep his anger in check and focus all his energies on his training. Nevertheless, the power of Viper Ouyang's signature Exploding Toad kung fu was founded upon a deep well of *neigong*, and such internal strength could only be built up little by little over a long period of time. Guo Jing knew that, for all the great progress he was making, he could not match Viper in that respect.

Their duel intensified when Guo Jing found an iron sword beside one of the dead bodies in the village and began practicing with the blade. Viper Ouyang's weapon of choice was his Serpent Staff, which housed two extremely venomous snakes in a secret compartment, but the original had been claimed by the waves during the duel at sea against Count Seven Hong, as they sailed from Peach Blossom Island, more than a year before. He had had a new one cast, sending his most trustworthy retainers to the Western Regions to seek out similar adders, but this replacement had been confiscated and later destroyed by Surefoot Lu some months ago. Now Viper was armed only with an ordinary iron staff, but, nonetheless, he was able to send the young man's sword flying again and again, thanks to his rich repertoire of moves. Had he still possessed the snakes, Guo Jing would have been undone in no time at all.

For the past few days, the peace of the deserted village had been disturbed by whinnying horses and boisterous soldiers, as the Great Khan's army marched home, eastward, but Guo Jing and Viper Ouyang were so engaged in their duel that they paid them no heed. At last, as dusk gave way to a crisp, clear night, the last troops passed through and tranquility returned.

Standing in a corner of the stone hut, Guo Jing tightened his grip on the sword's hilt as he watched the Venom. Nothing you do with your staff tonight will prise this blade from my hands, the young man silently promised his opponent. Though he knew he did not yet have the ability to get the better of the martial Master, he was eager to try out his newly acquired techniques.

"Scoundrel, where do you think you're going?"

Viper Ouyang and Guo Jing regarded each other in shock at the sound of a familiar voice. The same thought crossed their minds: What's Zhou Botong the Hoary Urchin doing this far west?

Guo Jing was about to rush out to greet his sworn brother when he heard hurried footsteps approaching the hut . . . Two people . . . One running ahead, the other stalking close behind.

With a wave of his hand, Viper whipped up a gust and extinguished the candle, plunging the room into total darkness. Presently, the door opened with a creak. A man charged inside, followed a moment later by Zhou Botong.

Viper noted with alarm that the first man, fleet and light on his feet, seemed to have outrun the Hoary Urchin, which meant his kung fu was comparable to that overgrown child's. Only a handful of martial masters were at the Urchin's level, and, if the man turned out to be Apothecary Huang or Count Seven Hong, then the Venom would need to formulate a plan of escape that very instant. The quietest ruffle followed by a barely audible tap interrupted Viper's thoughts. The man must have jumped up onto the rafters.

"I love hide-and-seek! Nothing makes the Hoary Urchin happier. You're not slipping away again."

The wooden door slammed shut, then a scuffle and a thump were heard. Viper Ouyang had been keeping a large rock by the doorway, which he used to secure the hut every night, for, if Guo Jing tried to move it out of the way, he was bound to make enough noise to wake the Venom from his dreams. It sounded like Zhou Botong had shifted the rock and propped it against the closed door.

"Oi, stinker, where are you?" Zhou Botong called, groping around in the pitch-dark room.

Guo Jing was about to point out where the man was hiding when a merry chortle rang out, then the scrambling of feet was followed by a *whoosh*, as grabbing hands parted the air. Zhou Botong had known all along that his playmate had leaped onto the roof beams; he had merely put on an act of fumbling around to lower the fellow's guard so he could mount a surprise assault.

The man on the rafters was truly agile. He flipped down in a somersault and crouched low in the north side of the room before Zhou Botong's fingers could reach him.

Muttering silly nothings to himself, the Hoary Urchin did not seem at all bothered that he had missed, though his movements were more cautious and considered than before. He listened intently, trying to determine the location of his prey. To his surprise, he heard three pairs of lungs at work, and recalled the light being put out as they approached the hut. Perhaps the people living here were too scared to reveal themselves? To reassure them, he yelled:

"Fret not, good folk. I'm here to catch a vagabond. I'll be out of your way as soon as I'm done."

Despite his jovial tone, Zhou Botong was paying close attention to the quiet murmur of the others' breathing. When it came to a martial man with advanced *neigong* skills, each breath was gentle but controlled, and, though each draw of air was effortless, it reached deep into the body. In comparison, an ordinary person's respiration sounded almost like a gasp—short, shallow and hoarse.

Zhou Botong noted the low, steady, measured exchange of air, coming from the east, the west and the north. Could there be two other kung fu masters in this tiny hut?

"You little cheat! You've placed your henchmen here!"

Guo Jing wanted to make himself known, but, when he considered how skilled the man being hunted was, he decided against it, mindful that the Venom was also skulking around. I'll keep quiet, for now, and offer help when Brother Zhou needs me, he said to himself.

The instant Zhou Botong detected the presence of other martial masters in the hut, he knew the situation was not to his advantage and started to tiptoe toward the door. "The hunter is now the hunted," he sighed.

Just then, war whoops and the thumping of hooves filled the air, like the surging high tide on mid-autumn night. Tens of thousands of soldiers, charging in the direction of the village.

"More of your lackeys? Pardon the Urchin for quitting our game—for now."

Zhou Botong picked up the rock that was blocking the door. But when everybody was expecting him to toss it aside and escape outside, the unpredictable man swirled around, lifting the stone higher with both hands, and hurled it toward the northern end of the hut.

By noting the path of the bluster whipped up by the flying rock, Viper Ouyang was able to determine the Hoary Urchin's precise position and deduce that he had left his right flank vulnerable. If he eliminated Zhou Botong now, he would not have to worry about the capricious Master joining forces with Guo Jing, and he could also rid himself a formidable rival before the Contest of Mount Hua. With that thought, Viper crouched low and thrust out both hands, sending a violent burst of Exploding Toad energy into Zhou Botong.

Though it was pitch black, Guo Jing recognized the *whoosh* of the wind accompanying the Venom's signature kung fu and knew that it was whipping into his sworn brother. Without a moment's hesitation, he lunged, letting fly with a Haughty Dragon Repents.

The man pursued by Zhou Botong had assumed the horse-riding stance the instant he sensed the rock hurtling toward him. Feet apart and knees bent, he flipped his palms out and thrust, and a potent stream of energy sent the heavy projectile flying back at his foe.

Although the four martial men had all launched their moves at slightly different times, their inner strength was more or less equal. Struck by these opposing forces, the rock crashed down onto a table in the middle of the room, smashing it into pieces.

The deafening boom amused Zhou Botong, and he squealed in laughter, only to find that he was unable to hear his own voice. A storm of screeching horses, clanging weapons and yelling soldiers had descended on the village. Guo Jing could make out from the clamor that a Khwarazmian unit in retreat was trying to use the settlement to make a last stand, but the Mongolian cavalry had caught up with them before they could position themselves. Iron-shod hooves made the earth tremble. Banners flapped audibly in the wind. Rallying calls and battle cries rang out against the thick hum of arrows in flight. The clash of metal on metal and the sound of sharp spearheads tearing flesh. But it was impossible to tell from the din just how many men were fighting around the stone hut.

3

The door flew open and a soldier burst in. Zhou Botong grabbed the man, flung him out, slammed the door shut and blocked it with the rock again, in one fluid movement.

Viper Ouyang decided there was no point remaining silent now that his failed attack had revealed his presence. "Hoary Urchin!"

Zhou Botong caught the muffled voice, but could not tell what was being said above the chaos outside, so he held his left palm close in a protective stance and groped for whoever had spoken with his other hand. Sensing the shift in the air, Viper shot his right arm out, hooked his fingers around Zhou Botong's wrist, and swung his knuckles in a backhanded slap with his left.

"Old Venom! You're here too!" Zhou Botong blocked the blow, swaying a little from the impact. He then swerved left to better position himself against his opponent, but this movement opened his back to the martial Master he had been stalking, who took his chance to launch a palm thrust from his hiding place. Zhou Botong threw his left fist backward in retaliation as he fended off Viper Ouyang with his right hand. He was in a buoyant mood. This was the first time since he had dreamed up the Competing Hands technique on Peach Blossom Island that he had found himself pitted against two top martial Masters at the same time. At last, he could test his creation's potency.

Just as his fist connected with his attacker's hand, Zhou Botong sensed someone rushing toward him from the east, someone who pushed his opponent's follow-up aside, absorbing the force of the strike.

"Brother Guo!"

"Guo Jing!"

"Qiu Qianren!"

The names were called out at the same time.

⁓

DURING THE battle at the Tower of Mist and Rain, when Viper Ouyang set his serpents on Guo Jing, the Quanzhen Immortals and their allies, Zhou Botong, who was petrified of snakes, clambered up onto the Tower's roof to avoid the creatures, refusing to come down even when he came under fire from hundreds of Song and Jin archers. Tired of warding off the downpour of arrows by hand, he lay down flat and covered himself with roof tiles. He made it through the night without getting shot or bitten, but, by the time the sun had risen and the fog had dispelled, he was alone—snakes, soldiers and his martial nephews, all gone.

Bored and with nothing in particular to do, Zhou Botong wandered aimlessly for several months, until he was accosted by a member of the Beggar Clan, who handed him a letter. Lotus had written to remind him that he had promised to do anything she asked of him, and she would like him to take the life of Qiu Qianren, leader of the Iron Palm Gang. She explained that there was a deep enmity between this man and Consort Liu of King Duan's court. If he succeeded in his mission, Lotus promised that he would no longer be hunted by that woman. If he failed, Consort Liu would seek him out to claim his hand in marriage, even if he fled to the sky's edge and the sea's end. Lotus concluded the letter with detailed directions to Iron Palm Mountain.

Zhou Botong had a vague recollection of running and yelling the words, "I'll do anything you ask of me . . ." the last time he had seen Lotus. Besides, Qiu Qianren had been colluding with the Jin Empire, and was a therefore a traitor to his country, so he saw no harm in doing away with him. He thought of his ill-fated dalliance with Consort Liu and how it had haunted him all these years. He knew he owed her a great debt and he felt he ought to do something for her. If he could resolve her feud with Qiu Qianren, and if she could free him of any further obligation, that would indeed be a most happy outcome. So, with the letter to guide him, the Urchin went straight to the home of the Iron Palm Gang.

At first, Qiu Qianren managed to hold his own, but, from the moment Zhou Botong brought out the Competing Hands technique, retreat was Qiu's only option. A duel between martial masters usually concluded when one side admitted defeat, but the Hoary Urchin ignored established practice and continued to harass his opponent. When Qiu Qianren asked him to explain his relentless pursuit, the normally verbose man could only stare at him, tongue-tied, spluttering nonsense. Of course, Qiu had no way of knowing that Zhou Botong would rather lose his head than say Consort Liu's name out loud.

And so, the contest continued. One dodged and parried, while the other doggedly gave chase, in a prolonged duel that took them farther and farther away from where they had begun. Zhou Botong's kung fu was more accomplished than Qiu's, but, even so, it was no mean feat to injure the leader of the Iron Palm Gang, let alone take his life.

Qiu Qianren had tried thousands of ways to give the implacable Urchin the slip, when a desperate idea came to him. Perhaps he could run to the cold and barren wilderness of the west.

Needless to say, he had misjudged Zhou Botong's character. The instant the Urchin caught on to Qiu's plan, he was giddy with anticipation, curious to see just how far the Iron Palm Water Glider would travel to evade him.

Before long, the two men had passed the last stronghold of the Central Plains and entered the vast desert to the west. The flat terrain offered little shelter, allowing Zhou Botong to track Qiu Qianren with ease. By now, they had come to an agreement: they would not be so unsporting as to attack while the other was sleeping, eating or relieving himself. Nonetheless, no matter what trickery Qiu Qianren attempted, the Hoary Urchin was a lingering specter, incessantly haunting his every step.

For Zhou Botong, his mission to kill Qiu Qianren had turned into an elaborate game of wits and strength, and the chase had become so diverting that, although he had his quarry cornered several times, he could not bring himself to take the man's life, for he knew how rare it was to encounter such an accomplished opponent. And that was how, by sheer coincidence, the pair found themselves in the stone hut where Guo Jing and Viper Ouyang had taken residence.

CORRALLED TOGETHER in a pitch-black room no more than two *zhang* square, the four men were not just robbed of their sight, for the battle raging outside now overwhelmed their hearing. Although Guo Jing, Zhou Botong and Qiu Qianren had cried out each others' names when they recognized each others' kung fu, they were unable to make out what was being said. All Viper Ouyang knew for sure was that the man who had come in first was Zhou Botong's foe, whereas Qiu Qianren was under the impression that the two Masters they had barged in on were in league.

When Guo Jing identified the fourth man in the room as Qiu Qianren, he paused, considering his next move, aware that his martial abilities still lagged behind those of the other three. Now that Zhou Botong was here, Guo Jing knew that together they would have a good chance of dispatching Viper Ouyang once and for all, and decided that he would keep the Venom occupied so his sworn brother could deal with Qiu Qianren first.

With this plan in mind, Guo Jing sent both palms slicing into the darkness, masking firm strikes as feints. His right struck empty air, but his left was met by an opposing hand. He instantly knew it belonged to Zhou Botong—after all, they had sparred countless times on Peach Blossom Island. Guo Jing was about to clasp his sworn brother's arm to make himself known, when the hand that had blocked his attack jerked back. In that same moment, a right-handed jab stabbed at his shoulder. The blow contained no inner strength, but still, a dull ache throbbed at the point of impact.

Of course, Zhou Botong knew full well that he had just struck Guo Jing, but he could not resist the call of his impish nature, following up with a thrust of his left palm.

"Brother Guo, are you testing my kung fu? Here comes the next move!" His words failed to reach his sworn brother's ears, drowned out by the warring armies outside.

Having been caught unawares once, Guo Jing was on his guard this time, and warded off Zhou Botong's hand with a flourish of his arm. Within moments, a dozen moves had been exchanged. Much impressed by the advancement of his little brother's martial skills over the past year, Zhou Botong chuckled in admiration. "Where did you learn this amazing kung fu?"

But how could Guo Jing hear him over the fierce battle outside?

"Fine! Keep your secret! What do I care?" Just as he was throwing this little tantrum, Zhou Botong sensed a rush of air at his back. "You can deal with those two on your own!" he said, and he hopped up onto the rafters with a tap of his foot.

While the two sworn brothers were brawling, Viper Ouyang and Qiu Qianren had traded enough moves to be able to identify each other by them. The two men had no quarrel, but they knew they would be competing for the title of Greatest Martial Master Under the Heavens at the upcoming Contest of Mount Hua, and the same thought flashed through their minds: If I can injure him now, I'll have one opponent less to contend with.

Spurred on by that conclusion, the two martial Masters threw themselves at each other without holding back, but they were soon distracted by tussling blasts of *neigong* power. They were both familiar with the Hoary Urchin's whimsical ways, so neither was at all surprised when he turned on Guo Jing. Indeed, they were secretly pleased to be gifted a chance to ambush Zhou Botong while he was otherwise occupied.

Just as the two men turned their attention to their new target, they sensed a soft, momentary flurry overhead and deduced that it was the wake left by Zhou Botong's flowing sleeves as he leaped up onto the roof beams, leaving his sworn brother to deal with two martial Masters alone.

Extricating himself from Zhou Botong's nonsense had been a trying task for Guo Jing; he had switched between four or five martial repertoires without any luck. Just as he thought he was finally free of the Urchin's attentions and could catch his breath, he realized with a groan that he now had to face two supreme Masters at the peak of their martial learning, when just one of them was more than he could handle. He pulled himself together and made a stand using the Competing Hands technique, holding the Venom back with this left arm and fending off the leader of the Iron Palm Gang with his right.

Zhou Botong was letting his imagination run away with him, following the commotion below through movements of the air, when it suddenly occurred to him that Guo Jing could get hurt. He scurried along the rafters to the far end of the hut, slid down the wall, and groped wildly at the darkness with both hands. His fingertips made contact with someone's back.

"Hmm . . . He's crouching . . ." Zhou Botong muttered to himself. Must be the Venom!

Viper Ouyang had expected Guo Jing to quickly crumble under the joint assault, but the boy had somehow managed to hold his own, which forced the Martial Great to resort once more to his Exploding Toad kung fu. Just as he was gathering his inner strength for the attack, Viper sensed someone behind him and swept his arm back to defend himself.

Guo Jing felt the pressure ease on one side and seized the chance to put Qiu Qianren on the defensive. Carving out some breathing space with a few swift palm strikes, he then retreated into a corner of the room, thankful for Zhou Botong's timely intervention. He would not have been able to deflect Viper's signature kung fu.

The melee grew ever more intense in the deafening darkness. One moment, Qiu Qianren would find himself staving off Zhou Botong; the next, he would be up against Guo Jing or Viper Ouyang.

The Hoary Urchin scrimmaged around in high spirits, throwing punches and palm strikes indiscriminately at anyone within reach. The brawl was more exhilarating than any fight he had experienced in his life.

Keen to add to the fun, he decided to hound Guo Jing again. "Let's play a new game, Brother. You against the four of us! So, now your opponents are my two hands, the smelly Old Toad and the Iron Palm stinker!"

It goes without saying that Guo Jing did not catch a word of what Zhou Botong was saying above the noise of the battle surrounding them. All he knew was that three martial Masters were attacking him at the same time, and there was nothing he could do but dodge the onslaught as best he could.

"Fret not, fret not! I'll come to your aid when you're in danger," Zhou Botong cried cheerfully to encouraged his little brother. But, in a scuffle this volatile, involving such skilled martial artists who could only discern each other's movements through changes in the air, a stray foot or fist was liable to be lethal, and no help could come fast enough.

Guo Jing was exhausted. He had beaten back another few dozen moves, but now Viper Ouyang and Qiu Qianren were starting to channel more and more of their deep reserves of *neigong* power into their strikes. The young man scampered to and fro as he repelled the incessant barrage, hoping to find an opportunity to hop up onto the rafters for a brief respite, and yet Zhou Botong had him trapped within a force field of palm thrusts.

"Brother Zhou! What's wrong with you? Why do you keep attacking me?" Guo Jing hissed, but his voice could not compete with the racket of the warring soldiers outside.

He scuttled back a few steps and tripped over the rock, which was lying in the wreckage of the table. Crashing to the floor, he managed to vault back onto his feet, but, before he could straighten up, he sensed a rush of air coming his way. Qiu Qianren's Iron Palm kung fu. The young man twisted round and grabbed the rock, lifting it over his chest. The instant Qiu Qianren's hand struck its surface, Guo Jing channeled all the inner strength pooled in his arms and thrust outward, meeting Qiu's power head-on through the stone.

But now Guo Jing could sense the air parting to his left. He let out a roar, directed yet more energy to his arms, and hurled the stone upward. Then he swerved to the side, only just evading Viper Ouyang's vicious palm strike.

The rock smashed through the roof, bringing down a torrent of tiles and rubble. The faint glow of starlight entered the small hut.

Zhou Botong scowled. "Ugh! What fun is it now we can see?"

4

BONE-WEARY, GUO JING STAMPED HIS FEET, SPRUNG UP WITH what little strength he still possessed, and left the hut through the hole in the roof. Viper Ouyang immediately prepared to leap after him in pursuit, but a hand closed around his left shin just as he took off.

"Don't go! Stay and play with me!" Zhou Botong wailed.

Viper kicked out with his right foot and the grip loosened, but he had lost his momentum and could not prevent himself from being drawn back down to the floor.

Seizing a chance to attack Viper at his most vulnerable, Qiu Qianren aimed a kick at the Martial Great's heart. Viper hunched his back and tucked in his chest, jabbing his index finger at his attacker's ankle as he did so.

A three-way scrap broke out. There was now enough light to discern shapes in the dark, and the fighting in the village was no longer as fierce as before. For the Hoary Urchin, deprived of the thrills of fighting deaf and blind, the melee had lost all its appeal. He adopted a more ferocious kung fu style and took out his disappointment on Viper Ouyang and Qiu Qianren, lashing out in a series of lethal assaults.

Guo Jing sprinted through battling soldiers and cavalrymen charging around on their steeds, desperate to leave behind the ringing of clashing steel and the blood-curdling screams as metal ripped through flesh, not stopping until he found himself in a grove some distance from the village. His body was gripped by muscle-splitting pains after the exertions of the night. He lay on the ground, hoping that his sworn brother had the skills to get himself out of trouble, and soon drifted into a deep sleep.

Guo Jing was woken by a strange sensation. Something soft, warm and a little moist had settled on his cheek. Was he being licked? A joyous whinnying greeted him as he opened his eyes. He jumped to his feet and threw his arms around Ulaan, who nuzzled him affectionately. Both man and horse were thrilled to be reunited after their long separation. Ulaan had been grazing in the grasslands surrounding the village while Guo Jing was being held hostage by Viper Ouyang, and had only wandered further afield to avoid the clash between the two armies.

The deserted settlement was now full of broken bows and snapped arrows, dying soldiers groaning in agony, and the corpses of horses and men who were past all suffering. Guo Jing had seen his share of gory deaths on the battlefield, but, as he led Ulaan through the carnage, he thought of Lotus, lost forever to this wilderness, and his heart filled with pain. He picked his way back to the stone hut, careful not to make a sound. He could hear no voices coming from inside, so he peered in through the gap between the door and the jamb. The hut was empty. He searched the small structure inside and out, but Zhou Botong, Viper Ouyang and Qiu Qianren were long gone, and there was nothing to indicate which direction they had taken.

Guo Jing stood in a daze for a time, then mounted Ulaan and galloped east to catch up with Genghis Khan's army.

BY NOW, the great cities of Khwarazm had either surrendered or been taken by the Mongolians, and the country's army of several hundred thousand had been routed. The majority of Shah Muhammad's followers had abandoned the haughty and brutal monarch, and only a small and pitiful band remained to escort him as he fled west. Genghis Khan ordered Subotai and Jebe to lead two divisions of ten thousand men to pursue the unseated ruler, while he brought the main army home in triumph.

Subotai and Jebe hunted the Shah beyond Moscow, as far as Kiev, on the River Dnieper, where they annihilated the allied forces of the Rus and the Cumans. The captured Grand Prince of Kiev was crushed to death along with eleven Russian princes. After this decisive defeat, known to history as the Battle of the Kalka River, a significant portion of the grasslands of the Rus groaned for years under the iron hooves of the Mongolian cavalry. Shah Muhammad lived out his days in flight, until he succumbed to illness on an island in the Caspian Sea.

GENGHIS KHAN had feared the worst when he heard Guo Jing had gone missing the day after they took Samarkand—for a lone man had little chance against an army, however broken and demoralized it may be. The young man's safe return was a great relief, and, needless to say, Khojin was ecstatic too.

Qiu Chuji traveled by Genghis Khan's side throughout the army's return journey, urging the conqueror again and again to show mercy. This line of conversation did not please the Great Khan, but he respected Qiu Chuji as a wise and enlightened man, and tried to abide by the Taoist's advice. As a result, countless lives were saved.

The march home was long, and when at last the army arrived on the banks of the Onon River, having traveled the tens of thousands of *li* that lay between Khwarazm and Mongolia, a great feast was held to celebrate the victory. And, the following day, Qiu Chuji, Surefoot Lu and the Beggar Clan members said their goodbyes and went south, back to the Central Plains.

Guo Jing had been inconsolable since Lotus's disappearance. He often went on long solitary rides with Ulaan and the condors, wandering the grasslands in a stupor, not speaking to anybody for days at a time. Khojin tried to offer him words of comfort, but he did not seem to hear them at all.

Months passed. The harsh autumn wind blew across the steppes again. The army had rested well over the summer, and Genghis Khan turned his mind once more to the South, summoning his generals to the golden *ger* to discuss strategy. The conqueror was too preoccupied by the conquest of the Jin Empire to notice Guo Jing's mood. Even when every other general offered their thoughts on how to bring down the Jurchens, the young man's silence did not strike him as out of the ordinary.

After the meeting, Genghis Khan rode alone to a small hillock near the camp to contemplate his next move. The following day, he gave his generals their orders: they would lead his troops along three different routes to attack the Jin. His two eldest sons, Jochi and Chagatai, were still in the west, bringing order to the newly annexed territories, so responsibility for the conquest fell on his younger sons. His heir and third son Ogedai was to lead the main army, while his fourth son Tolui and Guo Jing were to command the left and right flanks respectively.

Genghis Khan dismissed the other generals and his personal guards, so he could speak with the three commanders alone. "The Jin's elite troops are garrisoned in Tong Pass, protected by the Qin Mountains to the south and the Yellow River to the north. It's not a stronghold we can seize quickly or easily. You've heard the different strategies presented. They all show promise, but, if we attack the pass head-on, we'll trap ourselves in a protracted siege. Seeing that we have formed an alliance with the Song Empire and seized the Jin's main capital, Zhongdu, I believe the best approach would be to enter the Jin's territory across the Song border at Tangzhou and Dengzhou, then make straight for their southern capital, Daliang."

Ogedai, Tolui and Guo Jing nodded in agreement at this shrewd plan.

Genghis Khan then turned to Guo Jing with a smile. "I've been very impressed with the way you drill and deploy your troops. What do you think we should do after we capture Daliang?"

Guo Jing gave the matter thought. After a long silence, he shook his head. "We don't attack the city."

Puzzled, Ogedai and Tolui stared at Guo Jing, waiting for further explanation, but it was Genghis Khan who spoke first. "Then what *do* we do?" A kindly smile hovered on the conqueror's lips.

"We attack by not attacking."

His answer left Ogedai and Tolui even more confused.

"We attack by not attacking," Genghis Khan repeated with a chuckle. "Very well put! Now tell your brothers what you mean."

"I believe the Great Khan's plan is to feign an attack on the capital to draw the Jin armies out of their strongholds, then crush them in one battle outside the city walls. The Jin Emperor lives in Daliang, but they don't have many soldiers stationed there. The moment they see our approach, they'll recall the elite forces at Tong Pass to relieve them.

"In Chinese military tactics, there is a saying: 'If an army marches day and night nonstop at double pace, journeying a hundred *li* to seize an advantage, it will merely result in the capture of the generals of the three main divisions. For the robust will arrive first, the weak will lag behind, and only one-tenth of the troops will reach their destination as planned.'

"Now, the distance between Tong Pass and Daliang is at least a thousand *li*. The relief force will be in a hurry, and they will be reluctant to stop for rest, so, by the time their men and horses get to the capital, they'll be worn out, whereas we would have been waiting in our camp outside the city walls. This one battle will destroy the Jin's best troops, and, with no one to defend the city, Daliang will open its gates. If we are impatient and try to place it under siege, then it is likely that we will end up trapped between the city's own garrison and the reinforcements from Tong Pass."

"Exactly!" Laughing, Genghis Khan applauded the young man's insight, then unfurled a map on his desk.

It was a survey of the area surrounding Daliang, with the anticipated movements of the two armies clearly marked out. It detailed how the Mongolian cavalry could attack from behind in order to strike at the core of the Jin forces, and how they could lure the troops out of Tong Pass, round up the weary reinforcements and annihilate them under the city walls—just as Guo Jing had described.

Ogedai and Tolui looked between their father and Guo Jing in amazement, while Guo Jing himself regarded the conqueror with admiration.

I wouldn't have come up with the strategy without *The Secret to Defeating the Jin*, which distills the wisdom of Chinese generals spanning several thousand years, he reflected. But, with the Great Khan, it's his innate brilliance as a commander that leads him to the same conclusion—he doesn't even know how to read or write.

"We will defeat the Jin on this campaign," Genghis Khan declared, taking three silk pouches from the inside pocket of his robe. "Take these and keep them safe on your person. After you've taken Daliang, the three of you are to meet at the Golden Chime Hall in the Jin Emperor's palace and open the pouches together. Then you must act according to the plans you find inside."

Guo Jing took the silk pouch, noting that the wax seal bore the Great Khan's insignia.

"You must not open them before you enter Daliang, and you are to check each other's pouches, to make sure the seal has not been tampered with, before you look at their contents."

The three young men bowed and said in one voice, "We shall obey the Great Khan's orders."

Genghis Khan turned to Guo Jing again. "Now, tell me how you manage to be so adept at marshalling troops, when you're so muddle-headed when it comes to everything else."

Guo Jing explained how he had studied every word of *The Secret to Defeating the Jin* on the long road to Samarkand. He then recounted Yue Fei's story at Genghis Khan's bidding, telling him how this patriotic General of the Song Empire had defeated the Jin forces in a decisive battle near the town of Zhuxian, and how his reputation on the battlefield had inspired such fear in the Jin soldiers that they referred to him as "Grand Lord Yue." He also told the conqueror that the legend of Yue Fei's military prowess was so rooted in the Chinese people's imagination that the saying "It is easier to crush a mountain than the Yue Family Army" was still in use.

Genghis Khan paced silently as he listened to Guo Jing, his hands clasped behind his back. "I wish I were born a hundred years earlier, so I could have met this hero on the field. Is there any adversary alive today that I can call an equal?" The conqueror heaved a lonely sigh.

5

GUO JING LEFT THE GOLDEN *GER* AND WENT TO LOOK FOR his mother Lily Li. He had been busy with the army and had not seen her of late, but, since he was due to set off for the South the next day, he wanted to spend at least a little time with her. He entered his mother's *ger*, only to find it empty, her clothes and belongings nowhere to be seen. He asked the old soldier keeping watch, and learned that she had moved to a different tent at the Great Khan's command.

When he reached her new home, he found a *ger* several times larger than the one he had just left. He parted the flies and was dazzled by the gilded and bejeweled decorations, for the colorful interior was filled with treasures plundered from the recent campaign.

Princess Khojin was sitting with Lily Li, who was sharing stories from Guo Jing's childhood. When she saw Guo Jing enter the tent, she stood up and greeted him with a shy smile.

"Ma, where do all these things come from?"

"The Great Khan said you earned him a great victory and they are your reward. I don't know what to do with them. We have always lived simply."

Guo Jing nodded at his mother's words as he noticed eight new serving maids in the *ger*—they must be slaves captured during the conquest.

Khojin stayed to chat for a short while before taking her leave. She imagined that Guo Jing must have many things to say to her before his departure and that he would soon come after her, but, though she waited and waited, he did not leave the *ger*.

Lily Li also found it odd that her son did not follow Khojin. "The Princess is waiting for you. Go and talk to her."

He mumbled a reply, but made no move to leave.

Sensing his indecision, she sighed. "I hope you will succeed in vanquishing the Jin. We've lived here in the north for twenty years, and, though the Great Khan has been very kind to us, I do miss my true home. When this campaign is over, we can return to Ox Village and live in your papa's house. I know you don't care for wealth or rank, so we don't need to come back here. The only thing that troubles me is the Princess. I don't know what would be best . . ."

"I've told Khojin everything. Lotus is dead, and I can never marry."

"The Princess may be understanding, but I'm worried about the Great Khan."

"What about him?"

"He has been exceptionally generous over the last few days, showering us with gold, silver and gems—more gifts than I can count. He says they're a reward for your contribution on the battlefield, but, having lived in his camp all these years, I'd like to think I'm familiar with his disposition. I sense an ulterior motive."

"What do you mean, Ma?"

"I'm a simple country woman and my world is very different from his . . . but he may be trying to coerce you into doing something."

"He wants to make me marry Khojin."

"I don't think the Great Khan knows you are against the match, so why would he pressure you? I suspect it has something to do with the campaign against the Jin. I think he fears you may turn against him."

"Why would I do that?" Guo Jing shook his head, unable to follow his mother's line of reasoning. "He knows I don't desire riches or power."

"Tell him I'm homesick and I'd like to go south with you tomorrow. We may be able to gauge his intentions from his response."

"Why didn't you say so earlier, Ma? I'd love to take you back to your home, and I'm sure the Great Khan will grant us permission."

Guo Jing rushed out of the *ger*, expecting to find Khojin waiting outside, but she was nowhere to be seen. Assuming that she had got bored of waiting, he headed for Genghis Khan's tent, but he returned soon afterward, utterly crestfallen.

"The Great Khan said no, didn't he?"

"I don't understand. Why does he want you to stay here?" Guo Jing waited for his mother's reply, but none came, so he went on. "First, he said, 'Wouldn't it be a fine thing to take your mother south in honor, after we've conquered the Jin?' So I told him you miss home very much and want to go back as soon as possible. Suddenly, he grew angry and kept shaking his head, refusing to hear any more on the matter."

Lily Li pondered this for a moment. "Tell me everything he's said to you today."

Guo Jing outlined the conversation in the golden *ger* earlier, telling her how they had discussed the invasion strategy and how Genghis Khan had given them the silk pouches.

"How I wish your second *shifu* or Lotus were still with us. They would figure out what's afoot. Something is making me uneasy, but I'm just a foolish old woman, I can't put my finger on it."

Guo Jing took out the pouch and turned it over in his hand. "The

Great Khan did have an odd look on his face when he handed me this, but I doubt it has anything to do with him refusing to let you go south with me."

Lily Li examined the fabric, then dismissed her maidservants. "Let's see what's inside."

"We can't! It's a capital crime to break the seal!"

She looked at her son with a chuckle. "Have you forgotten that your ma is from Lin'an? Our city is known for producing the best silk brocade under the heavens. I can pick the fabric apart and darn it back together without leaving any trace—it's a skill I learned as a child. We don't have to break the seal."

Guo Jing watched as his mother separated each strand of silk with a fine needle to make an opening and removed the paper inside. She unfolded the note and showed it to him, her eyes locked on his. They had yet to read it, but they could already feel their blood growing cold.

It was a command from Genghis Khan, instructing Ogedai, Tolui and Guo Jing to hasten south with their armies to capture their next target: Lin'an. With the fall of the Song capital, Mongolia would have conquered all the known kingdoms under the heavens. If Guo Jing were instrumental in this conquest, the note promised, he would be named the Prince of the Song under the Great Mongolian Empire, and he would rule the current Song territory from Lin'an. If Guo Jing were to turn traitor, by defying orders or deserting his troops, Ogedai and Tolui had the authority to have him beheaded and his mother would be sentenced to death by flaying. The message was written in the new Mongolian script, which Guo Jing had learned to read.

Guo Jing relayed the note's content and a heavy silence filled the *ger*.

"Ma, if we hadn't seen this . . ." His voice faltered. He dreaded to think what would have happened, but, when he spoke again, he sounded confident and certain. "I am a subject of the Great Song Empire. I cannot betray my country."

"What should we do?"

"Head south. Tonight. It will be a tough journey, Ma."

"I'll be fine. Don't worry about me. Go and get ready. Be careful—don't let anyone get wind of our plan."

Guo Jing returned to his *ger*, took off the rich robes of a *Noyan* commander and changed into an ordinary fur coat. He packed a few changes of clothes, leaving behind the valuables bestowed on him by Genghis Khan, including the golden dagger crowned with a tiger's head, from which his title Prince of the Golden Blade was derived. He then selected eight horses, in addition to Ulaan, for the journey, so they could switch mounts at regular intervals to maintain a swift pace and shake off any pursuing forces. On his way back, he passed by his mother's old *ger* and was struck by a pang of sorrow—he could never again set foot in the land of his childhood.

It was almost dark when Guo Jing arrived at his mother's new *ger*, and the scene he found inside made his heart leap into his throat. Clothes and personal belongings were strewn over the floor. His mother was nowhere to be seen and his calls went unanswered. A sense of dread rose in Guo Jing. He rushed out of the tent, only to be dazzled by countless torches.

"The Great Khan summons the Prince of the Golden Blade!" Guo Jing recognized Tchila'un's voice immediately.

Now that his eyes had adjusted to the torchlight, he saw a battalion of soldiers lined up behind Genghis Khan's most trusted general, each carrying a long spear. He appraised the situation with apprehension. His kung fu should allow him to break through, but how could he flee on his own when his mother had been taken by the Great Khan? And so he followed Tchila'un to the golden *ger*, which was protected by rows and rows of archers and guards armed with halberds.

"The Great Khan insists that you be restrained," Tchila'un added. "Please do not take offense, my Prince."

Guo Jing nodded and crossed his wrists behind his back. Once he was bound, he strode inside.

Dozens of giant tallow candles burned brilliantly, making the interior as bright as day. The moment Genghis Khan saw Guo Jing, he smacked the desk before him and roared, "I raised you and gave you my daughter. How dare you betray me!"

Guo Jing saw the open pouch and knew there was no denying his crime. Standing tall, he said, "I am a subject of the Great Song Empire. How could I follow your command and attack my own people?"

Incensed by his defiant stance, the conqueror bellowed, "Take him out and cut off his head!"

Guo Jing knew that, even with his martial knowledge, physical resistance was futile, since his hands were bound by thick ropes and he was watched over by eight executioners armed with sabers. "You made a pact with the Song to attack the Jin together, and now you're planning to renege on your word and break faith with an ally. Is that the behavior of a hero?"

Angered by Guo Jing's words, Genghis Khan kicked over his golden desk. "The alliance is over as soon as we crush the Jin. We can then take the Song without breaking our promise. Off with his head!"

Although the generals were on good terms with Guo Jing, they were too intimidated by the Great Khan to speak up for the young man. Guo Jing started to make his way outside, without waiting for the guards to manhandle him.

"Stop!" Tolui was galloping over, dressed only in leather trousers, his naked torso exposed to the night air—he must have been in bed when the news reached him.

"Father!" Tolui pleaded as he stormed into the golden *ger*. "My *anda* Guo Jing won a great victory for us. He has also saved your life and mine, over the years. He may have committed a capital crime, but we cannot behead him."

This reminder softened the conqueror's resolve somewhat. "Bring him back!" he barked, and Guo Jing was escorted into the tent again.

Genghis Khan eyed the defiant young man. "What good is holding the Song Empire close to your heart? You've told me the story of General Yue Fei. For all his loyalty, he ended up being executed by his own countrymen. If you subjugate the Song for me, I give you my word—with everyone here before us as witness—I shall name you the Prince of the Song and make you the ruler of all territory belonging to the kingdom. You are of the South, and, as the overlord of the South, you will treat your own people well. You won't be betraying your country or your blood by serving me."

"I dare not defy the Great Khan's orders, but, if you want me to attack my homeland, you can cut me with a thousand sabers and shoot me with ten thousand arrows, and still I will refuse."

"Bring his mother!"

At Genghis Khan's command, Lily Li was led from the rear of the tent by two guards.

"Ma!" Guo Jing managed two steps toward his mother before his path was blocked by sabers. For the first time, he wondered how they were found out, for there had been no one else in the *ger* when they made their plans.

"If you do as I say, you and your mother will enjoy prestige and honor. Otherwise, a saber will fall and she'll be cut in two— because of *your* choice—and you, her son, will be the cause of her death."

Genghis Khan's threat shook Guo Jing to the core. Staring at his feet, the young man tried to work out the right course of action. Then Tolui spoke again.

"*Anda*, you were born and grew up here in Mongolia. You are just like every other Mongolian. Your father was murdered because corrupt Song officials conspired with the Jurchens. It was they who made your mother homeless. If Father hadn't taken you in, would you be standing here today? You cannot be the cause of your mother's death. I urge you to think again. Accept the Great Khan's command, and you can make sure the people of the Song are treated well and have a chance to live in peace again."

The words of agreement were on the tip of Guo Jing's tongue, but, as he looked into his mother's eyes, the principles she had instilled in him flashed through his mind, followed by the scenes of carnage and destruction the Mongolians had left in their wake as they conquered the nations of the Western Regions. He did not know what choice he should make.

Genghis Khan fixed Guo Jing with tiger-like eyes, waiting for him to speak. The hundred or so gathered in the golden *ger* were also watching the young man with bated breath.

Guo Jing took a step forward and stammered, "I—I . . ." and then nothing else followed.

"Great Khan." It was Lily Li who spoke. "May I speak with my son? I think he is struggling to wrap his head around the matter."

"By all means!" Genghis Khan was delighted.

Lily Li made her way over to Guo Jing, took him by the arm, and together they sat down in a quiet corner of the golden *ger*. She pressed him close to her and said softly, "Twenty years ago, there was a blizzard in Ox Village in Lin'an. You were in my belly then. That day, your father met Reverend Qiu Chuji, and he gave us two daggers—one for your father, and one for your uncle Yang." She reached into the inside pocket of his robe, took out the blade and pointed at the two characters carved into its hilt. "Reverend Qiu named you Guo Jing, and Uncle Yang's son Yang Kang. Do you know why?"

"He wanted us to always remember the humiliation of the year Jingkang, when our capital Kaifeng was sacked by the Jurchens."

"That's right. It's a cruel shame Yang Kang grew up to call the Jin Prince his father. He brought ruin unto himself and tainted Uncle Yang's reputation as a hero and a patriot." She heaved a sigh. "Why do you think I put up with the bitter cold of these northern lands to bring you up? Do you think I endured disgrace and hardship to raise a traitor, so you can break your father's heart in the Yellow Spring below?"

"Ma!" Tears ran down Guo Jing's face.

Genghis Khan, Tolui and the generals did not understand Chinese, so they had no idea what Lily Li had said, but, judging from Guo Jing's reaction, they assumed, to their relief, that she had persuaded him to save her life.

"A lifetime passes in the twinkling of an eye," she went on. "It is a trifling matter how long we live or when we die. As long as we have no cause to rue our behavior or our deeds, then we have made a worthy journey through the world. If people disappoint us or let us down, dwell not on what they have done wrong. Remember what I have taught you."

Lily Li gazed tenderly into Guo Jing's eyes. "Son, take good care of yourself." She slipped the dagger behind Guo Jing's back, cut the ropes around his wrists, and then twisted it round, plunging its point into her own breast. She performed this series of actions with such swift determination that, by the time Guo Jing could move to stop her, the keen blade was buried in her flesh, all the way to the hilt.

"Seize him!" Genghis Khan shouted.

The eight executioners guarding Guo Jing cast their weapons aside and pounced on the young man barehanded. They were afraid of accidentally hurting the Prince of the Golden Blade as they tried to restrain him.

Overwhelmed with grief, Guo Jing clasped his mother to his bosom and swept his right foot at his assailants. Two were sent flying. He thrust his left elbow back, cracking it into another's chest. With a roar, the generals in the *ger* joined the tussle, launching themselves at Guo Jing. He stepped aside, grabbed the fabric of the tent and yanked. Half the *ger* collapsed in an instant, trapping everyone inside. All except Guo Jing, who fled into the night with his mother's body.

"MA!" GUO JING cried again and again, but he received no answer. He held a finger under her nose and there was no movement of air.

A bugle sounded the call to arms. Soon, the camp was a boiling mass of shouting men and snorting horses. Torches flickered into life like so many stars. Guo Jing ran without thinking where he was headed, and, before long, he found himself surrounded. Despite his extraordinary kung fu, he was one man against an army of more than a hundred thousand. If he had Ulaan with him, he might have had a chance of breaking free, but, on foot and laden with his mother's lifeless form, he had no hope.

Unless . . . Guo Jing began to sprint at his fastest pace. If he could get to the cliffs, he could gain some time to try to devise an escape plan, for no one in the army knew lightness *qinggong* and none would be able to scale the sheer rock face. Suddenly, he heard soldiers chanting ahead of him, then a huge warhorse charged in his direction, carrying a ruddy-faced, white-bearded general. It was Tchila'un. Guo Jing swerved away from the warrior's swinging saber and ran full pelt into the waiting troops.

Surprised by Guo Jing's charge, the soldiers shouted in alarm, but the young man took no notice of them. Once he was among them, he grabbed the shin of the warrior closest to him, and, with a tap of his foot against the ground, flipped onto the man's horse. He then hurled the soldier from the saddle, snatched up his spear and laid his mother's body over the horse's back, in one fluid motion.

Leveling the spear, Guo Jing galloped away from Tchila'un's men, though in a direction that took him farther from the cliffs. With General Boroqul's men joining in the pursuit, he was not allowed a moment to think about his route, for he was quickly encircled again, with several thousand soldiers to the south closing off his escape options.

By the time Guo Jing had successfully charged through Boroqul's riders, he was covered in blood. He knew he was able to face down so many men by himself in part because the soldiers were unwilling to fight one of their own, but what he did not realize was that Genghis Khan had forbidden the use of arrows, insisting that he be taken alive.

Guo Jing pushed on, fighting back fresh tears brought on by the stiff, cold reality in his arms. He was at last making headway toward the South, but he was still in the heartlands of Mongolia, tens of thousands of *li* from the Central Plains, with just one spear and a standard warhorse for the journey. He could not see how he could shake off the pursuing troops and return to his homeland, especially as he would soon be robbed of the cloak of darkness.

As dawn broke, a plume of dust appeared in the distance and Guo Jing picked up the sound of horses thundering his way. He pulled at the reins and turned his mount east, but the creature, having battled and galloped through the night, buckled and went down on its fore-legs, unable to stand up again. Guo Jing slipped out of the saddle and leveled the spear at the incoming soldiers, still clinging to his mother's body.

As the riders drew near, a hum penetrated the dust cloud and, the next thing Guo Jing knew, an arrow buried itself in the shaft of his spear, sending a numbing tremor up his arm. The spearhead fell to the ground as a second arrow sang through the air, aimed for his chest. He flung the spear shaft away and grabbed the bolt with both hands. Then he noticed that the arrowhead had been snapped off. He looked up to see a lone general riding over, the riders under his command hanging back. It was his old archery teacher Jebe.

"*Shifu*, have you come to take me back?"

"Yes."

Guo Jing knew he had little hope of getting away and he found some comfort in the thought that someone important to him would earn the reward for his capture.

"Allow me to bury my mother." He looked around and saw an earthen mound to his left. He carried her body over to it, dug a pit with the broken spearhead and laid her down tenderly. The dagger was still lodged deep in her chest and he could not bring himself to pull it out. He kowtowed several times, then scooped up earth with both hands and scattered it over her body. Even now, he was strug-gling to believe that his mother, who had sacrificed so much to bring him up, would be laid to rest in this wilderness, far, far away from her home . . . He crumpled to the ground and broke down in tears.

Jebe dismounted and knelt beside Guo Jing, bowing four times before the grave. Once he had paid his respects, he handed his bow, arrows and spear to the grieving young man, then went to fetch his horse and put the reins into his hands.

"Go! We will likely never meet again."

"*Shifu!*"

"You risked your life to save mine when you were just a child. Shouldn't I do the same? Am I not a man of honor?"

"But, *Shifu*, it's a grave offense to defy the Great Khan's command."

"I've won enough battles to keep my head on my neck—I'll just get a taste of the punishment staffs. Now hurry and go!"

Still Guo Jing hesitated.

Jebe gestured at the warriors behind him. "These men served under you on our campaign to Khwarazm. I didn't bring my own troops in case they had other ideas. Go and ask them—ask them if they'd exchange you for riches and glory."

The soldiers dismounted when they saw Guo Jing approach. Prostrating themselves before him, they spoke in one voice: "We wish the *Noyan* a safe journey south."

Guo Jing cast his eye around and recognized each and every face. These men had rushed headlong into death beside him on the battlefield, charging fearlessly through enemy lines without a second thought. "When the Great Khan learns that you have let me go, he will show no mercy."

"We will always be the General's men," a soldier shouted, to a chorus of agreement.

Sighing, Guo Jing waved them farewell and climbed into the saddle. Just as he was about to urge the horse forward, he noticed a cloud of dust moving furiously toward them.

All those present were alarmed by the new arrivals, Jebe in particular. He was already facing serious repercussions for letting Guo Jing go, and, if anything flared up between his men and those approaching, he would be responsible for causing a fight between brothers-in-arms.

"Guo Jing! Go!" Jebe urged.

"Do not hurt the Prince!" The cry from the incoming rider

surprised everybody. They were now close enough for Guo Jing to make out the Fourth Prince's banner.

Tolui emerged from the swirling dust and made straight for Guo Jing. His mount was lathered in red sweat. It was Ulaan.

"*Anda*, they didn't hurt you, did they?" he asked as he jumped to the ground.

"No, *Shifu* was going to bring me in." The lie was for Jebe's sake.

Tolui shot the General a glare. "Take Ulaan and go, *anda*!" He pointed to the saddlebag. "In here are two thousand *taels* of gold. We shall meet again, Brother."

Guo Jing leaped onto Ulaan. "Please ask Khojin to take care of herself—I hope she'll find a suitable husband. She shouldn't to tie herself to me."

"She will never agree to marry anyone else." Tolui heaved a deep sigh. "I know she'll head south to look for you. I'll make sure she's safe on the journey—"

"No, she shouldn't search for me. How do you find one person under this vast sky? It will only bring sorrow if we meet again."

The sworn brothers regarded each other in silence. Eventually, Tolui said, "You should go, but let me ride with you for a while."

They turned their horses toward the south and traveled side by side for more than thirty *li*.

"*Anda*, you should turn back now," Guo Jing said, looking back over his shoulder. "'A send-off spanning a thousand *li* still ends in a parting.'"

"Just a little farther."

Ten *li* later, they dismounted and said their goodbyes with a tearful hug.

Tolui watched as Guo Jing rode away, until he was no more than a speck on the horizon, and continued to stare after him as he disappeared into the boundless desert. Haunted by sorrow and a sense of loss, the Mongol Prince could not tear his eyes away from the southern skies.

CHAPTER ELEVEN

GOOD AND EVIL, RIGHT AND WRONG

I

FOR DAYS, ULAAN GALLOPED SOUTH WITH GUO JING ON HIS back, barely stopping to rest. They only eased off when they had covered enough distance that no pursuing force could hope to catch them. As they approached the Central Plains, the days grew warmer and the grass greener and more lush. But each city they passed was scarred by war, with corpses and bones piled high by the roadside. Guo Jing was shocked by the horrific sights and sounds along the way.

Resting at a dilapidated pavilion, he found himself studying the scrawls left by travelers on the walls, and one message in particular caught his eye.

A Tang dynasty poet wrote:
Running water murmurs in the slanting sun,
No sign of dogs or livestock, just croaking crows.
Thousands of villages but not one cooking fire,
No sign of habitation, just flowers wild.

Once glorious like the finest brocade, the mountains and rivers of our
Central Plains are now ruined by fierce battles waged by foreign brutes.
The people suffer greatly, their misery far beyond the weight carried
by these words.

Sorrow welled up in Guo Jing as he stared at the characters. He began to weep.

He had been riding without a destination, without a purpose. In one year, he had lost his mother, Lotus and his *shifus*—the people dearest to him in this world. They had been snatched away from him, one by one. Viper Ouyang killed his *shifus* and Lotus. He ought to take revenge, but, at the thought of retribution, the horrors of the Khwarazmian massacres flooded his mind. In his quest to avenge his father, he had caused the death of tens of thousands of innocents who had no connection to his personal feud. How could he ever make peace with that in his heart? Maybe it was wrong to seek redress?

Overwhelmed by the bereavements he had suffered, Guo Jing began to question and doubt all that he had known, believed and lived for.

I've spent my life working on my kung fu, but what was the point of all that training? he asked himself. I couldn't protect my mother. I couldn't protect Lotus. What purpose has my martial knowledge served? I tried so hard to be a good person, but did that make anybody happy? Mother died because of me. Lotus died because of me. Khojin will be miserable for the rest of her life because of me. So many people have suffered—all because of me.

No one could dispute the villainy of Wanyan Honglie and Shah Muhammad of Khwarazm, but what about Genghis Khan? He killed Wanyan Honglie, which should make him a good man, and yet he ordered me to conquer the Song Empire. He gave my mother and I refuge for twenty years, then drove her to take her own life.

Yang Kang and I made our pledge of brotherhood, agreeing to share our blessings and to bear each other's troubles, but we never lived by it—we were never of one heart. Sister Mercy Mu is a good person, so why is she so steadfast in her love for Yang Kang? Tolui and I are *anda*, we have been sworn brothers in the truest sense, and yet, if he leads his troops south, are we to face one another on the battlefield? Are we to fight to the death? No! No! We all have a mother, and they risked everything to carry us in their bellies for nine moons. Our mothers sacrificed everything to raise us. How can I kill a mother's son and break her heart? I can't bear the thought of killing Tolui, and neither could he bring himself to take my life. But how can I stand by and let him slaughter my people—the people of the Song Empire?

What's the point of learning kung fu? To fight, to kill. Everything I've done over the past twenty years is wrong. I've worked hard and strived to learn, to train. And the result? I bring harm to the people around me. If I'd known, I would have refused to learn even the simplest move. But, if I hadn't trained in the martial arts, what would I have done? What is the point of me living in this world? How should I spend the next decades before I die? Is it better to go on living or to die young? I'm already plagued by so many troubles and worries, and they're only going to grow. But what would be the point of Ma bringing me into this world if I die young? What would be the point of her putting in so much effort to raise me?

These questions whirled round and round in Guo Jing's head, and the more he tried to find answers, the more confused he became. For days now, he had found no appetite at mealtimes, and sleep had not come to him at night. He wandered the wilderness, grappling with these matters at all hours.

Ma and each and every one of my *shifus* taught me to honor my word and to always keep faith, he said to himself. And so, even though I loved Lotus with all my heart, I did not turn my back on my troth-plight to the Great Khan's daughter. But what did that lead to? Death. The unjust and untimely deaths of Lotus and my mother. And did my stubbornness make anyone happy? Not Genghis Khan, not Tolui, not Khojin.

The Seven Heroes of the South lived by the principles of righteous loyalty, but none of them came to a good end. *Shifu* Hong is generous to all, and yet he is saddled with injuries that are slow to heal. Viper Ouyang and Qiu Qianren have done many terrible things, but they still roam free and unburdened. Does the Way of the Heavens exist? Is the Lord of the Heavens blind? Does He care about justice? Does He care about good and evil?

Was I right to plead for the Samarkandians? Should I have let the Khan have his way?

Guo Jing brooded over these issues as he roamed through the wastelands, drifting without purpose. Ulaan trailed after him, stopping every so often for a mouthful of fresh grass.

I traded Lotus's life to save theirs. I didn't know a single soul in that city of several hundred thousand—I shared no ties, no bonds, no kinship with any of them, men or women, old or young. For Lotus, I'd happily give my life. It's a choice I would never rue. And yet, I asked the Great Khan to spare those wretched Samarkandians and almost lost my head in the process. My brothers-in-arms begrudged me for it too. They risked their lives to take the city, but a few words from me snatched away their chance to plunder it.

My desire to help those strangers cost Lotus her life, and I nearly paid with mine too. For their sake, I offended the Great Khan, my soldiers and my good friends. Was I an idiot? Yes, what I did was stupid—but was it something I had *to do?*

My six shifus, Master Hong and my mother all taught me to act with righteousness, to uphold justice, to help those in need. They taught me to put others first, so I'd never stand by and refuse to offer a helping hand to those in danger just because it was not to my benefit. They taught me to be prepared to give my life to stop those who would inflict harm on the defenseless.

The Jurchens invaded my homeland and butchered my people. It's my duty to resist them—whether I live or die as a result, whether my actions get me into more trouble or not, should never be my concern. If the Great Khan sacks Lin'an, he'll be killing the Song people. I'd give up Lotus, I'd give up my life to save as many as I could. That would be the right thing to do.

A great man's heart should be bounteous and compassionate. As *Shifu* Count Seven Hong has said to me many times: "Death is no hindrance to an act righteous and just." Of course, that's how it should be, but Khwarazm has nothing to do with the Song Empire, the people of Samarkand aren't Han Chinese like me. They speak a different language. They write in a different script. Even their facial features and the color of their eyes and hair are different from mine. What have they got to do with me? Why could I not stomach the sight of them being slaughtered by Mongolian soldiers? Why did I feel like that? Was I utterly, utterly in the wrong? Am I only to give my life to save those dear to me—my parents, my *shifus*, my friends and my beloved Lotus? Should I not bother with those who bear no relation to me?

When Viper Ouyang and his nephew's raft fell apart at sea, *Shifu* chose to help those scoundrels, without a second thought. He simply did what he felt he should do, not caring whether his actions would serve him well. Unlike the Venom. *Shifu* saved his life, but that heartless ingrate did not hesitate to deal his rescuer a death blow. *Shifu* nearly died from his injuries, but he never once regretted pulling them from the water and from the clutches of death.

I remember when he told us: "When we see someone in trouble, we should always help them, regardless of the consequences for ourselves. When we talk about acting with righteousness and upholding justice, we're talking about what's good and evil, what's right and wrong, and that is key to the moral code of *xia*—doing what's just, doing what's true, doing what's right, doing what's humane, doing what brings peace to our hearts. If we weigh whatever we do in terms of success and failure, gains and losses, benefits and costs—that's just business, it's not altruism or being charitable, or doing good deeds. When we do good, it may not be in our best interests, but that doesn't matter, because the point of our existence is to act 'righteous and just.'"

Yes, that's it! I see now what *Shifu* was trying to tell me. I should help my own people. I should help those of different tribes. I should do what I feel needs to be done, help anyone in need—it doesn't matter who they are or whether my actions are to my advantage or not.

If I were dying of thirst in the desert and a shepherd from Samarkand rode by on his camel, would he give me water from the plentiful supply he had? I think he would overlook the fact that we were total strangers and offer me a drink, because it would be an act "righteous and just."

I saved the people of Samarkand, but my choice condemned Lotus. Should I have acted otherwise? No! I didn't kill Lotus. It was Viper Ouyang. He chased her into the swamp. I risked my life searching for her, but I couldn't find her—I couldn't save her. I'd give my life so she could live again, but she didn't know that when she died. Now that her spirit is in the heavens, she knows. She knows that I only failed to ask Genghis Khan to cancel my betrothal to Khojin because I was begging him to spare hundreds of thousands of Samarkandians who were about to be exterminated. She knows she's the one I want to marry. She knows! She knows!

The thought that Lotus's spirit, whether in the heavens above or in the netherworld below, knew what was in his heart and that he had always been true to her, offered some solace to Guo Jing, for it meant that they had at last resolved the misunderstanding that had torn them apart. Of course, he would have much preferred that she were still alive.

I wish Lotus were still here, he sighed. She could hate me, resent me—I don't mind. She could spurn me, ignore me—I'd accept that. She could marry another man—I'd give her my blessing. As long as she was here, alive!

At last, the tangled thoughts that had so troubled Guo Jing were beginning to straighten out.

2

ARRIVING IN A SMALL TOWN NEAR THE CITY OF JINAN, in Shandong province, Guo Jing found himself a table at a tavern, in the hope of dulling his grief with drink. Just as he was gulping down his third cup, a burly man rushed through the doors.

"Tartar scum!" he shouted, jabbing a finger into Guo Jing's face. "You murdered my family. I'll kill you!" The finger was swiftly followed by a punch.

Taken aback, Guo Jing raised his left hand, caught the man's wrist and guided his fist away to one side. The reflexive defensive move slammed the fellow facedown into the floor—he clearly knew no martial arts at all. Guo Jing was extremely sorry that he had given this man a bloody forehead and extended a hand to help him up.

"Brother, you're mistaking me for someone else."

"Tartar scum!" the man yelled even louder. A dozen or so townspeople charged into the tavern and started raining blows on Guo Jing in a scrum of fists and feet.

Over the past few days, Guo Jing had come to the conclusion that kung fu brought only harm and destruction, and had made up his mind not to raise a hand against anyone. So he swerved and dodged from side to side, refusing to launch a single counterstroke at these aggressive strangers, none of whom had any martial training. But, as more and more angry men poured in, filling the little tavern, quite a number of punches and kicks began to land on his body. Guo Jing knew he had to get away from the mob before the situation got out of hand. Just as he gathered his strength to clear a path out of the tavern, he heard a familiar voice from beyond the doorway.

"Guo Jing, what are you doing here?"

The young man looked through the crowd to see strands of a long, flowing beard fluttering over plain Taoist robes—Eternal Spring Qiu Chuji!

"Elder Qiu!" he cried out in joy. "I don't know why they're attacking me."

Qiu Chuji parted the hostile horde and pulled Guo Jing out from their midst. The two martial men sped off using lightness *qinggong*, leaving the brawlers panting far behind.

Ulaan found his master by following his whistles, and it did not take long for the three of them to reach the uninhabited wilderness beyond the town. The young man recounted how he had been set upon for no reason whatsoever, but Qiu Chuji just laughed at his confusion.

"You're dressed in Mongolian clothes. The townsfolk took you for one of *them*."

The Taoist went on to explain that the Mongolians and the Jurchens had been waging war throughout Shandong. At first, the people aided the Mongols, for they had long suffered under the Jin, but soon they discovered that all soldiers are equally savage. They had merely swapped one tyranny for another—villages were still being burned, people were still being slaughtered, women were still being taken, anything of value was still being plundered . . . So, whenever the locals found Mongolian riders separated from their fellows, they would tear into the stragglers, beating them to death.

"Why didn't you fight back? You're bruised and swollen all over."

Guo Jing heaved a sigh and told Qiu Chuji about Genghis Khan'ssecret plan for the conquest of the Song Empire, which had led to his mother's suicide and his escape from Mongolia.

"We must hurry south and warn the Imperial Court. We need to prepare our defenses."

"What good will that do? When two armies meet, there won't just be mountains of dead soldiers—countless lives and homes will also be destroyed."

"The people's suffering will be greater if our Song Empire falls to the Mongols."

Guo Jing considered Qiu Chuji's response. "There are many things I struggle to fathom. Could I ask the Reverend to enlighten me?"

The Taoist monk took the young man by the hand, led him to a nearby scholar tree and invited him to sit down in its shade. "I shall do what I can."

The concerns Guo Jing had been wrestling with for the past days poured out of him, in particular his confusion over what was right and wrong, and the moral pitfalls of practicing the martial arts. When he was done, the young man exhaled deeply and added, "I have decided never again to raise a hand against another person. I wish I could unlearn what I've learned, but it's hard to make the muscles forget. Just now, without even thinking about it, I cracked open a poor fellow's head."

"You're mistaken, Guo Jing. When the existence of the Nine Yin Manual became known in the *wulin*, decades ago, many martial masters died trying to obtain it. As you know, that was why the Contest of Mount Hua was held. My *shifu*, Wang Chongyang the Double Sun Immortal, prevailed over the other Greats and won custodianship of the Manual. He had originally planned to destroy it, but he changed his mind, saying, 'Water can carry a boat, but it can also capsize it. Let the world decide whether they will use it for good or evil.'

"Literary flair, military wisdom, hardy soldiers, sharp weapons—they can all be of great benefit to humankind, but they can also bring calamity upon us. If you are compassionate and stout of heart, then, the stronger your kung fu, the more good you can do. Why would you wish to cast off your knowledge?"

"I am sure the Reverend knows best," Guo Jing said, mulling over the Taoist's words. "The greatest martial artists of our age are the Heretic of the East, the Venom of the West, the King of the South and the Beggar of the North. It's no mean feat to even approach their level, and yet, if one manages to do so, what good will it bring—for oneself and for the people?"

Qiu Chuji considered how best to respond. "Apothecary Huang's peculiar conduct is rooted in his disdain for convention and worldly ways," he said, after a long pause, "but he is not often given the chance to explain or justify himself. However, he is also known to act willfully, with little regard for others, and that I cannot condone. Viper Ouyang has done many wicked deeds and we need say no more about him. King Duan was a generous and benevolent ruler who could have done much good for the people, but he chose to renounce the world and live as a recluse because of an affair of the heart, which is not exactly the behavior of one who possesses true compassion and staunch principles. The one I wholly admire and would happily prostrate myself before is Count Seven Hong—he truly does uphold justice and help those in need. The second Contest of Mount Hua is almost upon us. It is possible that someone out there may surpass Chief Hong's martial achievements, but the heroes under the heavens will still honor him above all others in the *wulin*— because none can fault him for his actions and his heart."

"Has *Shifu* recovered from his injuries? Do you know if he'll compete on Mount Hua?"

"I haven't seen Chief Hong since returning from the Western Regions, but, whether or not he takes part in the Contest, I am sure he will be there. I am on my way to the mountain myself, in fact. Why don't you come with me?"

"Pardon me, Elder Qiu, but I do not wish to go to a place where the only talk is of kung fu." Guo Jing was feeling so disillusioned that the mere thought of the Contest made him apprehensive.

"Where will you go next?"

"I don't know."

Qiu Chuji was unsettled by Guo Jing's low spirits and withered expression, which were those of a man who had suffered a grave illness and lost all will to live. He tried to console the young man and cheer him up, but the only response he managed to solicit was a weary shake of the head.

He doesn't want to listen to me, the Taoist thought with a sigh, but he'll probably heed his *shifu* Count Seven Hong. If I can persuade him to come to Mount Hua, a reunion with Chief Hong will spur him on and lift him out of this rut. But how do I get him to join me? . . . Yes, maybe this will work!

Qiu Chuji looked Guo Jing in the eye and said, "If you truly wish to set aside your martial skills, I believe it is possible."

"Really?"

"There is a man who mastered the Nine Yin Manual without any conscious effort on his part, but, in order to stay true to the vow he made, he forced himself to forget everything—"

"Of course! Brother Zhou! He can teach me his method!"

Guo Jing jumped up in excitement, but then it struck him how rude he had been—Zhou Botong was Qiu Chuji's martial uncle, so, by calling him brother, he had just claimed to be the Taoist's senior.

Noticing the young man's sheepish expression, Qiu Chuji smiled. "Uncle Zhou cares little for hierarchies and honorifics. Call him what you like, I don't mind."

"Where is he?"

"He'll most certainly come to Mount Hua."

"I will join you, then."

When they reached the next town, Guo Jing bought a horse for Qiu Chuji and they rode side by side westward, arriving at the foot of Mount Hua in a matter of days.

3

ONE OF THE FIVE MOUNTAINS THAT CHINESE EMPERORS HAD since time immemorial made pilgrimage to, Mount Hua was known as the Mountain of the West because it occupied the most westerly location among its fellow peaks. The ancients matched the Five Mountains to the Five Classics of the Confucian canon, and Mount Hua, with its sheer crags and jagged tors, was compared to the *Spring and Autumn Annals*, which had the most austere content out of all the Classics, being a chronicle of major events in the State of Lu.

Qiu Chuji and Guo Jing began their ascent from the south, where the start of the trail was marked by the Mountain Herb Pavilion. Twelve enormous dragon-vine trees had taken root beside this open structure. Coiled and intertwined, their gnarly branches twisted toward the heavens like flying dragons, reminding Guo Jing of the Dragon Soars in the Sky technique from the Dragon-Subduing Palm. He even started to see connections between the rugged contours of the ancient bark and the key tenets of the Nine Yin Manual, and found himself dreaming up a fist-fighting repertoire of twelve moves based on their stark, knotty outlines. He was drawn into the mental exercise, until a sudden thought stole into his mind: Why am I dreaming up new ways to hurt people? I'm supposed to be setting aside my kung fu!

While Guo Jing berated himself for his lack of resolve, he heard Qiu Chuji say, "To us Taoists, Mount Hua is of great spiritual importance. These twelve dragon-vine trees are said to have been planted by our Ancient Grandmaster Chen Tuan."

"Is he the Immortal who slept for many years?"

"Quite so! Ancient Grandmaster Chen Tuan, or Master Xiyi, as he was sometimes honored, was born toward the end of the Tang dynasty and lived under five ruling families—Liang, Tang, Jin, Han and Zhou. Each time he heard about a dynastic change, he shut the doors of his house and lay down in sorrow. Rumor had it that he was deep in slumber, but, in fact, he was so concerned about the chaos and disturbances under the heavens and the sufferings of the common people that he kept himself indoors. And yet, when he heard the news that Emperor Taizu, the founding father of our Song Empire, had ascended the throne, he roared with laughter. So elated was he that he fell off his donkey and announced that peace had come to the world. Emperor Taizu was benevolent and compassionate; the people did indeed live well under his rule."

"If Ancient Grandmaster Chen Tuan were alive today, he would probably close his doors again, for years," Guo Jing said, shaking his head sadly.

Sighing, Qiu Chuji replied, "The Mongolians have taken control of the north, and now they've turned their sights on the South. Our Song Emperor and his officials are corrupt and inept. They see no way to turn the situation around, but we are full-blooded men, we cannot just give up, even when all seems lost. Master Xiyi was as wise as he was enlightened, but to stand aside and shy away from the cause of one's worries is not an act befitting a truly compassionate and righteous man, nor the behavior of one who lives according to the moral code of *xia*."

The two men left their horses at the base of the mountain and made their way up on foot. They passed through Peach Grove Plain, crossed Xiyi Gorge and continued on their way up Sal Tree Plain. Mount Hua lived up to its treacherous reputation, and the path grew more perilous with each step they took toward the summit. When they came to the Gate of Western Mysteries, the route was so steep that one had to hoist oneself up with the help of a metal cable, but Qiu Chuji and Guo Jing scaled the severe incline with ease, using lightness kung fu. After another seven *li*, they arrived at Green Branches Plain. Beyond this rare stretch of flat terrain, vertiginous rocks rose up, looking for all the world as though they had been splintered from the peak with sharp blades, and a giant boulder blocked the way to the northern escarpment.

"This is Turn Around Rock," Qiu Chuji explained. "From here to the summit, the trail is even more dangerous. Travelers would be wise to heed its advice at this point."

A small stone pavilion stood ahead of them, far in the distance. The Taoist monk pointed it out. "That's Wager Pavilion. Legend has it that Emperor Taizu played a game of Go, there, with Chen Tuan, with Mount Hua as the stake. The Emperor lost, and the people of this place have been exempt from sending silver and grain to the court ever since."

"Genghis Khan, the Shah of Khwarazm, the Emperors of the Song and the Jin—they gamble with each other for mastery of the world, and we common people are just the many stones they toy with on the Go board."

"Indeed." Qiu Chuji nodded in agreement. "Guo Jing, it makes me very happy to hear that you've been thinking about such matters, and that you're no longer the unworldly, rather ignorant boy you once were. As you have wisely observed, these kings, rulers and generals wager their subjects and their kingdoms, and when they lose, they don't just lose their lands, they lose their heads, and in the process bring immeasurable pain to the people."

The conversation lapsed as the two men navigated the Thousand *Chi* Precipice and the Hundred *Chi* Crevice, for so narrow were these passes that they could only progress by squeezing themselves through them sideways.

Guo Jing marveled at the dizzying landscape. If someone were to waylay us here, he said to himself, we'd have no room to maneuver or defend ourselves.

Just as that notion entered his head, a man called out to them from up ahead. "Qiu Chuji, we spared you at the Tower of Mist and Rain. Why are you here on Mount Hua?"

The Taoist dashed forward a few steps and took cover in a slight recess along the cliff wall. Marginally less exposed, he looked up to see Hector Sha, Tiger Peng, Lama Supreme Wisdom and Browbeater Hou blocking the precipitous path to the summit. He had expected Viper Ouyang and Qiu Qianren to make an appearance, but had reasoned that since Zhou Botong, Count Seven Hong and Apothecary Huang would also be present, he would not have to worry about them. What he had not foreseen was that mediocre martial artists like Hector Sha would also make the journey, and that they would be so contemptible as to ambush him during his ascent through unfavorable terrain.

Qiu Chuji was now standing in a less precarious spot, but it would not take much to send him plummeting into the ravine ten thousand *zhang* below. To grasp the advantage of making the first move, the monk drew his sword with a *sha!* and thrust its point at Browbeater Hou in a White Flash Pierces the Sky.

The Three-Horned Dragon was not only the weakest of Qiu

Chuji's assailants, he had also lost an arm to Apothecary Huang in Ox Village. Nevertheless, he was able to twist away from the ferocious lunge and fend it off with his pitchfork.

As the two weapons clashed, Qiu Chuji's strength surged to the tip of his blade. Using the point of contact as a pivot, the Taoist sprung up and vaulted over Browbeater Hou's head, a leap that also sent him sailing clear of Tiger Peng and Lama Supreme Wisdom's combined pincer assault.

Their weapons fell on the cliff face instead. Sparks flew as metal grated on rock.

Seeing his companions fail to hold back Qiu Chuji, despite their three to one advantage, Hector Sha swerved this way and that using Shape Changing kung fu to block the Taoist monk's advance. Qiu flashed his sword, forcing Sha to retreat farther and farther back. The Dragon King was determined to stand in the Quanzhen Master's way, but he too was impeded by the loss of an arm, which had been hacked off at Iron Spear Temple to stem the spread of Viper Ouyang's venom.

At last, Qiu Chuji managed to push past his opponent, but Hector Sha gave chase, refusing to give him a moment's respite. Tiger Peng had now rejoined the fray, jabbing at Qiu with his Scribe's Brushes, while Lama Supreme Wisdom clashed and clanged his cymbals.

Guo Jing could see that Qiu Chuji was increasingly hard-pressed. He knew he ought to step in, but, at the same time, he was revolted by the fierce fighting—surely it would be immoral to involve himself in such a scrap. He turned his back on the skirmish and climbed down the pass with the help of a vine, looking for a different route to the summit. As he walked away, two questions echoed in his mind: Should I help Elder Qiu? Should I raise my fists again? The more he agonized over what he ought to do, the more befuddled he became. If I don't help him and he ends up injured or worse, would it be my fault? If I help him and throw his attackers off the cliff, would that be right or wrong?

He was now so far from the scuffle that he could no longer hear the clash of weapons. Sitting down on a boulder, he stared blankly at the majestic prospect, trying to settle on the right course of action.

Guo Jing focused on his dilemma, with no sense of how much time was passing, until a rustle from a nearby clutch of trees jolted him back to the present. He looked over to find a man with long white hair and a ruddy complexion peering at him—Graybeard Liang the Ginseng Codger—then turned back to survey the view once more.

Putting Guo Jing's blank reaction down to his confidence in his superior martial skills, Old Liang ducked back among the trees. He was ruffled to be so ignored, though he could not deny that the boy was indeed more than a match for him. He watched from his hiding place with bated breath, expecting Guo Jing to come for him at any moment, but the frowning young man just mumbled to himself, listless and lost, as if he had been possessed by demons.

Why's he acting so strange? Graybeard Liang wondered. He decided to give Guo Jing a little prod.

Not daring to draw near, he threw a stone at the boy's back. Guo Jing merely turned a fraction to the side to evade the projectile. He did not acknowledge the culprit with so much as a glance.

Taking courage from this, the old man drew nearer. "Guo Jing, what are you doing here?"

"I'm wondering if it's right to inflict harm on another with my kung fu," came the honest answer.

It took a moment for the Ginseng Immortal to grasp the significance of this response. The boy really is a fool, he thought with excitement, taking a couple more steps forward.

"Certainly not! It's deeply wrong to use one's martial skills to hurt others."

"You think so too? I really want to purge everything I know from my head and my body."

Old Liang kept his eyes locked on Guo Jing, who was gazing at the sky, and said in his most soothing tone, "I've been trying to forget my martial knowledge too. I can help you, if you like." As he spoke, he crept up to a spot right behind the young man.

Taking no notice of his furtive approach, Guo Jing replied, "Great! Tell me what I should do."

"I know an excellent way."

The Ginseng Immortal seized Guo Jing, locking two major pressure points, Celestial Pillar, at the nape of his neck and Spirit Hall, near the right shoulder blade. By the time the young man had registered the contact, his whole body had gone numb and he had lost control of his limbs.

Graybeard Liang sniggered. "You'll know no kung fu when I'm finished with you." Then he clamped his teeth over Guo Jing's throat, breaking the skin. He lapped up the blood, careful not to waste a single drop, for it had been fortified by the vital fluid of the python he had spent many years cultivating with precious medicinal herbs.

Your kung fu improved so much after you drank my snake's blood, whereas I'm still stuck at the same level. Old Liang sucked harder at the memory of that fateful night. I'm going to take back what's mine—I'll drink you dry! He slurped away, too worked up to give any thought to whether the python blood was still potent after two years in the boy's veins.

Stars danced before Guo Jing's eyes. Whether from pain or from blood loss, he was not certain, but he knew he ought to resist. He summoned his strength, but, with the two acupoints sealed, he could not channel his energy at all. He watched as crimson webs spread across the whites of his attacker's eyes and a feral snarl took over the man's face.

He's going to bite through my windpipe! The young man's body screamed as Old Liang's teeth sank deeper into his flesh.

Guo Jing no longer had the mental capacity to agonize over whether or not it was acceptable to use his martial knowledge. Instinct took over. Drawing on the Transforming Muscles, Forging Bones technique from the Nine Yin Manual, he sent a blast of elemental *qi* from his Elixir Field to the two vital points in his enemy's control. The force disrupted the joints in Graybeard Liang's thumbs and index fingers, making his hands slip off the vital points.

Guo Jing dipped his chin, hunched his shoulders and tugged in his stomach sharply. This series of subtle movements generated an explosive burst of energy from his waist, far more powerful than anything the arms or legs could muster. It rocked the older man's footing and tossed him up into the air.

Over Guo Jing's head and over the cliff edge.

Graybeard Liang's spine-chilling cries echoed between the bare crags, amplified by the sheer rocky surfaces. Guo Jing stared into the depths in shock, trying to come to terms with what he had done.

I have killed yet another person with my martial learning . . . But, if I hadn't reacted that way, I'd be dead. It's not right to take his life, but am I supposed to do nothing and let him kill me?

Accepting that he had no answer to this, Guo Jing leaned over the edge and looked down into the gorge. He was so high up that he could not see all the way to the bottom—it was impossible to determine the Ginseng Codger's final resting place.

GUO JING sat back down, still in a daze. After a while, he remembered the wound on his neck and tore a strip from his robe. He had just finished bandaging when—*clack . . . clack clack*—he heard a series of intermittent, arrhythmic taps coming from behind him.

As he turned, a strange sight came into view. It was a moment before he registered the figure as human.

But it was upside down, as though doing a handstand.

The man clutched a round stone in each hand. With each "step," he struck them against the rocky ground, which accounted for the clacking sounds.

Astonished that anybody would choose to move around in such a curious manner, Guo Jing squatted down and tilted his head to get a better look at the man's face.

Viper Ouyang!

He backed away, eyeing the Martial Great with caution, convinced that some infernal plot was unfolding—the timing of the Venom's appearance, so soon after the unpleasant encounter with Graybeard Liang, and the peculiar manner of his entrance were too strange to be a coincidence.

Viper bent his arms, then straightened them out, springing onto a boulder. He landed on his head, pressed his arms to his sides and extended his feet into the sky in a headstand. His body was as stiff as a corpse.

Intrigued, Guo Jing could not resist asking about the meaning of this series of bizarre moves. "Master Ouyang, what are you doing?"

But the martial Master did not grant him an answer. He looked as if he had not heard a word he had said. Guo Jing retreated a few more paces and held his left arm over his chest to guard it. Thus protected, he observed the Venom from a safe distance. He waited for some time, long enough to drink a pot of tea, and yet Viper did not move from that awkward stance. The young man was eager to get to the bottom of this perplexing display, but it was hard to read the Martial Great's face because of his inverted posture. So, Guo Jing turned his back on the Venom and bent over to look through his parted legs. Now that he was oriented the same way, he noticed that his nemesis was sweating profusely. He seemed to be in great discomfort.

He must be practicing some strange *neigong* technique. Just as the thought presented itself to Guo Jing, Viper stretched his arms out until they leveled with his shoulders and began to rotate, pirouetting on his head like a spinning top. He whirled faster and faster, his sleeves flapping noisily in the gust whipped up by his movement.

He is indeed practicing internal kung fu, Guo Jing said to himself. What a curious technique that it requires him to be upside down like this!

Suddenly, it struck him that Viper Ouyang was at his most vulnerable right now, for, when cultivating advanced inner-strength skills, one had to center all the energy in the body, to the point where there was nothing left to defend against even the smallest external provocation. It was customary to ask teachers or friends accomplished in the martial arts to stand guard, or to find a secluded place, to avoid being disturbed.

Yet, it seemed to Guo Jing that the Venom was practicing here alone, neglecting to take any of the usual precautions. It was especially baffling that he would do so on Mount Hua, at a time when the greatest martial Masters under the heavens were assembling in that very place. Most heroes of the *wulin* were at odds with Venom of the West, and there were probably enough plots against his person brewing on an ordinary day, let alone on the eve of the second Contest. What had made him so brazen as to train by himself? In his current state, it would take no more than a simple punch or a regular kick from a well-built man without any knowledge of kung fu to cause him grievous internal injuries. Right now, Viper Ouyang was a piece of meat lying on the chopping block, waiting for the carver's knife.

As that image flashed by, Guo Jing thought of Lotus and his *shifus*. Killed or murdered at the hands of this unscrupulous man. This was the chance for revenge he had been dreaming of. What was he waiting for? He took a couple of steps toward the man who had taken so much from him, but, all of a sudden, he saw Graybeard Liang plunging to his death in his mind's eye again.

Laden with guilt, the young man halted, unable to steel his heart to take yet another life.

By now, the Venom had started to slow down, and he soon came to a complete stop. He held the inverted position for some time before flipping upright in a half somersault. Drawing himself up to his full height, he walked back the way he had come—on his feet, this time—gazing straight ahead.

Guo Jing tiptoed after the Martial Great, burning with curiosity.

4

Guo Jing followed Viper Ouyang up a verdant slope to a slate ridge, where the Venom stopped at the mouth of a cave and spoke in a gruff tone. "*Hahoramanpayas sinajaya sagara.* Your interpretation of this line is wrong. It doesn't work in practice."

Sheltering behind a boulder, Guo Jing was astonished to hear him quoting from the final passage of the Nine Yin Manual. He recalled how he had set down this portion of the text without altering a single character because Count Seven Hong feared that the Venom might be able to understand the mysterious language it was written in.

Who was he talking to?

A light, melodious voice drifted from the cave. "My interpretation isn't the problem. It's you. Your kung fu isn't up to the task. No wonder you failed."

Lotus!

Guo Jing nearly cried out her name. The very person he had mourned night and day for months. How did she survive the swamp? Am I dreaming? Is this an illusion? Am I so maddened by grief that I'm hearing voices?

Viper's harsh tones cut through the storm of questions in Guo Jing's head.

"I tried what you described. There can't be any mistake on my part, but the flow in the Conception Vessel and the Yang Link Meridian won't reverse."

"Force is futile in kung fu when you haven't reached the necessary level."

That is Lotus's voice! There's no doubt about it, Guo Jing told himself, trembling with excitement. Light-headed and overjoyed, he had somehow torn open the bite wound in his agitation and blood was seeping from the bandage, but the pain did not bother him in the slightest.

"The Contest begins at midday tomorrow. I don't have time for this. Explain the rest of the passage now!"

Guo Jing now understood why Viper Ouyang had risked practicing *neigong* in the open earlier without taking any of the usual precautions.

A peal of laughter beat back the Martial Great's wrath. "Have you forgotten your pact with my Guo Jing? He promised to spare your life three times—on the condition that it would be up to *me* whether or not I was willing to teach you."

An indescribable warmth spread through the young man's heart at the sound of his beloved's voice uttering the words "my Guo Jing." He wanted to jump up and shout at the top of his lungs to let out the euphoria inside.

"We may have an agreement, but the situation changes things." Viper dropped the stones he had held in his hands while he was walking upside down and strode into the cave.

"Have you no shame? I won't tell you anything!"

"We shall see . . ."

A wild cackle, followed by a scream and the sound of fabric ripping.

Guo Jing rushed into the cave, holding his left palm before him in defense. Once more, he acted out of instinct. There was no time to consider the moral implications of using his kung fu.

"Lotus, I'm here!"

The fingers of Viper's left hand were wrapped around the end of the Dog-Beating Cane, while his right hand reached for Lotus's shoulder. She thrust the bamboo stick forward and it slid out of the Venom's grasp at an angle.

Flick the Mangy Dog Away, a move from the Dog-Beating repertoire, known only to the Chief of the Beggar Clan.

The Venom applauded the nimble maneuver, but, now that Guo Jing was here, he knew he could not continue to coerce Lotus into sharing her knowledge. After all, he was a grandmaster of the martial arts, and it was not befitting for a man of his status to be caught breaking his word. The last thing he needed was to be grilled by the boy over his failure to honor their pact. He shook out his sleeve with a wave of his arm to hide his burning cheeks and shot out of the cave, disappearing down the slope in the blink of an eye.

Quivering with joy, Guo Jing hurried over to Lotus and clasped her hands between his. "I've missed you so much!"

She pulled away and shot him a black look. "Who are you? Why do you take my hands?"

"I—I am Guo Jing . . . You—"

"I don't know who you are." She cut him off and stalked out of the cave.

Guo Jing hastened after her, bowing as he spoke: "Lotus! Lotus! Hear me out!"

"*Huh!* Who are you to me? How dare you address me by my given name!"

Guo Jing opened his mouth to answer, but no words came out.

Lotus stole a glance at him. She had never seen him so haggard and withered, and a pang of pity hit her. But as she recalled how he had chosen time and again to turn his back on her—and their future together—she felt her heart harden and she walked away with a *pah!*

Panicking, Guo Jing caught her flowing sleeve to hold her back. "Allow me to say one thing," he begged in a faltering voice.

"Go on."

"When I found your golden hair band and your sable coat in the swamp, I thought you—"

"There, you've said your *one* thing." She pulled the fabric out of his grasp and headed down the crest to find the way to the summit.

Guo Jing found himself in a familiar bind. He was desperate to explain himself, but he did not know how to put all that he had been feeling into words, and he could see that Lotus was determined to cut all ties with him. Fearing that, if he let her out of his sight, he would never see her again, he trailed after her in silence.

Lotus marched away in agitation, her robe fluttering in the wind. This unplanned reunion was stirring up memories and feelings from the past few months that she would rather forget. The great dangers she had faced, casting off her golden hair band, her pearl brooch and her sable coat in the marsh to throw Viper Ouyang off her trail. The misery of traveling thousands of *li* eastward on her own, without any company, then falling grievous sick in Shandong, when all she wanted was to be home with her father on Peach Blossom Island. The bitter reality of being bedridden, with nothing to occupy her but thoughts of how faithless and heartless Guo Jing had been, and how she wished her parents had not brought her into this world and exposed her to such anguish. And the despair when Viper Ouyang captured her in southern Shandong and dragged her along to Mount Hua so she could explain the Nine Yin Manual.

These unpleasant ghosts of the recent past shadowed Lotus as she picked her way along the dangerous pass, as did the light scuffle of Guo Jing's footsteps. She sped up, only to hear him pick up his pace; the opposite happened when she slowed down. Losing patience with him, she whipped around and snapped, "Why are you following me?"

"I will follow you always. I will never leave you again this lifetime."

Lotus responded with a sneer. "Why would the Prince of the Golden Blade, the son-in-law of the great Genghis Khan, wish to follow this poor nobody?"

"How could I have anything more to do with that man when he caused the death of my mother?"

Guo Jing's reply made Lotus flush red with fury. "There I was thinking you hadn't forgotten about me entirely, but it turns out you only came looking for me because you've been kicked out by Genghis Khan. Now that you're neither a prince nor the conqueror's son-in-law, you remember this poor nobody. Do you think I'm so base and low that I'm happy to be at your beck and call when you need me, and cast aside when you don't?" Tears of anger rolled down her cheeks.

The sight of her crying sent Guo Jing into a blind panic. He wanted to explain himself, he wanted to say something to comfort her, but no words would come to him. He stood there, mouth agape, until he eventually managed to say, "Do what you want with me. Hit me. Kill me. I'm right here, Lotus."

"Why would I want to do that?" she said feebly, heartsick. "Can't you pretend we've never met? . . . I beg you. Stop following me."

All color drained from Guo Jing's face. "Tell me how I can convince you that I am true of heart."

"You'll make up with me today, but, when Princess Khojin turns up tomorrow, you'll cast me to the back of your mind. Nothing you do or say will convince me that you'll be constant. Unless you're dead, maybe."

Hot blood surged in Guo Jing's chest. Nodding at her words, he strode toward the brink. They had reached one of the most perilous sections of Mount Hua, known as the Cliff of Sacrifice. To leap from here would break every bone in his body. Seeing that he was taking her words literally, in his usual pig-headed way, she lunged, grabbing the back of his robe to hoist herself up. With a tap of her foot on his shoulder, she propelled herself over his head and landed between him and the precipice.

"I know you don't care for me! Now you won't even let a few words said in anger pass. I'll say this once—you don't have to upset me like this. Just don't ever come near me again."

Lotus was visibly shaking, her face white as snow. Perched on the very brink above the jagged rocks below, she resembled a white camellia shivering in a storm.

Guo Jing was ready to jump, but, seeing Lotus balancing so precariously, he stepped back. "Don't stand so close to the edge."

His apparent concern made Lotus's heart ache. "Who wants your false words and false feelings?" she hissed. "When I was alone and

sick in Shandong, why didn't you come to see me? When I failed to
shake off the pesky Old Toad, why didn't you come to rescue me?
My ma didn't want to have anything to do with me. She passed on
from this world, leaving me behind. My pa doesn't want me—he
never bothered to look for me. And you don't want me either! No
one in this world wants me. No one cares for me!" She stamped
her foot and sobbed helplessly, the bitter heartbreak and disillusion
built up over the past year pouring out with her tears.

Guo Jing agreed with every statement she had made. In fact, he
despised himself more with each word wrung from her shivering
frame. As Lotus braced herself against a sudden gust of wind, he took
off his outer robe, but, before he could wrap it around her, he heard
a familiar voice.

"Who's making our Miss Huang cry?"

A man with flowing hair and a beard to match appeared next to
them, but Guo Jing did not spare the newcomer a single glance.

Still in a foul mood, Lotus greeted him sharply. "Hoary Urchin!"
she snapped. "I sent you to kill Qiu Qianren. Have you brought me
his head?"

"Good Miss Huang, tell me who upset you?" Zhou Botong asked,
trying to divert her attention from his failed mission. "The Urchin
will make them pay."

"Him." She jabbed her finger at Guo Jing. Keen to ingratiate himself, Zhou Botong boxed his sworn brother about the ears without
giving the young man any warning.

The smacks landed loudly on Guo Jing's cheeks, almost knocking the light from his eyes. He was so consumed by Lotus's presence
that he had failed to see the attack coming.

"Dear Miss Huang, was that enough? If not, I'll cuff him a few
more times."

Lotus's fury melted away at the sight of the fiery, hand-shaped
marks on each side of Guo Jing's face. She felt a spark of rekindled
tenderness, but it was short-lived, quickly consumed by an overwhelming displeasure that found an easy target in Zhou Botong.

"I'm upset with him. What's that got to do with you? Who says you can beat him up? I sent you to kill Qiu Qianren. Why haven't you done so?"

Zhou Botong stuck out his tongue and sighed. That kiss on the arse had fallen woefully wide of the mark. He had no wish to face Lotus's ire any longer than was necessary, and, while he turned over in his head excuses to slip away, he heard the clash of weapons, along with faint shouting, coming from somewhere behind them.

"Hark! It must be Qiu Qianren. I'll finish him off," he cried, hot-footing it in the direction of the distant commotion.

If Qiu Qianren had been responsible for the muted clamor from afar, Zhou Botong would in fact have bolted in the opposite direction. After Guo Jing had at last managed to extricate himself from the scuffle in the deserted village in the Western Regions, Viper Ouyang too had abandoned the fight, leaving Qiu Qianren alone to deal with Zhou Botong's harassment.

As the leader of one of the largest martial groups in the *wulin*, Qiu Qianren knew he would not live down the humiliation of being captured by the Hoary Urchin, but he was worn out physically and mentally by his attempts to evade him. He resigned himself to the harsh truth that he would have to take desperate measures to preserve his dignity and free himself from the ordeal. Catching a glimpse of several venomous snakes coiled up together in the sand, he recognized that they were an extremely deadly species. One bite would be enough, and, as it would also numb the body, it would be among the least painful ways to die. He reached out and pinched one of the serpents seven inches below its head, snatching it up.

"Zhou Botong, you've won!" he cried, aiming the fangs at his wrist, ready to end his life.

But, the instant the Urchin made out the scaly creature held between Qiu's fingers, he let out a yelp and scurried away.

It was a short while before Qiu Qianren realized that the exaggerated reaction was brought about by the snake—and that the tables had been decisively turned. He armed himself with a second serpent and raced after his tormentor, yelling to catch his attention.

Zhou Botong, convinced that his organs were about to burst open from fright, ran as fast as his legs would allow. As it happened, Qiu Qianren's lightness kung fu was more advanced than that of his erstwhile pursuer—after all, it was the reason he was honored in the *wulin* as the Iron Palm Water Glider. He could easily have overtaken the Urchin, but he was still wary of him after suffering at his hands for so long. And so, one fled and the other gave chase, and the game continued until the sky grew dark. In the failing light, Zhou Botong managed to lose his tail, but, in fact, Qiu had allowed him to escape so he could make his own retreat.

The next day, Zhou Botong stole a fine horse and galloped east, hoping to shake Qiu Qianren off once and for all.

LOTUS'S EYES followed Zhou Botong as he scuttled away, then her gaze shifted to Guo Jing. After a while, she glanced down at her feet and sighed.

"Lotus."

"Mm."

Catching her barely perceptible response, Guo Jing readied himself to apologize once more and beg her forgiveness, but he knew how inarticulate he was and he could not risk angering her further by saying the wrong thing. So, they just stood looking each other on the exposed crag, while the wind blew about them. The sound of Lotus sneezing reminded Guo Jing that he had been about to put his robe around her. She accepted the garment without resistance nor any acknowledgment, her head bowed, not favoring him with so much as a glance.

Merry chortles interrupted their awkward standoff. Zhou Botong's voice could be heard again, crying, "Marvelous! Marvelous!"

Lotus took Guo Jing's hand and said softly, "Let's see what's going on."

The young man burst into joyful tears, too relieved to muster a reply.

Chuckling, Lotus dabbed his eyes with her sleeve. "Look at yourself. People will think you're crying because I slapped you."

"Nothing would make me happier."

She flashed him a radiant smile.

The young lovers had finally set aside their differences. Hand in hand, they headed away from the precipice. It did not take them long to find Zhou Botong. He was lounging on a boulder, his hands resting on his belly and his foot on his knee, looking distinctly pleased with himself. Qiu Chuji stood beside him, gripping the hilt of his sword. Hector Sha, Tiger Peng, Lama Supreme Wisdom and Browbeater Hou were present too, and the four of them were all in the process of launching an offensive with their weapons or shrinking away from an attack. They each maintained a different posture, but the one thing they had in common was that they were all frozen stiff, as though carved of wood or shaped from clay. The Hoary Urchin had locked their movements via their acupoints.

"*Huh!* Last time you smelly vagabonds fell into my hands, you stopped listening to me when you realized my little balls of grime weren't deadly poison. Well, well, let's see how defiant you are today." Zhou Botong had not yet decided how to deal with them, but he knew Lotus would be full of ideas. "Good Miss Huang, I present these stinking thieves to you," he said, hailing the new arrivals.

"What am I supposed to do with them?" She eyed the capricious man. "So . . . you don't want to kill them, but you don't want to let them go either, am I right? And you're not sure how to keep them in line. Now, if you call me Big Sister three times, I'll tell you what to do."

The Hoary Urchin did as he was asked, accompanying two cries of "Big Sister!" with a bow, before choosing to finish with a flourish, exclaiming, "Dear Auntie!"

Tickled to be addressed as an elder by her senior, Lotus pointed at Tiger Peng, struggling to supress a smile. "Search him."

Zhou Botong found Peng's secret weapon, a ring studded with pins laced with venom, along with two small bottles of antidote.

"He pricked and poisoned your martial nephew Ma Yu with that. You should do the same to him."

Tiger Peng and his fellows might have been immobilized, but there was nothing wrong with their hearing. Lotus's words sent their frightened spirits flying out of their bodies, and, the next thing they knew, they were being stung repeatedly by the toxic ring.

"Now they'll do anything you tell them to. Just make sure you don't lose the antidote."

Chuckling, the Urchin cocked his head to one side and wondered what other tricks he could pull on the four men. He scratched around his body, harvesting a good deal of detritus, which he mixed with the antidote and rubbed into little balls. These he stuffed back into the bottles, which he then handed to Qiu Chuji.

"Take these scoundrels back to the Zhongnan Mountains and lock them up in the Chongyang Temple for twenty years. If they behave themselves on the way there, you can give them one of these miraculous pills. If they don't, give them another taste of their own poison—no need to be merciful."

Qiu Chuji bowed, accepting the task.

"Well said, Old Urchin." Lotus flashed him a broad grin. "You've really come along, this past year!"

Puffed up by her praise, Zhou Botong released the men's vital points. "Off you go to Chongyang Temple. If you change your ways in good faith, maybe you'll become men, after all. But, if you don't do as you're told . . ." He sniggered. "We Quanzhen monks kill without batting an eye and tear out flesh without creasing our brows. We'll neutralize the poison in your body, then cut you up to make meat-balls. Enough to feed the whole monastery. Then we'll see if you can still get up to mischief!"

The captured men vowed to be good. Stifling a smile, Qiu Chuji took his leave, escorting the four rogues down Mount Hua with his sword in his hand.

Lotus chuckled. "When did you learn to scold like that? It started out promising, but then it just got ridiculous."

Zhou Botong threw his head back and laughed. In that moment, he caught from the corner of his eye a flash of white light from the peak to his left—sunlight reflecting off a fine blade.

"Oooh, what's that?"

Guo Jing and Lotus turned in the direction he was indicating, but they did not spot anything.

"I'll take a look," the Urchin said, charging full pelt uphill. He wanted to get away before Lotus could ask him about Qiu Qianren again.

Now that they were finally alone, the young couple could not wait to discuss all they had experienced in the time they were apart. They sat down at the entrance to a shallow cave and talked until the sun dipped behind the mountains to the west—and still they had more to share. Guo Jing took a dried flatbread from his knapsack and tore a piece off for Lotus.

"Remember the scrambled version of the Nine Yin Manual you set down for the Venom?" Lotus giggled as she chewed. "Following your good example, I've also been inventing interpretations for him. He lapped them up without ever doubting their veracity—he's been practicing earnestly for months. I told him that this advanced kung fu has to be cultivated upside down, and he followed my ramblings to the letter, walking around on his hands, forcing his *qi* to circulate in reverse. I have to give the Old Toad some credit, though—he's now able to flip the flow in the Yin Link, Yang Link, Yin Heel and Yang Heel meridians at will. I wonder what it would be like if he managed to invert every energy channel."

"So *that's* why he was walking on his hands just now. It can't be easy."

"Have you come to win the honor of the Greatest Martial Master Under the Heavens?" Lotus asked, after a brief silence.

"Don't make fun of me. I'm here to ask Brother Zhou to teach me how to unlearn my kung fu," Guo Jing said, and he outlined for her the issues that he had been contemplating of late.

Lotus tilted her head to one side, considering his words. "It probably is better to forget it all," she said with a sigh. "It's true that, as our martial prowess grows, we also become less happy, whereas, when we were young and knew nothing, we lived without a care in the world." Somehow, it did not occur to her that this was just the inevitable result of growing up, and had nothing to do with one's martial ability. She paused, then changed the subject. "Viper Ouyang said that the Contest starts tomorrow. Papa will surely be there. Since you're not taking part, we should help him claim the title."

"I don't ever want to say no to you, Lotus, but I do think our *shifu* deserves it more—for his compassion and his principles."

Lotus had been resting against Guo Jing, but now, vexed by his implied criticism of her father, she pushed him away. He was flustered by her sudden anger, but, when she spoke, there was a hint of laughter in her voice.

"Well, I can't deny that *Shifu* Hong has treated us well. How about we help no one?"

"Your papa and our *shifu* are both men of honor and virtue. They wouldn't want us plotting anything behind their backs."

"So I'm a conniving villain now, am I?" She fixed him with a stony glare.

"Forgive me!" he cried in panic. "I'm not good with words. I didn't mean to upset you."

"You're going to upset me again and again, in the years to come," she replied, trying to swallow a giggle.

Guo Jing looked at her and scratched his head, unable to catch her meaning.

"If you don't cast me aside again, we'll have plenty of time together, so who knows how many more silly things you'll say to me?"

Thrilled by her talk of a future together, he took her hands tenderly in his. "Why would I ever cast you aside?"

"It wouldn't be the first time. But I suppose you'll come running back to me when your Princess gets tired of you."

The joke cut Guo Jing to the quick, bringing to mind his mother's death. The moon had just risen, casting a silver glow on everything it touched. Lotus saw his expression and realized she had spoken out of turn.

"Let's not bring up the past anymore. I'm very happy being with you right now. You may kiss my cheek, if you'd like."

The young man blushed, but dared not accept the invitation. Lotus gave him an abashed smile and turned the conversation back to the Contest. "Who do you think will win tomorrow?"

"It's hard to say. Do you think Reverend Sole Light will take part?"

"Uncle Sole Light has left behind the troubles of this world. Surely he won't be competing for the title."

Guo Jing bobbed his head in agreement. "Your papa, *Shifu* Hong, Brother Zhou, Qiu Qianren and Viper Ouyang—they each have their signature skill to rely on. I wonder if *Shifu* has recovered or if his kung fu is still affected . . ." His concern for Count Seven was evident in his voice.

"The Hoary Urchin would be the strongest if he used techniques from the Nine Yin Manual, but he won't, and that leaves him the weakest of the five."

As the young lovers continued to talk—about the Contest and anything else that sprang to mind—Lotus began to feel drowsy, dozing off in Guo Jing's embrace. It was rare for her to remove the Hedgehog Chainmail, so she had developed a special way of leaning into him to save him from being pricked. She had not reclined like this for a long time, and it filled her heart with a contentment beyond description. Guo Jing too was feeling heavy-eyed, but soon the light scratching of footsteps jolted him awake.

5

A SHADOWY FIGURE SHOT PAST THE MOUTH OF THE CAVE, followed a moment later by another, their robes flapping behind them in a gale of their own making. Guo Jing immediately recognized Zhou Botong as the one on the run, thanks to his distinctive lightness *qinggong*, and, a moment later, he managed to place the man in pursuit . . . Qiu Qianren! The young man was mystified. The last time he had come across the two of them together, far out in the Western Regions, the leader of the Iron Palm Gang had been fleeing from Brother Zhou. How had they come to switch roles? He had no idea that Qiu had discovered the Hoary Urchin's fear of snakes.

He nudged Lotus and whispered in her ear, "Look!"

She lifted her head to see Zhou Botong scurrying around in the moonlight, casting fearful glances over his shoulder.

"Qiu, you old scoundrel!" he cried. "I've got lackeys here to catch your snakes. You'd better run, before it's too late!"

Qiu Qianren just laughed. "Do you take me for a gullible child?"

"Brother Guo! Miss Huang! Help me!"

Lotus held Guo Jing back, to keep him from rushing out to his sworn brother's aid, and said under her breath, "Don't move yet."

The Urchin was running in circles, yelling at the top of his lungs. "Stinking lad! Cruel wench! If you don't come out right away, I'll curse eighteen generations of your ancestors!"

Lotus stood up, laughing. "Go on, then. Curse my papa. See how far it gets you.

Qiu Qianren was holding a serpent in each hand. Zhou Botong felt his knees give way at the sight of their flickering tongues.

"Good Miss Huang, quickly! Quickly! I'll curse eighteen generations of my own ancestors if you help me now!"

With Guo Jing and Lotus poised to step in, Qiu Qianren knew

he needed to make himself scarce before the three of them banded together against him. It would be best to lie low until noon the next day, when the Contest began, for he did not fear facing any of them in single combat. He tapped both feet against the ground and lunged forward, thrusting the snakes at Zhou Botong's face.

The Urchin flicked his sleeves to fend off the creatures and threw himself sideways. Just then, he heard a quiet rustling sound pass overhead, and, a moment later, something chilly landed on the nape of his neck. It wriggled into his collar and slid down his spine, squirming around in his clothes, slippery and slimy.

"I'm dead! I'm dead!" he shrieked, his terrified spirits taking flight. He dared not reach into his undershirt to remove the unwitting stowaway, so he ran in circles, jumped around and flipped back and forth. Suddenly, he froze. His body went numb and he flopped to the ground, convinced that the snake had sunk its fangs into his back.

Guo Jing and Lotus rushed over, fearing the worst. Qiu Qianren was mystified by Zhou Botong's fit, but it gave him a chance to sneak away. As he strained his eyes in the gloom to find the trail down the mountain, a dark profile emerged from the trees.

"Qiu Qianren, you won't get away this time."

The figure was silhouetted by the moon, its face shrouded in shadow. The guttural voice, cold as ice, was menacing enough to give even Qiu Qianren the shivers.

"Who are you?" he hissed.

The newcomer ignored his question and approached Zhou Botong, who was still curled up on the ground, convinced that he was bound for the netherworld.

"Master Zhou, have no fear. It's not a snake."

In his fuzzy state, Zhou Botong felt himself being lifted up. The voice startled him and he sprang to his feet, only to sense the cold-blooded creature writhing against his back.

"It bit me again! It's a snake. It's a snake!"

"It's a gold wah-wah. Not a snake."

By now, Guo Jing and Lotus were able to make out the man's

features in the moonlight. It was the fisher, one of Reverend Sole Light's four disciples. Holding the Urchin steady, he reached inside his collar and pulled out the golden salamander. The fisher then explained that he had found a pair of the amphibians in a brook earlier and had been keeping them inside his robe. One had escaped and found its way up a tree, a few moments earlier, before falling on Zhou Botong. These creatures were not known to bite, but, if the fisher had appeared any later, the Hoary Urchin would likely have fainted from fright.

Somewhat calmer now, Zhou Botong parted his eyelids to take a peek at the fellow propping him up. He thought his deliverer looked familiar, but his wits were too scattered to allow him to place his face. Hearing footsteps, he turned toward the sound and was surprised to find Qiu Qianren stumbling back from a threatening presence. He peered at this approaching figure, and, once more, his soul and spirits took flight.

Consort Liu, from King Duan's palace in Dali!

UNTIL THIS moment, Qiu Qianren had been confident that the Contest was his to lose. Of all the heroes of the *wulin* likely to attend, he considered only Zhou Botong to be his martial superior. If his snakes could scare the volatile man into fleeing Mount Hua, he reasoned, then there would be no one left to stand in his way. He had never imagined that Madam Ying would be present. The sight of her brought back memories of the frenzied, reckless way she had attacked him on Blue Dragon Shoal—if this raving crone pounced on him now, the others would probably follow suit, and there was little chance of him coming out of the encounter alive.

"You killed my baby son!" the woman screeched.

The toddler's mother! . . . But how does she know it was me? I disguised myself in the uniform of an imperial guard and covered my face with a mask. Qiu Qianren was shaken. He had thought King Duan would sacrifice his training to save the life of his own child, leaving him with one fewer competitor to contend with for the Greatest Martial Master title, but the stony-hearted sovereign had thwarted his plan by refusing to heal the boy . . .

"Mad hag, I'm warning you . . ."

"Give me back my son!"

"What does it have to do with me?"

"I didn't see your face that night, but your laugh was seared into my memory. Go on, laugh! Let me hear it again!"

Qiu Qianren eyed Madam Ying's outstretched arms and edged two steps back. He remembered her acting like this on the barge, lunging at him and trying to lock him in her arms so she could take her savage revenge. He leaned a fraction to one side, held out his right palm and smacked his left against it. The impact sent his right hand flying at an angle into Madam Ying's lower abdomen. Yin and Yang Unite as One—one of the thirteen deadly moves of the Iron Palm repertoire.

Madam Ying thought she could dodge the ferocious attack using her Weatherfish Slip kung fu, but Qiu Qianren was too fast. Before she could even shift her footing, his palm was within half a *chi* of her belly. Realizing she might yet again fail to exact vengeance, she steeled herself to stomach the blow. She had in mind one last desperate gambit—to drag him over the brink. They would plunge to their deaths together. Just as she was readying herself to pounce and clamp her arms around him, a fist flew past her ear, stirring up a gust that lashed her face like a barbed whip. It forced Qiu Qianren to withdraw his lethal strike so his hands were free to deal with the new threat coming at his flank.

"Not you again, Hoary Urchin!" he growled.

For it was Zhou Botong who had stepped in, deploying a technique from the Nine Yin Manual to deflect Qiu's lethal Iron Palm strike. In doing so, he had been careful to position himself in such a way that he had his back to the woman and would not need to look her in the eye.

"You're no match for him. Get out of here! Go! I'm going too . . ."

Zhou Botong forced the words out between gritted teeth, his body tense as he drew back, poised to bolt downhill, as far away from his old lover as possible.

"Zhou Botong, why won't you avenge your son?"

Stunned, Zhou froze on the spot. "What? I had a son?"

"Yes—Qiu Qianren killed our son."

Never in his wildest dreams had Zhou Botong imagined that their brief dalliance could have resulted in a child. He was struck dumb by the news, unsure how to respond to the revelations. Forgetting his opponent, he turned and saw a monk with the face of King Duan standing with his four disciples beside the woman he knew as Consort Liu.

Qiu Qianren, meanwhile, having spun away from Zhou Botong's attack, now found himself with his back less than three *chi* from the sheer drop. And before him stood a crowd that wanted him dead. The martial Master had never been in a more precarious situation. His only hope was to talk his way out of it. He clapped his hands together and put on a show of bombast: "I came to Mount Hua to fight for the title of the Greatest Martial Master Under the Heavens, and yet you are conspiring together to eliminate me on the eve of the Contest. Who would have thought that such exulted heroes of the *wulin* would resort to so base a scheme?"

Zhou Botong could not dispute his logic. "As you wish. I will take your life after the Contest instead."

"I will not wait another day!" Madam Ying hissed.

Lotus was also vexed by his concession. "Old Urchin, we keep faith with those who keep faith, and we punish those who break it. We all have a reason to fight him—he can have no complaints."

The blood drained from Qiu Qianren's face. He was surely doomed. But he had one last trick up his sleeve. "On what grounds are you calling for my death?" he asked, fixing his gaze on each of them in turn.

It was the scholar, Reverend Sole Light's disciple, who answered. "The evil deeds you have committed are reason enough."

Qiu Qianren threw his head back and let out a grating laugh. "When it comes to martial prowess, I cannot stand against your superior numbers, but, when we speak of good and evil, let one who among you has never killed nor done wrong come forth. I shall bare my neck and accept my fate like a man."

Letting out a sigh, Sole Light was the first to step back. He sat cross-legged on the ground, with his head bowed. The rest stood in silence, thinking about the times they had erred. Not one of them had an answer for Qiu Qianren's challenge.

The monk's four disciples—the fisher, the logger, the farmer and the scholar—had ordered the deaths of numerous individuals when they served the Kingdom of Dali. Although they had adhered to the principles of justice during the proceedings, they could not rule out the possibility that mistakes had been made and innocent men condemned. Zhou Botong and Madam Ying exchanged glances; neither could shed the lingering guilt over what had happened between them. Guo Jing had slain many on the battlefield during the Khwarazm campaign, and he had been reproaching himself for it ever since. As for Lotus, she recalled the many worries she had subjected her father to in recent years, and regretted her deeply unfilial behavior. Then there were those she had cheated, deceived, swindled and tricked—more than she could count.

Qiu Qianren had not dared to hope that his plan would work so well. His foes were all bereft of speech, too shamed by their own misdeeds to raise a hand against him. He strode toward Guo Jing, and the young man turned aside and stepped out of his way. Qiu Qianren picked up his pace to put as much distance as possible between them, only for a switch of bamboo to come flying at him from a cluster of rocks, whacking him in the face.

So swift and sudden was this makeshift weapon that, in the split second it took Qiu Qianren to raise his left palm and twirl his wrist to try to push it aside, it jolted out of reach, returning just as quickly to threaten three major vital points on his chest. The bamboo stick continued to whip into Qiu Qianren like a storm, impossible to block or avoid, forcing him to withdraw to the very edge of the cliff. And now its master emerged from his craggy hideout.

"*Shifu!*" Guo Jing and Lotus cried at the same time.

Count Seven Hong, the Divine Vagrant Nine Fingers.

"You stinking beggar," Qiu Qianren said, glowering. "Have you come to pass sentence on me too? There's still a day to go before the Contest."

"I'm here to rid the world of evil. Not to compare kung fu."

"Oh, indeed, great hero. Here stands your villain. But who are you to take my life? Can you claim to be innocent of all wrongdoing?"

"Aye! This Old Beggar has taken two hundred and thirty-one lives to date, and they were all miscreants. Corrupt officials, local tyrants, double-crossers, oath breakers. The Beggar Clan investigated each one thoroughly, gathering evidence, and each case was scrutinized twice over to ensure no one was wronged and there were no miscarriages of justice. Only then would I execute the trespasser. I might be a glutton and a buffoon, and sometimes a little muddled-headed when it comes to details, but I have never killed a person that did not deserve their fate. Qiu Qianren, you will be number two hundred and thirty-two!"

Count Seven Hong's tirade had left Qiu Qianren speechless, and now the Divine Vagrant proceeded to list the man's crimes.

"Qiu Qianren, your *shifu* Shangguan Jiannan was a great hero, a true patriot, a man of integrity who devoted his entire life to serving his country. And yet, when you inherited the leadership of the Iron Palm Gang, you consorted with the Jurchen invaders and betrayed your homeland. How will you face your *shifu* when you leave this life behind?

"You have come to Mount Hua to fight for the greatest honor the *wulin* can bestow. *Huh!* For shame! Even if you prove to be more skilled than each and every one of us, no hero under the heavens will ever crown a traitor."

Qiu Qianren was dumbstruck by the Beggar's fierce castigation. Memories from the past decades gushed forth into his mind. He thought of the principles and morals his *shifu* had tried to instill in him. He could hear his *shifu's* last words and final biddings from his deathbed, as he passed on the maxims and rules of the Iron Palm Gang to the man he was entrusting with its leadership. He recalled his *shifu's* exhortations to act in the best interests of their country and their people, and remembered his explanation for the Gang's name. It was not just the name of a kung fu technique. It was a reminder to its members that they should root out evil with an iron will and strike down wickedness with a firm and steady hand. Qiu at last realized how, as he had aged and his martial skills had developed, he had strayed further and further from the tenets of the Iron Palm Gang—to serve the country with loyalty, to destroy the country's enemies and to reclaim the country's lost lands. He could see that he had sunk lower and lower, accepting followers that were increasingly vulgar and morally wanting, to the point that the few remaining upstanding members distanced themselves from the group. The Iron Palm Gang had become a cohort of outlaws, traitors and wrongdoers undertaking cruel deeds at the bidding of corrupt men.

Qiu Qianren looked up at the bright moon overhead. Pinned in place by Count Seven's blazing glare, he knew he had been acting contrary to the demands of honor and dignity for most of his life. A cold sweat of shame and regret covered his skin.

"Chief Hong, thank you for your admonition." And, with those words, Qiu Qianren turned and leaped from the precipice.

Count Seven Hong had been expecting Qiu to lash out to silence him, and had been holding the bamboo cane in readiness, for any blow was likely to be deadly. It had not occurred to him that the proud man would be driven to suicide by remorse. Before the Beggar could react, a gray shadow swooped in and a hand shot out. Sole Light was now right on the brink, still sitting in the same position with his legs crossed, but he had one arm curled around Qiu Qianren's shins, pulling him back.

"*Sadhu, sadhu!* Boundless is the bitter sea, look behind you for the shore," the monk said. "Since you rue your past ills, it is not too late to be a new man."

Qiu Qianren knelt before the former King of Dali. There were a thousand things he wanted to say, but it was all lost in a wail of anguish and a flood of tears.

Watching the broken, sobbing man, Madam Ying saw her chance and removed a sharp dagger from the inside pocket of her robe.

"No!" Zhou Botong put his hand over her wrist to forestall her attack.

"What do you think you're doing?"

Zhou Botong had been trembling with fear ever since he had set eyes on the woman, and, hearing her snap at him, all he could think of was to run away. Yelping, he flew down the mountain.

"Where are you going?" Madam Ying shouted, giving chase.

"My tummy hurts. I need to go!"

His answer stopped her in her tracks, but she soon resumed the pursuit, sprinting at her fastest pace.

"*Aiyooo!*" the Hoary Urchin yelled, terrified. "Don't come any closer! I've soiled myself. It stinks!"

But Madam Ying had been searching for this man for twenty years, and she knew, if he slipped away this time, she would likely never see him again. What did she care if he had emptied his bowels? In fact, Zhou Botong had lied about the bad stomach, hoping to scare her into keeping her distance so he could get away. Shrieking as he ran, he suddenly realized his trousers *were* weighed down, after all, the fabric sticking to his legs, warm and wet.

Guo Jing and Lotus watched the odd couple disappear around a rocky bend and exchanged wry smiles. They turned to see Reverend Sole Light speaking under his breath to Qiu Qianren, as the penitent man nodded earnestly along to what he was being told.

The monk continued to impart his wisdom for a long time, before at last standing up. "Let's go," he said.

The young lovers stepped forward to bow to the Martial Great, then inclined their heads toward his four disciples.

With a kindly smile, Sole Light placed one hand on Guo Jing's head and the other on Lotus's. "Brother Seven, it gives me great joy to see you so hale and hearty. And I must congratulate you on accepting such a brilliant pair of disciples."

Bowing, the Beggar returned the courtesy. "I am happy to see the Reverend in good health. Thank you for saving the lives of these two little ones."

"Water runs far in mountains tall, our paths shall cross again." The monk touched his palms together in a Buddhist gesture of respect, then set off downhill.

"Are you leaving now? The Contest is tomorrow."

Sole Light looked back at Count Seven Hong with a smile. "This old monk leads a simple life, unfettered by worldly trappings. It is not my place to contend with the foremost heroes under the heavens. I came to resolve the wrongs and entanglements that have tied us down for so long, and, thanks be to good fortune, I have succeeded. But, Brother Seven, you deserve the honor. Who in this world can compare to you? There is no need to be humble." He made another obeisance, took Qiu Qianren by the hand and resumed his descent. His four disciples bent low in deference and followed their Master.

As the scholar walked past Lotus, he noticed the color in her cheeks and the joyful spark in her eyes, and recited with a smile:

> *"In the damp lowlands are carambola trees,*
> *Supple and luxuriant are their branches."*

Catching the joke made at her expense, Lotus also replied in verse:

> *"Chickens rest in the roost in the wall,*
> *The day has reached eventide."*

Laughing heartily, the scholar put his hands together to take his leave.

"Lotus, what was that about?" Guo Jing could not make head nor tail of the exchange.

"Quotes from *The Book of Songs*."

"Oh." Knowing nothing about poetry, Guo Jing chose not to pursue that line of conversation.

Lotus noted his reaction with a smile. Chancellor Zhu is indeed perceptive, she said to herself. He has seen clearly into my heart and cited this poem because it is known to be a love song about a young woman's feelings for her unmarried sweetheart. The final line of each stanza is especially apt:

> *In delight, envy your wanting for awareness.*
> *In delight, envy your wanting for kindred.*
> *In delight, envy your wanting for household.*

They do suit Guo Jing—a headstrong and artless boy, without the ties of kin or the bonds of marriage. It does work well . . .

"Oh no!" Lotus suddenly cried out loud.

"What is it?"

"I just thought of the next lines of the poem I quoted." She gave a sheepish grin.

> "*Goats and oxen come down the hill.*
> *Goats and oxen make their way home.*

"I wanted to call Chancellor Zhu a four-legged beast, but I now realize I included Uncle Sole Light in the insult . . . and that's terribly rude of me!"

The convoluted jibe did not interest Guo Jing, so he cast his mind back to what Count Seven Hong had said when reprimanding Qiu Qianren. He sensed that the Beggar's words could help him to at last untangle the jumble of questions that had been troubling him.

Shifu said he had killed two hundred and thirty-one trespassers, each of them a villain, Guo Jing reminded himself. Because *Shifu's* conscience is clear, when he chastised Qiu Qianren, he exuded a might that could not be challenged, even though their martial skills are on a par. Qiu Qianren's malevolent heart could not withstand the force of justice that *Shifu* embodies. And I can aspire to be like *Shifu*—I can use my kung fu to do good, to uphold righteousness. I don't have to discard what I've learned.

In fact, Qiu Chuji had tried to explain this same simple truth to Guo Jing, but his words did not carry the same weight as Count Seven Hong's, and the barbaric massacres of the Khwarazm campaign and his mother's suicide had been too fresh in the boy's mind. Applying Count Seven's remarks to the questions he had been grappling with, Guo Jing at last found some measure of peace, secure in his belief that he should follow in his *shifu's* footsteps.

Guo Jing and Lotus approached Count Seven and paid their respects with a bow. After they had parted in Jiaxing, the Beggar had followed Apothecary Huang back to Peach Blossom Island to recuperate from the internal injuries he had suffered at Viper Ouyang's hands. Thanks to the isolated location and the Heretic's help, he was able to use the advanced *neigong* technique outlined in the final passage of the Nine Yin Manual to reconnect the flow of energy along his meridians, and, within half a year, he had fully recovered. It took just another six months for him to fully regain his martial ability. Apothecary Huang had returned to the mainland once Count Seven's condition was stable, traveling north in search of Lotus, but the Beggar had only recently left the island. He had since met with Surefoot Lu, who told him all about Guo Jing and Lotus's adventures.

After they had heard each other's news, Guo Jing said, "*Shifu*, you should rest—it's nearly dawn. The Contest will be starting soon, and it will be exhausting."

"Believe it or not, I've grown more competitive with age," Count Seven said with a chuckle. "My heart pounds with excitement at the thought of sparring with the Heretic of the East and the Venom of the West. Lotus, did you know that your papa has made great progress in recent years? Who do you think will emerge victorious from our duel?"

"You and Papa have always been evenly matched, but, now that you know the secret method from the Nine Yin Manual, Papa won't be able to beat you. When we see him, I'll tell him to withdraw, so we can go back to Peach Blossom Island sooner."

Discerning her true meaning from her tone, Count Seven let out a belly laugh. "There's no need to worry, lass. I won't be using the techniques from the Manual. This Old Beggar has his principles. I won't fight with anything that isn't rightfully mine. I'll only use my own kung fu when I face Old Heretic Huang."

This was exactly what Lotus had hoped he would say. "*Shifu*, don't be upset if you can't beat Papa. I'll make it up to you by cooking a hundred different dishes—including some new ones that I've just invented. Whether you win or lose, you'll be just as happy."

The gourmand's mouth watered at the prospect, but he still feigned disapproval. "This girl has a black heart. First you provoke me, now you try to bribe me. You just want your papa to win!"

Grinning broadly, Lotus was about to argue back when Count Seven Hong shot to his feet, his eyes fixed on something behind her. "Old Venom, you're early!"

Guo Jing and Lotus scrambled up to stand beside their *shifu* and saw Viper Ouyang's towering form standing right where they had been sitting. They were shocked that they had not detected his arrival, so light and soundless was his approach.

CHAPTER TWELVE

CONTEST OF MOUNT HUA

I

"WE EARLY ARRIVALS CAN START FIRST," VIPER OUYANG SAID. His voice betrayed no emotion. "Old Beggar, do we fight to win, or to the death?"

"Both. And there's no need to rein yourself in."

"Excellent!"

Viper had been standing with his left arm behind his back, and now, with a flourish, he brought out the Serpent Staff and slammed the butt down on the rocky ground. "Here, or somewhere more spacious?"

Lotus cut in before Count Seven Hong could reply. "Why Mount Hua? You should fight on a boat."

"Huh?" The Beggar was baffled.

"So Master Ouyang can demonstrate yet again how he requites kindness with spite, and hit you with a sneaky blow from behind."

Count Seven chuckled at Lotus's barbed reference to the battle at sea that had seen him injured at Viper Ouyang's hands. "I'll fall for a trick once, but never again. Don't expect me to go easy on you this time, Old Venom."

Viper did not show the slightest reaction to their taunts. He bent slightly at the knees, switched the Serpent Staff to his right hand and summoned his internal strength to his left palm, ready to unleash his Exploding Toad kung fu.

Meanwhile, Lotus presented the Dog-Beating Cane to Count Seven. "*Shifu*, show him the might of Dog-Beating kung fu and the full power of the Nine Yin Manual. A scoundrel like him doesn't deserve to be treated with respect."

I mustn't wear myself out wrangling with the Venom, Count Seven said to himself, as he accepted the emblem of the Beggar Clan Chief with a nod. Or I won't be able to take on Old Heretic Huang when he arrives.

With that thought, he launched two consecutive moves with such rapidity that they formed a pincer attack—a Strike Grass, Startle Snake from the left, and a Flick Grass, Find Serpent from the right.

Count Seven Hong had never used the Dog Beater against Viper Ouyang, but the Venom was wary of it all the same, having experienced its speed and unpredictability in Lotus's hands.

From the storm whipped up by the bamboo cane, Viper knew he had to tread carefully. He hefted the Serpent Staff, blocking one blow head-on while sidestepping the other, then speared the staff at Count Seven's upper abdomen.

Viper Ouyang was now using a third incarnation of the Serpent Staff, having been deprived of the previous two. This one was crowned with a snarling face more chilling than before, but the adders it concealed were newly trained. They had not yet attained the agility or ferocity in combat of their distinguished forebears.

Count Seven Hong and Viper Ouyang had first faced one another at the original Contest of Mount Hua, when they had vied for martial supremacy and the chance to own the Nine Yin Manual. Their next encounter came on Peach Blossom Island, in a trial to determine whether Guo Jing or Gallant Ouyang would win Lotus's hand. Both bouts, although fierce, were simply about winning—there was nothing more at stake. Their third battle, however, came at sea, on a blazing ship, with their lives hanging by a thread, yet even then Count Seven had restrained himself and refrained from launching deadly moves. He had even intervened to save the Venom from being scourged by a red-hot anchor chain, only for Viper to return the favor by setting his serpents on him and striking him in the back. Count Seven very nearly succumbed to the injuries he had sustained, and it had taken him two years to make a complete recovery. He had never suffered a more costly defeat or experienced a closer brush with mortality. How could he let such an affront go unpunished at their fourth confrontation? This time, both men resolved to unleash the full extent of their martial might, holding nothing back. The slightest misstep would mean instant death.

Time seemed to stand still as two hundred quick-fire moves were exchanged amid a rapid succession of leaps and somersaults. Suddenly, the moon disappeared, leaving the sky darker than ever. As their eyes adjusted to the gloom, the two Martial Greats circled each other warily, weapons held high to guard their torsos, keeping the urge to attack in check—for the moment.

The young couple began to edge closer to the fight, ready to rush to Count Seven's aid, if need be. Guo Jing's face was drawn with worry. *Shifu* has just spent two years recuperating, while the Venom was free to continue his training. The thought made his heart hammer in his chest. So Viper may be more powerful than *Shifu* now . . . What a fool I was to spare that villain's life even once!

He wondered if he should step in, but Count Seven had made himself clear—he would fight the Venom one-on-one. Guo Jing's first instinct was to obey his *shifu*, but doubts continued to gnaw at him. What if Viper injures *Shifu* again? Who else can stand against this monster? How many more good people will he hurt?

By now, Guo Jing felt he was coming to a more nuanced understanding of how one should keep faith and maintain integrity. It wasn't enough just to live up to your words and beliefs in a literal sense—you also had to consider the context and the consequences. He now saw how stupid he had been—stubborn, inflexible and pig-headed.

Energized by this insight, he felt a rush of warmth filling his core. With the combatants now reconciled to the darkness, the duel was showing the first tentative signs of warming up again. Following its progress through the swishing sounds made by the Dog-Beating Cane and the Serpent Staff as they cut through the air, Guo Jing held one palm before the other, listening closely, poised to help his Master.

Lotus's voice rang out in the dark: "Viper Ouyang! You made a pact with Guo Jing. You vowed not to use force on me, and, in return, Guo Jing agreed to spare your life three times. But you broke your word. Yesterday, in the cave. Any other hero of the *wulin* would be consumed by shame at the mere thought of it. Only you would be thick-skinned enough to show your face at a contest for the ultimate honor in the martial world the very next day."

Viper had more unscrupulous deeds to his name than he could count, but he took great pride in his reputation as a man who honored his promises. If he had only had more time to learn the Manual's secrets, he would not have overlooked his agreement with Guo Jing and tried to coerce Lotus into sharing her knowledge with him.

His ears burned with shame. He did not enjoy being called out in this way, and, for a brief moment, his focus wavered. The Serpent Staff stalled in the air, and he nearly took a hit from the Dog Beater.

But Lotus wasn't finished with him yet. "Surely it's a serious loss of face for a Martial Great to be shown mercy by a junior? Not just once, but three times! And, to make matters worse, you reneged on the oath you made to that very same young man. Are you really trying to make the jaw of every *jianghu* hero ache from laughter? Well, well, Old Venom. There's one title you do deserve—the Thickest Skin Under the Heavens!"

Viper seethed with rage. He realized she was trying to rile him and disrupt his control of his internal energy flow. The smallest mistake could spell defeat. He tried to block out her taunts, but it became increasingly difficult as her claims grew more and more scandalous. She went on to attribute a string of notorious deeds to his name, even though he had had nothing to do with any of them.

The list of offenses swelled until he was being painted as the source of all evil, personally responsible for every abomination under the heavens.

Well aware that Viper lacked any kind of moral compass, Lotus feared that he would not be sufficiently ruffled by being linked with even the most nefarious acts. She decided to whittle away at his indomitable reputation instead, with stories that cast the conceited martial Master as subservient to those he considered beneath him. There was the time she had seen him begging Lama Supreme Wisdom to spare his life, the time she had heard him calling Hector Sha "Dearest Uncle," and the time he had hailed Tiger Peng as "Father," groveling at his feet for the formula behind the poison that gave his secret weapon its potency.

At first, Viper Ouyang ignored her slanders, but they were soon so outrageous that he could not help being drawn into a battle of words. Sensing that her provocations were hitting the mark, Lotus redoubled her efforts. She recalled how she had happened across him recommending his services to Wanyan Honglie. How he had implored the Jin Prince for the chance to lead his personal guard, and stood sentry outside his chamber every night to convince him. The three confrontations with Guo Jing in the Western Regions scarcely needed embellishing, but she could not resist adding a little spice. She recounted with relish how Guo Jing had spared Viper from being buried alive by sand, frozen to death in an ice block, and drowned in a cesspool. She gleefully detailed how the Martial Great had stripped naked and jumped off the snow-capped peak overlooking Samarkand, watched by hundreds of thousands of soldiers, and how he had been stung on the buttocks by three arrows mid-flight. She urged him to remove his trousers at the very summit of Mount Hua and reveal these battle scars for all to see.

The martial Master had never been so abused in his life, and nor had he been so tested by a fight—both physically and mentally. If he were to prevail, he would have to use the kung fu from the Nine

Yin Manual, even though he was yet to master the reversal of every energy flow.

Suddenly, the Serpent Staff came alive in his hands, keening as it sliced through the air, and Count Seven found himself confronted with a fighting style unlike any he had ever known. Alarmed, the Beggar stilled his mind and reined in the Dog Beater to focus on defending himself as he studied the Venom's unorthodox moves.

"*Yosiya babashiji shiramanbi.*"

Viper's head jerked imperceptibly at the sound of Lotus's voice. But he could not recall a single line from the Manual that matched the nonsensical words she had just chanted.

"What does that mean?" he demanded.

How was he to know that it was her own fabrication, as she rolled her tongue to imitate the Sanskrit-inspired phrases? She followed it with a series of random, meaningless sounds, her tone twisting and turning—snapping in anger, then pleading with sincere conviction; sighing in amazement, then singing with joy. She rounded off her performance by crying out several times with increasing urgency, inflecting her voice with a questioning tone.

Viper Ouyang tried desperately to ignore her, but in the end he gave in. "What are you asking me?"

Lotus answered in the same made-up language.

Puzzled, the Venom attempted to respond with a few snatches of the jumble of characters Guo Jing had written down for him. Instantly, a muddle of voices, shapes, kung fu moves and martial mnemonics surged and swelled in urgent waves around his brain. The heavens swirled and the earth swiveled, and all of a sudden he had no idea where he was or what he was doing.

Count Seven spotted a gap in the offensive patterns of Viper's staff and—"*Ha!*"—he thwacked the Dog Beater down on the crown of his head.

The strike was imbued with all the Beggar's mighty internal strength, and the heavy blow further scrambled the Venom's wits. So confused was the Martial Great that he would have mixed up something as simple as the seven meats and eight vegetables if he were asked—or was it the other way round? With a howl of rage and confusion, he scampered off, holding his staff upside down.

"Where are you going?" Guo Jing asked, making a lunge for the fleeing man.

Viper sprang clear, turned three somersaults in a row, then half rolled and half crawled behind a towering rock, disappearing from view in the blink of an eye.

2

"I WOULDN'T HAVE BEATEN THE VENOM WITHOUT YOUR help," Count Seven said to Lotus, his tone somewhat subdued. "However, master and disciple working together like that against a lone opponent isn't particularly honorable."

"But you taught me that kung fu!"

"What you've just demonstrated can't be taught—you have to be born with it. And there's only one rascal of a man who could sire a little imp like you."

A booming voice answered Count Seven. "Old Beggar, have you taken to calling people names behind their back?"

"Papa!" Lotus ran toward the man who was striding up the rocky mountain path. The light of dawn cast a soft glow on his green robe and plain scholar's headscarf.

Apothecary Huang, Heretic of the East and Lord of Peach Blossom Island.

Lotus threw herself into her father's arms and hugged him tightly. It had been a year since they had last seen each other. Apothecary Huang could see that his little girl had blossomed into a graceful young woman. The resemblance to her late mother was so strong that he sensed an undercurrent of grief surging to the surface, in spite of his joy at their reunion.

"Heretic Huang, remember what I told you on Peach Blossom Island?" Count Seven said, after hailing the new arrival. "Your lovely daughter is quick-witted and armed with a bellyful of plots. You'll never have to worry about her, because she'll always come out on top. No one can hope to outwit her. Tell me, was this Beggar right?"

Smiling, Apothecary Huang extricated himself from his daughter's embrace, took her by the hand and approached Count Seven Hong. "My sincere congratulations on defeating the Venom. It lifts a heavy weight off your heart and mine."

The Beggar bowed low. "Now it's our turn. Come, come, let's get started. The moment I set eyes on your daughter, I think of her cooking and the worms in my belly squirm with excitement. I don't care which of us is named the Greatest. The sooner we're done, the sooner I get to taste her food and my mouth can stop watering."

Lotus giggled. "*Shifu*, I said I'd only cook for you if you lose."

"Pah! Shameless little wench. Are you trying to threaten me?" Count Seven hissed in mock reproof.

"Old Beggar, your injury has cost you two years of training. I fear we may no longer be evenly matched." Apothecary Huang tried to keep his tone matter of fact. "And, Lotus, you must treat your *shifu* to the greatest dishes under the heavens, regardless of the result."

"Such words befit the status of a grandmaster! I knew the Lord of Peach Blossom Island couldn't be as petty as the young lass, here." Count Seven hefted the Dog-Beating Cane. "Come! Let's begin!"

Apothecary Huang shook his head. "You have just had a long battle with the Venom. I refuse to take advantage of your weakened state. We shall wait until noon, so you have time to restore your energy."

Count Seven understood his logic, but was raring to go nonetheless. Apothecary Huang sat on a rock, paying him no heed.

"Papa, *Shifu*, I have a suggestion—you can fight now and it will still be fair."

The two Martial Greats eyed the young woman expectantly.

"It is the Contest of Mount Hua today, and a winner must be determined. But, if you were to duel directly, whatever the outcome, it might cause a rift in your friendship. I propose, instead of fighting each other, you both take on Guo Jing. Papa will go first, then *Shifu* when he has recovered his strength. Whoever requires the least moves to beat Guo Jing will be named the victor."

The Beggar laughed. "Very clever!"

"Papa and Guo Jing are both fresh, and when Guo Jing challenges you, *Shifu*, you'll have both completed one fight. Now, that's fair, isn't it?"

Apothecary Huang nodded. "Come, Guo Jing. Would you like to use a weapon?"

"No," the youth replied.

But Lotus wasn't quite done yet. "There's still one question to resolve. What if neither of you manages to subdue Guo Jing within three hundred moves?"

Count Seven gave a hearty laugh. "Old Heretic, for a moment, I envied you for having such a devoted daughter, committed to helping you win the ultimate honor. But she has just demonstrated an eternal truth—they always put their sweetheart first! She concocted the whole scheme to present that silly lad of hers with the title of Greatest Martial Master Under the Heavens!"

Apothecary Huang had always doted on Lotus and he did not mind granting his daughter her wish. "If we old men fail to overcome the boy in three hundred moves, what right do we have to be hailed as the Greatest?"

Nodding in agreement, Count Seven gave Guo Jing a shove. "Well? What are you waiting for?"

The young man stumbled, unsure how he should proceed. He had no desire to win any titles, but he was in a position to influence the outcome. Who deserves the honor more? he asked himself. Should he help either one of them to claim it?

The Heretic was also presented with a dilemma. I can hold back to help the boy last three hundred moves, but what if the Beggar takes his duel seriously? Then I'd be handing him the title! Hmm . . . Let me gauge Guo Jing's ability first, then I can decide on a course of action.

"First move!" Apothecary Huang twirled his left palm and aimed an angled slash at Guo Jing's shoulder.

Guo Jing raised his right arm to block the strike. The impact sent a shudder through him, almost knocking him off his feet.

He laughed inwardly at himself, shaking his head. How silly I was, thinking I'd need to hold back. I have no hope of withstanding a hundred moves, let alone three hundred, even with all my training!

His mind made up, Guo Jing now gave the duel his undivided attention. He would favor neither martial Master and concentrate instead on lasting as long as he could.

And yet, after the initial exchanges, it was Apothecary Huang who was feeling apprehensive. He had put two-thirds of his strength into his moves so far, but still found himself hemmed in by Guo Jing's offensive patterns. When did this silly boy reach such an advanced level? he asked himself. If it continues like this, he might even beat me outright!

His pride stung, Apothecary Huang launched into one of his most prized martial inventions, Cascading Peach Blossom Palm, flitting in and around Guo Jing, his palms a waspish blur, as he fought to regain the upper hand. And yet, a dozen kung fu repertoires and more than a hundred moves later, he was still unable to bring the fight under his control. Fearful of being overwhelmed, he was forced to resort to a low trick to land a kick to his opponent's left shin and buy himself a little time.

Shame on me! Apothecary Huang let out a breath of relief as the glancing blow sent Guo Jing scuttling back two steps. The Heretic piled on the pressure, launching a series of unrelenting attacks intended to overwhelm the young man, like blasting winds and crashing waves might swamp a boat at sea. But Guo Jing was unshakeable in his defense, maintaining the duel's balance of power without once showing the slightest weakness or sign of fatigue.

"Two hundred and three, two hundred and four..."

Apothecary Huang was getting flustered. What if the Beggar crushes Guo Jing within a hundred moves? He altered his combat style yet again, unleashing a succession of swift palm strikes that fluttered hither and thither like butterflies' shadows.

The phenomenal speed of this assault dazzled Guo Jing. It felt as though he was being crushed under the weight of a mountain. Starbursts filled his vision. His breathing was rapid and shallow.

Sensing that Guo Jing was at last succumbing, Apothecary Huang intensified his lightning barrage. Lotus was counting faster and faster too.

Guo Jing's lips were dry, his tongue was on fire, his arms and legs achy and sore. He was hanging on through sheer force of will.

"Three hundred!"

The Heretic leaped back, his expression betraying a momentary loss of composure.

Guo Jing was reeling, seeing double. Now that the fight was over, he found his body whirling leftwards of its own accord. Turning through a dozen involuntary rotations, he could tell that just a few more would send him crashing to the ground. He stamped his left foot down with the full force of Thousand *Jin* Load kung fu, managing to stall the spinning for a split second. But the aftershock of Apothecary Huang's *neigong* was still roiling in his system, and, moments later, he was overcome once more. This time, to keep himself steady, he bent from the waist and thrust down with his right hand. Pushing with all his strength, he employed a variation of Dragon in the Field to rachet himself the other way. After twenty rotations, his mind at last began to settle.

"Father," he said, bowing before Apothecary Huang, "if you had made one more move, you'd have knocked me over."

"I like how you address my papa," Lotus remarked with a giggle.

Apothecary Huang was thoroughly impressed by the way Guo Jing had found his feet after being turned about by the Five Spins of the Mysterious Gates, a kung fu which had taken him nigh on twenty years to perfect.

"Old Beggar, the title is yours." He cupped his hands in respect and turned to leave.

"Not so hasty. We don't know for sure yet," Count Seven said. "Will you lend Guo Jing your iron *xiao* flute?"

Apothecary Huang had snapped his jade flute in two when he thought Lotus had drowned at sea, and he now carried a plainer specimen, made of iron, in its place. He pulled it from his belt and handed it to the young man.

Count Seven nodded encouragingly. "Take it. I'll fight with my bare hands."

"Huh?" Guo Jing gaped at his *shifu*.

"I taught you your palm kung fu. You won't get far using that. Steady! Here comes the first move!" Quick as a flash, Count Seven locked Guo Jing's wrist with his left hand, then seized the iron flute. The young man let it slip out of his grasp, offering no resistance. He had no idea what he was supposed to do with the musical instrument.

"Stupid boy, this is a martial contest!" Count Seven slapped the *xiao* into Guo Jing's open palm with his left hand, then immediately reached for it with his right. This time, Guo Jing evaded his groping hand with a neat twirl.

"One." That was the signal for Lotus to begin the count.

Guo Jing had never been adept at armed combat, and the techniques he had been taught by the Six Freaks of the South were not particularly sophisticated. But, when he had found the sword in the deserted village in the Western Regions, he had developed their repertoires using insights gleaned from the Nine Yin Manual, coming up with methods for staving off the *neigong* power imbued in each swing of the Venom's staff. Now he applied all he had learned to his handling of the iron *xiao*, and it was proving just as effective against Count Seven's palm thrusts.

The Beggar was pleased to see his disciple crafting such a watertight defense. The lad has improved no end, he observed with pride. The hours I spent training him certainly weren't wasted... But, if I beat him within two hundred moves, I'll be showing the Old Heretic up. I know! I'll wait until we reach the two-hundred mark before I get too heavy-handed.

He settled into Haughty Dragon Repents, the first of the Eighteen Dragon-Subduing Palms, and began to cycle through the whole repertoire in all its nine variations. Each thrust ripped noisily through the air, as Guo Jing was enveloped within the fleeting shadows of the Beggar's two hands.

And yet, Count Seven Hong had made a strategic error. If he had been ruthless from the start, he could have routed Guo Jing, for the young man's skills with a weapon lagged some way behind his palm kung fu. In choosing to begin his offensive in earnest after two hundred moves, he was both underestimating Guo Jing's stamina and overestimating his own.

Aged twenty, Guo Jing was at his physical peak, and his already formidable internal energy had been enriched at the source thanks to the Transforming Muscles, Forging Bones technique from the Nine Yin Manual. Count Seven was not only several decades older, he had also just recovered from a crippling internal injury that was compounded by a deadly snakebite. Even though his kung fu had been restored, it was a trauma that had shaken his very core—the deep well from which the Dragon-Subduing Palm drew its power.

By the time he had worked his way through the ninth round of the Dragon-Subduing Palm, Count Seven had unleashed one hundred and sixty-two palm strikes. Though they were still fierce and sharp, their impact was reduced, and their aftereffects did not linger so long in Guo Jing's system. For him, the first two hundred moves were a period of adjustment, allowing him to settle on an effective response. Though the defensive sword strokes he was sketching with the iron flute were merely an adequate deterrent, the counterattacks he was launching with his left hand were growing in efficacy. Count Seven soon recognized the problem facing him. With his dwindling strength, he could not hope to win out through brute force alone. But he might stand a chance if he could outwit the boy . . . And so, the Beggar spread his arms wide, leaving his chest undefended.

Shifu has never shown me this! Startled by the unfamiliar technique, Guo Jing hesitated. He could easily thrust his weapon into

Count Seven's upper abdomen or chest, but how could he deal his teacher what would surely be a lethal blow?

"You've fallen for my trick!" Count Seven's left foot flew up, kicking the iron *xiao* out of Guo Jing's hand. Laughing in triumph, he flipped his right palm and sliced it down at an angle, striking the young man on his left shoulder.

Count Seven only channeled four-fifths of his strength into the blow, thinking it would be enough to knock Guo Jing off his feet and secure his victory, without actually injuring the boy. But Guo Jing had grown stouter and hardier over the past year, living in the saddle, at the mercy of gales and snowstorms. The pain was severe, but, though he staggered back from the impact, he did not fall.

Surprised to see Guo Jing still standing, the Beggar was quick to offer a word of advice. "Breathe in and out three times, slow and steady, so you won't get an internal injury."

Guo Jing did as he was told. Once the roiling sensation in his chest had eased, he bowed to his Master. "*Shifu*, you have won."

"No, I haven't. You could've struck me in the belly, but you chose not to. I doubt the Heretic will accept such a result. Carry on!"

Deprived of his weapon, Guo Jing now began to employ Luminous Hollow Fist to counter Count Seven's palm thrusts.

When developing this kung fu on Peach Blossom Island, Zhou Botong had drawn on concepts from the *Classic of the Way and Virtue*. In this Taoist canon, it is said that, "Strong armies can be crushed, strong trees can be snapped. Tough strength has its downsides, supple weakness has its upsides." The *Classic* also states that, "Nothing is more supple or weak than water, yet nothing surpasses its ability to attack the tough and strong, and nothing can be its substitute. The weak overcomes the strong, the supple conquers the firm. Everyone under the heavens knows it, though no one can put it into practice."

Inspired by these notions, as well as the ancient saying, "The supple can overcome the firm," Luminous Hollow Fist allowed one to cultivate a supple control of strength that offered a means to curb the power of the Dragon-Subduing Palm, a kung fu that was its opposite in every way—direct, forthright and unyielding. In theory, at least. In practice, it came down to martial ability; even Zhou Botong would struggle to subdue a master of Count Seven Hong's stature.

But the Hoary Urchin had more than one trick up his sleeve, and he had also taught his sworn brother his second great innovation, Competing Hands. Using this unique technique, Guo Jing was able to launch moves from Luminous Hollow Fist with his right hand and moves from Dragon-Subduing Palm with his left.

As the duel wore on, Guo Jing began, without any conscious effort on his part, to meld the firm with the supple, so yin and yang were in support of each other. The results were phenomenal. None of Count Seven's strikes could find a way though, and Guo Jing was quite capable of holding his own.

The excitement in Lotus's voice was becoming more and more evident as they approached the three-hundredth move.

"Two hundred ninety-nine!"

Count Seven's competitive instincts would not let him submit without one last throw of the dice. He let rip with a Haughty Dragon Repents, crying "Watch out!" as he channeled his inner strength to his arms. After all, the Beggar only wished to beat his student, not to hurt him.

Guo Jing felt a mighty force, with the power to topple mountains and overturn seas, sweep into him. He knew he could not counter this level of ferocity with Luminous Hollow Fist, so instead he traced a circle with his right arm. *Whoosh!* He too sent forth a Haughty Dragon Repents.

Their hands met with a *pang!* Their bodies shuddered.

Apothecary Huang and Lotus gasped and rushed over to check on them. Their palms seemed to have fused together.

Guo Jing was willing to concede, but he knew that, if he withdrew his strength too soon, he would end up absorbing the brunt of the attack. The only way to avoid injury was to hold Count Seven's force at bay with his own *neigong* until the sting was drawn from it. When it was safe to disengage, he would gladly accept defeat.

Count Seven, meanwhile, had not imagined that his opponent would have the skill to counter his Haughty Dragon Repents head-on, for it was a move he had spent a lifetime perfecting. Delighted by this unexpected proof of his student's talent, the Beggar decided that the day should belong to Guo Jing. It would be his pleasure to help the boy consolidate his reputation in the *wulin*. With that thought, Count Seven began to withdraw the flow of his inner strength.

3

THREE CHILLING HOWLS ECHOED BETWEEN THE CRAGS. Guo Jing, Lotus and the two Martial Greats stared about in alarm. All at once, in a whirl of robes, a figure materialized before their eyes, suddenly in their midst. Instead of walking on his feet, he had covered the distance from his hiding place in three acrobatic flips.

Viper Ouyang, the Venom of the West, had returned. His clothes were torn and tattered. Streaks of blood ran down his face.

"I have mastered the secret method of the Nine Yin Manual. I am the Greatest Martial Master Under the Heavens!" he declared, swinging the Serpent Staff.

Count Seven Hong snatched up the Dog-Beating Cane and lunged to meet the sweeping blow that was arcing toward the four of them. The stalemate with Guo Jing had ended the instant they sensed Viper's presence.

Just a handful of moves was enough to leave Count Seven shocked to the core by what he was witnessing from his opponent. Viper's kung fu had always been peculiar, but his behavior now was both freakish and erratic. One moment he dragged his fingers down his own cheek, the next he kicked his own buttocks with his heel. Each swipe of his staff juddered midcourse before continuing along an entirely unexpected new path. It was impossible to anticipate where each blow would land. The Beggar weaved a tight net of defense with the Dog Beater, too perturbed to risk any kind of countermove.

Pak, pak, pak! Viper cuffed himself on the ear three times and let out a howl. He then took two round stones from the inside pocket of his robe, put them on the ground and placed his hands over them. He flipped into a handstand, then began scuttling around on all fours.

Count Seven was mystified. Why are you crawling around like a dog? Have you forgotten that my cane kung fu was devised for beating curs like you? Chuckling inwardly, he speared his weapon into the Venom's flank.

Viper flipped and rolled, trapping the Dog Beater under him. He kept on turning, claiming more of the cane and forcing Count Seven to loosen his grip. Then he sprang up and kicked both feet out in quick succession. Count Seven had no choice but to let go and back away.

Apothecary Huang, Guo Jing and Lotus were stunned. Lotus had retrieved the iron *xiao* flute when it was torn from Guo Jing's grasp, and now she handed it to her father. Thus armed, Apothecary Huang lunged, placing himself between the Venom and Count Seven.

Viper pounced, his clawed fingers groping for the flute. "King Duan, I do not fear your Yang in Ascendance!" he shouted.

He's not right in the head, the Heretic thought as he eyed this wild reaction. The Venom had always been savage in combat, but there was now a feral edge to his aggression that Huang had not detected in their previous encounters, and he had no idea what could have brought about such a transformation.

In fact, not even the Venom himself understood the source of his odd behavior. He had not realized the Nine Yin Manual he had studied so assiduously was made up. Its nonsensical content had already set his head spinning long before Lotus put in motion her plot to lead him astray through deliberate misguidance. From the start, he had accepted every word as the undisputed truth, and blundered blindly from one false promise to the next in his desperation to master the techniques in the shortest possible time. And, if that was not bad enough, he had been whacked on the head while in this deluded state by Count Seven Hong.

Though he had been on an erroneous path from the very beginning, Viper's firm martial foundation had allowed him to somehow forge a way through, and now his attacks were so erratic and unpredictable that the two other Martial Greats present could only look on, mouths agape.

In just a few dozen moves, Viper had Apothecary Huang on the run, and it was Guo Jing's turn to enter fray. But one look at the young man was enough to reduce the Venom to tears.

"My boy! You died such a terrible death!"

He cast the Serpent Staff aside and threw his arms wide to envelop Guo Jing, filling the air with his heart-rending wails. The addled martial Master had clearly confused him with his late nephew, Gallant Ouyang.

Guo Jing launched a palm thrust to keep the distraught man at bay, but Viper simply turned the blow aside with his left wrist, locked his fingers over the attacking arm and pulled Guo Jing into an embrace. The young man struggled with all his might, but Viper's grasp was too strong—he could barely move.

Count Seven rushed in to jab the Phoenix Tail pressure point at the base of the Venom's spine, but it had no effect whatsoever. The inversed meridian flow had shifted the position of every acupoint in Viper's body.

Lotus crept up, hoping to hit Viper on the head with a rock. The deranged martial Master balled his right hand into a fist and threw an uppercut, sending the stone flying into the air. Guo Jing seized his chance, taking advantage of the distraction to ease himself out of Viper's grip and leap out of reach.

Their embrace broken, the Venom seemed to forget about him instantly, focusing instead on a renewed tussle with the Heretic. This time, Apothecary Huang was fighting barehanded, his iron flute tucked into his belt. Every move Viper made was more outlandish than the last. Sometimes he was upside down, sometimes he was the right way up. He even supported himself with just one hand, holding his body stretched out parallel to the ground, while his free hand thrust and probed, weaving one complex pattern after another.

Apothecary Huang was too busy defending himself to pay much attention to these unusual stances, but the other three were awed by the display.

Lotus could not bear to see her father so hard-pressed. "*Shifu*, we shouldn't have to follow the *wulin* rules when dealing with a mad man like him. Let's help Papa!"

Count Seven's expression was grim. "I'd agree with you on any other day, but today is the Contest of Mount Hua. Only single combat is permitted. If we gang up on the Venom, we'll be mocked by every hero of the *jianghu*."

Even as they deliberated, Viper's onslaught was growing ever more frenzied. Foaming at the mouth, he had now taken to charging into his opponent with his head lowered. The demented way he threw himself into each attack forced Apothecary Huang to fall farther and farther back.

Suddenly, Viper paused, twitching and shuddering, his eyes rolling in his head, before lurching forward without warning to launch a fresh tide of relentless, maddened fury. But, this time, he left his upper body undefended.

Only the truly insane fight with so little regard for their own well-being, Apothecary Huang said to himself, sensing an opportunity to neutralize his opponent once and for all. He flexed the fingers of his right hand in a Supernal Flick, aiming for the Welcome Fragrance pressure point on the side of the Venom's nose.

Apothecary Huang's lunge was impossibly quick, far outstripping the human eye, but just as his fingertip grazed Viper Ouyang's nose, the man twisted around and sunk his teeth into the offending digit.

Horrified, the Heretic groped for the Venom's temple, aiming for the Great Sun point, but the Venom simply brushed his hand away and bit down harder.

Guo Jing pounced on Viper Ouyang and snaked his arm around his neck in a wrestling move he had learned growing up on the

Mongolian steppe. The Venom let his jaw slacken and swiveled out of the headlock.

"Well done, Guo Jing!" Lotus cried, applauding. "That's what a good son-in-law should do!"

Apothecary Huang also granted Guo Jing a smile, impressed by his swift and selfless intervention.

But now Lotus was forced to rush to Guo Jing's aid as Viper Ouyang turned his vicious moves on him. Sensing her approach, the Venom snapped around and clawed at her face with both hands. In the glaring sunlight, the snarl on his blood-stained features was a terrifying sight. Lotus stumbled back with a yelp, while Guo Jing threw a palm strike to draw the Venom's attention. The young man paid a price for his gallantry—after just a dozen exchanges, he had taken blows on the shoulder and the leg.

"Guo Jing, get back, let me try." Count Seven stepped forward, barehanded this time. He had now observed Viper Ouyang's peculiar kung fu long enough to identify a rough pattern. These mercurial new moves resembled the Venom's most frequently employed palm techniques, but they were often inverted—what had been high was now low, and left had been swapped with right. Although the reversals were not so straightforward in every case, the Beggar now had a general idea of what the Venom might do next, and was able to launch a counterstroke once every three moves.

Apothecary Huang kept his eyes trained on the duel while Lotus bandaged his finger with a handkerchief. He also recognized familiar elements in Viper's movements, and, once he started to spot gaps in his attack, he began to call them out:

"Brother Seven, kick him at Jumping Round, in the buttocks!"

"Uppercut to the Great Tower Gate, in the stomach!"

"Backhand slash to Celestial Pillar, at the back of the neck."

With Apothecary Huang's help, Count Seven Hong was at last fighting Viper Ouyang on an equal footing, but it was humiliating that it had required their combined efforts to get him to this point.

Little by little, the Beggar was taking control of the fight, and, to all watching, it seemed certain that, in a few more moves, he would emerge victorious. Suddenly, he heard Viper hawking up phlegm in his throat and, moments later, the fruits of the Venom's labors came flying at his face. He twisted aside, avoiding the spittle, but the Venom had anticipated his reaction and was hacking his palm down to shut off his escape, while coughing up and sending forth another gob of expectorate.

Count Seven was now caught between Viper's strange kung fu and the disgusting projectile heading his way. He would prefer not to be hit by the sputum, seeing as it was dispatched with a martial Master's internal force. If it hit him in the eye, the main concern, other than the pain would be the opportunity it would give Viper to sneak up on him. With great reluctance, Count Seven snatched the slobber in his right hand, then thrust his left in retaliation. Viper dredged up yet more mucus—he had now added shooting phlegm from his lips to his martial repertoire—while continuing to throw punches and palm strikes.

Count Seven burned with fury at this insulting attack. The slimy sensation in his right hand was becoming unbearable, but he did not want to wipe the gunk onto his clothes.

"This is yours!" the Beggar cried, lurching forward to smear it over the Venom's face. The move contained a hidden, lethal sting.

Despite his confused state of mind, Viper Ouyang was physically more alert and responsive than ever. He turned his head by a fraction, evading the Beggar's swipe with ease. Count Seven flipped his palm over and thrust, aiming a finger jab at his opponent's face. Viper bared his teeth, ready to snap his jaw shut.

The very move that had caught Apothecary Huang unawares. Though absurd and undignified, it was executed with such rapidity that it was impossible to avoid.

Apothecary Huang, Guo Jing and Lotus saw what was coming. Count Seven's hand was less than an inch from Viper's mouth. They stood transfixed as the Venom parted his lips, revealing two rows of white teeth gleaming in the sun.

"Watch out!"

"Oh no!"

All four of them, Viper included, had forgotten one thing. Count Seven Hong had two titles. Beggar of the North was one. The other was Divine Vagrant Nine Fingers. Years ago, thanks to his gluttony, he lost track of time and failed to save the life of a good man of the *jianghu*. To punish himself for his lack of self-control, he cut off the forefinger—which is associated with the appetite—of his right hand.

Viper's bite was quick and precise. *Clack!* His jaw snapped shut on . . . nothing. Of course, the story of the Beggar's missing finger was well known throughout the *wulin*, but, in such an intense contest, one that had seen Viper pouncing and prowling like a mad tiger, how could he be expected to recall such a minor detail?

And small errors of this kind were often what determined the outcome of a duel between great Masters of equal standing—otherwise the fight would last for days. Taking advantage of the split second it took Viper to react to his misjudgment, Count Seven launched a Hearty Laughter, poking the Earth Granary vital point at the corner of the Venom's mouth with his middle finger.

Viper Ouyang felt the hit on this major pressure point of the Stomach Meridian, but his inverted energy flow meant that the attack only caused a slight numbness in his body. In no time at all, he had regained his full range of motion and was able to retaliate with a palm strike to the Beggar's shoulder.

Fortunately for Count Seven Hong, the acupoint jab had succeeded in curtailing Viper's strength to some extent, and he managed to dissipate the brunt of the blow's remaining *neigong* energy by flipping backward along its path. It was not an elegant retreat, but it bought the Beggar enough time and space to launch one final, desperate counterattack. Digging his right heel into the ground to anchor himself, he let fly with a Dragon in the Field.

The powerful strike forced the Venom to stagger back several steps, tottering unsteadily like a drunkard. When he finally secured his footing, he threw his head back and cackled at the sky.

Count Seven had escaped unscathed, but he was numb and sore. As an experienced grandmaster, he knew it was time to withdraw from the fight and admit defeat. He wrapped his palm over his fist and said, "Brother Ouyang, this Old Beggar concedes. The day is yours. You are the Greatest Martial Master Under the Heavens."

Viper let out another laugh and threw his arms up in feverish excitement. He turned to Apothecary Huang. "King Duan, do you concede?"

The Heretic was reluctant to accept that he had been bested, especially by a man who had clearly lost his wits. He realized that, if they allowed Viper Ouyang to claim the title, he and the Beggar would be the laughing stock of the *wulin*, but neither of them stood a chance against the crazed martial Master, so he had no choice but to nod grudgingly.

"My son, are you happy? Your papa is invincible! No one can match your papa's kung fu!" Once again, Viper was mistaking Guo Jing for Gallant Ouyang. In his confusion, he had also revealed a long-hidden secret: Gallant was known publicly as his nephew, but he was in fact Viper's own issue—the secret love child of a liaison with his sister-in-law.

"We can't beat you," Guo Jing said, for it was the truth and he could not deny that Viper deserved the honor.

Viper greeted his submission with gleeful laughter, before turning to Lotus. "Are you pleased, dear daughter?"

Lotus had not stopped thinking of ways to tackle the madman in their midst. Now, at last, she felt an idea was within her grasp. The confused questions, the odd expressions, the waving arms and tapping feet, his shadow dancing about in the same manic way . . . it all pointed to one thing . . .

"Who says you're the Greatest?" Lotus said. "There's still someone you can't beat."

Viper Ouyang thumped his chest and roared in fury. "Who? Who is this person? Tell him to come here and fight me now!"

"He's very skilled. You don't stand a chance."

"Who is he? Tell him to come now!"

"Viper Ouyang."

The Venom scratched his head. ". . . Viper . . . Ouyang?"

"Yes. Viper Ouyang. Your kung fu is excellent, but you can't beat Viper Ouyang."

The name whirled round and round the Venom's chaotic mind. "Viper Ouyang" sounded so familiar. He felt it was someone he knew intimately . . . but, then again . . . he was not sure who he was anymore . . .

"Who am I?" he blurted out.

"You are you. Think! Who are you?"

A chill went through Viper's heart. He asked himself as Lotus had suggested, and felt his tangled thoughts growing more and more knotted and the answer ever more elusive.

The questions of "Who am I?", "What was I before I was born?", "What will become of me when I die?", which had haunted philosophers through the ages, had, on occasion, kept Viper Ouyang awake at night too. And, in his current confused state, they were enough to send him into a stupor.

The Venom looked around blankly, muttering, "Me? Who am I? Where am I? What's happened to me?"

"Viper Ouyang wants to fight you. He wants your Nine Yin Manual."

"Where is he?"

Lotus pointed at his shadow. "There. Behind you."

The Venom spun round. With the sun on his back, a crisp silhouette of his body was cast on the cliff wall. He punched. He thrust his palm. The dark shape on the rock face mirrored his exact movements. He sent a flying kick, striking his foot into the rock. He pulled back in great pain, startled.

"What . . . He . . ." the Martial Great stammered.

"He hit back," Lotus observed, her tone matter of fact.

The Venom crouched and launched his palms at the shadow. The inky double responded simultaneously with the same kung fu.

He felt a solid force resisting him and his opponent did not quail in the slightest. Panicked, he delivered a rapid-fire barrage—left, right, left, right. The darkened figure responded in kind, matching strength with strength. When he channeled more power into each blow, his adversary retaliated with equal force.

Recognizing that he was up against a truly formidable foe, the Venom turned side on to his opponent to better guard his frame. Now that he was facing the sun, his shadow was behind him.

"Where are you going?" He spun round and leaped at the fleeing silhouette with the sun on his back.

On this stretch of cliff wall, his shadow looked as if it were standing up straight. The Venom swung his right palm and it landed square on his opponent, but so intense was the pain that he thought his bones had been crushed.

"Good kung fu!" the Venom cried, letting fly with his left foot.

His foe intercepted him with the same move, and agonizing pain followed.

Viper Ouyang dared not launch another attack. He turned and fled, running in the direction of the sun. After a short while, he was relieved to discover that he had lost sight of his enemy. He looked back to see if the man was truly gone, only to find him hot on his heels, trailing after him in a most curious manner. He had never seen anybody move like that before, and he was filled with abject terror.

"You're the Greatest! You've won! I submit to you!"

Receiving no response, the Venom took off again. A moment later, he glanced back over his shoulder. To his horror, he saw that the man was stalking his every step—he just would not let him be. The Venom tried shoving him away. He tried beating him back. But his relentless foe simply would not give up.

Howling in terror, Viper Ouyang raced downhill as fast as he could, his cries echoing between the many peaks of Mount Hua: "I submit to you! Stop chasing me!"

4

VIPER OUYANG'S CRIES AND PLEAS WERE FAINT NOW, YET they still echoed up from the gorge from time to time. He must have covered several *li* already. His voice, like a wolf's howl or the shriek of a ghost on the wind, sent a chill to one's core that not even the warm sunlight could dispel.

Saddened to see their peer and a fellow martial Master laid so low, Apothecary Huang and Count Seven Hong shared a sigh.

"His end is coming . . ."

The Beggar's remark caused Guo Jing to jerk his head and he began to mutter to himself: "You mean me? . . . Who am I?"

"You are Guo Jing!" Lotus exclaimed immediately. "Think about anything but yourself." Given his bull-headed nature, she feared that he would refuse to let go of the question and suffer the same fate as Viper Ouyang.

Her reminder snapped Guo Jing out of his trance. ". . . Right! *Shifu*, Lord Huang, let's make our way down."

"Lord Huang?" Count Seven snorted. "Do you want to be cuffed on the ears again? Stupid lad!"

"Guo Jing, remember how you addressed Papa earlier . . ." Lotus said with a blush and a bashful smile.

"Father!" the young man blurted out, after a brief pause.

Laughing in approval, Apothecary Huang took Lotus by the hand, then offered his free arm to Guo Jing.

"Brother Seven, the martial arts do indeed present all of us with myriad paths, and none of them are finite. The Old Venom's kung fu is truly astonishing and humbling, but, with the passing of the Double Sun Immortal Wang Chongyang, it would seem that there is no one truly worthy of the title of Greatest Martial Master Under the Heavens."

"Well, there's one Greatest Under the Heavens I can vouch for," Count Seven said. "Lotus and her cooking."

The young woman giggled into her hand. "Spare me your flattery. I'll make some tasty dishes once we've made our way down."

After they had settled into a guest house at the foot of Mount Hua, Lotus busied herself with the evening's feast, choosing the best seasonal, local ingredients and preparing them with great care. Count Seven Hong gorged himself until his belly could hold no more. That night, Guo Jing shared a room with his *shifu*, but, when he opened his eyes in the morning, his bed was empty. There were three characters traced in grease on the table:

Fare thee well

Whether they were written with a chicken drumstick or a pig's trotter, it was impossible to tell.

Downhearted, Guo Jing went to see Apothecary Huang and Lotus to inform them of Count Seven's departure.

"This has always been Brother Seven's way," Huang said. "One may only catch a glimpse of the divine dragon's head or its tail—never its full glory." He turned to Guo Jing. "Would you like to come with me to Peach Blossom Island? I am hoping you will invite your first *shifu*, Ke Zhen'e, to officiate the marriage ceremony. I understand Master Ke is now the person closest to you, after your mother's passing."

Overwhelmed by opposing feelings of grief and joy, Guo Jing had trouble putting his thoughts into words, so he settled for bobbing his head in enthusiastic agreement.

Lotus loved teasing Guo Jing when he was dumbstruck, but, this time, she glanced at her father and swallowed her jibe.

The Heretic had little patience for silly banter and he did not like making small talk. After traveling with the young couple for a few days, he decided to make his own way.

"Papa is so understanding," Lotus said with a laugh. "He knows we can't be free and at ease in his company, and neither can he with us!" She proceeded to list the sights she wanted to see along the way—the majestic mountains and the grand lakes and rivers. She suggested a route from west to east, starting from the regions of East Jingzhaofu and Nanjing and taking in the cities of Luoyang and Kaifeng; after that, they would head south and roam around the areas of Huainan, Jiangnan and finally West Zhe, before heading to the coast for passage to Peach Blossom Island.

"What do you think, Guo Jing? The two of us together, happy and carefree. Isn't this how life should be?"

BEFORE THEY set off, Guo Jing purchased a horse for himself, so Lotus could ride alone on Ulaan. The first half of the trip took them through Jin territory, but, since the Jurchens had been crushed by the Mongolians at every turn in recent years, they had lost control of much of the land to the east of Tong Pass that Lotus was interested in exploring. The young lovers were able to make their way in peace, without being troubled by Jin soldiers along the way.

As they approached Guangde, in East Jiangnan, a familiar caw sounded in the air. Guo Jing looked up to see the white condors winging their way south. He had fled Mongolia in such a frantic state that he had given up hope of ever seeing them again. Thrilled, he whistled for the birds' attention. They swooped down and greeted their masters with affectionate nuzzles. As Guo Jing stroked their backs, he noticed a small roll of leather fastened to the male condor's foot. He untied it. A few lines in Mongolian had been scratched onto its surface with the point of a dagger.

Our armies are marching to conquer the Great Song. My father knows that you have returned to the South, but has not changed his mind about the campaign. I know you are loyal to your country and would brave death to defend it. I have been the cause of your mother's tragic end, and I am too ashamed to see you again. I have traveled to the extreme west to seek my eldest brother's protection and will not return to this land of old for the rest of my days. As the proverb says, the camel may be strong, but it cannot carry a thousand men—to bear such a weight is to die in vain. I hope you will cherish yourself and live a long life with infinite blessings.

The note was not addressed to anyone and it contained no signature, but it was clear that Princess Khojin had intended it for Guo Jing. He translated the message for Lotus.

"'The camel cannot carry a thousand men.' What an odd thing to say!"

"It's a Mongolian saying, similar to the Chinese phrase, 'A single log cannot support a tall tower.'"

Lotus nodded. "It's always been clear the Mongolians would invade the Song, but, for her to put it in writing, she must be very fond of you indeed."

AFTER A few more days on the road, Guo Jing and Lotus crossed into western Two Zhes and rode into Changxing, on the southern shore of Lake Tai. Surrounded by fertile farmland, it should have been a prosperous town, but its proximity to the border between the Jin and the Song in the Huainan and Jiangnan regions had convinced many of its inhabitants to flee south, abandoning their fields and their homes.

The young couple passed through the desolated town and its outlying villages, taking a path that led them up a mountain. The grass and weeds along the trail were so overgrown that they reached the horses' bellies. Ahead of them was a dense and dark forest that betrayed no sign of human activity.

All of a sudden, the condors screeched in anger. They plunged straight down from on high and vanished into the trees.

Knowing that something must have provoked the birds, Guo Jing and Lotus spurred their mounts into the woods. Soon, they found the raptors wheeling aggressively over a man who was trying to ward them off with a steel saber. Lotus was first to recognize him. Elder Peng, the disgraced Beggar Clan member! They had not expected to chance upon him here, of all places.

He was hacking viciously at the air with the blade, but the birds were not deterred. The female condor dived, snatched up Peng's headscarf with her talons and pecked at the crown of his head. Peng swung his weapon again, and a cloud of white feathers rained down on him.

The hairless patch on his head reminded Lotus of the bloody scalp torn off by the female condor after the wreck at Blue Dragon Shoal. She remembered the wound to the condor's breast, which they had found when the two birds returned to Uncle Sole Light's mountain sanctuary from Peach Blossom Island. Perhaps Elder Peng fired the arrow? That would explain their hostility toward him.

"Hey! Look over here!" she cried.

The sudden appearance of the Beggar Clan Chief sent Elder Peng's quaking spirits beyond the highest heavens. He turned and bolted. The male condor swooped down and pecked at his head. Peng swung the saber into the air to protect himself. Spotting that he had left his flank undefended, the female condor flew in from the side and struck his left eye with her beak.

Peng shrieked, tossed his blade aside and dived into a bush. He crawled deep into the spiky shrubbery, caring little for his torn skin so long as the thorns kept the birds at bay. The condors circled overhead, refusing to let him out of their sight.

Guo Jing whistled a command, calling the birds off. "Let him be. He's blind in one eye." Then he heard a mewling sound coming from a thicket behind him. He dismounted and waded through the undergrowth. A baby was lying on its back on the ground, and, next to it, a pair of feet were poking out from the bushes. He parted the vegetation to find an unconscious young woman, her wrists and ankles bound.

"Mercy!" Lotus helped her friend into a sitting position and cut the ropes restraining her. Then she massaged Mercy's acupoints and pressed a finger to her philtrum to bring her around.

Guo Jing, meanwhile, had plucked up the child. The infant gazed at him with bright eyes, not at all afraid of the stranger.

Mercy gradually came to and tried to focus on the concerned faces before her. "Big Brother Guo . . . Sister Huang . . . ?" A distinct tremor in her feeble voice.

"Sister Mu, why are you here? Are you hurt?" Guo Jing asked.

Realizing she was not dreaming, Mercy pushed herself up higher and reached out for her babe. Holding him close, she collected herself and began to recount all that had happened to her since they had last seen each other in Peach Spring.

Mercy had already told the story of how she had lost her honor to Yang Kang in a moment of weakness on Iron Palm Mountain. Not long after they had parted, she discovered that she was with child, and her only wish at that moment was to return to Ox Village in Lin'an. She attempted the journey alone, dragging her increasingly cumbersome body thousands of *li* east from Hunan, all the way to the outskirts of Changxing, where she found she could go no farther. Taking shelter in an abandoned forester's hut, she gave birth to her son. She had no desire to mix with other people, so she lived off the land, hunting and foraging for sustenance. Fortunately, the baby was healthy and well behaved. He gave her great comfort and brought joy into her otherwise lonely and miserable existence.

She had been gathering firewood, just now, when she came across Elder Peng. He was taken by her looks and tried to force himself upon her. She fought back, but, though her kung fu was advanced enough to keep her safe in most situations, it was of little use against Peng. After all, he had once been one of the Four Elders of the Beggar Clan, and his martial skills were considerable, on a par with those of Surefoot Lu and Elder Jian. On top of that, he was a master of the dark art of mind entrapment, capable of controlling another simply by staring into their eyes.

The last thing Mercy remembered was being overpowered and tied up, before she passed out from fear and fury at the horrors that she was about to endure. It was fortuitous that Guo Jing and Lotus happened to be in the area, and that Peng had somehow drawn the ire of the condors, otherwise she would not have been able to escape the ordeal.

Guo Jing and Lotus spent that night in Mercy's hut. When Lotus mentioned what had happened to Yang Kang, Mercy's tears fell like rain. Her reaction was testament to the deep affection she still had for the faithless Prince, and Lotus decided to withhold from her the whole truth. She dreaded to think how Mercy would feel if she knew that Yang Kang had remained loyal to the Jin Empire to the bitter end and never stopped thinking of Wanyan Honglie as his father, or that he had played a part in the murder of five of Guo Jing's *shifus*.

And so Lotus just told her that Yang Kang had been poisoned by Viper Ouyang at Iron Spear Temple in Jiaxing. When she uttered those words, a voice cried inside her: *I'm not lying, it was the Venom's poison that killed him* . . . She could not bring herself to admit that he had come into contact with such a lethal substance only because of her—for she had revealed his crimes, including the killing of Gallant Ouyang, and, when he had tried to silence her, he had struck a part of the Hedgehog Chainmail that was tainted by the toxin.

The child's features reminded Guo Jing of Yang Kang, and he sighed as he recalled his failure to live up to the pledge of brotherhood he had made with the infant's father.

"Brother Guo, may I ask you to name my boy?" Mercy said, drying her tears.

Guo Jing considered her request. "His father and I swore we would be brothers," he said at last, "but things did not turn out as we had hoped, in part because I did not fulfill my duty as a friend. This is my deepest regret. I hope this child, when he grows up, will make good his father's mistakes, and act with compassion and integrity. Lotus, I'm not good with words—help me, please?"

Lotus turned to Mercy to see what she thought of this idea.

"Sister, please give my child a name that will express what Brother Guo has said."

A moment later, Lotus said, "What if his given name was Penance, and his courtesy name Amend, as a reminder to repent and change his ways when he errs?"

"Thank you. I pray he will live up to your hopes for him."

Lotus invited Mercy to come with them to Peach Blossom Island, while Guo Jing suggested that he take little Penance on as his disciple, so the boy could learn kung fu.

Mercy was moved by their offers, and she knew that Guo Jing and Lotus truly meant well, but being in their presence never failed to shine a light on her own misfortunes and solitude, bringing a dull ache to her heart and making it hard for her to accept their kindness.

She tried to smile. "My boy is blessed to have Brother Guo for his *shifu*. Please accept our obeisance." With baby Penance in her arms, she kowtowed to Guo Jing. "He is still too young to travel, but, one day, he shall present himself to his *shifu* and *shimu*."

The next morning, Guo Jing and Lotus once more asked Mercy to join them on their journey, but she insisted that she would make her own way back to her village in Lin'an. Before they left the hut, Guo Jing took out the gold ingots Tolui had given him and pressed most of them onto her.

Thanking him for his generosity, Mercy then accompanied the young couple as far as the edge of the forest. "I will take Penance to Iron Spear Temple," she said as they parted, "so he can visit his father's grave."

5

ONE NIGHT, AFTER LOTUS HAD MADE THEM SUPPER IN THEIR guest house, Guo Jing fell into a particularly somber mood. His mind kept straying back to Khojin's letter, which he carried in his inside shirt pocket, and to his childhood with Tolui and Khojin, filling him with nostalgia for all the games they had played on the Mongolian steppe. He had never had romantic feelings for the young woman, but he could not shake a lingering sense of guilt. After all, he was the reason she was spending the best years of her youth in a self-imposed exile in the far west, away from all that she had known and loved, and with only her brother Jochi for company.

The thought of the inevitable Mongol invasion dragged Guo Jing's spirits down even further. Hundreds of thousands of common people would suffer the brutality of war because the Song Emperor was unworldly, his officials incapable, his soldiers and generals corrupt and unwarlike. The Song had no hope of holding back Genghis Khan's riders, and, if he informed the court of the invasion, they would likely surrender without putting up even a show of a fight.

Lotus sat quietly beside Guo Jing, mending clothes by lamplight, and left him to his brooding.

"What do you think Khojin meant by this?" Guo Jing said, out of the blue. He read from her letter: "'I have been the cause of your mother's tragic end, and I am too ashamed to see you again.'"

"Well, it was her father who . . ." Lotus's voice trailed off.

Guo Jing's only response was a guttural *Mm.* He was running through the events of that terrible day in his head. Suddenly, he leaped to his feet, striking the table. "It all makes sense now!"

His abrupt movement made Lotus jump and she pricked herself with the sewing needle. A bead of blood formed on her fingertip. "What do you mean?"

"Mother and I were alone in the *ger* when we unpicked the Great Khan's silk pouch and made the decision to go home. I never understood how Genghis Khan discovered our plans. Now I do—it was Khojin!"

"Why would she do that? Wasn't she devoted to you?"

"She wanted to make me stay. She must have seen us picking apart the silk pouch and packing our things. So, she told her father, thinking he would find some way to convince me not to leave. She had no idea that we were committing a capital crime . . ." He heaved a weary sigh.

"Why don't you go and find her?"

"Why would I want to do that? I only ever cared for her as my little sister."

Satisfied with his answer, Lotus gave Guo Jing a sweet smile.

THE NEXT morning, Guo Jing and Lotus headed south, with the intention of stopping in Huzhou for the night. They stayed in the city's grandest inn, the Merchant's Guesthouse, and, at dusk, they joined the other guests in the dining hall for supper. At the table next to theirs were seven or eight men who spoke with Shandong accents, sharing tales of the Qingzhou Patriotic Army's struggle against the Jin. Guo Jing was fascinated by their conversation, and called for five *jin* of wine and eight dishes to be sent to their table, so he could approach the men to find out more.

It turned out they were silk merchants from Qingzhou who had fled south to avoid the chaos of war. They had come to the Two Zhes because they knew the area well, having traveled there frequently to conduct business. Impressed by the generous spread of food that appeared on their table, and by Guo Jing's courteous manners, they told the young man all they knew about the situation in their hometown.

Qingzhou, in Yidu prefecture, was an important city in Shandong. The Jurchens' hold on the region had been weakened by the defeats they had suffered at the hands of the Mongolians, and the local Han population had seized the opportunity to rise against them, taking back a sizeable swathe of land. They had called themselves the Patriotic Army, naming Li Quan from Weizhou as their leader.

Li Quan and his wife, Yang Miaozhen, were both formidable warriors. She was known as Pear Blossom Spear, and there was a local saying that described her prowess: "For twenty years unmatched under the heavens." Li Quan's older brother, Li Fu, was also a renowned fighter. The Jin troops sent to face them were routed, scattering like fallen petals flushed by spring torrents. Patriots traveled from all over Shandong to pledge their allegiance, and the group's reputation spread far and wide.

The Patriotic Army secured a string of decisive victories, forcing the Jin armies in Huainan and Shandong to withdraw to the west. The last time the Song people had enjoyed success on this scale against the Jurchens was more than a century ago, in the days of Generals Yue Fei, Liu Qi and Yu Yunwen.

The Imperial Court at Lin'an was thrilled. Chancellor Shi Miyuan named Li Quan Commander-in-Chief of Jingdong. Although the territory was still under the Jin's jurisdiction, the Song Empire continued to appoint an official to govern the region—in name only. The Song now had an army north of the Yangtze, headquartered in Chuzhou, and its presence was invigorating news for those subjects in the Jin-annexed regions nearby who had remained loyal.

Though it received official recognition, as well as funds and grain from court, the Patriotic Army was not trusted by those in power. After Li Quan quelled a Jin incursion south of the River Huai, threatening the Song's heartlands along the Yangtze, he was rewarded with two grand titles: Military Commissioner of the Peace Preserving Army and Deputy Commissioner of Frontier Appeasement at Jingdong. But, at the same time, General Xu Guo was appointed Military Commissioner of East Huai, with power over Li Quan and orders to keep the upstarts under control.

Xu Guo had won battles against the Jin at the border strongholds of Xiangyang and Zaoyang, but as a commander he was rude and prejudiced. Each time the Patriotic Army fought alongside the Song Empire's regular army, Xu Guo would favor his own soldiers and mete out harsh punishments to Li's men.

Ultimately, this sealed his fate. During a battle with Mongolian riders who had come to claim Jin territory around Qingzhou, the rear guard of the Patriotic Army mutinied while Li Quan was leading from the front. They killed Xu Guo's entire family and forced the General to commit suicide.

Lotus was intrigued by the tales told by the Qingzhou merchants. "Guo Jing, I'd like to see for myself how unmatched this Pear Blossom Spear really is."

"Yes! And we should help them reclaim more of our land from the Jin."

Guo Jing and Lotus altered their travel plans there and then, and headed north for Shandong the next morning. When they arrived in Qingzhou, they sought an audience with the formidable couple to offer their assistance in repelling the Song's enemies.

Having been a court official for some time now, Li Quan had acquired a haughty manner, putting too much store by his own importance. He did not want to waste his time exchanging pleasantries with a simple youth and a pretty girl who did not seem to have anything concrete to offer. He brushed them off with perfunctory words of thanks and a vague promise that he would summon them if he had trouble holding back the enemy.

Li Quan sent for food and wine for his guests, then turned away to attend to army business at the dining table. For weeks now, he had been plagued by conflicts between elements of his Patriotic Army and the Song court's regular troops. He issued orders for the arrest of the soldiers who had clashed with men of the Patriotic Army and the expulsion of those who were occupying the treasure house.

Guo Jing and Lotus were disappointed that the warrior they had heard so much about was turning out to be a terrible leader. His first priority had not been the city's defenses, but petty punishments against those who disagreed with his subordinates. It was clear that the guardians of this city were not a united front. They were even more alarmed when they witnessed the offhand way Li Quan treated information about enemy movements in the region.

"How many men? Mongols or Jurchens? Not the Mongols? Can't be. Where's their vanguard now?"

The answer was given in similar broad strokes, to the extent that it was impossible to tell if the scout's report was genuine or made up. The exchange ruined Guo Jing and Lotus's appetite. After a quiet discussion, they took their leave, and Lotus set off on Ulaan for a quick reconnaissance of the surrounding area.

At sundown, Guo Jing waited outside the north gate for her return. He rushed forward when he saw a cloud of dust rising from the horizon—Ulaan was galloping at full speed. Lotus tugged at the reins the moment she spotted Guo Jing.

"Mongolians, at least a hundred thousand." Her face was pale, her voice strained with tension. "How can we resist them?"

"That many?" Guo Jing bowed to Lotus. "You must have a plan, my strategist."

Lotus shook her head. "I've been thinking this over since Samarkand. In single combat, no more than two or three people under the heavens can match you. We don't have much to worry about in a fight against a few dozen men, maybe even a hundred. But, with tens of thousands out there, what can the two of us do to make a difference?"

"The Song Empire has enough subjects and soldiers to resist the Mongolians. If we were of one heart, we'd have nothing to fear. But the traitors at court are cowardly and corrupt. Every decision they make is a disaster for the people and the country. And the so-called Patriotic Army busy themselves with infighting, when our true enemies are almost at the city gates!"

"Well, we'll just have to kill as many Mongolians as we can. If the worst happens, we can ride away on Ulaan . . . We can't burden ourselves with all the worries of the world."

"That's not right, Lotus. We've studied General Yue Fei's *The Secret to Defeating the Jin*, and we should follow his example and repay our country with loyalty. He gave our people a taste of victory, and we can use his methods to defeat the Mongolians. Even if nothing comes of it, we should do everything in our power to help. If we die on the battlefield, we will have lived up to the principles our parents and *shifus* instilled in us."

"I knew this day would come eventually. Very well! Live together, die together!"

Now that they had confirmed their resolve to defend their country at all costs, Guo Jing and Lotus felt more at ease. They headed back into the city, found an inn and drank as they discussed the coming invasion and the prospect of separation in life and in death, their hearts closer than ever before.

At the second watch of the night, their conversation was interrupted by heart-rending wails from beyond the city walls.

"They're here!" Lotus cried.

The young couple hurried to position themselves on the battlements of the north gate. Streams of refugees—men and women, young and old—were making for the city.

Faced with endless skirmishes between different factions of the Song military, many of Qingzhou's residents had chosen to camp in the wilderness surrounding the city, but, now that the Mongols were here, they had no choice but to seek safety within the city walls.

An officer rode up to the north gate and ordered the guards to make sure it remained shut and barred—under no circumstances should they allow anyone inside. Moments later, a company of archers manned the ramparts at Li Quan's command. Arrows nocked, bows drawn, they took aim at their fellow countrymen, shouting at them to get back.

"The Mongols are here!" Screams and shouts filled the air, but the north gate remained shut.

From their elevated vantage point, Guo Jing and Lotus could just about make out the faint glow of a fiery dragon slithering in their direction through the dark of the night.

The Mongolian vanguard.

Guo Jing knew from experience that Genghis Khan's army would be with them by dawn. And he was well acquainted with the conqueror's siege craft—he would send prisoners to scale the walls ahead of his warriors. But what really troubled the young man was the prospect of a first wave of bloodshed before the Mongols even arrived. The blood of the people of Qingzhou—those outside the walls pitted against those inside for a chance to be protected by the city's fortifications.

Now was the moment to act. Guo Jing waved his arms for attention and projected his voice: "If Qingzhou falls, we all die. If you're a real man, join me and fight!" He jumped from the ramparts to find a way to force open the gates.

"Arrest him!" the officer shouted, upon hearing Guo Jing's call to arms, for he was a loyal follower of Li Quan. Before any of his men could carry out his orders, Guo Jing grabbed him by the front of his robe, dragged him out of the saddle and mounted his warhorse.

"Open the gate!" he demanded, towering over the officer.

The bulk of the Patriotic Army rank and file had joined up because they believed in retaking lost Song land, and they were repulsed by the idea of keeping their fellow countrymen out. After all, many had friends and family in the crush beyond the walls, and it was impossible to remain unmoved by their despairing cries. Not a single soldier gave any thought to rescuing their leader.

Fearful for his life, the officer relented. The gates were flung open and the refugees poured in like a swelling tide.

Guo Jing grabbed a spear and placed the officer under Lotus's watch, ready to ride out to intercept the enemy.

"Wait!" Lotus stopped him. She made their captive strip off his armor, then strapped it onto Guo Jing herself, taking the chance to whisper in his ear: "Say you have an imperial mandate to lead the army out." She then flicked the officer's pressure points to lock his movements and left him at the foot of the ramparts.

"I was sent by His Majesty the Song Emperor to defend this city and its people. Fight with me!" Guo Jing cried, amplifying his voice with *qi* from the Elixir Field. His words cut through the din, loud and clear. For a moment, the people of Qingzhou fell silent, then they erupted in cheers. No one had time to consider whether or not he was telling the truth, for their enemies would be upon them in a matter of hours. Moreover, with clashes between the Patriotic Army and the regular army a daily occurrence, the soldiers were used to conflicting orders. They were not going to question a leader that gave them hope.

Guo Jing mustered six or seven thousand volunteers, but even the soldiers among them were disorganized and ill-trained. How could this ragtag band possibly stand against elite Mongol riders?

A sudden situation calls for surprise, an army in danger calls for deceit.

With this maxim from *The Secret to Defeating the Jin* in mind, Guo Jing sent three thousand men to conceal themselves behind a hill to the east. He ordered them to wave their standards and shout at the top of their voices when the cannons fired to give the signal—but to make certain that only the banners were visible. A similar battalion was sent with orders to do the same behind the hill on the west when the cannons sounded for a second time. He then gave detailed instructions to the artillery teams. Reassured by confident and clear commands, the unit captains took their men to their positions.

When first light came, it was heralded by the beating of drums and the calls of a thousand bugles, soon followed by a dust storm kicked up by countless galloping horses. The Mongols had arrived.

By now, all the refugees had entered the city. Lotus rode up to Guo Jing, armed with a spear, in time to hear him issue his final command before the battle began: "Keep all four gates open! Everyone must remain inside. If anyone is caught disobeying this order, off with their head!"

The jingle of horse bells announced the arrival of Li Quan and Yang Miaozhen. Li, clad in full armor, carried a saber, while Yang held her Pear Blossom Spear. The burnished spear point glittered in the sunlight. She looked every inch the warrior of legend that had first captured Lotus's imagination.

When the first unit of Mongol riders charged toward Qingzhou, they were surprised to find that the city gates had been thrown open. Stranger still, their approach was barred not by a waiting army, but by two teenagers standing side by side, their only support, a middle-aged couple. The commander of the thousand-strong detachment halted his men and sent his fastest rider to report this unexpected situation to his superior.

Hearing the news, the divisional general rode to the frontline to see for himself, and immediately recognized Guo Jing among those standing outside the walls. He had admired the clever strategies deployed by the young commander when taking cities on the road to Samarkand, culminating in the fearless descent into the capital itself, and he knew the youth had never lost a battle.

The veteran soldier studied the view that the open gates offered him into the city, eyeing the empty streets of Qingzhou with caution, then cupped his hands in greeting. "Prince of the Golden Blade."

Guo Jing returned the salute, but did not speak.

The Mongolian wheeled his horse around and hurried back to inform the general in overall command of the campaign. An hour or so later, a yak's-tail banner came into view, carried by an elite mounted unit in fine iron armor.

It was Tolui, the fourth son of Genghis Khan.

"Guo Jing, *anda*!"

"Brother Tolui!"

In the past, the sworn brothers would have leaped from their saddles and folded their arms around each other in a warm embrace, but now they pulled their horses to a stop when they were still five *zhang* apart.

"*Anda*, you have come to invade my homeland," Guo Jing stated dispassionately.

Tolui tried to explain. "I am here under Father's orders. I do not have a choice. Please forgive me."

Guo Jing scanned the horizon. Flags swirled like clouds, sabers sparkled like fresh snow. If they charge at us now, we'll all die here today. He fixed his gaze on Tolui once more. "Very well. Come and take my life."

The Mongolian Prince was taken aback by Guo Jing's tone. I cannot match his talent on the battlefield, he told himself. And our ties are as close as ties of flesh and blood. Am I really supposed to destroy such a bond?

Watching from afar, Li Quan and Yang Miaozhen were stunned to see their visitor conversing with the Mongol commander. They did not know what to make of it. Lotus, meanwhile, gave the signal for the cannons to fire from the city walls.

Boom! War cries erupted from the hill to the east.

All color drained from Tolui's face.

The cannons sounded again. Banners were raised above the slopes to the west.

We're surrounded! Tolui realized with horror. He knew that there were only several thousand fighting men in Qingzhou, and, under normal circumstances, they would represent no threat at all, but, with Guo Jing on their side, he could not afford to be careless. He bid his *anda* farewell and gave the order for the army to retreat and set up camp thirty *li* from the city.

With Tolui gone, Lotus allowed herself a smile at his expense. "Congratulations! You've tricked them with an empty city."

Her words did nothing to dispel the grim look on Guo Jing's face. He knew it was a hollow victory. "Tolui is patient and determined. He'll be back tomorrow. What do we do then?"

"There is one way . . . but, you're sworn brothers. You may not wish to . . ."

". . . You want me to assassinate him?"

"He is Genghis Khan's youngest son and also his favorite. His status is far above that of an ordinary general. If the Fourth Prince dies, the army will withdraw."

Guo Jing did not know how to respond. He rode back into the city with his head bowed.

Awed by the exchange they had just witnessed, and by the way Guo Jing had sent an army into retreat single-handedly, Li Quan and Yang Miaozhen invited the young couple back to their residence to celebrate.

Guo Jing was in low spirits. He insisted that the Mongolians would return the next day and asked Li about his plans for defending the city.

"You are good friends with the Mongolian commander," the Patriotic Army General ventured. "Perhaps you can agree terms for laying down our arms to save the city."

"*Pah!*" Guo Jing spat. "If you want to surrender, negotiate your own terms, but you won't save a single life that way."

Embarrassed, Li Quan and Yang Miaozhen made their excuses and withdrew from the feast.

Guo Jing was all too familiar with the Mongolian attitude toward those who yielded—mercy did not come into it. As dusk fell, his ears seemed to become more sensitive to the sobs and wails that could be heard throughout the city. He could already see the brutal fate awaiting its people. Qingzhou's streets would be awash with blood, every living soul inside its walls butchered.

The massacre of Samarkand came back to him, turning his stomach, and he struck the dining table. "Ancient heroes sacrificed their kin to safeguard their principles. I can give up one friendship to save a city."

6

CHANGING INTO BLACK CLOTHES TO BLEND INTO THE NIGHT, Guo Jing and Lotus rode north for the Mongolian camp. They tethered their horses a few *li* short of it and made the final approach on foot. At the perimeter of the camp, they captured two sentries, locked their acupoints and stripped them of their armor. Thus disguised, it did not take them long to reach Tolui's *ger*, since Guo Jing knew the habits of the Mongol army inside out.

It was now completely dark. Guo Jing and Lotus crept up to the sizeable tent and peered through a gap in the felt.

Tolui was pacing around in a state of restless agitation, muttering: "Guo Jing, *anda* . . ."

Lotus clamped her hand over Guo Jing's mouth just as he parted his lips to speak. Only then did the youth realize his mistake—Tolui was talking to himself!

"A true man is resolute. Get it done," Lotus urged him under her breath.

Just then, they heard pounding hooves approaching. The rider dismounted just a few feet from the entrance to the *ger*. Guo Jing knew only messengers bearing the most urgent dispatch would remain in the saddle all the way up to a commander's tent.

"Let's hear the news first," he said.

A herald clad in yellow prostrated himself before Tolui. "Fourth Prince, I have orders from the Great Khan."

"Speak."

Rising to his knees, the herald presented Tolui with a roll of parchment, then began to chant. Though the Mongolian script was widely used in Genghis Khan's court, the conqueror himself could neither read nor write, so his edicts and messages were often passed on verbally as well as in writing. With more complex matters like military orders, the words were arranged into songs to make them easier to commit to memory, and the messengers were tested again and again before they set off, to ensure accurate delivery.

Only three lines had been sung, and Tolui was already in tears. Guo Jing also felt his heart skip a beat. Genghis Khan had fallen ill after the successful conquest of Tangut, and his health had failed to improve in the weeks that followed. He was asking Tolui to return by the swiftest horse.

The message ended thus:

I have missed Guo Jing greatly. If you discover his whereabouts in the South, you must entreat him to come north to bid me a final farewell. All his offenses are forgiven.

Guo Jing cut the *ger* open with his dagger and stepped inside. "I'll come with you, *anda*."

Tolui was startled by the intrusion, but, when he realized it was Guo Jing, he hurried over to give his sworn brother a hug.

The messenger kowtowed before Guo Jing. "Prince of the Golden Blade, the Great Khan speaks of you every day. Please, visit him in the golden *ger*."

Hearing himself addressed by his former title, Guo Jing was reminded of all the misunderstandings that had blighted his relationship with Lotus. He ducked out through the gap he had made, took her hand and led her into the *ger*. "We'll go together and we'll come back together."

TOLUI ORDERED the retreat that night, and the army set off the following morning. Guo Jing and Lotus traveled side by side, as the two condors wheeled overhead.

"Li Quan is weak," Guo Jing said with a sigh. "What fire he had in him has gone out. He will surrender when the Mongolians return." His prediction was proved accurate when Qingzhou was besieged again, some months later.

Worried that he would not make it in time to see his father, Tolui entrusted the army's return to his deputy, and gathered the swiftest horses to race back with Guo Jing and Lotus. The three of them reached Genghis Khan's camp in Tangut in less than a month. The Prince was relieved to see the nine-tail banner hoisted high over the golden *ger*. The Great Khan was still alive.

Tolui dismounted by the entrance to the tent and rushed inside.

Guo Jing reined in his horse some distance away. He was deeply conflicted about seeing Genghis Khan again. The man had raised him like his own son, recognized his talent and given him opportunities, but he had also driven his mother to suicide in pursuit of his limitless ambitions and put whole cities to the sword to soothe his injured pride. Guo Jing felt both love and disgust for the conqueror, and the weight of these opposing emotions weighed heavy upon him.

A fanfare dragged him back to the present. A company of archer-bodyguards lined up in two rows before the golden *ger*. Wrapped in black sable, Genghis Khan emerged, holding on to Tolui for support. His stride was as long and bold as before, but it was plain for all to see that he was no longer steady on his feet.

Guo Jing dismounted and prostrated himself before the great warrior.

Hot tears streamed down Genghis Khan's face. "Get up! Get up!" he said with a tremor in his voice. "You're back, Guo Jing, my boy. You've both come back. This is excellent! I have thought of you every day," he added, patting Tolui on the shoulder.

Guo Jing rose to his feet and met the Great Khan's gaze. He was shocked to see the change in him. The conqueror's hair was now completely white, his face marred by deep grooves of wrinkles, his cheeks sallow and sunken. It was clear that he had little time left, and much of Guo Jing's resentment drained away.

Genghis Khan put his free hand on Guo Jing's shoulder and looked back and forth between him and Tolui. Then he heaved a sigh and gazed into the distance, lost in thought. The young men remained silent, not wishing to interrupt his reverie.

At length, Genghis Khan breathed a heavy sigh and began to speak. "When Jamuka and I first declared ourselves *anda*, how could I have known that I would have to kill him myself? In a few days' time, I will join him, returning to the yellow earth . . . Who has won? Who has lost? What difference does it make, in the end?" He squeezed both young men on the shoulder. "You two must always stay on good terms. Do not turn against each other. If you don't wish to marry Khojin, Guo Jing, you don't have to. You are Han, you will never be Mongolian. This is something I have come to understand of late. We may be of different tribes, but we must still remain on good terms—until death—like a family. When my *anda* Jamuka died, our feud was over for him, but not for me—whenever I think of our broken pledge of brotherhood, I am kept awake all night."

Tolui and Guo Jing thought of their recent confrontation before the walls of Qingzhou. Neither was proud of that encounter.

Genghis Khan had not been standing long, but he already felt drained of all strength. As he was preparing to go inside, they caught sight of a knot of riders heading for the golden *ger*. The man leading the group wore a white robe fastened with a gold belt, in the style of the Jin Empire's court dress. The sight of a rival emissary energized the aged Khan somewhat.

The man dismounted, hurried toward the golden *ger* and prostrated himself some distance away, clearly afraid to come any closer. "The ambassador of the Jin Empire begs an audience with the Great Khan."

"The Jin refuse to yield. Why have they sent you?" Genghis Khan said haughtily.

"Our humble state has offended the celestial might of the Great Khan, and we deserve to die ten thousand deaths for this transgression. We have come to present a gift of one thousand pearls, passed down from our ancestors, in the hope that the Great Khan will show mercy. They are the most important treasures of our state, and we beg the Great Khan to accept them."

The emissary rose to his knees. He produced a bundle from his knapsack and unwrapped it to reveal a jade plate, onto which he emptied a pouch of glittering pearls. Still kneeling, he shuffled forward and he offered them up to the conqueror with both hands.

Genghis Khan cast a glance from the corner of his eye. The pearls were perfectly round, and each was roughly the size of the tip of his little finger. To find one such specimen would be hard enough, and yet in their midst was a single mother pearl, many times larger than the rest. Together, they gave off a soft, warm glow, casting a rainbow halo over the jade plate.

Not long ago, Genghis Khan would have been pleased by such a gift, but now he just frowned.

He jerked his head toward one of his personal guards, ordering the soldier to take the plate.

The ambassador could not hide his delight. "Every man in our humble state would be forever grateful if the Great Khan were to accept our peace offering."

"Who says I'm accepting anything? I will send an army to crush your Jin Empire this very instant. Seize him. Now!"

The guards rushed over to restrain the messenger.

"A thousand pearls cannot give me even one more day on this earth." Sighing, Genghis Khan took the jade plate from the guard and hurled it to the ground. It shattered, sending pearls rolling in every direction.

A good portion of them were picked up by soldiers in the days to follow, but many remained hidden among the long grass. Herdsmen were said to continue to find pearls on this site for hundreds of years thereafter.

GENGHIS KHAN returned to his golden *ger* in low spirits. At dusk, he sent for Guo Jing and took him riding in the open country. They had been in the saddle for more than ten *li* when the sound of raptors cawing in the skies above reached their ears. Guo Jing's white condors were soaring overhead.

Genghis Khan unslung his iron bow, nocked an arrow and fired.

"No!" Guo Jing cried, but it was too late. The bolt was already shooting toward the female condor. He knew she would not escape with her life—the conqueror was known for his aim and the strength of his arm. But, at the moment of impact, the bird simply

veered to one side and knocked the arrow off course with her wing. Her mate screeched in fury and dived at Genghis Khan.

"Shoo!" Guo Jing lashed at the bird with his whip.

Sensing the urgency of his master's command, the condor aborted his attack. He beat his wings, crowed with displeasure, and flew off with his female companion.

Gloom shrouded Genghis Khan. He might have retained some of his agility, but his strength had waned. He cast his bow and quiver to the ground. "Never have I failed to bring down a condor. My time must be up."

Guo Jing wanted to say something to console him, but no words came to mind. The Great Khan spurred away, heading north. Fearing for the aged warrior's well-being, Guo Jing urged Ulaan to follow him. They caught up with Genghis Khan in the blink of an eye, as though they had been soaring on the wind.

Genghis Khan slowed his mount to a trot, halted and looked around him. "This vast Empire I have built is unrivaled throughout history. From the heart of our kingdom, you can ride in any direction—east, south, west, north—and it will take a whole year to reach the border, even with the fastest horses. Tell me, of all the heroes past and present, who has come close to what I've achieved?"

Guo Jing considered how he should respond. "No one since time began has come close to the Great Khan's military prowess, but your might—the might of just one man—was built upon a mountain of white bones and a sea of widows' and orphans' tears."

Genghis Khan's face darkened with rage and he raised his whip, ready to strike Guo Jing, but the young man did not flinch, staring defiantly back at him instead. The whip faltered in the air and the blow never fell.

"What do you mean?"

Guo Jing knew it was dangerous to provoke the conqueror, but he told himself he had little to lose. *It's not likely I'll see him again after this trip. I should tell him plainly what I think.*

"Great Khan, you have treated me as your kin, cared for me and given me rank and riches, and I have also honored you as family, respected you, loved you. I'd like to ask you one question: when we die and return to the earth, how much space do we take up?"

"About this much." Genghis Khan swirled his whip around to demonstrate.

"In that case, what is the point of occupying so much land, killing so many people and sowing so much misery?" Genghis Khan had no answer for that, so Guo Jing went on. "Since times of old, heroes were looked up to while they lived and admired by those that came after them because they did good deeds for the people and fought to protect them. As I see it, having blood on one's hands does not make one a hero."

"Are you saying that I will be forgotten? That I have lived a life unworthy?"

"No one can deny that you have done great things. You persuaded the Mongolians to stop fighting among themselves. People of a hundred different states and tribes now live in peace under your rule, and each of them owes you a debt of gratitude. But, wherever you rode on your conquests, you left a pile of corpses as high as any mountain. Do your achievements outweigh your sins? Do they justify all the blood that has been shed? That is much harder to answer."

Genghis Khan was a proud man, and, because of the power he wielded, it had been decades since anyone had dared to present him with the brutal truth in such a forthright manner. He found it impossible to argue with what Guo Jing was saying. He felt as though he had been galloping at speed and had tugged at the reins to bring his mount to a sudden halt, and, as he looked back at the trail of dust in his wake, he had no idea where he had come from, where he was going or why he was even there. A choking, gurgling sound rose in his throat. Blood sprayed from his lips, staining the ground.

Guo Jing could see how hard his words had hit the dying man, and he reached out to steady him. "Great Khan, let's turn back. You need rest. Pardon me for speaking out of turn."

Genghis Khan gave the young man a faint smile, his complexion a waxy yellow. "No one around me is as bold as you. They dare not give me the honest truth." His face then lit up with all the stubborn pride of a great warrior. "I have seen every land under the heavens during my lifetime and conquered more kingdoms than I can name, and yet, to you, I am no hero. *Huh!* That is truly the talk of a child!" And, with a crack of his whip, he galloped away.

That night, Genghis Khan breathed his last in the golden *ger*. As he lay dying, he was heard to murmur, "Hero . . . hero . . ."

Perhaps he was pondering Guo Jing's words.

Once Guo Jing and Lotus had paid their respects to the Great Khan's body, they bid Tolui farewell and returned to the Central Plains. On their way south, they came across skulls and bones scattered among the tall grass, as they passed through lands laid waste through war, and, each time, they sighed and told themselves they were lucky to have each other. But they could not help but ask when the common people would enjoy true peace and at last be free of the evils of this world.

> *Embers in the flames of war,*
> *Few homes left in villages poor.*
> *No rush to cross the river at dawn,*
> *The flawed moon sinks into cold sand.*

THE END

Further deeds of Guo Jing, Lotus Huang and other martial masters of the wulin *are told in* The Return of the Condor Heroes.

Appendix

NOTES ON THE TEXT

Page numbers denote the first time these concepts or names are mentioned in the book.

P. 7 COUNTING RODS

Counting rods are portable collections of small sticks of similar sizes that were used for calculating numbers in ancient China. They can be made of wood, bamboo, bone, ivory, jade or metal. The earliest known set was discovered in a tomb dating back to the Warring States period (fifth century B.C–221 B.C.), meaning that this calculation system has been in use for more than two thousand years. This computation tool was eventually replaced by the abacus. A variation of the rods' arrangement, called Suzhou numerals, is still occasionally being used today to record numbers in more traditional settings and can sometimes be seen in wet markets in Hong Kong.

P. 8 THE HEAVEN UNKNOWN TECHNIQUE

In modern mathematical terms, it presents an exploration to solve multivariable equations of higher degrees. Heaven, Earth, Man and

Matter in historical Chinese computational canons are the equivalent of x, y, z and w in algebra.

Li Ye (1192–1279) was one of the first mathematicians to write and publish a methodical discourse on this Chinese system of algebra for multivariable equations. The earliest known record of this technique can be dated back to the Northern Song (960–1127), and the nineteen unknowns quoted by Lotus Huang were cited by Li Ye in his writings from a now-lost treatise he had come across.

P. 9   NINE HALLS DIAGRAM / SCRIPT OF RIVER LUO

Often rendered as Lo Shu or Luo Shu in English, the Script of River Luo is a diagram passed down from ancient times to explain the changes, connections and interactions between the heavens, the earth and all that lies within, from which the Eight Trigrams were believed to be derived. In the myths, a divine turtle appeared in the Luo River when the legendary Emperor Yu the Great was fortifying its flood defenses. On its shell were markings in nine groups, each with a different number of dots. From studying their distribution and arrangement, Yu derived nine strategies for governing and managing the world. The Script of River Luo is a cornerstone of Chinese mathematics and divination, including geomancy, or feng shui. In numerical terms, it can be represented by an associative magic square of three by three, in which the sum of any line, whether vertical, horizontal or diagonal, is always fifteen. This configuration is also referred to as a Nine Halls Diagram.

4	9	2
3	5	7
8	1	6

P. 22   WATER, FIRE, WOOD, METAL, EARTH, RAHU AND KETU

The stars Water, Fire, etc. are the planets Mercury, Mars, Jupiter, Venus and Saturn respectively, while Rahu and Ketu are referred to as shadow planets, the former being the ascending lunar node and the latter the descending lunar node in Vedic astrology. Rather than being physical entities in space, Rahu and Ketu are the points of intersection between the paths of the sun and the moon as they move on the celestial sphere.

P. 22   THE PROBLEM OF DISTRIBUTING SILVER, ETC.

In modern mathematical terms, this question relates to the study of higher order arithmetic series—adding infinitely to a given starting quantity—which is a major field of calculus. This problem and its solution were first published in 1303, in a book called *Siyuan yujian*, or *Jade Mirror of the Four Unknowns*, by the Yuan dynasty mathematician Zhu Shijie (1249–1314), one of the most important figures in the history of mathematics.

P. 22   THE PROBLEM OF THE GHOST VALLEY SAGE

The mathematical questions and concepts mentioned in this chapter were worked on and developed by Chinese scholars roughly contemporary to the setting of the story. This example is an exploration of number theory in pure mathematics, an area in which Song dynasty mathematicians attained an in-depth knowledge, and is now commonly known as the Chinese remainder theorem.

P. 27   TIANBAO ERA / EMPEROR XUANZONG OF TANG / NOBLE CONSORT YANG / LI LINFU / YANG GUOZHONG

The Tianbao era refers to the years 741 to 756, the third and final regnal period of Emperor Xuanzong (685–762), the seventh ruler of the Tang dynasty (618–907). He was on the throne for forty-three years, from 713 to 756, and the first three decades of his reign were considered to be the dynasty's golden age, as well as a high point in Chinese history. In his latter years in power, however, he became reliant on self-serving officials, notably Chancellor Li Linfu, allowing them to run the country while he preferred to enjoy the company of Noble Consort Yang. His affection for Yang also resulted in her relations gaining power at court.

Though his neglect of state affairs culminated in the An Lushan Rebellion (755–763), leading to his abdication and Noble Consort Yang's death, and to seven years of domestic warfare that blighted the reigns of two further Emperors and weakened the dynasty, Xuanzong's doomed devotion to Noble Consort Yang was immortalized in various classics of Chinese literature that have subsequently inspired many stage and screen adaptations. In the popular imagination, he is better known as Emperor Ming of Tang.

Noble Consort Yang (719–756), whose full name was Yang Yuhuan, was one of the four beauties of ancient China. Her cousin Yang Guozhong (died 756) utilized his connection to her to improve his position in court, and eventually brought down and supplanted his one-time collaborator, Chancellor Li Linfu. He was blamed, together with Noble Consort Yang, for causing the An Lushan Rebellion, which resulted in the Emperor fleeing the capital. Yang Guozhong was killed by soldiers of the Imperial Guard, while Emperor Xuanzong was forced into ordering Noble Consort Yang to be strangled.

Li Linfu (683–753), whom Yang Guozhong succeeded, was Chancellor for eighteen years, from 734 to 752. It is believed that he maintained power by flattering the Emperor and blocking potential challengers from reaching positions of influence.

P. 27 DALI KINGDOM / NANZHAO / GELUOFENG

Situated in the region of Yunnan today, the Dali Kingdom (937–1253) was an independent state that existed around the same time as the Song Empire (960–1279). Their kings declared obedience to the Song and acted as military commissioners for their more powerful neighbor.

Nanzhao was the self-governing state in the same area preceding the establishment of the Dali Kingdom, and the height of its influence came during the eighth and ninth centuries.

Geluofeng (712–779, reigned 748–779) was the fifth king of Nanzhao. Like his forebears, he accepted the dominance of the Tang Empire, but, a few years after he ascended the throne, he gave his support to the Tubo Kingdom in their struggle against the Tang. Later, with the Tang in the grip of internal turmoil during the An Lushan Rebellion, Geluofeng enlarged the Nanzhao state, annexing parts of modern-day Sichuan and Guizhou. When the situation in the Tang Empire stabilized, however, he declared that Nanzhao would always be a friend of the Tang.

P. 27 TUBO KINGDOM

Tubo was a Tibetan kingdom that prospered during the seventh and ninth centuries, with economic and diplomatic ties to the dynasties that ruled over the territories covering both China and India today. It was often engaged in conflicts with the Tang Empire, and, by the middle of the eighth century, it was one of the largest empires in Asia, reaching beyond the Tibetan Plateau to encompass areas of modern-day Qinghai, Xinjiang, Sichuan and Yunnan.

P. 28 GOATS ON THE HILL

As touched upon throughout the story and in the notes of Volume I, *A Hero Born*, there is a specific genre of poetry in Chinese literature known as *ci*, or lyric poetry. These verses are written to fit a specific tune or melody, like song lyrics, and they follow strict rules that specify not only the length of each line and the rhyme scheme, but also the tone pitch of each character within the line. The tunes are now mostly lost, with only their titles known to us, though it is occasionally possible to reconstruct some semblance of the underlying harmony through the sonic quality of the words. "Goats on the Hill" is one such tune title, and many poets have set lyrics to variations of this melody over the centuries.

The author noted that, in the early summer of 2000, when he traveled to Lijiang in Yunnan and attended a concert of music from the Tang and Song dynasties, one of the songs performed was "Goats on the Hill," with the words "*Mountains huddled, / Torrents bubbled...*" as sung by the logger in this volume. He wrote that, although he knew the poem was believed to have been written by the Yuan dynasty writer Zhang Yanghao (1270–1329)—who was born decades after our tale's setting—he decided to include it anyway, allowing himself a minor anachronism for the sake of the story. When revising the novel for the final time, he added his reimagination of how some of the songs could have been passed down in the Dali Kingdom, inspired by his visit to Yunnan.

P. 56 CAPPED MEN

According to Confucian tradition, when men came of age at twenty, they would go through a capping ceremony at which they would acquire a courtesy name, officially entering adulthood.

P. 65 *TRIRATNA*

Sanskrit for the Three Jewels or Three Treasures of Buddhism—the Buddha, the one who has attained full enlightenment; the dharma, the teachings of the Buddha; and the sangha, the monastic community practicing the dharma.

P. 70 SEMI-PROCESSED JADE PLAQUE XUAN PAPER

Soft, with a fine texture, but robust all the same, Xuan paper has been used for painting and calligraphy for more than a thousand years, and is still made by hand today, following traditional techniques. Although it is sometimes called rice paper in English, and often includes some proportion of rice straw in its composition, the unique ingredient that gives it the desirable qualities of being resistant to creasing, moths and mold is the bark of the blue sandalwood tree. It is named after Xuanzhou, the area from which it was sold.

Xuan paper is usually categorized into three main types, according to the different ratios of key ingredients and to the processes it is subjected to: the raw paper has the highest water absorbency and is most suitable for expressive inkwash; the ripe paper takes the least water and is used for *gongbi*-style painting, with its fine and detailed brushstrokes; and the half-ripe or semi-processed paper is a happy medium between the two. Jade plaque is a type of half-ripe paper, named for its white and smooth appearance.

P. 70 KUMARAJIVA OF THE KINGDOM OF KUCHA

The monk Kumarajiva (344–413) was one of the most important translators of Buddhist texts from Sanskrit into Chinese. His translations stand out thanks to their smooth flow and the clarity with which they convey complex meanings. To this day, his versions are recited and studied not only by believers, but also by scholars of Buddhism, literature and translation. It is not uncommon to hear his turns of phrase from the Diamond Sutra or the Lotus Sutra quoted offhand in modern everyday situations, so embedded in the Chinese culture and language are his works.

P. 96 MUTTON-FAT WHITE JADE FROM KHOTAN

Khotan, in the southwestern region of modern-day Xinjiang, has been an important source of nephrite jade throughout the history of China. The highest-quality stones come from the rivers originating in the Kunlun Mountains, though few outstanding pebbles or boulders can be found today. The most precious light-colored variety is known as mutton-fat white jade because of its resemblance to its namesake.

P. 117 *APSARAS / DEVAS / YAKSAS*

Apsaras are celestial singers, musicians and dancers; *devas* are a class of beings who live longer than humans and have deific powers; *yaksas* are spirits related to nature, which are usually benevolent, but can also be mischievous. These divine beings are common to both Hinduism and Buddhism.

P. 123 DUAN ZHIXING

A real historical figure, Duan Zhixing (1149–1200) ruled the Dali Kingdom from 1172 until his death in 1200. Although his father, Duan Zhengxing (posthumous title: Zhengkang), did abdicate to become a monk, the tale of Duan Zhixing being reborn as Reverend Sole Light is a fictional invention.

P.144 A CURIOUS FORM OF SANSKRIT INFLECTED BY THE CHINESE LANGUAGE

The incomprehensible passage at the end of the Nine Yin Manual, which also appeared in volumes II and III, was inspired by a book called *Mongol-un nigucha tobchiyan*, or *The Secret History of the Mongols*. It was believed to have been completed by 1240, written either in the Mongolian script then transliterated phonetically into Chinese characters, or directly in Chinese characters to emulate the sounds of the Mongolian language. It tells the life story of Genghis Khan, from his origins and childhood all the way to his death, and is one of the most important accounts in the Mongolian language of the founding of the Mongol Empire.

This book exists in two versions: in its "phonetic" form and as a translation in Chinese prose. It was the "phonetic" text, in which Chinese readers without knowledge of Mongolian will simply find a jumble of random characters they recognize but cannot make sense of, that inspired the invented language of the Nine Yin Manual.

The collection of characters that make up the final "Sanskrit" passage of the Nine Yin Manual are in fact entirely made up by the author, though similar combinations are seen in Chinese trans-literation of Buddhist chants, which are recorded in Sanskrit. The lines that appear in this English translation are based on Mandarin pronunciations of the Chinese characters, which are then converted into spellings that recall the form of romanized Sanskrit, while maintaining some semblance of what the made-up text sounds like in Chinese.

P. 162 BIANLIANG

Bianliang, which also appears as Daliang in this volume, is the city now known as Kaifeng. It was the capital of the Song Empire between 960 and 1127, until the Jurchen invasion forced the Imperial Court to relocate south to Lin'an. It was one of the largest cities in the world in the eleventh century, with a population of at least half a million residents, and, by some estimates, twice that number. The five-meter long scroll painting by Zhang Zeduan (1085–1145), "Along the River During the Qingming Festival," depicts its vibrant street life, and many of its details are corroborated by surviving contemporary accounts. Marco Polo also wrote about this metropolis when he visited China in the late thirteenth century.

P. 213 LYCHEE PORK KIDNEY, ETC.

Some of the delicacies mentioned by Count Seven Hong are from *Wulin jiushi*, or *Old Affairs of Wulin* by Zhou Mi (1232–98). They were served to Emperor Gaozong of Song at a banquet at the home of General Zhang Jun, in 1151.

Old Affairs of Wulin, completed in around 1290, after the establishment of the Yuan dynasty, records all aspects of urban life in Lin'an during the Southern Song era, as experienced by the common people as well as by those at court, offering great insight into the customs of the day, especially those related to entertainment and performance. *Wulin* here refers to the hills around West Lake, and was used as an alternative name for Lin'an, which is known today as Hangzhou.

P.233 CHANCELLOR LIN XIANGRU / GENERAL LIAN PO

Chancellor Lin Xiangru and General Lian Po served the state of Zhao in the third century B.C., during the Warring States period (fifth century B.C.–221 B.C.)

Lin Xiangru was initially a retainer of the palace eunuch Miao Xian, but his eloquence twice spared Zhao humiliation at the hands of the more powerful and aggressive Qin state, and he was promoted by the King of Zhao to the highest position in court, rising above General Lian Po.

Offended that a low-born man who had never risked his life for his country on the battlefield was so honored, the General made it known that he would insult Lin should they meet. In order to avoid a confrontation, Lin feigned illness to stay away from court, and, whenever he saw General Lian on the street, he would ask his entourage to take his palanquin by another route.

Lin's followers were ashamed to see the man they admired bow to General Lian's threats, assuming that he feared the military man, but Lin explained that he was placing the country's survival before his personal honor, for the only reason the Qin had not sent troops to Zhao was that they were wary of both him and General Lian. If the two of them were engaged in petty wrangling against each other, they would leave their state vulnerable. When Lin's words reached the General's ears, he hurried to Lin's mansion carrying sharp brambles on his unclothed back to beg for punishment and forgiveness. The two men became friends for life.

P. 303   GENERAL WANG YANZHANG

Wang Yanzhang (863–923) was a famous general of the Later Liang state (907–23), known for his prowess on the field and his loyalty to his country. He was captured by Later Tang (923–37) forces and subsequently beheaded when he refused to defect.

Later Liang was one of the states of the turbulent Five Dynasties and Ten Kingdoms period (907–79) that preceded the founding of the Song dynasty.

P. 314   LITTLE ISLAND OF FLEABANE AND GOOSEFOOT

The Island of Fleabane and Goosefoot, or Penglai in Mandarin transliteration, is one of the five mythical mountains in the Eastern Sea, home to celestial immortals. The Little Island of Fleabane and Goosefoot of Xincheng Town was once a part of Nengren Temple (founded in 503), and is now a park open to the public in modern-day Jiaxing.

P. 330   BIAN ZHUANGZI SLAYED THE WAR-WEARIED TIGERS

Bian Zhuangzi was an official of the state of Lu (1043–249 B.C.), known for his courage. He once came upon two tigers feeding on an ox carcass and unsheathed his blade, ready to claim them. However, he was stopped and told to wait, for the tigers would likely fight each other over the food before long. Bian followed the advice and held back until one tiger had killed the other, then entered the fray and slayed the surviving but injured animal with ease, becoming known as the man who took on two tigers. This story was recorded in the *Record of the Grand Historian* by Sima Qian, and became a metaphor for taking action strategically at the right moment for optimal results.

P. 352 TONG PASS

With the Yellow River to its north and the Qin Mountains to its south, Tong Pass is one of the most important military strongholds in the history of China. Its unique geographical position allowed it to defend Chang'an (modern-day Xi'an) from attacks coming from the east. If they could breach it, armies coming from the west could capture the key cities of the plains of northern China—from Luoyang and Kaifeng all the way to Beijing—with relative ease. However, as long as the soldiers garrisoned there did not sally out to engage the enemy, it was nigh on impregnable, and it was said that two soldiers behind its walls could hold back a company of a hundred.

P. 360 KHWARAZM

Khwarazm, also known as Chorasmia, lies in the territories of modern Turkmenistan, Uzbekistan and Kazakhstan. Its Shahs ruled over Central Asia and Iran between the eleventh and thirteenth centuries, until the Mongolians conquered the Khwarazmian Empire. Situated at the crossroads of the caravan routes along the Silk Road, the region was vital to trade between the Asian and European continents.

P. 360 ALA AD-DIN MUHAMMAD

The real historical figure Muhammad II of Khwarazm, who reigned from 1200 to 1220, was the penultimate Shah of the Khwarazmian Empire. His rejection of Genghis Khan's attempt to establish trade relations—by arresting the first envoy for spying and executing the second—is believed by historians to have been a cause of the brutal invasion by the Mongolians.

P. 366 THE HEAVENS LOOK ASKANCE, ETC.

The real historical figure Qiu Chuji's journey to the west at the invitation of Genghis Khan is well documented. His disciple Li Zhichang wrote a detailed diary of the trip, which took place between 1220 and 1223, named *Changchun zhenren xiyouji*, or *The Travels of Immortal Eternal Spring to the West*. The text survives to this day, and it is a valuable account of Central Asia at the time, describing its geography, the lives of ordinary people and conditions for travelers. It also sheds light on the Mongolian administration and offers a candid portrait of Genghis Khan.

The letter quoted here is the actual message the conqueror sent the Taoist monk, written on the first day of the fifth lunar moon of the year 1219, which is May 12 in today's calendar.

P. 401 SAMARKAND

Situated in modern Uzbekistan, Samarkand—also spelled as Samarqand—is one of the oldest cities of Central Asia with great commercial importance, lying at the junction of trade routes from China and India. It was destroyed by Genghis Khan in 1220.

P. 402 CLOUD LADDERS

Hinged folding ladders used for scaling city walls. They were a common siege weapon in medieval China, and some designs included a compartment at the base to provide soldiers with shelter from projectiles hurled from the walls as they approached.

P. 432 A DECADE PLAGUED BY WAR, ETC.

The verses on these pages are original poems written by the real historical figure Qiu Chuji.

P. 489 FIVE CLASSICS OF THE CONFUCIAN CANON

The Five Classics are: the *Book of Songs*, a collection of verses meant to be sung; the *Book of Documents*, a collection of speeches and other texts by rulers and important ministers; the *I'Ching* or *Book of Changes*, a system of divination; the *Book of Rites*, descriptions of social forms and ritual matters; and *Spring and Autumn Annals*, a chronicle of the state of Lu between 722 B.C. and 479 B.C. Most of these texts were written before Confucius's lifetime (551–479 B.C.), and the versions that survive today were mostly compiled—or even composed—during the Han period (206 B.C.–220 A.D.), when Confucianism became the official state philosophy.

P. 491 A GAME OF GO

Also called *weiqi*, this Chinese board game for two players is set on a grid of nineteen by nineteen lines. Each side has one hundred and eighty pieces in the shape of flat round pebbles, which are called stones, one set black, the other white. Crudely speaking, the aim is to remove the opponent's stones by encircling them. It is a game of strategy and patience, and one is often required to sacrifice one's own stones in order to come out on top at the end. It is regarded as a way to cultivate wisdom, rather than a simple pastime, and is one of the four arts—together with calligraphy, painting and the playing of the *qin* zither—that should be mastered by a literati or by anyone who wishes to be considered learned.

P. 560 LI QUAN / YANG MIAOZHEN

Li Quan (1190–1231) was a rebel leader who joined the anti-Jin resistance army founded by Yang An'er, the elder brother of his wife, Yang Miaozhen. All three are real figures from history.

JIN YONG (1924–2018) (pen name of Louis Cha) is a true phenomenon in the Chinese-speaking world. Born in Mainland China, he spent most of his life writing novels and editing newspapers in Hong Kong. His enormously popular martial-arts novels, written between the late 1950s and 1972, have become modern classics and remain a must-read for young readers looking for danger and adventure. They have also inspired countless T.V. and video-game adaptions. His death in October 2018 was met with tributes from around the globe.

Estimated sales of his books worldwide stand at 300 million, and if bootleg copies are taken into consideration, that figure rises to a staggering one billion. International recognition came in the form of an O.B.E. in 1981, a Chevalier de la Légion d'Honneur (1992), a Chevalier de la Légion d'Honneur (2004), an honorary fellowship at St Antony's College, Oxford, and honorary doctorates from Hong Kong University and Cambridge University, among others.

GIGI CHANG translates from Chinese into English. Her translations include classical Chinese dramas for the Royal Shakespeare Company and contemporary Chinese plays for London's Royal Court Theater, Hong Kong Arts Festival and Shanghai Dramatic Arts Center.

SHELLY BRYANT divides her year between Shanghai and Singapore, working as a writer, researcher and translator. Her translation of Sheng Keyi's *Northern Girls* was long-listed for the Man Asian Literary Prize in 2012.

THE RETURN OF THE CONDOR HEROES

CHINA, 1237 A.D.

Genghis Khan is dead. The Mongolians, led by the conqueror's third son, Ogedai, have vanquished the Jurchen Jin Empire, and now turn their armies on their ally the Great Song Empire. A dozen years have passed since the second Contest of Mount Hua.

A new generation of martial artists are vying for recognition in the *jianghu*, but as the fall of their country looms closer, the making of a hero depends on more than mere kung fu skills.

A chance meeting with his father's sworn brother Guo Jing lifts Penance Yang from a life of vagrancy and initiates him into the martial world to which his parents Yang Kang and Mercy Mu once belonged.

Placed under the care of the Quanzhen Sect at their base in the Zhongnan Mountains, Penance stumbles across the mysterious history behind the founding of this most respected martial school and embarks on a journey during that forces him to come to terms with his family's past as well as secrets of his own heart.